VIZ GRAPHIC NOVEL

MAISON IKKOKU™ VOLUME TWELVE

HOUNDS OF WAR

STORY AND ART BY

RUMIKO TAKAHASHI

CONTENTS

This volume contains MAISON IKKOKU PART EIGHT #1 through #6 in their entirety.

STORY AND ART BY • RUMIKO TAKAHASHI

ENGLISH ADAPTATION BY • GERARD JONES

Director of Sales & Marketing/Oliver Chin
Translation/Mari Morimoto
Touch-Up Art & Lettering/Bill Spicer
Cover Design/Hidemi Sahara
Editor/Trish Ledoux
Assistant Editor/Bill Flanagan

Managing Editor/Hyoe Narita
Editor-in-Chief/Satoru Fujii
Publisher/Seiji Horibuchi

Printed in Canada

Published by Viz Communications, Inc.
P.O. Box 77010
San Francisco, CA 94107

10 9 8 7 6 5 4 3 2
First printing, July 1999
Second printing, December 1999

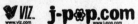

Get your Free Viz Shop-By-Mail Catalog!
(800) 394-3042
or Fax (415) 348-8936

MAISON IKKOKU GRAPHIC
NOVELS TO DATE

MAISON IKKOKU
FAMILY AFFAIRS
HOME SWEET HOME
GOOD HOUSEKEEPING
EMPTY NEST
BEDSIDE MANNERS
INTENSIVE CARE
DOMESTIC DISPUTE
LEARNING CURVES
DOGGED PURSUIT
STUDENT AFFAIRS
THE HOUNDS OF WAR
GAME, SET, MATCH.

PART ONE

THE CHRYSANTHEMUM AND THE BUILDING BLOCK

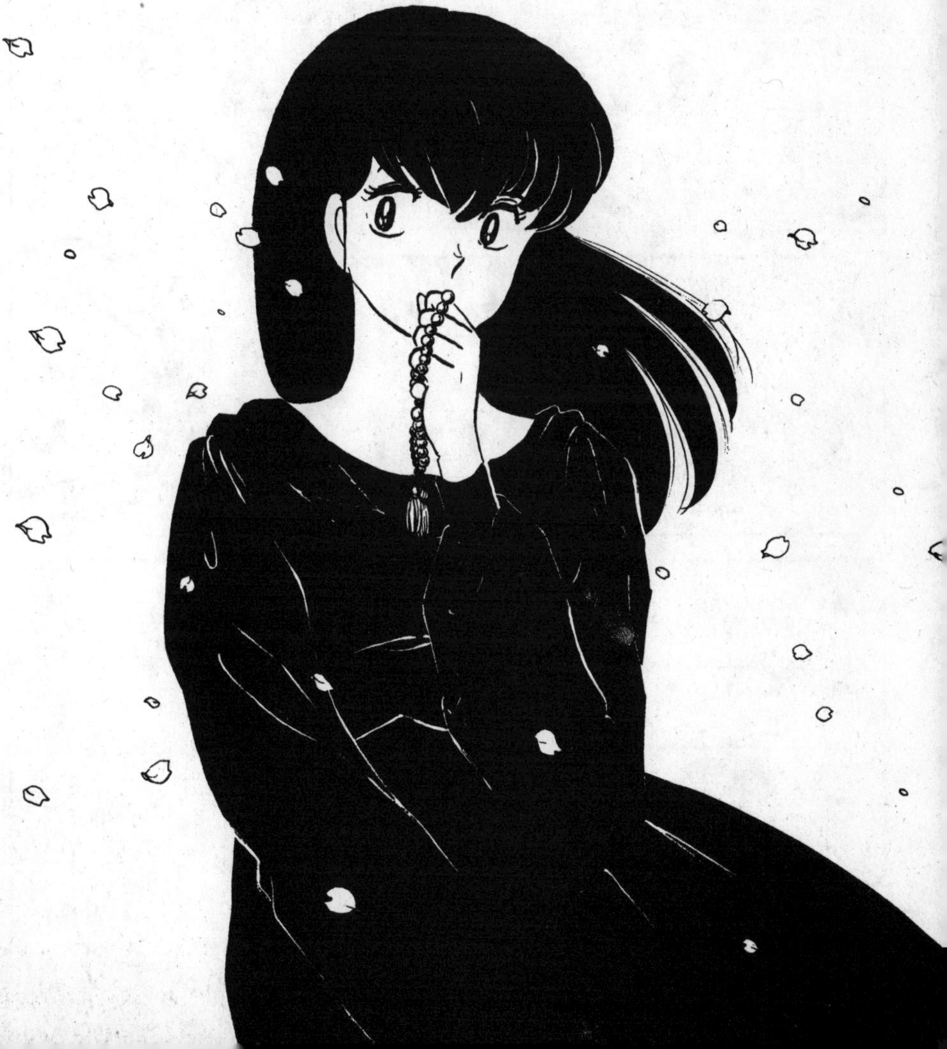

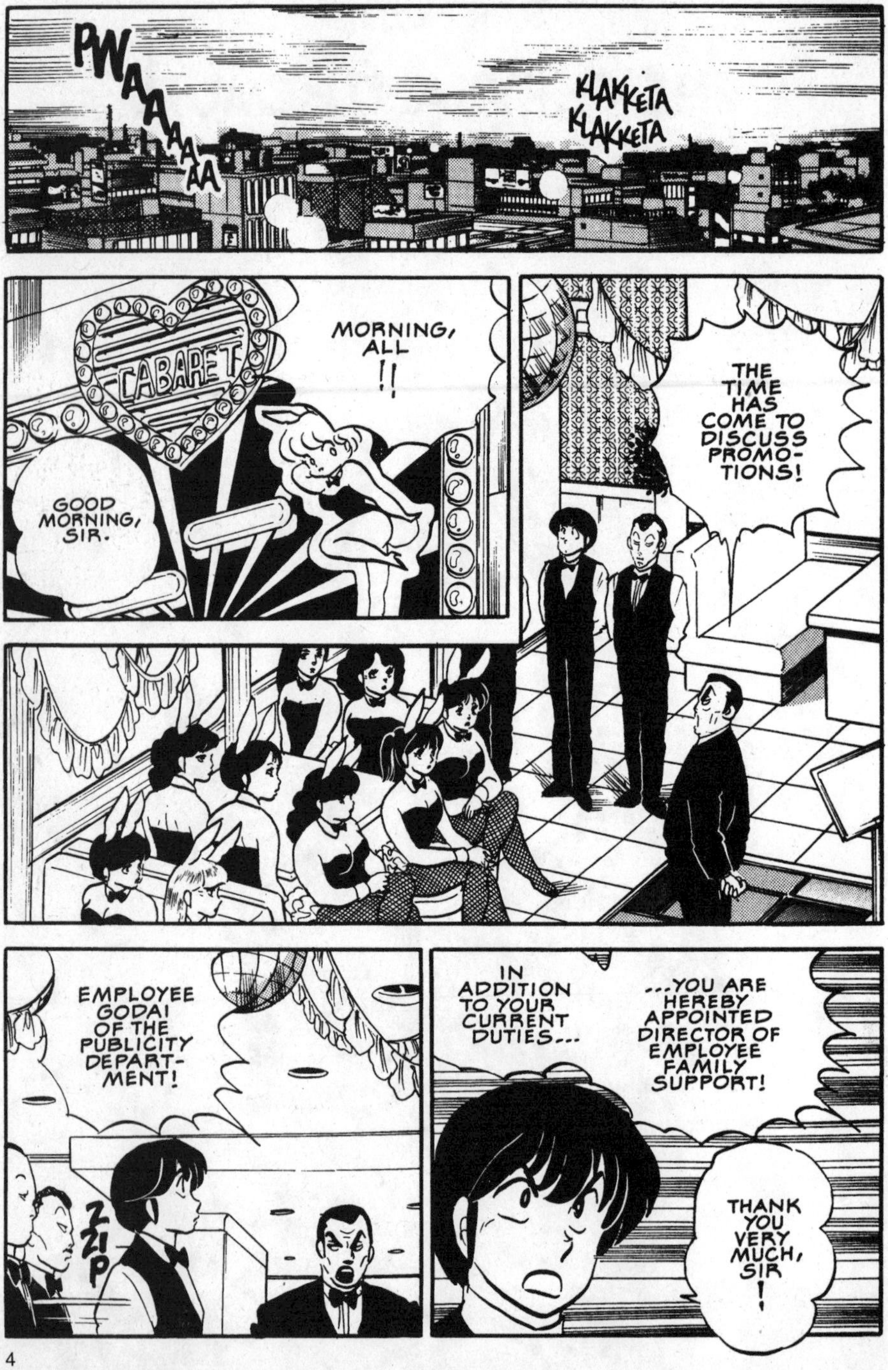
PWAAAAAAA
KLAKKETA KLAKKETA
MORNING, ALL!!
GOOD MORNING, SIR.
THE TIME HAS COME TO DISCUSS PROMO-TIONS!
EMPLOYEE GODAI OF THE PUBLICITY DEPART-MENT!
ZZIP
IN ADDITION TO YOUR CURRENT DUTIES...
...YOU ARE HEREBY APPOINTED DIRECTOR OF EMPLOYEE FAMILY SUPPORT!
THANK YOU VERY MUCH, SIR!

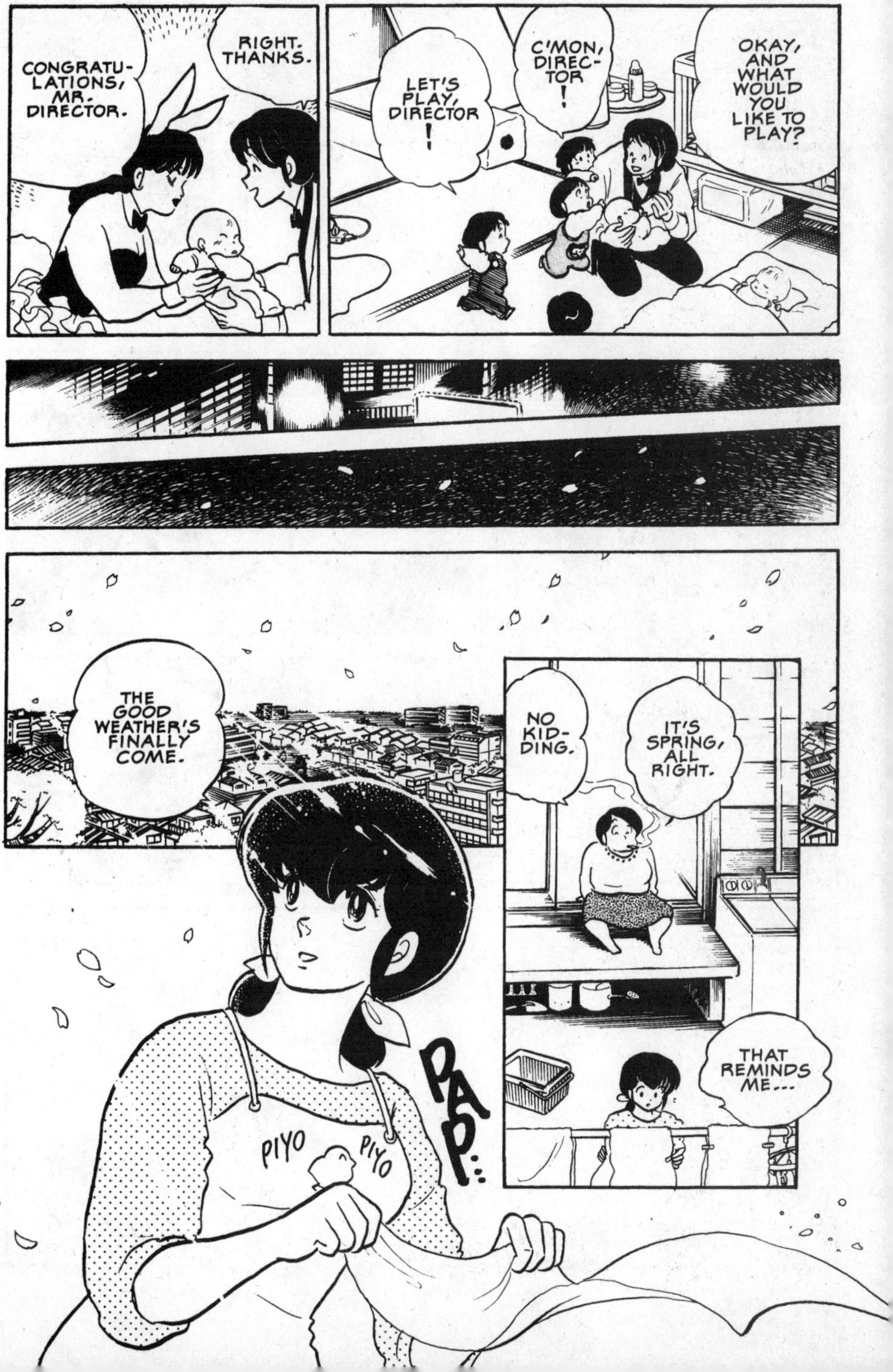
CONGRATULATIONS, MR. DIRECTOR.
RIGHT. THANKS.
LET'S PLAY, DIRECTOR!
C'MON, DIRECTOR!
OKAY, AND WHAT WOULD YOU LIKE TO PLAY?
THE GOOD WEATHER'S FINALLY COME.
PIYO PIYO
PAP...
NO KIDDING.
IT'S SPRING, ALL RIGHT.
THAT REMINDS ME...

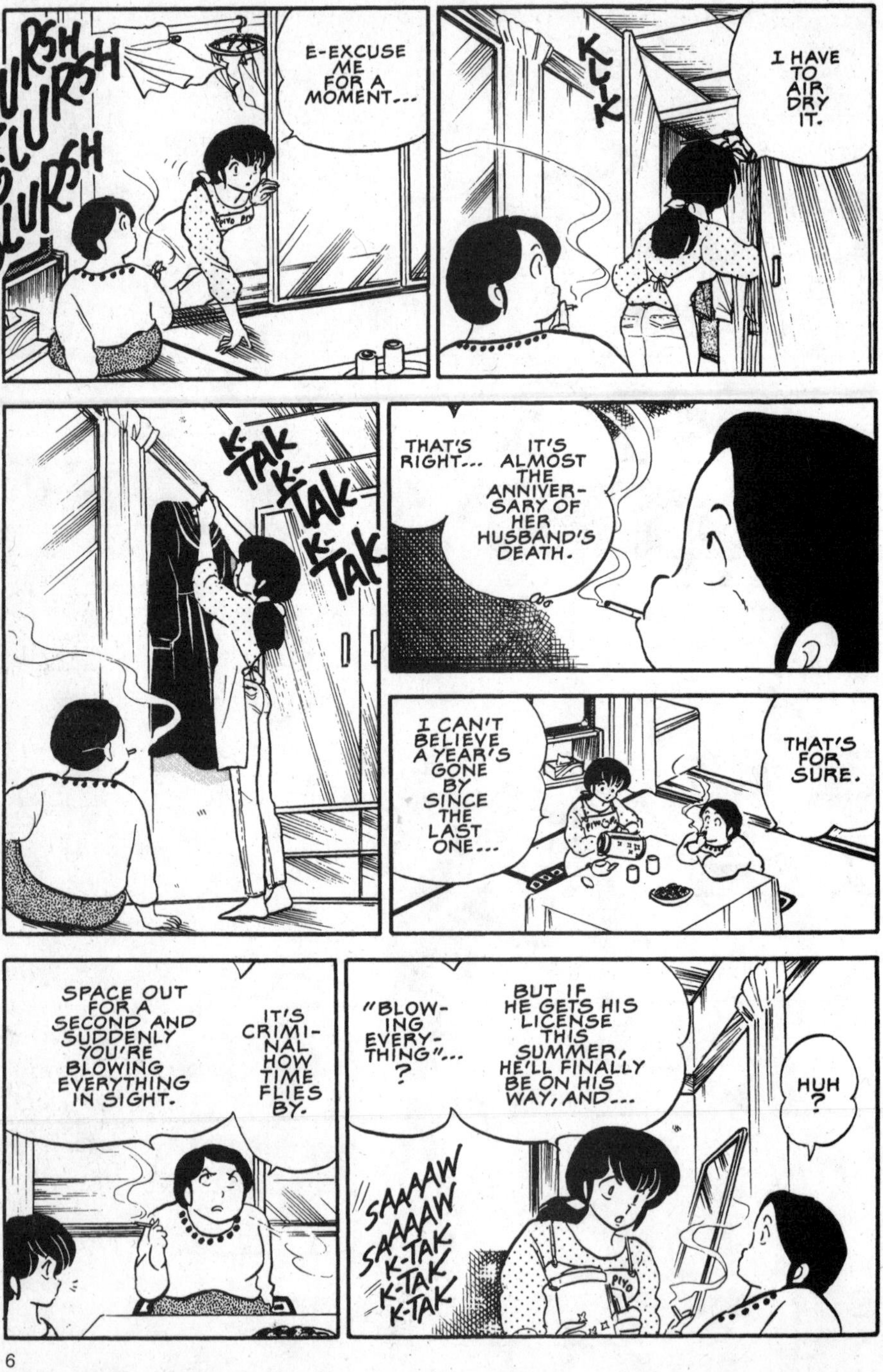
GLURSH GLURSH GLURSH
E-EXCUSE ME FOR A MOMENT...
KLIK
I HAVE TO AIR DRY IT.
K-TAK K-TAK K-TAK
THAT'S RIGHT...
IT'S ALMOST THE ANNIVERSARY OF HER HUSBAND'S DEATH.
I CAN'T BELIEVE A YEAR'S GONE BY SINCE THE LAST ONE...
THAT'S FOR SURE.
SPACE OUT FOR A SECOND AND SUDDENLY YOU'RE BLOWING EVERYTHING IN SIGHT.
IT'S CRIMINAL HOW TIME FLIES BY.
"BLOWING EVERYTHING"...?
BUT IF HE GETS HIS LICENSE THIS SUMMER, HE'LL FINALLY BE ON HIS WAY, AND...
HUH?
SAAAAW SAAAAW K-TAK K-TAK K-TAK

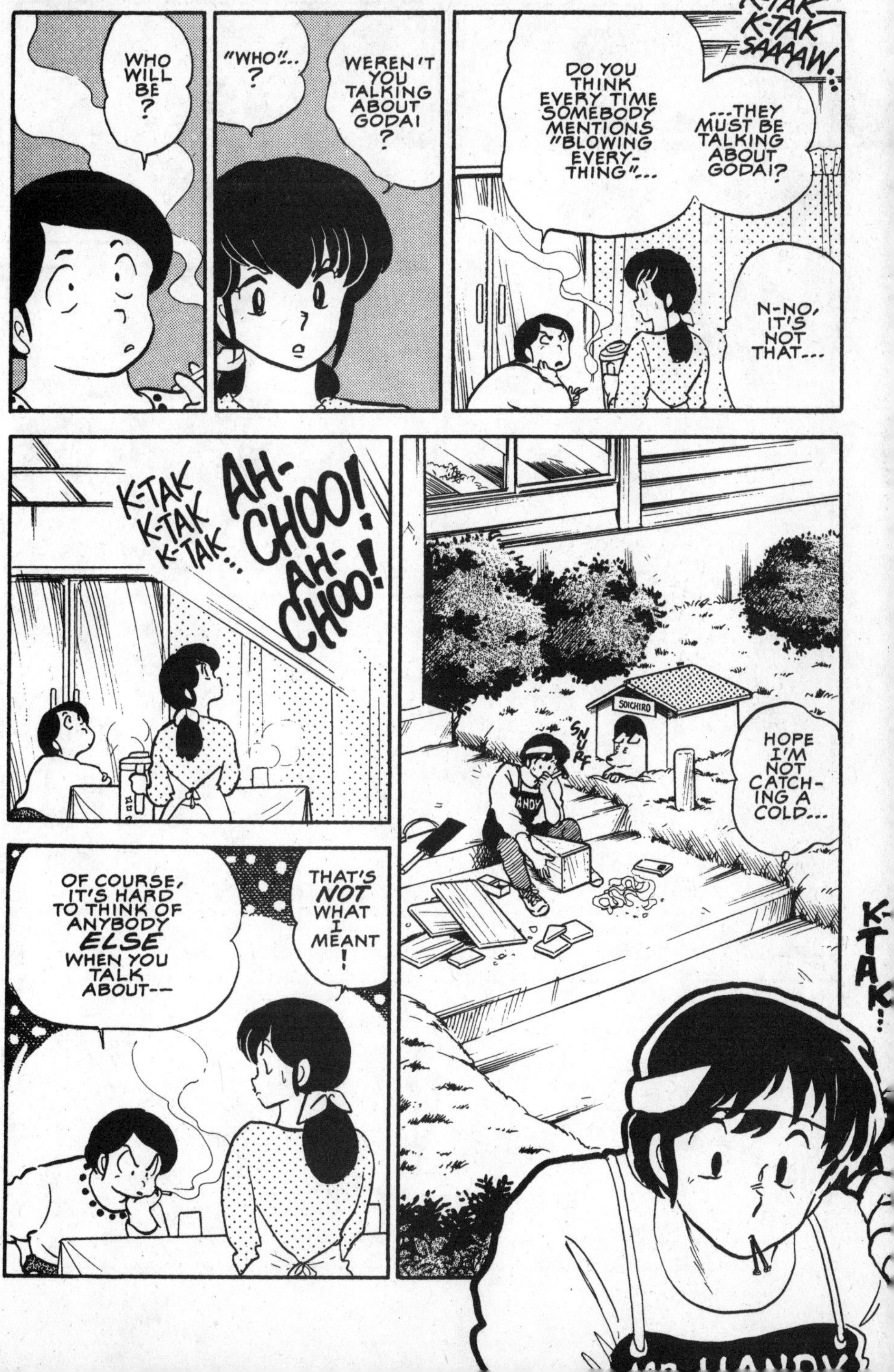
WHO WILL BE ?
"WHO"... ?
WEREN'T YOU TALKING ABOUT GODAI ?
K-TAK K-TAK SAAAAW...
DO YOU THINK EVERY TIME SOMEBODY MENTIONS "BLOWING EVERYTHING"...
...THEY MUST BE TALKING ABOUT GODAI?
N-NO, IT'S NOT THAT...
K-TAK K-TAK K-TAK...
AH-CHOO! AH-CHOO!
OF COURSE, IT'S HARD TO THINK OF ANYBODY ELSE WHEN YOU TALK ABOUT--
THAT'S NOT WHAT I MEANT !
SOICHIRO
SNUFF
HOPE I'M NOT CATCHING A COLD...
K-TAK K-TAK...

WHAT ARE YOU DOING OUT HERE, ANYWAY?

BUILDING BLOCKS?

K-TAK K-TAK K-TAK

UH-HUH.

WAITAMINNIT... YOU'RE BABY-SITTING... AT THE STRIP CLUB?!

OH MY.

K-TAK

THEY DON'T HAVE ANY DECENT TOYS OR ANY-THING...

...SO I FIGURED I'D MAKE THEM MYSELF.

R. HANDY

HOW MUCH EXTRA YOU GETTIN'?

HUH?

SHPAA

S HANDY

DON'T TELL ME YOU'RE DOING IT FREE?

THIS ISN'T ABOUT MONEY!

I'M SURE THE CHILDREN WILL BE THRILLED.

MR. HANDY

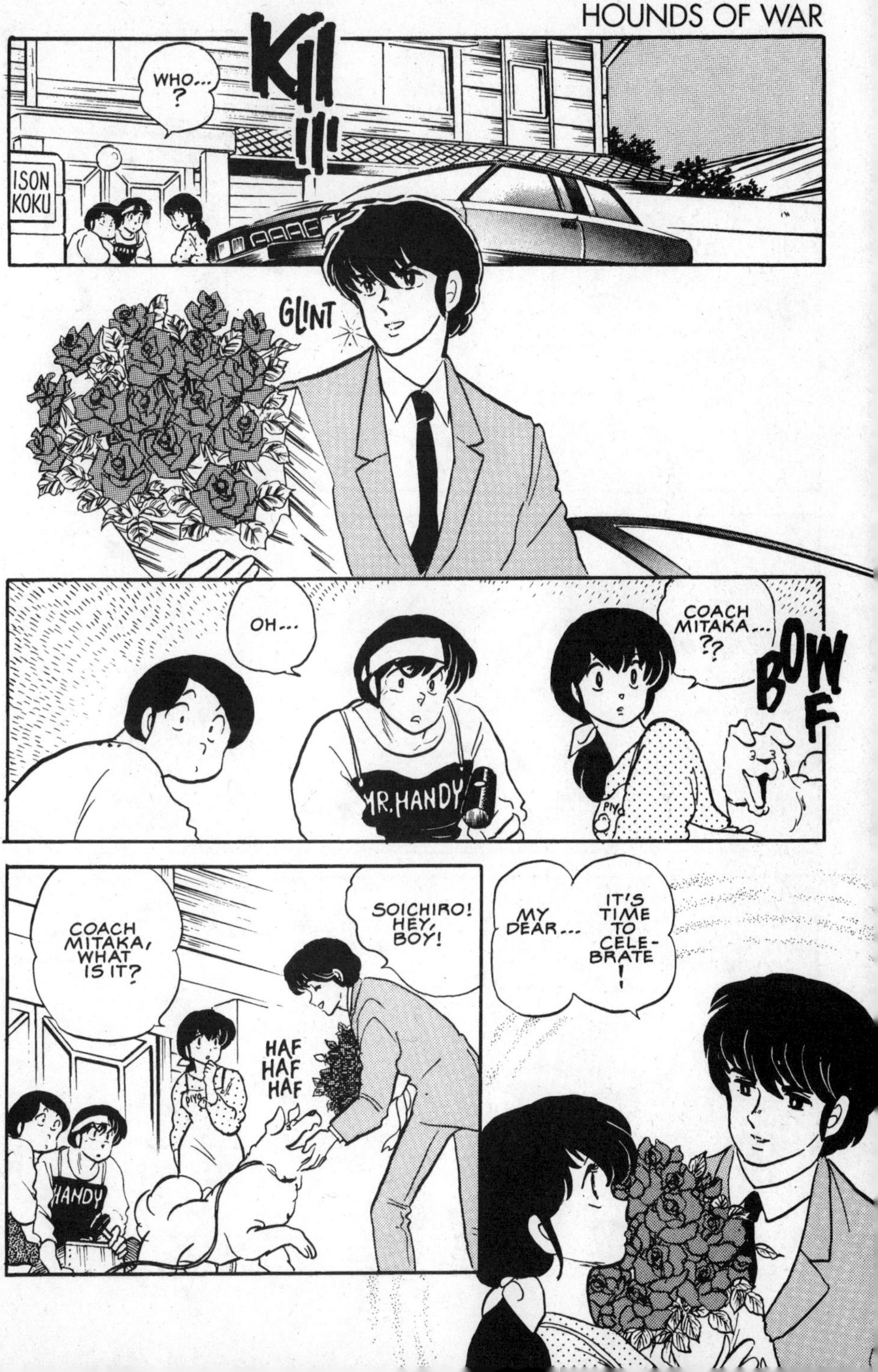
WHO... ?
KII
ISON
KOKU
GLINT
OH...
MR. HANDY
COACH MITAKA... ??
BOWF
COACH MITAKA, WHAT IS IT?
SOICHIRO! HEY, BOY!
HAF HAF HAF
HANDY
MY DEAR...
IT'S TIME TO CELE-BRATE!

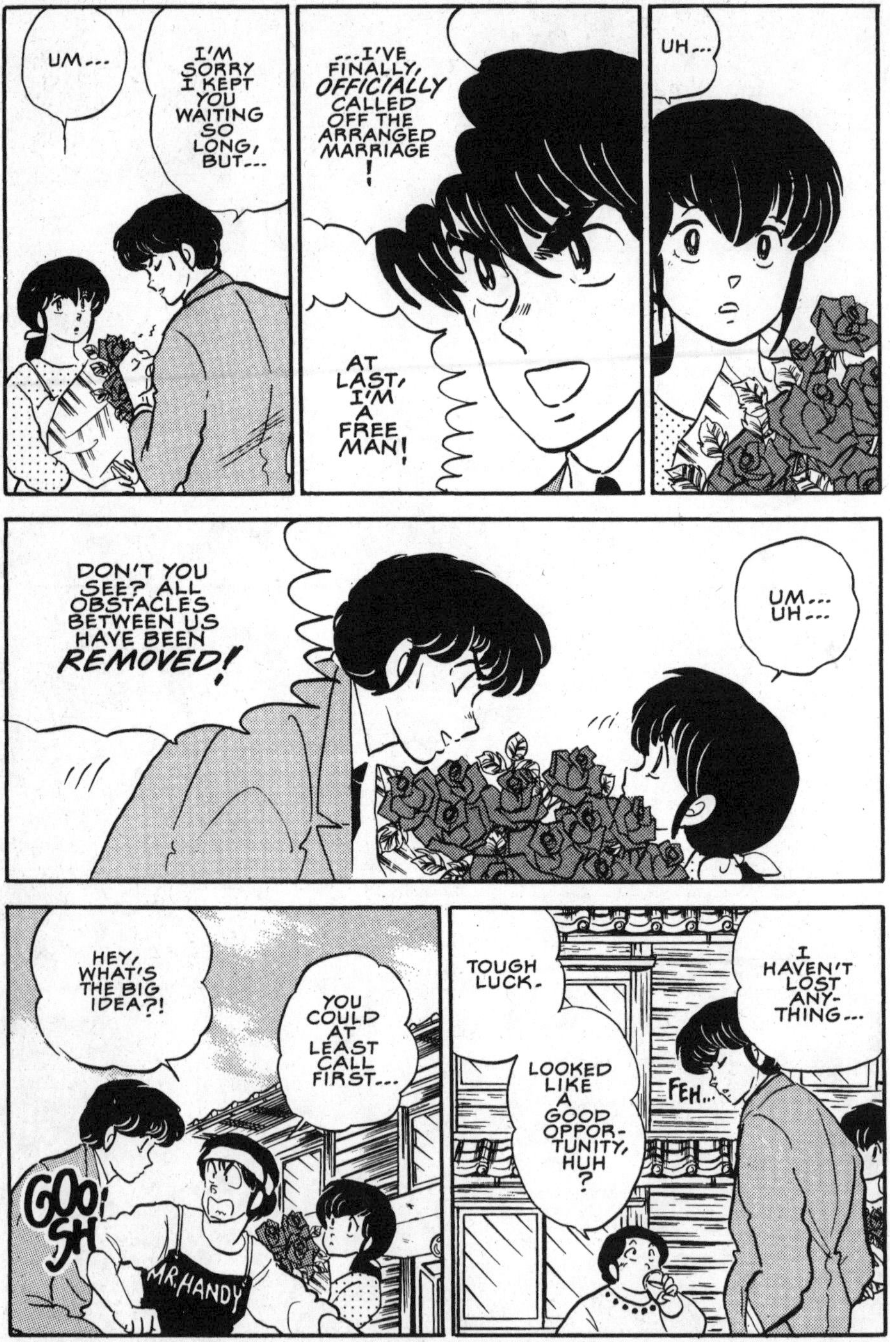
UM...
I'M SORRY I KEPT YOU WAITING SO LONG, BUT...
...I'VE FINALLY, OFFICIALLY CALLED OFF THE ARRANGED MARRIAGE!
AT LAST, I'M A FREE MAN!
UH...
DON'T YOU SEE? ALL OBSTACLES BETWEEN US HAVE BEEN REMOVED!
UM... UH...
HEY, WHAT'S THE BIG IDEA?!
YOU COULD AT LEAST CALL FIRST...
GOOSH
MR. HANDY
TOUGH LUCK.
LOOKED LIKE A GOOD OPPORTUNITY, HUH?
FEH...
I HAVEN'T LOST ANYTHING...

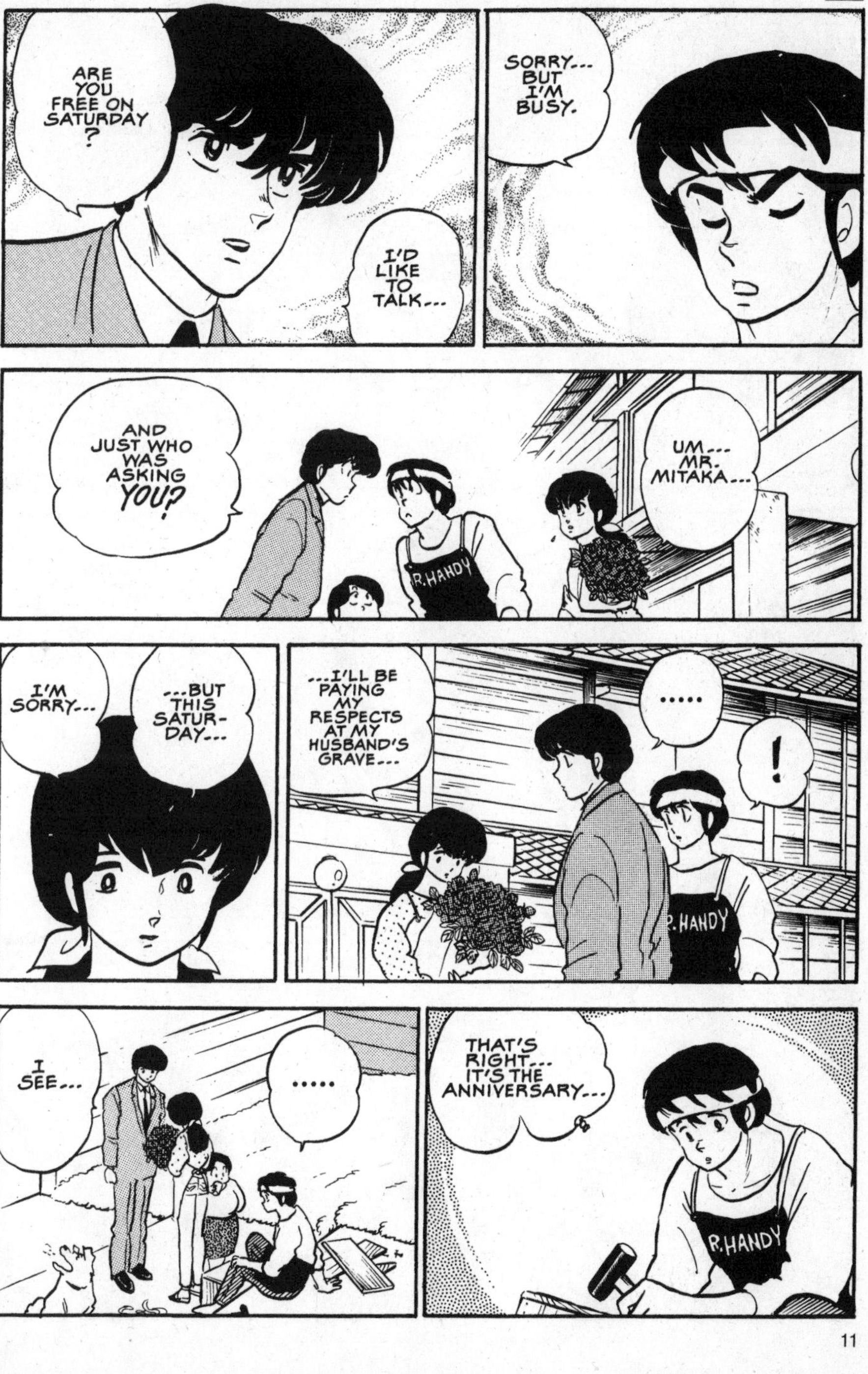
ARE YOU FREE ON SATURDAY?
I'D LIKE TO TALK...
SORRY... BUT I'M BUSY.
AND JUST WHO WAS ASKING YOU?
R. HANDY
UM... MR. MITAKA...
I'M SORRY...
...BUT THIS SATURDAY...
...I'LL BE PAYING MY RESPECTS AT MY HUSBAND'S GRAVE...
.....
!
R. HANDY
I SEE...
.....
THAT'S RIGHT... IT'S THE ANNIVERSARY...
R. HANDY

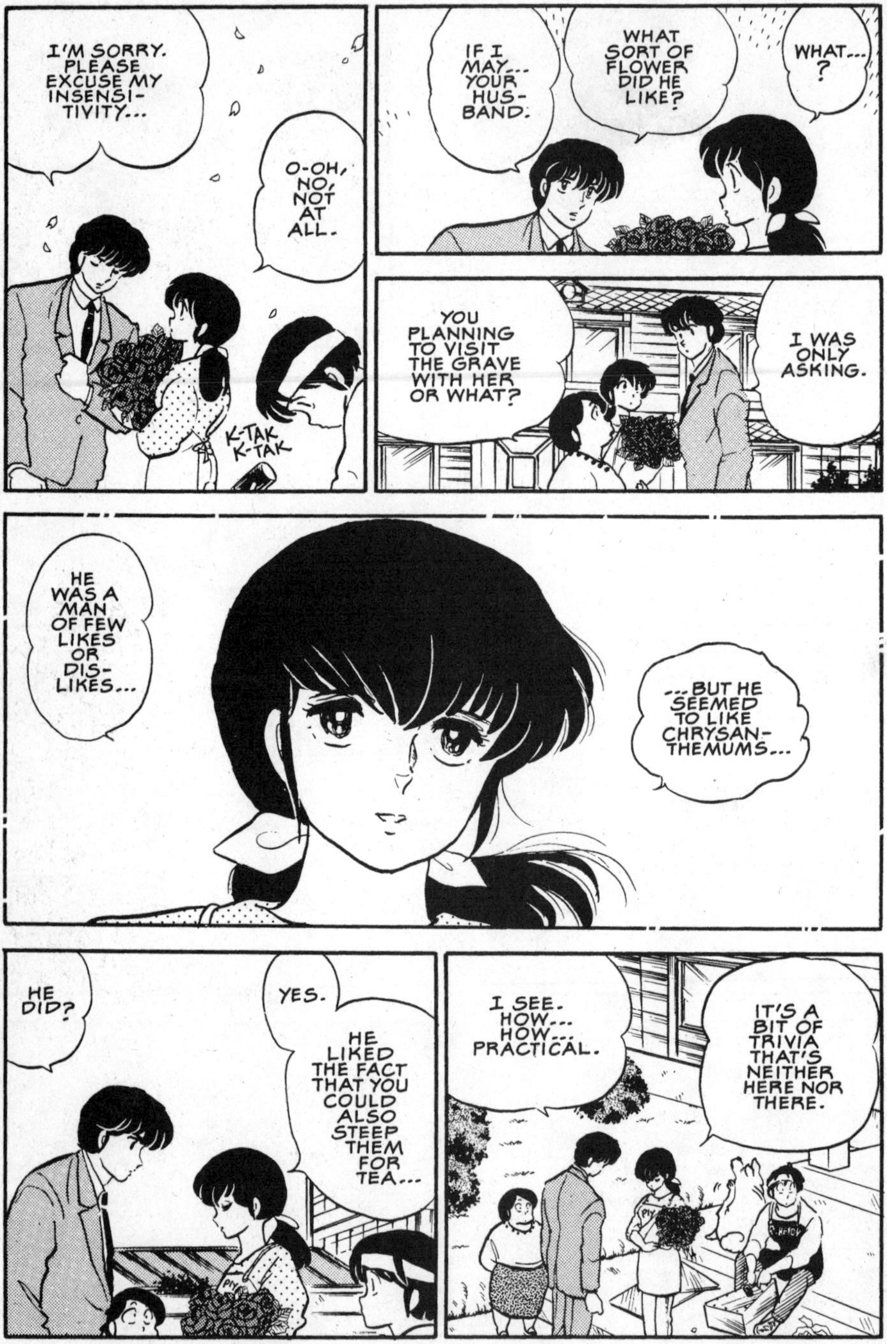
I'M SORRY. PLEASE EXCUSE MY INSENSI-TIVITY...
O-OH, NO, NOT AT ALL.
K-TAK K-TAK
IF I MAY... YOUR HUS-BAND.
WHAT SORT OF FLOWER DID HE LIKE?
WHAT...?
YOU PLANNING TO VISIT THE GRAVE WITH HER OR WHAT?
I WAS ONLY ASKING.
HE WAS A MAN OF FEW LIKES OR DIS-LIKES...
...BUT HE SEEMED TO LIKE CHRYSAN-THEMUMS...
HE DID?
YES.
HE LIKED THE FACT THAT YOU COULD ALSO STEEP THEM FOR TEA...
I SEE. HOW... HOW... PRACTICAL.
IT'S A BIT OF TRIVIA THAT'S NEITHER HERE NOR THERE.

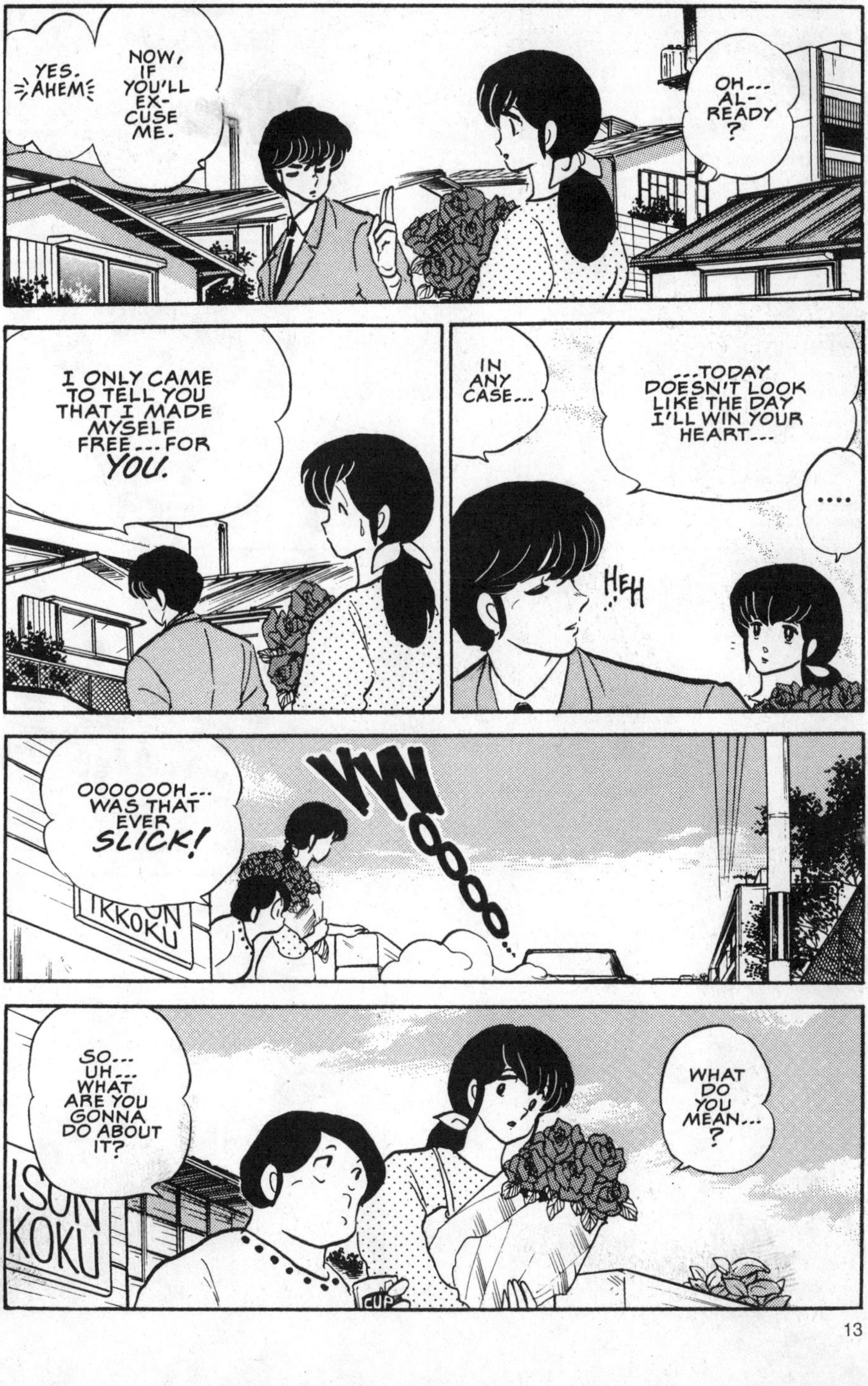
YES. AHEM
NOW, IF YOU'LL EXCUSE ME.
OH... AL-READY?
I ONLY CAME TO TELL YOU THAT I MADE MYSELF FREE... FOR YOU.
IN ANY CASE...
...TODAY DOESN'T LOOK LIKE THE DAY I'LL WIN YOUR HEART...
HEH
....
OOOOOOH... WAS THAT EVER SLICK!
VVWOOOOO...
SO... UH... WHAT ARE YOU GONNA DO ABOUT IT?
WHAT DO YOU MEAN...?

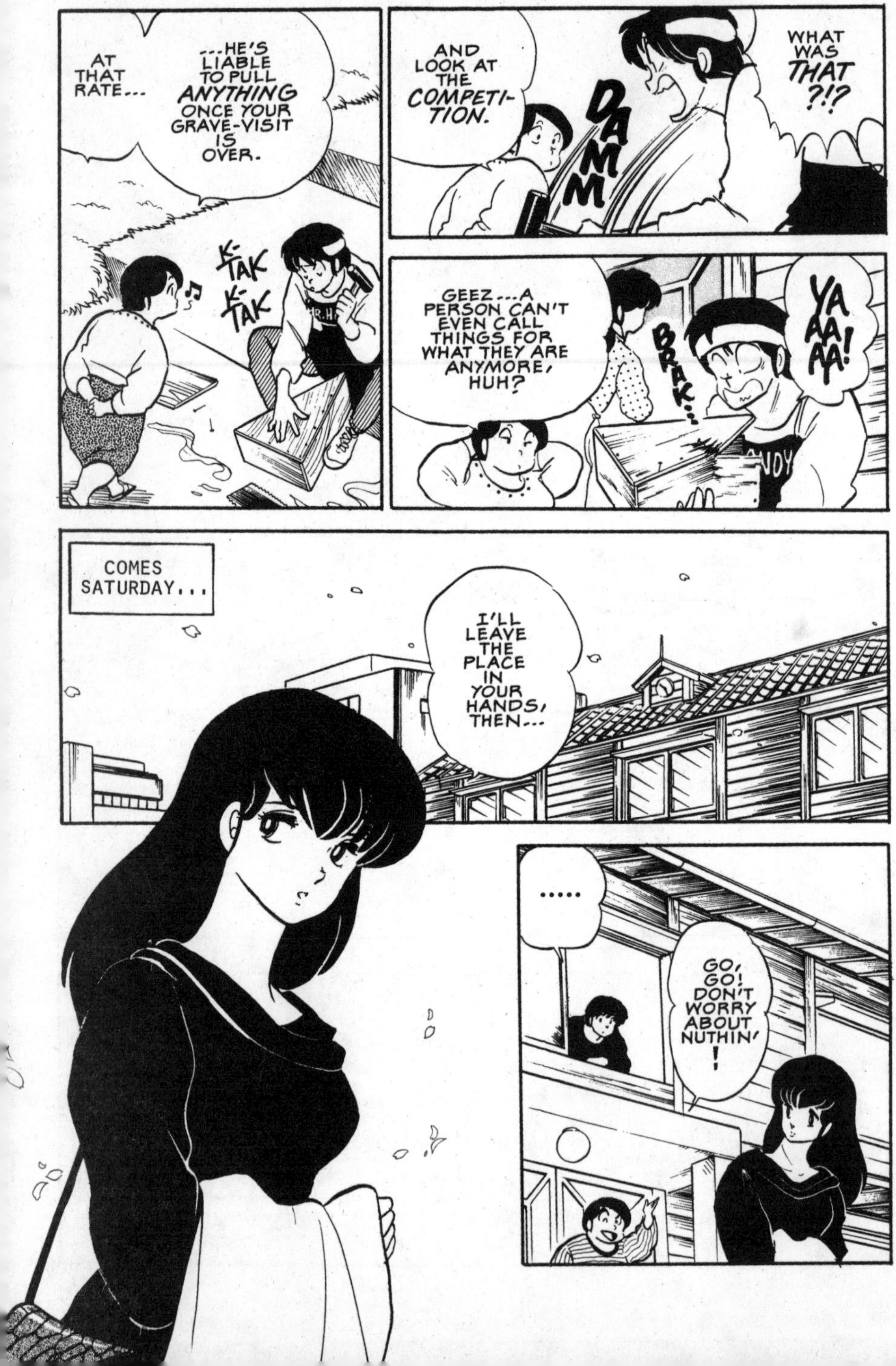
AT THAT RATE...
...HE'S LIABLE TO PULL ANYTHING ONCE YOUR GRAVE-VISIT IS OVER.
K-TAK K-TAK
AND LOOK AT THE COMPETITION.
DAMM
WHAT WAS THAT?!?
GEEZ...A PERSON CAN'T EVEN CALL THINGS FOR WHAT THEY ARE ANYMORE, HUH?
BRAK...
YAAAAA!
COMES SATURDAY...
I'LL LEAVE THE PLACE IN YOUR HANDS, THEN...
.....
GO, GO! DON'T WORRY ABOUT NUTHIN'!

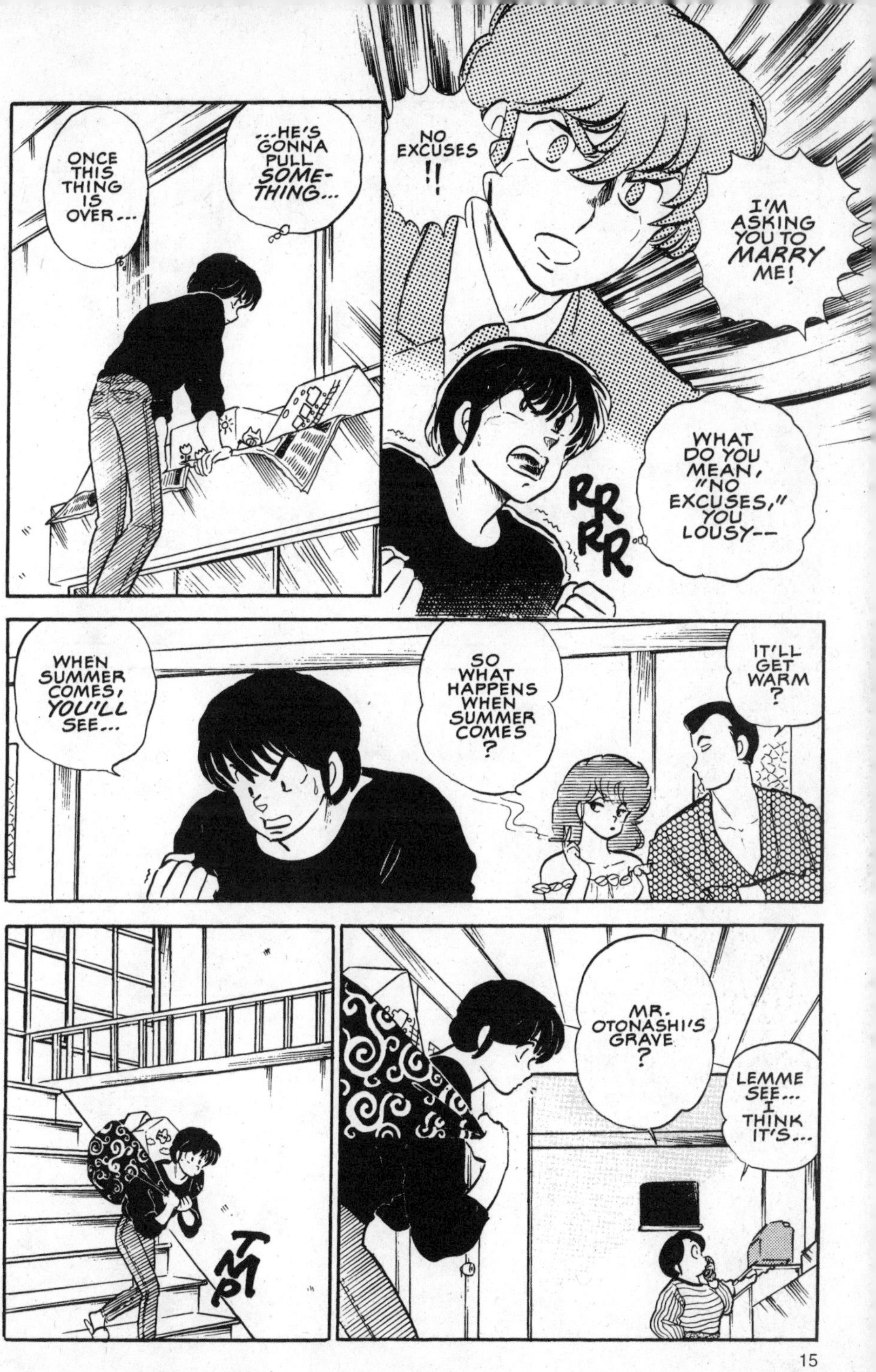

ONCE THIS THING IS OVER...
...HE'S GONNA PULL SOMETHING...
NO EXCUSES !!
I'M ASKING YOU TO MARRY ME!
RRRR
WHAT DO YOU MEAN, "NO EXCUSES," YOU LOUSY--
WHEN SUMMER COMES, YOU'LL SEE...
SO WHAT HAPPENS WHEN SUMMER COMES ?
IT'LL GET WARM ?
TMP
MR. OTONASHI'S GRAVE ?
LEMME SEE... I THINK IT'S...

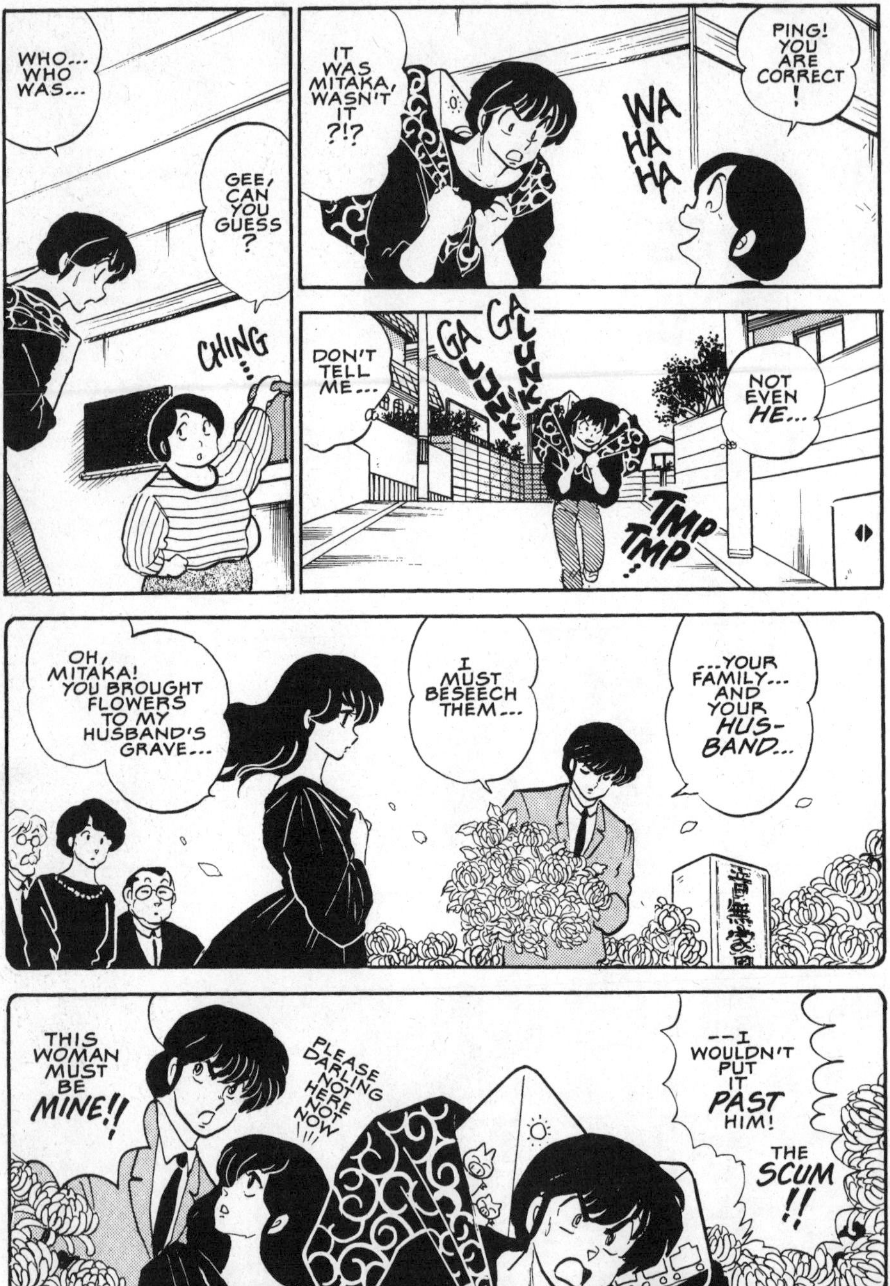
WHO... WHO WAS...
GEE, CAN YOU GUESS?
CHING...
IT WAS MITAKA, WASN'T IT ?!?
WA HA HA
PING! YOU ARE CORRECT!
DON'T TELL ME...
GA GA LUNK LUNK
NOT EVEN HE...
TMP TMP...
OH, MITAKA! YOU BROUGHT FLOWERS TO MY HUSBAND'S GRAVE...
I MUST BESEECH THEM...
...YOUR FAMILY... AND YOUR HUSBAND...
THIS WOMAN MUST BE MINE!!
PLEASE DARLING NOT HERE NOT NOW!!!
--I WOULDN'T PUT IT PAST HIM!
THE SCUM!!

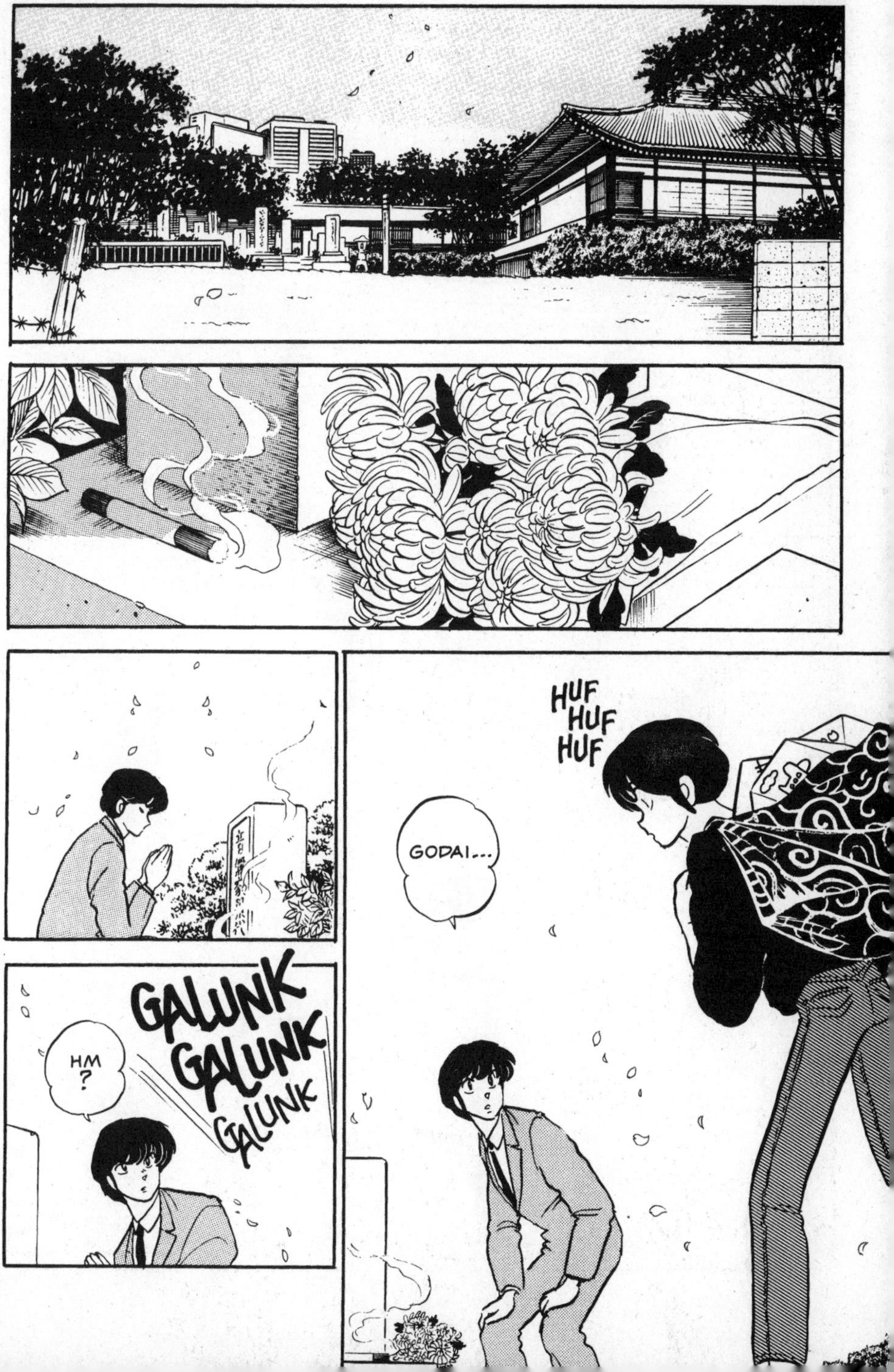
HUF
HUF
HUF
GODAI...
GALUNK
GALUNK
GALUNK
HM ?

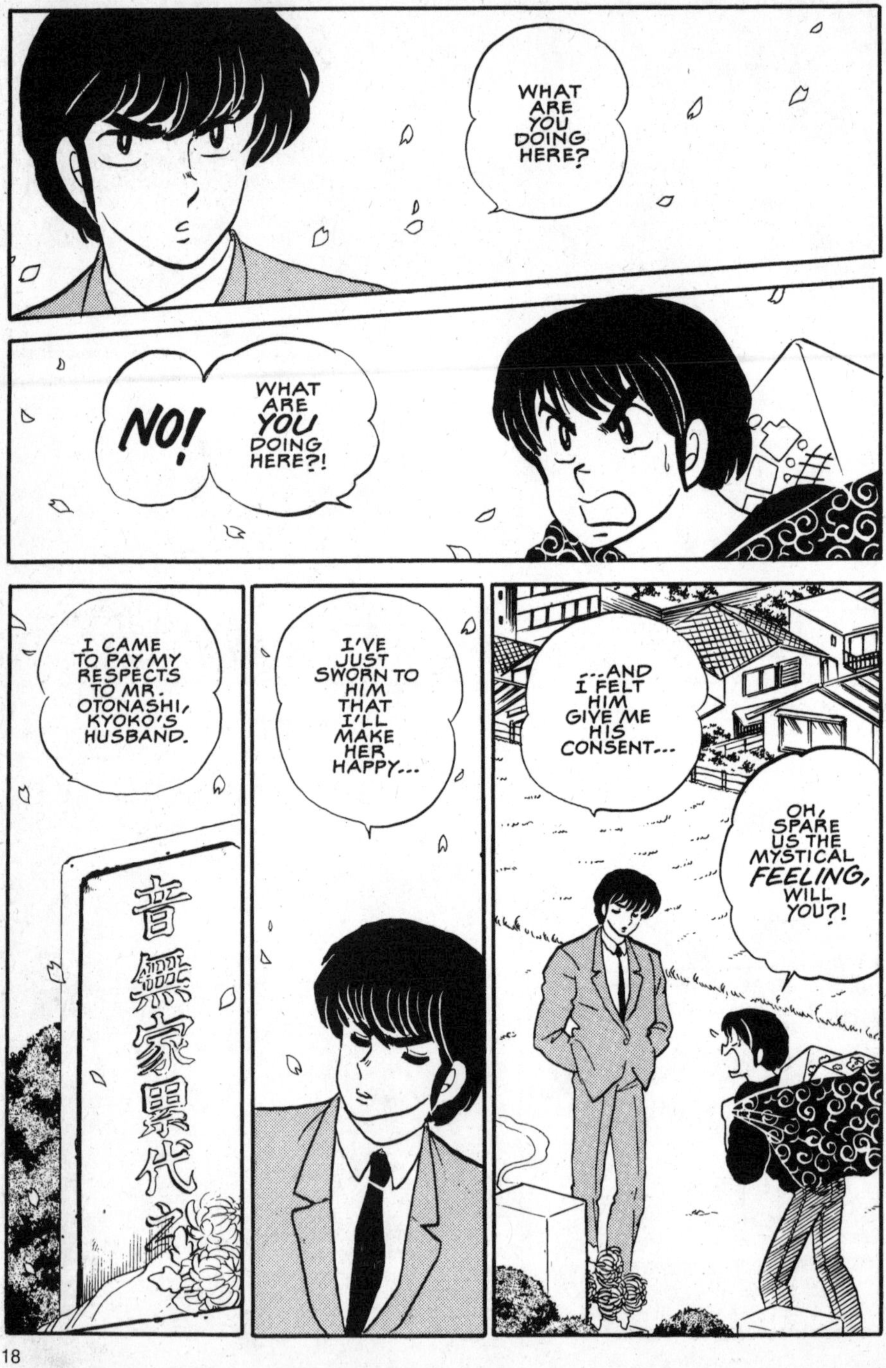
WHAT ARE YOU DOING HERE?
NO! WHAT ARE YOU DOING HERE?!
I CAME TO PAY MY RESPECTS TO MR. OTONASHI, KYOKO'S HUSBAND.
音無家累代之
I'VE JUST SWORN TO HIM THAT I'LL MAKE HER HAPPY...
...AND I FELT HIM GIVE ME HIS CONSENT...
OH, SPARE US THE MYSTICAL FEELING, WILL YOU?!

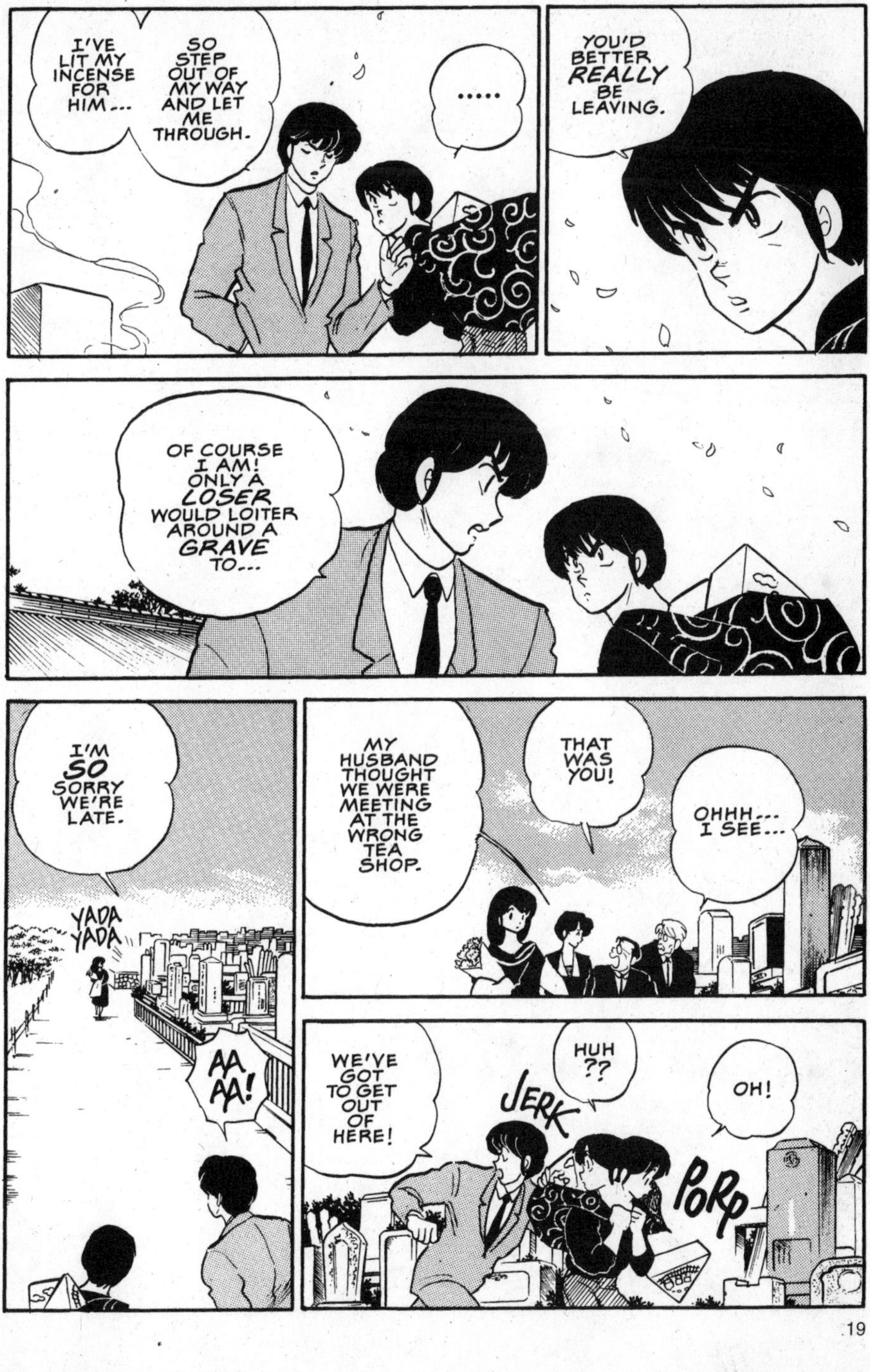
I'VE LIT MY INCENSE FOR HIM...
SO STEP OUT OF MY WAY AND LET ME THROUGH.
.....
YOU'D BETTER REALLY BE LEAVING.
OF COURSE I AM! ONLY A LOSER WOULD LOITER AROUND A GRAVE TO...
I'M SO SORRY WE'RE LATE.
YADA YADA
AAAA!
MY HUSBAND THOUGHT WE WERE MEETING AT THE WRONG TEA SHOP.
THAT WAS YOU!
OHHH... I SEE...
WE'VE GOT TO GET OUT OF HERE!
JERK
HUH ??
OH!
PORP

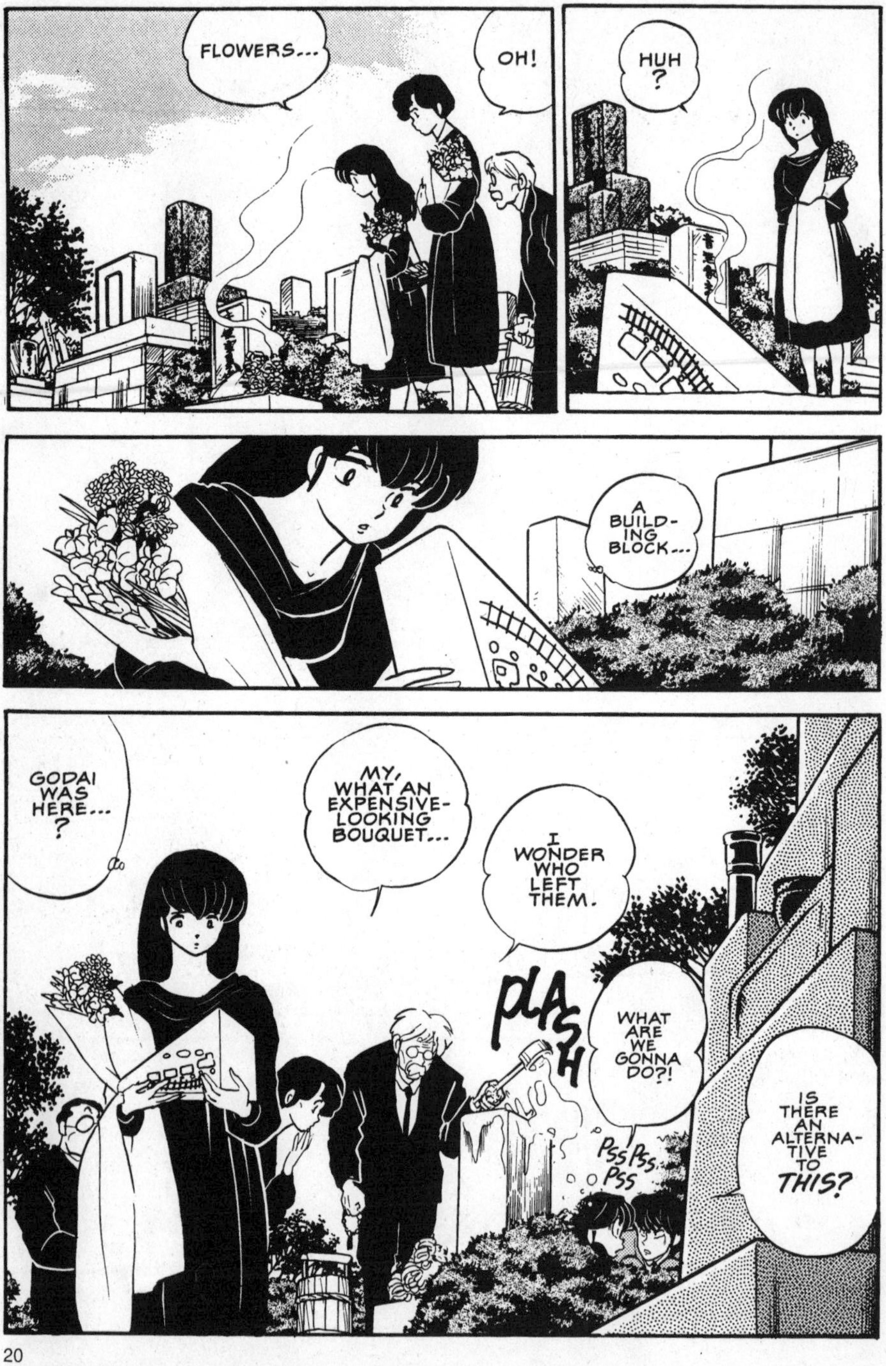
FLOWERS...
OH!
HUH?
A BUILDING BLOCK...
GODAI WAS HERE...?
MY, WHAT AN EXPENSIVE-LOOKING BOUQUET...
I WONDER WHO LEFT THEM.
PLASH
WHAT ARE WE GONNA DO?!
PSS PSS PSS
IS THERE AN ALTERNATIVE TO THIS?

PART TWO

BACK FROM THE GRAVE

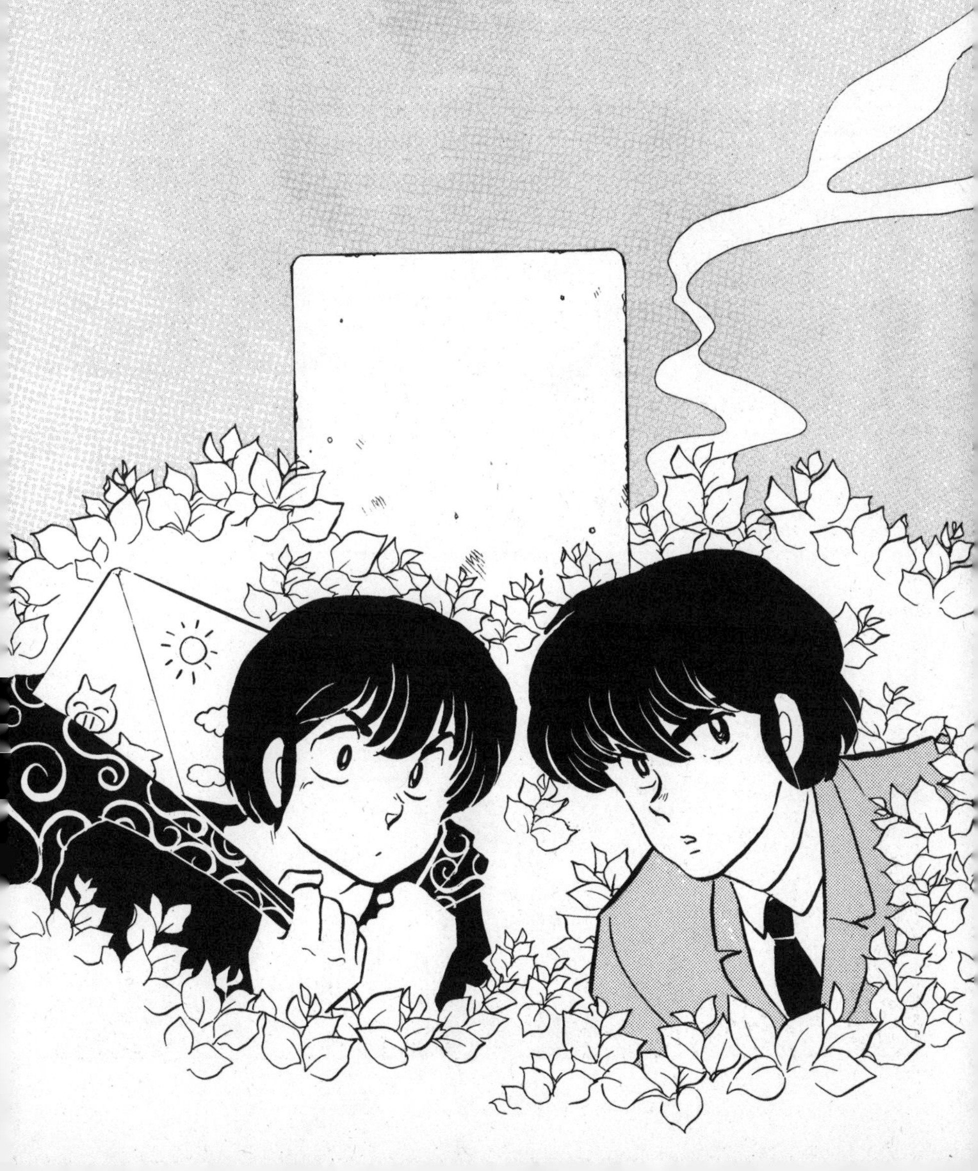

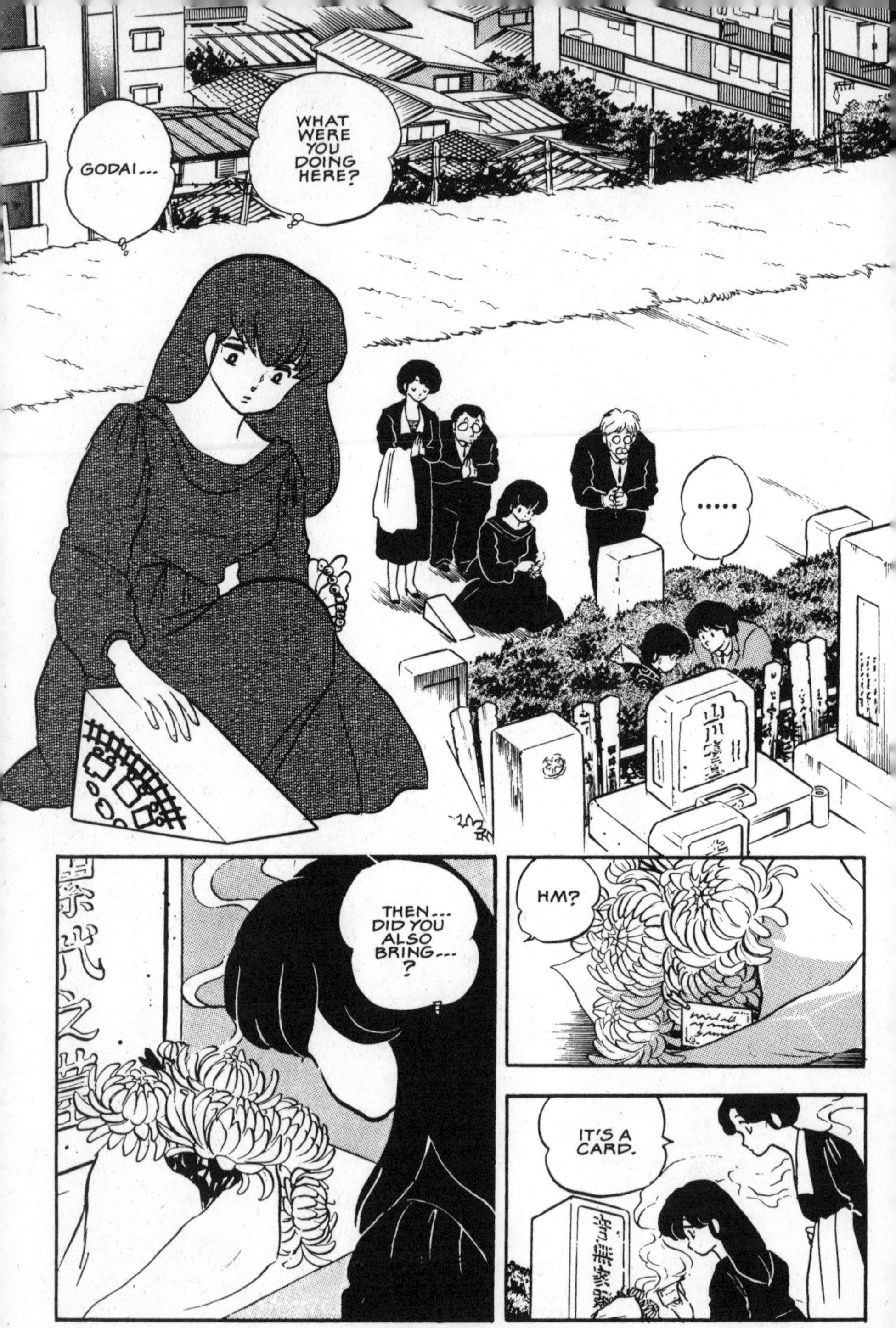
GODAI...
WHAT WERE YOU DOING HERE?
......
THEN... DID YOU ALSO BRING...?
HM?
IT'S A CARD.

IT WAS MITAKA...?

With all my heart. S. Mitaka

WELL.

ISN'T THAT THE TENNIS COACH...?

IS HE A FRIEND OF YOURS, KYOKO??

!

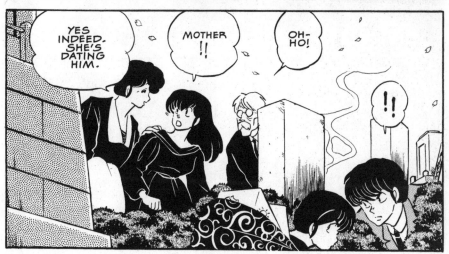

YES INDEED. SHE'S DATING HIM.

MOTHER!!

OH-HO!

!!

!!

HE'S THE COACH AT A TENNIS SCHOOL I'M ATTENDING... THAT'S ALL.

I SEE.

OH, LISTEN TO HER!

"THAT'S ALL," SHE SAYS!

WHAT?!?

.....

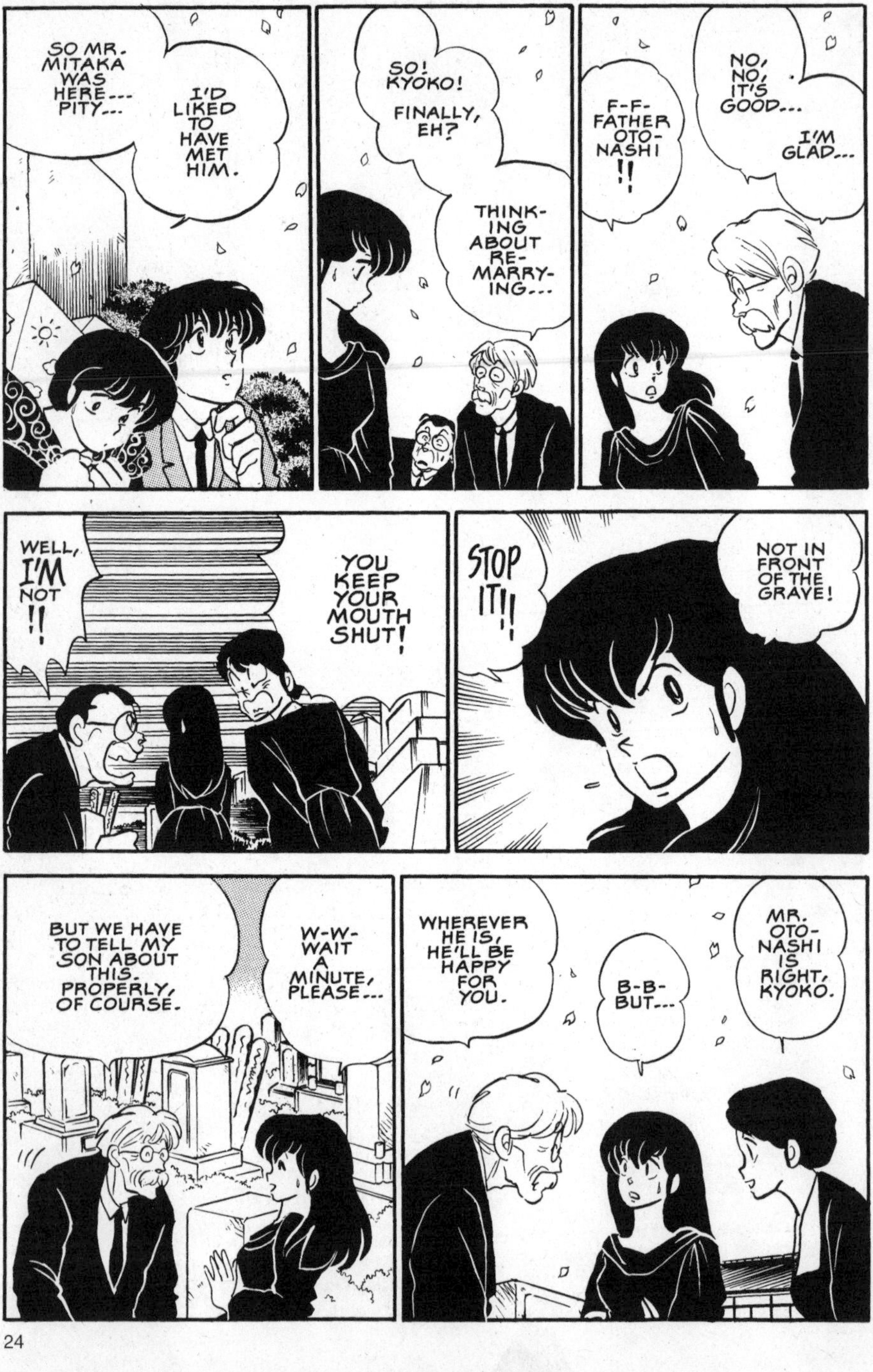
SO MR. MITAKA WAS HERE... PITY...
I'D LIKED TO HAVE MET HIM.
SO! KYOKO! FINALLY, EH?
THINKING ABOUT RE-MARRYING...
F-F-FATHER OTO-NASHI !!
NO, NO, IT'S GOOD... I'M GLAD...
WELL, I'M NOT !!
YOU KEEP YOUR MOUTH SHUT!
STOP IT!!
NOT IN FRONT OF THE GRAVE!
BUT WE HAVE TO TELL MY SON ABOUT THIS. PROPERLY, OF COURSE.
W-W-WAIT A MINUTE, PLEASE...
WHEREVER HE IS, HE'LL BE HAPPY FOR YOU.
B-B-BUT...
MR. OTO-NASHI IS RIGHT, KYOKO.

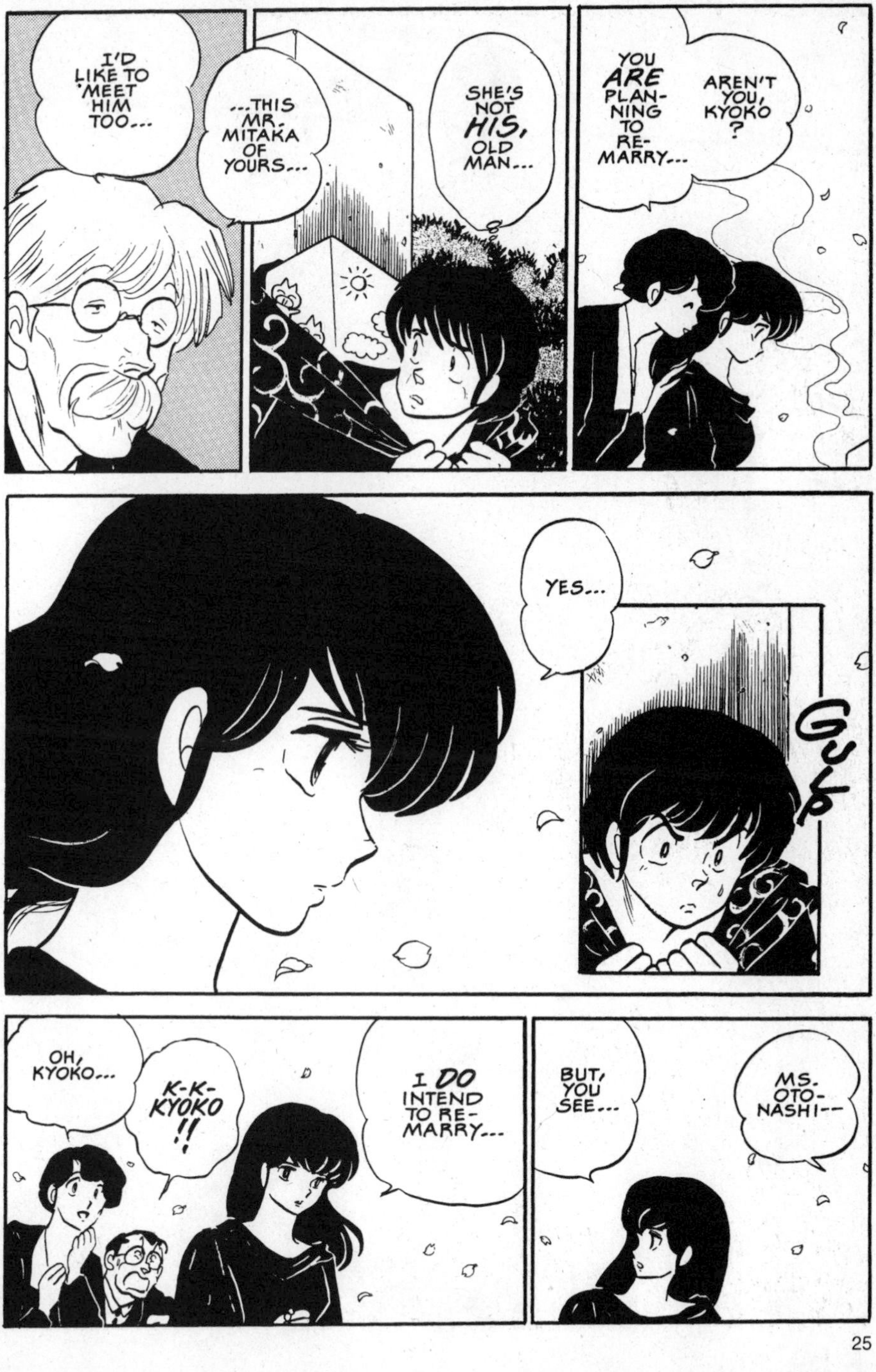
I'D LIKE TO MEET HIM TOO...
...THIS MR. MITAKA OF YOURS...
SHE'S NOT HIS, OLD MAN...
YOU ARE PLAN-NING TO RE-MARRY...
AREN'T YOU, KYOKO?
YES...
GULP
OH, KYOKO...
K-K-KYOKO!!
I DO INTEND TO RE-MARRY...
BUT, YOU SEE...
MS. OTO-NASHI--

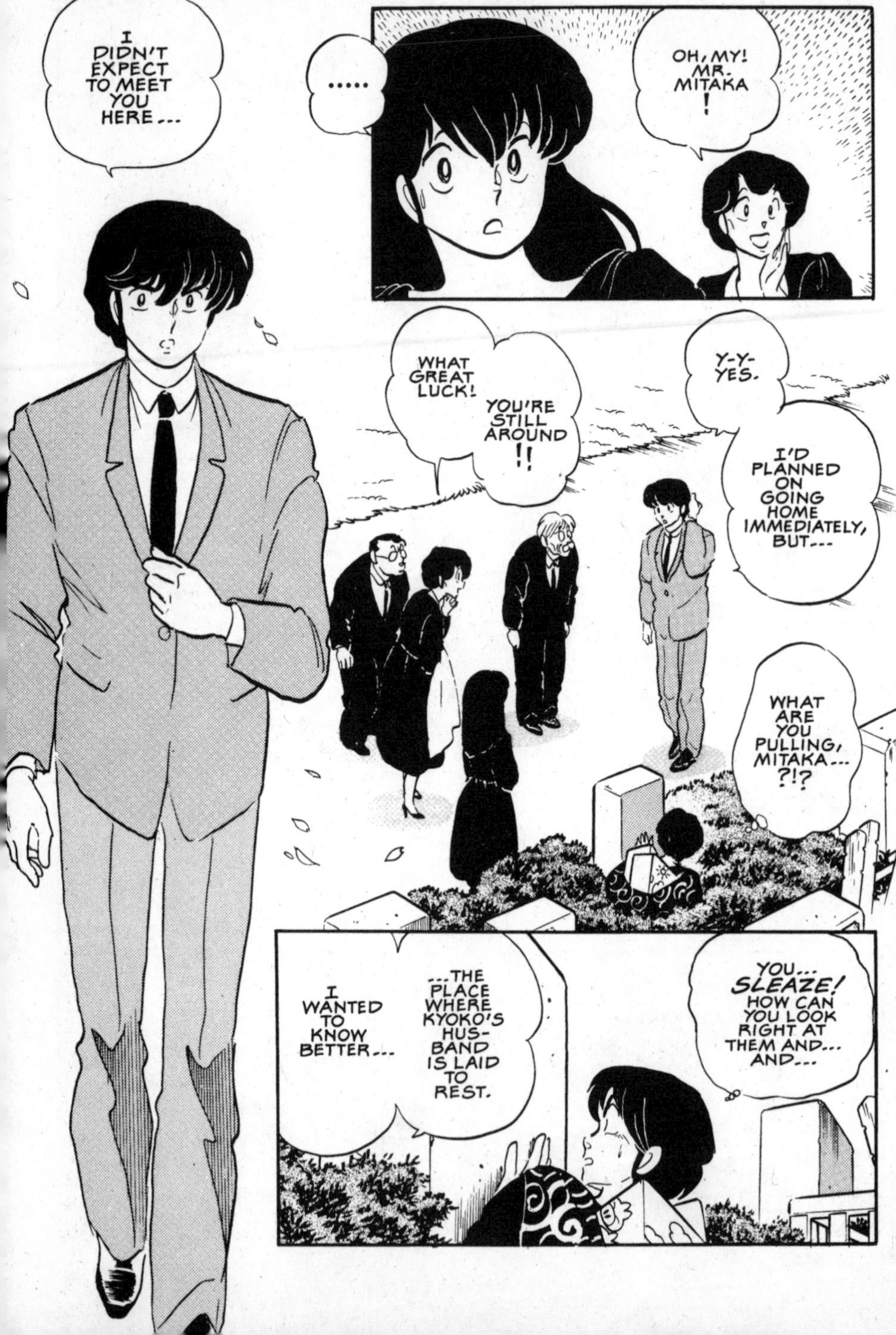
I DIDN'T EXPECT TO MEET YOU HERE...
.....
OH, MY! MR. MITAKA!
WHAT GREAT LUCK!
YOU'RE STILL AROUND!!
Y-Y-YES.
I'D PLANNED ON GOING HOME IMMEDIATELY, BUT...
WHAT ARE YOU PULLING, MITAKA...?!?
I WANTED TO KNOW BETTER...
...THE PLACE WHERE KYOKO'S HUS-BAND IS LAID TO REST.
YOU... SLEAZE! HOW CAN YOU LOOK RIGHT AT THEM AND... AND...

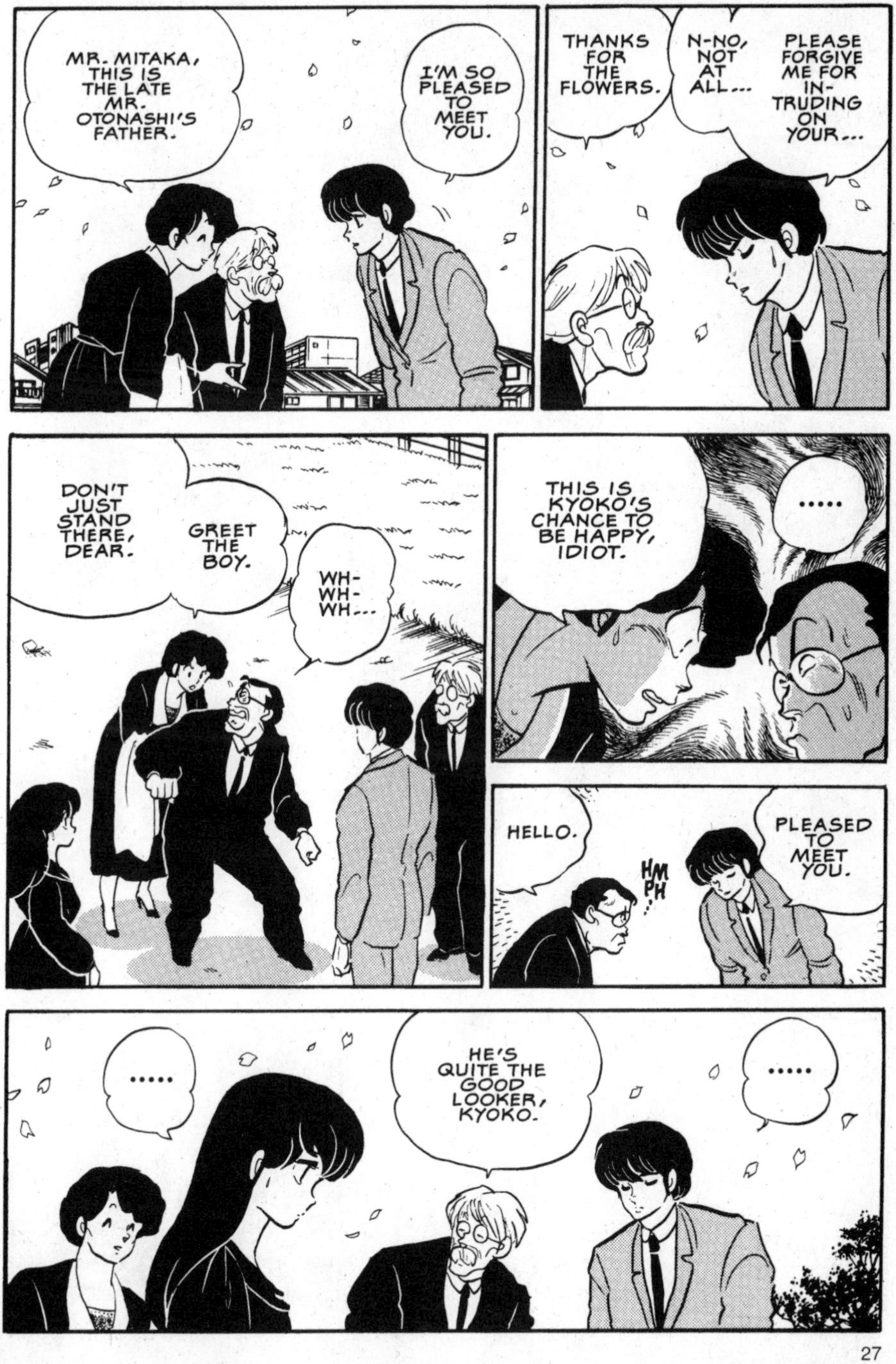
MR. MITAKA, THIS IS THE LATE MR. OTONASHI'S FATHER.
I'M SO PLEASED TO MEET YOU.
THANKS FOR THE FLOWERS.
N-NO, NOT AT ALL...
PLEASE FORGIVE ME FOR IN-TRUDING ON YOUR...
DON'T JUST STAND THERE, DEAR.
GREET THE BOY.
WH-WH-WH...
THIS IS KYOKO'S CHANCE TO BE HAPPY, IDIOT.
.....
HELLO.
HMPH
PLEASED TO MEET YOU.
.....
HE'S QUITE THE GOOD LOOKER, KYOKO.
.....

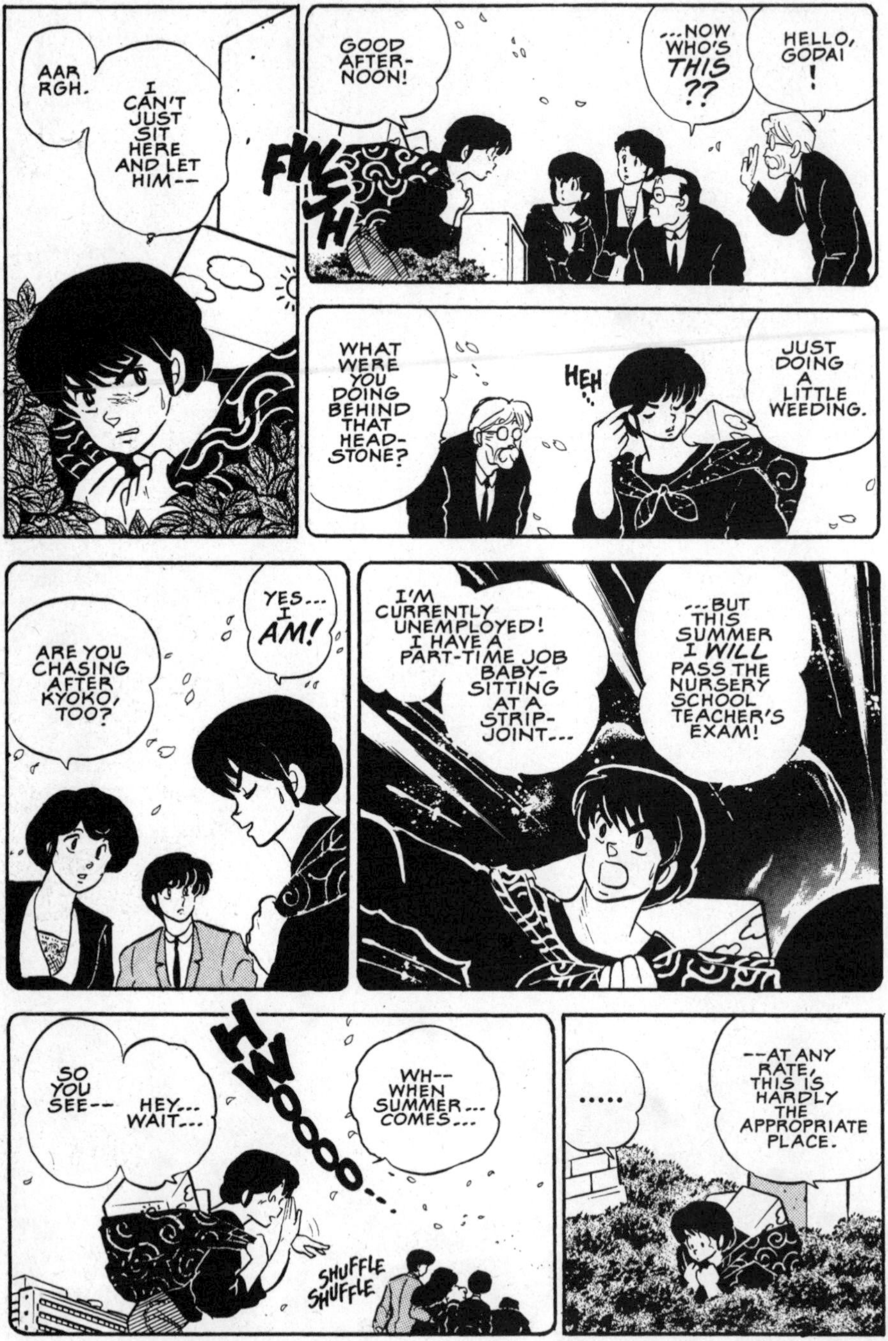
AAR RGH.
I CAN'T JUST SIT HERE AND LET HIM--
GOOD AFTER-NOON!
FWASH
...NOW WHO'S THIS ??
HELLO, GODAI !
WHAT WERE YOU DOING BEHIND THAT HEAD-STONE?
HEH
JUST DOING A LITTLE WEEDING.
ARE YOU CHASING AFTER KYOKO, TOO?
YES... I AM!
I'M CURRENTLY UNEMPLOYED! I HAVE A PART-TIME JOB BABY-SITTING AT A STRIP-JOINT...
...BUT THIS SUMMER I WILL PASS THE NURSERY SCHOOL TEACHER'S EXAM!
SO YOU SEE--
HEY... WAIT...
HWOOOOO...
WH-- WHEN SUMMER... COMES...
SHUFFLE SHUFFLE
.....
--AT ANY RATE, THIS IS HARDLY THE APPROPRIATE PLACE.

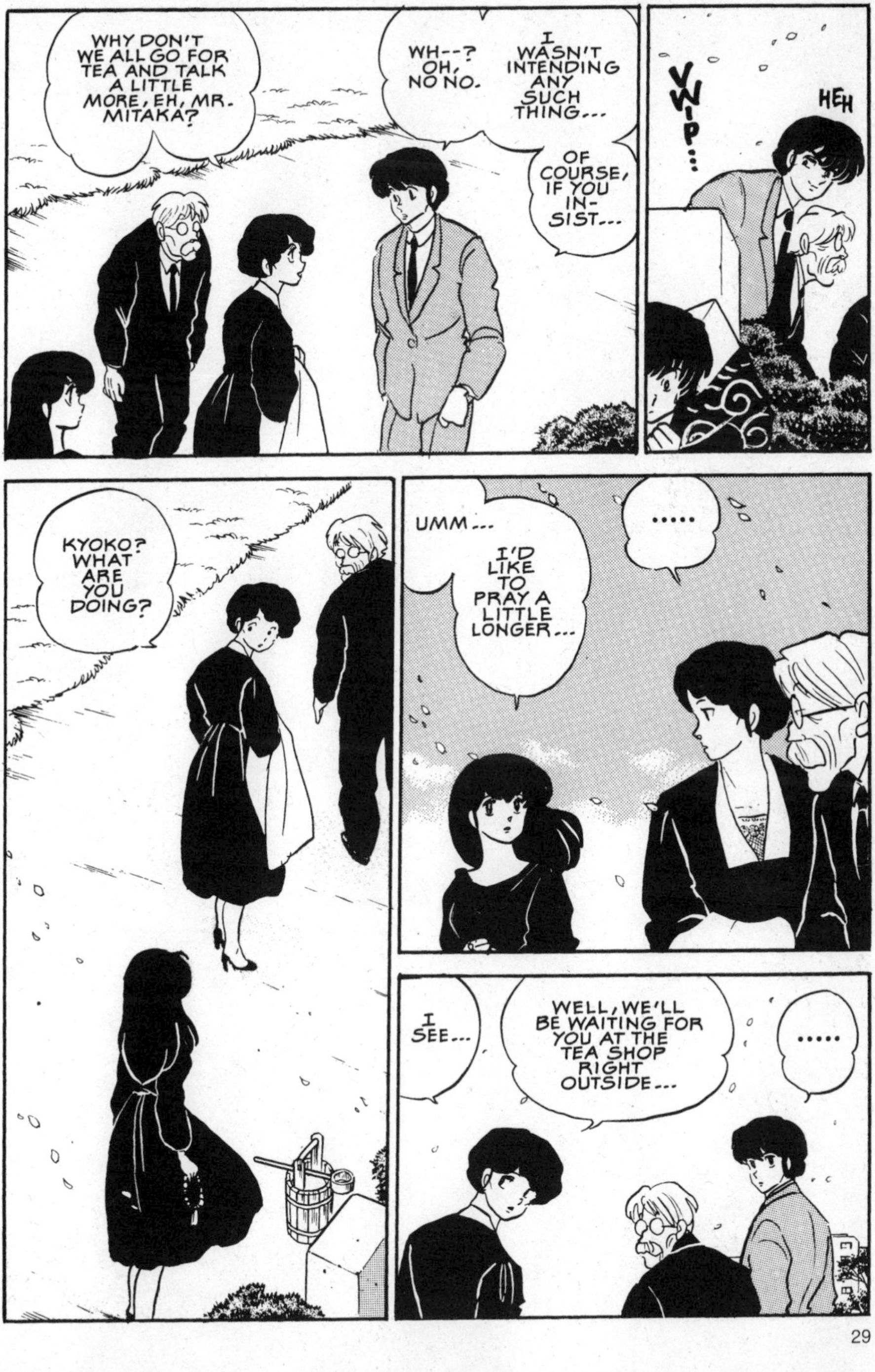
WHY DON'T WE ALL GO FOR TEA AND TALK A LITTLE MORE, EH, MR. MITAKA?
WH--? OH, NO NO.
I WASN'T INTENDING ANY SUCH THING...
OF COURSE, IF YOU IN-SIST...
VWIP...
HEH
KYOKO? WHAT ARE YOU DOING?
UMM...
I'D LIKE TO PRAY A LITTLE LONGER...
.....
I SEE...
WELL, WE'LL BE WAITING FOR YOU AT THE TEA SHOP RIGHT OUTSIDE...
.....

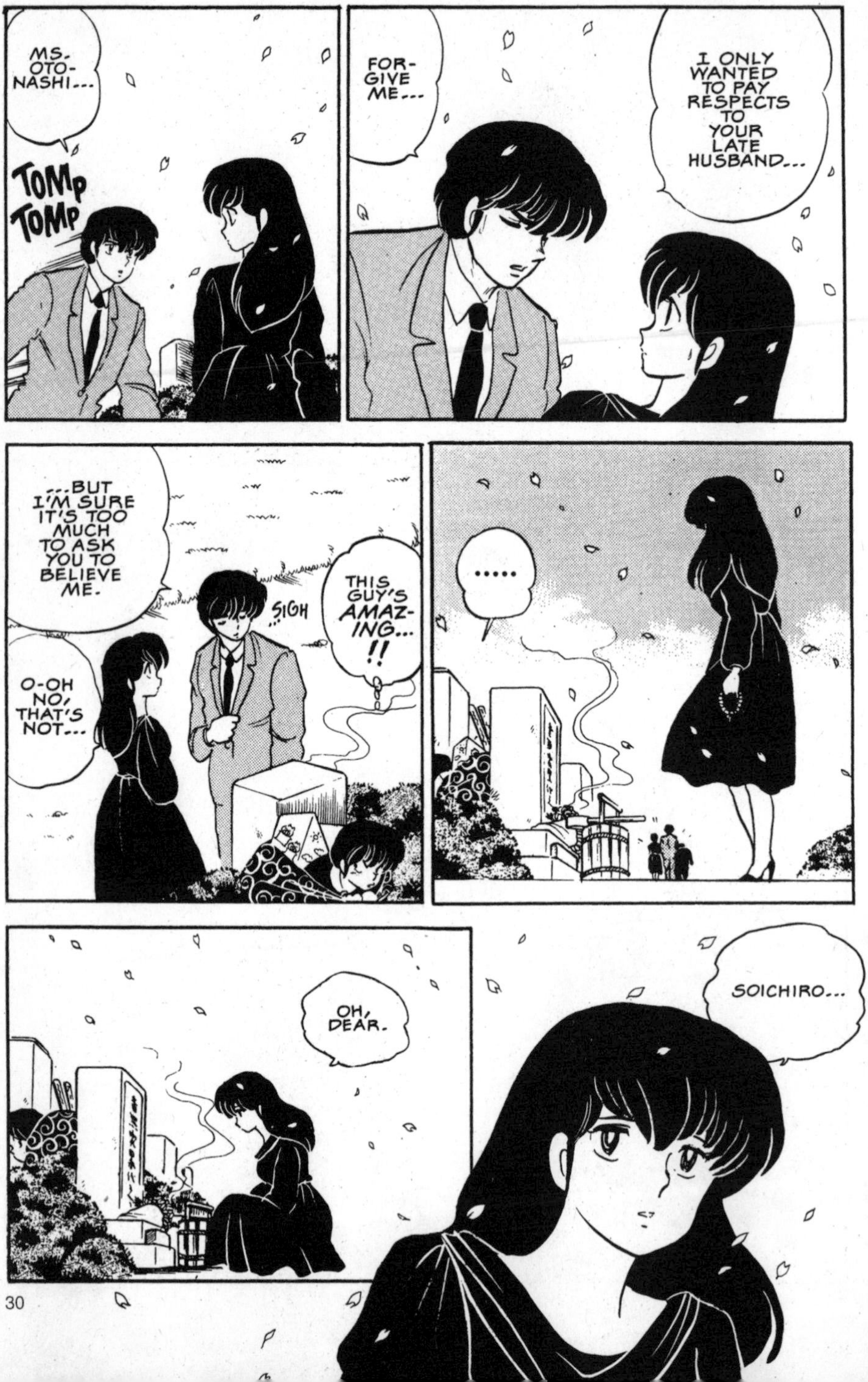
MS. OTO-NASHI...
TOMP TOMP
FOR-GIVE ME...
I ONLY WANTED TO PAY RESPECTS TO YOUR LATE HUSBAND...
...BUT I'M SURE IT'S TOO MUCH TO ASK YOU TO BELIEVE ME.
SIGH
THIS GUY'S AMAZ-ING...!!
O-OH NO, THAT'S NOT...
......
OH, DEAR.
SOICHIRO...

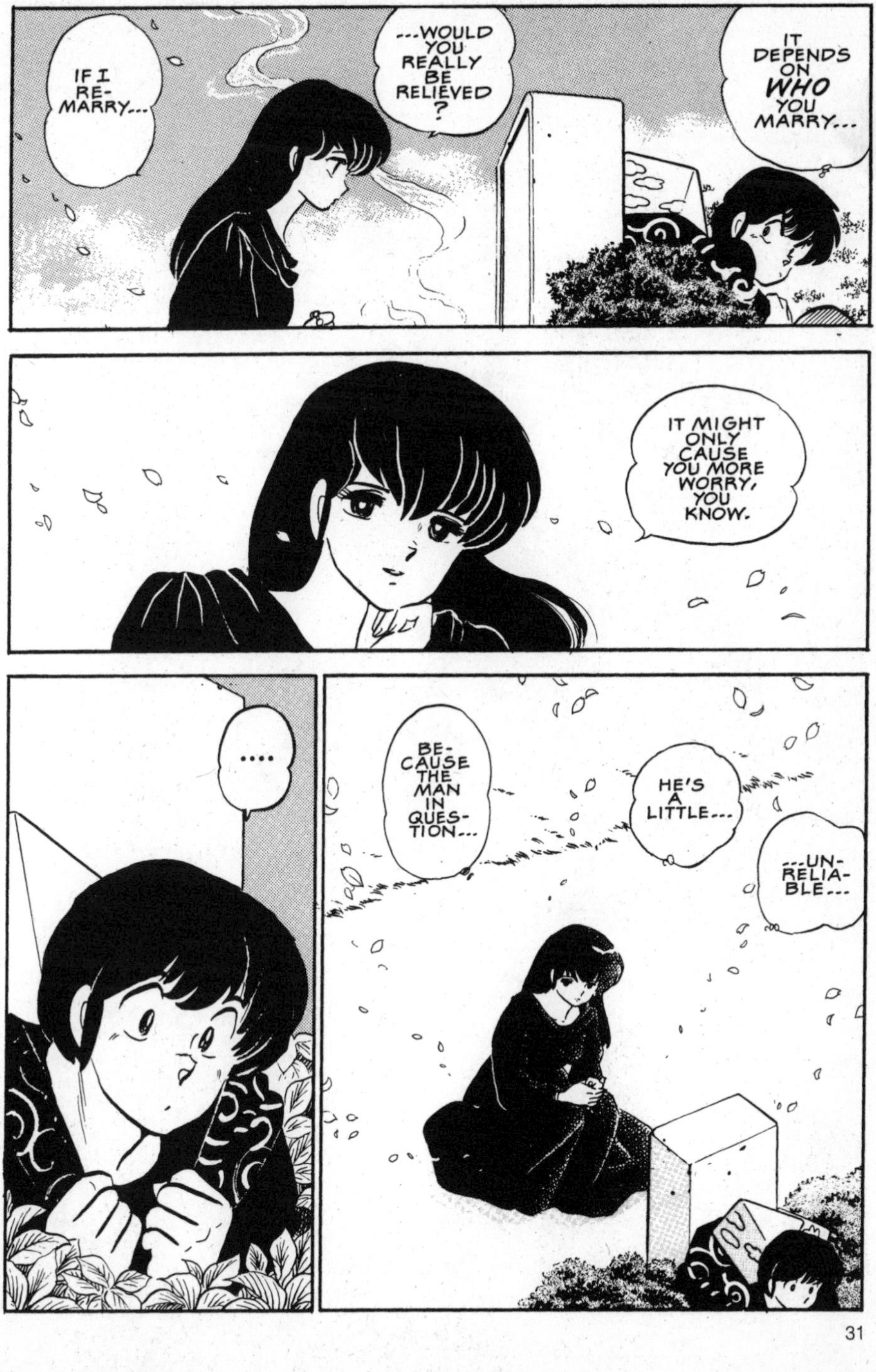
IF I RE-MARRY...
...WOULD YOU REALLY BE RELIEVED?
IT DEPENDS ON WHO YOU MARRY...
IT MIGHT ONLY CAUSE YOU MORE WORRY, YOU KNOW.
....
BE-CAUSE THE MAN IN QUES-TION...
HE'S A LITTLE...
...UN-RELIA-BLE...

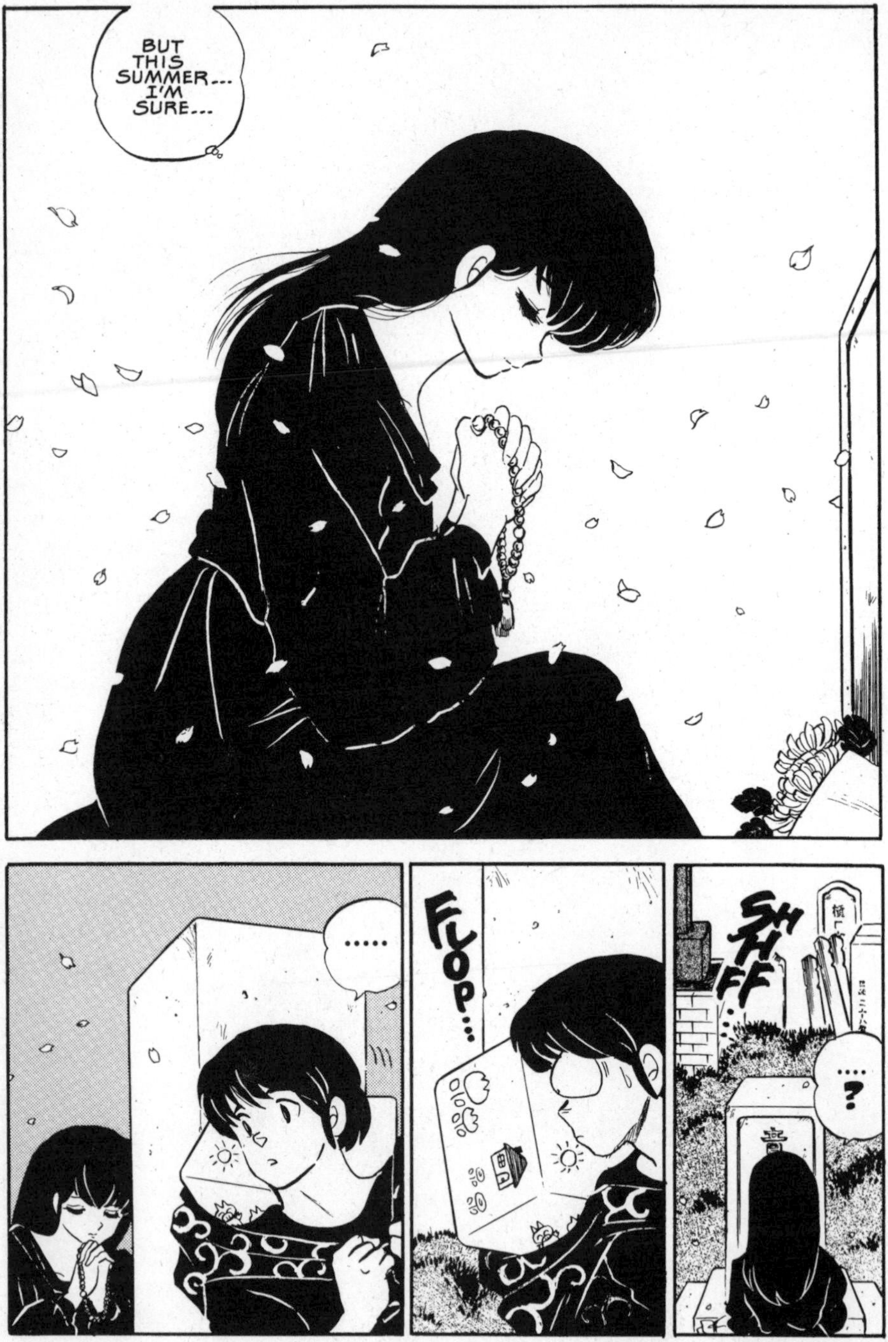
BUT THIS SUMMER... I'M SURE...
.....
FLOP...
SHHFF
....?

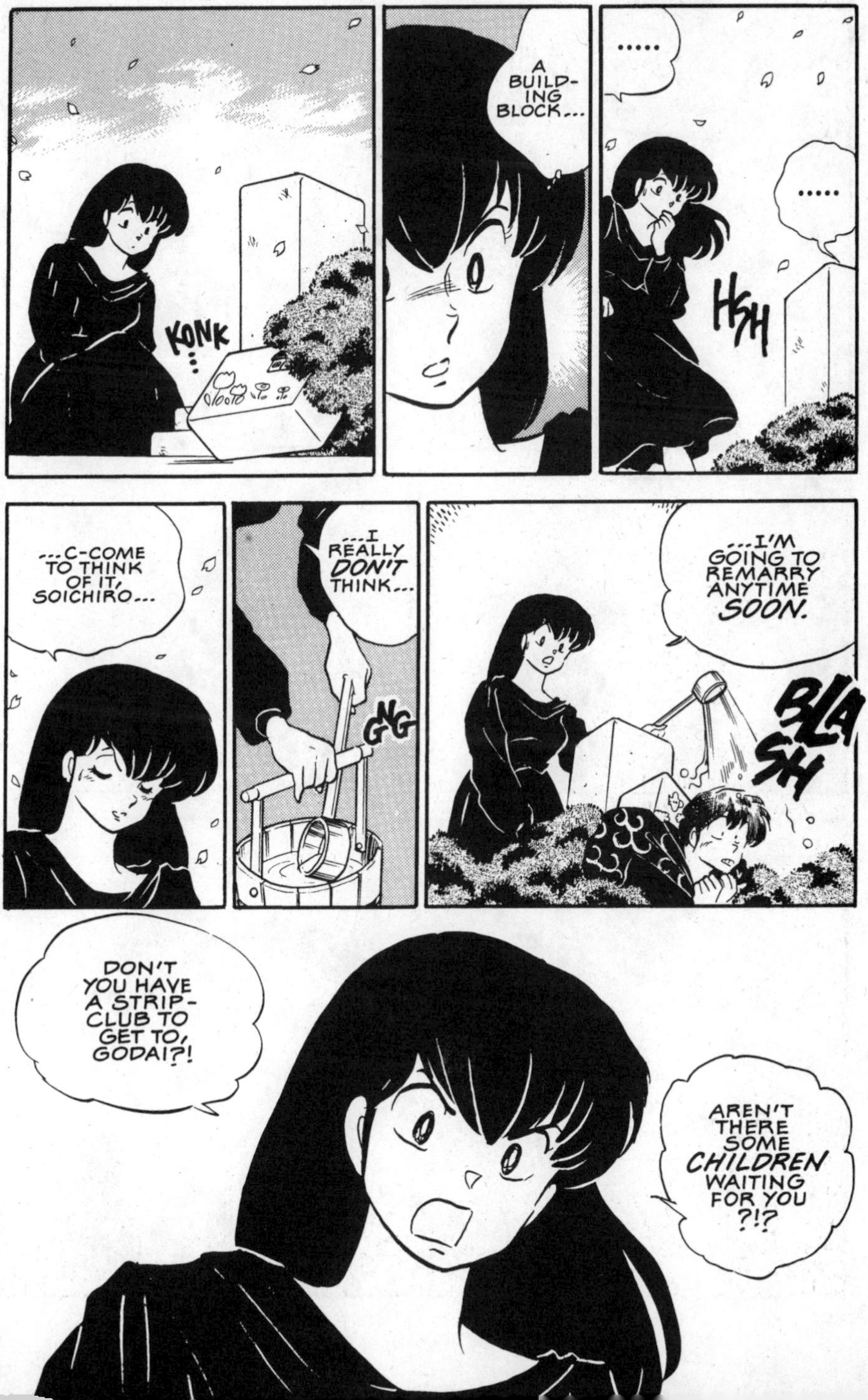
KONK
A BUILD-ING BLOCK...
......
......
HSH
...C-COME TO THINK OF IT, SOICHIRO...
...I REALLY DON'T THINK...
GNG
...I'M GOING TO REMARRY ANYTIME SOON.
BLASH
DON'T YOU HAVE A STRIP-CLUB TO GET TO, GODAI?!
AREN'T THERE SOME CHILDREN WAITING FOR YOU?!?

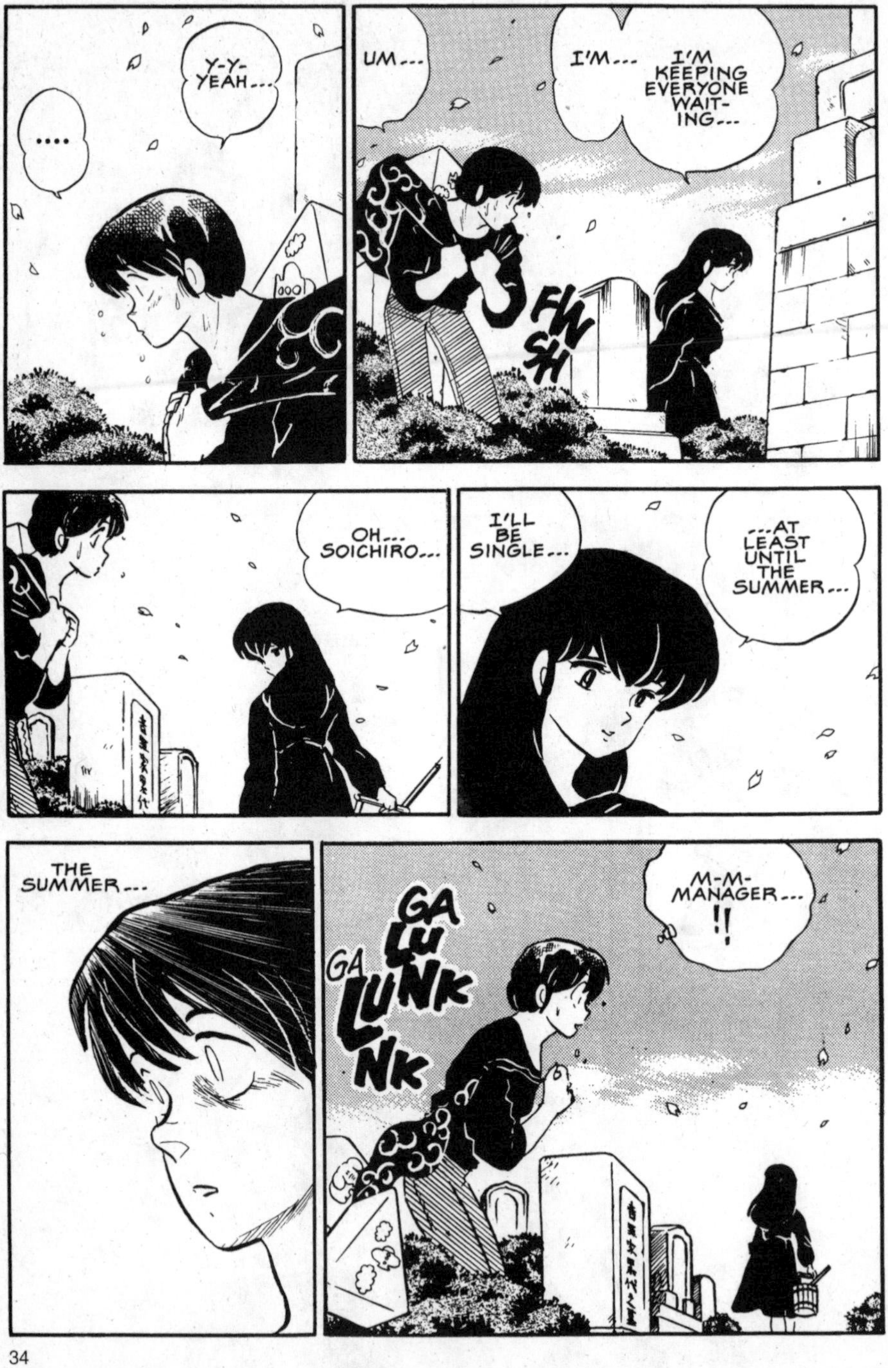
.....
Y-Y-YEAH...
UM...
I'M... I'M KEEPING EVERYONE WAITING...
FWSH
OH... SOICHIRO...
I'LL BE SINGLE...
...AT LEAST UNTIL THE SUMMER...
THE SUMMER...
GA LUNK GA LUNK
M-M-MANAGER... !!

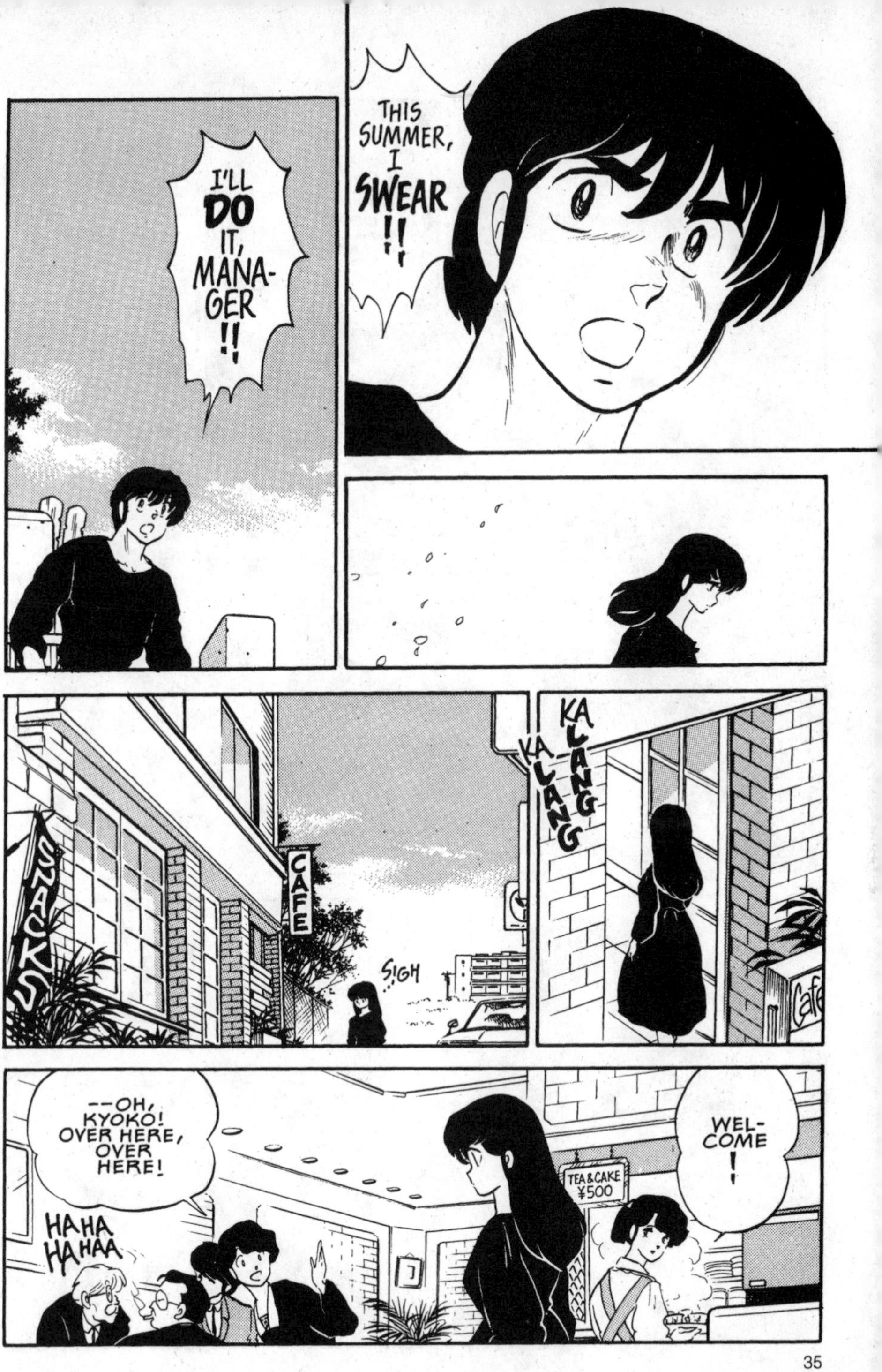
I'LL DO IT, MANAGER!!
THIS SUMMER, I SWEAR!!
SNACKS
CAFE
SIGH
KA LANG KA LANG
Cafe
--OH, KYOKO! OVER HERE, OVER HERE!
HA HA HA HAA
TEA & CAKE ¥500
WELCOME!

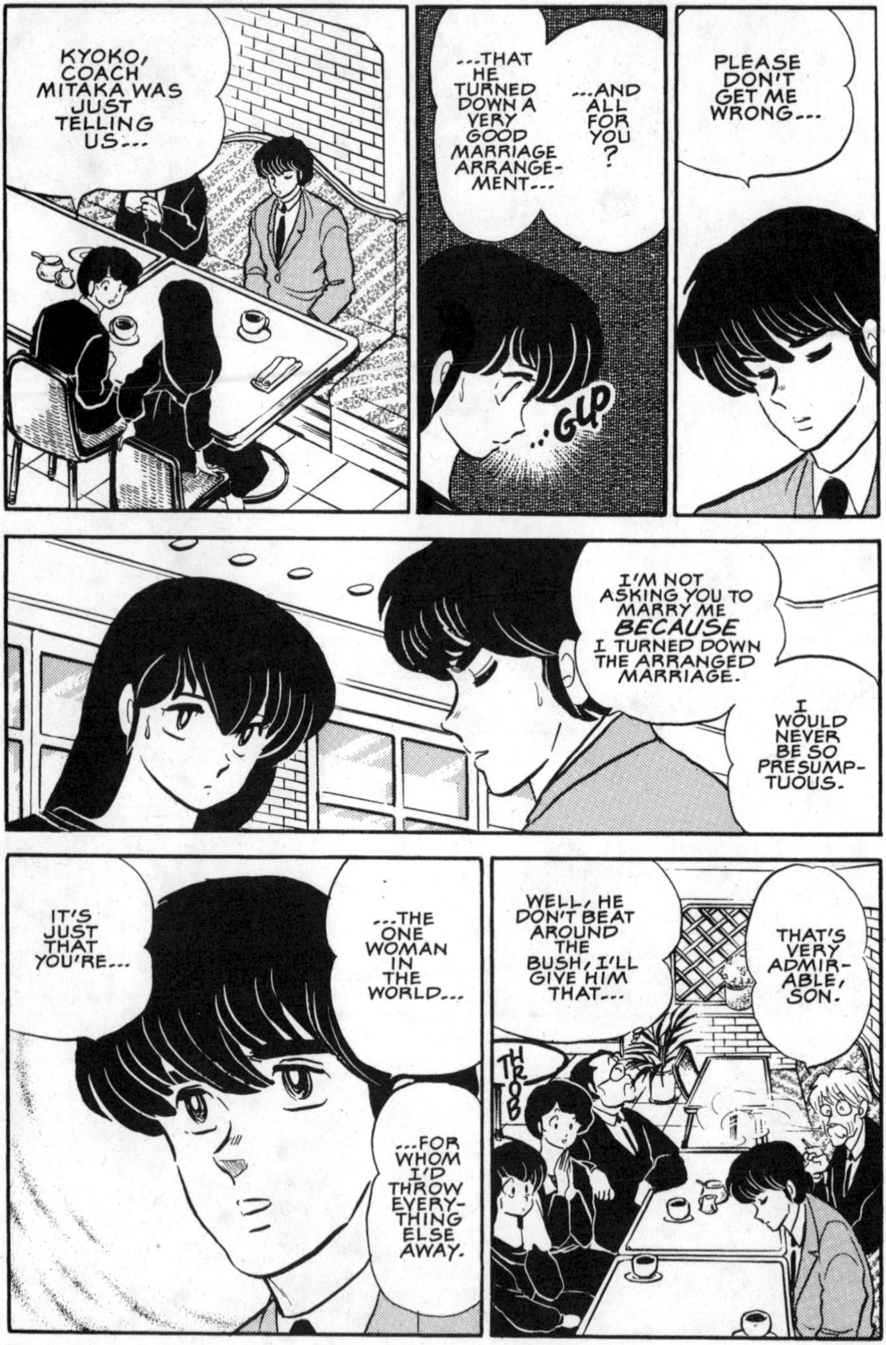
KYOKO, COACH MITAKA WAS JUST TELLING US...
...THAT HE TURNED DOWN A VERY GOOD MARRIAGE ARRANGE-MENT...
...AND ALL FOR YOU?
...GLP
PLEASE DON'T GET ME WRONG...
I'M NOT ASKING YOU TO MARRY ME BECAUSE I TURNED DOWN THE ARRANGED MARRIAGE.
I WOULD NEVER BE SO PRESUMP-TUOUS.
IT'S JUST THAT YOU'RE...
...THE ONE WOMAN IN THE WORLD...
...FOR WHOM I'D THROW EVERY-THING ELSE AWAY.
WELL, HE DON'T BEAT AROUND THE BUSH, I'LL GIVE HIM THAT...
THAT'S VERY ADMIR-ABLE, SON.
THROB

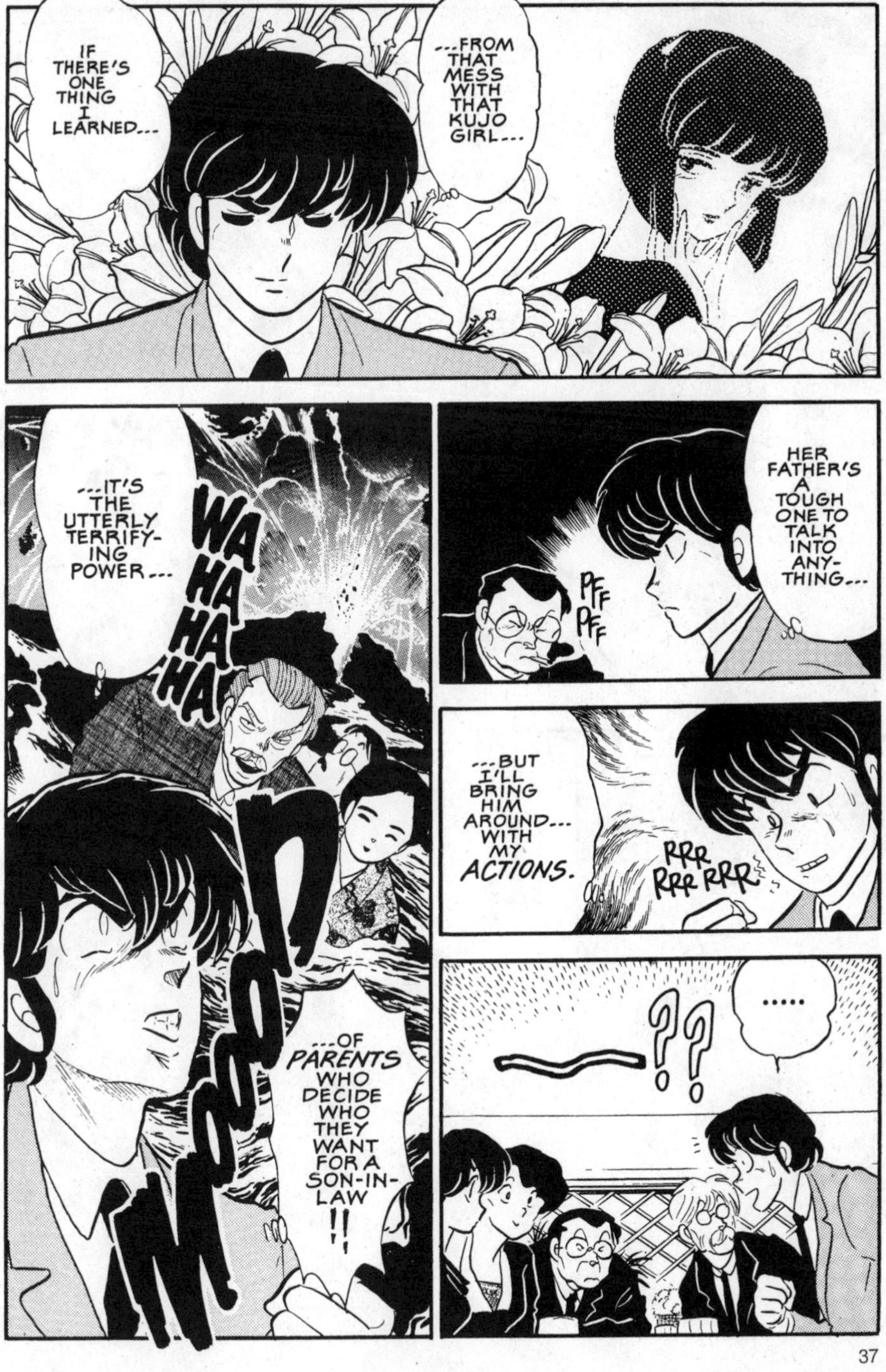
IF THERE'S ONE THING I LEARNED...
...FROM THAT MESS WITH THAT KUJO GIRL...
...IT'S THE UTTERLY TERRIFYING POWER...
WA HA HA HA HA
...OF PARENTS WHO DECIDE WHO THEY WANT FOR A SON-IN-LAW!!
HER FATHER'S A TOUGH ONE TO TALK INTO ANYTHING...
PFF PFF
...BUT I'LL BRING HIM AROUND... WITH MY ACTIONS.
RRR RRR RRR
.....
??

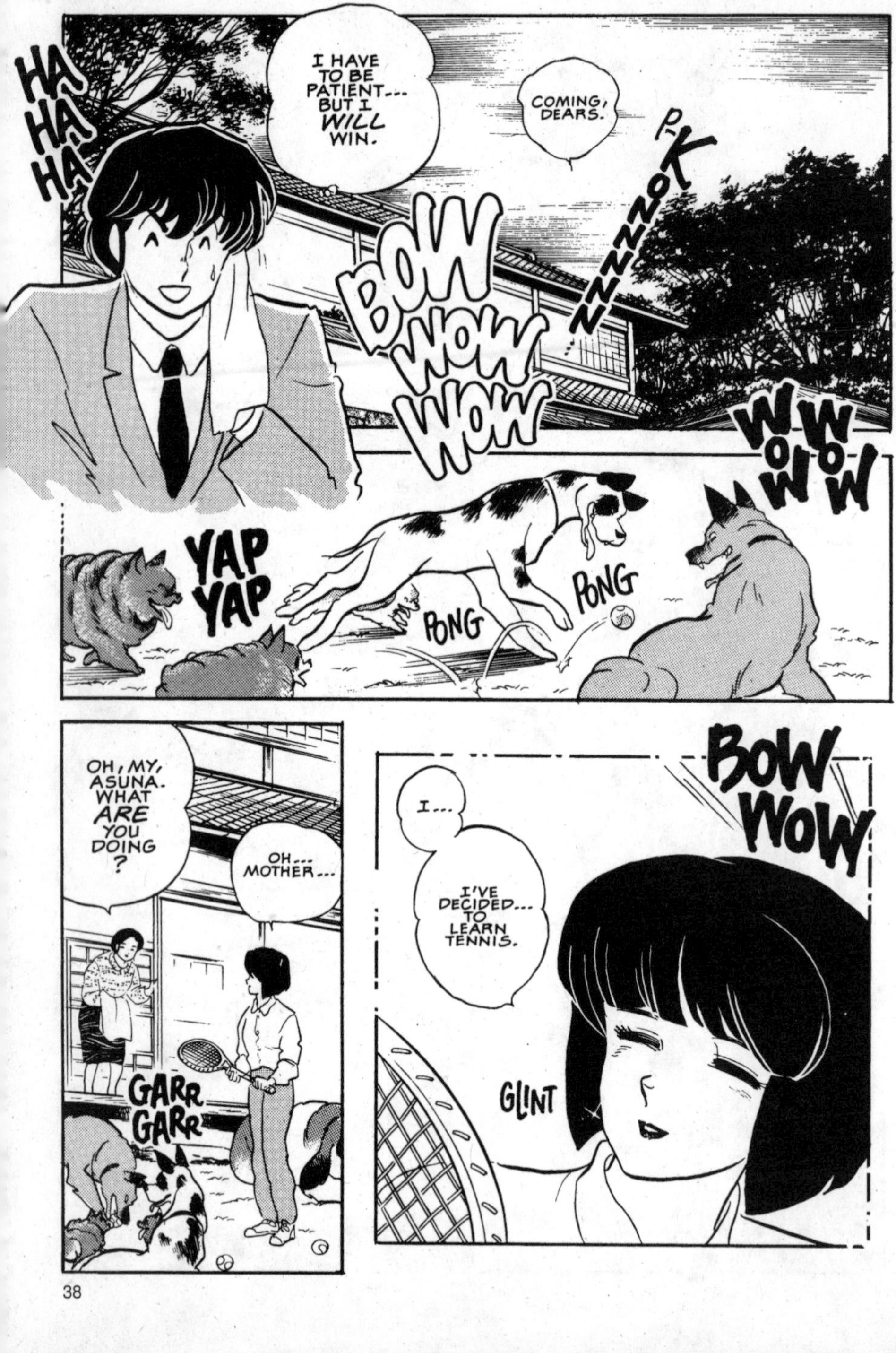
HA HA HA
I HAVE TO BE PATIENT... BUT I WILL WIN.
COMING, DEARS.
P-KONNNNNN
BOW WOW WOW
WOW WOW WOW
YAP YAP
PONG
PONG
OH, MY, ASUNA. WHAT ARE YOU DOING?
OH... MOTHER...
GARR GARR
I...
I'VE DECIDED... TO LEARN TENNIS.
BOW WOW
GLINT

PART THREE

NEVER LET YOU GO

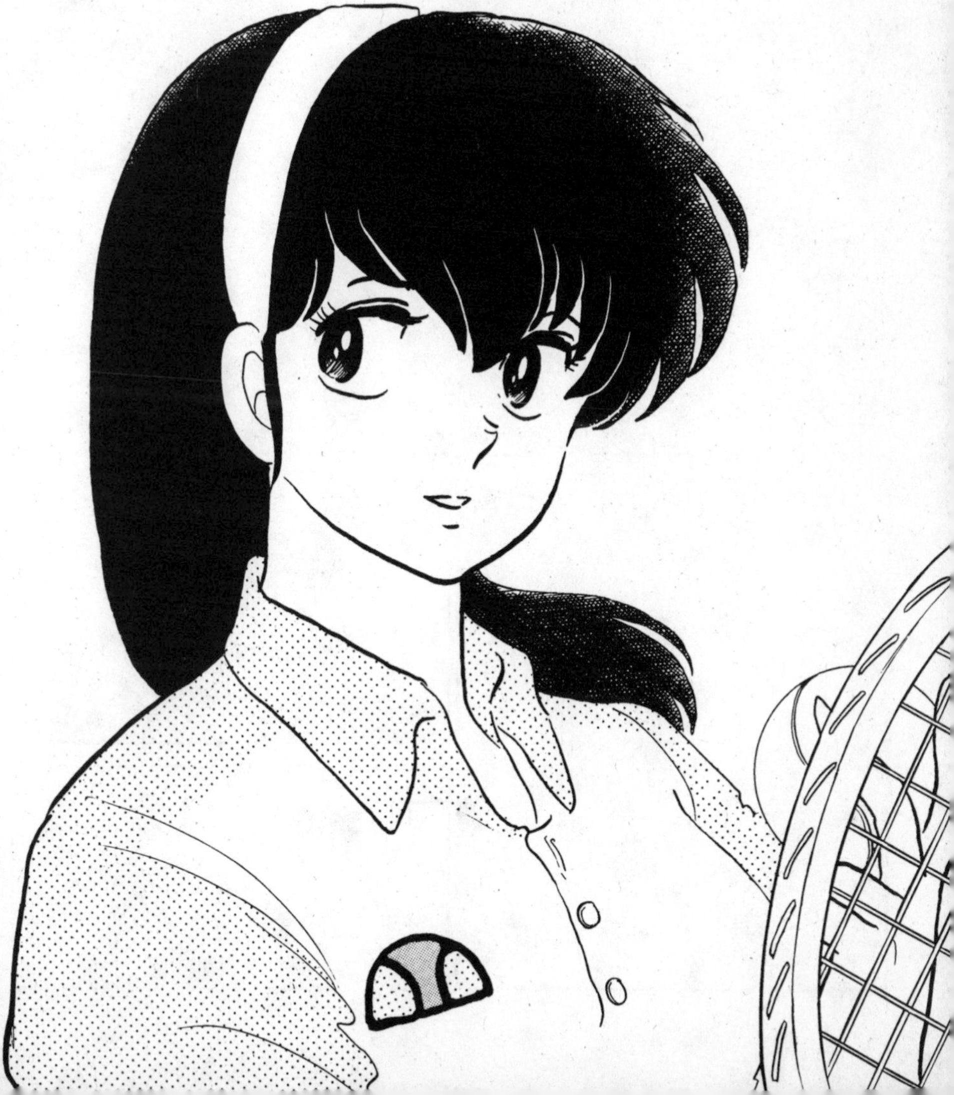

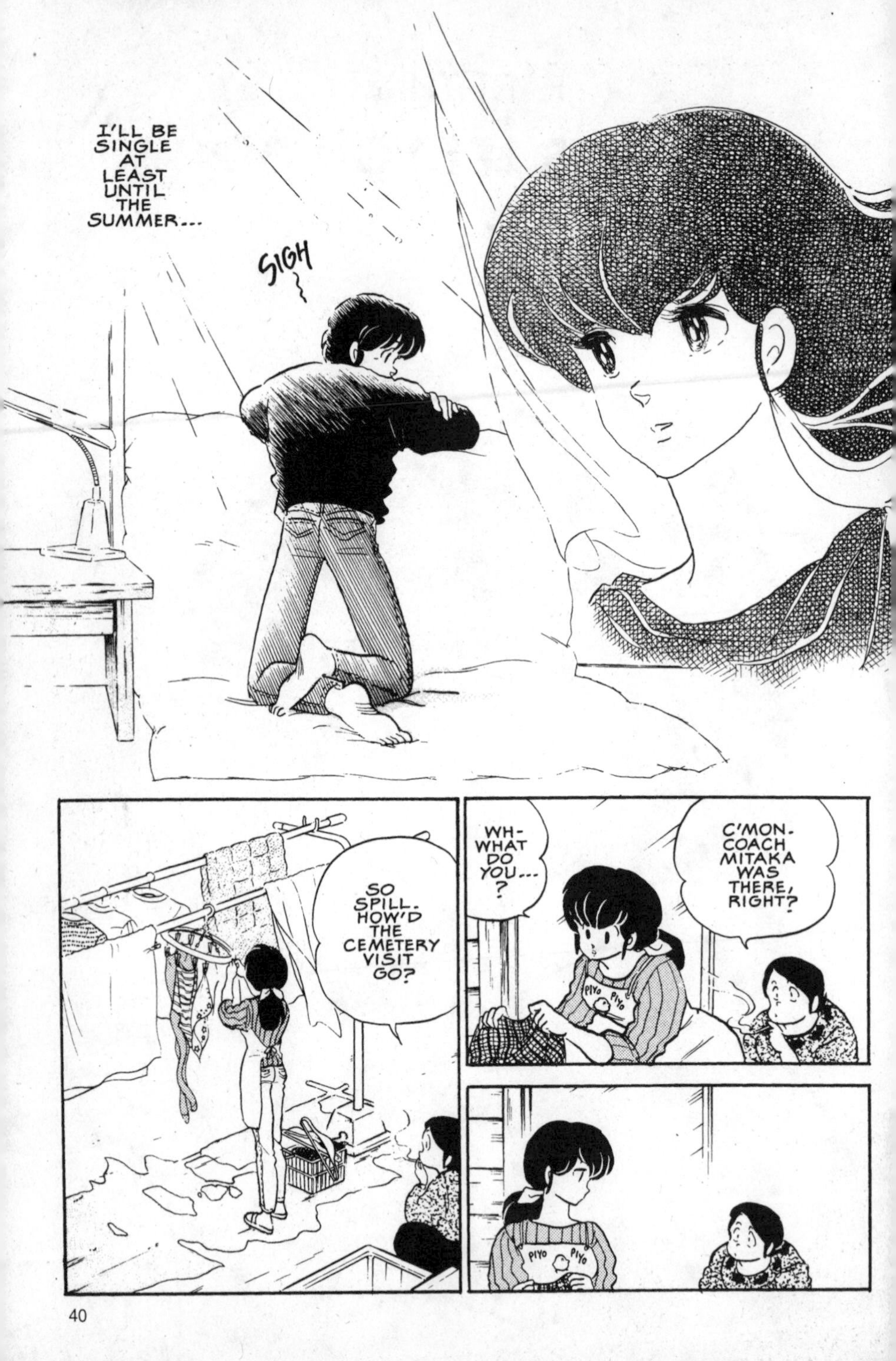
I'LL BE SINGLE AT LEAST UNTIL THE SUMMER...
SIGH
SO SPILL. HOW'D THE CEMETERY VISIT GO?
WH-WHAT DO YOU...?
C'MON. COACH MITAKA WAS THERE, RIGHT?
PIYO PIYO
PIYO PIYO

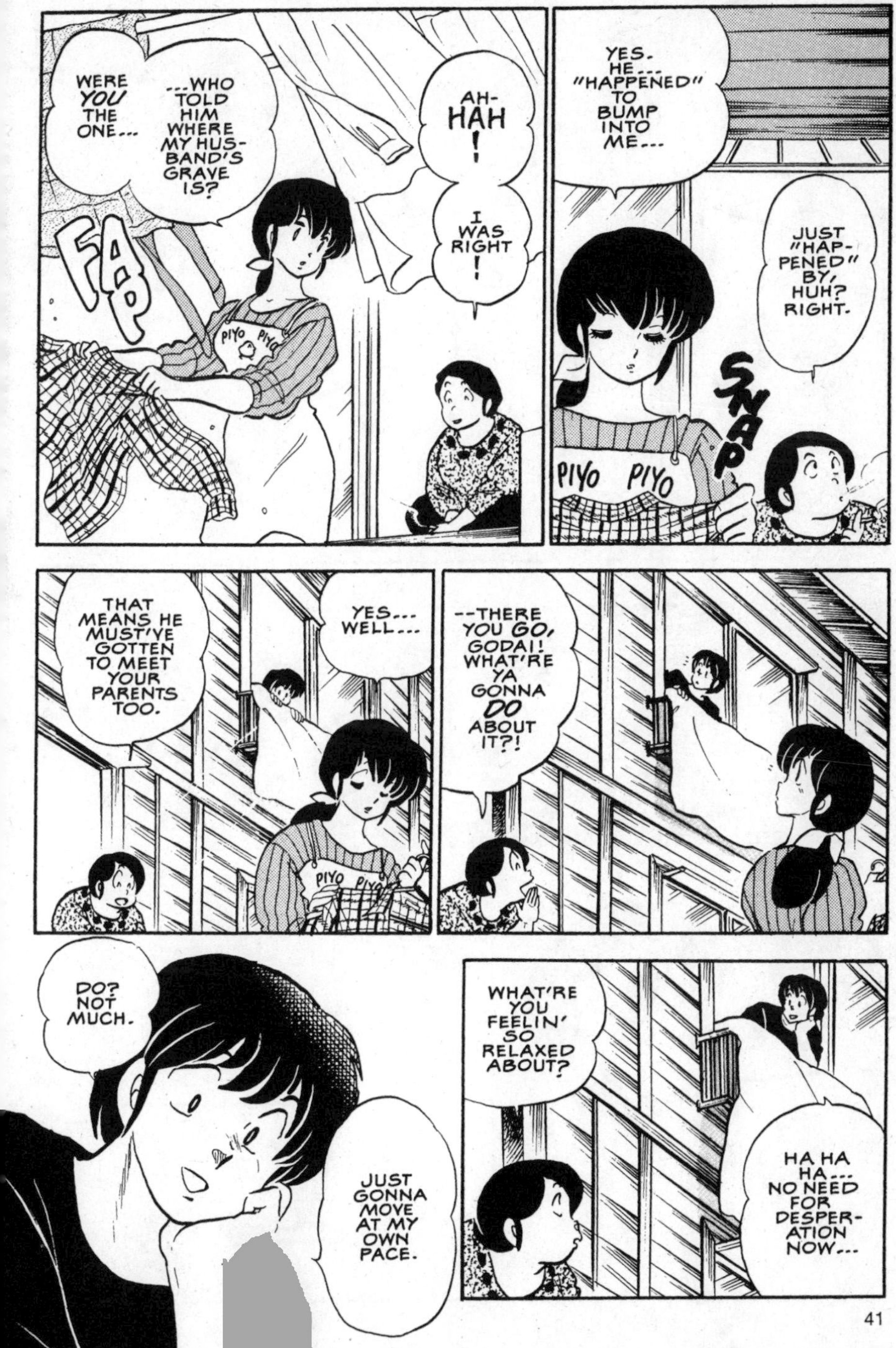
WERE YOU THE ONE...
...WHO TOLD HIM WHERE MY HUS-BAND'S GRAVE IS?
FAP
AH-HAH!
I WAS RIGHT!
YES. HE... "HAPPENED" TO BUMP INTO ME...
JUST "HAP-PENED" BY, HUH? RIGHT.
SNAP
PIYO PIYO
THAT MEANS HE MUST'VE GOTTEN TO MEET YOUR PARENTS TOO.
YES... WELL...
--THERE YOU GO, GODAI! WHAT'RE YA GONNA DO ABOUT IT?!
DO? NOT MUCH.
JUST GONNA MOVE AT MY OWN PACE.
WHAT'RE YOU FEELIN' SO RELAXED ABOUT?
HA HA HA... NO NEED FOR DESPER-ATION NOW...

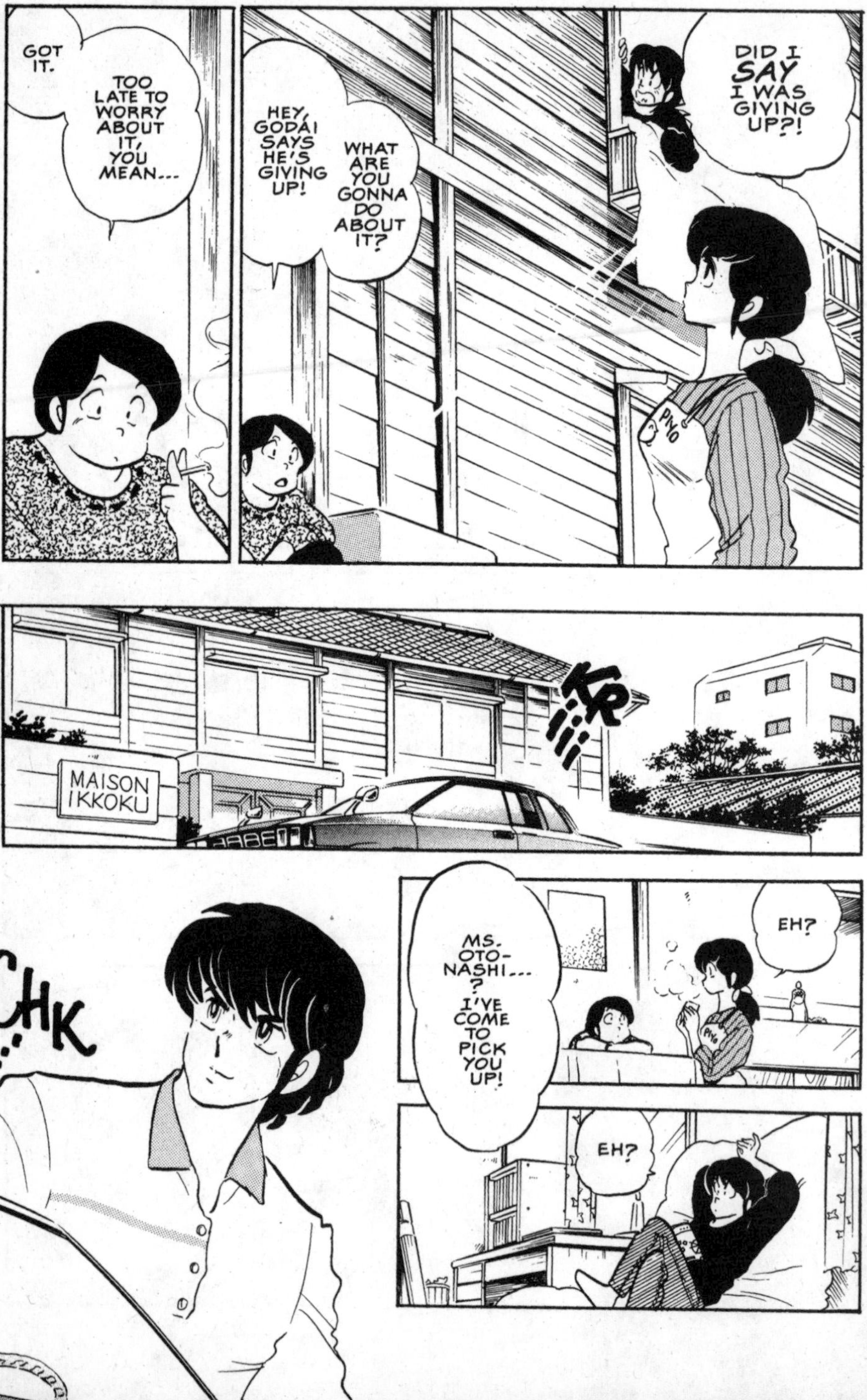
GOT IT.
TOO LATE TO WORRY ABOUT IT, YOU MEAN...
HEY, GODAI SAYS HE'S GIVING UP!
WHAT ARE YOU GONNA DO ABOUT IT?
DID I SAY I WAS GIVING UP?!
MAISON IKKOKU
KRIII
CHK...
MS. OTO-NASHI...? I'VE COME TO PICK YOU UP!
EH?
EH?

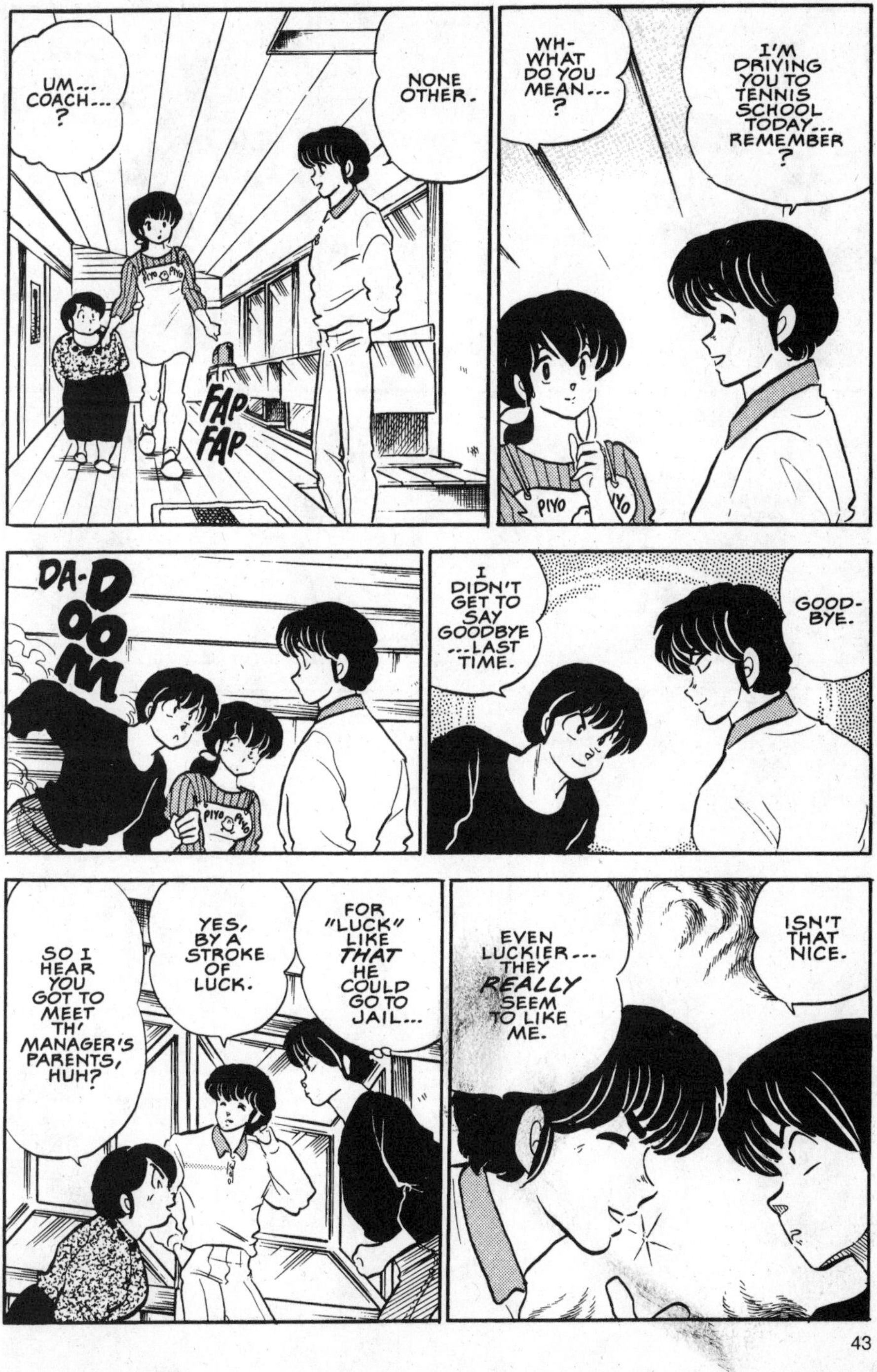
UM... COACH... ?
NONE OTHER.
FAP FAP
WH-WHAT DO YOU MEAN... ?
I'M DRIVING YOU TO TENNIS SCHOOL TODAY... REMEMBER ?
DA-DOOM
I DIDN'T GET TO SAY GOODBYE ...LAST TIME.
GOOD-BYE.
SO I HEAR YOU GOT TO MEET TH' MANAGER'S PARENTS, HUH?
YES, BY A STROKE OF LUCK.
FOR "LUCK" LIKE THAT HE COULD GO TO JAIL...
EVEN LUCKIER... THEY REALLY SEEM TO LIKE ME.
ISN'T THAT NICE.

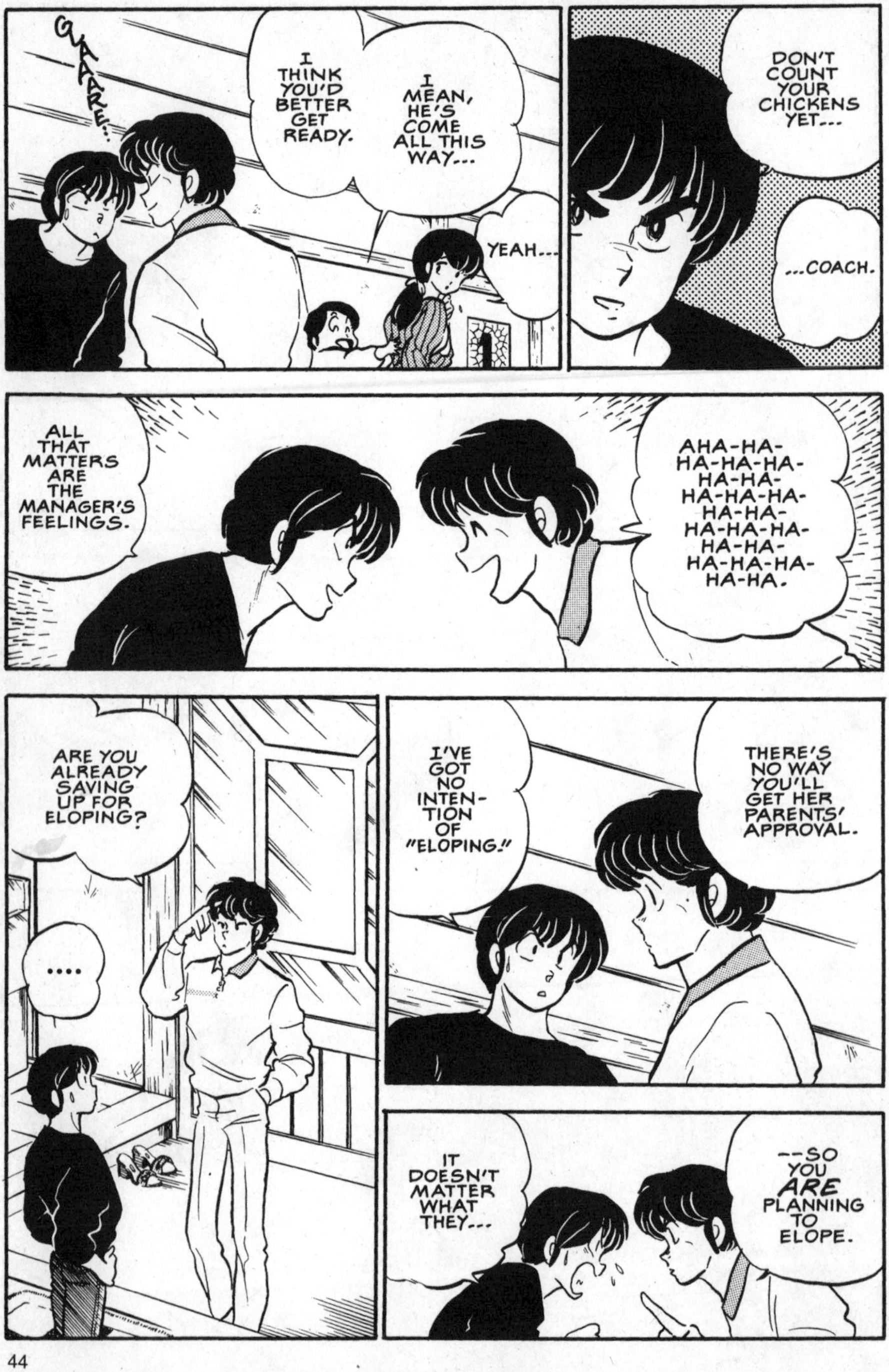
GLAAARE...
I THINK YOU'D BETTER GET READY.
I MEAN, HE'S COME ALL THIS WAY...
YEAH...
DON'T COUNT YOUR CHICKENS YET...
...COACH.
ALL THAT MATTERS ARE THE MANAGER'S FEELINGS.
AHA-HA-HA-HA-HA-HA-HA-HA-HA-HA-HA-HA-HA-HA-HA-HA-HA-HA-HA-HA-HA-HA.
ARE YOU ALREADY SAVING UP FOR ELOPING?
....
I'VE GOT NO INTEN-TION OF "ELOPING!"
THERE'S NO WAY YOU'LL GET HER PARENTS' APPROVAL.
IT DOESN'T MATTER WHAT THEY...
--SO YOU ARE PLANNING TO ELOPE.

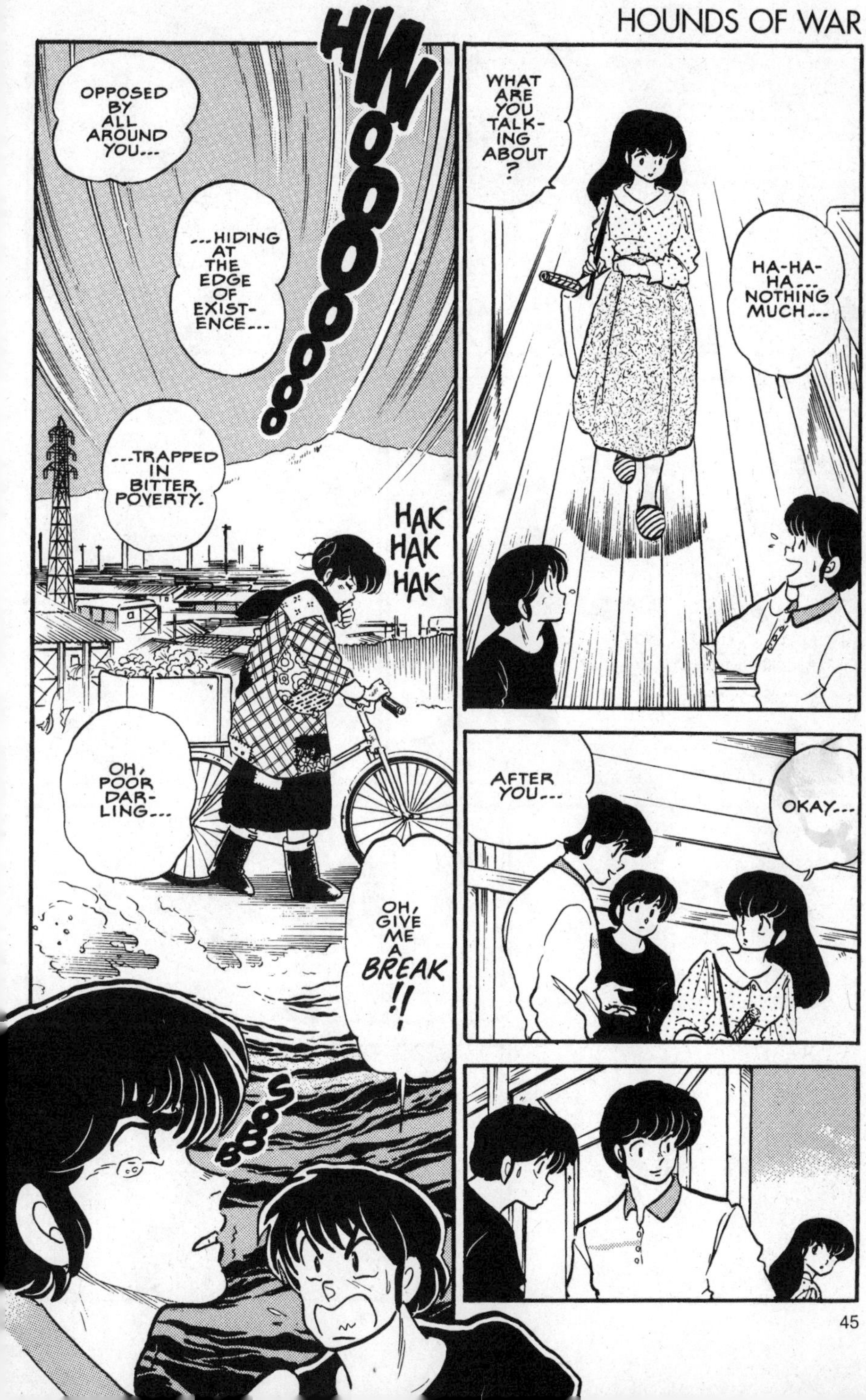
OPPOSED BY ALL AROUND YOU...
HWOOOOOOOOO
...HIDING AT THE EDGE OF EXISTENCE...
...TRAPPED IN BITTER POVERTY.
HAK HAK HAK
OH, POOR DARLING...
OH, GIVE ME A BREAK!!
SOBB
WHAT ARE YOU TALKING ABOUT?
HA-HA-HA... NOTHING MUCH...
AFTER YOU...
OKAY...

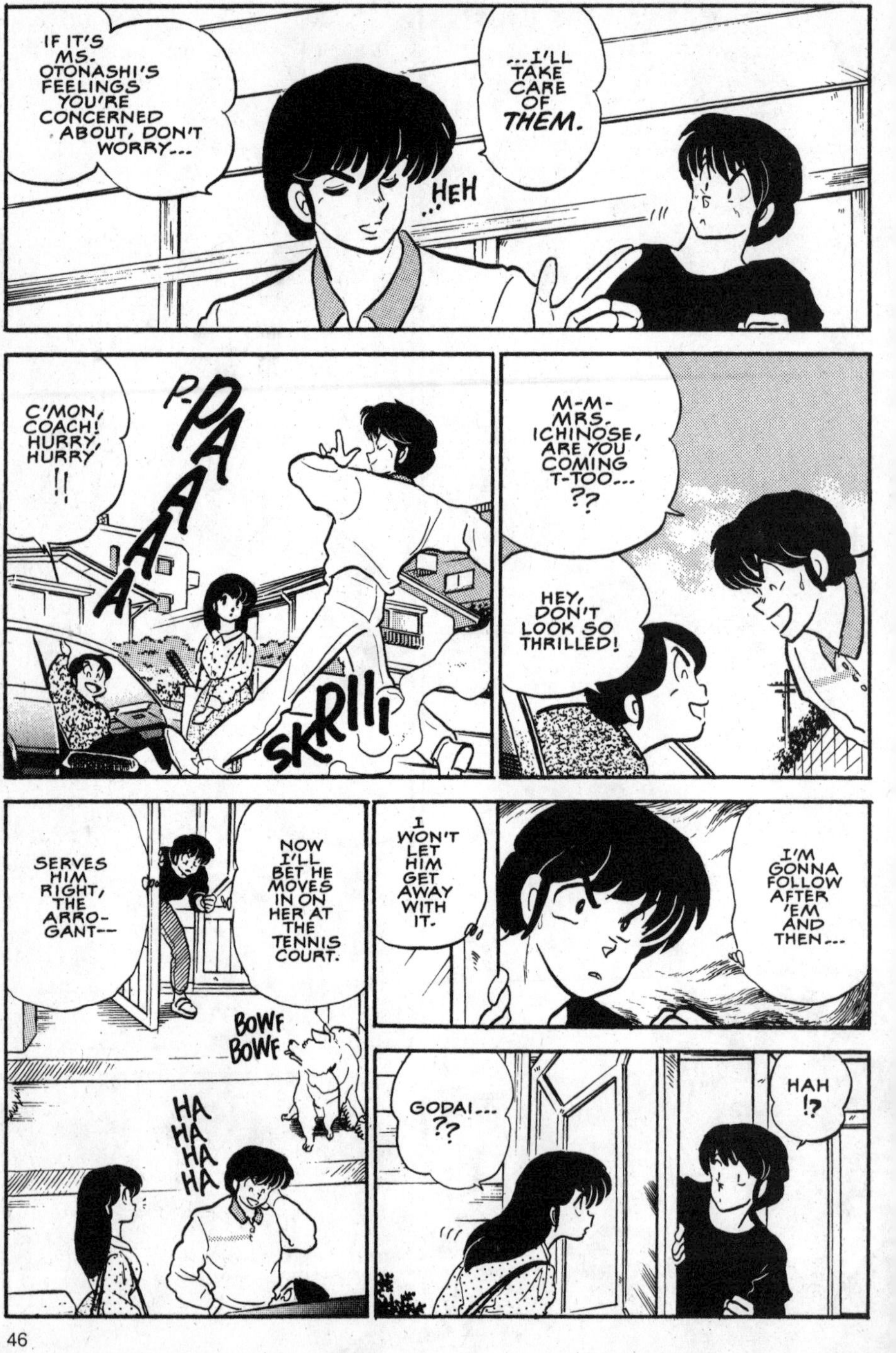

IF IT'S MS. OTONASHI'S FEELINGS YOU'RE CONCERNED ABOUT, DON'T WORRY...
...I'LL TAKE CARE OF THEM.
...HEH
C'MON, COACH! HURRY, HURRY!!
P-PAAAAA
SKRIII
M-M-MRS. ICHINOSE, ARE YOU COMING T-TOO...??
HEY, DON'T LOOK SO THRILLED!
SERVES HIM RIGHT, THE ARRO-GANT--
NOW I'LL BET HE MOVES IN ON HER AT THE TENNIS COURT.
BOWF BOWF
I WON'T LET HIM GET AWAY WITH IT.
I'M GONNA FOLLOW AFTER 'EM AND THEN...
HA HA HA HA HA
GODAI...??
HAH!?

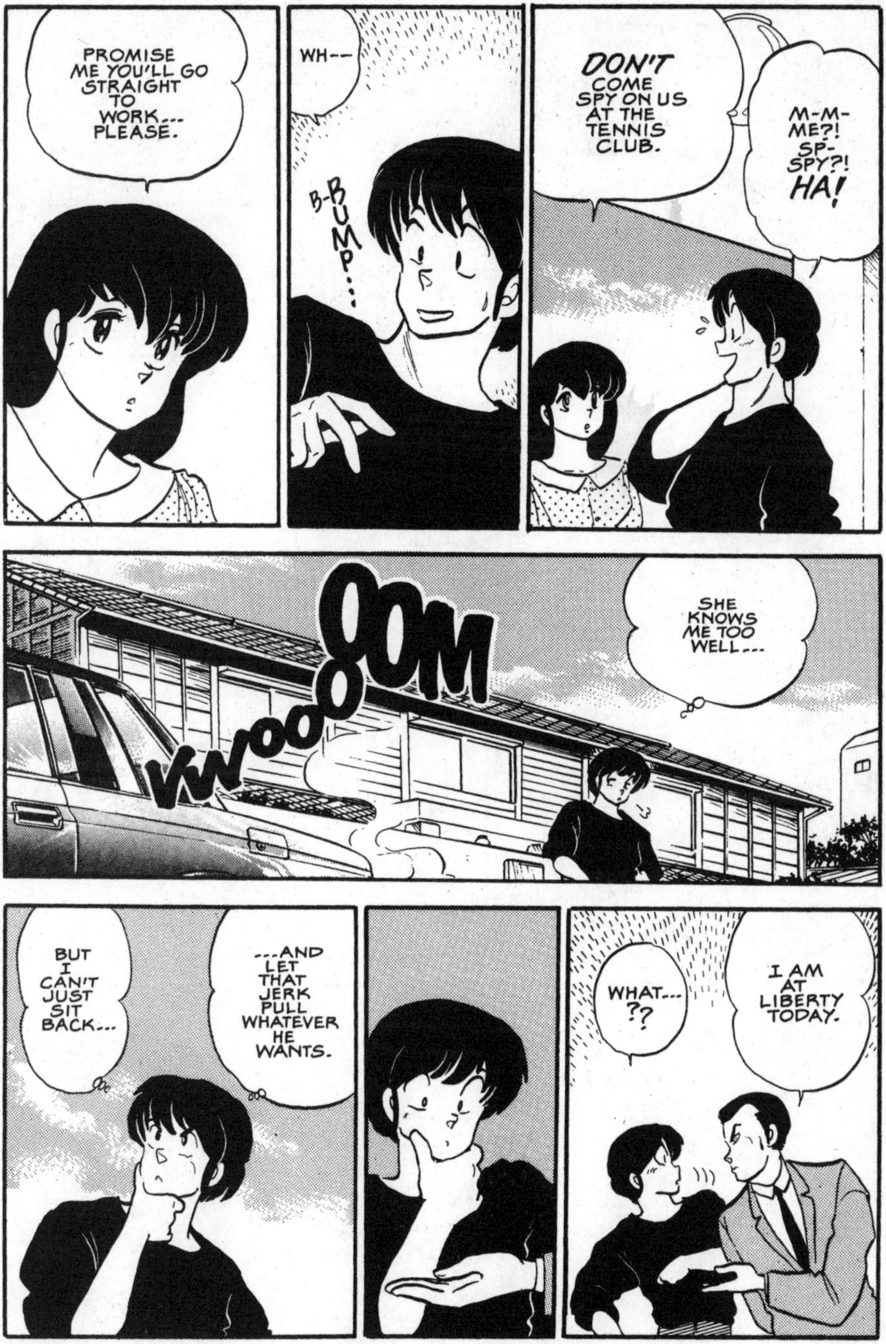
PROMISE ME YOU'LL GO STRAIGHT TO WORK... PLEASE.
WH--
B-BUMP...
DON'T COME SPY ON US AT THE TENNIS CLUB.
M-M-ME?! SP-SPY?! HA!
VWOOOOOOM
SHE KNOWS ME TOO WELL...
BUT I CAN'T JUST SIT BACK...
...AND LET THAT JERK PULL WHATEVER HE WANTS.
WHAT... ??
I AM AT LIBERTY TODAY.

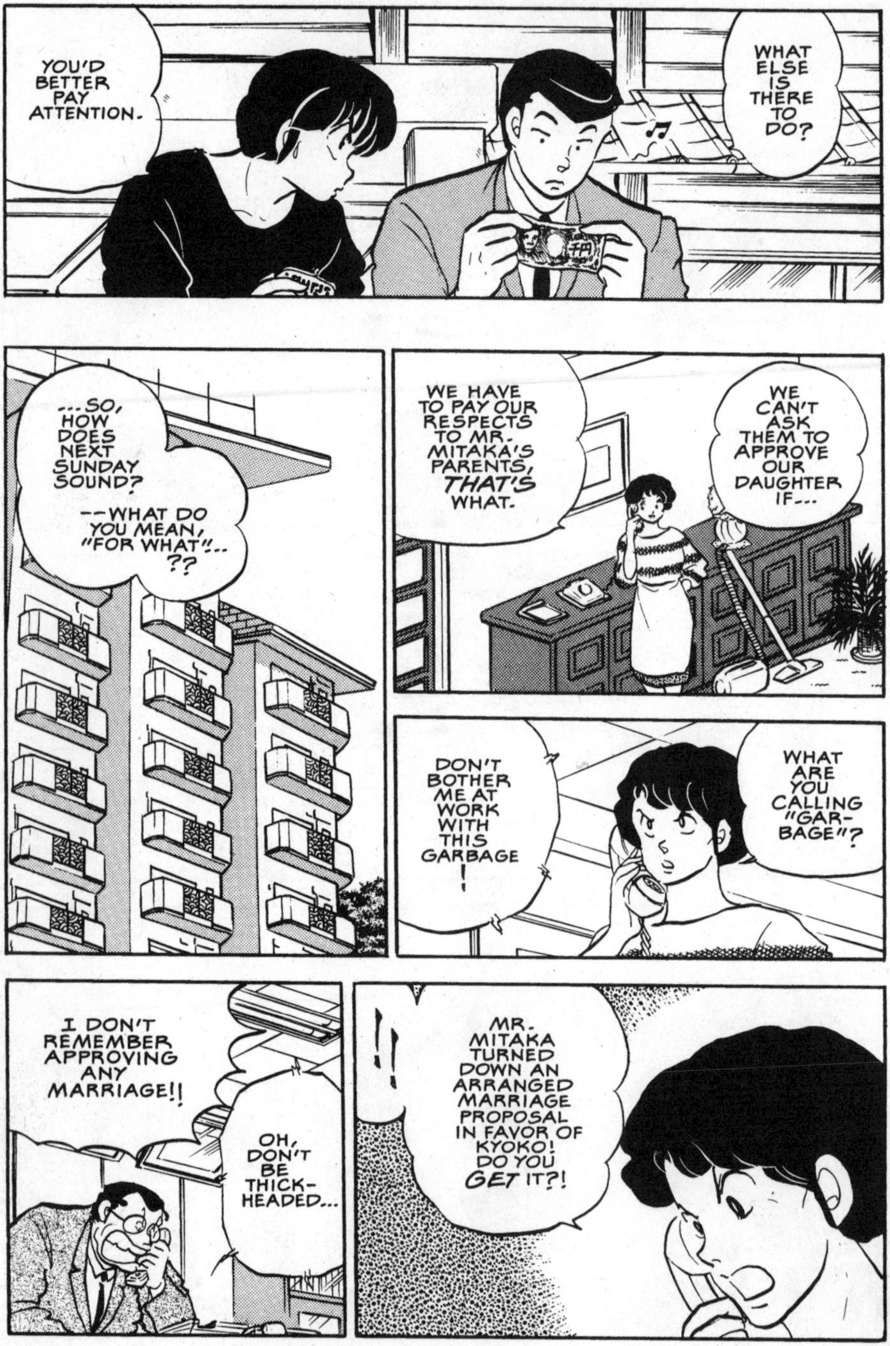
YOU'D BETTER PAY ATTENTION.
WHAT ELSE IS THERE TO DO?
...SO, HOW DOES NEXT SUNDAY SOUND?
--WHAT DO YOU MEAN, "FOR WHAT"...??
WE HAVE TO PAY OUR RESPECTS TO MR. MITAKA'S PARENTS, *THAT'S* WHAT.
WE CAN'T ASK THEM TO APPROVE OUR DAUGHTER IF...
DON'T BOTHER ME AT WORK WITH THIS GARBAGE!
WHAT ARE YOU CALLING "GARBAGE"?
I DON'T REMEMBER APPROVING ANY MARRIAGE!!
OH, DON'T BE THICK-HEADED...
!!
MR. MITAKA TURNED DOWN AN ARRANGED MARRIAGE PROPOSAL IN FAVOR OF KYOKO! DO YOU *GET* IT?!

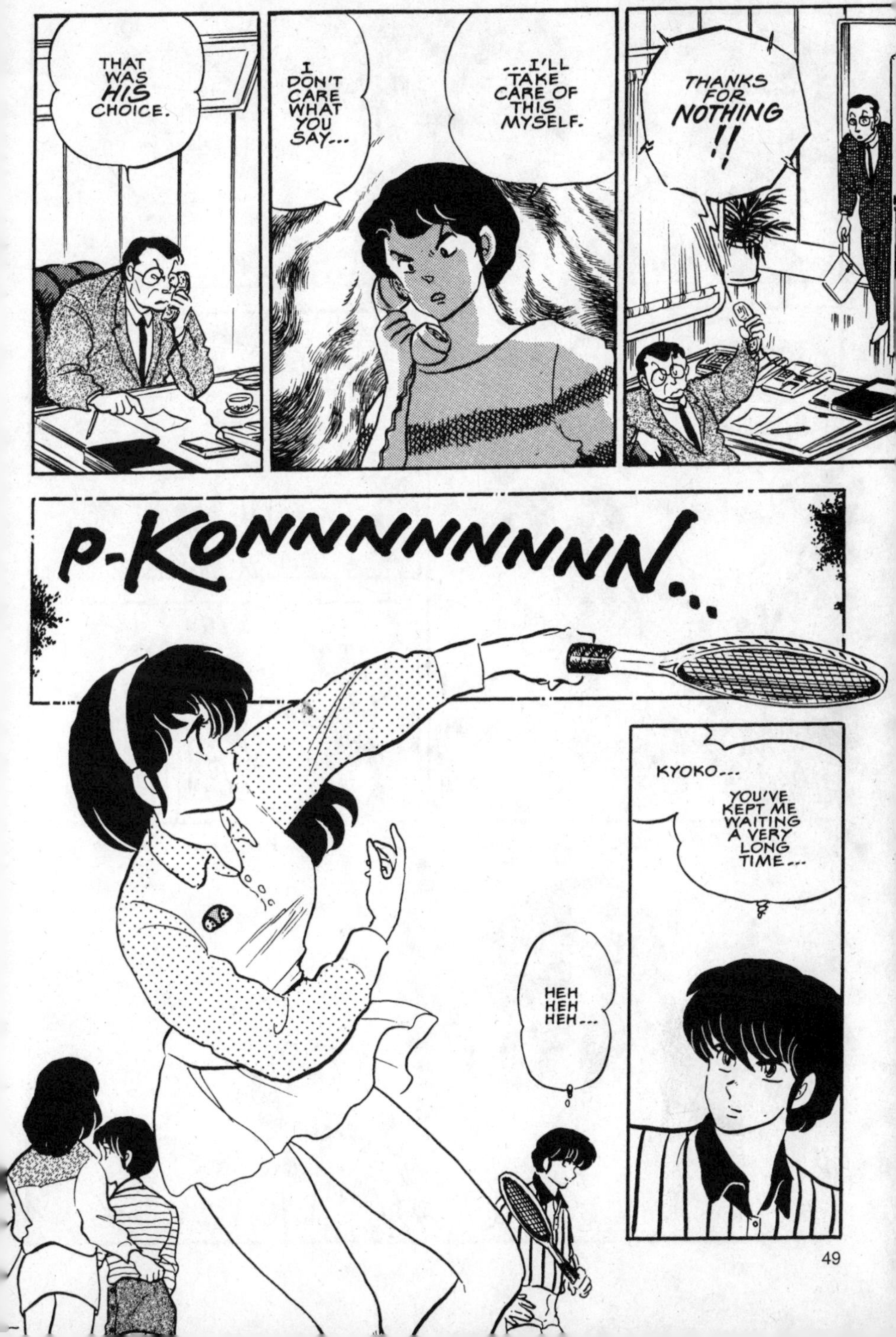
THAT WAS HIS CHOICE.
I DON'T CARE WHAT YOU SAY...
...I'LL TAKE CARE OF THIS MYSELF.
THANKS FOR NOTHING !!
P-KONNNNNNNN...
HEH HEH HEH...
KYOKO...
YOU'VE KEPT ME WAITING A VERY LONG TIME...

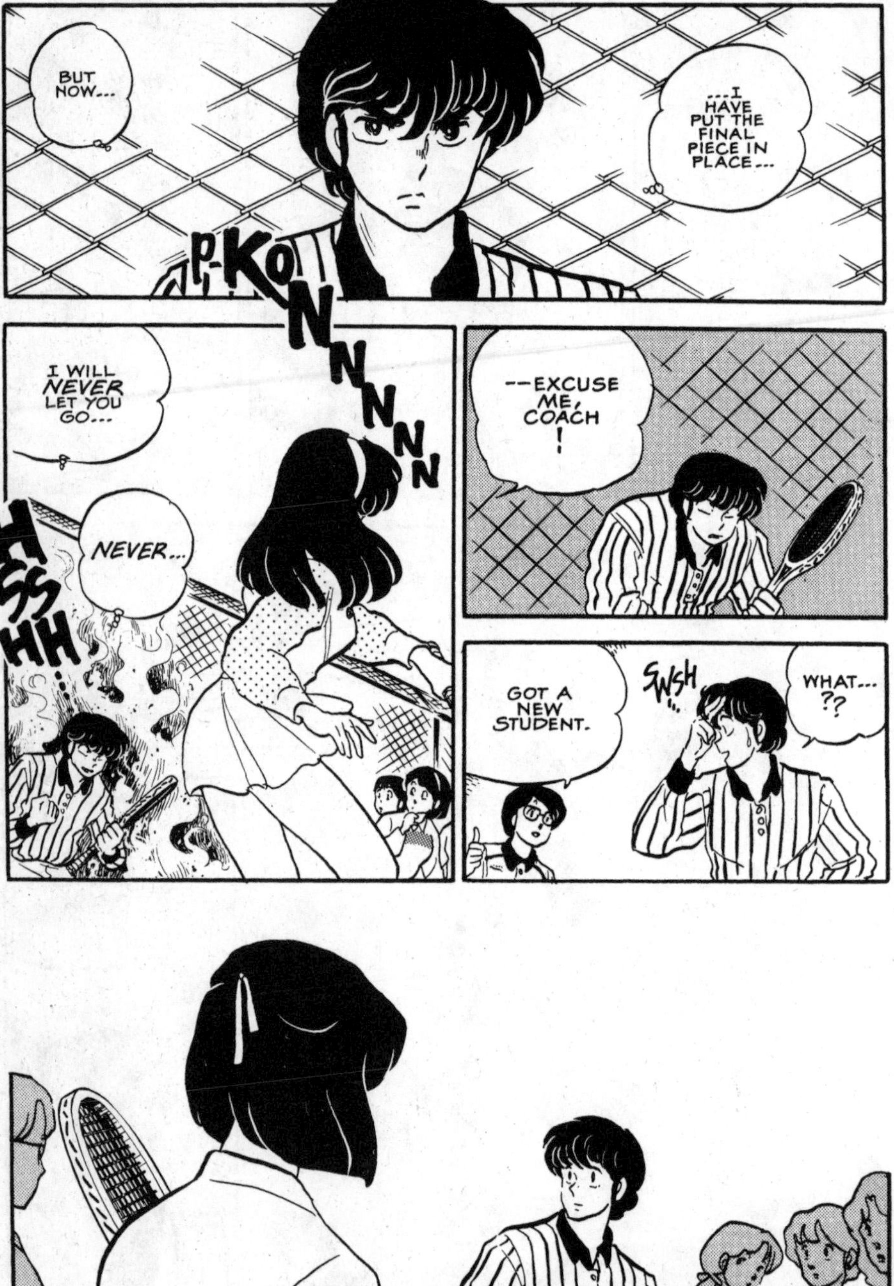
BUT NOW...
...I HAVE PUT THE FINAL PIECE IN PLACE...
P-KONNNNNNN
I WILL NEVER LET YOU GO...
NEVER...
HISSHH...
--EXCUSE ME, COACH!
GOT A NEW STUDENT.
SWSH
WHAT...??

I AM A TER- RIBLE PLAYER.

BUT I LOOK FORWARD EAGERLY TO YOUR INSTRUC- TION.

...BLUSH

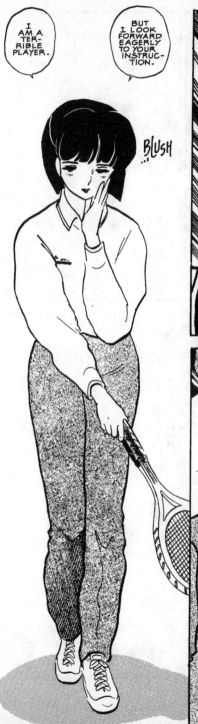

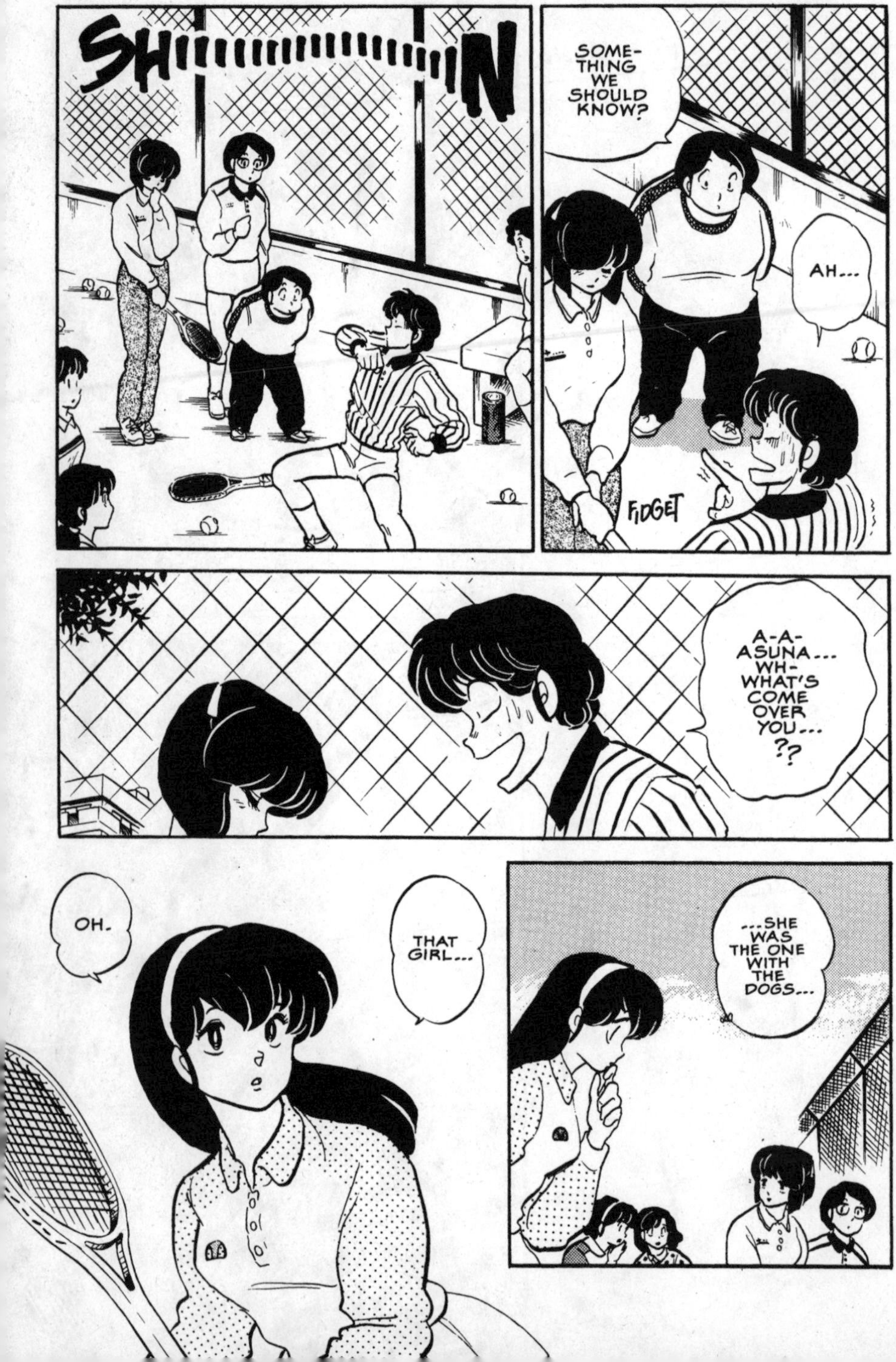
SHIIIIIIIIIIIIIIIIIN
SOME-THING WE SHOULD KNOW?
AH...
FIDGET
A-A-ASUNA... WH-WHAT'S COME OVER YOU...??
OH.
THAT GIRL...
...SHE WAS THE ONE WITH THE DOGS...

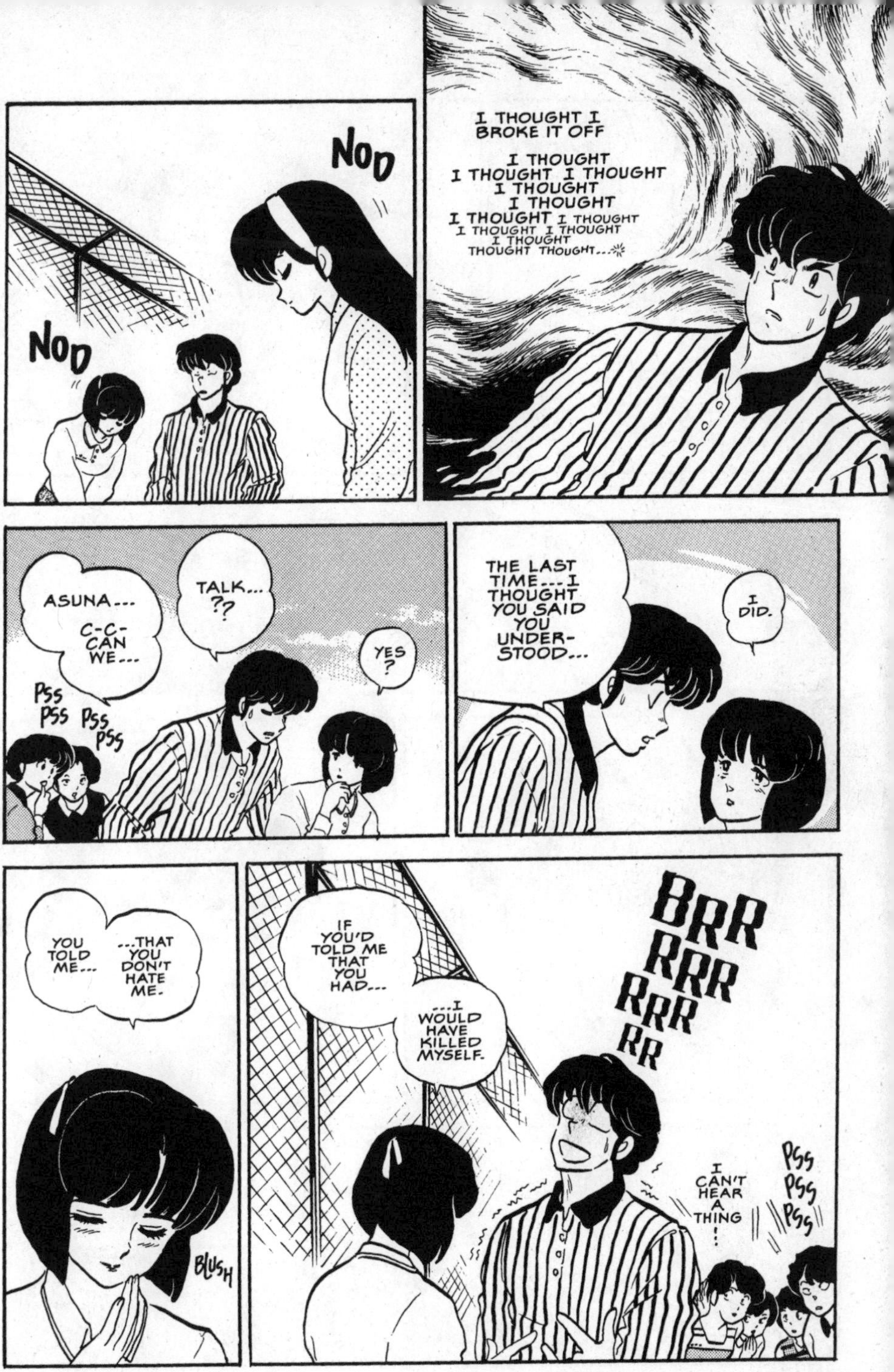

NOD
NOD
I THOUGHT I BROKE IT OFF
I THOUGHT I THOUGHT I THOUGHT I THOUGHT I THOUGHT I THOUGHT I THOUGHT I THOUGHT I THOUGHT I THOUGHT THOUGHT THOUGHT...
ASUNA... C-C-CAN WE...
TALK... ??
YES?
PSS PSS PSS PSS
THE LAST TIME... I THOUGHT YOU SAID YOU UNDER-STOOD...
I DID.
YOU TOLD ME...
...THAT YOU DON'T HATE ME.
BLUSH
IF YOU'D TOLD ME THAT YOU HAD...
...I WOULD HAVE KILLED MYSELF.
BRRRRRRRRRR
I CAN'T HEAR A THING!
PSS PSS PSS

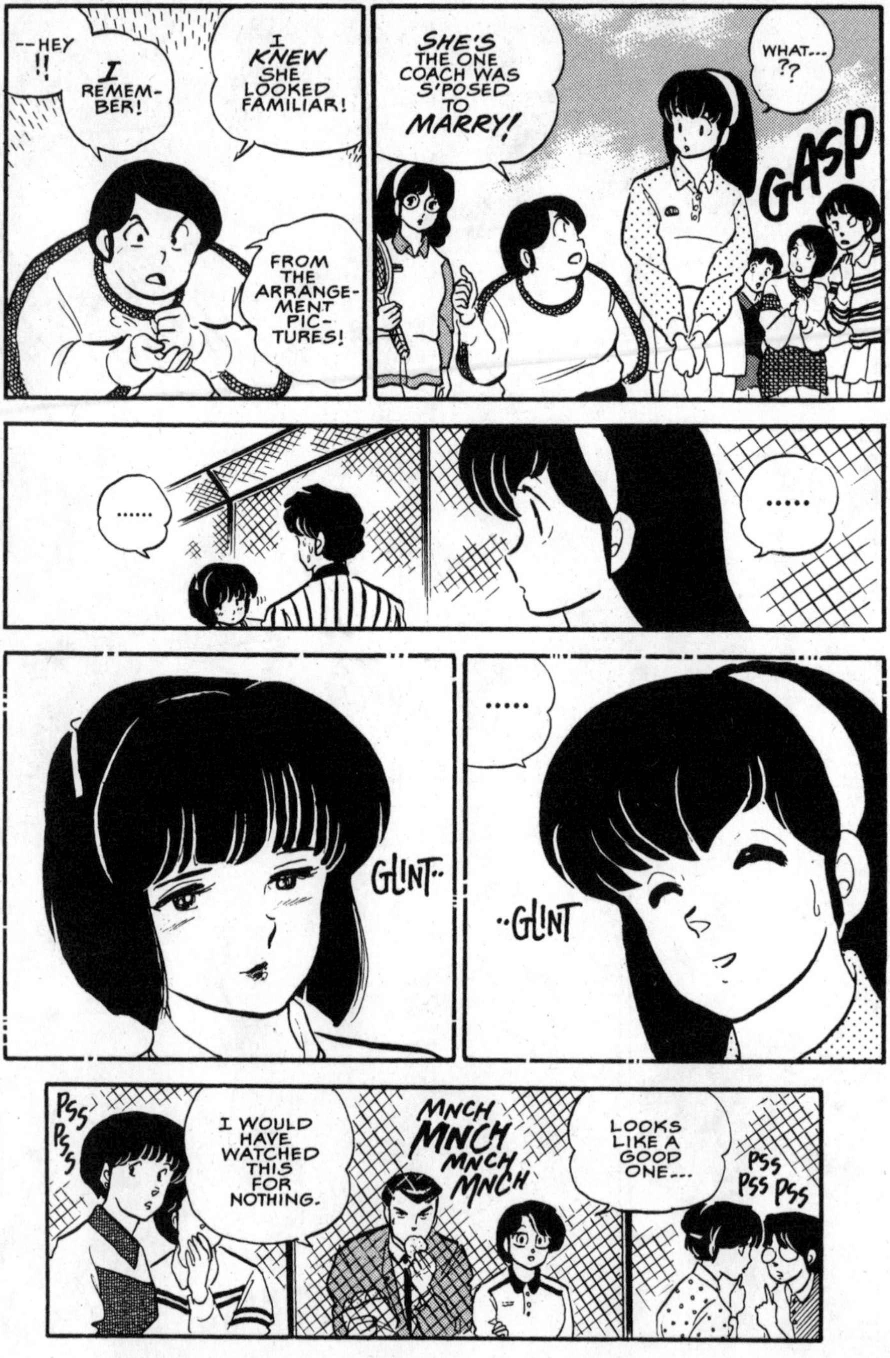
--HEY !!
I REMEMBER!
I KNEW SHE LOOKED FAMILIAR!
FROM THE ARRANGEMENT PICTURES!
SHE'S THE ONE COACH WAS S'POSED TO MARRY!
WHAT... ??
GASP
......
......
GLINT..
.....
..GLINT
PSS PSS
I WOULD HAVE WATCHED THIS FOR NOTHING.
MNCH MNCH MNCH MNCH
LOOKS LIKE A GOOD ONE...
PSS PSS PSS

PART FOUR
THE AGE OF INNOCENCE

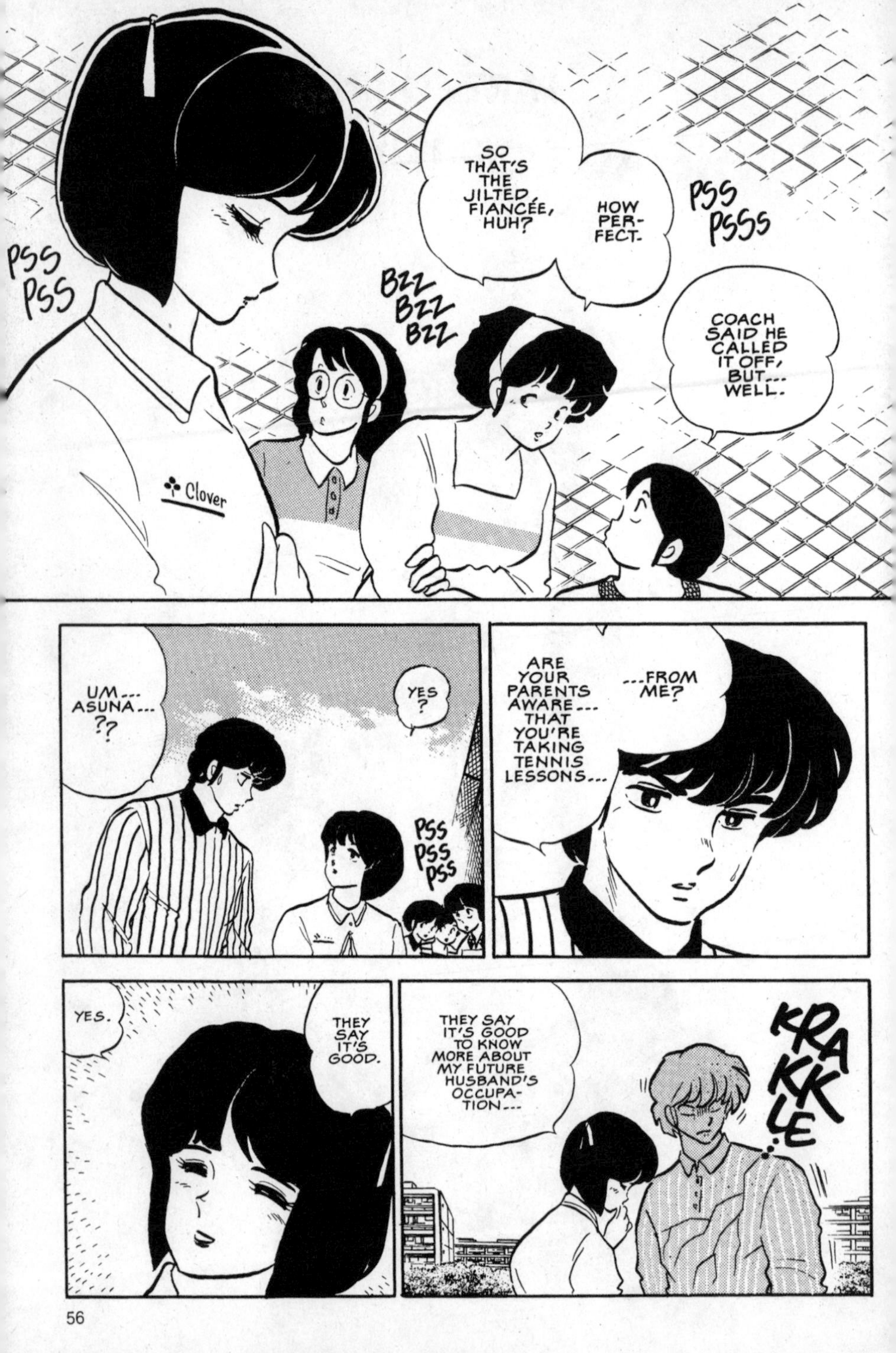

PSS PSS
BZZ BZZ BZZ
SO THAT'S THE JILTED FIANCÉE, HUH?
HOW PER-FECT.
PSS PSSS
COACH SAID HE CALLED IT OFF, BUT... WELL.
Clover
UM... ASUNA... ??
YES?
PSS PSS PSS
ARE YOUR PARENTS AWARE... THAT YOU'RE TAKING TENNIS LESSONS...
...FROM ME?
YES.
THEY SAY IT'S GOOD.
THEY SAY IT'S GOOD TO KNOW MORE ABOUT MY FUTURE HUSBAND'S OCCUPA-TION...
KRAKKLE

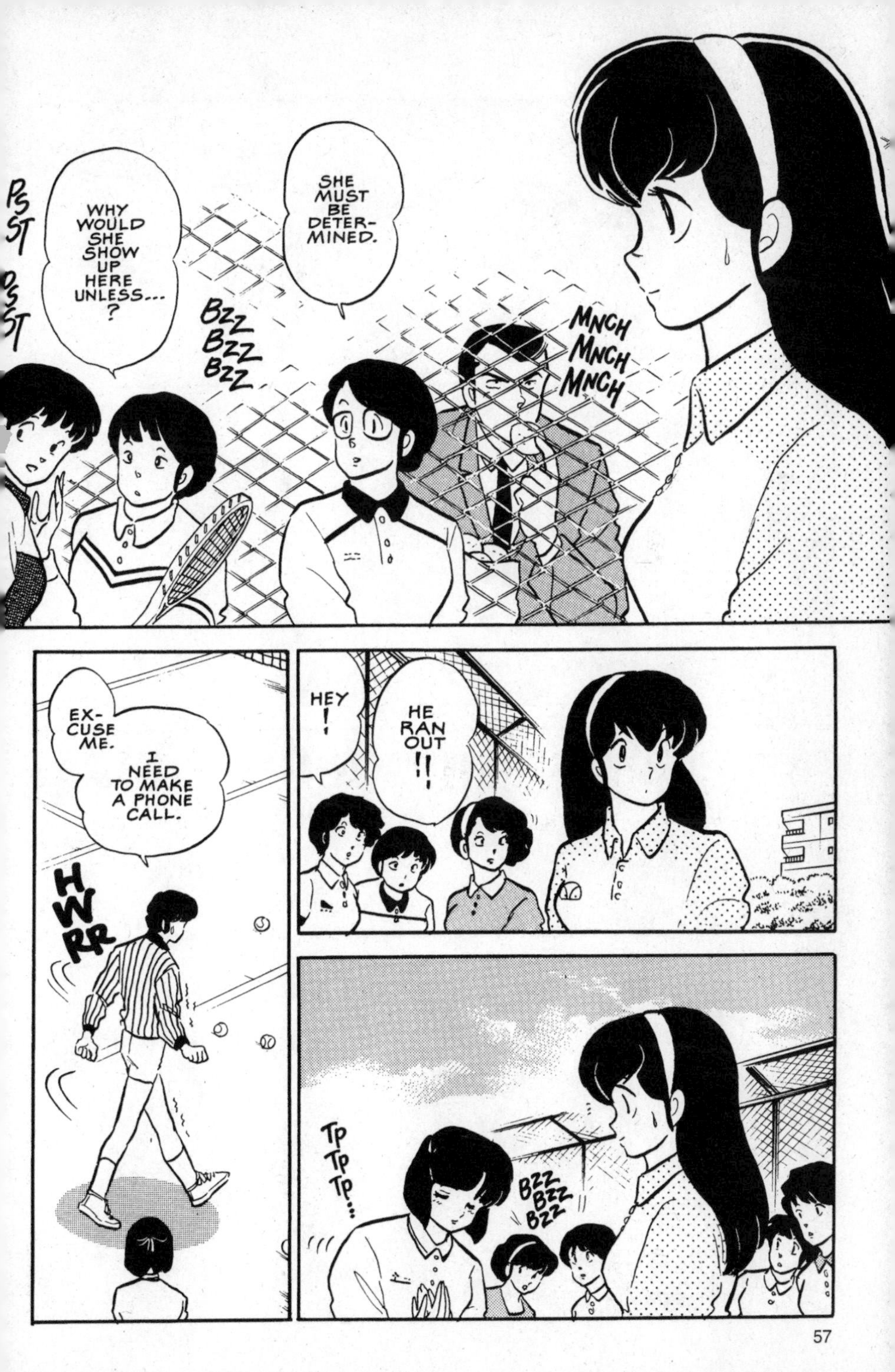
PSST PSST
WHY WOULD SHE SHOW UP HERE UNLESS...?
SHE MUST BE DETER-MINED.
BZZ BZZ BZZ
MNCH MNCH MNCH
EX-CUSE ME.
I NEED TO MAKE A PHONE CALL.
HWRR
HEY!
HE RAN OUT!!
TP TP TP...
BZZ BZZ BZZ

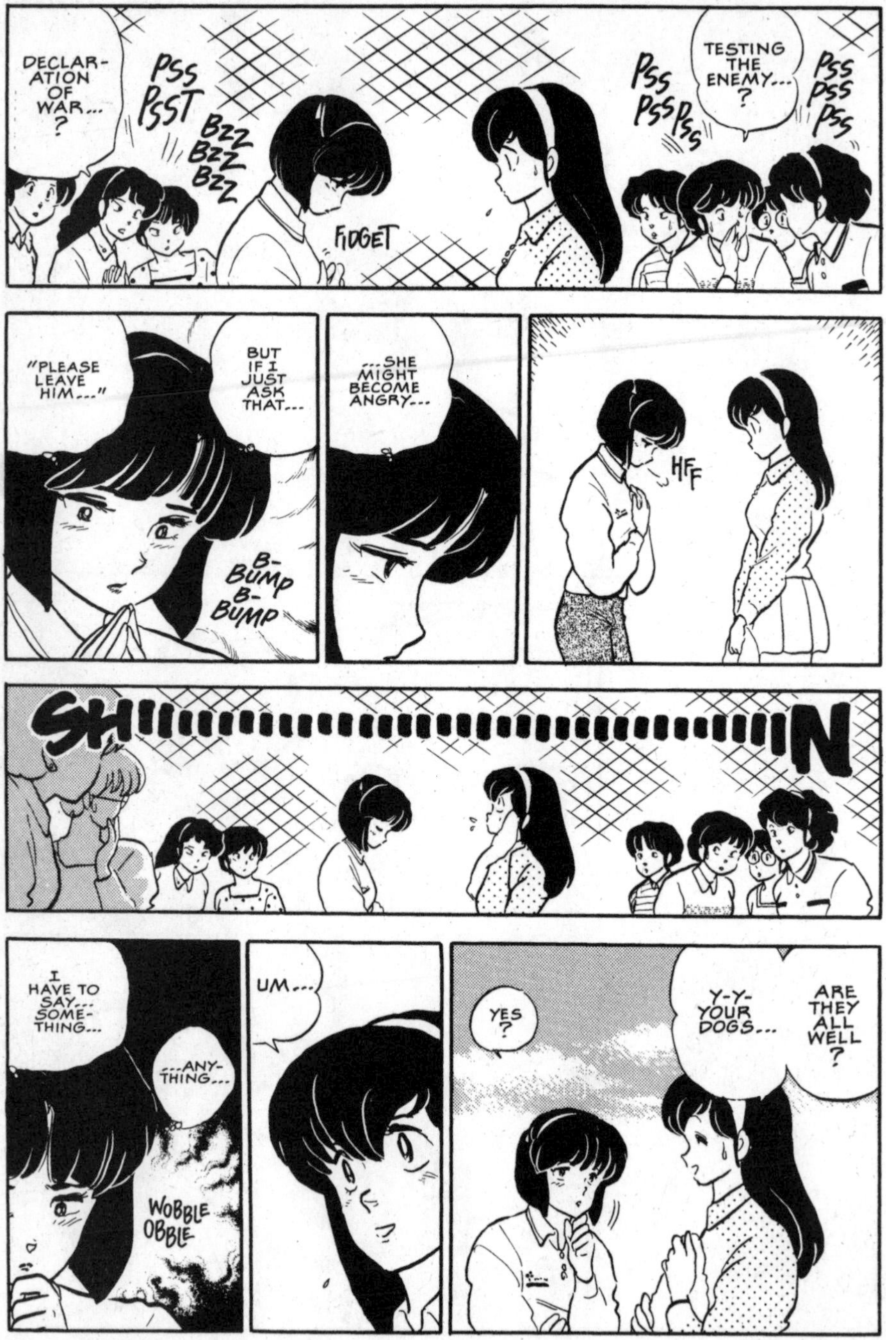
DECLARATION OF WAR...?
PSS PSST
BZZ BZZ BZZ
FIDGET
PSS PSS PSS
TESTING THE ENEMY...?
PSS PSS PSS
"PLEASE LEAVE HIM..."
BUT IF I JUST ASK THAT...
B-BUMP B-BUMP
...SHE MIGHT BECOME ANGRY...
HFF
SHIIIIIIIIIIIIIIIIIIIIIIIIIIIIIIIIIIIIIIIN
I HAVE TO SAY... SOMETHING...
...ANYTHING...
WOBBLE OBBLE
UM...
YES?
Y-Y-YOUR DOGS...
ARE THEY ALL WELL?

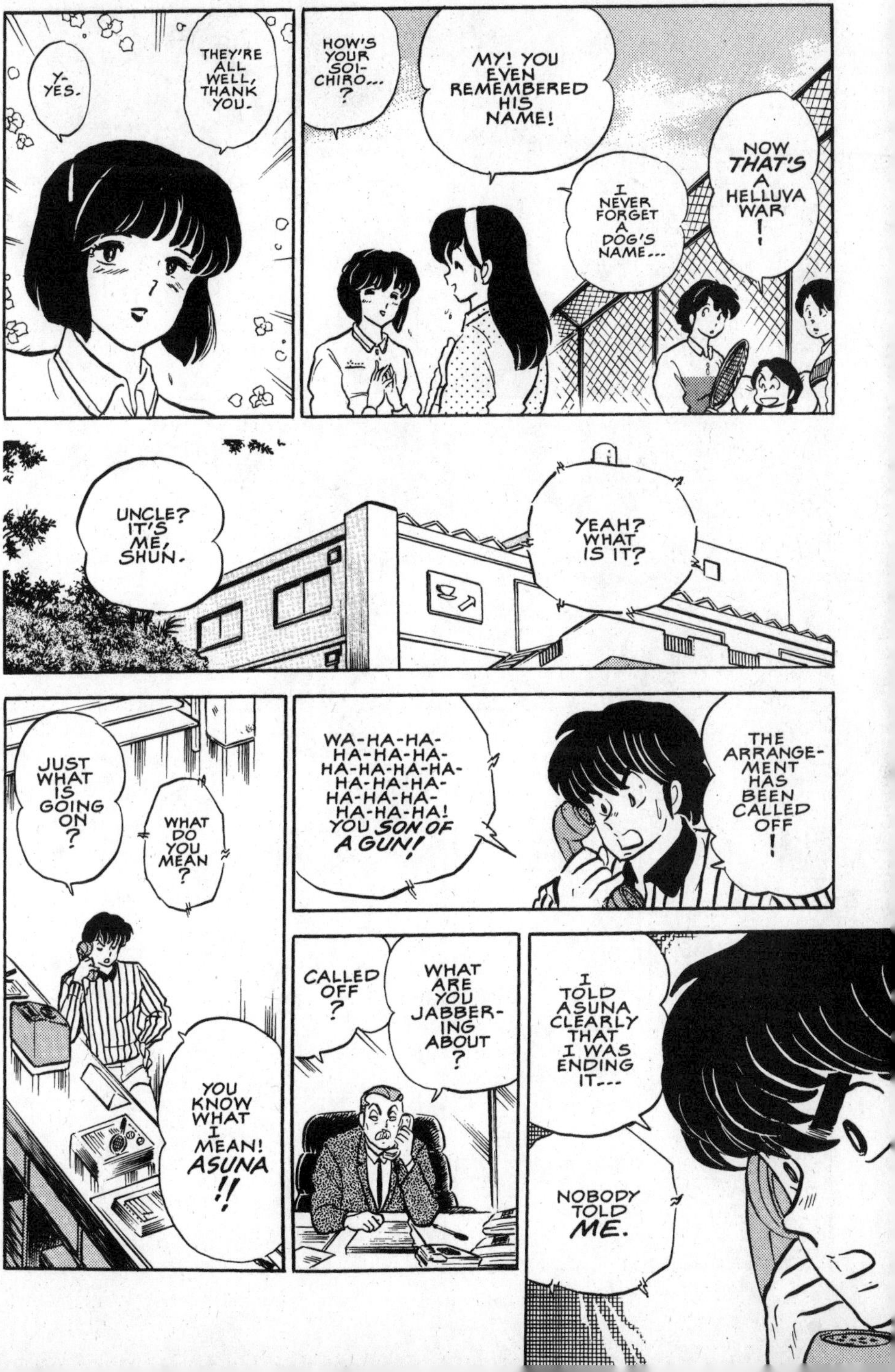
Y-YES.
THEY'RE ALL WELL, THANK YOU.
HOW'S YOUR SOI-CHIRO...?
MY! YOU EVEN REMEMBERED HIS NAME!
I NEVER FORGET A DOG'S NAME...
NOW THAT'S A HELLUVA WAR!
UNCLE? IT'S ME, SHUN.
YEAH? WHAT IS IT?
JUST WHAT IS GOING ON?
WHAT DO YOU MEAN?
YOU KNOW WHAT I MEAN! ASUNA!!
WA-HA-HA-HA-HA-HA-HA-HA-HA-HA-HA-HA-HA-HA-HA-HA-HA-HA-HA-HA! YOU SON OF A GUN!
THE ARRANGEMENT HAS BEEN CALLED OFF!
CALLED OFF?
WHAT ARE YOU JABBERING ABOUT?
I TOLD ASUNA CLEARLY THAT I WAS ENDING IT...
NOBODY TOLD ME.

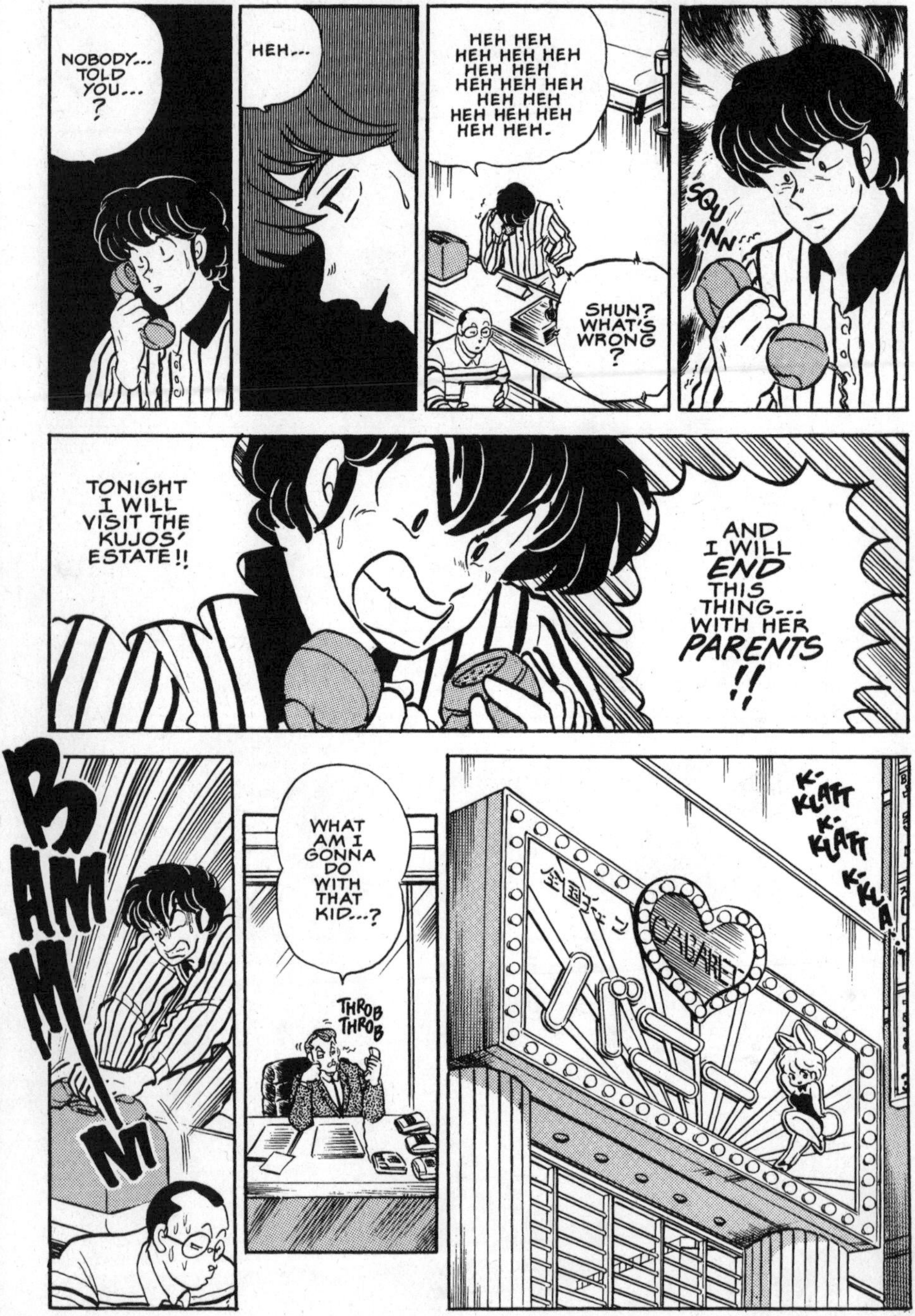
NOBODY... TOLD YOU... ?
HEH...
HEH HEH HEH HEH HEH HEH HEH HEH HEH HEH HEH HEH HEH HEH HEH HEH HEH HEH HEH.
SHUN? WHAT'S WRONG ?
SQUINN
TONIGHT I WILL VISIT THE KUJOS' ESTATE!!
AND I WILL END THIS THING... WITH HER PARENTS !!
BAMMM
WHAT AM I GONNA DO WITH THAT KID...?
THROB THROB
K-KLATT K-KLATT K-KLA...

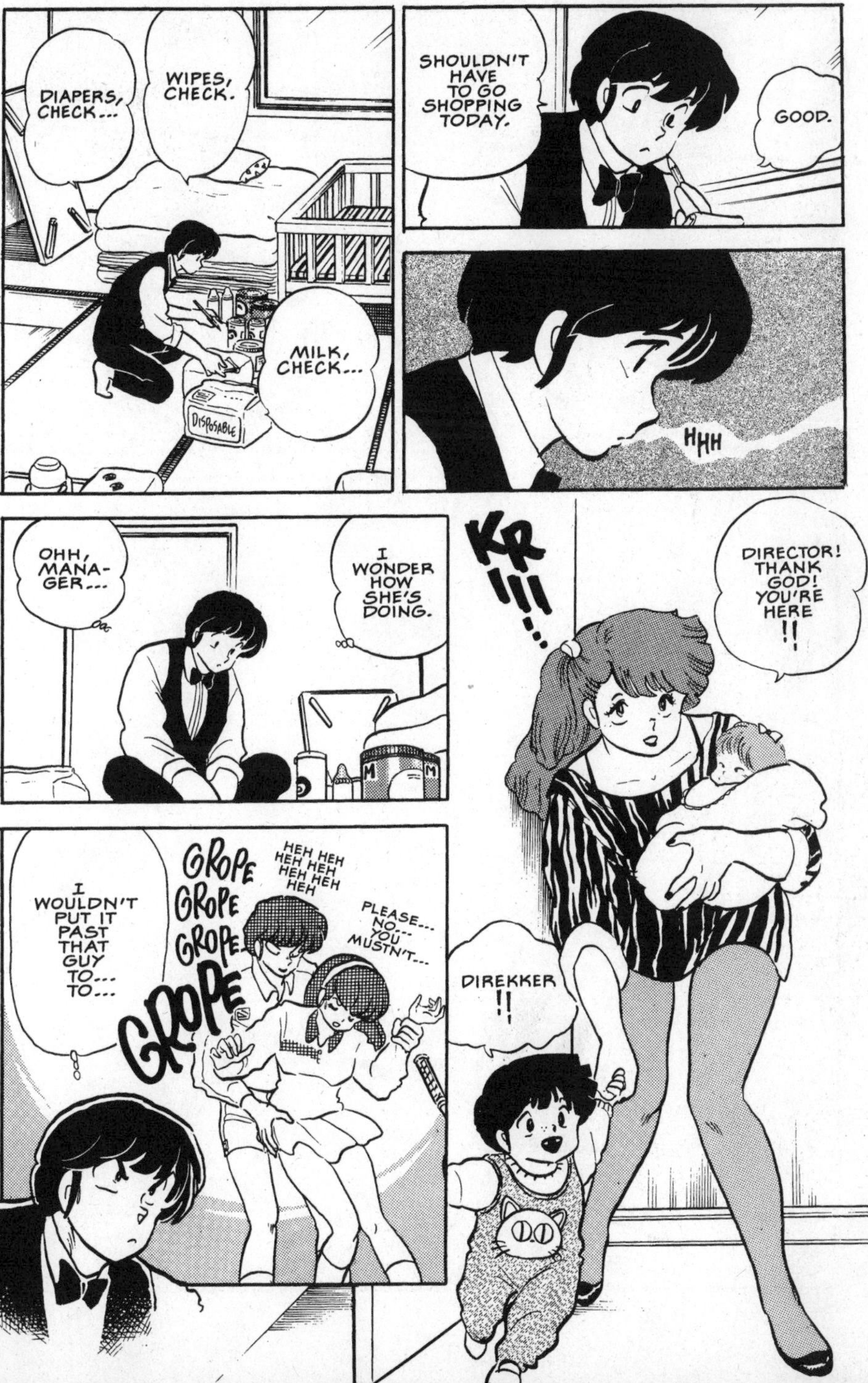
DIAPERS, CHECK...
WIPES, CHECK.
MILK, CHECK...
SHOULDN'T HAVE TO GO SHOPPING TODAY.
GOOD.
HHH
OHH, MANAGER...
I WONDER HOW SHE'S DOING.
I WOULDN'T PUT IT PAST THAT GUY TO... TO...
GROPE GROPE GROPE
HEH HEH HEH HEH HEH HEH HEH
PLEASE... NO... YOU MUSTN'T...
GROPE
KR!!!...
DIRECTOR! THANK GOD! YOU'RE HERE!!
DIREKKER!!
DISPOSABLE

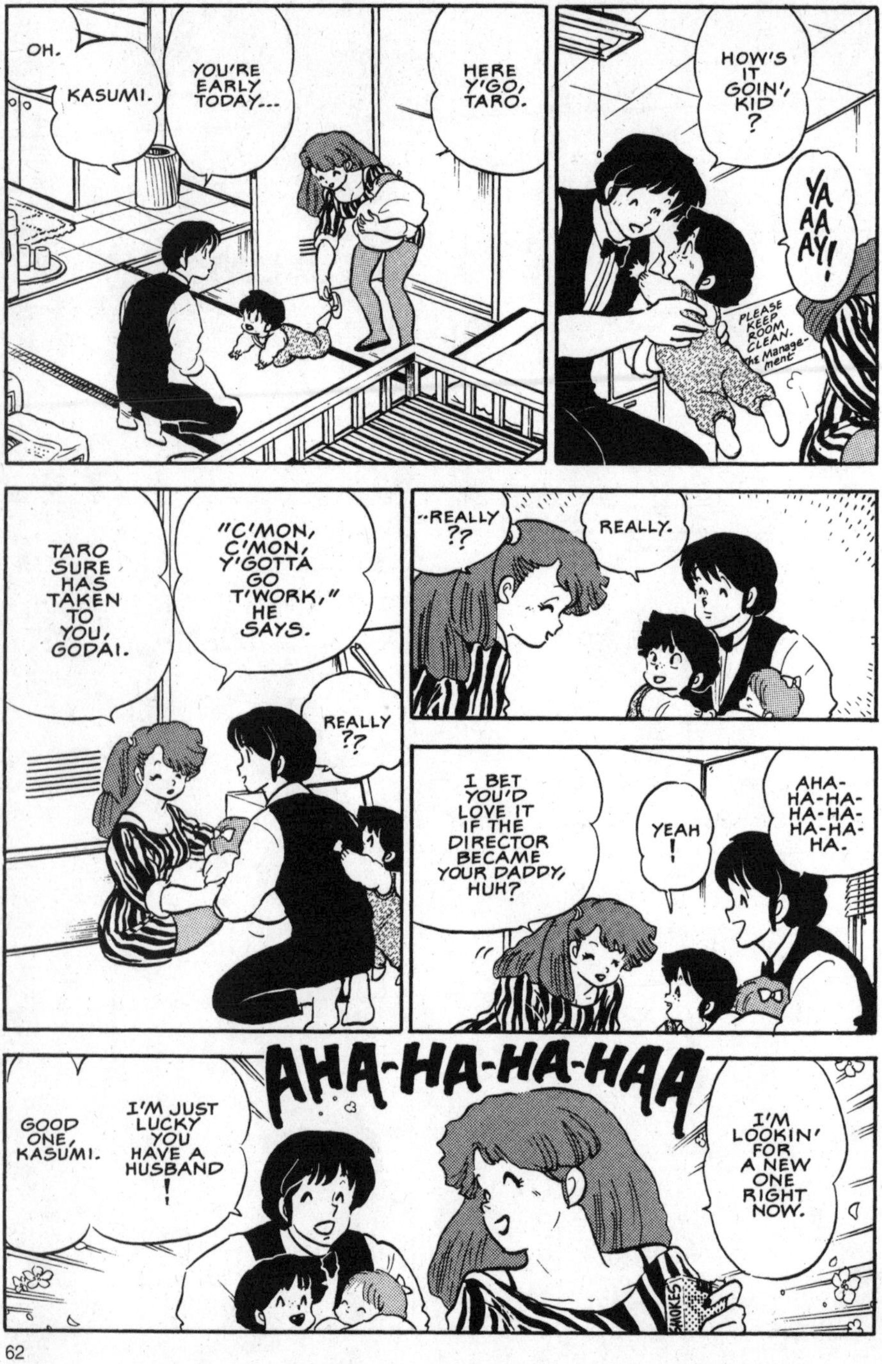
OH.
KASUMI.
YOU'RE EARLY TODAY...
HERE Y'GO, TARO.
HOW'S IT GOIN', KID?
YAAAAY!!
PLEASE KEEP ROOM CLEAN. The Management
TARO SURE HAS TAKEN TO YOU, GODAI.
"C'MON, C'MON, Y'GOTTA GO T'WORK," HE SAYS.
REALLY??
..REALLY??
REALLY.
I BET YOU'D LOVE IT IF THE DIRECTOR BECAME YOUR DADDY, HUH?
YEAH!
AHA-HA-HA-HA-HA-HA-HA.
GOOD ONE, KASUMI.
I'M JUST LUCKY YOU HAVE A HUSBAND!
AHA-HA-HA-HAA
I'M LOOKIN' FOR A NEW ONE RIGHT NOW.
SMOKES

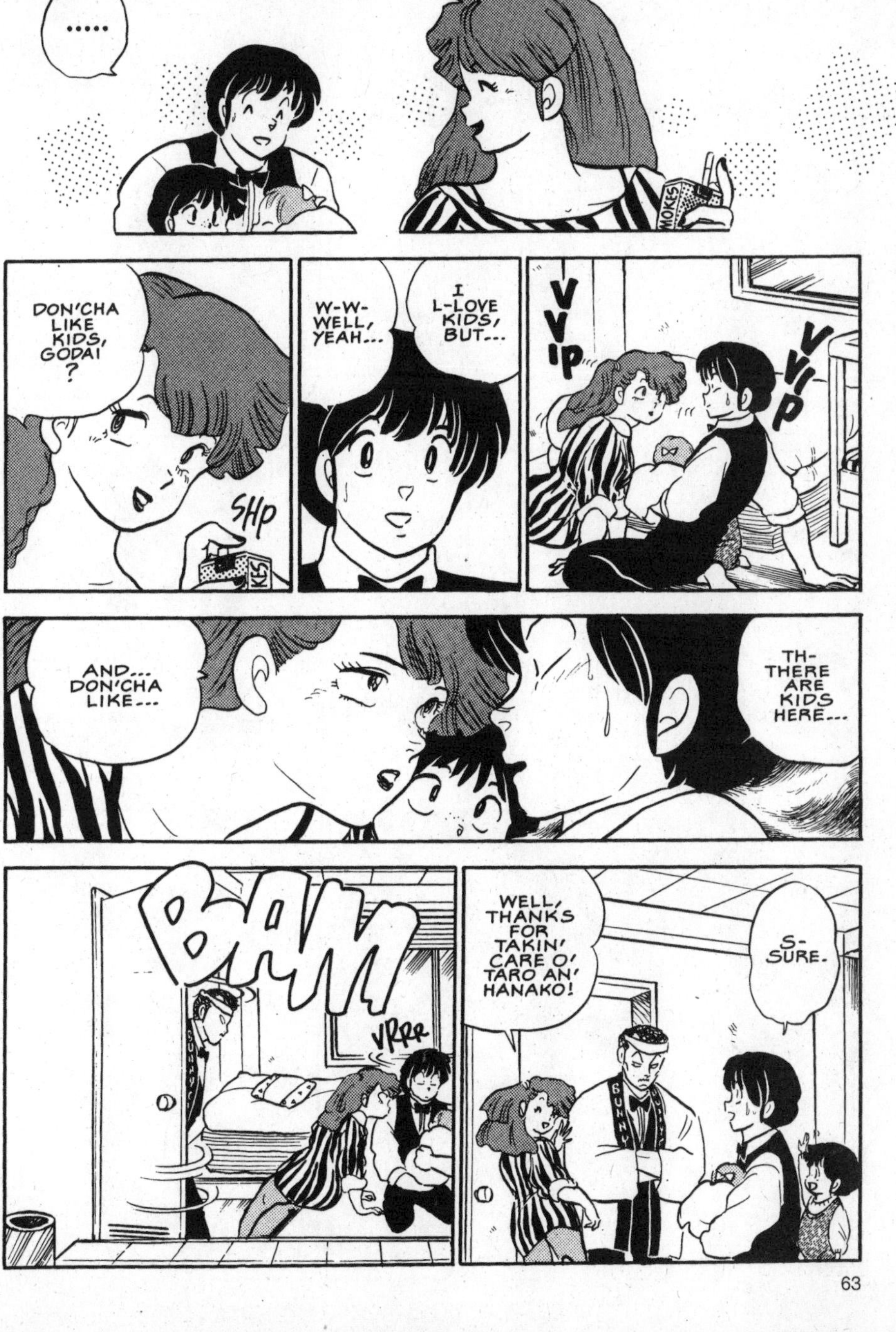
......
DON'CHA LIKE KIDS, GODAI?
SHP
W-W-WELL, YEAH...
I L-LOVE KIDS, BUT...
VVIP
VVIP
AND... DON'CHA LIKE...
TH-THERE ARE KIDS HERE...
BAM
VRRR
WELL, THANKS FOR TAKIN' CARE O' TARO AN' HANAKO!
S-SURE.

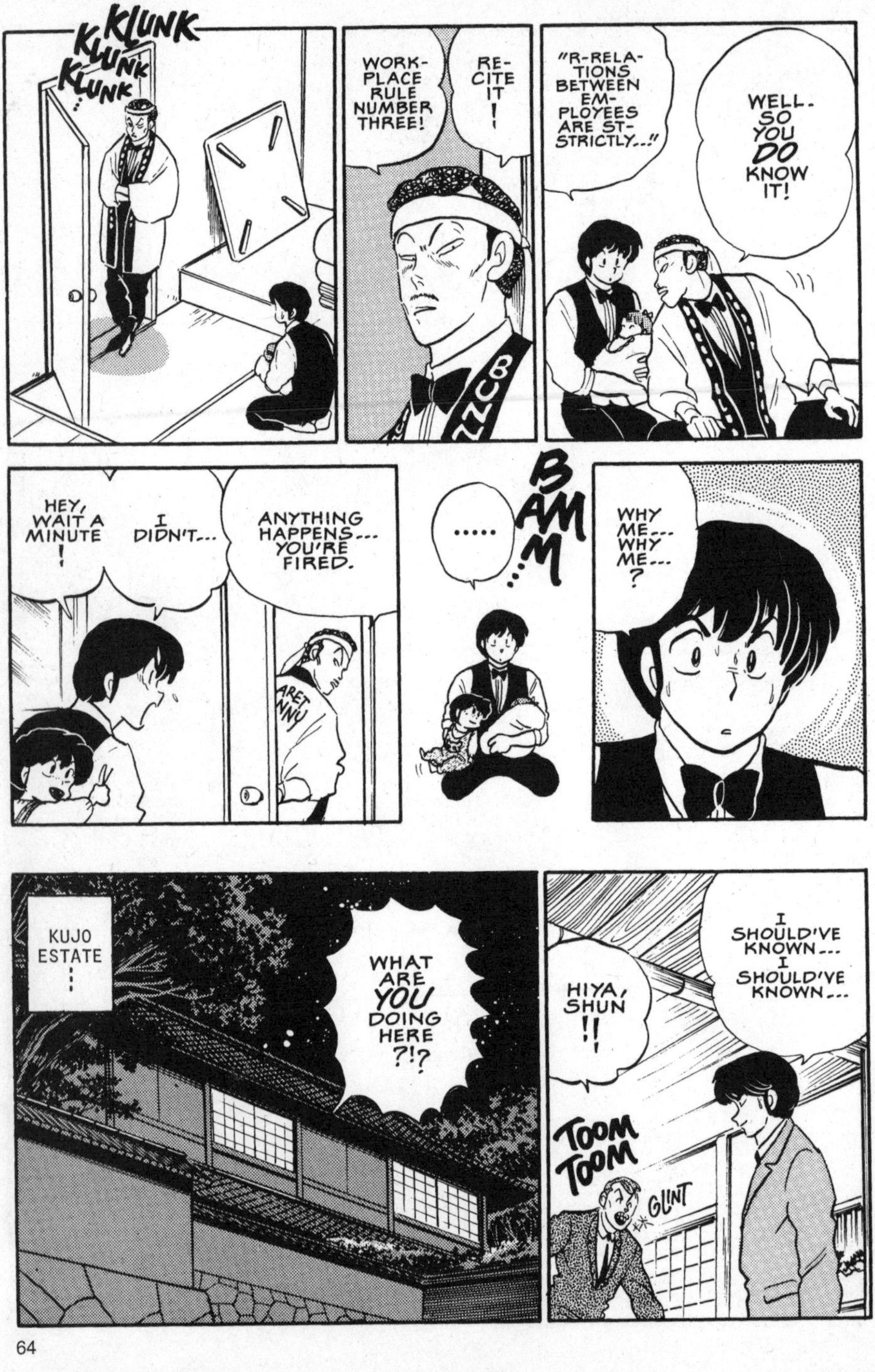
KLUNK
KLUNK
KLUNK
WORK-PLACE RULE NUMBER THREE!
RE-CITE IT!
"R-RELATIONS BETWEEN EM-PLOYEES ARE ST-STRICTLY...!"
WELL. SO YOU DO KNOW IT!
HEY, WAIT A MINUTE!
I DIDN'T...
ANYTHING HAPPENS... YOU'RE FIRED.
.....
BAM...
WHY ME... WHY ME...?
KUJO ESTATE...
WHAT ARE YOU DOING HERE?!?
HIYA, SHUN!!
I SHOULD'VE KNOWN... I SHOULD'VE KNOWN...
TOOM TOOM
GLINT

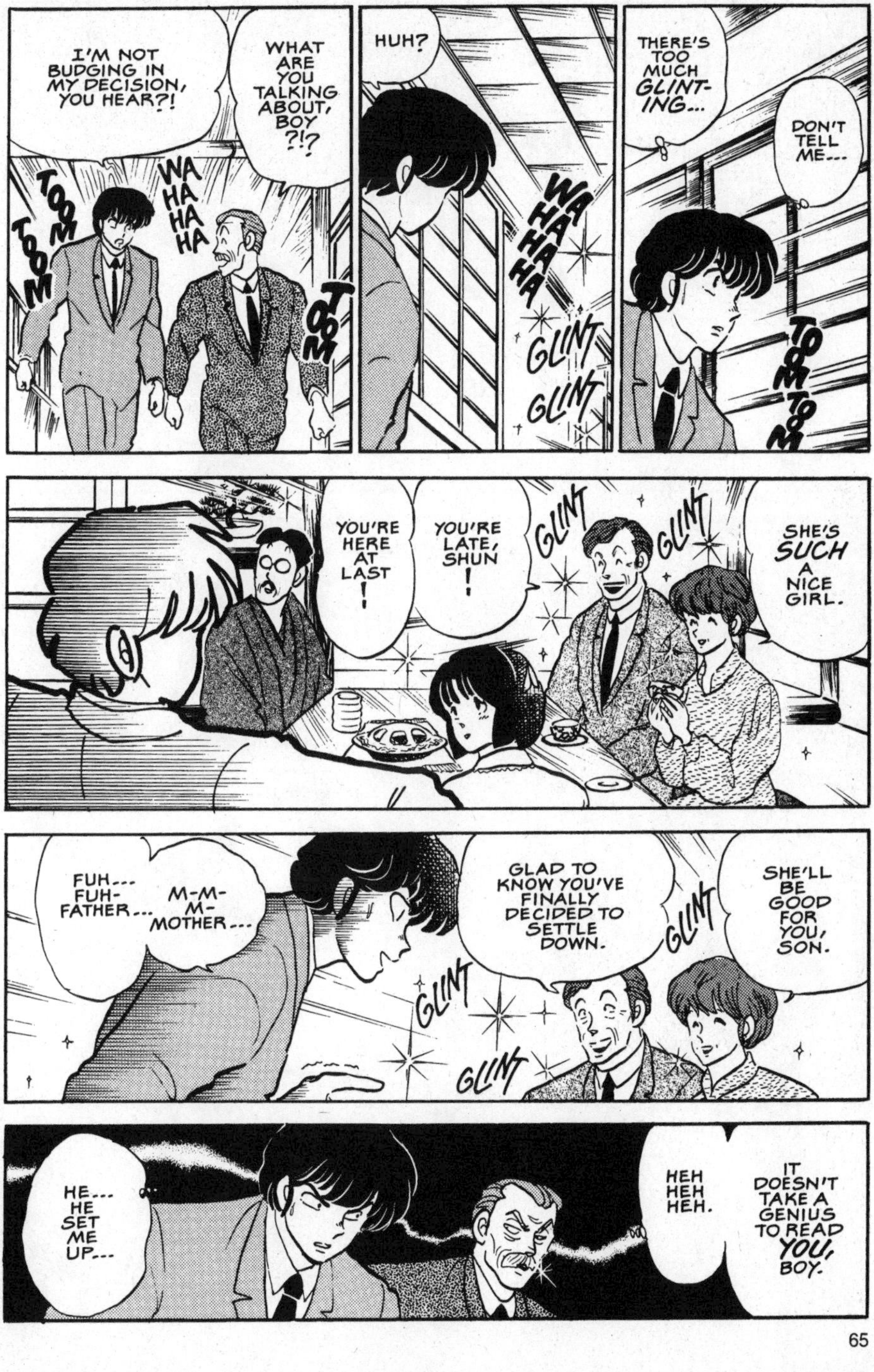
I'M NOT BUDGING IN MY DECISION, YOU HEAR?!
WHAT ARE YOU TALKING ABOUT, BOY ?!?
TOOM TOOM
WA HA HA HA
TOOM
HUH?
WA HA HA HA
GLINT
GLINT
THERE'S TOO MUCH GLINTING...
DON'T TELL ME...
TOOM TOOM
YOU'RE HERE AT LAST!
YOU'RE LATE, SHUN!
GLINT
GLINT
SHE'S SUCH A NICE GIRL.
FUH... FUH- FATHER... M-M-M- MOTHER...
GLAD TO KNOW YOU'VE FINALLY DECIDED TO SETTLE DOWN.
GLINT
SHE'LL BE GOOD FOR YOU, SON.
GLINT
GLINT
HE... HE SET ME UP...
HEH HEH HEH.
IT DOESN'T TAKE A GENIUS TO READ YOU, BOY.

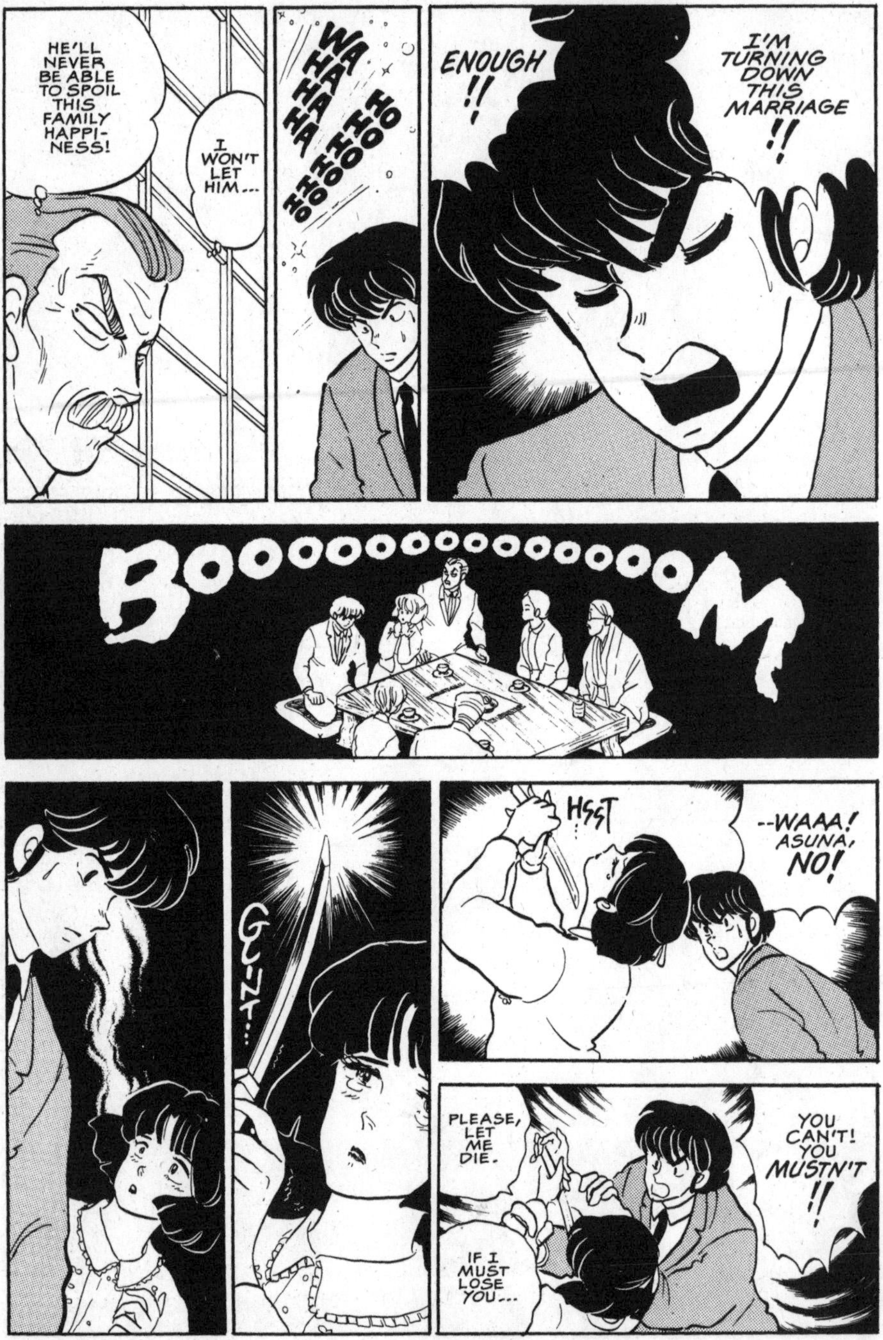
HE'LL NEVER BE ABLE TO SPOIL THIS FAMILY HAPPINESS!
I WON'T LET HIM...
WAHAHAHAHA
HOHOHOHOHO
ENOUGH !!
I'M TURNING DOWN THIS MARRIAGE !!
BOOOOOOOOOOOOOOM
GLINT...
HSST
--WAAA! ASUNA, NO!
PLEASE, LET ME DIE.
IF I MUST LOSE YOU...
YOU CAN'T! YOU MUSTN'T !!

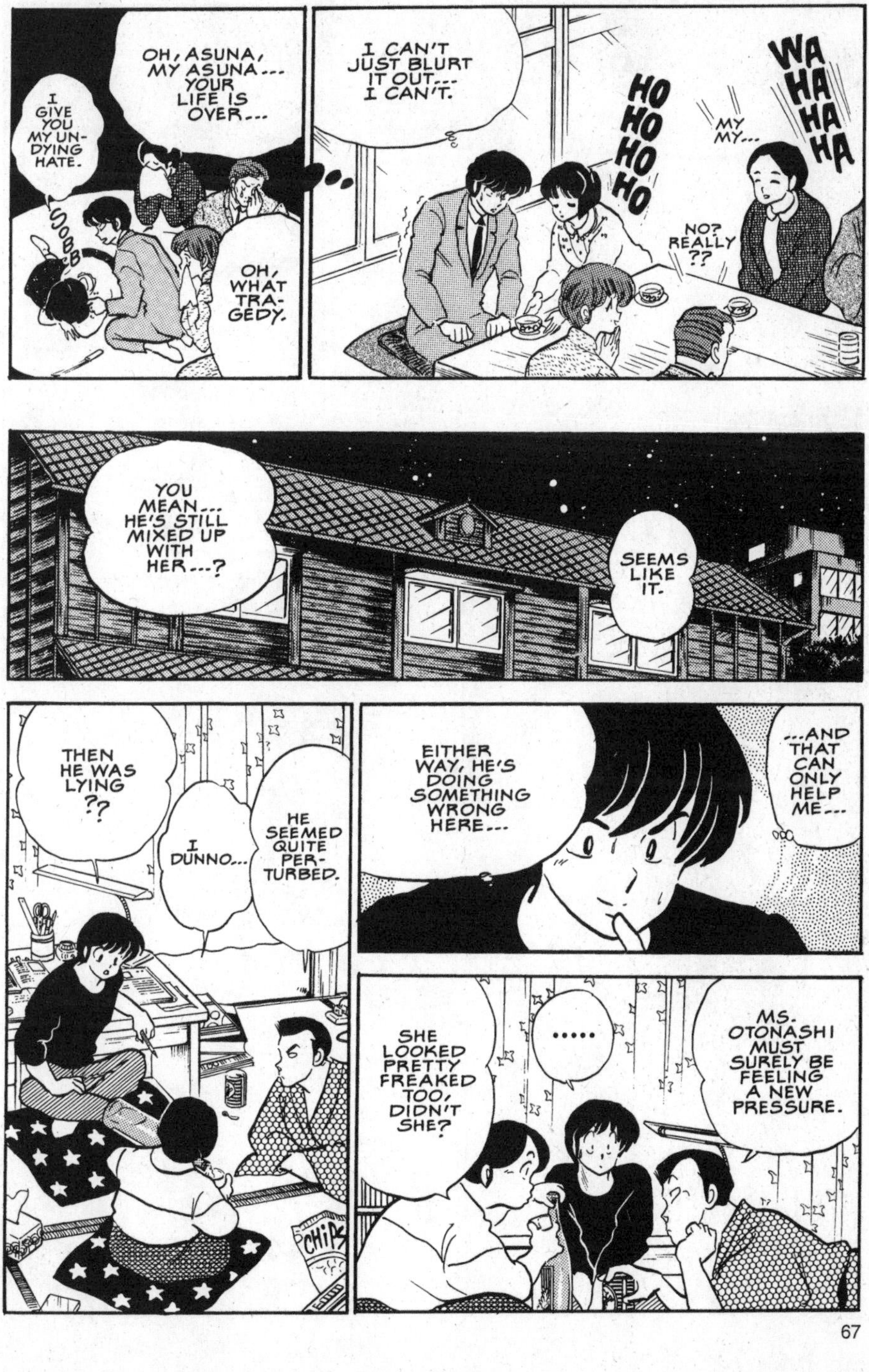
OH, ASUNA, MY ASUNA... YOUR LIFE IS OVER...
I GIVE YOU MY UN-DYING HATE.
SOBB
OH, WHAT TRA-GEDY.
I CAN'T JUST BLURT IT OUT... I CAN'T.
HO HO HO HO HO
WA HA HA HA HA
MY MY...
NO? REALLY ??
YOU MEAN... HE'S STILL MIXED UP WITH HER...?
SEEMS LIKE IT.
THEN HE WAS LYING ??
I DUNNO...
HE SEEMED QUITE PER-TURBED.
CHIPS
EITHER WAY, HE'S DOING SOMETHING WRONG HERE...
...AND THAT CAN ONLY HELP ME...
SHE LOOKED PRETTY FREAKED TOO, DIDN'T SHE?
.....
MS. OTONASHI MUST SURELY BE FEELING A NEW PRESSURE.

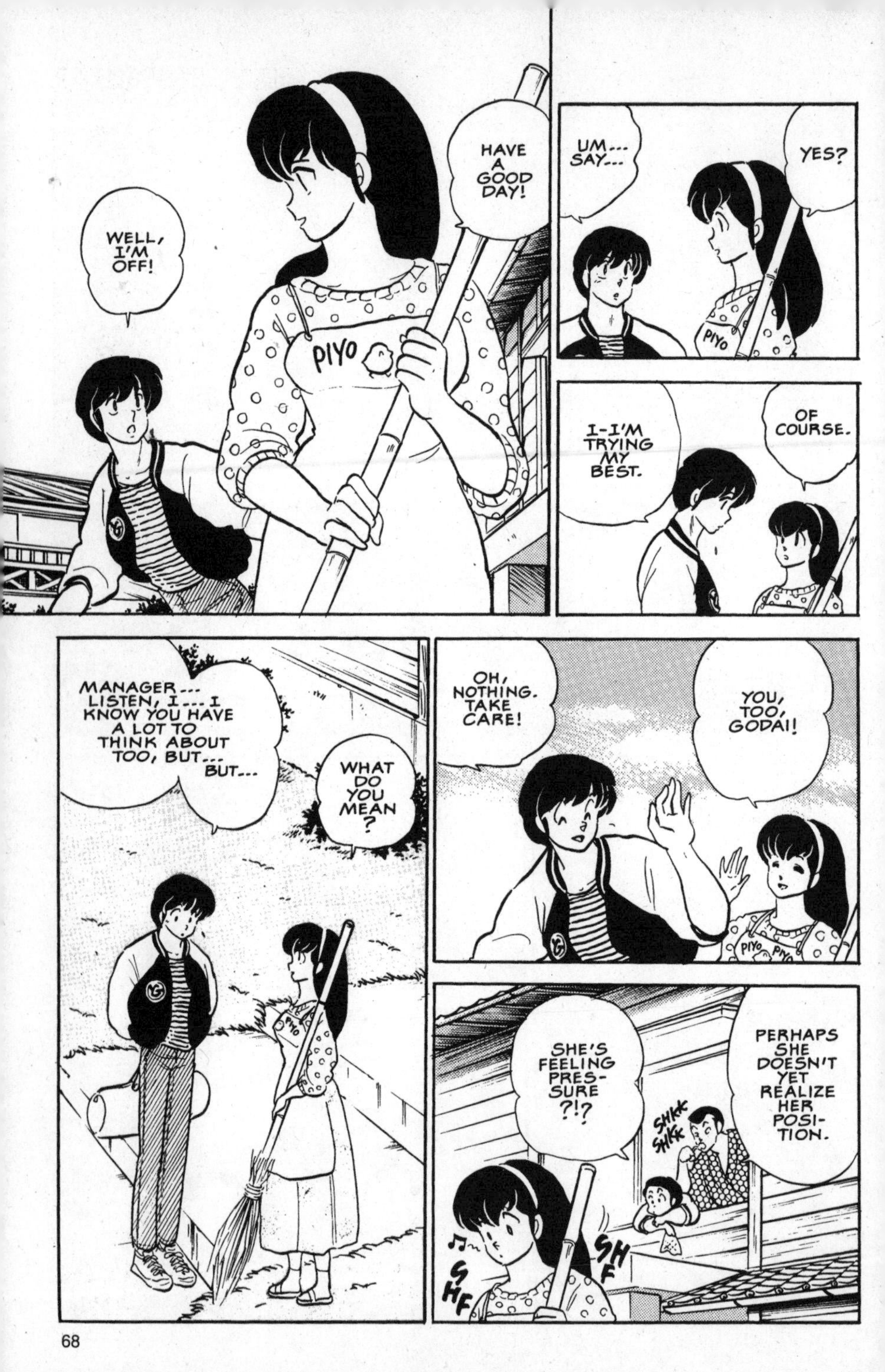
WELL, I'M OFF!
HAVE A GOOD DAY!
PIYO
UM... SAY...
YES?
PIYO
I-I'M TRYING MY BEST.
OF COURSE.
MANAGER... LISTEN, I... I KNOW YOU HAVE A LOT TO THINK ABOUT TOO, BUT... BUT...
WHAT DO YOU MEAN?
PIYO
OH, NOTHING. TAKE CARE!
YOU, TOO, GODAI!
PIYO PIYO
SHE'S FEELING PRES-SURE ?!?
PERHAPS SHE DOESN'T YET REALIZE HER POSI-TION.
SHKK SHKK
SHF
SHF

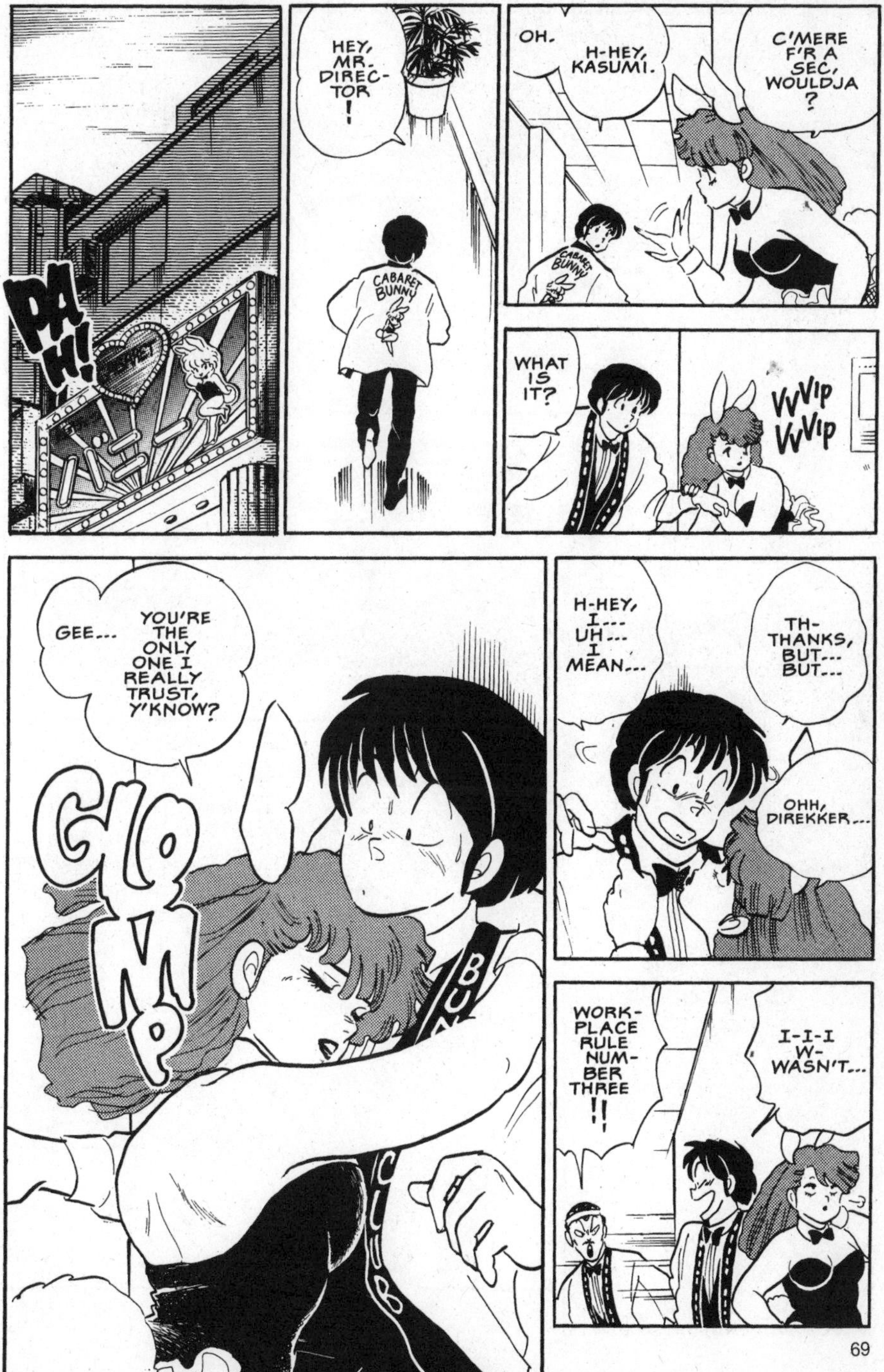
PA-H!
HEY, MR. DIRECTOR!
OH.
H-HEY, KASUMI.
C'MERE F'R A SEC, WOULDJA?
WHAT IS IT?
VVVIP VVVIP
GEE... YOU'RE THE ONLY ONE I REALLY TRUST, Y'KNOW?
GLOMP
H-HEY, I... UH... I MEAN...
TH-THANKS, BUT... BUT...
OHH, DIREKKER...
WORK-PLACE RULE NUM-BER THREE!!
I-I-I W-WASN'T...

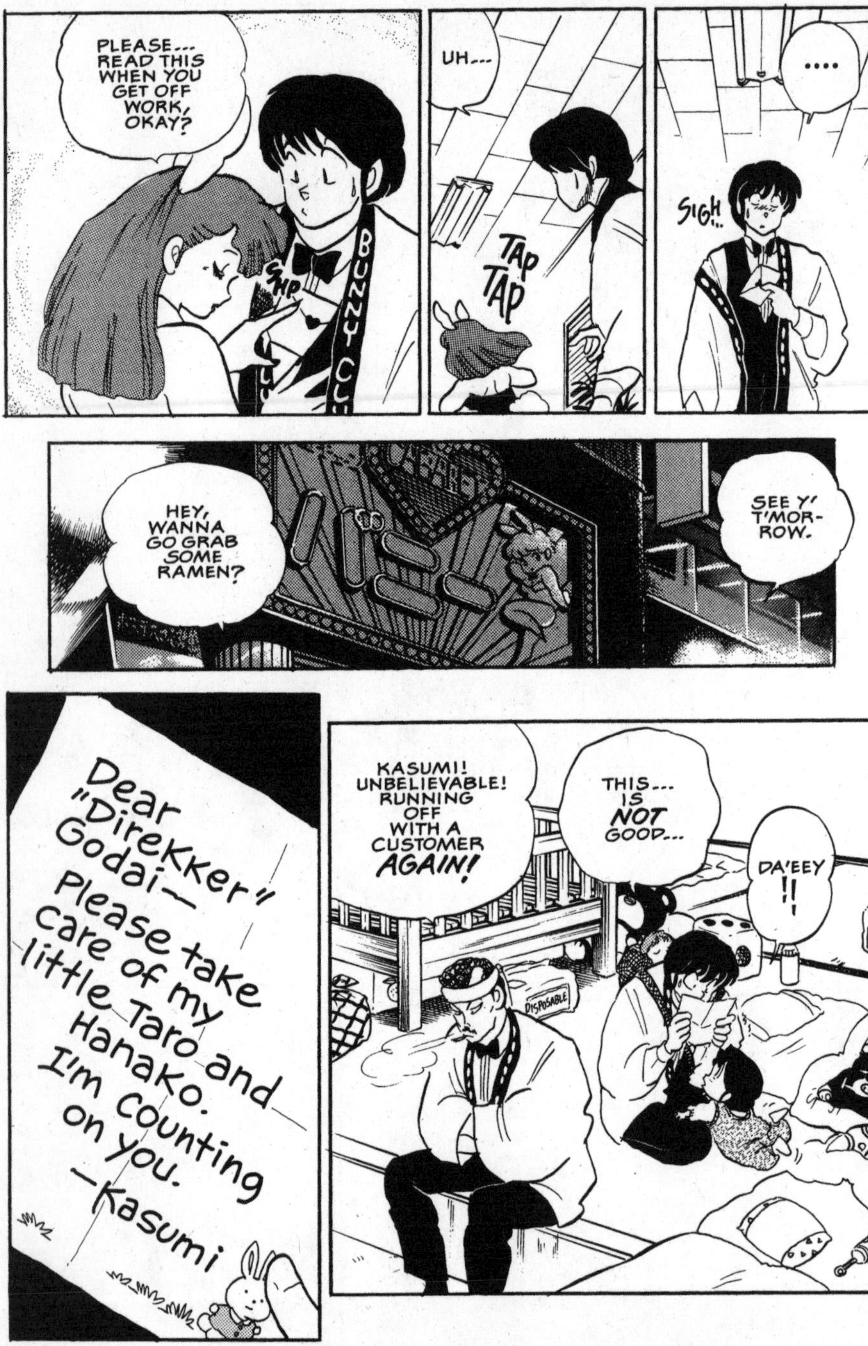
PLEASE... READ THIS WHEN YOU GET OFF WORK, OKAY?
SHP
BUNNY CLU
UH...
TAP TAP
....
SIGH!..
HEY, WANNA GO GRAB SOME RAMEN?
SEE Y' T'MOR-ROW.
Dear "Direkker" Godai~ Please take care of my little Taro and Hanako. I'm counting on you. —Kasumi
KASUMI! UNBELIEVABLE! RUNNING OFF WITH A CUSTOMER AGAIN!
THIS... IS NOT GOOD...
DA'EEY !!
DISPOSABLE

PART FIVE
THE TROUBLE WITH GIRLS...
AND BOYS

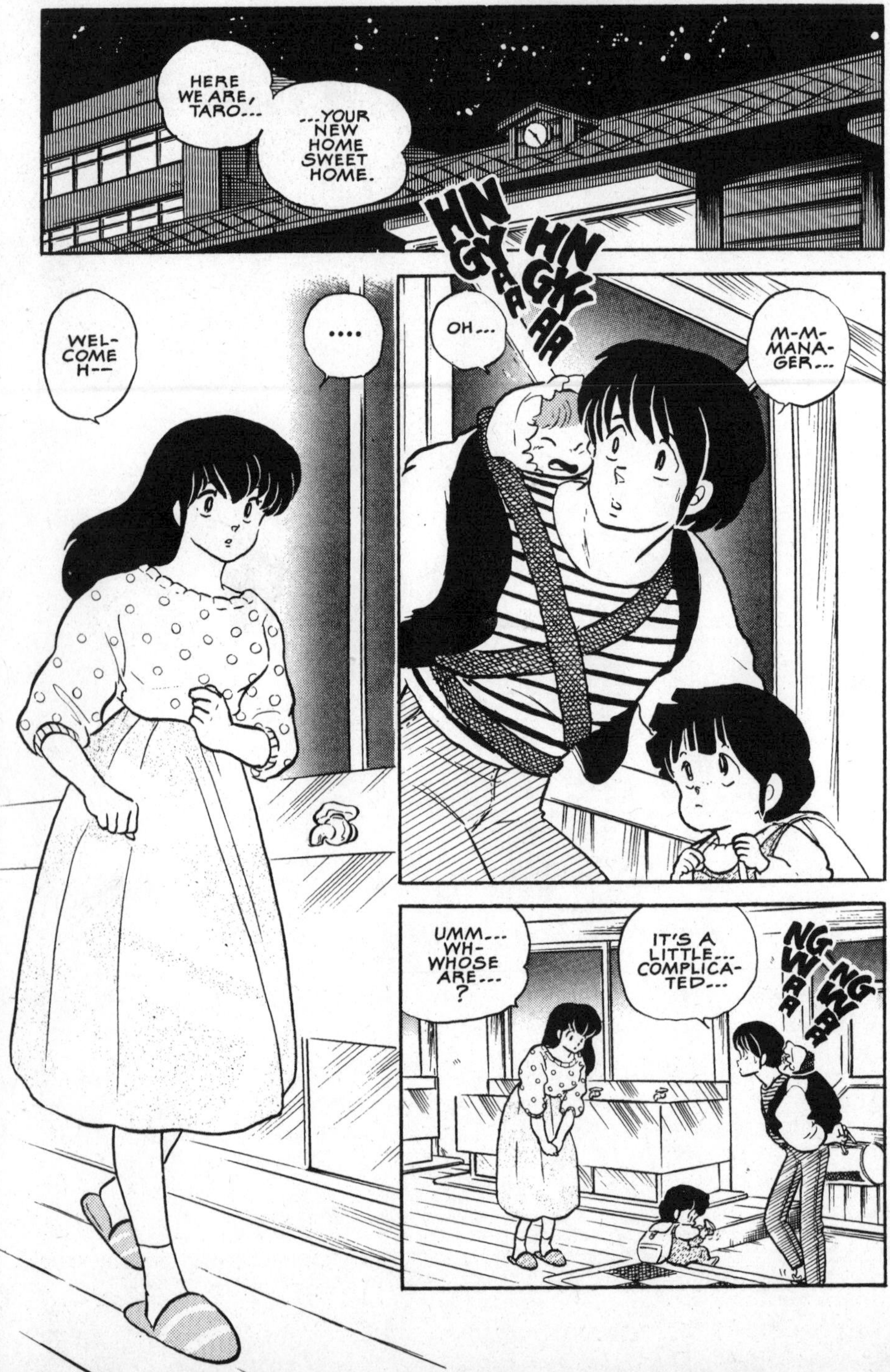
HERE WE ARE, TARO...
...YOUR NEW HOME SWEET HOME.
HNGYAA
HNGKAAA
WEL-COME H--
....
OH...
M-M-MANA-GER...
UMM... WH-WHOSE ARE...?
IT'S A LITTLE... COMPLICA-TED...
NG-WAA
NG-WAA

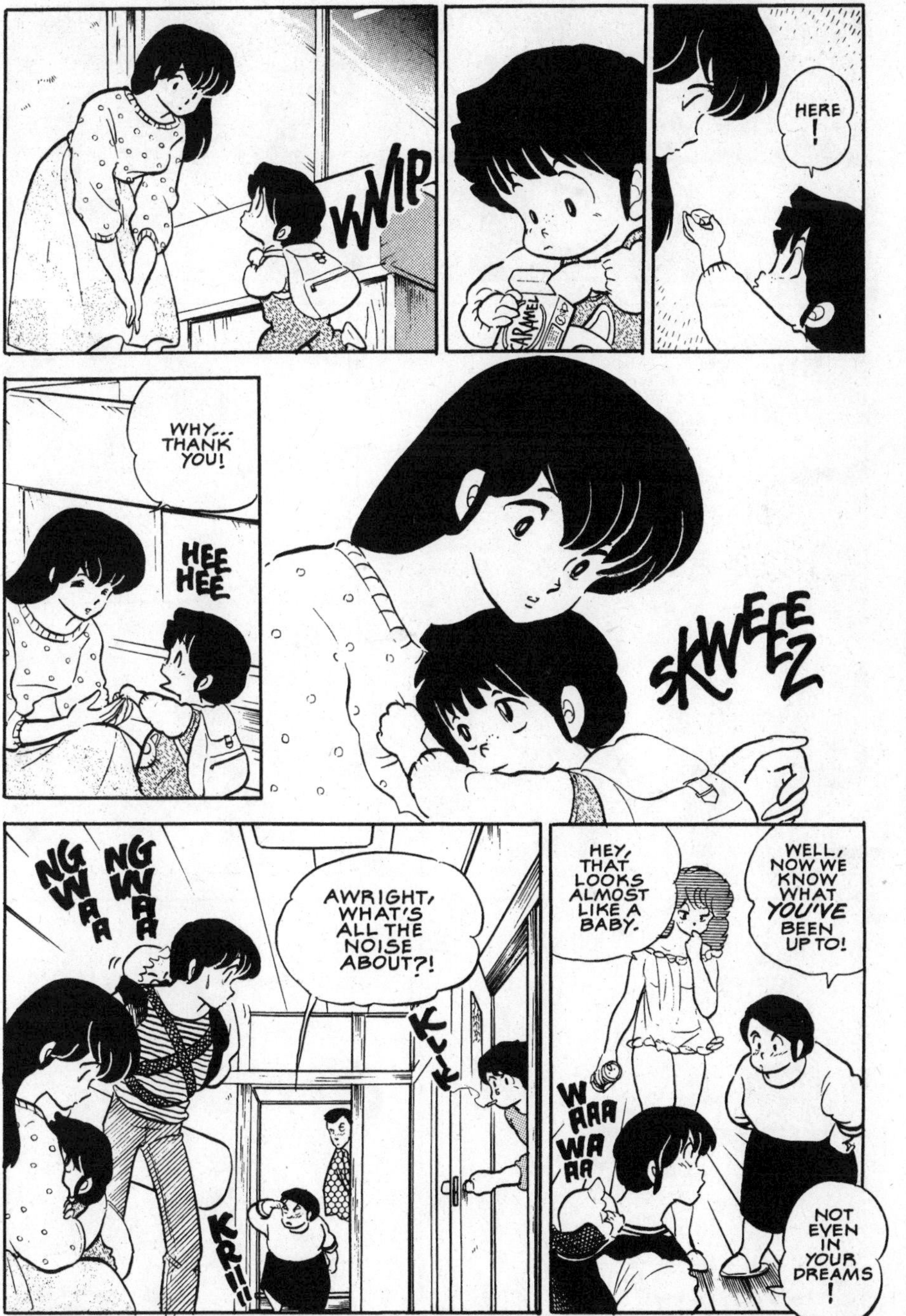
WHIP
CARAMEL
HERE!
WHY... THANK YOU!
HEE HEE
SKWEEZ
NG WAA NG WAA
AWRIGHT, WHAT'S ALL THE NOISE ABOUT?!
KLIK
KRII
HEY, THAT LOOKS ALMOST LIKE A BABY.
WELL, NOW WE KNOW WHAT YOU'VE BEEN UP TO!
WAAA WAAA
NOT EVEN IN YOUR DREAMS!

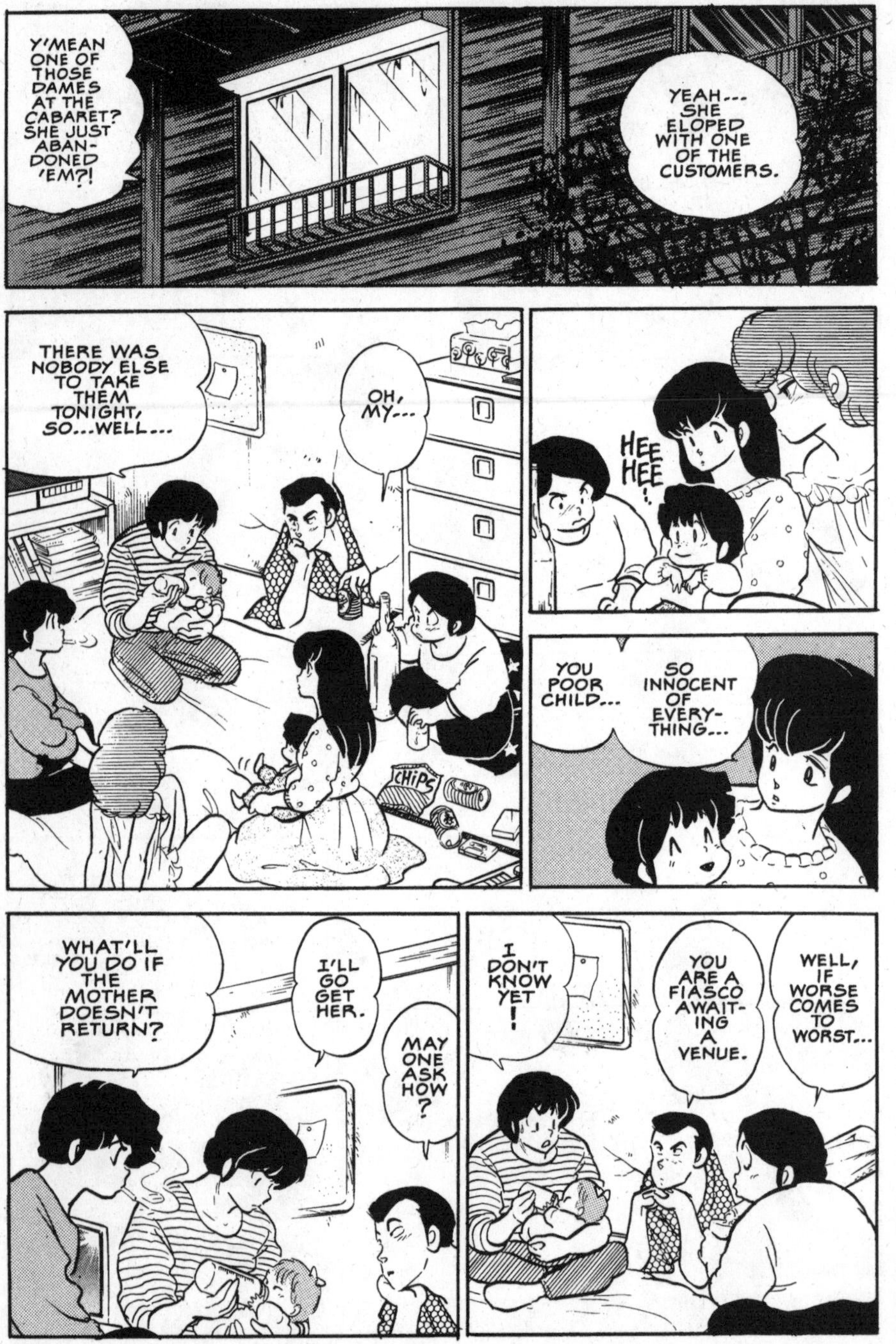
Y'MEAN ONE OF THOSE DAMES AT THE CABARET? SHE JUST ABAN-DONED 'EM?!
YEAH... SHE ELOPED WITH ONE OF THE CUSTOMERS.
THERE WAS NOBODY ELSE TO TAKE THEM TONIGHT, SO...WELL...
OH, MY...
CHIPS
HEE HEE
YOU POOR CHILD...
SO INNOCENT OF EVERY-THING...
WHAT'LL YOU DO IF THE MOTHER DOESN'T RETURN?
I'LL GO GET HER.
MAY ONE ASK HOW?
I DON'T KNOW YET!
YOU ARE A FIASCO AWAIT-ING A VENUE.
WELL, IF WORSE COMES TO WORST...

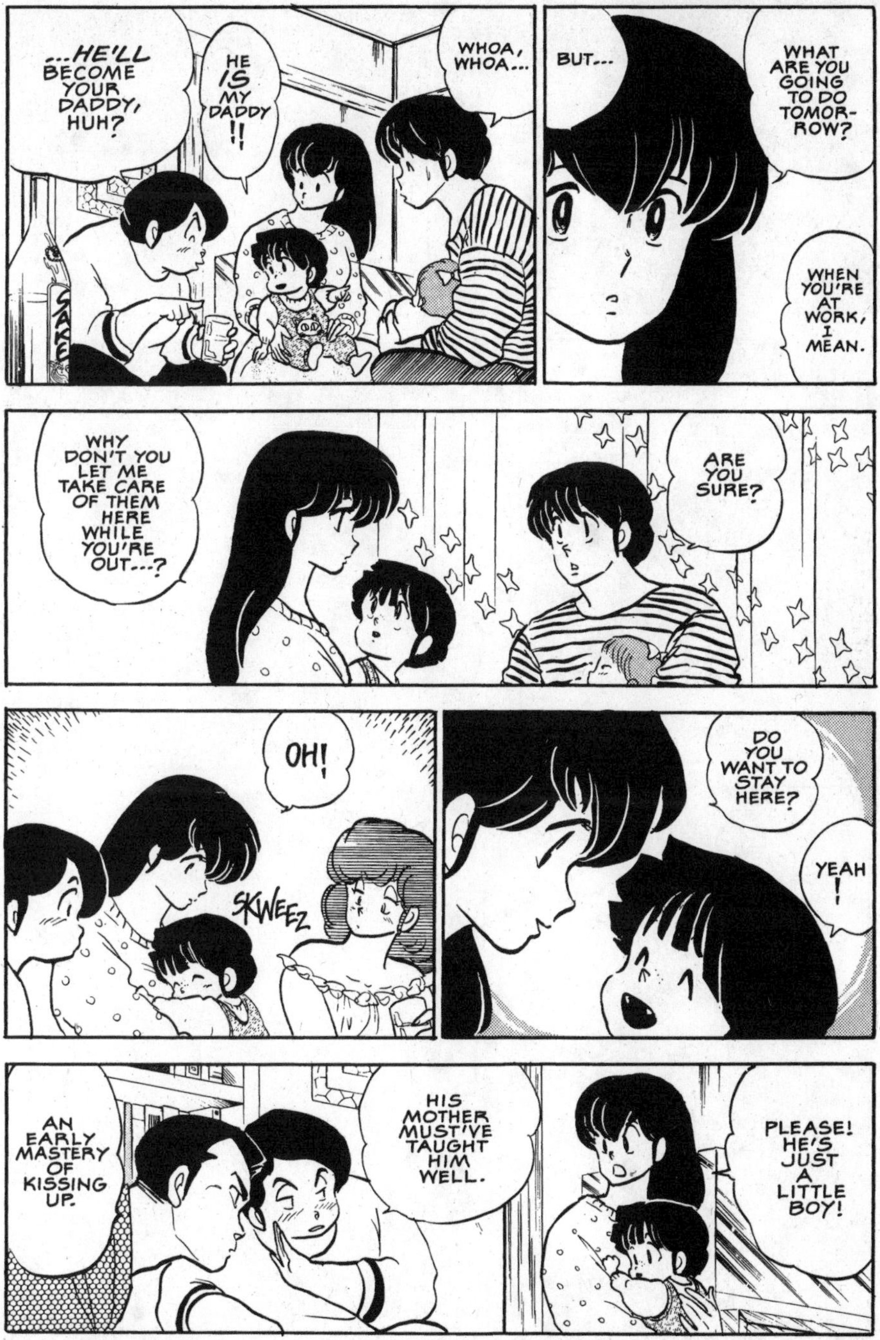
...HE'LL BECOME YOUR DADDY, HUH?
HE IS MY DADDY!!
WHOA, WHOA...
BUT...
WHAT ARE YOU GOING TO DO TOMORROW?
WHEN YOU'RE AT WORK, I MEAN.
WHY DON'T YOU LET ME TAKE CARE OF THEM HERE WHILE YOU'RE OUT...?
ARE YOU SURE?
OH!
SKWEEZ
DO YOU WANT TO STAY HERE?
YEAH!
AN EARLY MASTERY OF KISSING UP.
HIS MOTHER MUST'VE TAUGHT HIM WELL.
PLEASE! HE'S JUST A LITTLE BOY!

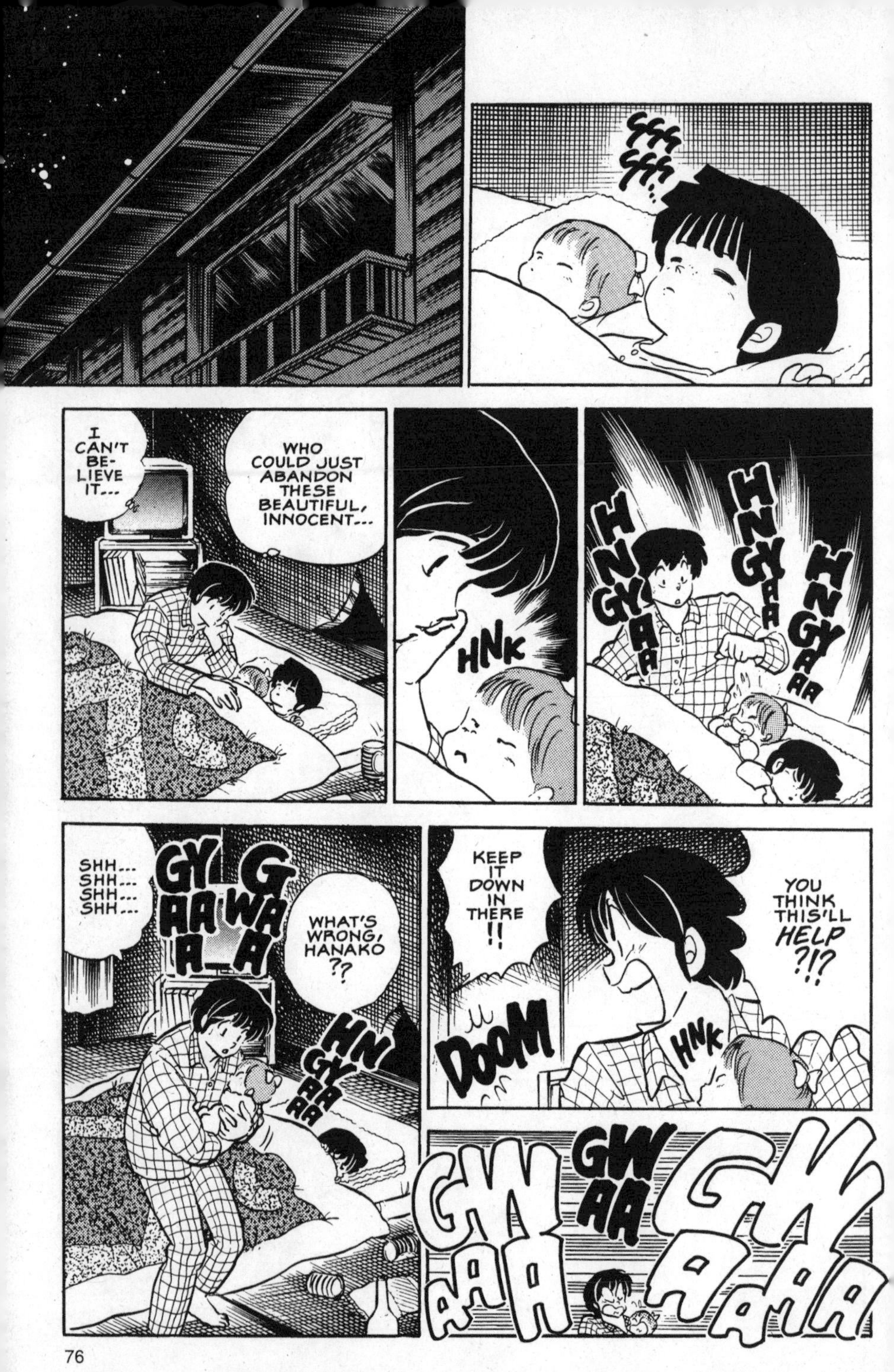
SSS SSS...
I CAN'T BELIEVE IT...
WHO COULD JUST ABANDON THESE BEAUTIFUL, INNOCENT...
HNK
HNGYAA
HNGYAA
HNGYAAA
SHH... SHH... SHH... SHH...
GYAAA
GWAA
WHAT'S WRONG, HANAKO??
HNGYAAA
KEEP IT DOWN IN THERE!!
YOU THINK THIS'LL HELP?!?
DOOM
HNK
GWAAA
GWAA
GWAAAA

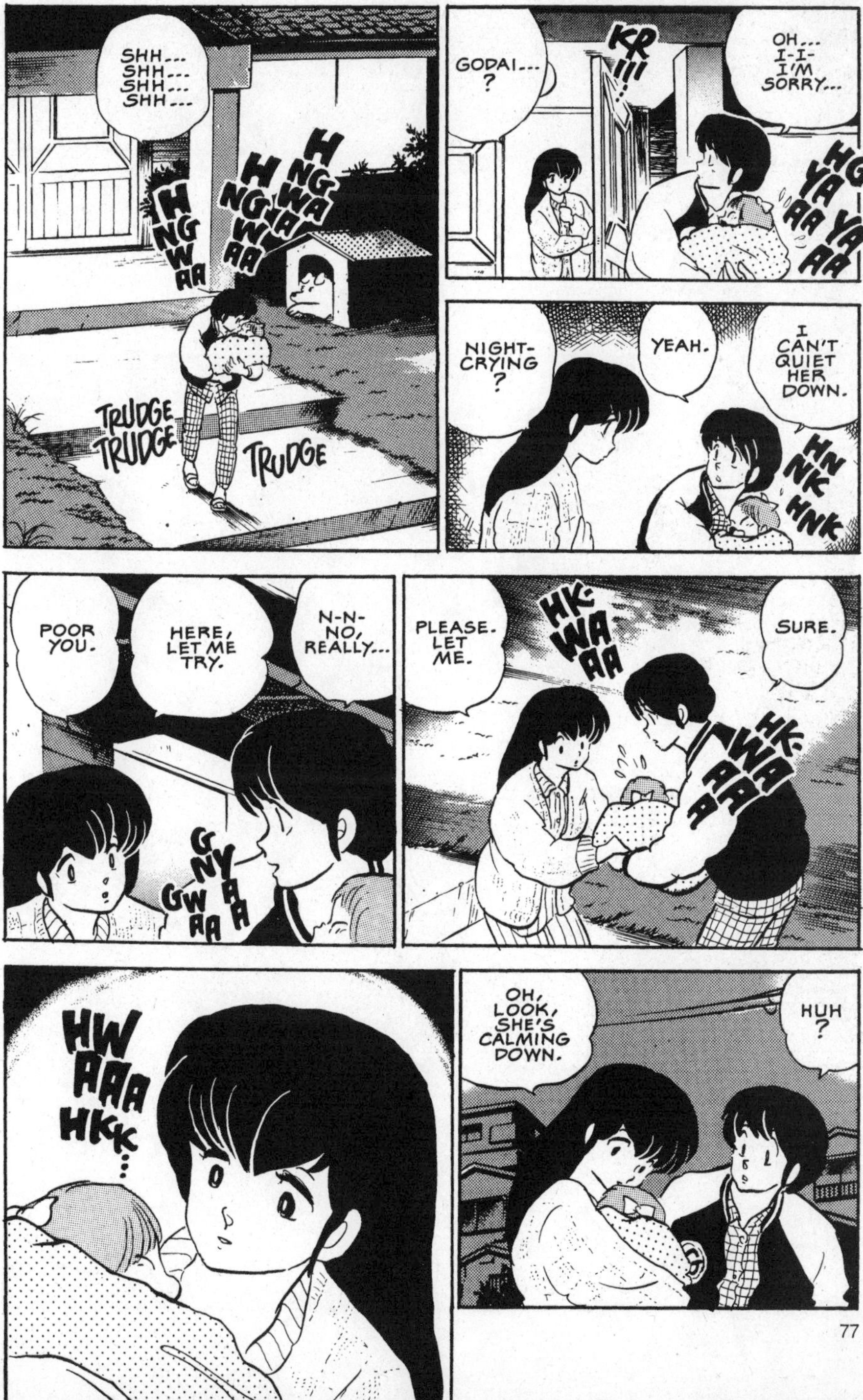
SHH...
SHH...
SHH...
SHH...
HNGWAA
HNGWAA
HNGWAA
TRUDGE
TRUDGE
TRUDGE
GODAI...?
KRIII
OH... I-I-I'M SORRY...
HG YA AA YA AA
NIGHT-CRYING?
YEAH.
I CAN'T QUIET HER DOWN.
HNK HNK
POOR YOU.
HERE, LET ME TRY.
N-N-NO, REALLY...
GNYAA GWAA
PLEASE. LET ME.
HK-WAAA
SURE.
HK-WAAAA
HWAAAHKK...
OH, LOOK, SHE'S CALMING DOWN.
HUH?

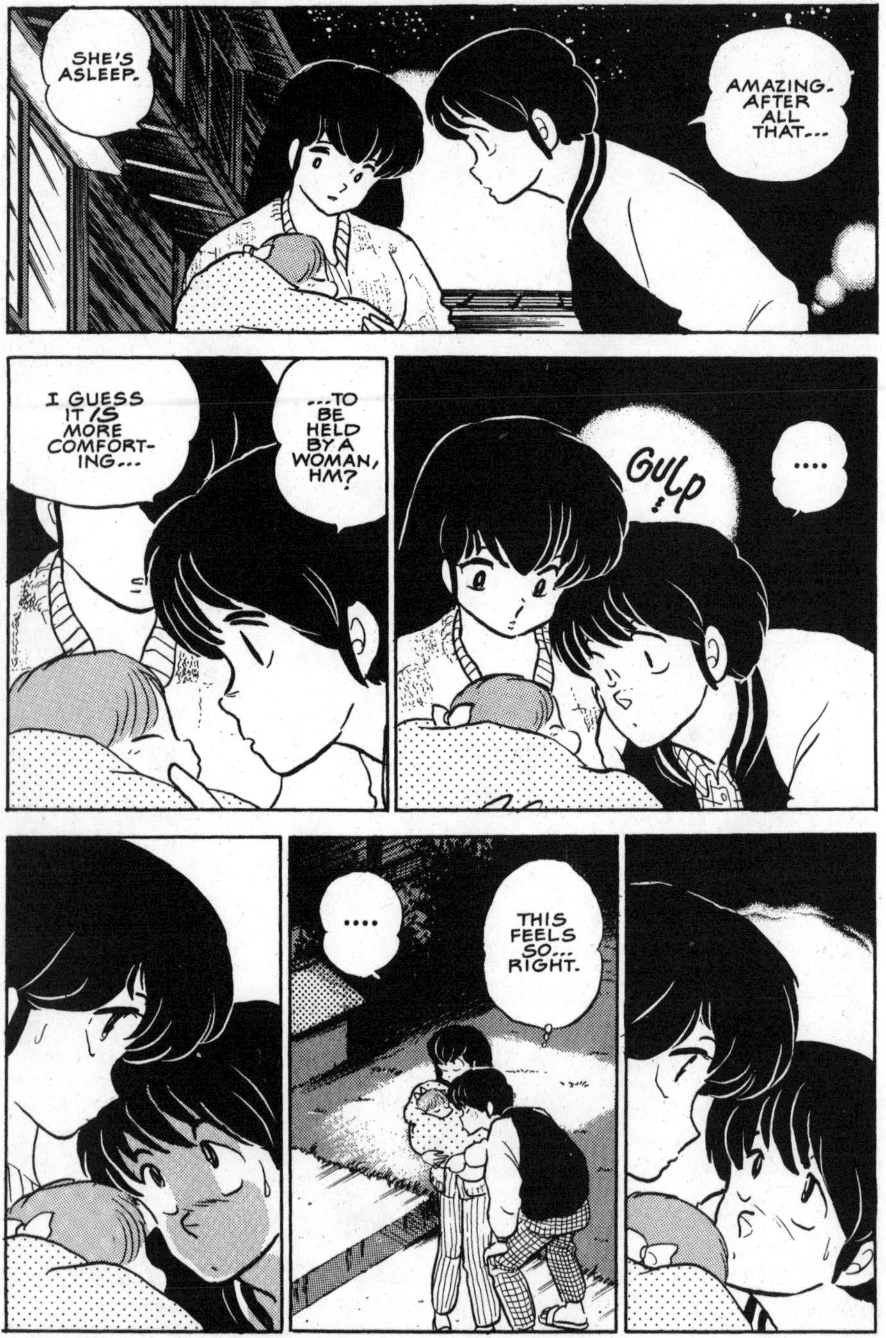
SHE'S ASLEEP.
AMAZING. AFTER ALL THAT...
I GUESS IT IS MORE COMFORTING...
...TO BE HELD BY A WOMAN, HM?
GULP
....
....
THIS FEELS SO... RIGHT.

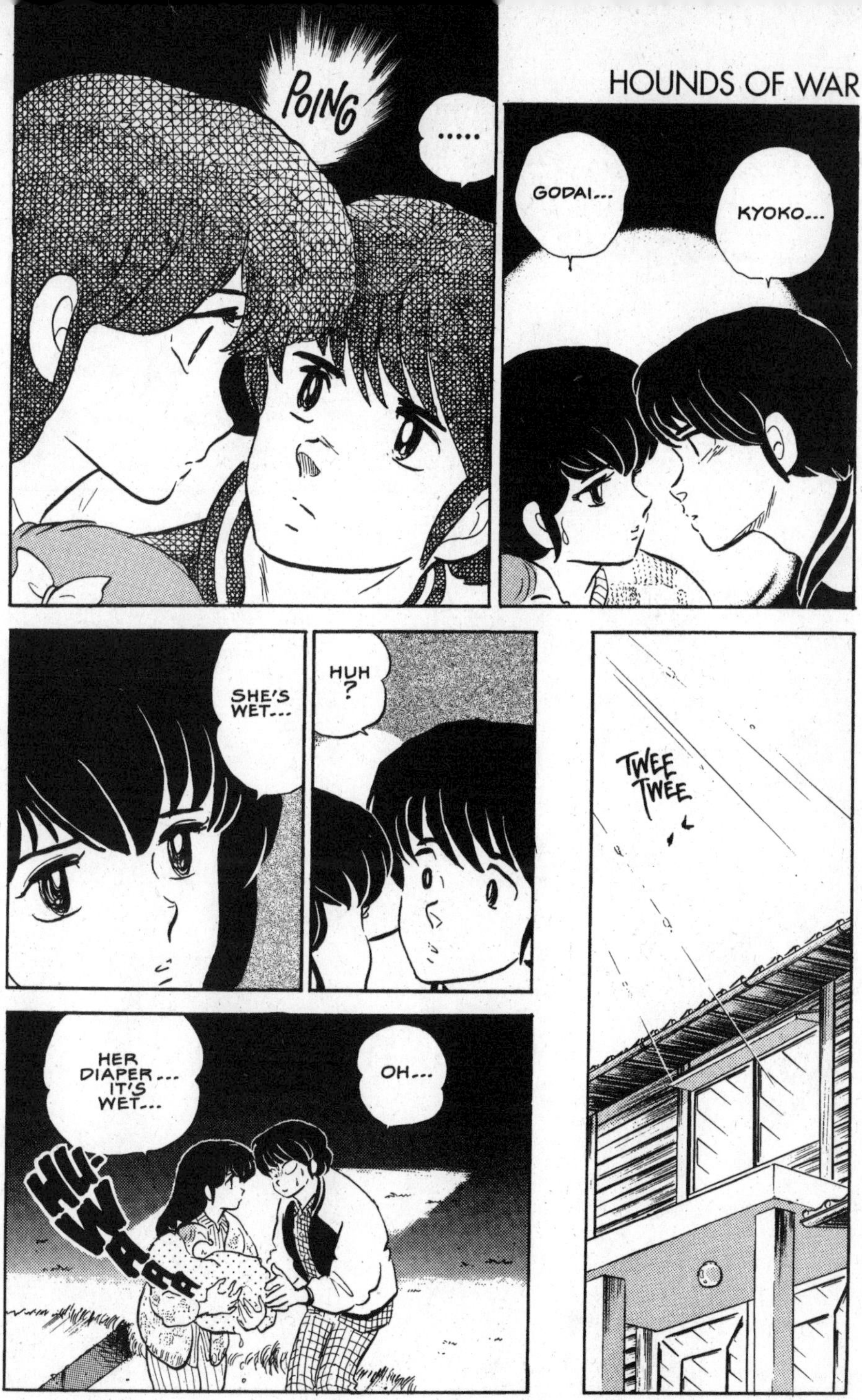
POING
......
GODAI...
KYOKO...
SHE'S WET...
HUH ?
HER DIAPER... IT'S WET...
OH...
HU WAAA
TWEE TWEE

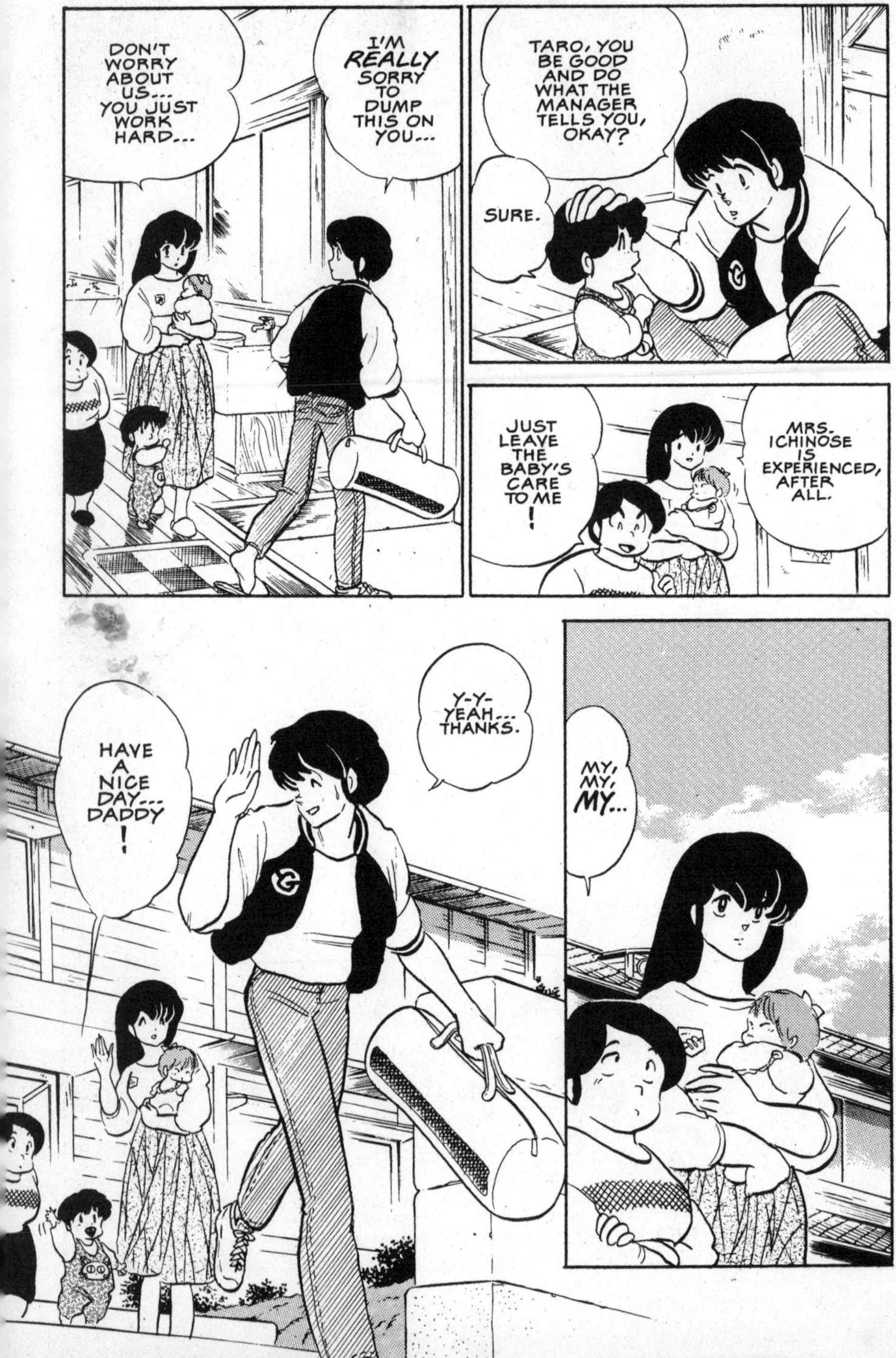
I'M REALLY SORRY TO DUMP THIS ON YOU...
DON'T WORRY ABOUT US... YOU JUST WORK HARD...
TARO, YOU BE GOOD AND DO WHAT THE MANAGER TELLS YOU, OKAY?
SURE.
JUST LEAVE THE BABY'S CARE TO ME!
MRS. ICHINOSE IS EXPERIENCED, AFTER ALL.
HAVE A NICE DAY... DADDY!
Y-Y-YEAH... THANKS.
MY, MY, MY...

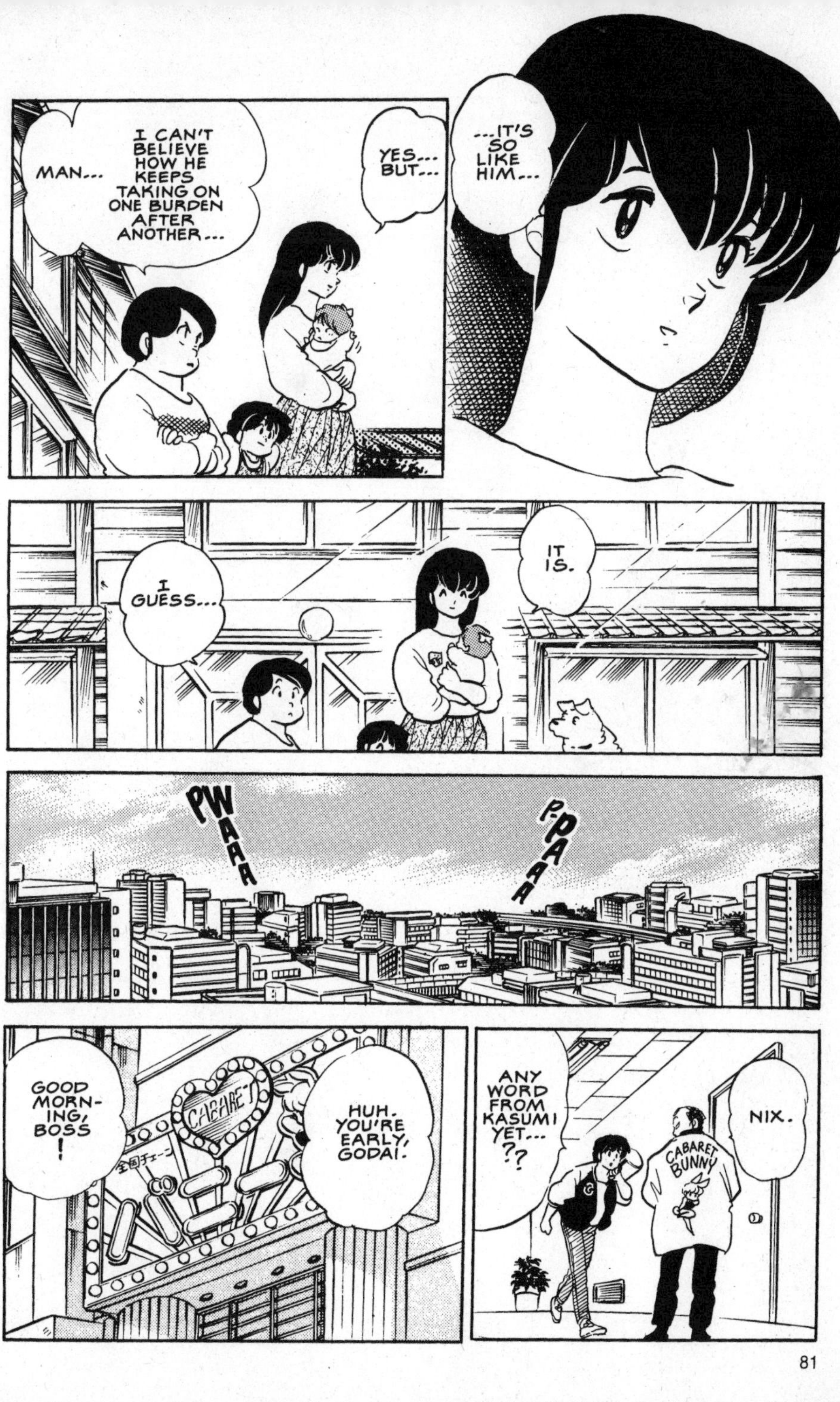
MAN... I CAN'T BELIEVE HOW HE KEEPS TAKING ON ONE BURDEN AFTER ANOTHER...
YES... BUT...
...IT'S SO LIKE HIM...
I GUESS...
IT IS.
PWAAAA
P-PAAAA
GOOD MORNING, BOSS!
CABARET
全国チェーン
HUH. YOU'RE EARLY, GODAI.
ANY WORD FROM KASUMI YET...??
CABARET BUNNY
NIX.

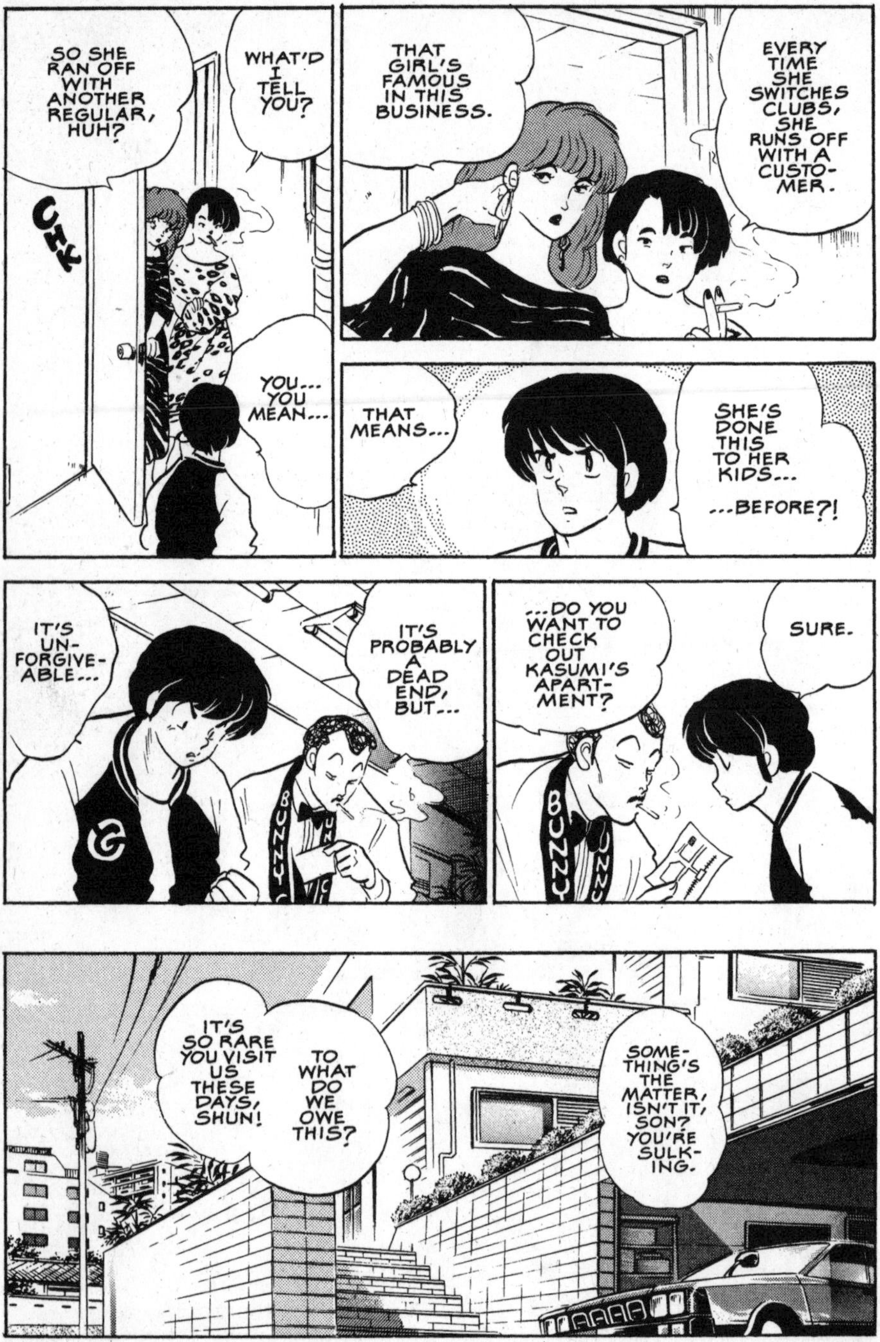
SO SHE RAN OFF WITH ANOTHER REGULAR, HUH?
WHAT'D I TELL YOU?
CHK
YOU... YOU MEAN...
THAT GIRL'S FAMOUS IN THIS BUSINESS.
EVERY TIME SHE SWITCHES CLUBS, SHE RUNS OFF WITH A CUSTO-MER.
THAT MEANS...
SHE'S DONE THIS TO HER KIDS...
...BEFORE?!
IT'S UN-FORGIVE-ABLE...
IT'S PROBABLY A DEAD END, BUT...
...DO YOU WANT TO CHECK OUT KASUMI'S APART-MENT?
SURE.
IT'S SO RARE YOU VISIT US THESE DAYS, SHUN!
TO WHAT DO WE OWE THIS?
SOME-THING'S THE MATTER, ISN'T IT, SON? YOU'RE SULK-ING.

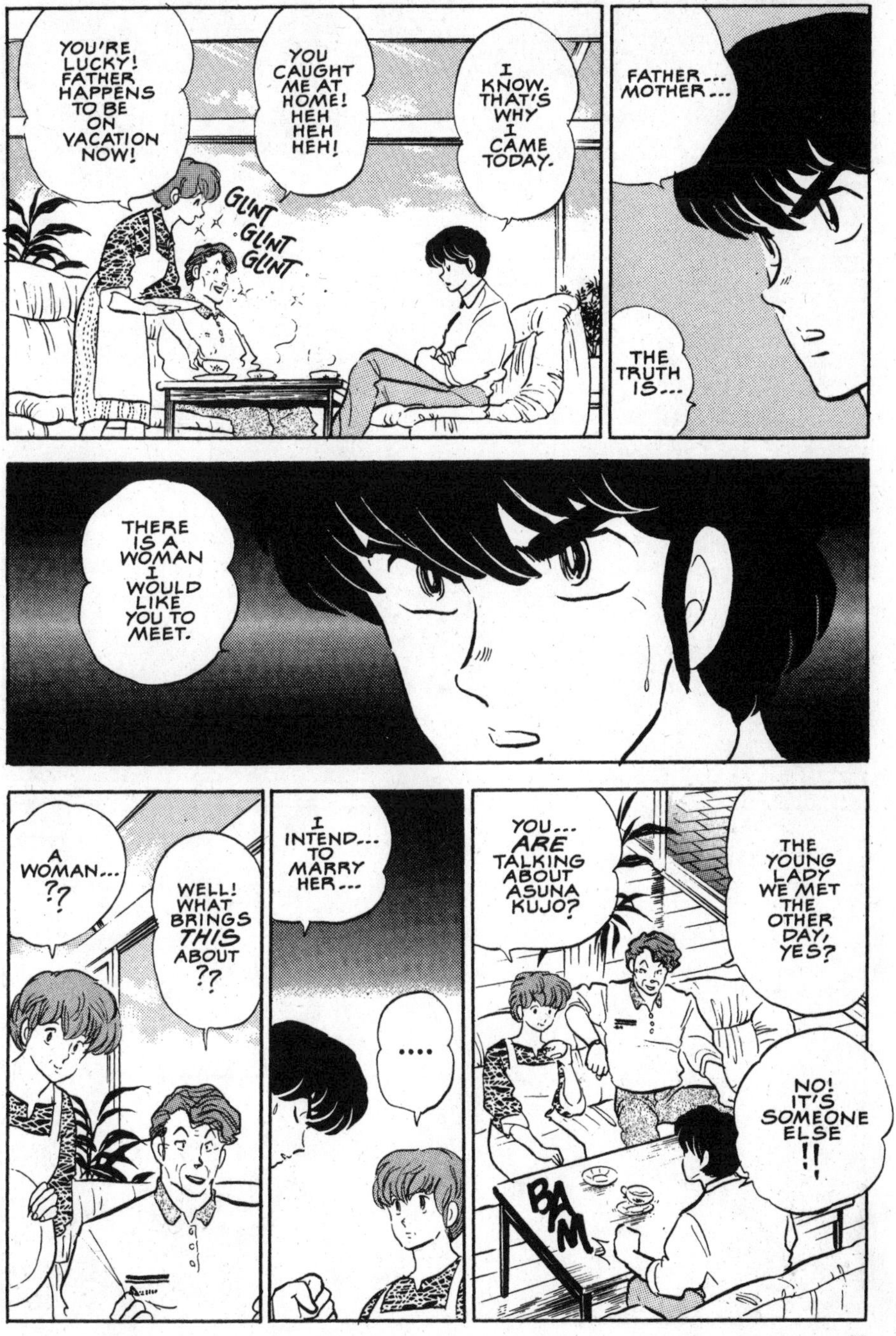
YOU'RE LUCKY! FATHER HAPPENS TO BE ON VACATION NOW!
YOU CAUGHT ME AT HOME! HEH HEH HEH!
GLINT GLINT GLINT
I KNOW. THAT'S WHY I CAME TODAY.
FATHER... MOTHER...
THE TRUTH IS...
THERE IS A WOMAN I WOULD LIKE YOU TO MEET.
A WOMAN...??
WELL! WHAT BRINGS *THIS* ABOUT??
I INTEND... TO MARRY HER...
....
YOU... *ARE* TALKING ABOUT ASUNA KUJO?
THE YOUNG LADY WE MET THE OTHER DAY, YES?
BAM
NO! IT'S SOMEONE ELSE!!

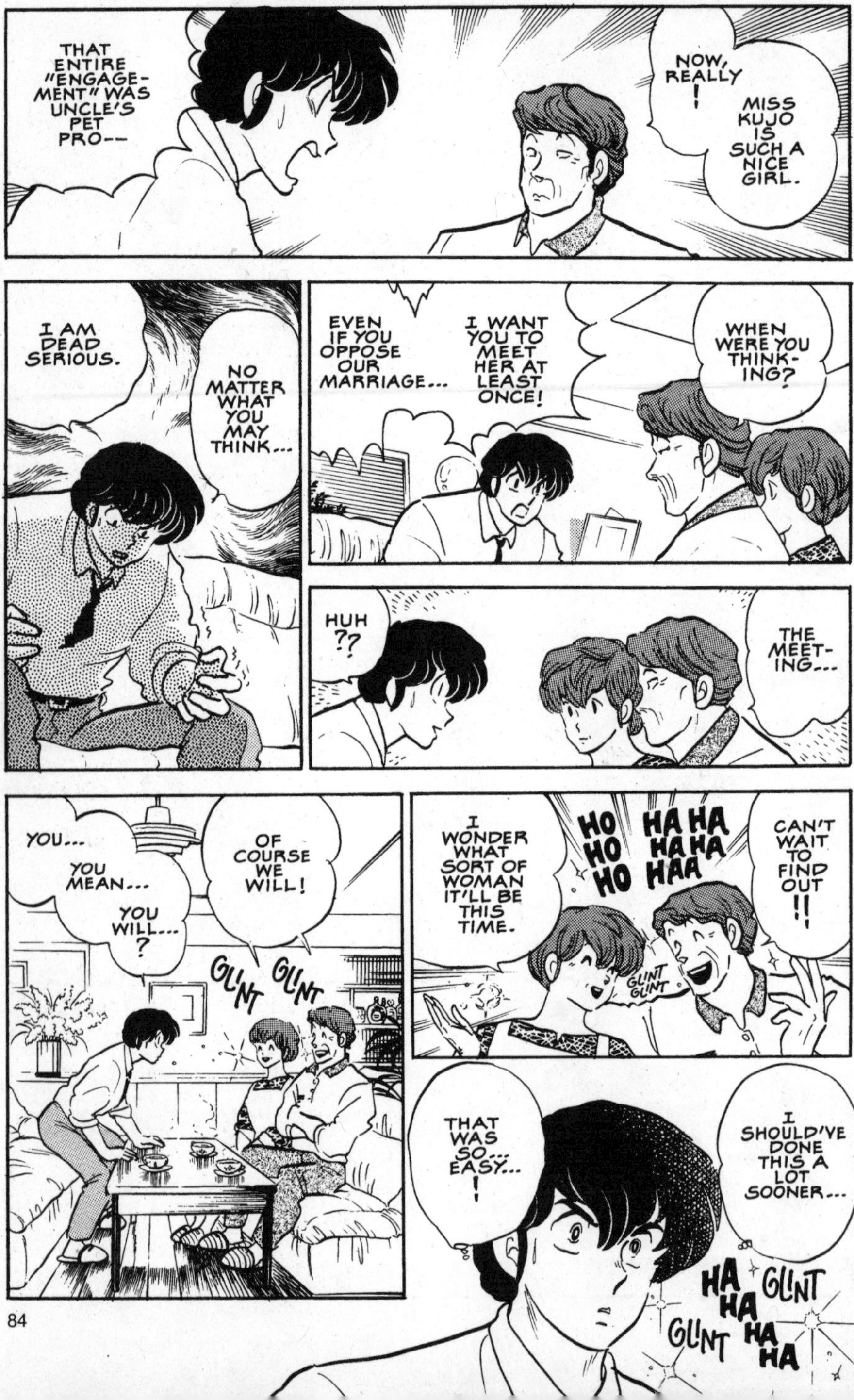
THAT ENTIRE "ENGAGEMENT" WAS UNCLE'S PET PRO--
NOW, REALLY!
MISS KUJO IS SUCH A NICE GIRL.
I AM DEAD SERIOUS.
NO MATTER WHAT YOU MAY THINK...
EVEN IF YOU OPPOSE OUR MARRIAGE...
I WANT YOU TO MEET HER AT LEAST ONCE!
WHEN WERE YOU THINKING?
HUH ??
THE MEETING...
YOU...
YOU MEAN...
YOU WILL...?
OF COURSE WE WILL!
GLINT GLINT
I WONDER WHAT SORT OF WOMAN IT'LL BE THIS TIME.
HO HO HO
HA HA HA HA HA HAA
GLINT GLINT
CAN'T WAIT TO FIND OUT!!
THAT WAS SO... EASY...!
I SHOULD'VE DONE THIS A LOT SOONER...
HA HA HA HA HA
GLINT GLINT

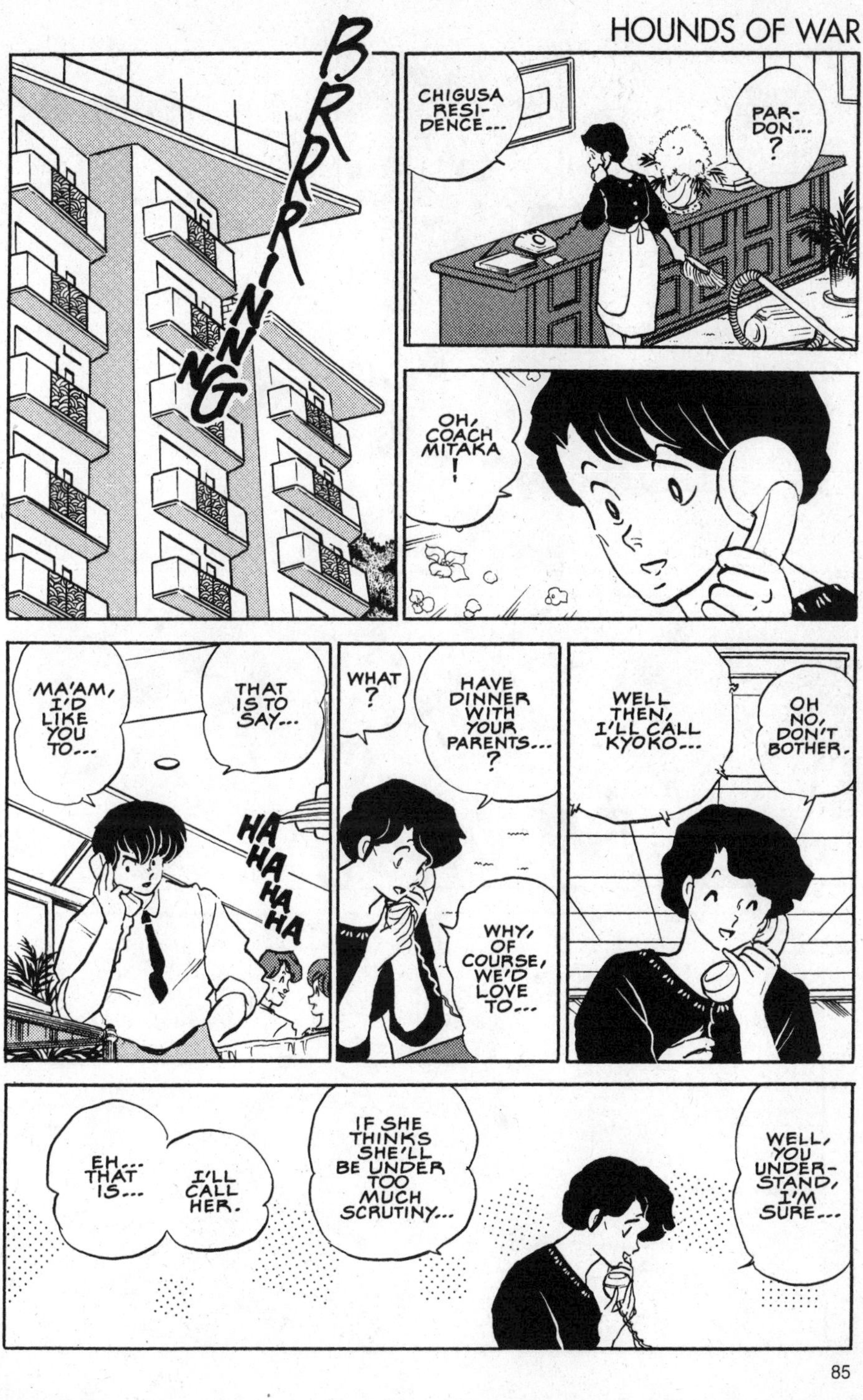
BRRRINNNG
CHIGUSA RESIDENCE...
PARDON...?
OH, COACH MITAKA!
MA'AM, I'D LIKE YOU TO...
THAT IS TO SAY...
HA HA HA HA
WHAT?
HAVE DINNER WITH YOUR PARENTS...?
WHY, OF COURSE, WE'D LOVE TO...
WELL THEN, I'LL CALL KYOKO...
OH NO, DON'T BOTHER.
EH... THAT IS...
I'LL CALL HER.
IF SHE THINKS SHE'LL BE UNDER TOO MUCH SCRUTINY...
WELL, YOU UNDERSTAND, I'M SURE...

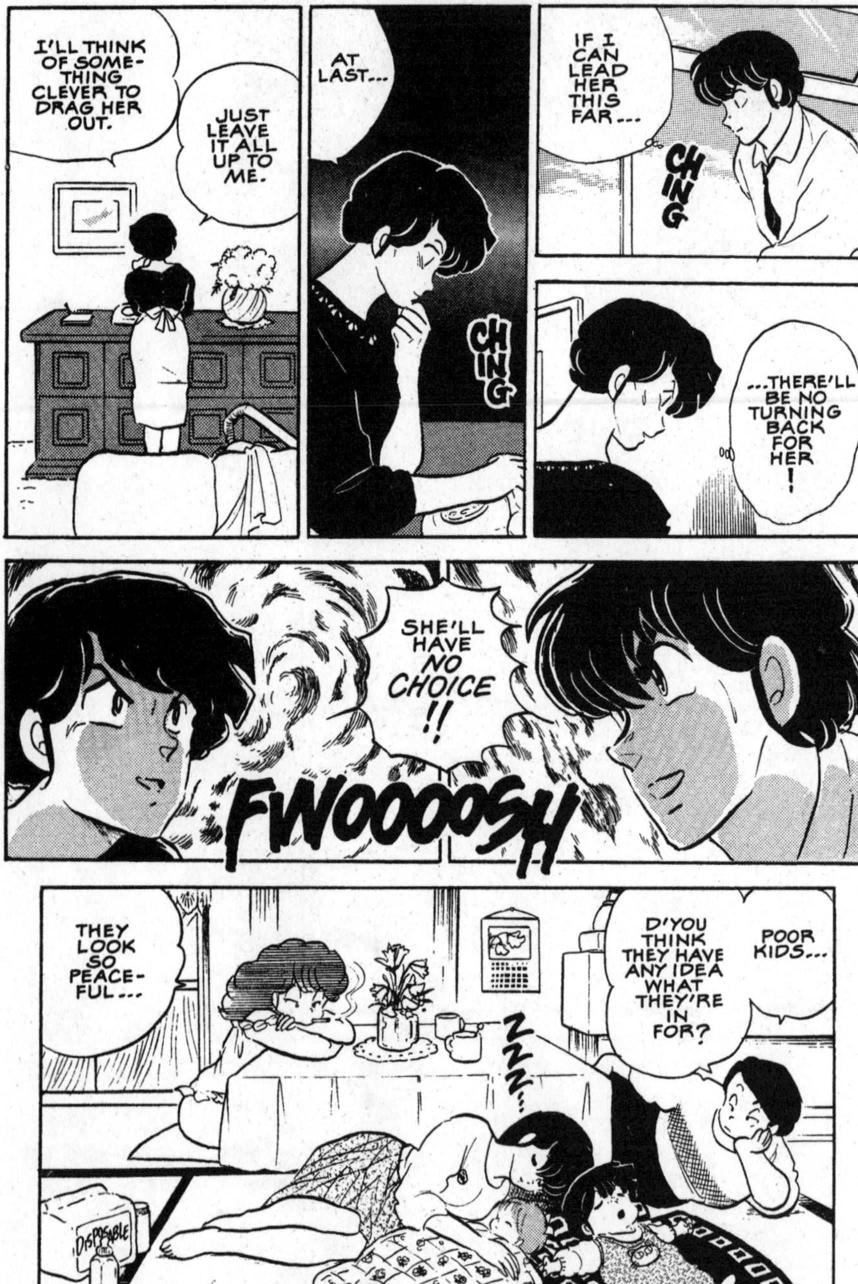
I'LL THINK OF SOME-THING CLEVER TO DRAG HER OUT.
JUST LEAVE IT ALL UP TO ME.
AT LAST...
CHING
IF I CAN LEAD HER THIS FAR...
CHING
...THERE'LL BE NO TURNING BACK FOR HER!
SHE'LL HAVE NO CHOICE!!
FWOOOOSH
THEY LOOK SO PEACE-FUL...
ZZZ...
D'YOU THINK THEY HAVE ANY IDEA WHAT THEY'RE IN FOR?
POOR KIDS...
DISPOSABLE

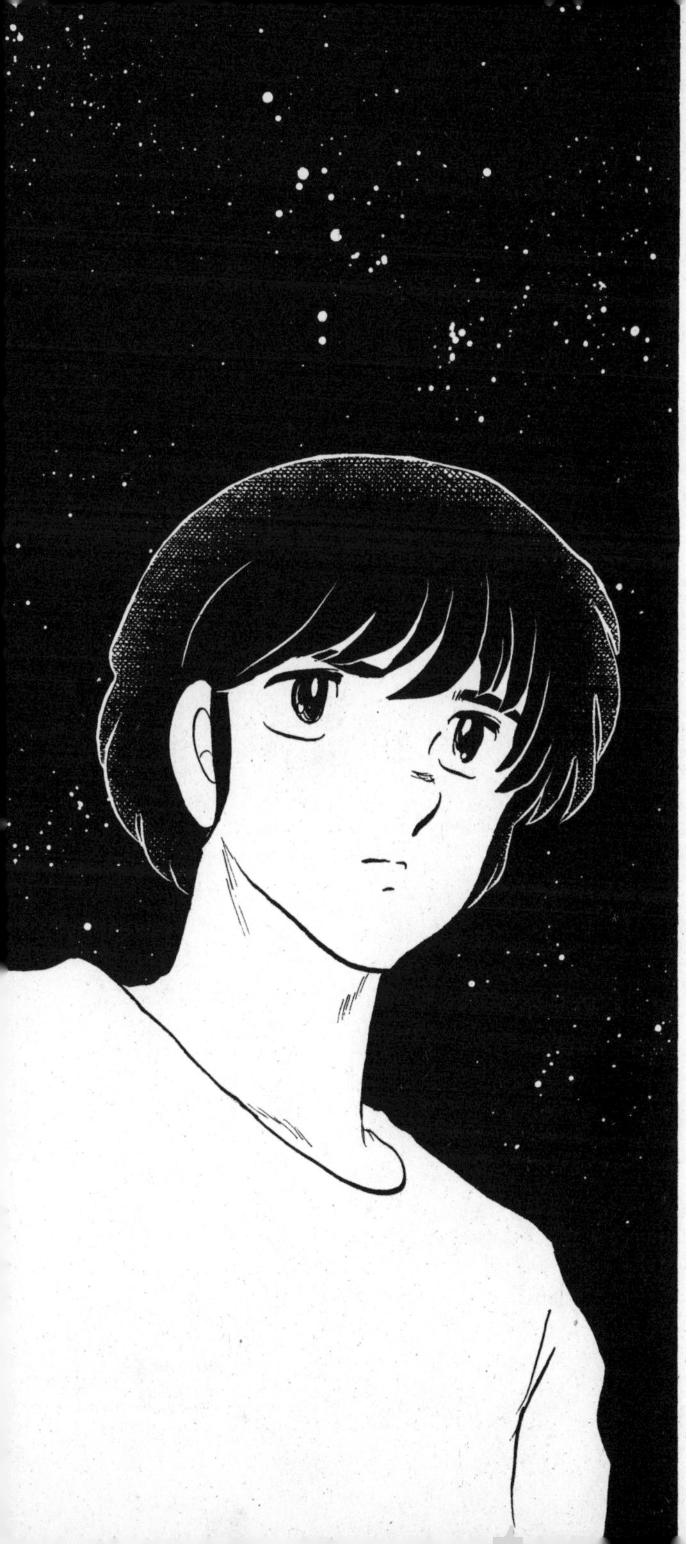

PART SIX
STARS IN YOUR EYES

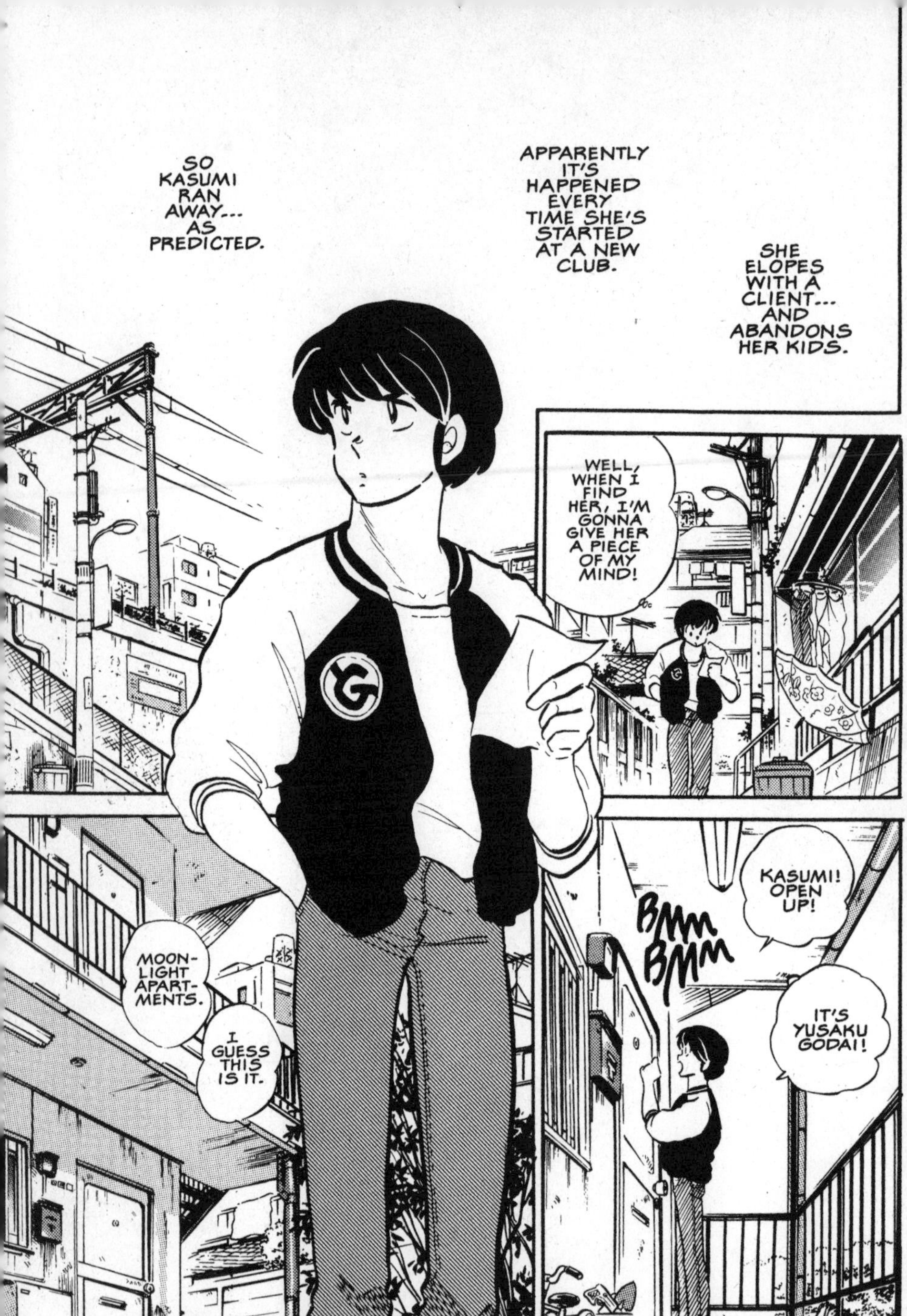
SO KASUMI RAN AWAY... AS PREDICTED.
APPARENTLY IT'S HAPPENED EVERY TIME SHE'S STARTED AT A NEW CLUB.
SHE ELOPES WITH A CLIENT... AND ABANDONS HER KIDS.
WELL, WHEN I FIND HER, I'M GONNA GIVE HER A PIECE OF MY MIND!
MOONLIGHT APARTMENTS.
I GUESS THIS IS IT.
BMM BMM
KASUMI! OPEN UP!
IT'S YUSAKU GODAI!

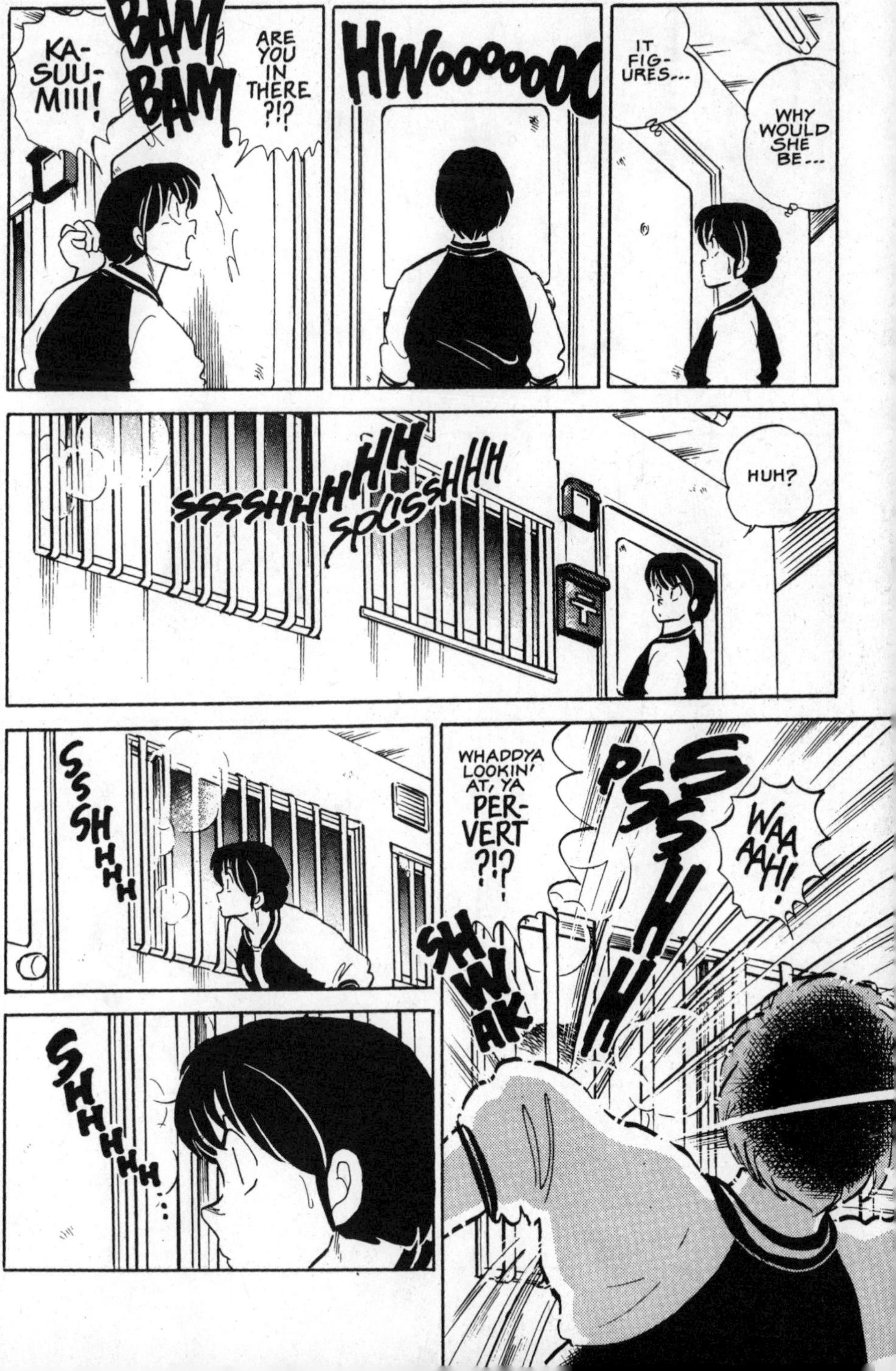
KA-SUU-MIIII!
BAM BAM
ARE YOU IN THERE ?!?
HWOOOOOOO
IT FIGURES...
WHY WOULD SHE BE...
SSSSHHHHHH
SPLISSHHHH
HUH?
SSSHHHH
SHHHHHH...
WHADDYA LOOKIN' AT, YA PER-VERT ?!?
PSSSHHHH
WAAAAH!
SHWAK

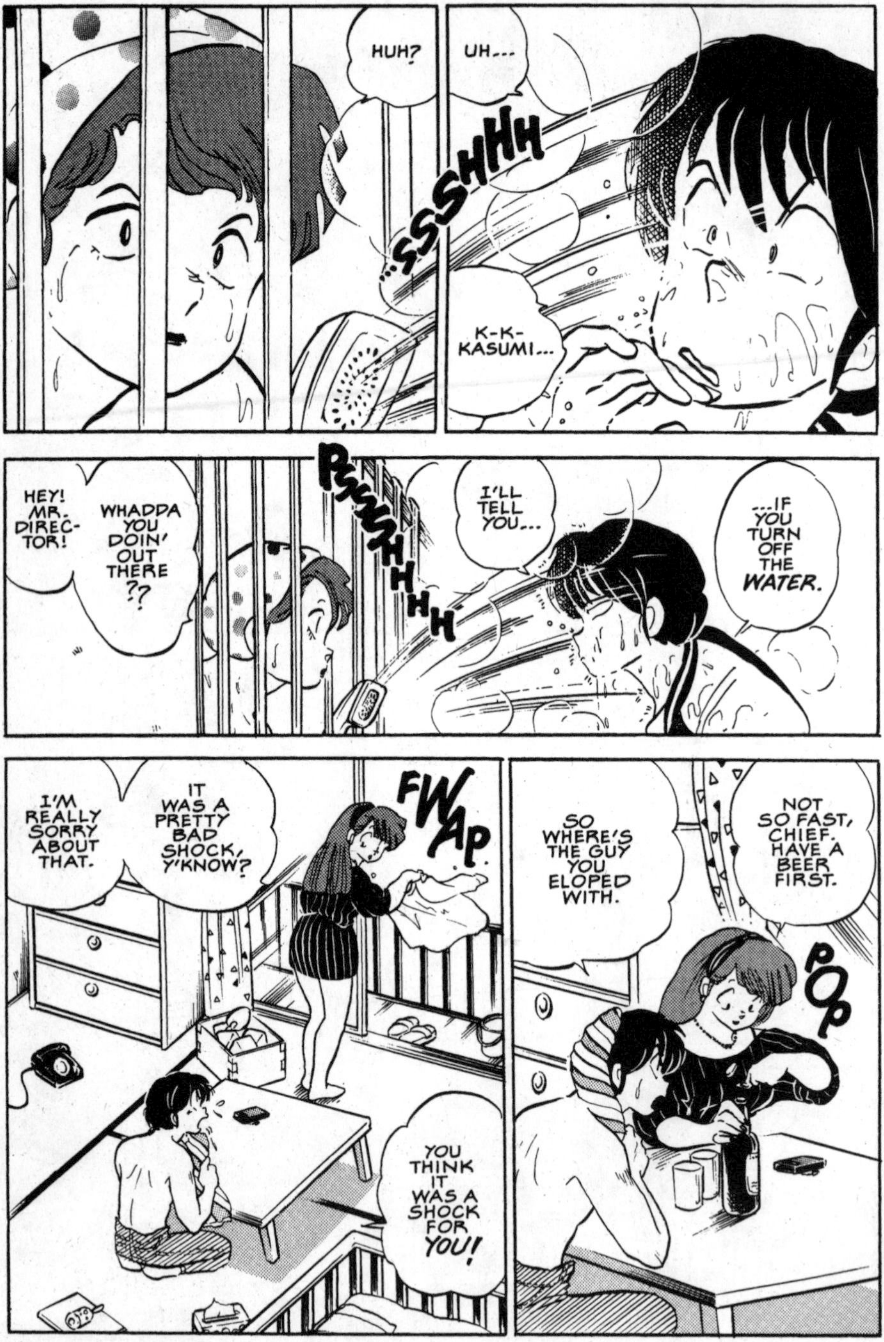
HUH?
UH...
SSSHHH
K-K-KASUMI...
HEY! MR. DIRECTOR!
WHADDA YOU DOIN' OUT THERE ??
PSSSHHHHH
I'LL TELL YOU...
...IF YOU TURN OFF THE WATER.
I'M REALLY SORRY ABOUT THAT.
IT WAS A PRETTY BAD SHOCK, Y'KNOW?
FWAP.
YOU THINK IT WAS A SHOCK FOR YOU!
SO WHERE'S THE GUY YOU ELOPED WITH.
NOT SO FAST, CHIEF. HAVE A BEER FIRST.
POP

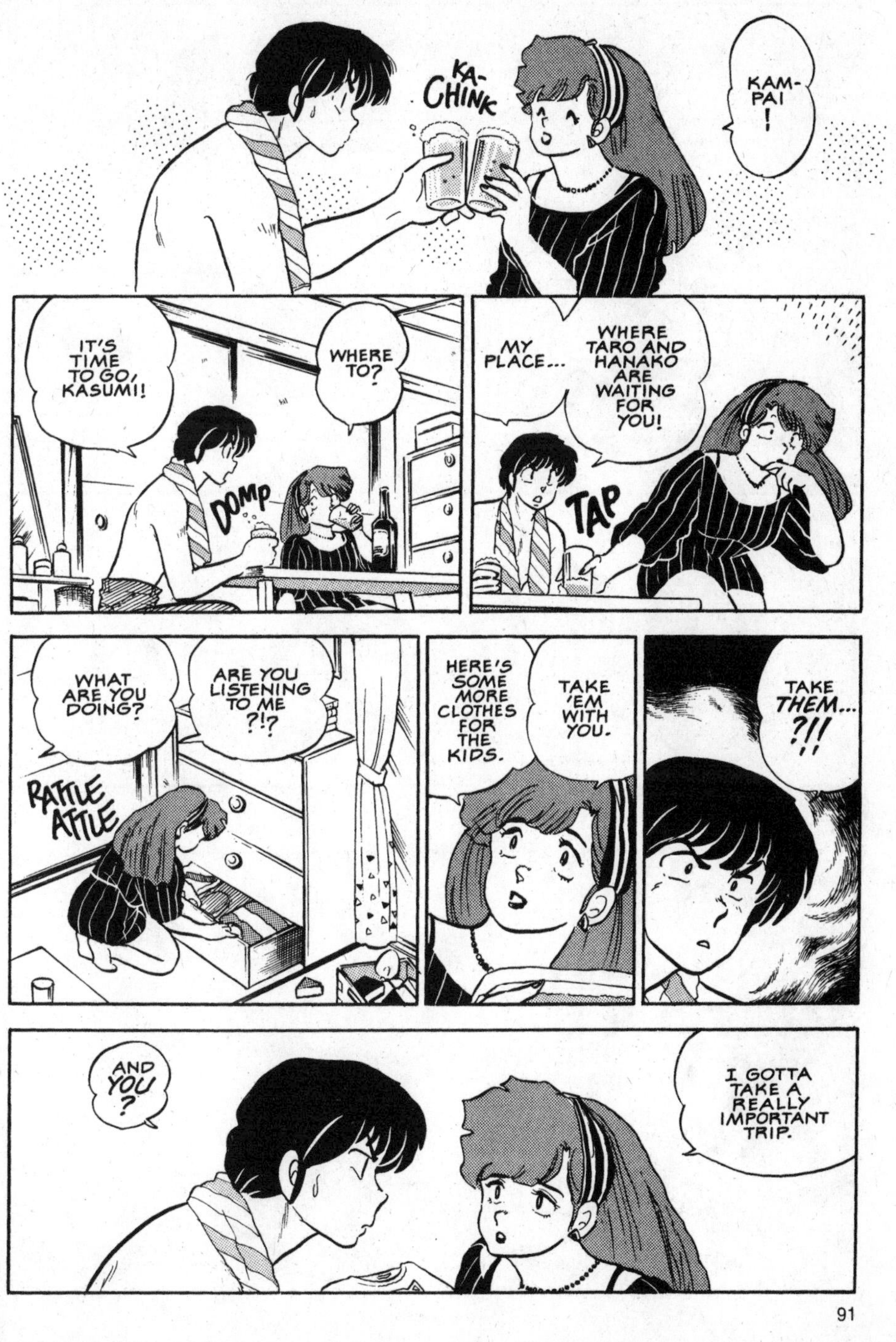
KA-CHINK
KAM-PAI!
IT'S TIME TO GO, KASUMI!
WHERE TO?
DOMP
MY PLACE...
WHERE TARO AND HANAKO ARE WAITING FOR YOU!
TAP
WHAT ARE YOU DOING?
ARE YOU LISTENING TO ME ?!?
RATTLE ATTLE
HERE'S SOME MORE CLOTHES FOR THE KIDS.
TAKE 'EM WITH YOU.
TAKE THEM... ?!!
AND YOU?
I GOTTA TAKE A REALLY IMPORTANT TRIP.

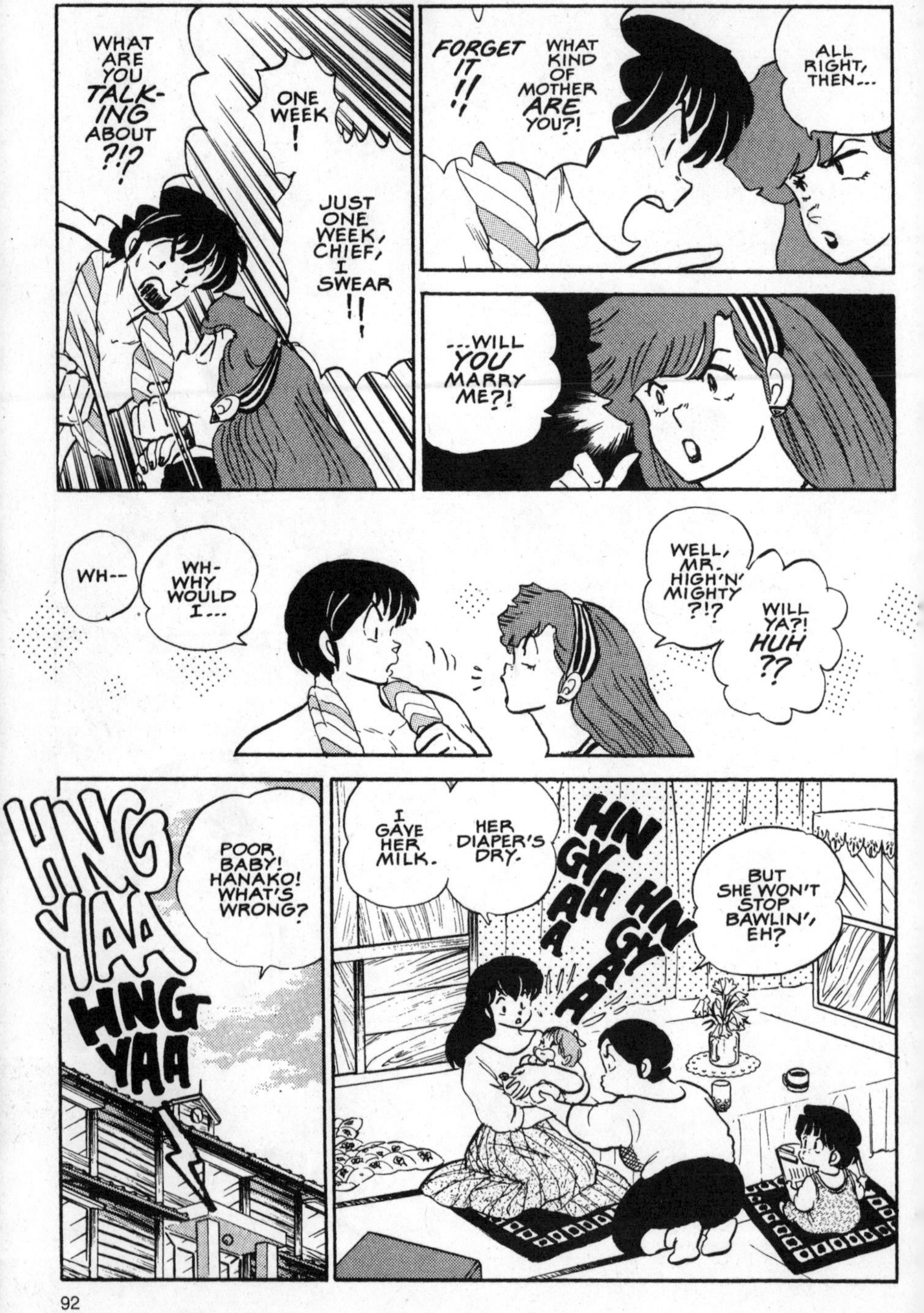
WHAT ARE YOU TALKING ABOUT ?!?
ONE WEEK!
JUST ONE WEEK, CHIEF, I SWEAR!!
FORGET IT!!
WHAT KIND OF MOTHER ARE YOU?!
ALL RIGHT, THEN...
...WILL YOU MARRY ME?!
WH--
WH-WHY WOULD I...
WELL, MR. HIGH'N' MIGHTY ?!?
WILL YA?! HUH??
HNG YAA
HNG YAA
POOR BABY! HANAKO! WHAT'S WRONG?
I GAVE HER MILK.
HER DIAPER'S DRY.
HN GYAAA
HN GYAAA
BUT SHE WON'T STOP BAWLIN', EH?

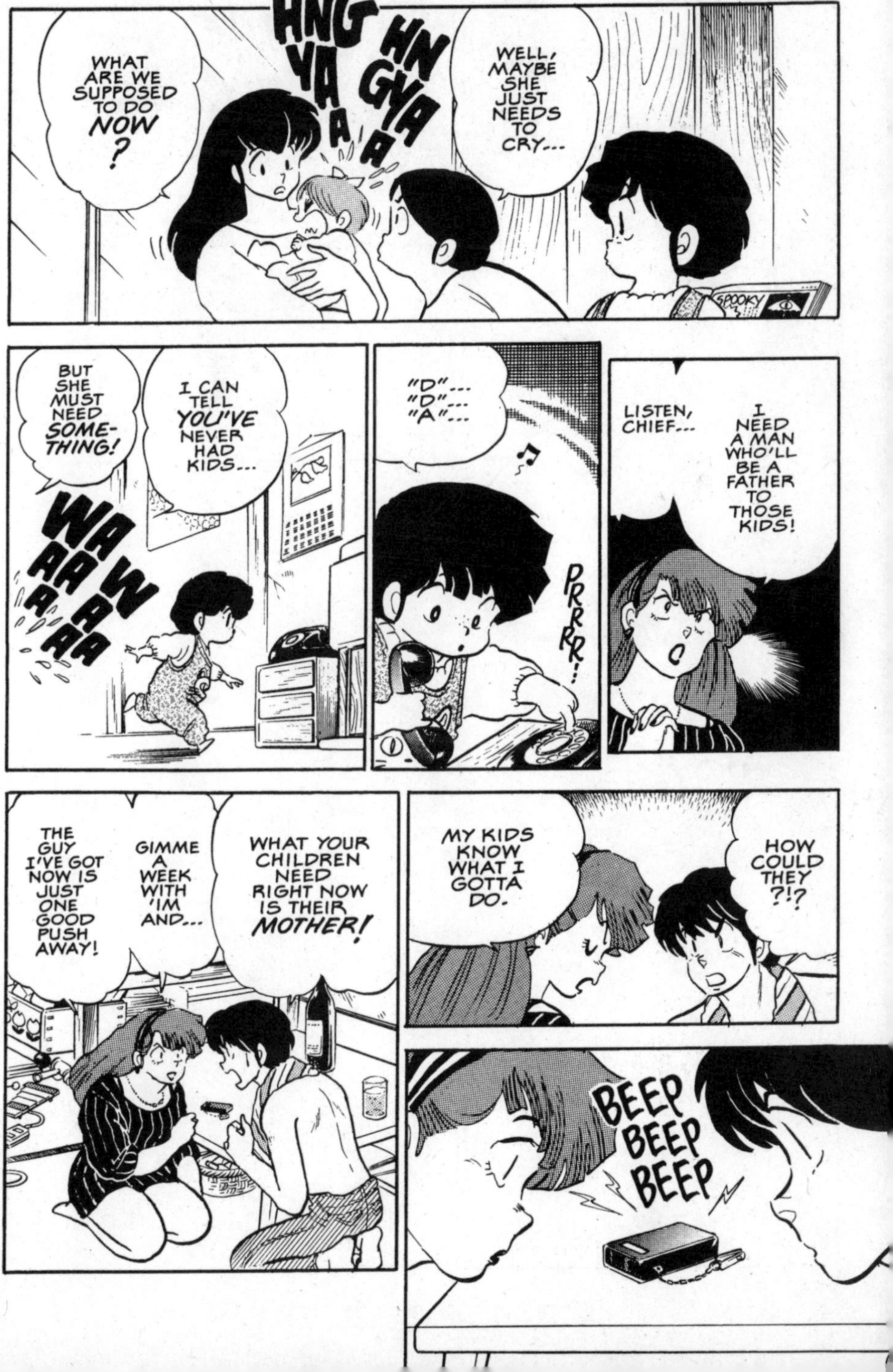
WHAT ARE WE SUPPOSED TO DO NOW?
HNG YAA
HN GYAA
WELL, MAYBE SHE JUST NEEDS TO CRY...
SPOOKY
BUT SHE MUST NEED SOMETHING!
I CAN TELL YOU'VE NEVER HAD KIDS...
WAAAA WAAAA
"D"... "D"... "A"...
PRRRR!
LISTEN, CHIEF...
I NEED A MAN WHO'LL BE A FATHER TO THOSE KIDS!
THE GUY I'VE GOT NOW IS JUST ONE GOOD PUSH AWAY!
GIMME A WEEK WITH 'IM AND...
WHAT YOUR CHILDREN NEED RIGHT NOW IS THEIR MOTHER!
MY KIDS KNOW WHAT I GOTTA DO.
HOW COULD THEY?!?
BEEP BEEP BEEP

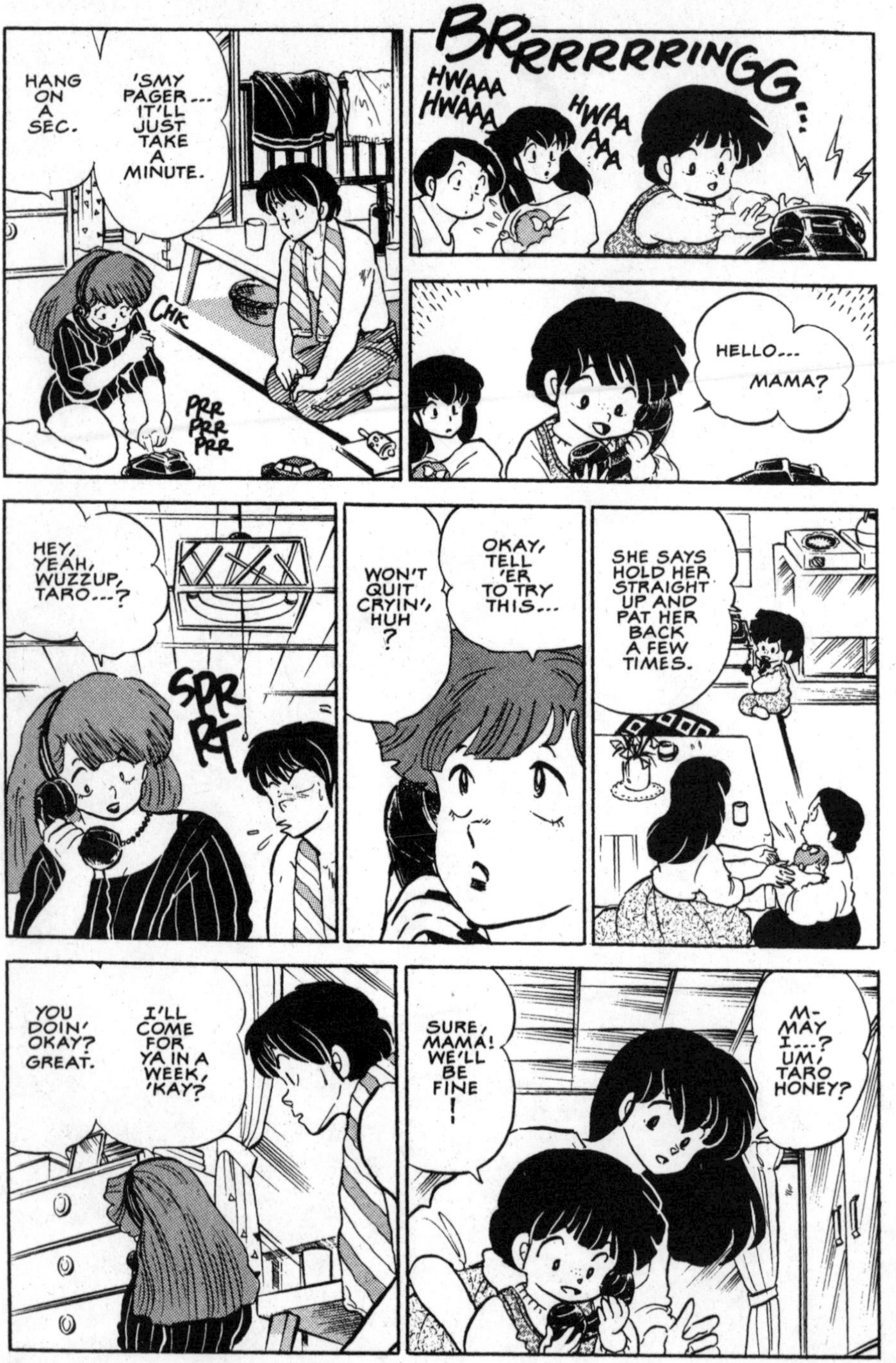
HANG ON A SEC.
'SMY PAGER... IT'LL JUST TAKE A MINUTE.
CHK
PRR PRR PRR
BRRRRRRRINGG!!
HWAAA HWAAA
HWAA AAA
HELLO... MAMA?
HEY, YEAH, WUZZUP, TARO...?
SPR RT
WON'T QUIT CRYIN', HUH?
OKAY, TELL 'ER TO TRY THIS...
SHE SAYS HOLD HER STRAIGHT UP AND PAT HER BACK A FEW TIMES.
YOU DOIN' OKAY? GREAT.
I'LL COME FOR YA IN A WEEK, 'KAY?
SURE, MAMA! WE'LL BE FINE!
M-MAY I...? UM, TARO HONEY?

ER... HELLO?

IS THIS TARO'S MOTHER?

HEY HEY HEY!

I'LL BET THIS IS THE BUILDING MANAGER!

LISTEN, I CAN'T THANK YOU ENOUGH FOR LOOKING AFTER MY KIDS!

NOW I'LL PUT 'IM ON FOR YA!

WHAT??

M-M-MANA-GER...?

GODAI?!

WHAT'S GOING ON?

I-I'LL EX-PLAIN LATER...

I'M ABOUT TO COME BACK, AND I'LL BE BRINGING...

HEY-- WAIT!!

VWISHH

STOP RIGHT THERE!!

CLANG CLANG CLANG

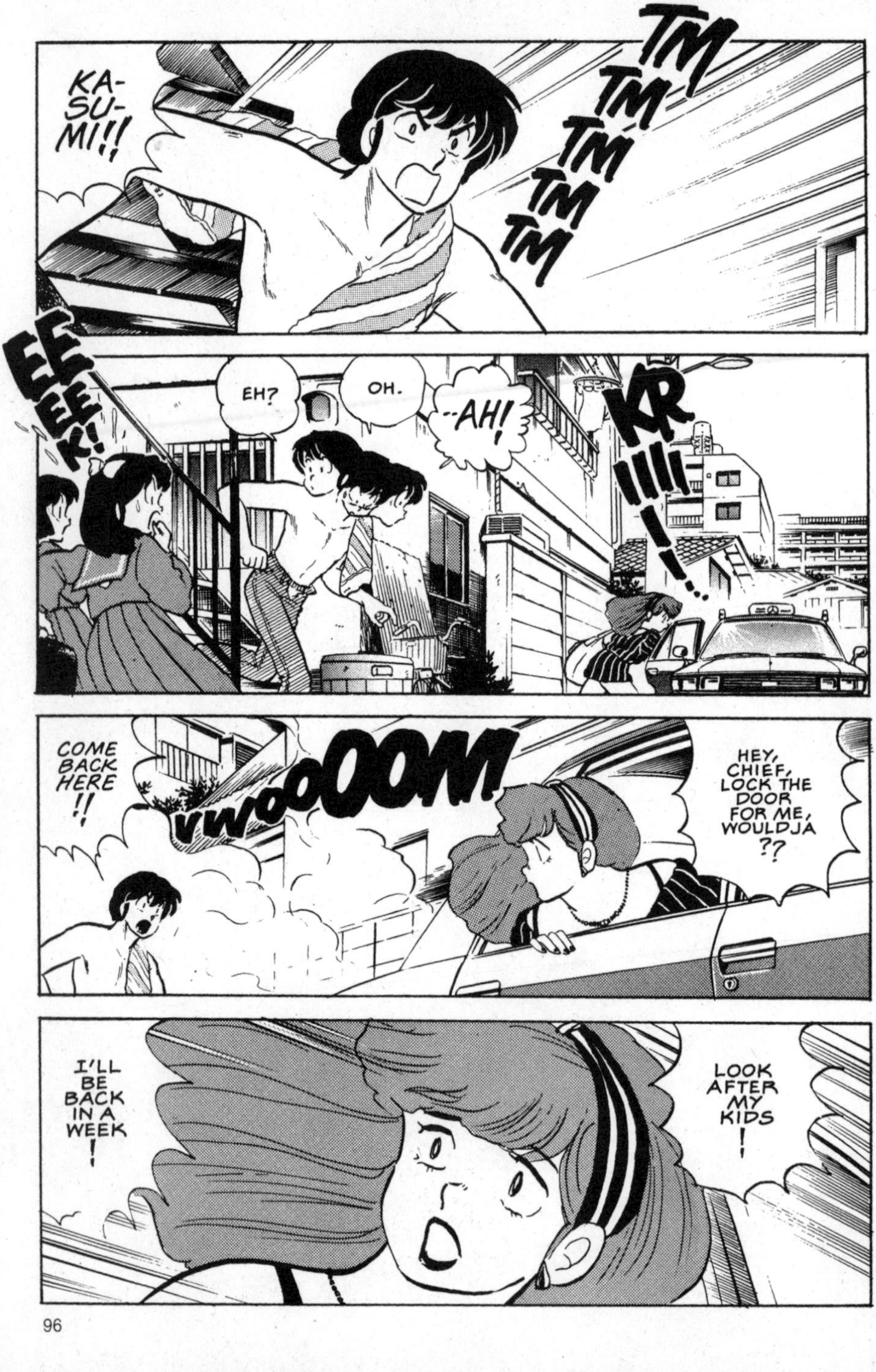
KA-SU-MI!!
TM TM TM TM TM TM
EEEEK!
EH?
OH.
--AH!
KR!!!!---...
COME BACK HERE!!
VWOOOOOM
HEY, CHIEF, LOCK THE DOOR FOR ME, WOULDJA??
I'LL BE BACK IN A WEEK!
LOOK AFTER MY KIDS!

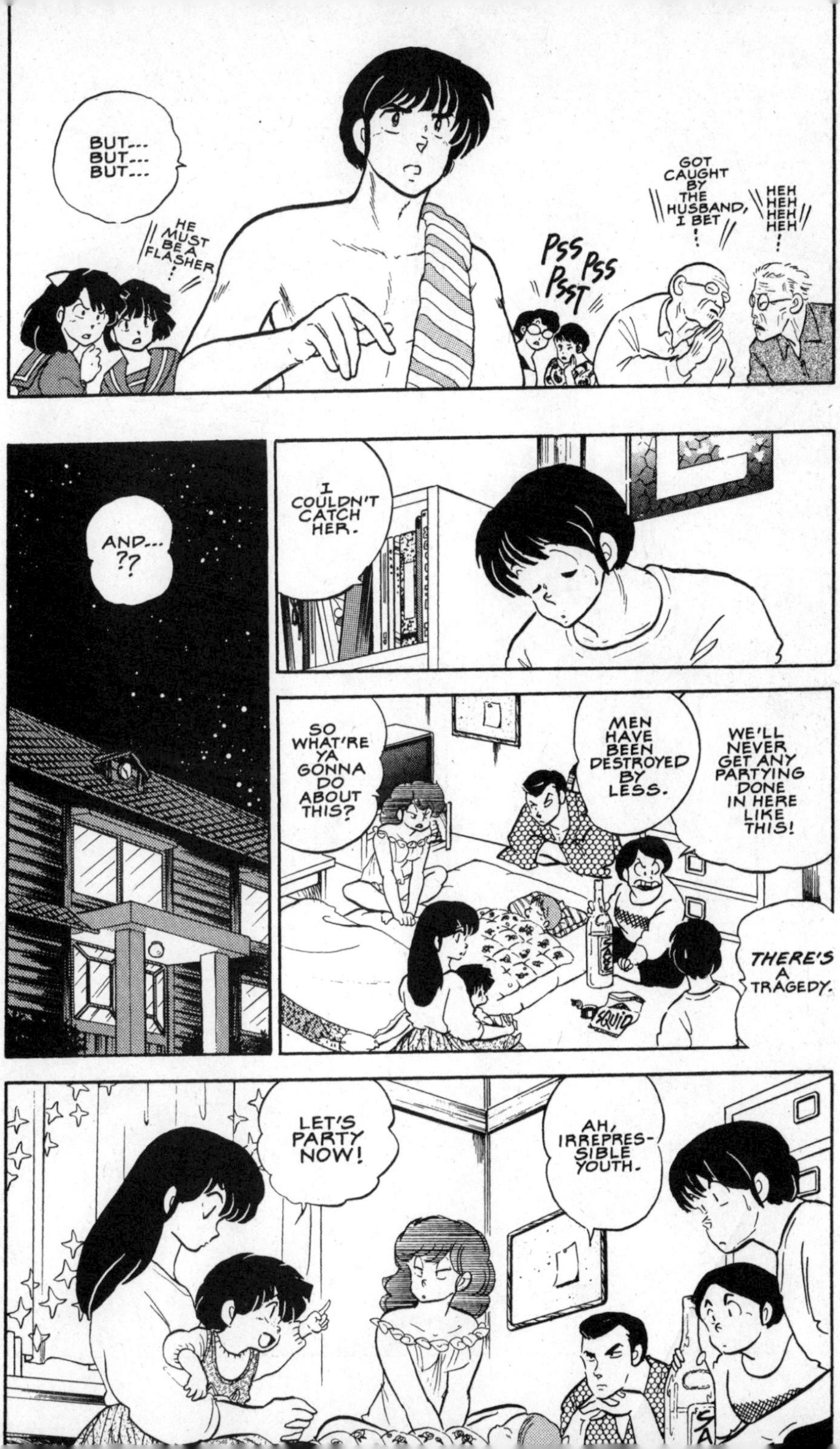
BUT... BUT... BUT...
HE MUST BE A FLASHER...
PSS PSS PSST
GOT CAUGHT BY THE HUSBAND, I BET!
HEH HEH HEH HEH!
AND... ??
I COULDN'T CATCH HER.
SO WHAT'RE YA GONNA DO ABOUT THIS?
MEN HAVE BEEN DESTROYED BY LESS.
WE'LL NEVER GET ANY PARTYING DONE IN HERE LIKE THIS!
SQUID
THERE'S A TRAGEDY.
LET'S PARTY NOW!
AH, IRREPRES-SIBLE YOUTH.

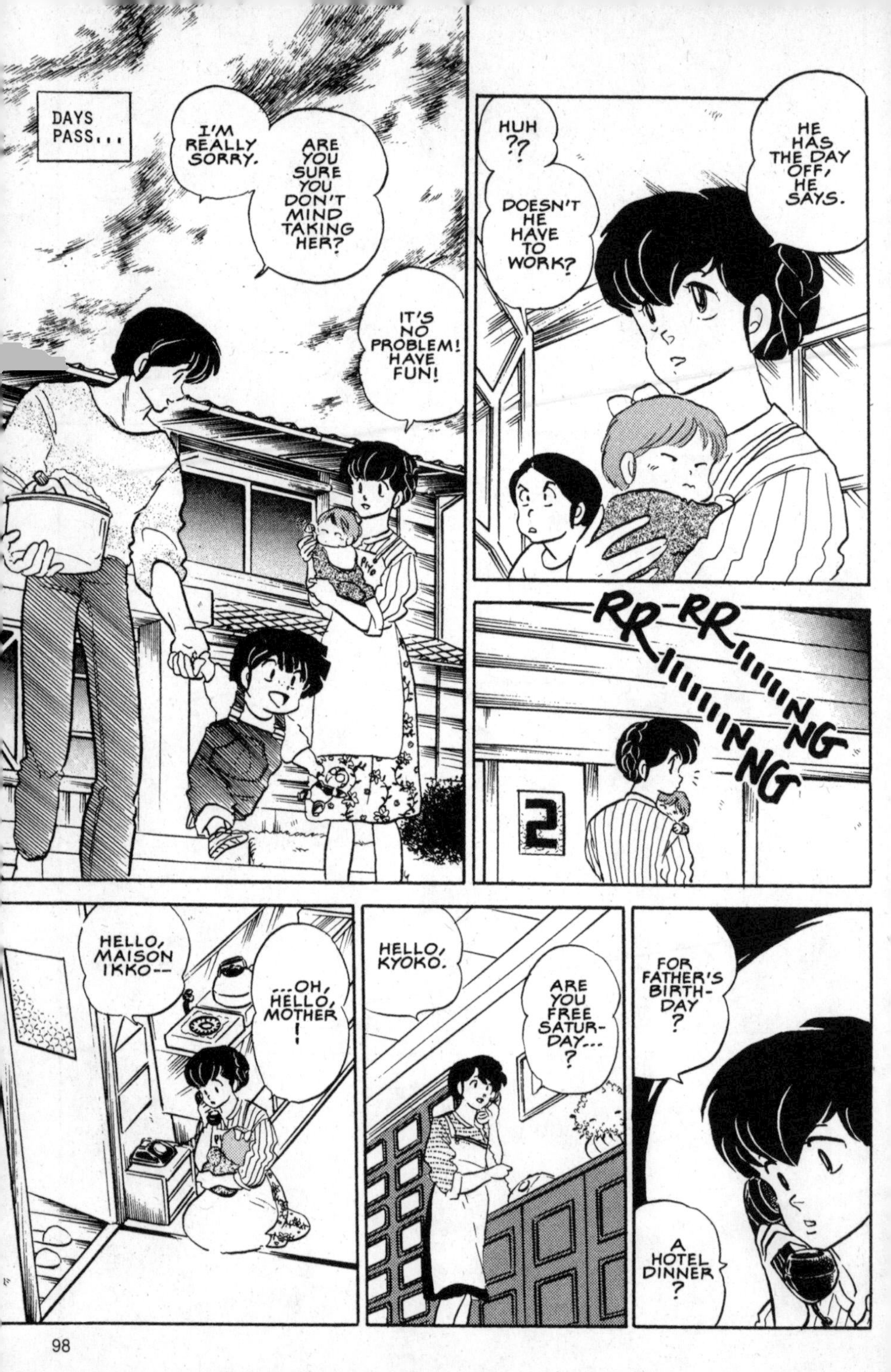
DAYS PASS...
I'M REALLY SORRY.
ARE YOU SURE YOU DON'T MIND TAKING HER?
IT'S NO PROBLEM! HAVE FUN!
HUH ??
DOESN'T HE HAVE TO WORK?
HE HAS THE DAY OFF, HE SAYS.
RR RR RIIIIIING NG IIIIIING NG
2
HELLO, MAISON IKKO--
...OH, HELLO, MOTHER !
HELLO, KYOKO.
ARE YOU FREE SATURDAY... ?
FOR FATHER'S BIRTHDAY ?
A HOTEL DINNER ?

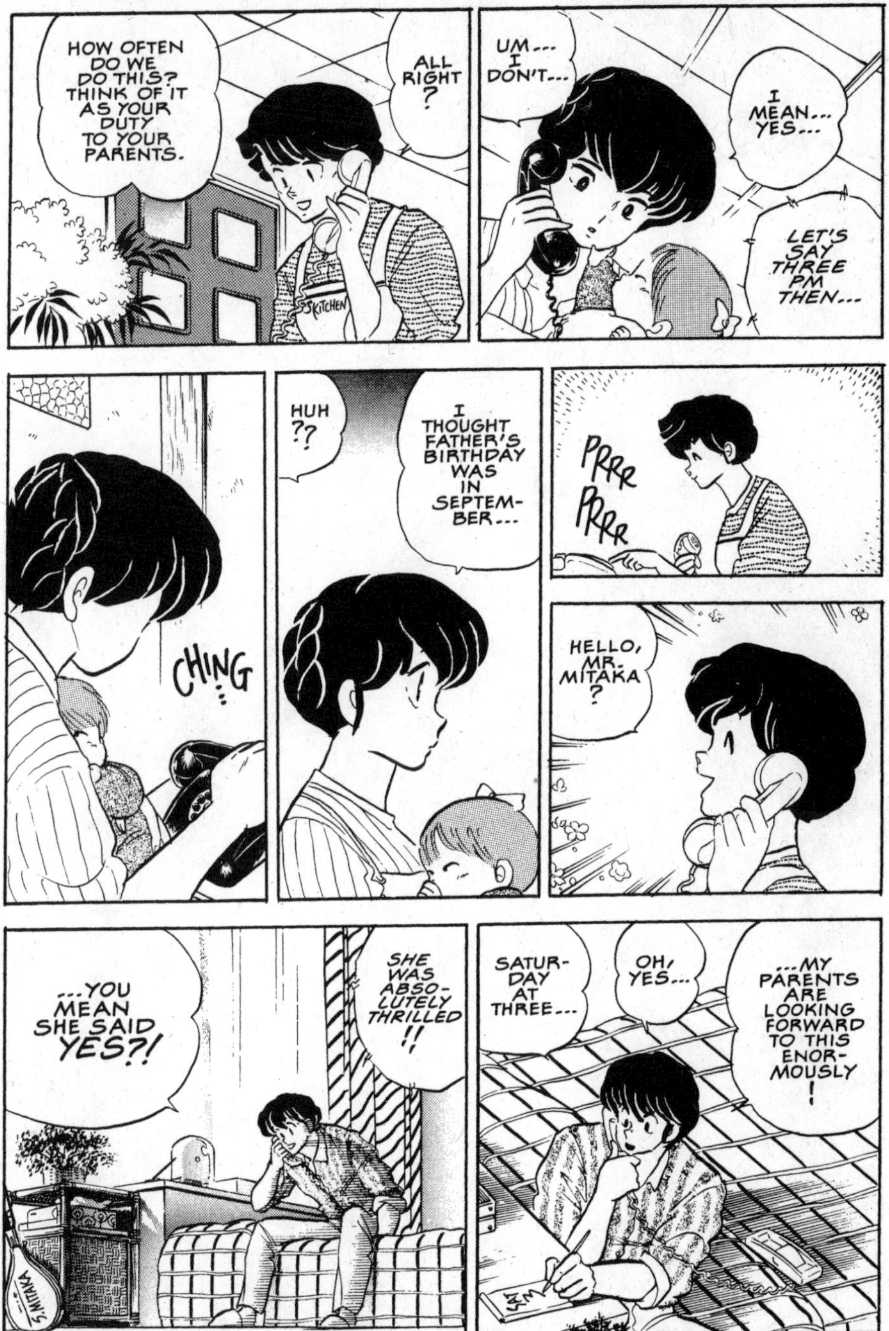
HOW OFTEN DO WE DO THIS? THINK OF IT AS YOUR DUTY TO YOUR PARENTS.
ALL RIGHT?
KITCHEN
UM... I DON'T...
I MEAN... YES...
LET'S SAY THREE PM THEN...
CHING
HUH ??
I THOUGHT FATHER'S BIRTHDAY WAS IN SEPTEMBER...
PRRR PRRR
HELLO, MR. MITAKA?
...YOU MEAN SHE SAID YES?!
SHE WAS ABSOLUTELY THRILLED!!
S. MITAKA
SATURDAY AT THREE...
OH, YES...
...MY PARENTS ARE LOOKING FORWARD TO THIS ENORMOUSLY!

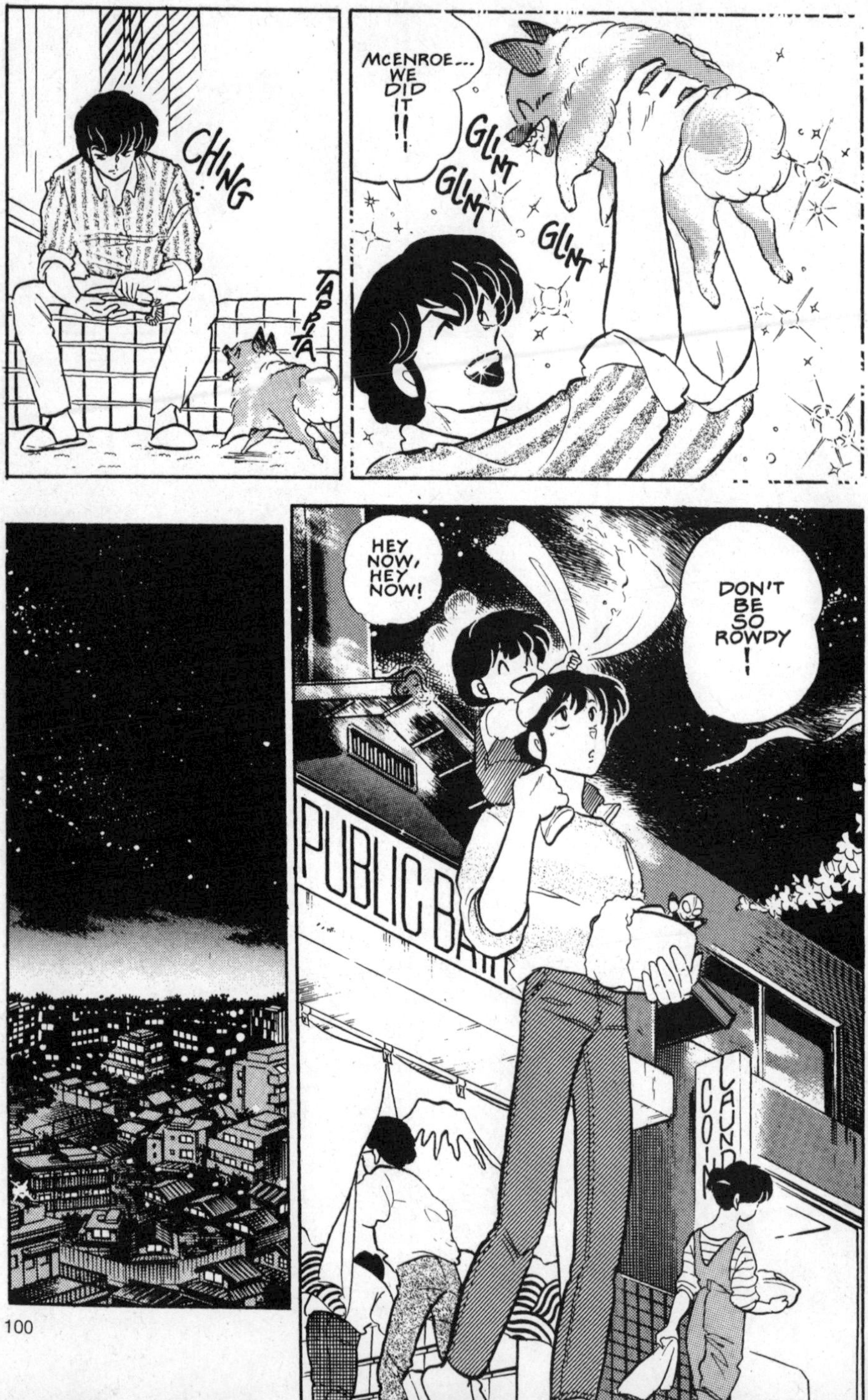
CHING
TAPPITA
MCENROE... WE DID IT!!
GLINT
GLINT
GLINT
HEY NOW, HEY NOW!
DON'T BE SO ROWDY!
PUBLIC

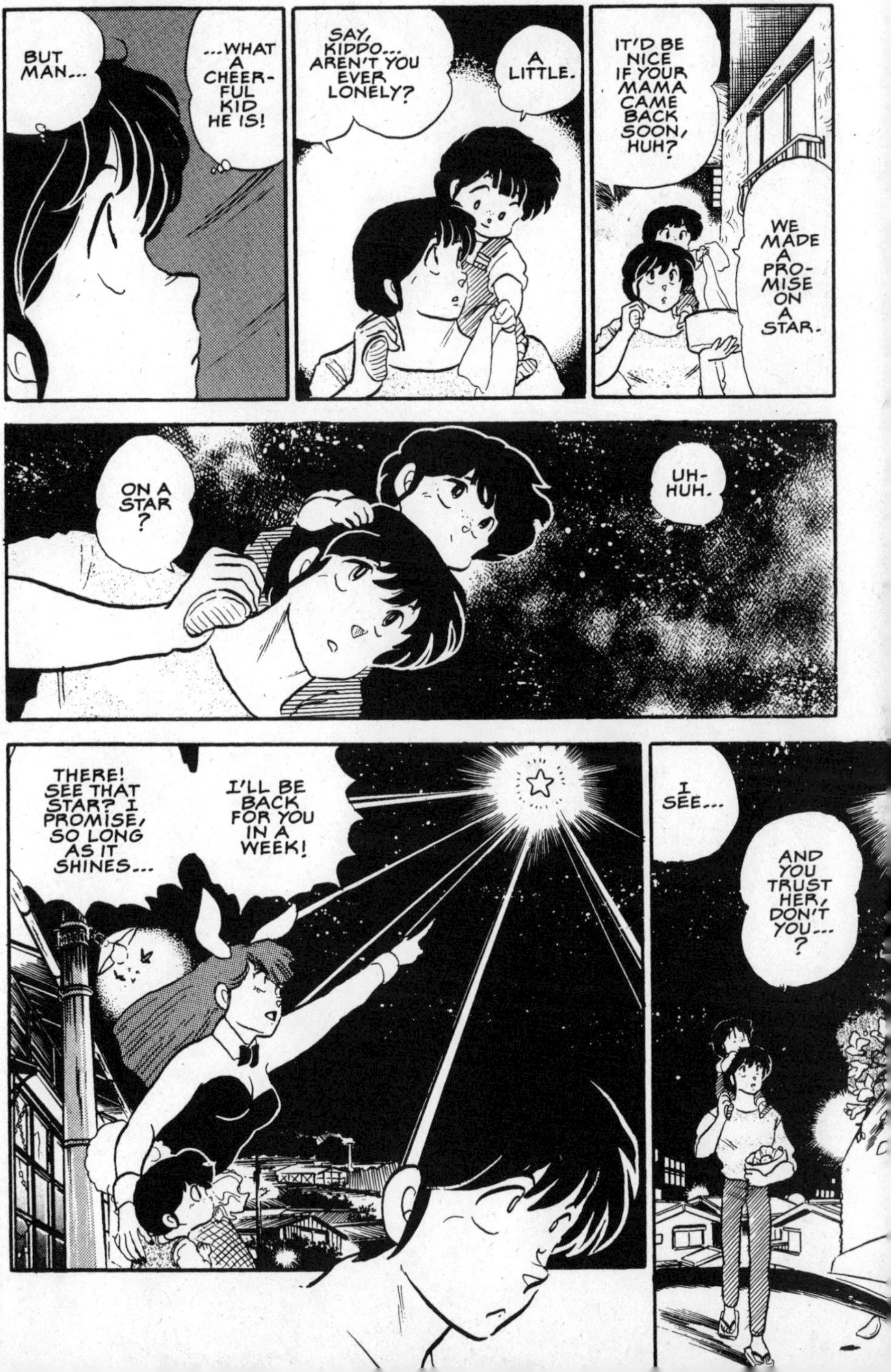
BUT MAN...
...WHAT A CHEERFUL KID HE IS!
SAY, KIDDO... AREN'T YOU EVER LONELY?
A LITTLE.
IT'D BE NICE IF YOUR MAMA CAME BACK SOON, HUH?
WE MADE A PROMISE ON A STAR.
ON A STAR?
UH-HUH.
THERE! SEE THAT STAR? I PROMISE, SO LONG AS IT SHINES...
I'LL BE BACK FOR YOU IN A WEEK!
I SEE...
AND YOU TRUST HER, DON'T YOU...?

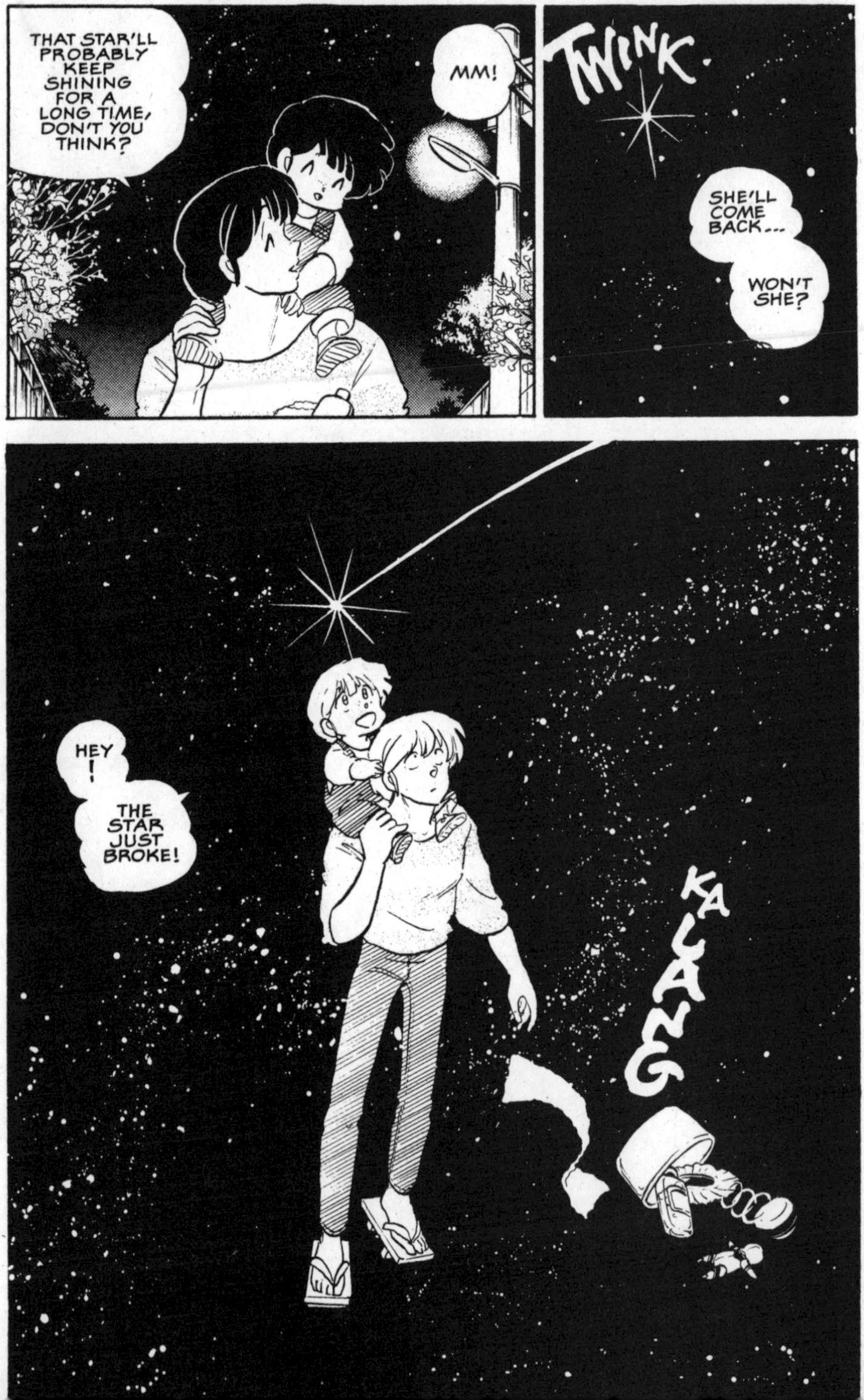
THAT STAR'LL PROBABLY KEEP SHINING FOR A LONG TIME, DON'T YOU THINK?
MM!
TWINK
SHE'LL COME BACK...
WON'T SHE?
HEY!
THE STAR JUST BROKE!
KALANG

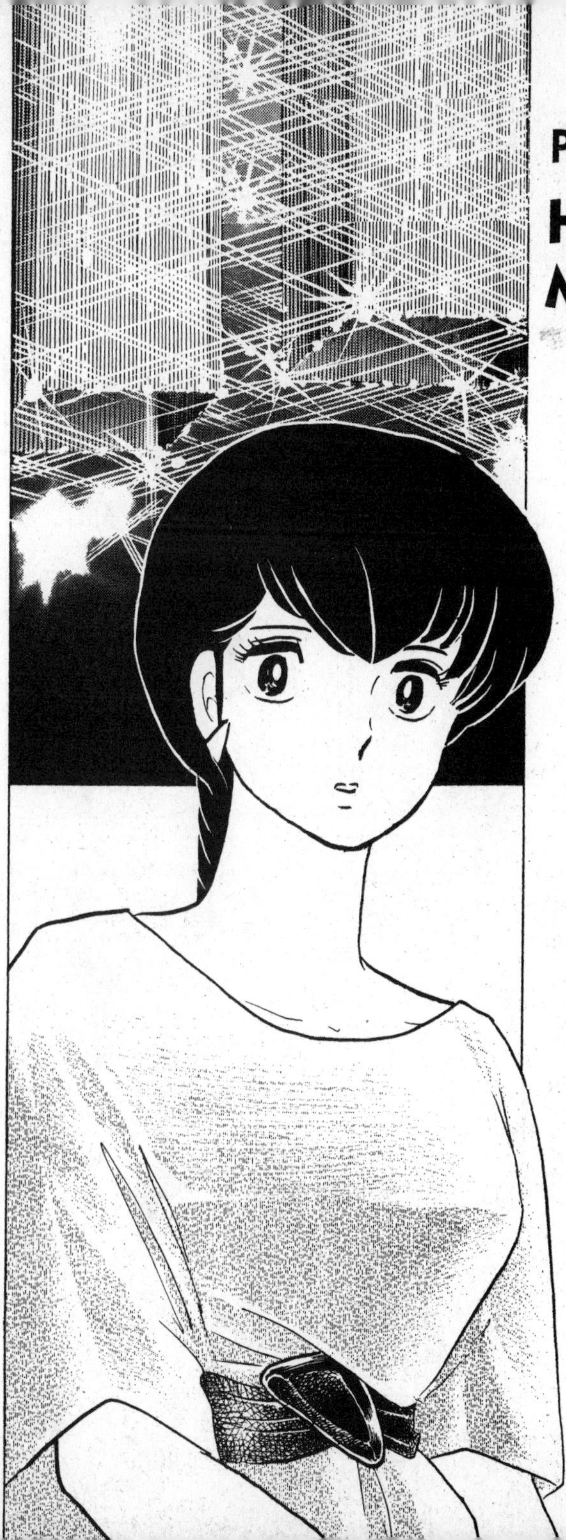

PART SEVEN

HELP ME!

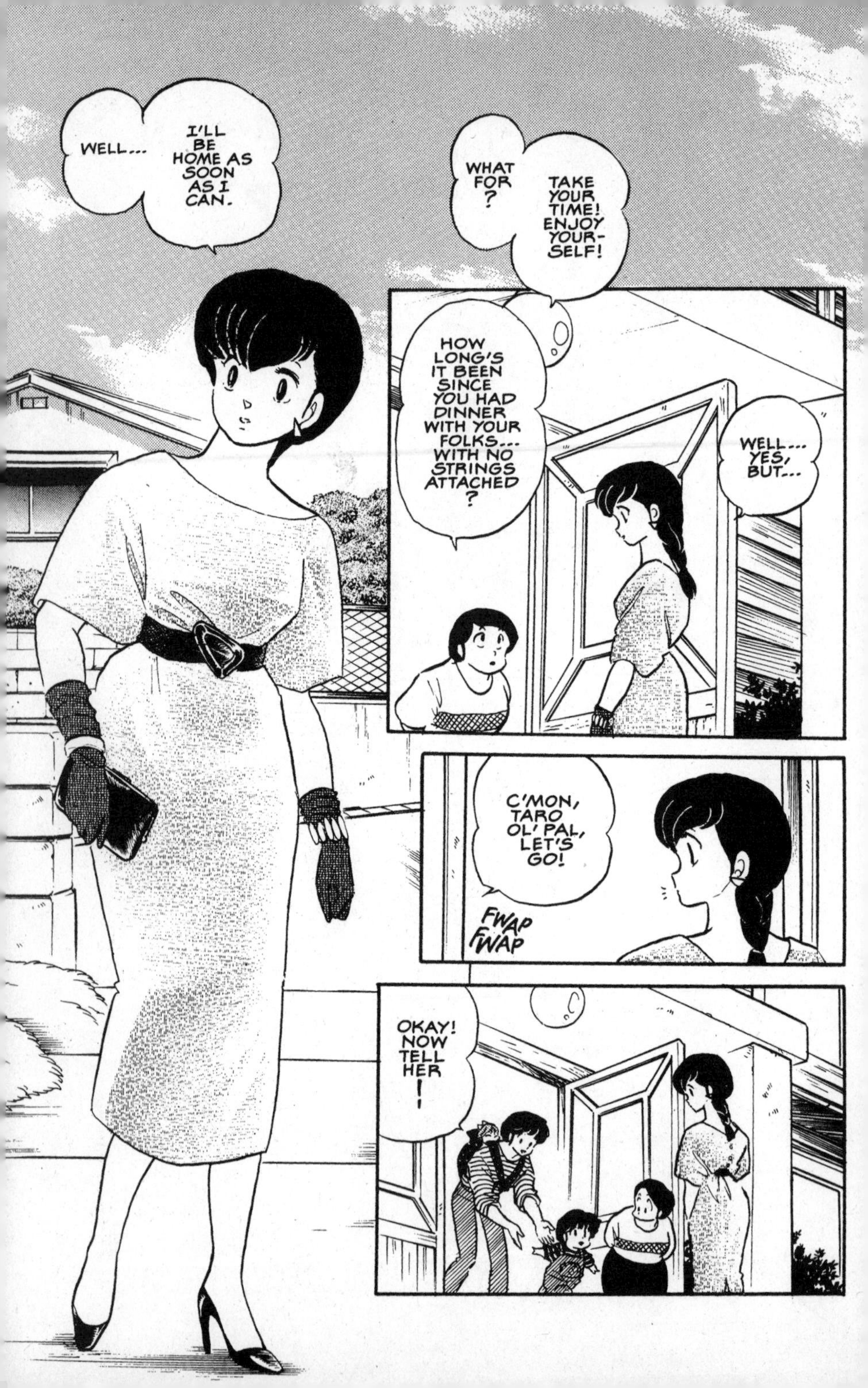
WELL... I'LL BE HOME AS SOON AS I CAN.
WHAT FOR? TAKE YOUR TIME! ENJOY YOURSELF!
HOW LONG'S IT BEEN SINCE YOU HAD DINNER WITH YOUR FOLKS... WITH NO STRINGS ATTACHED?
WELL... YES, BUT...
C'MON, TARO OL' PAL, LET'S GO!
FWAP FWAP
OKAY! NOW TELL HER!!

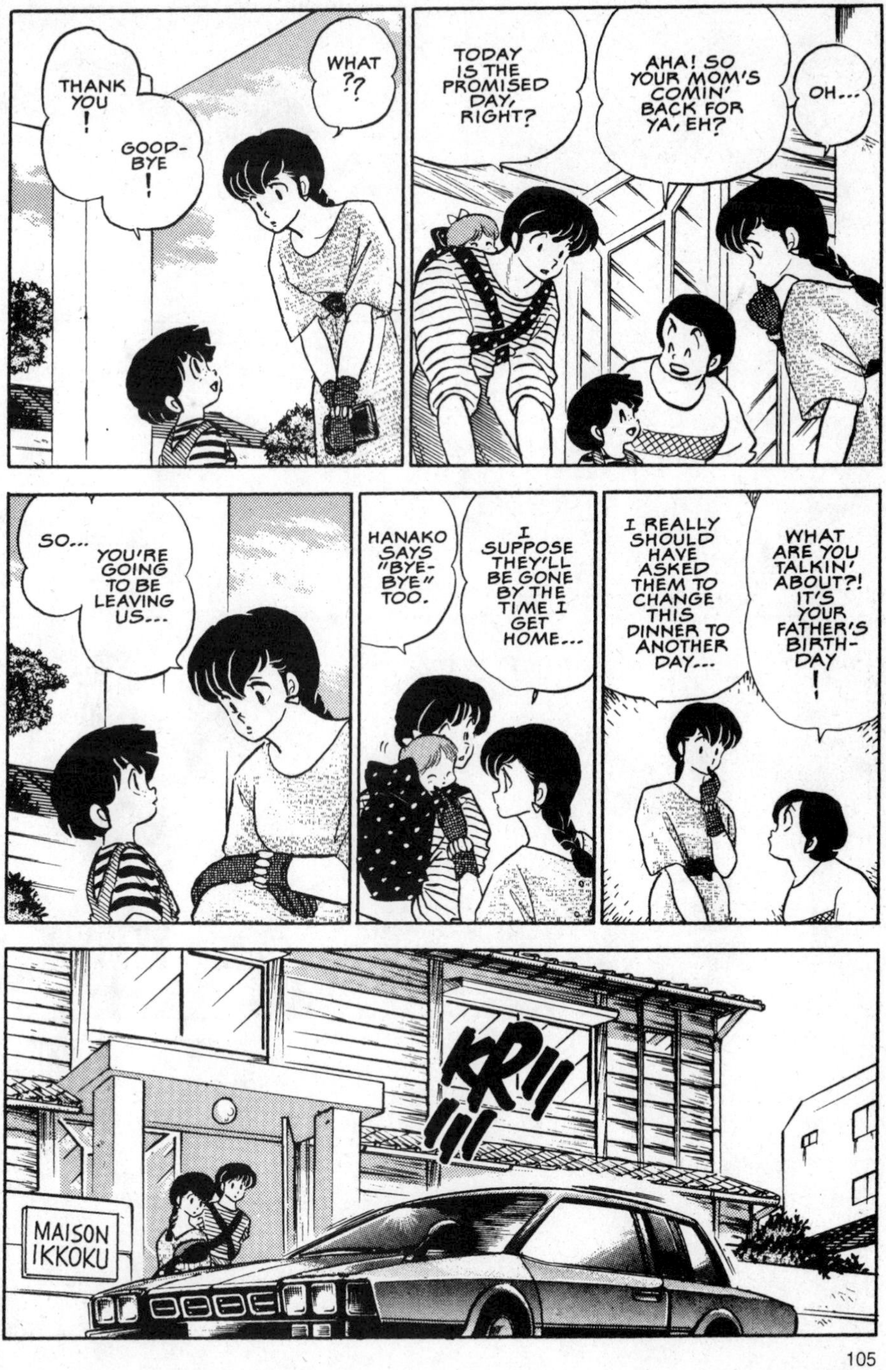
THANK YOU!
GOOD-BYE!
WHAT??
TODAY IS THE PROMISED DAY, RIGHT?
AHA! SO YOUR MOM'S COMIN' BACK FOR YA, EH?
OH...
SO... YOU'RE GOING TO BE LEAVING US...
HANAKO SAYS "BYE-BYE" TOO.
I SUPPOSE THEY'LL BE GONE BY THE TIME I GET HOME...
I REALLY SHOULD HAVE ASKED THEM TO CHANGE THIS DINNER TO ANOTHER DAY...
WHAT ARE YOU TALKIN' ABOUT?! IT'S YOUR FATHER'S BIRTHDAY!
KRII III
MAISON IKKOKU

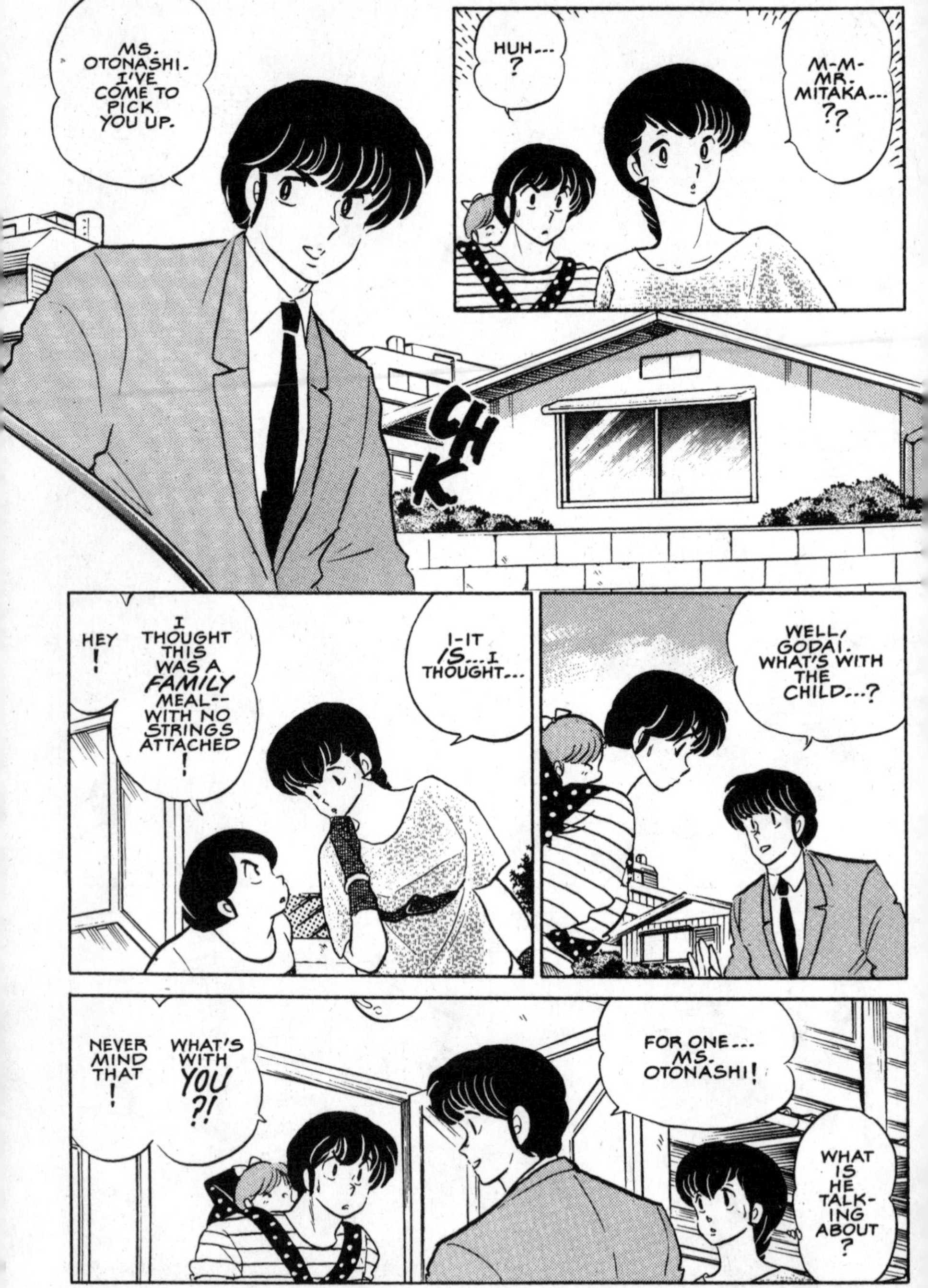
MS. OTONASHI. I'VE COME TO PICK YOU UP.
CHK
HUH...?
M-M-MR. MITAKA...??
HEY!
I THOUGHT THIS WAS A FAMILY MEAL--WITH NO STRINGS ATTACHED!
I-IT IS...I THOUGHT...
WELL, GODAI. WHAT'S WITH THE CHILD...?
NEVER MIND THAT!
WHAT'S WITH YOU?!
FOR ONE... MS. OTONASHI!
WHAT IS HE TALKING ABOUT?

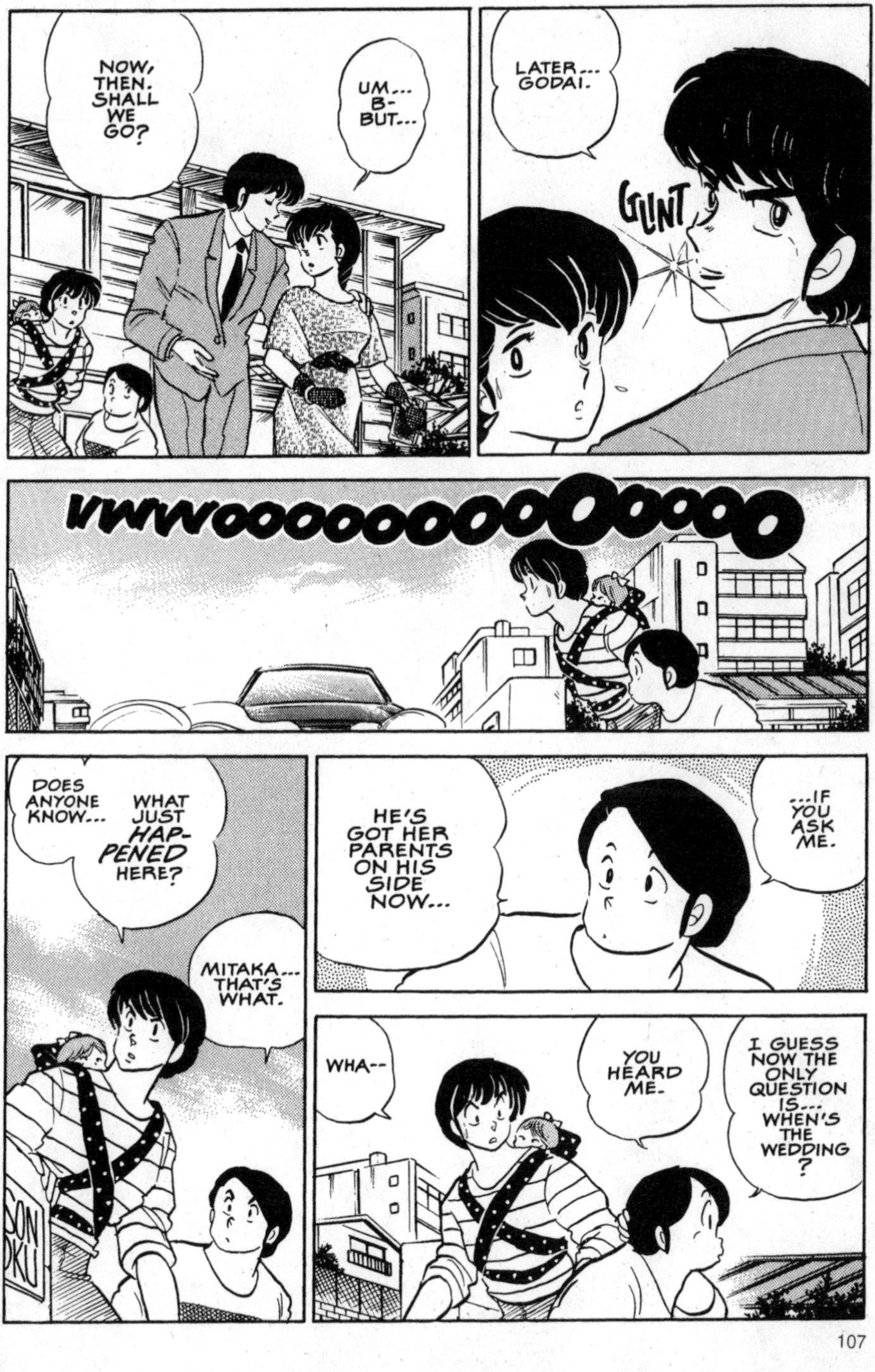
NOW, THEN. SHALL WE GO?
UM... B- BUT...
LATER... GODAI.
GLINT
VVVVOOOOOOOOOOOOOOO
DOES ANYONE KNOW...
WHAT JUST HAPPENED HERE?
MITAKA... THAT'S WHAT.
HE'S GOT HER PARENTS ON HIS SIDE NOW...
...IF YOU ASK ME.
WHA--
YOU HEARD ME.
I GUESS NOW THE ONLY QUESTION IS... WHEN'S THE WEDDING?

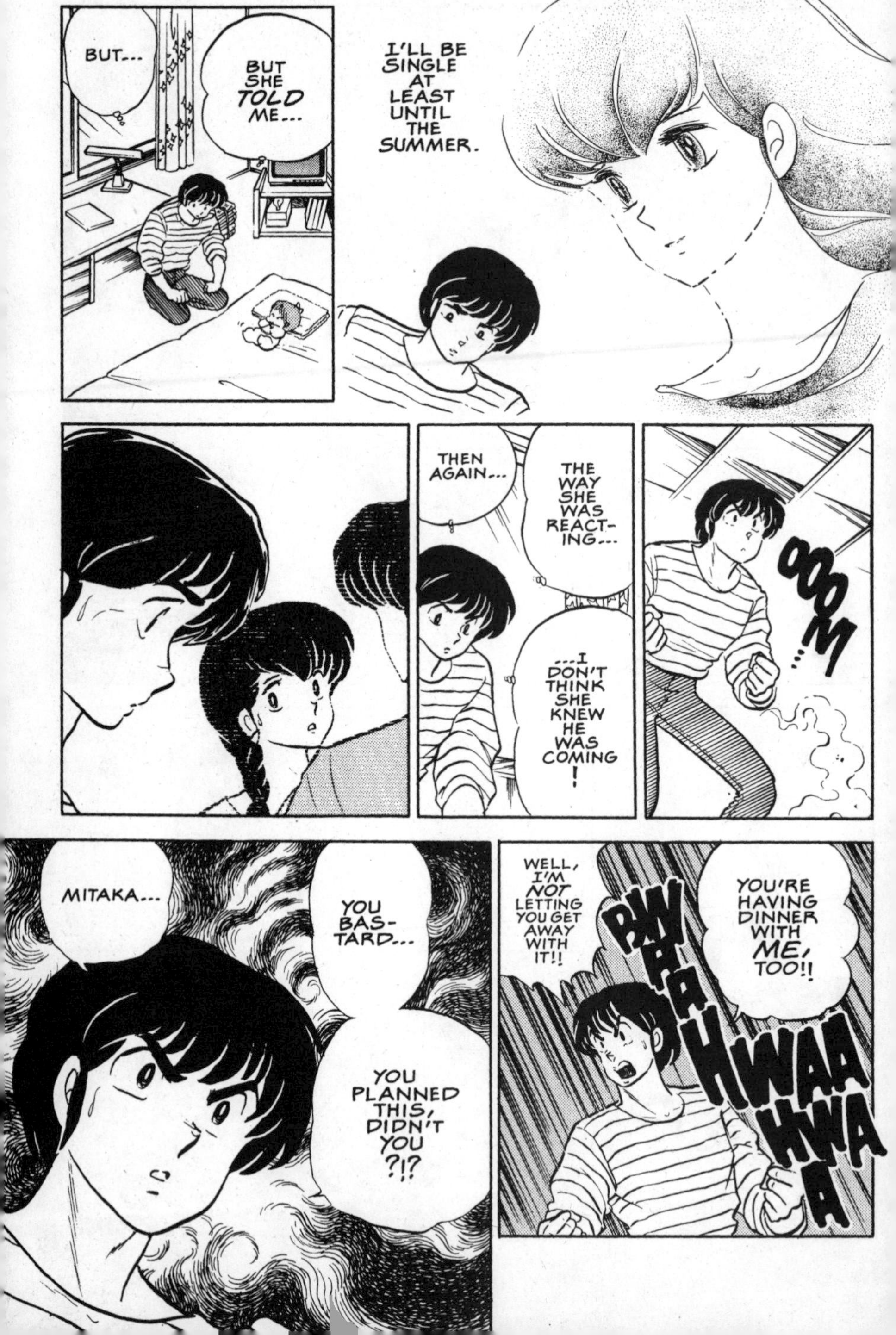
BUT...
BUT SHE TOLD ME...
I'LL BE SINGLE AT LEAST UNTIL THE SUMMER.
THEN AGAIN...
THE WAY SHE WAS REACT-ING...
...I DON'T THINK SHE KNEW HE WAS COMING!
OOOM...
MITAKA...
YOU BAS-TARD...
YOU PLANNED THIS, DIDN'T YOU ?!?
WELL, I'M NOT LETTING YOU GET AWAY WITH IT!!
YOU'RE HAVING DINNER WITH ME, TOO!!
BWAHAHAHWAAHWAA

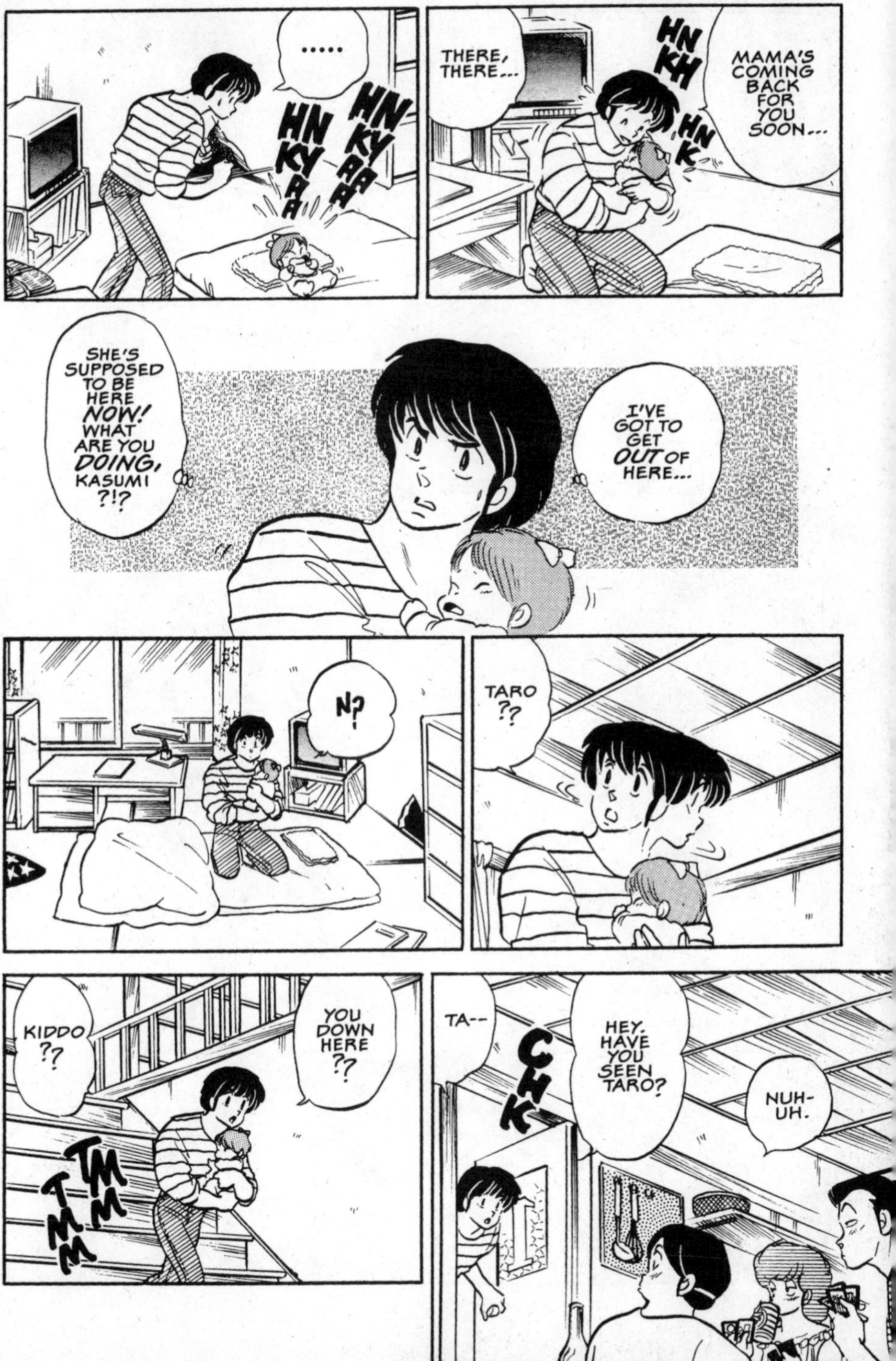
......
HN KYAA
HN KYAA
THERE, THERE...
HN KH
HN K
MAMA'S COMING BACK FOR YOU SOON...
SHE'S SUPPOSED TO BE HERE NOW! WHAT ARE YOU DOING, KASUMI ?!?
I'VE GOT TO GET OUT OF HERE...
N?
TARO ??
KIDDO ??
YOU DOWN HERE ??
TMM TMM TMM
TA--
CHK
HEY. HAVE YOU SEEN TARO?
NUH-UH.

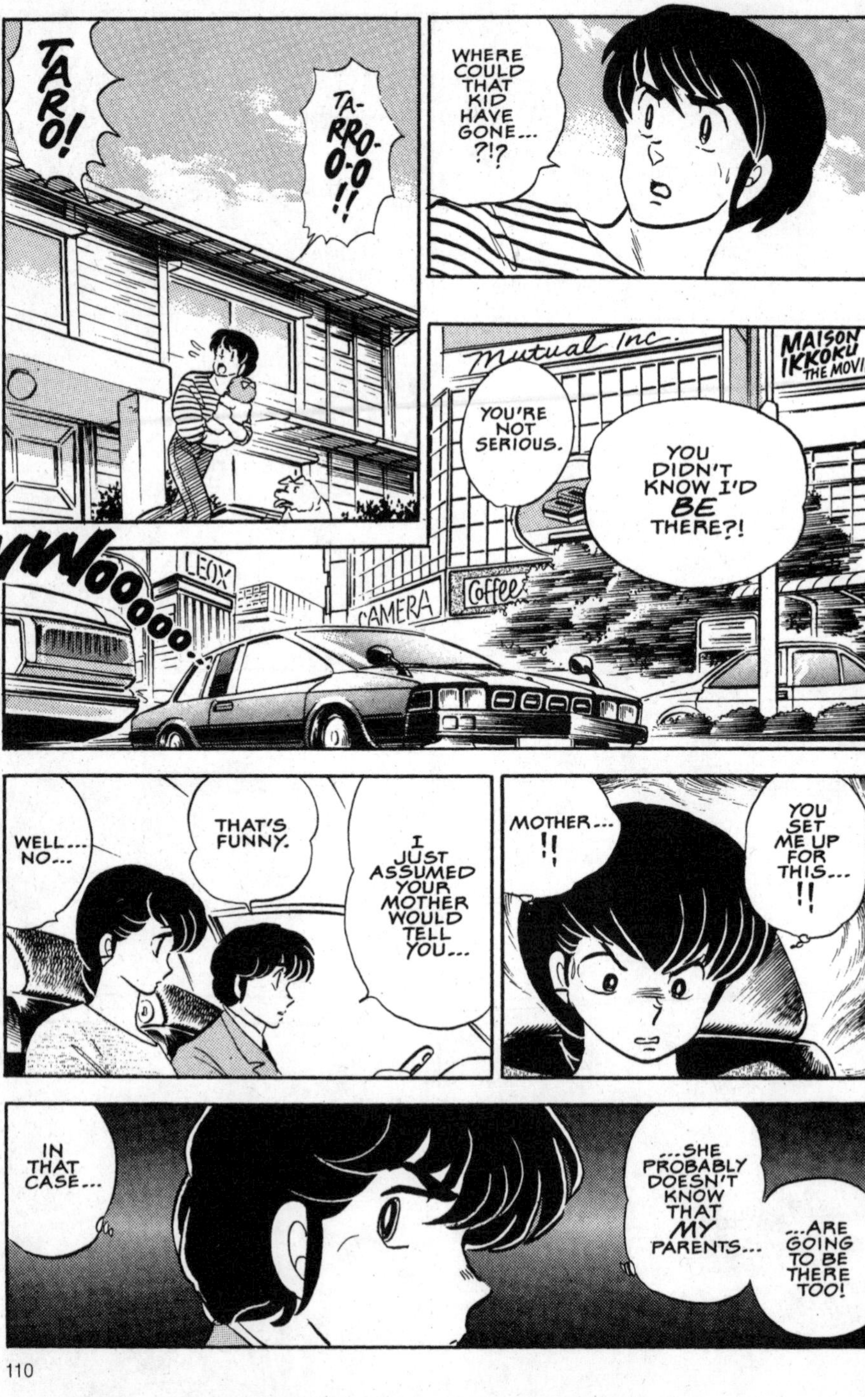
TARO!
TA-RRO-O-O!!
WHERE COULD THAT KID HAVE GONE...?!?
MUTUAL INC.
MAISON IKKOKU THE MOVIE
LEOX
CAMERA
Coffee
VWOOOOOO...
YOU'RE NOT SERIOUS.
YOU DIDN'T KNOW I'D BE THERE?!
WELL... NO...
THAT'S FUNNY.
I JUST ASSUMED YOUR MOTHER WOULD TELL YOU...
MOTHER...!!
YOU SET ME UP FOR THIS...!!
IN THAT CASE...
...SHE PROBABLY DOESN'T KNOW THAT MY PARENTS...
...ARE GOING TO BE THERE TOO!

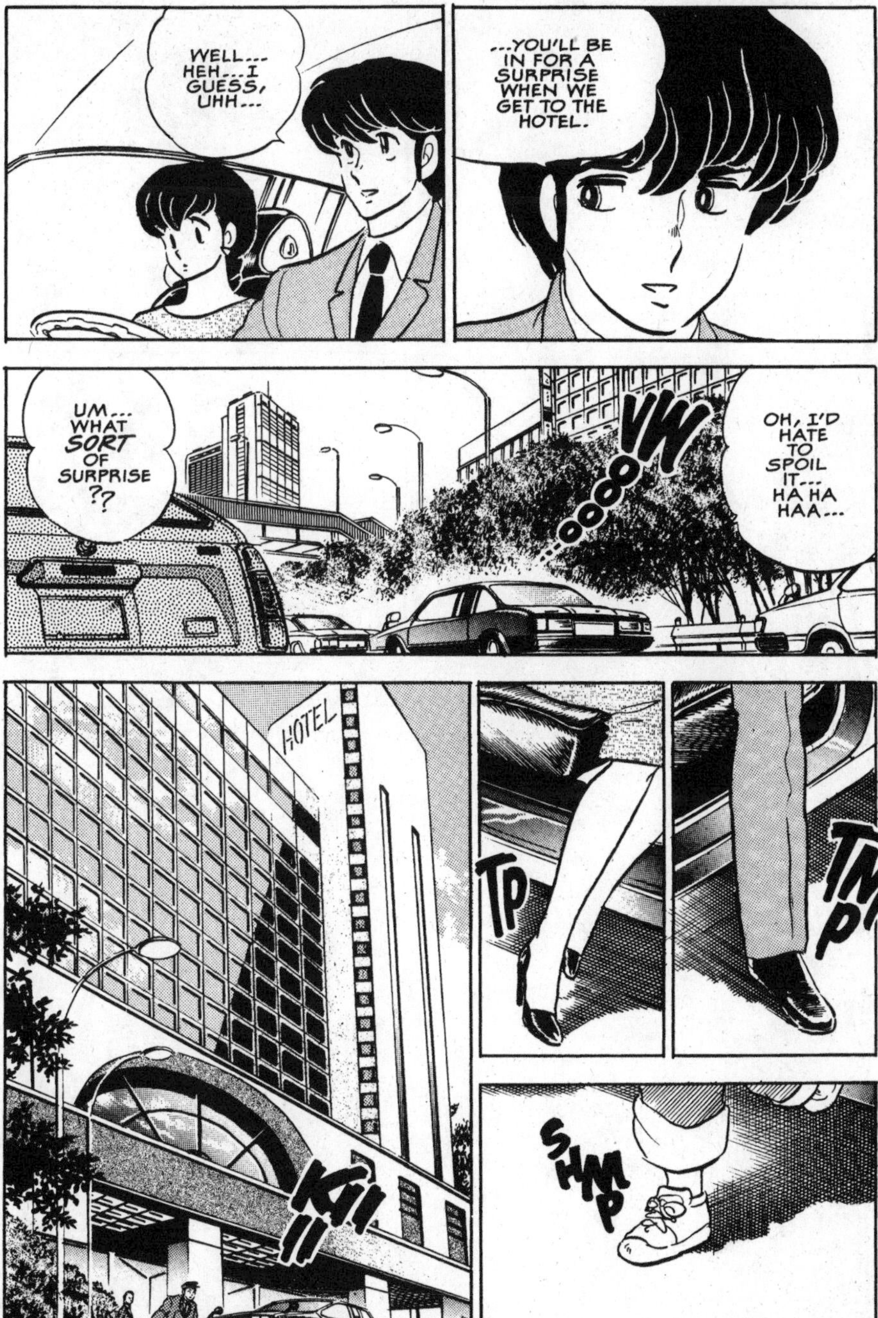
WELL... HEH... I GUESS, UHH...
...YOU'LL BE IN FOR A SURPRISE WHEN WE GET TO THE HOTEL.
UM... WHAT SORT OF SURPRISE ??
VWOOOOO
OH, I'D HATE TO SPOIL IT... HA HA HAA...
HOTEL
KII
TP
TMP
SHMP

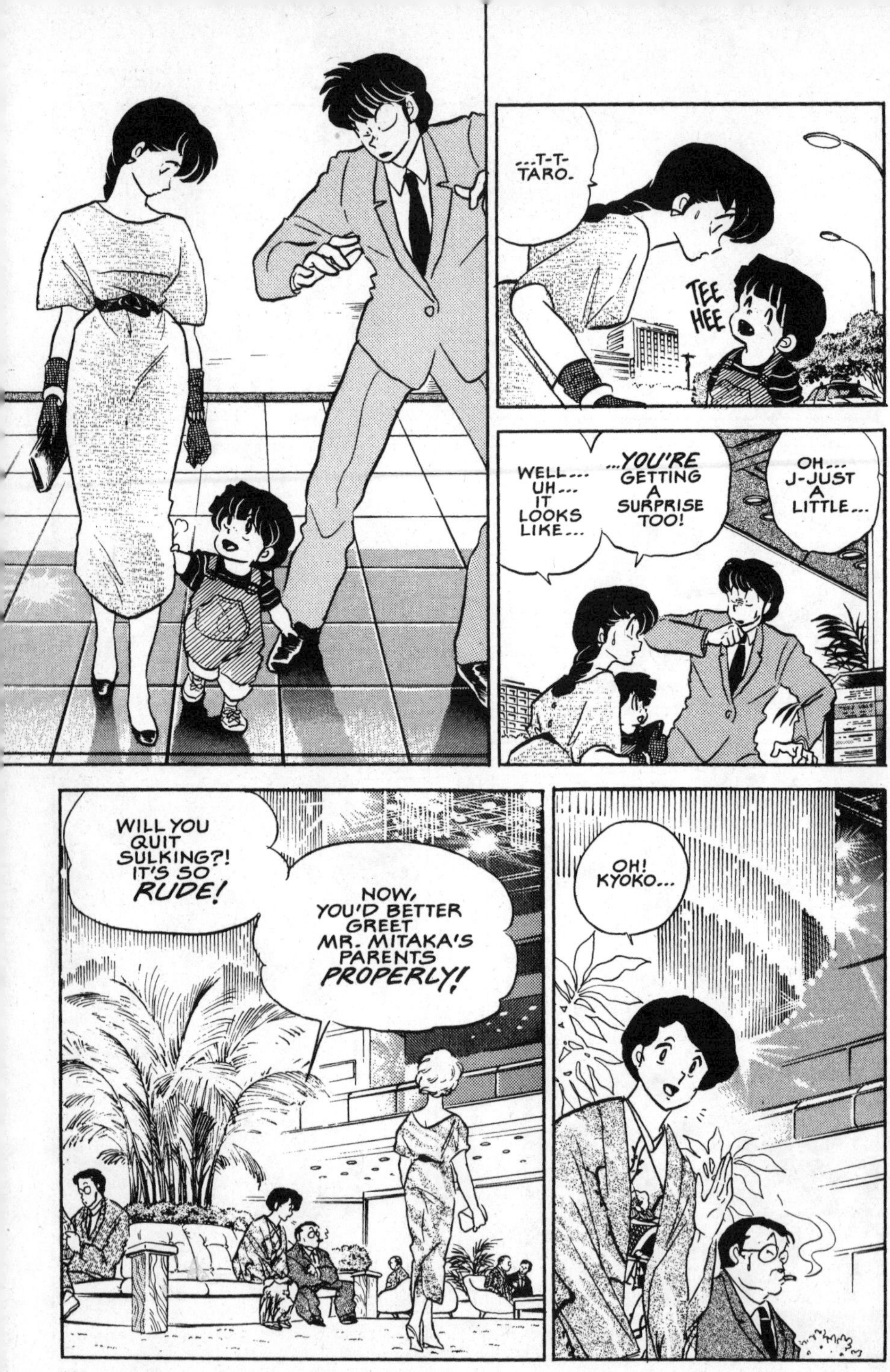

...T-T-TARO.
TEE HEE
WELL... UH... IT LOOKS LIKE...
...YOU'RE GETTING A SURPRISE TOO!
OH... J-JUST A LITTLE...
WILL YOU QUIT SULKING?! IT'S SO RUDE!
NOW, YOU'D BETTER GREET MR. MITAKA'S PARENTS PROPERLY!
OH! KYOKO...

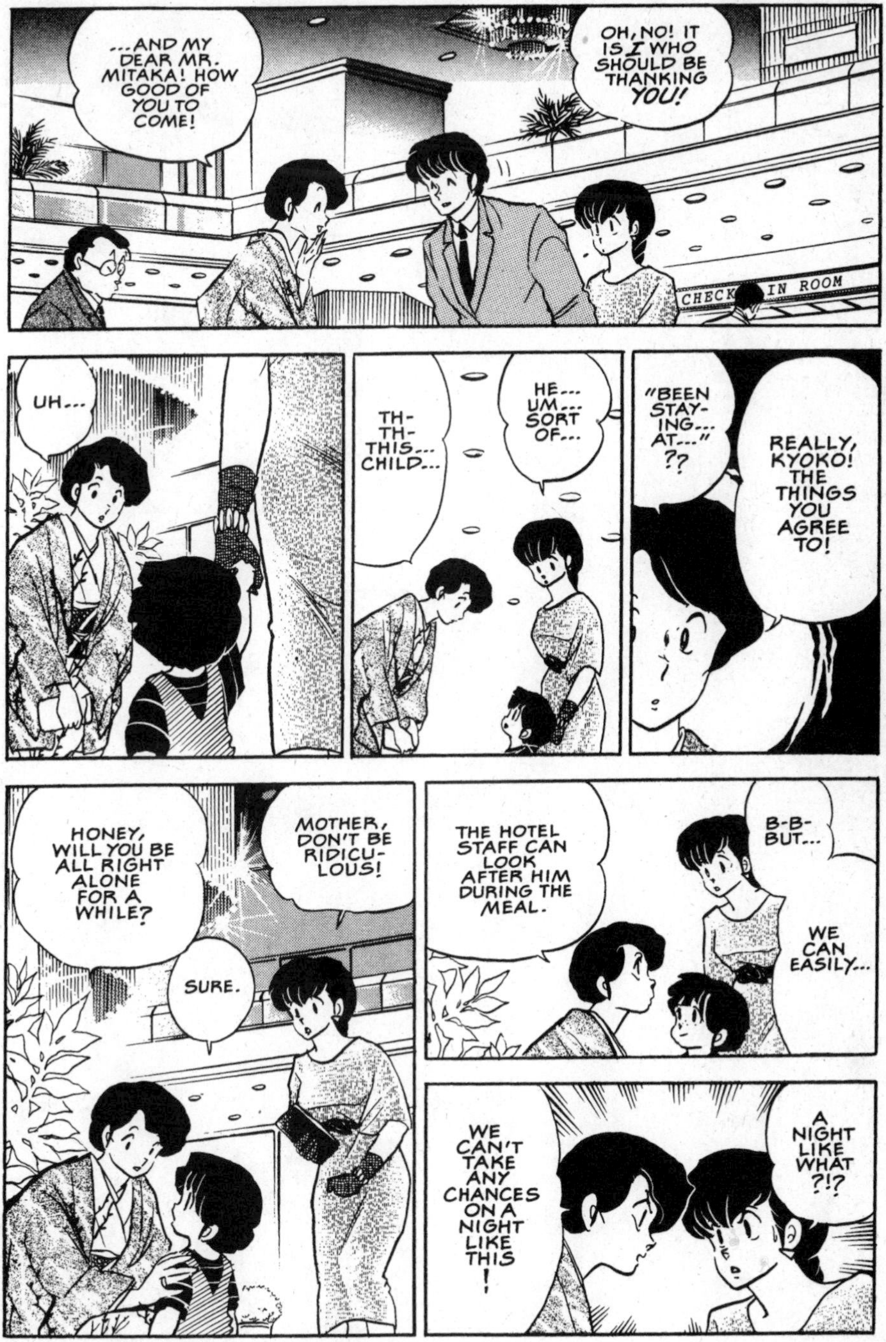
...AND MY DEAR MR. MITAKA! HOW GOOD OF YOU TO COME!
OH, NO! IT IS I WHO SHOULD BE THANKING YOU!
CHECK IN ROOM
UH...
TH-TH-THIS... CHILD...
HE... UM... SORT OF...
"BEEN STAYING... AT..." ??
REALLY, KYOKO! THE THINGS YOU AGREE TO!
HONEY, WILL YOU BE ALL RIGHT ALONE FOR A WHILE?
SURE.
MOTHER, DON'T BE RIDICULOUS!
THE HOTEL STAFF CAN LOOK AFTER HIM DURING THE MEAL.
B-B-BUT...
WE CAN EASILY...
WE CAN'T TAKE ANY CHANCES ON A NIGHT LIKE THIS!
A NIGHT LIKE WHAT ?!?

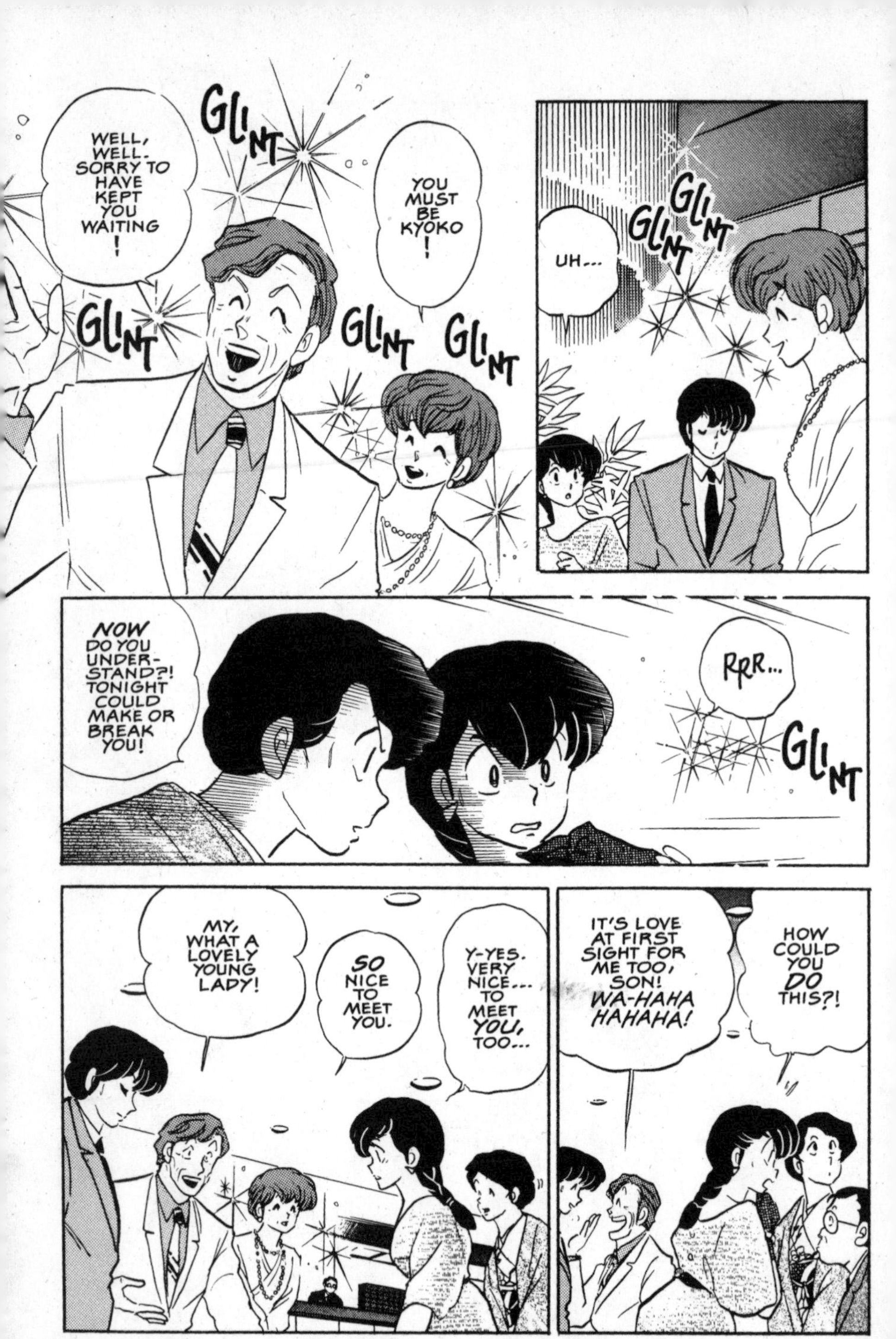
GLINT
WELL, WELL. SORRY TO HAVE KEPT YOU WAITING!
GLINT
YOU MUST BE KYOKO!
GLINT GLINT
GLINT GLINT
UH...
NOW DO YOU UNDER-STAND?! TONIGHT COULD MAKE OR BREAK YOU!
RRR...
GLINT
MY, WHAT A LOVELY YOUNG LADY!
SO NICE TO MEET YOU.
Y-YES. VERY NICE... TO MEET YOU, TOO...
IT'S LOVE AT FIRST SIGHT FOR ME TOO, SON! WA-HAHA HAHAHA!
HOW COULD YOU DO THIS?!

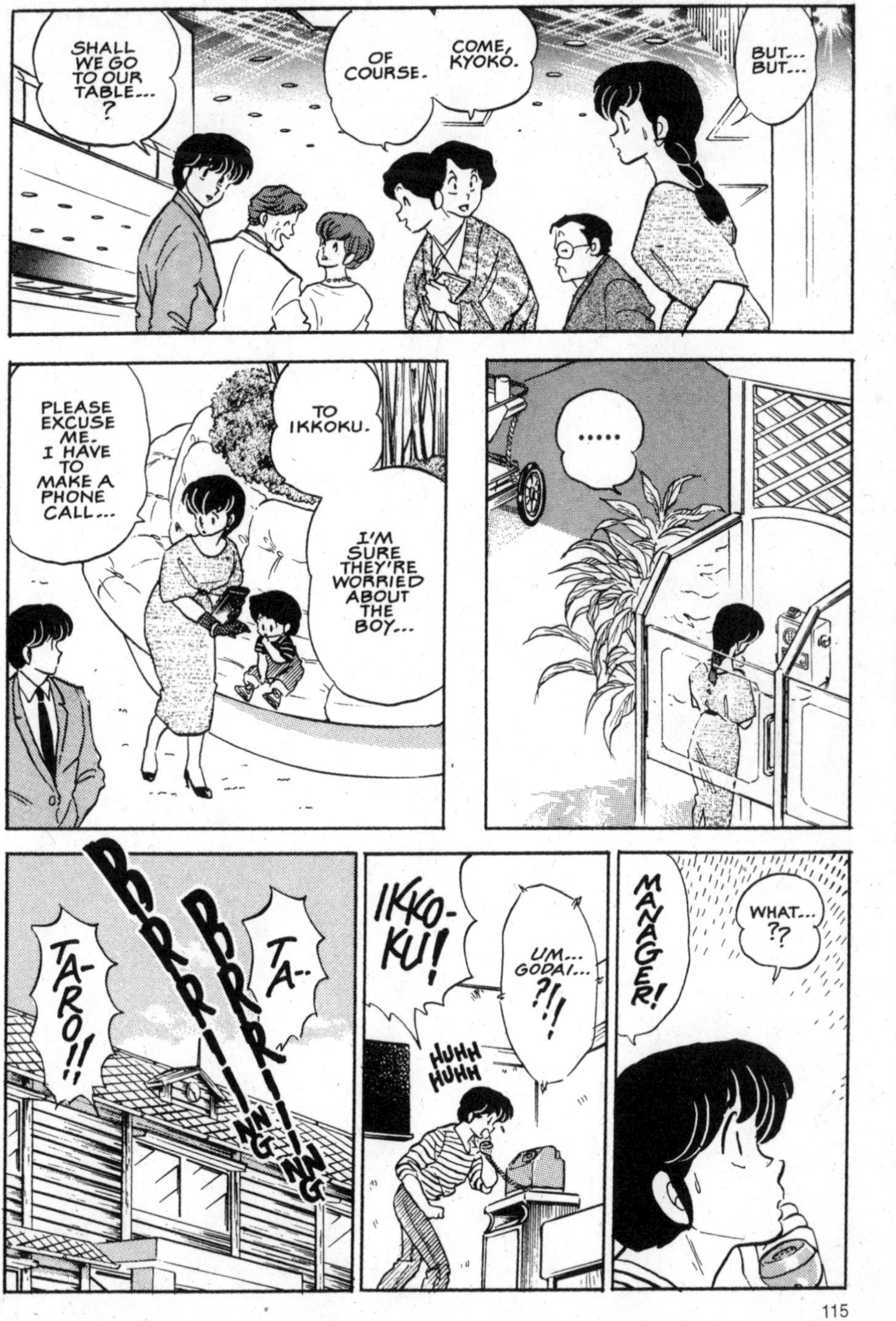
SHALL WE GO TO OUR TABLE...?
OF COURSE.
COME, KYOKO.
BUT... BUT...
PLEASE EXCUSE ME. I HAVE TO MAKE A PHONE CALL...
TO IKKOKU.
I'M SURE THEY'RE WORRIED ABOUT THE BOY...
.....
BRRRIIIING
TA-RO!!
BRRRIIIING
TA-..
IKKO-KU!
UM... GODAI...?!!
HUHH HUHH
MANAGER!
WHAT...??

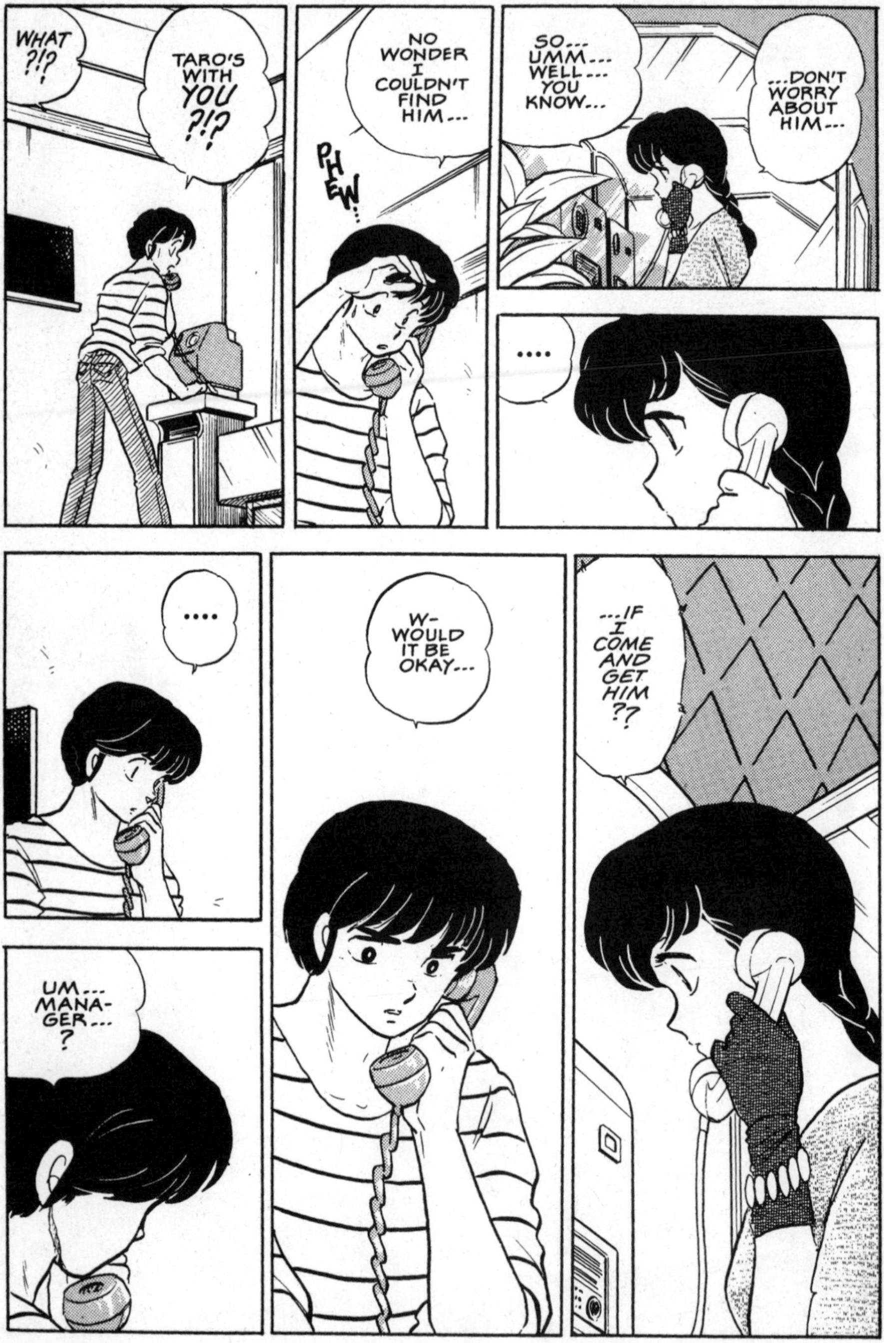
WHAT ?!?
TARO'S WITH YOU ?!?
PHEW..
NO WONDER I COULDN'T FIND HIM...
SO... UMM... WELL... YOU KNOW...
...DON'T WORRY ABOUT HIM...
....
....
W-WOULD IT BE OKAY...
...IF I COME AND GET HIM ??
UM... MANAGER... ?

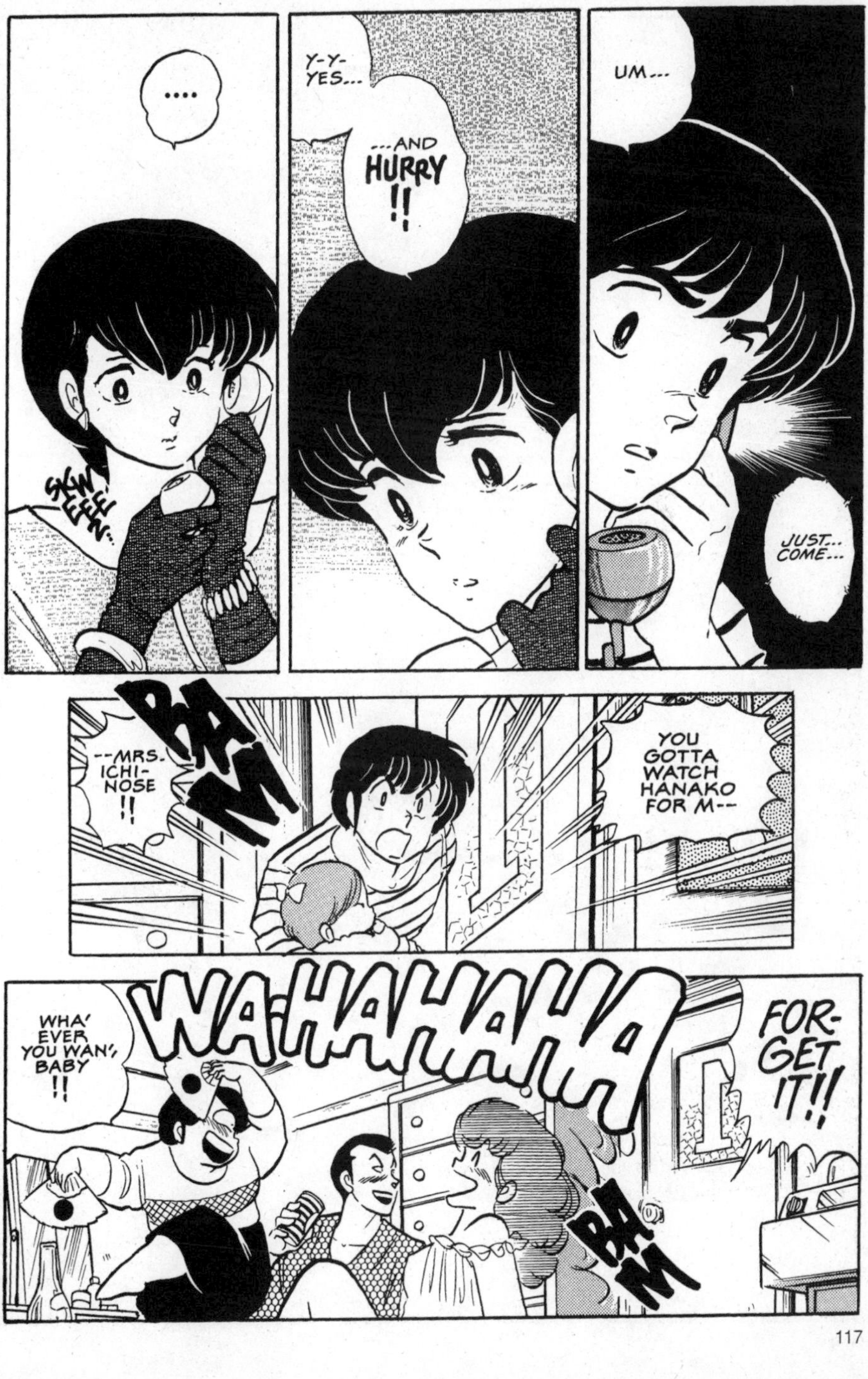
....
SKWEEEN
Y-Y-YES...
...AND HURRY!!
UM...
JUST... COME...
BAM
--MRS. ICHINOSE!!
YOU GOTTA WATCH HANAKO FOR M--
WAHAHAHA
WHA'EVER YOU WAN', BABY!!
FOR-GET IT!!
BAM

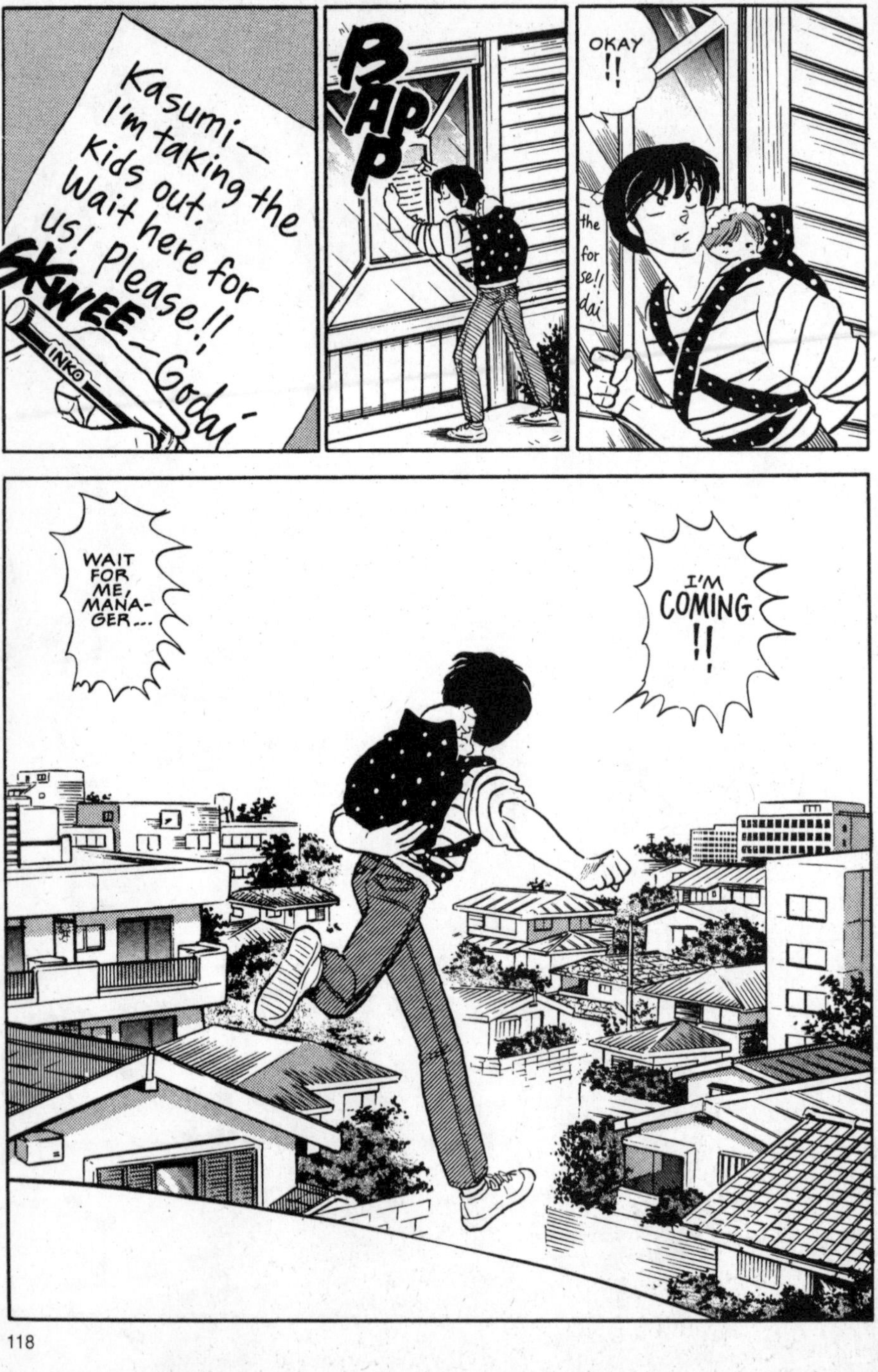
Kasumi— I'm taking the kids out. Wait here for us! Please!! —Godai
SKWEE
INKO
BAP
OKAY !!
WAIT FOR ME, MANA-GER...
I'M COMING !!

PART EIGHT
TREACHEROUS NIGHT

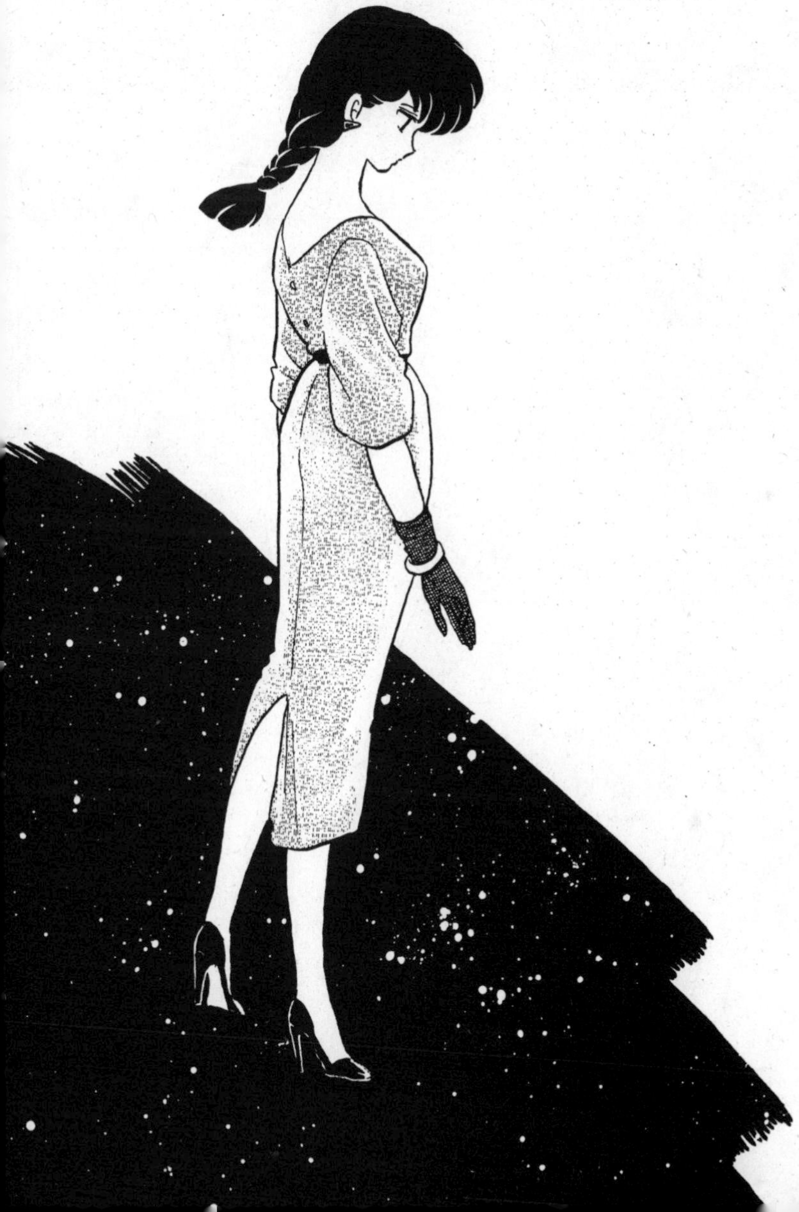

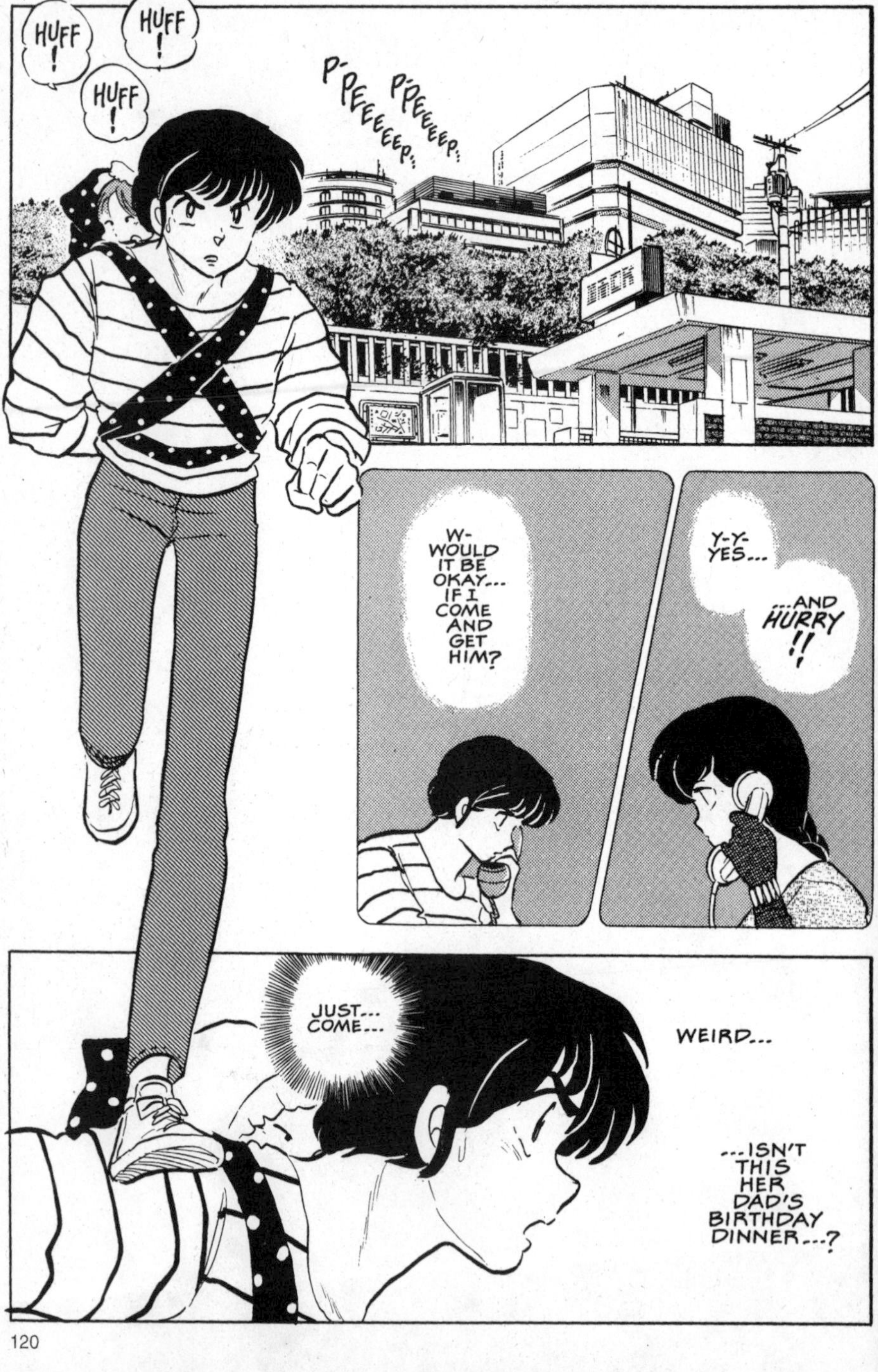
HUFF!
HUFF!
HUFF!
P-PEEEEEEP...
P-PEEEEEP...
W-WOULD IT BE OKAY... IF I COME AND GET HIM?
Y-Y-YES...
...AND HURRY!!
JUST... COME...
WEIRD...
...ISN'T THIS HER DAD'S BIRTHDAY DINNER...?

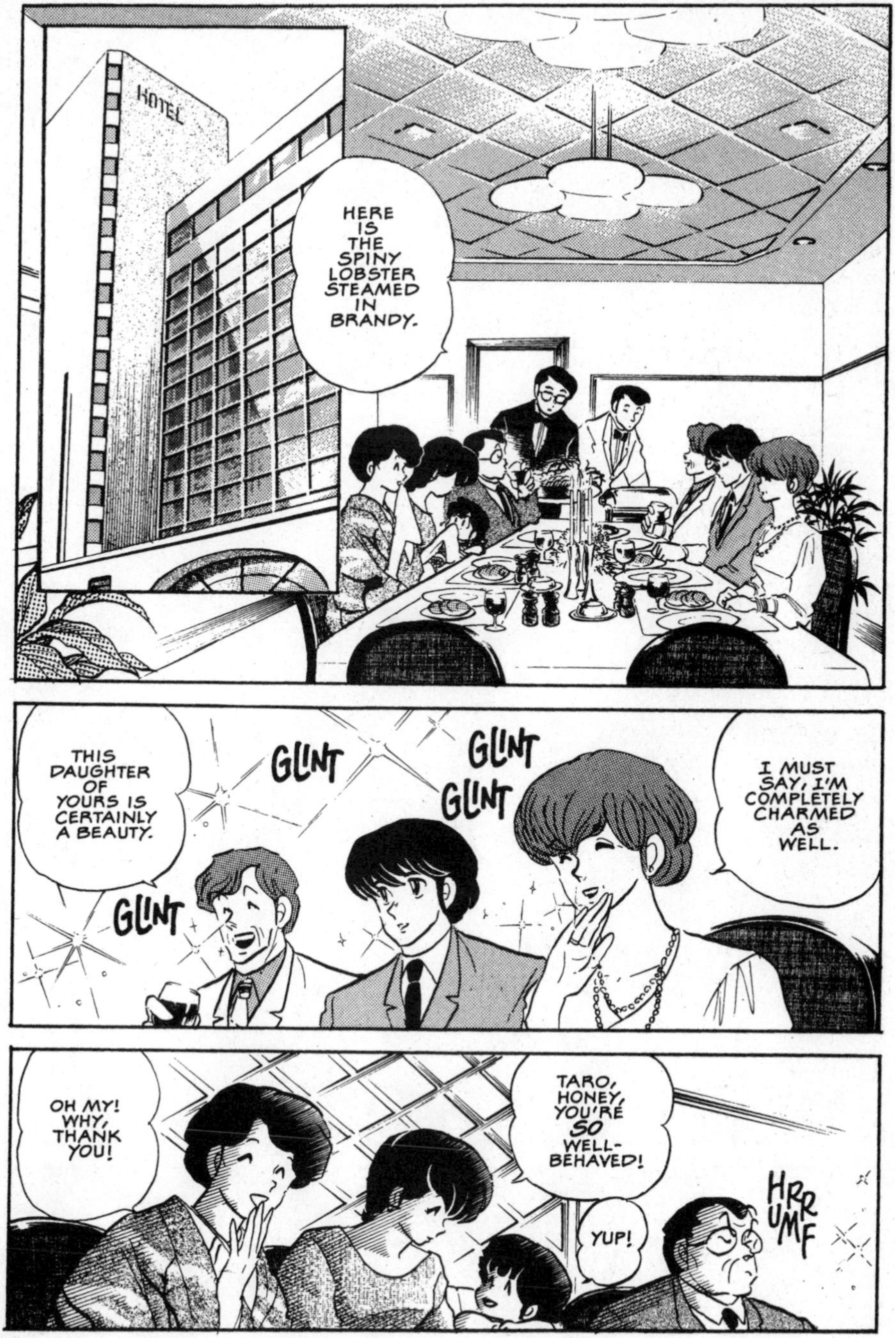
HOTEL
HERE IS THE SPINY LOBSTER STEAMED IN BRANDY.
THIS DAUGHTER OF YOURS IS CERTAINLY A BEAUTY.
GLINT
GLINT
GLINT
GLINT
I MUST SAY, I'M COMPLETELY CHARMED AS WELL.
OH MY! WHY, THANK YOU!
TARO, HONEY, YOU'RE *SO* WELL-BEHAVED!
YUP!
HRRUMF

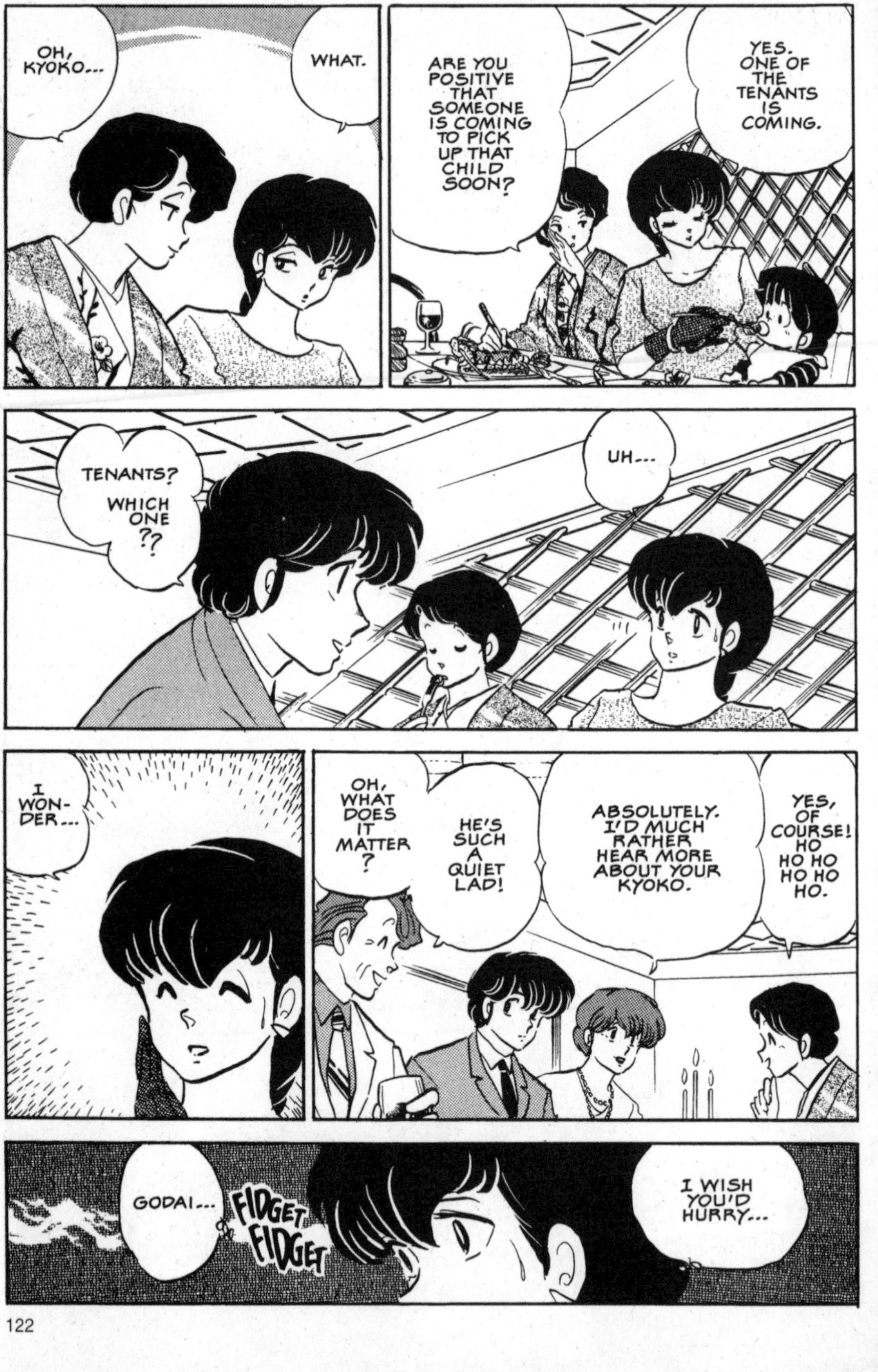

OH, KYOKO...
WHAT.
ARE YOU POSITIVE THAT SOMEONE IS COMING TO PICK UP THAT CHILD SOON?
YES. ONE OF THE TENANTS IS COMING.
TENANTS? WHICH ONE??
UH...
I WONDER...
OH, WHAT DOES IT MATTER?
HE'S SUCH A QUIET LAD!
ABSOLUTELY. I'D MUCH RATHER HEAR MORE ABOUT YOUR KYOKO.
YES, OF COURSE! HO HO HO HO HO HO.
GODAI...
FIDGET FIDGET
I WISH YOU'D HURRY...

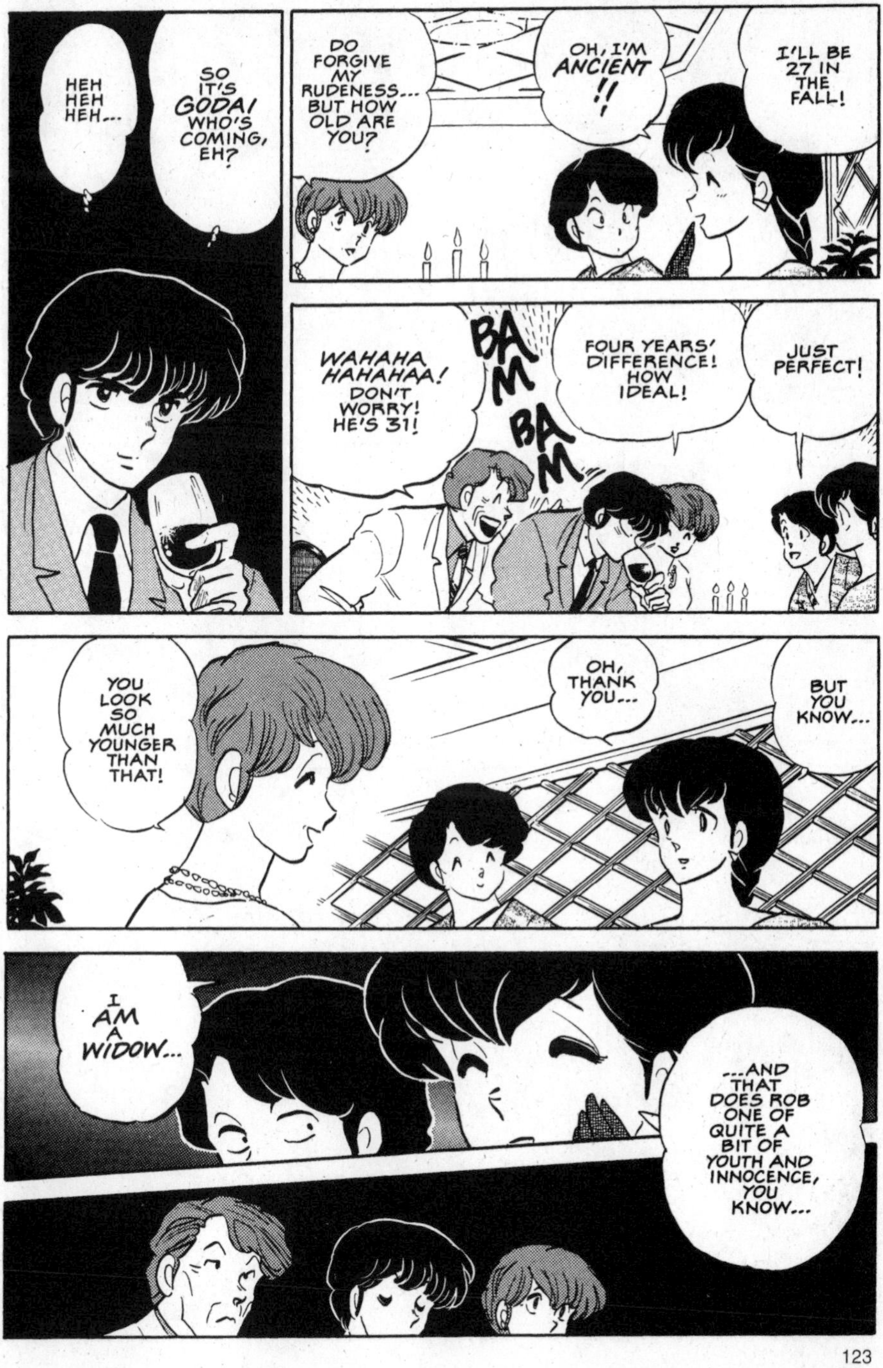
HEH HEH HEH...
SO IT'S GODAI WHO'S COMING, EH?
DO FORGIVE MY RUDENESS... BUT HOW OLD ARE YOU?
OH, I'M ANCIENT !!
I'LL BE 27 IN THE FALL!
WAHAHA HAHAHAA! DON'T WORRY! HE'S 31!
BAM BAM
FOUR YEARS' DIFFERENCE! HOW IDEAL!
JUST PERFECT!
YOU LOOK SO MUCH YOUNGER THAN THAT!
OH, THANK YOU...
BUT YOU KNOW...
I AM A WIDOW...
...AND THAT DOES ROB ONE OF QUITE A BIT OF YOUTH AND INNOCENCE, YOU KNOW...

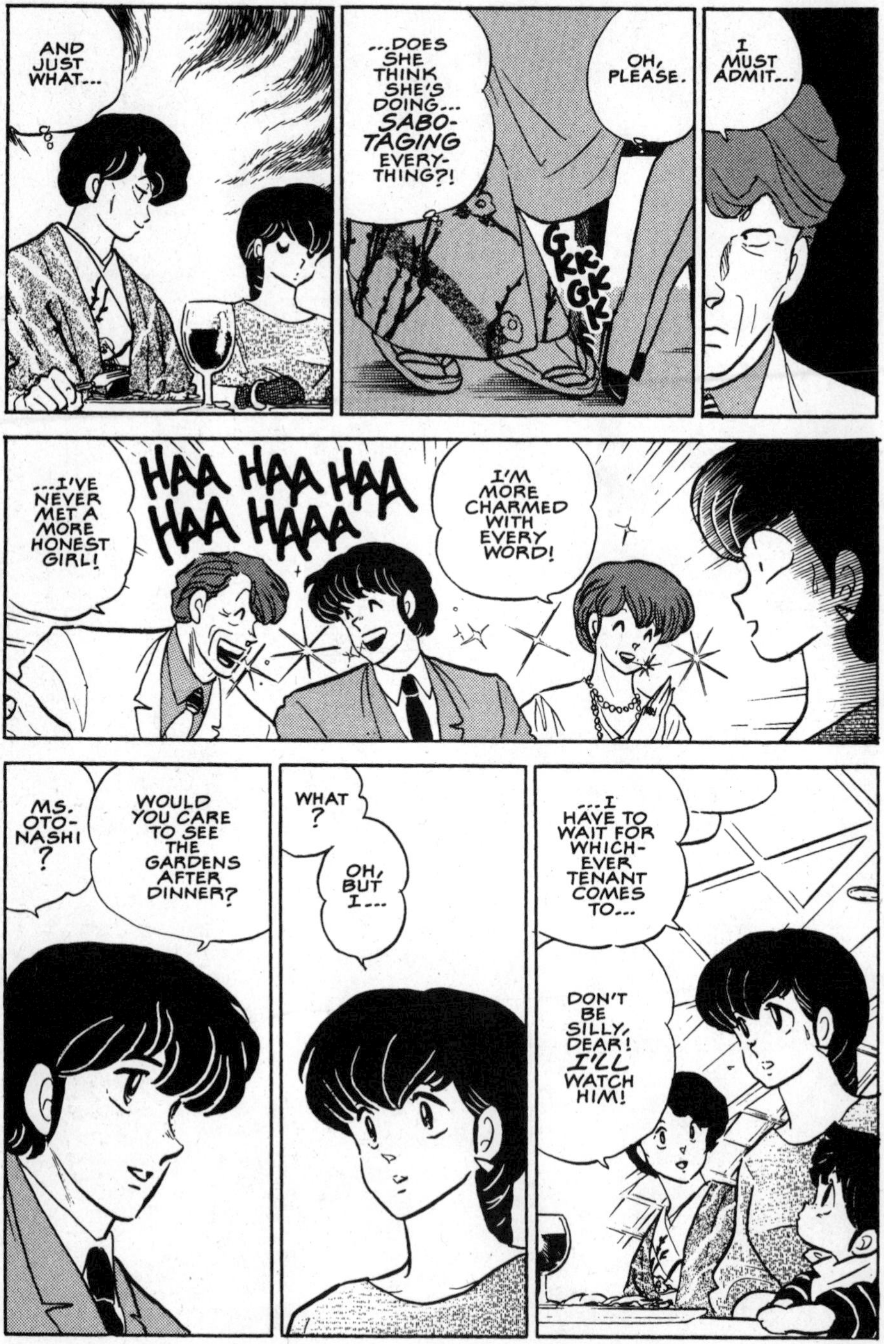
AND JUST WHAT...
...DOES SHE THINK SHE'S DOING... *SABOTAGING* EVERYTHING?!
GKK GKK
OH, PLEASE.
I MUST ADMIT...
...I'VE NEVER MET A MORE HONEST GIRL!
HAA HAA HAA HAA HAA HAAA
I'M MORE CHARMED WITH EVERY WORD!
MS. OTONASHI?
WOULD YOU CARE TO SEE THE GARDENS AFTER DINNER?
WHAT?
OH, BUT I...
...I HAVE TO WAIT FOR WHICHEVER TENANT COMES TO...
DON'T BE SILLY, DEAR! *I'LL* WATCH HIM!

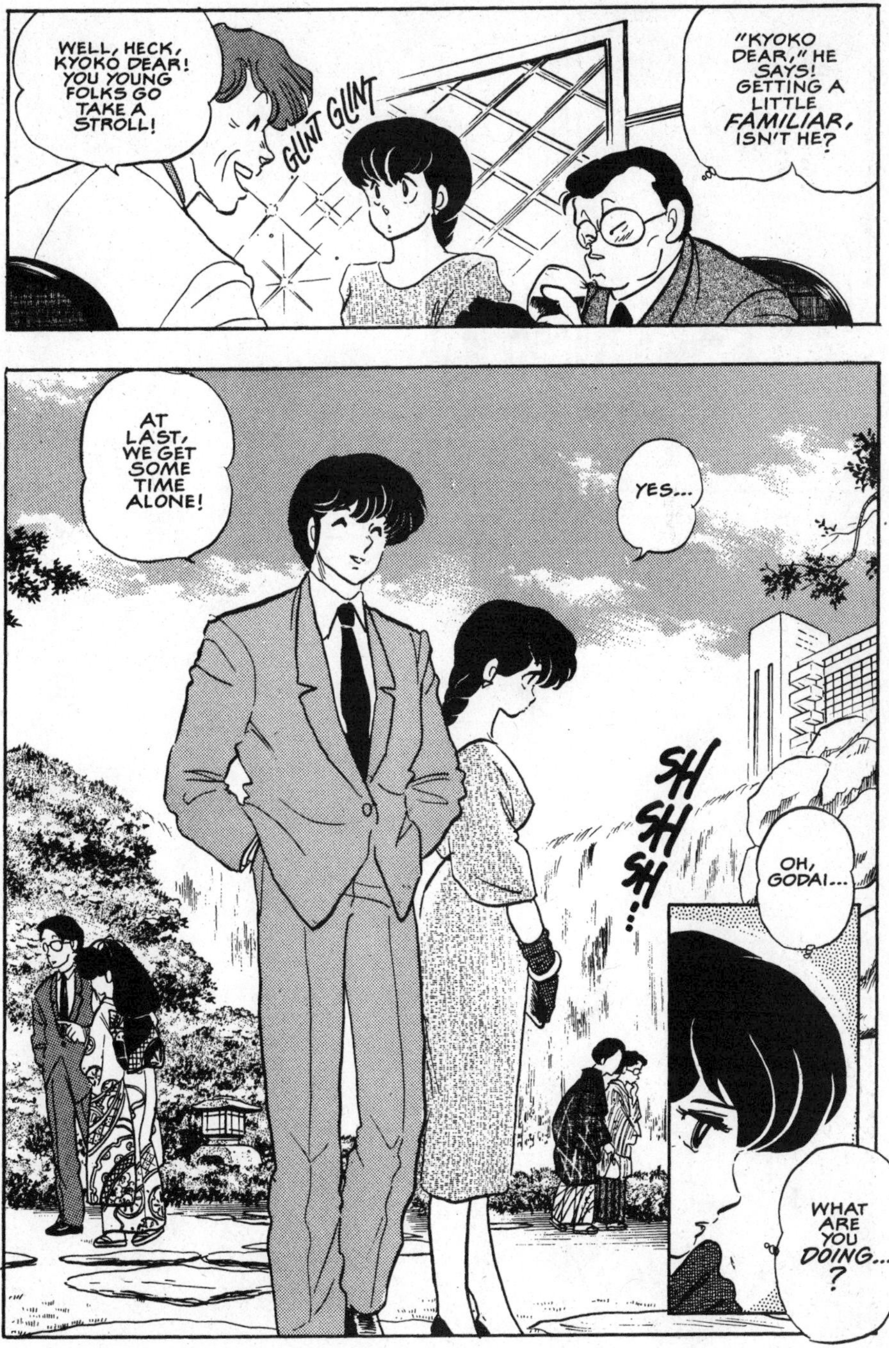
WELL, HECK, KYOKO DEAR! YOU YOUNG FOLKS GO TAKE A STROLL!
GLINT GLINT
"KYOKO DEAR," HE SAYS! GETTING A LITTLE FAMILIAR, ISN'T HE?
AT LAST, WE GET SOME TIME ALONE!
YES...
SH SH SH...
OH, GODAI...
WHAT ARE YOU DOING...?

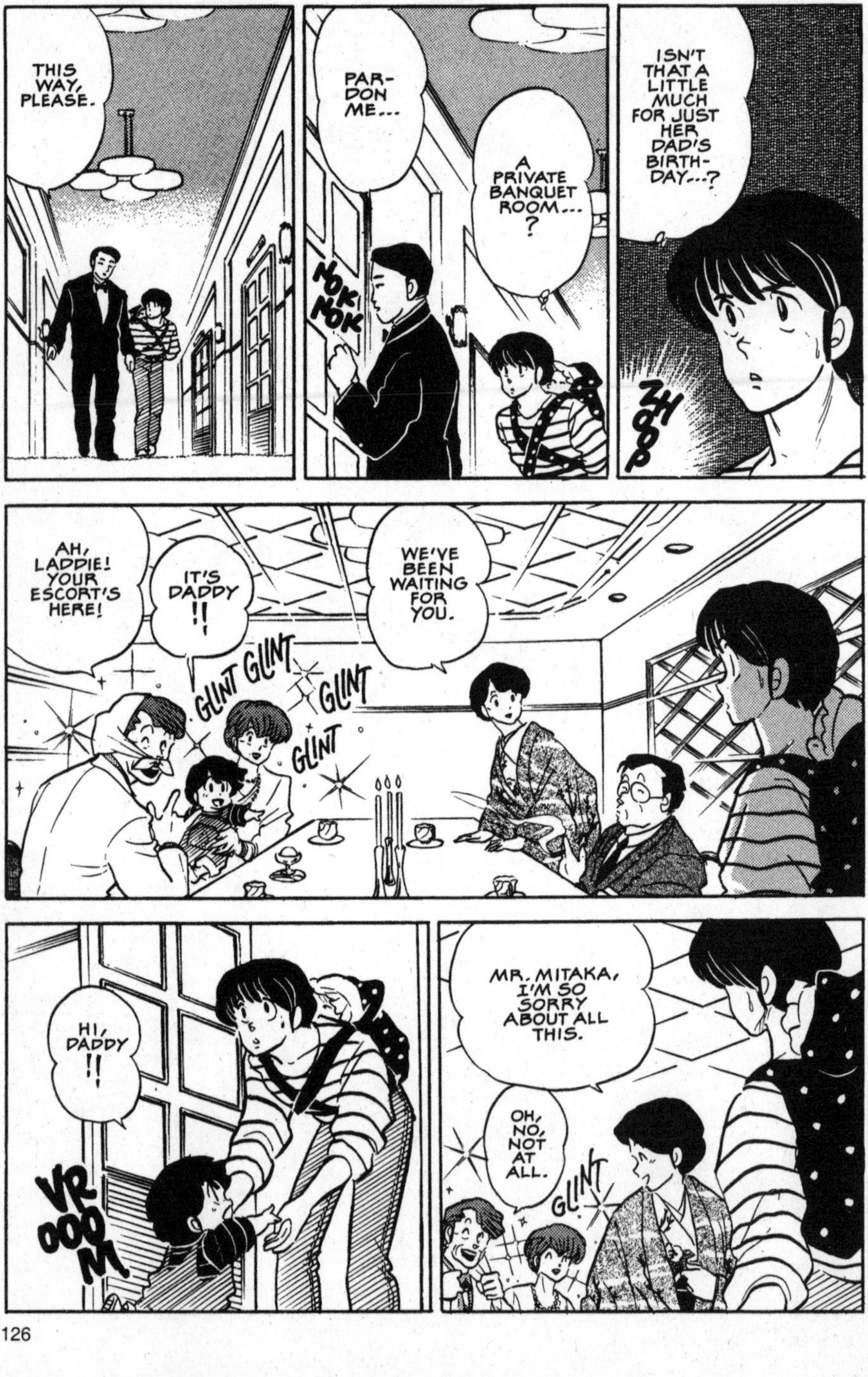
THIS WAY, PLEASE.
PARDON ME...
NOK NOK
A PRIVATE BANQUET ROOM...?
ISN'T THAT A LITTLE MUCH FOR JUST HER DAD'S BIRTHDAY...?
ZHOOP
AH, LADDIE! YOUR ESCORT'S HERE!
IT'S DADDY!!
GLINT GLINT
GLINT
GLINT
WE'VE BEEN WAITING FOR YOU.
HI, DADDY!!
VROOOOM
MR. MITAKA, I'M SO SORRY ABOUT ALL THIS.
OH, NO, NOT AT ALL.
GLINT

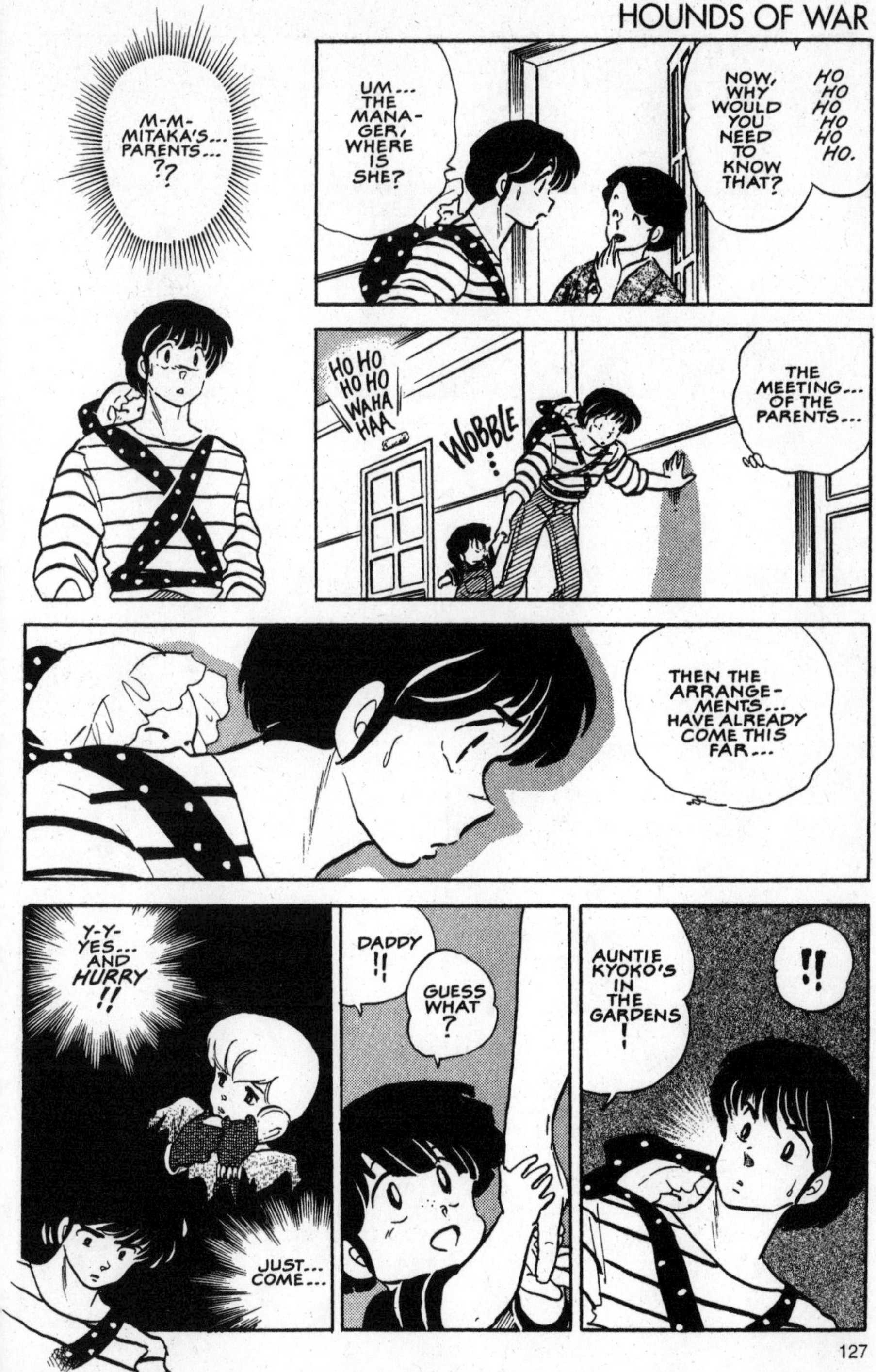
M-M-MITAKA'S... PARENTS...??
UM... THE MANAGER, WHERE IS SHE?
NOW, WHY WOULD YOU NEED TO KNOW THAT?
HO HO HO HO HO HO.
HO HO HO HO WAHA HAA
WOBBLE...
THE MEETING... OF THE PARENTS...
THEN THE ARRANGEMENTS... HAVE ALREADY COME THIS FAR...
Y-Y-YES... AND HURRY!!
JUST... COME...
DADDY!!
GUESS WHAT?
AUNTIE KYOKO'S IN THE GARDENS!
!!

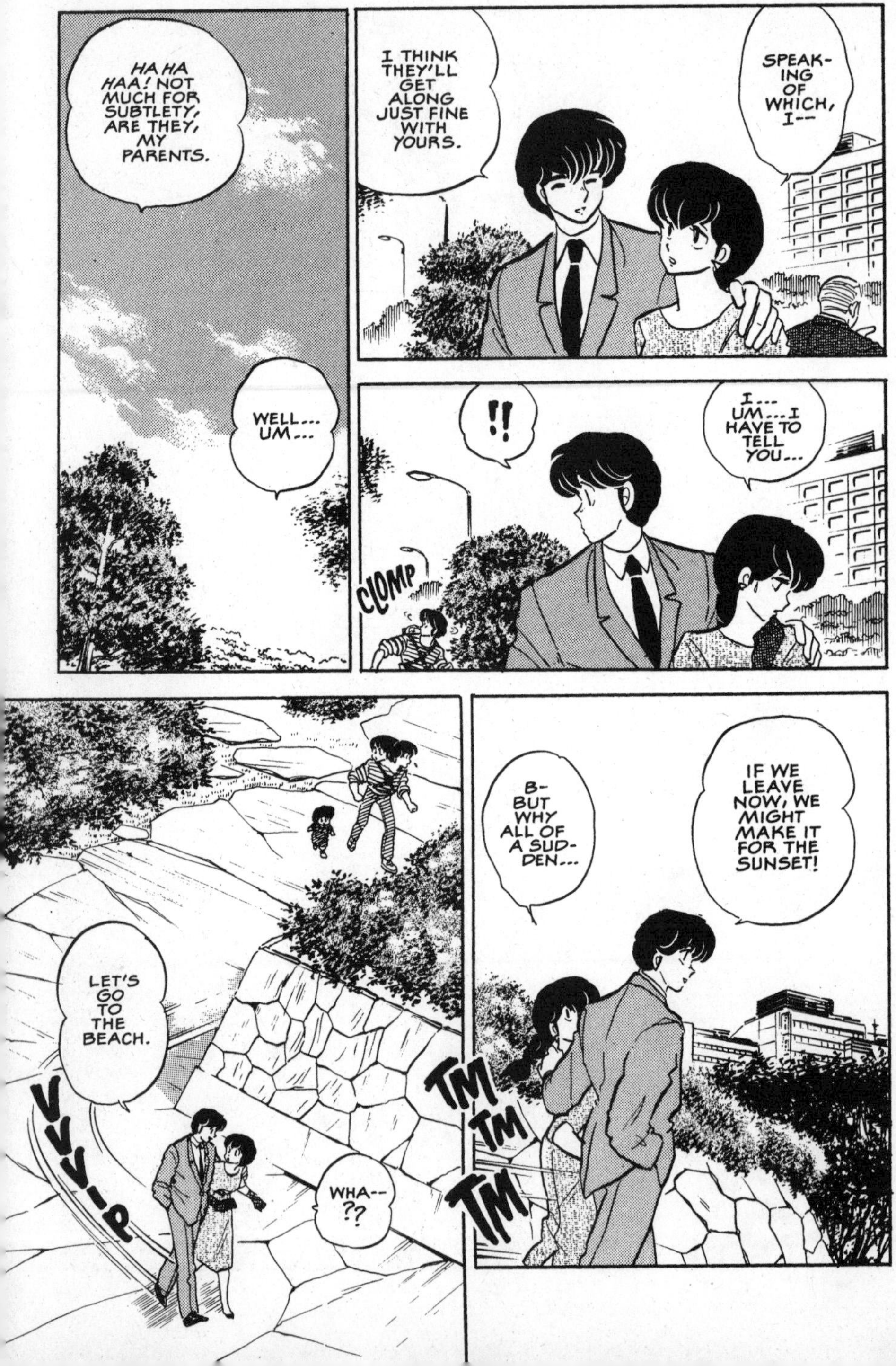
HA HA HAA! NOT MUCH FOR SUBTLETY, ARE THEY, MY PARENTS.
WELL... UM...
I THINK THEY'LL GET ALONG JUST FINE WITH YOURS.
SPEAKING OF WHICH, I--
CLOMP
!!
I... UM... I HAVE TO TELL YOU...
LET'S GO TO THE BEACH.
VVVIP
WHA--??
B-BUT WHY ALL OF A SUDDEN...
IF WE LEAVE NOW, WE MIGHT MAKE IT FOR THE SUNSET!
TM TM TM

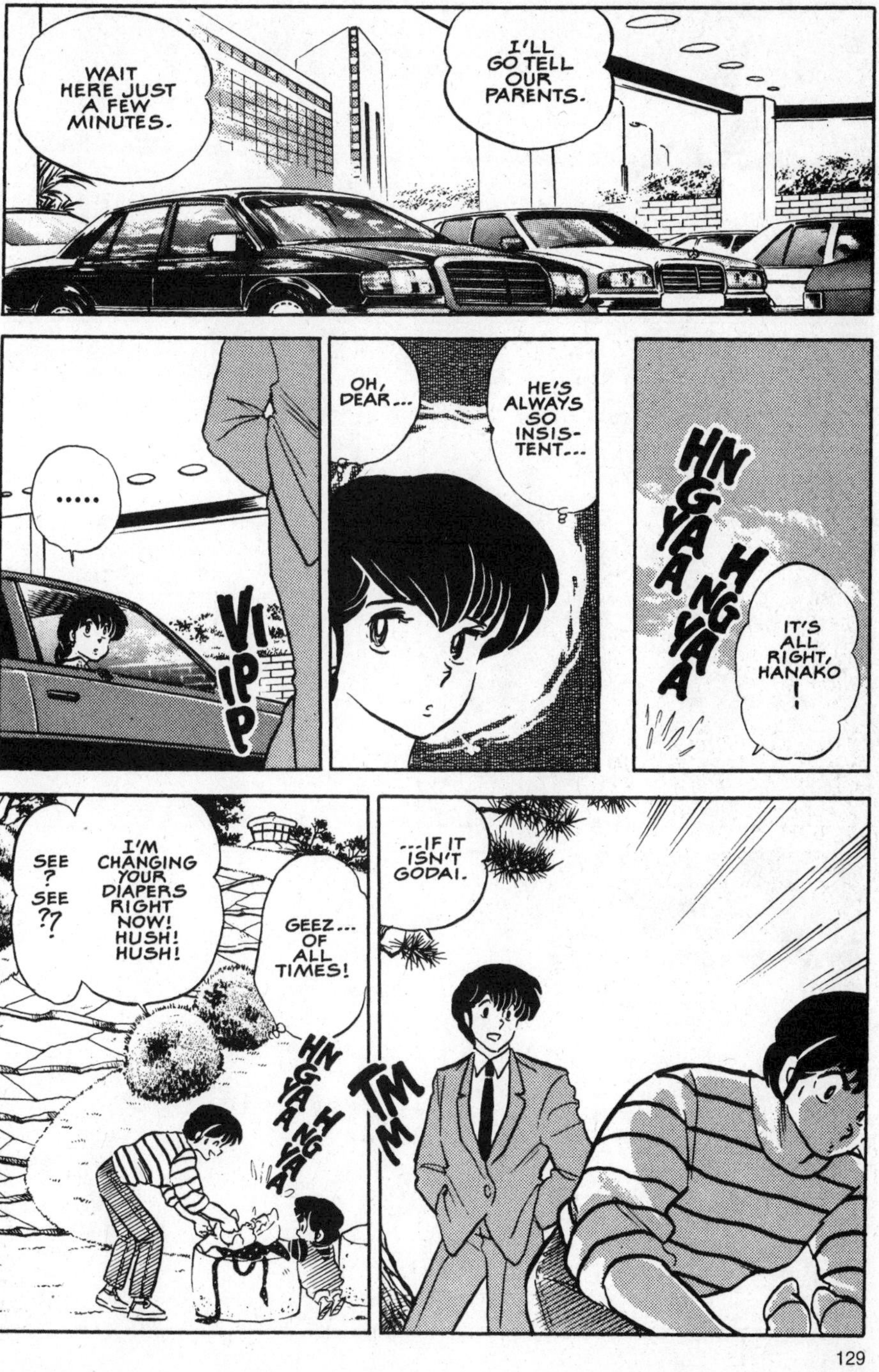
WAIT HERE JUST A FEW MINUTES.
I'LL GO TELL OUR PARENTS.
.....
VIIPIP
OH, DEAR...
HE'S ALWAYS SO INSIS-TENT...
HN GYAA
HNGYAA
IT'S ALL RIGHT, HANAKO!
SEE? SEE??
I'M CHANGING YOUR DIAPERS RIGHT NOW! HUSH! HUSH!
GEEZ... OF ALL TIMES!
HN GYAA
HNGYAA
TMM
...IF IT ISN'T GODAI.

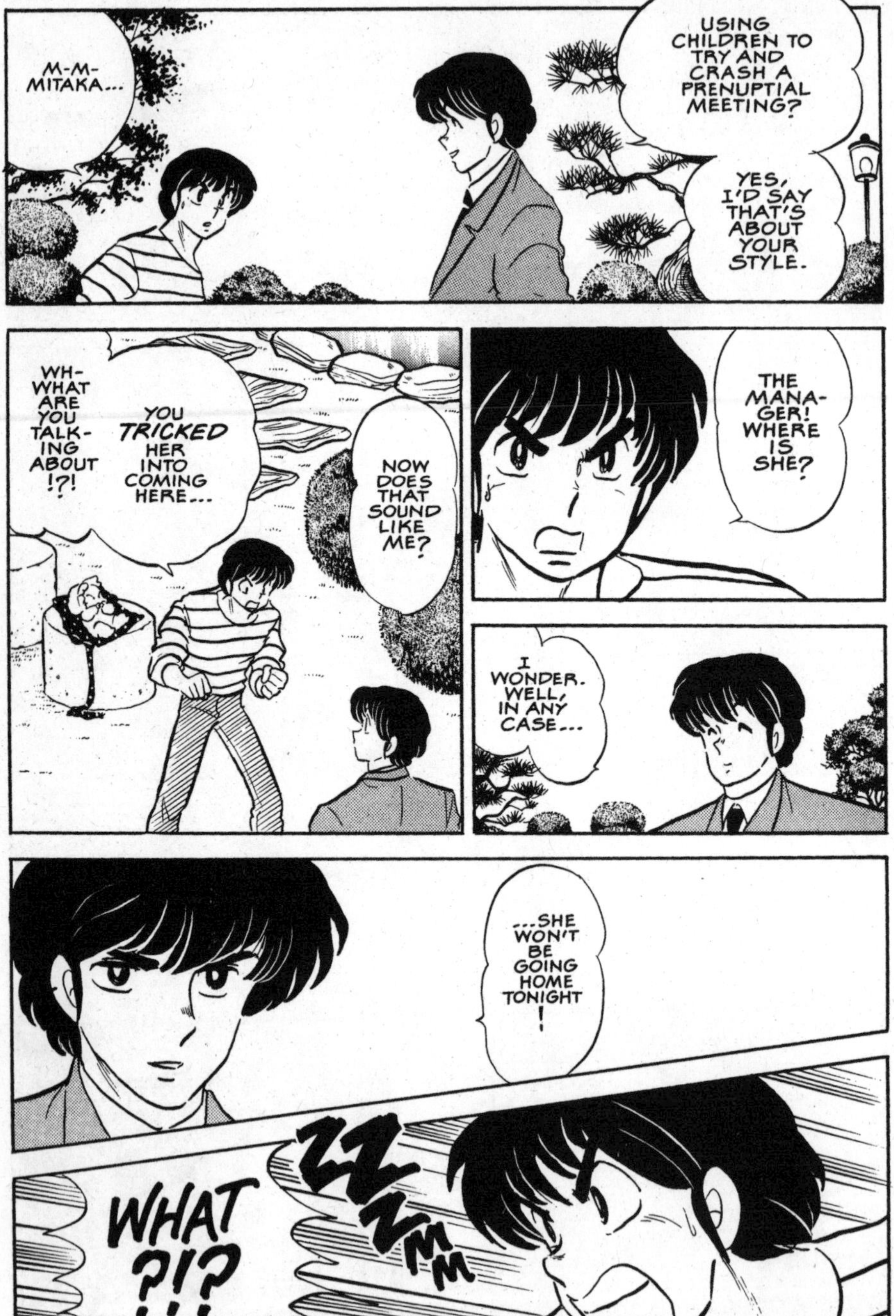
M-M-MITAKA...
USING CHILDREN TO TRY AND CRASH A PRENUPTIAL MEETING?
YES, I'D SAY THAT'S ABOUT YOUR STYLE.
WH-WHAT ARE YOU TALKING ABOUT !?!
YOU *TRICKED* HER INTO COMING HERE...
NOW DOES THAT SOUND LIKE ME?
THE MANAGER! WHERE IS SHE?
I WONDER. WELL, IN ANY CASE...
...SHE WON'T BE GOING HOME TONIGHT!
WHAT ?!?
ZZZMMM

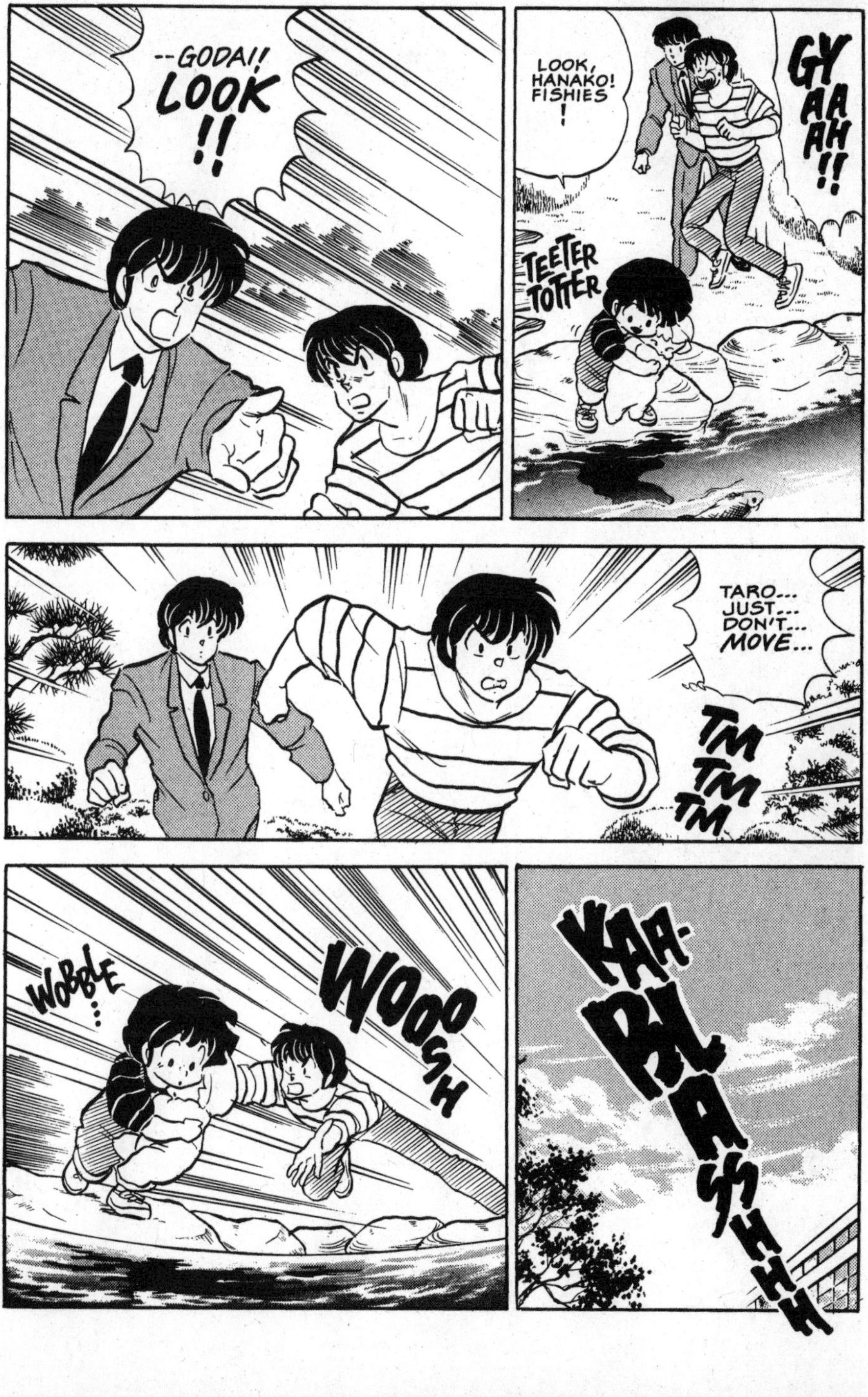
--GODAI!! LOOK !!
LOOK, HANAKO! FISHIES!
GYAAH!!
TEETER TOTTER
TARO... JUST... DON'T... MOVE...
TM TM TM
WOBBLE...
WOOOSH
KAA-BLAASHHHHH

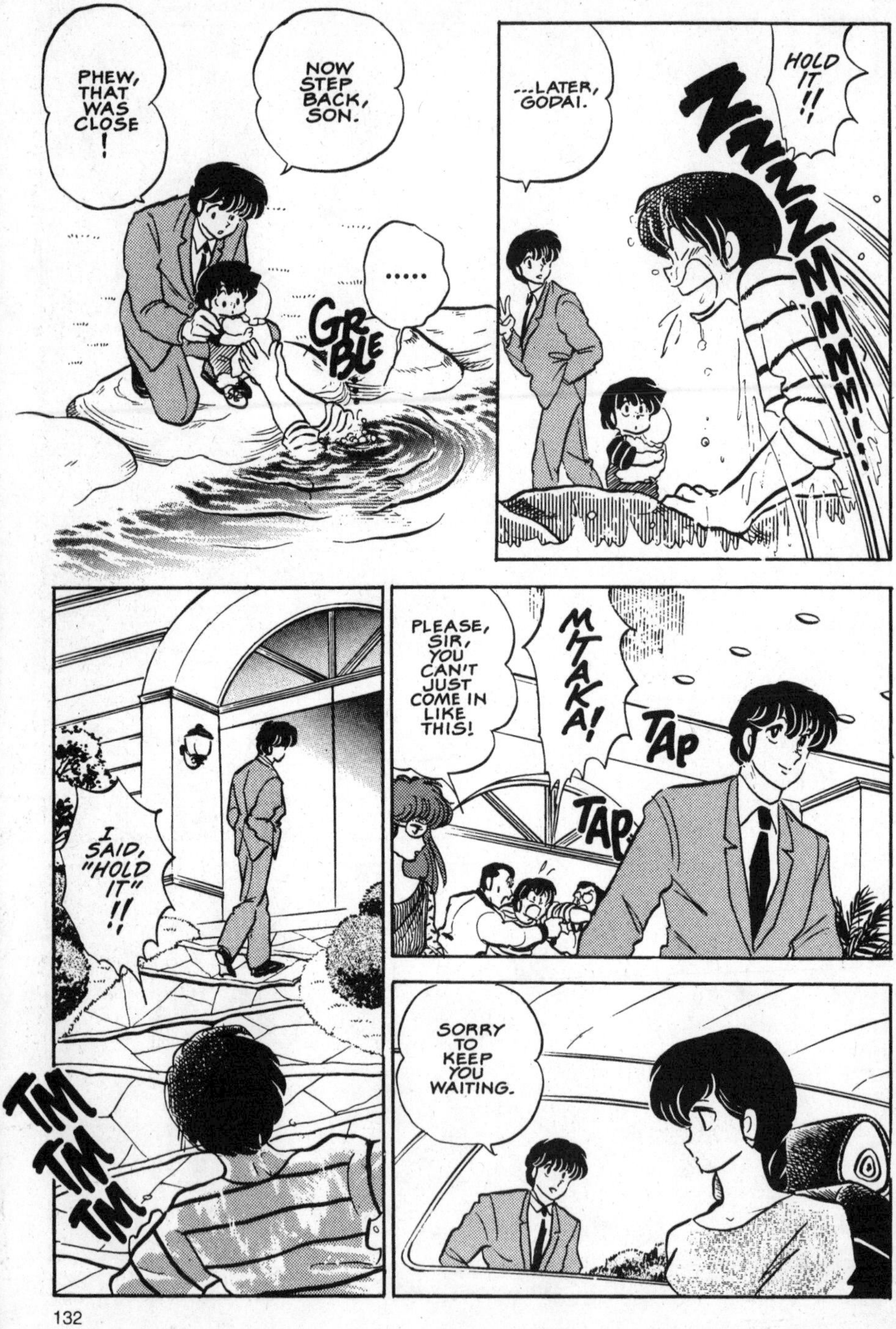
PHEW, THAT WAS CLOSE!
NOW STEP BACK, SON.
.....
GRBLE
...LATER, GODAI.
HOLD IT!!
NNNNNMMMMM!!...
I SAID, "HOLD IT"!!
TM TM TM
PLEASE, SIR, YOU CAN'T JUST COME IN LIKE THIS!
MITAKA!
TAP
TAP
SORRY TO KEEP YOU WAITING.

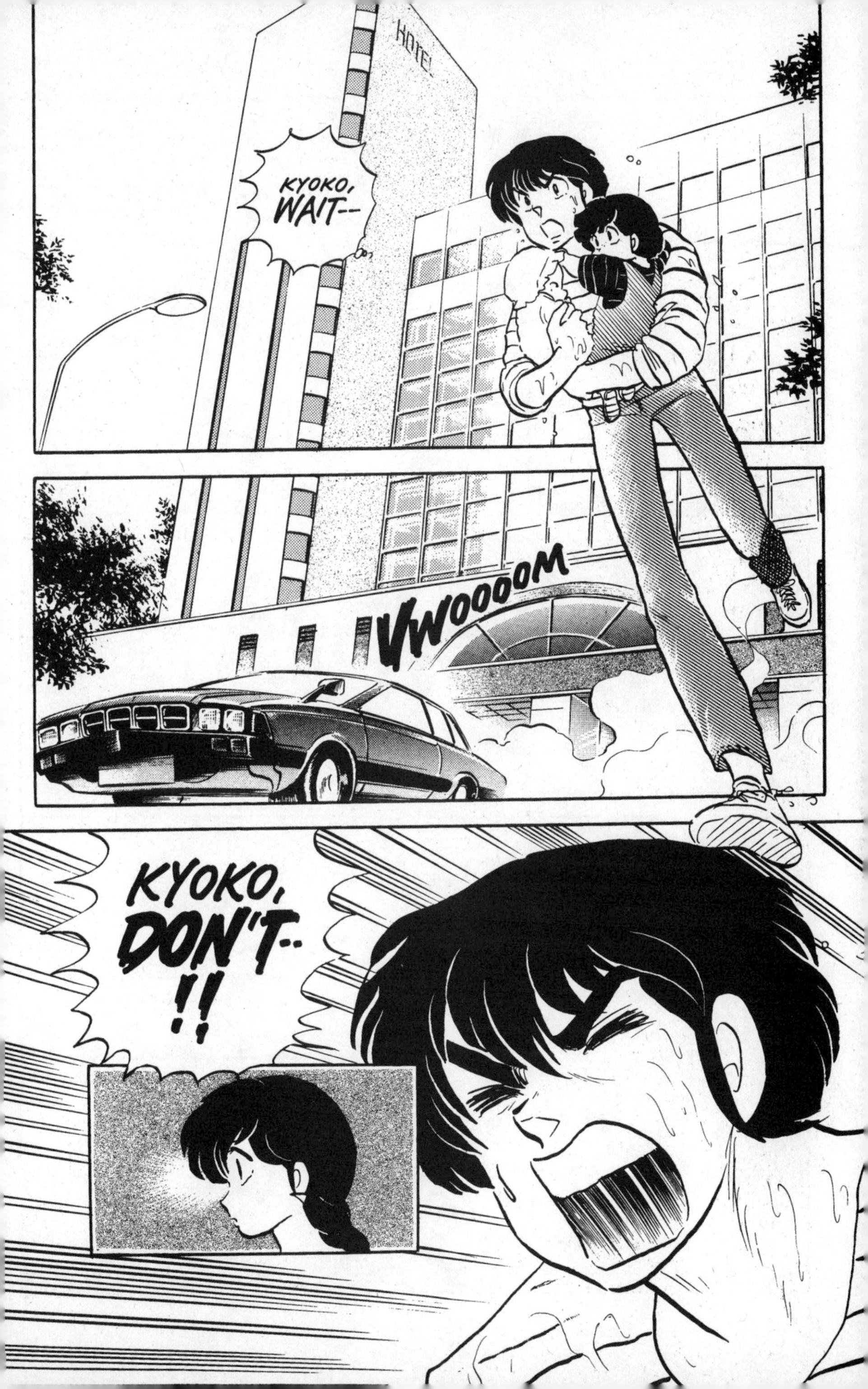
HOTEL
KYOKO, WAIT--
VWOOOOM
KYOKO, DON'T-- !!

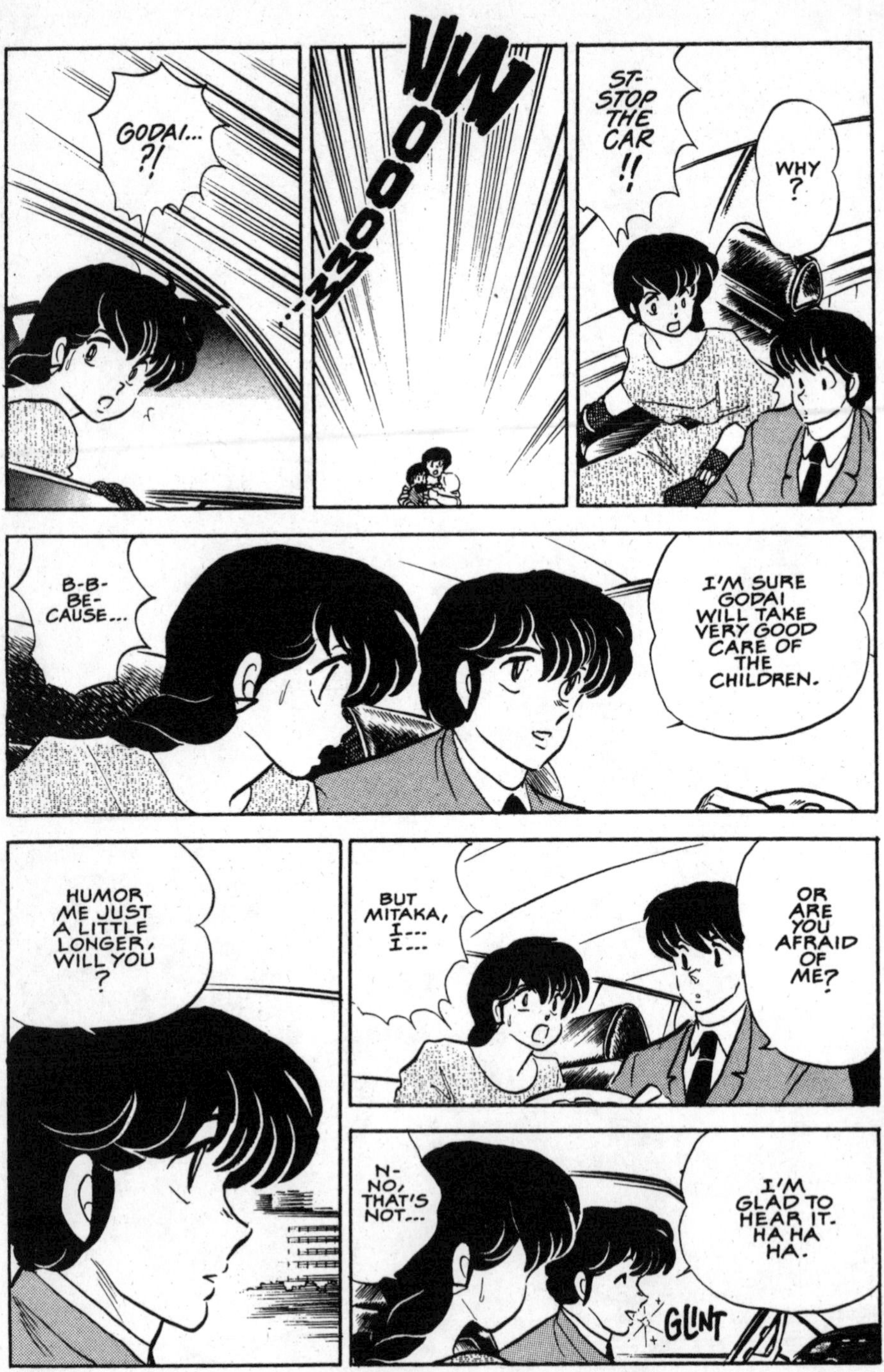
GODAI... ?!
VVVROOOOMM...!!
ST-STOP THE CAR!!
WHY?
B-B-BE-CAUSE...
I'M SURE GODAI WILL TAKE VERY GOOD CARE OF THE CHILDREN.
HUMOR ME JUST A LITTLE LONGER, WILL YOU?
BUT MITAKA, I... I...
OR ARE YOU AFRAID OF ME?
N-NO, THAT'S NOT...
I'M GLAD TO HEAR IT. HA HA HA.
GLINT

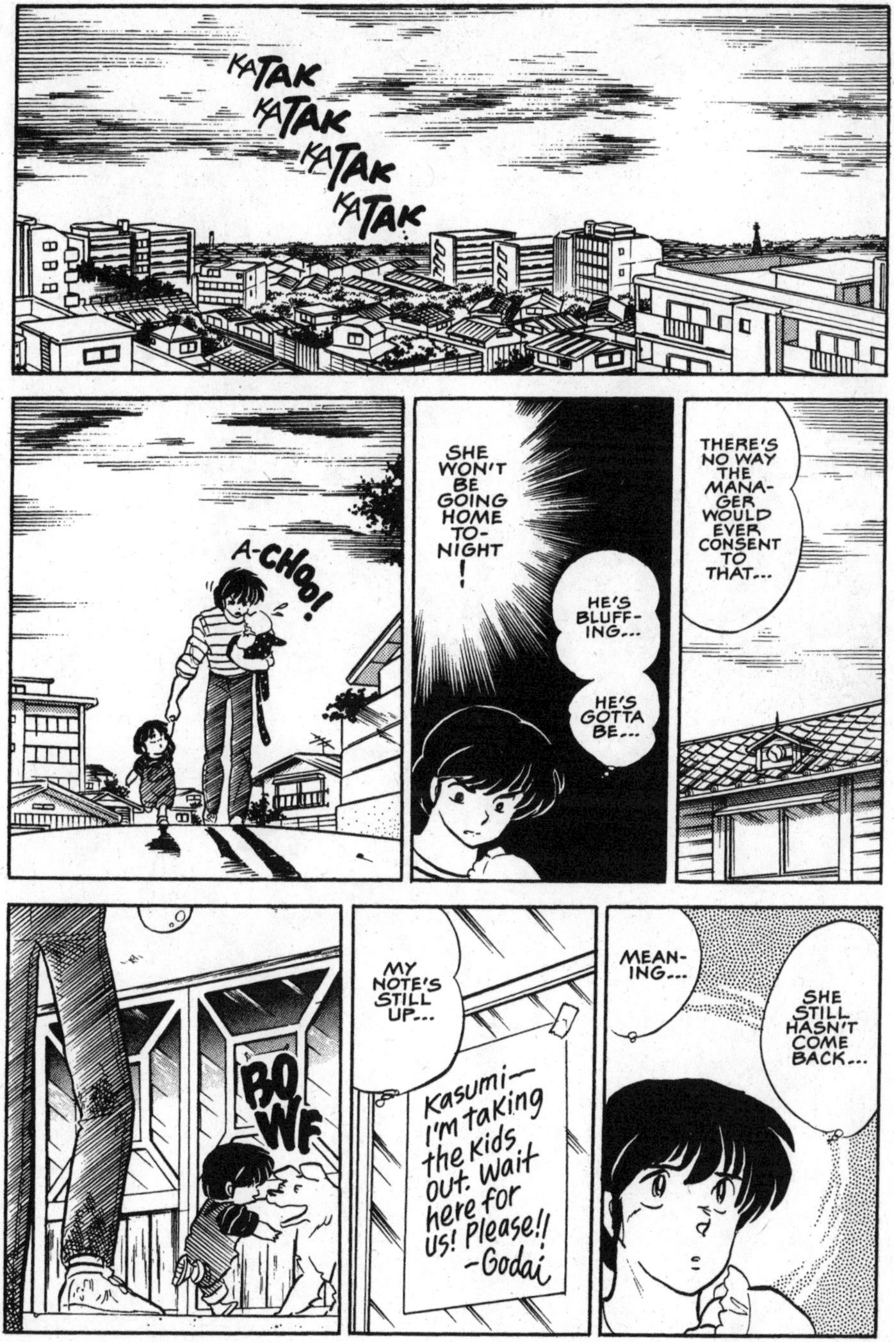
KATAK
KATAK
KATAK
KATAK
A-CHOO!
SHE WON'T BE GOING HOME TO-NIGHT!
HE'S BLUFF-ING...
HE'S GOTTA BE...
THERE'S NO WAY THE MANA-GER WOULD EVER CONSENT TO THAT...
BOWF
MY NOTE'S STILL UP...
Kasumi— I'm taking the kids out. Wait here for us! Please!! -Godai
MEAN-ING...
SHE STILL HASN'T COME BACK...

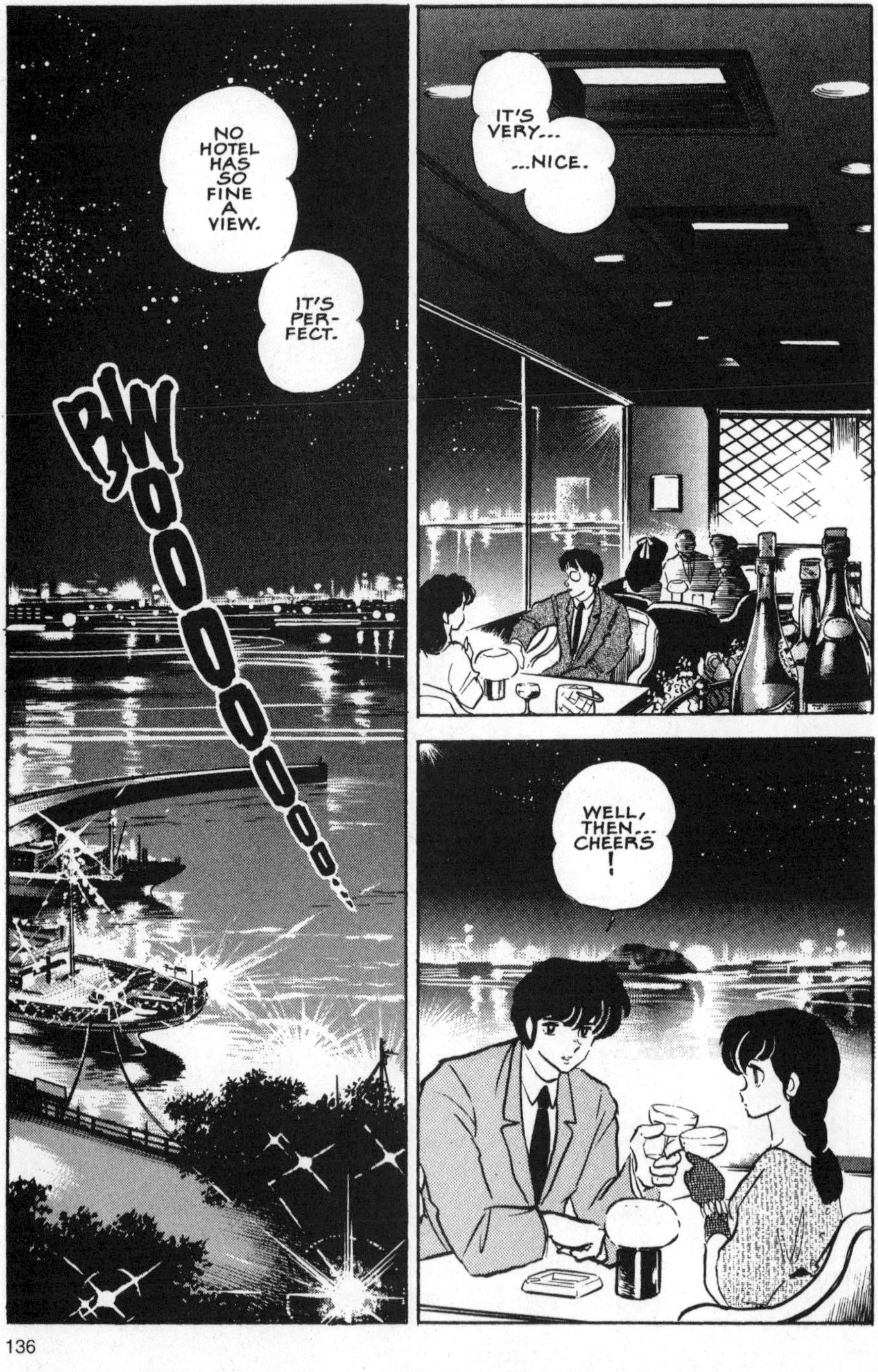
NO HOTEL HAS SO FINE A VIEW.
IT'S PER-FECT.
BWOOOOOOOOOOO...
IT'S VERY...
...NICE.
WELL, THEN... CHEERS!

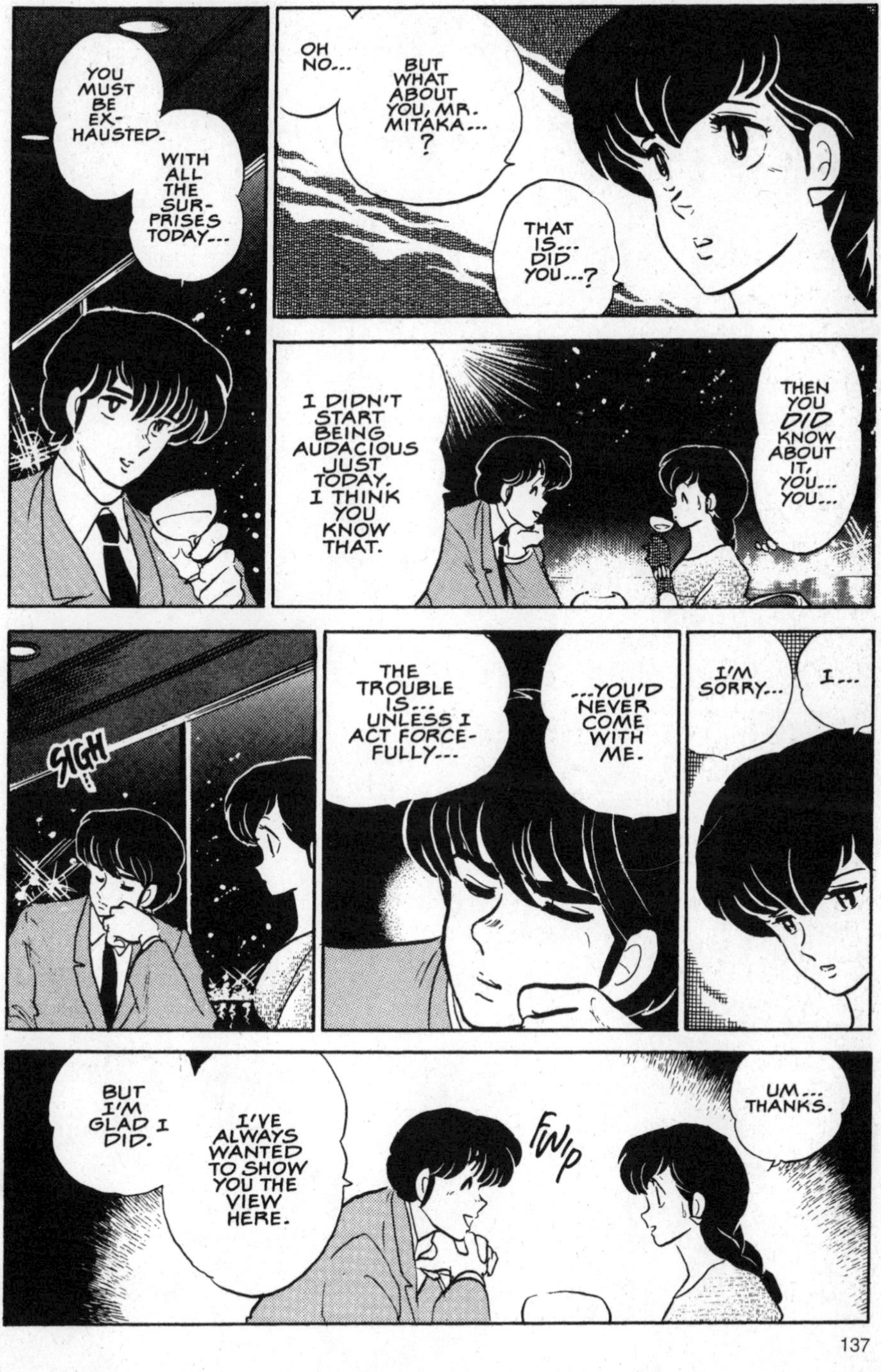
YOU MUST BE EX-HAUSTED.
WITH ALL THE SUR-PRISES TODAY...
OH NO...
BUT WHAT ABOUT YOU, MR. MITAKA...?
THAT IS... DID YOU...?
I DIDN'T START BEING AUDACIOUS JUST TODAY. I THINK YOU KNOW THAT.
THEN YOU DID KNOW ABOUT IT, YOU... YOU...
SIGH
THE TROUBLE IS... UNLESS I ACT FORCE-FULLY...
...YOU'D NEVER COME WITH ME.
I'M SORRY...
I...
BUT I'M GLAD I DID.
I'VE ALWAYS WANTED TO SHOW YOU THE VIEW HERE.
FWIP
UM... THANKS.

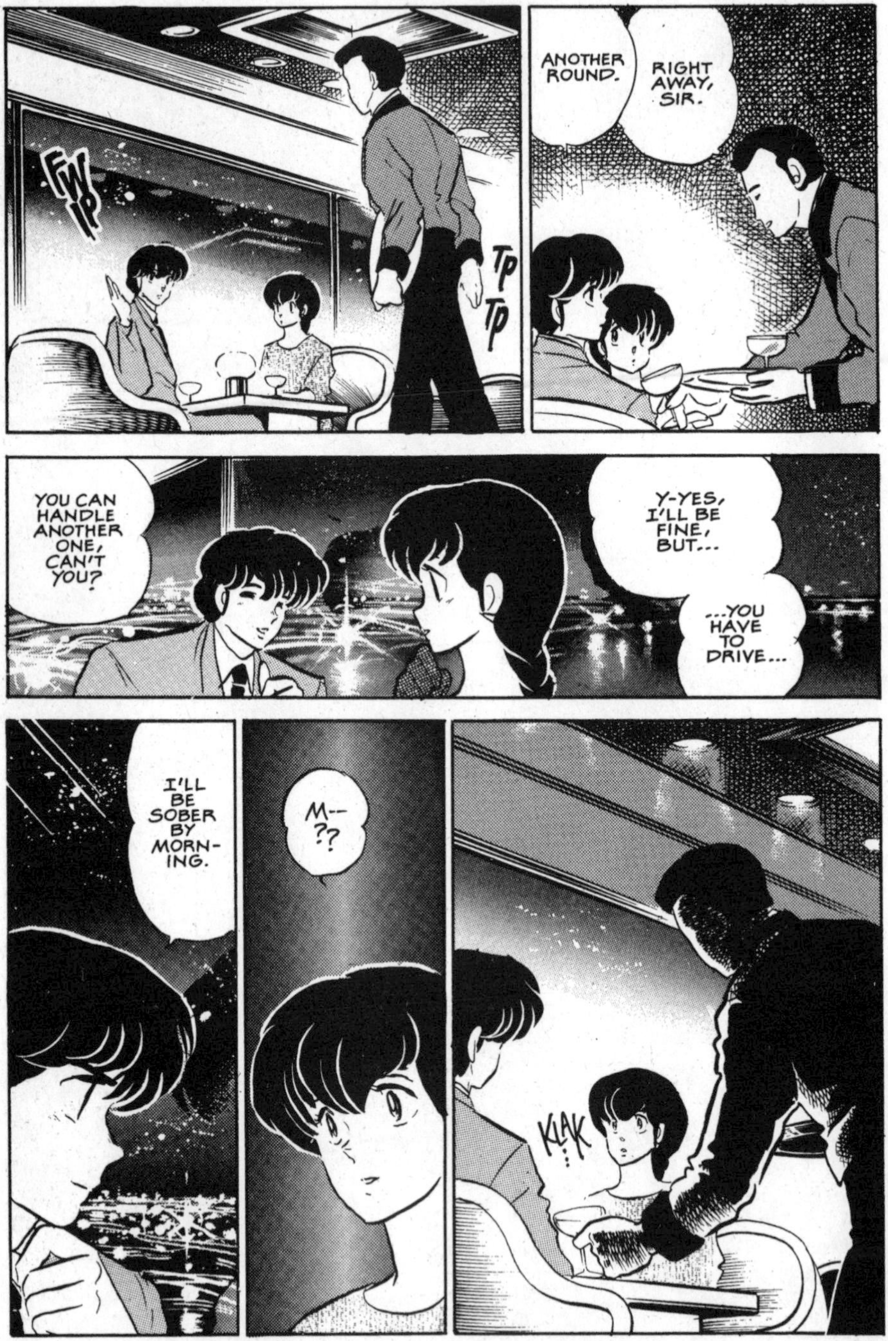
FWIP
TP TP
ANOTHER ROUND.
RIGHT AWAY, SIR...
YOU CAN HANDLE ANOTHER ONE, CAN'T YOU?
Y-YES, I'LL BE FINE, BUT...
...YOU HAVE TO DRIVE...
I'LL BE SOBER BY MORNING.
M-- ??
KLAK...

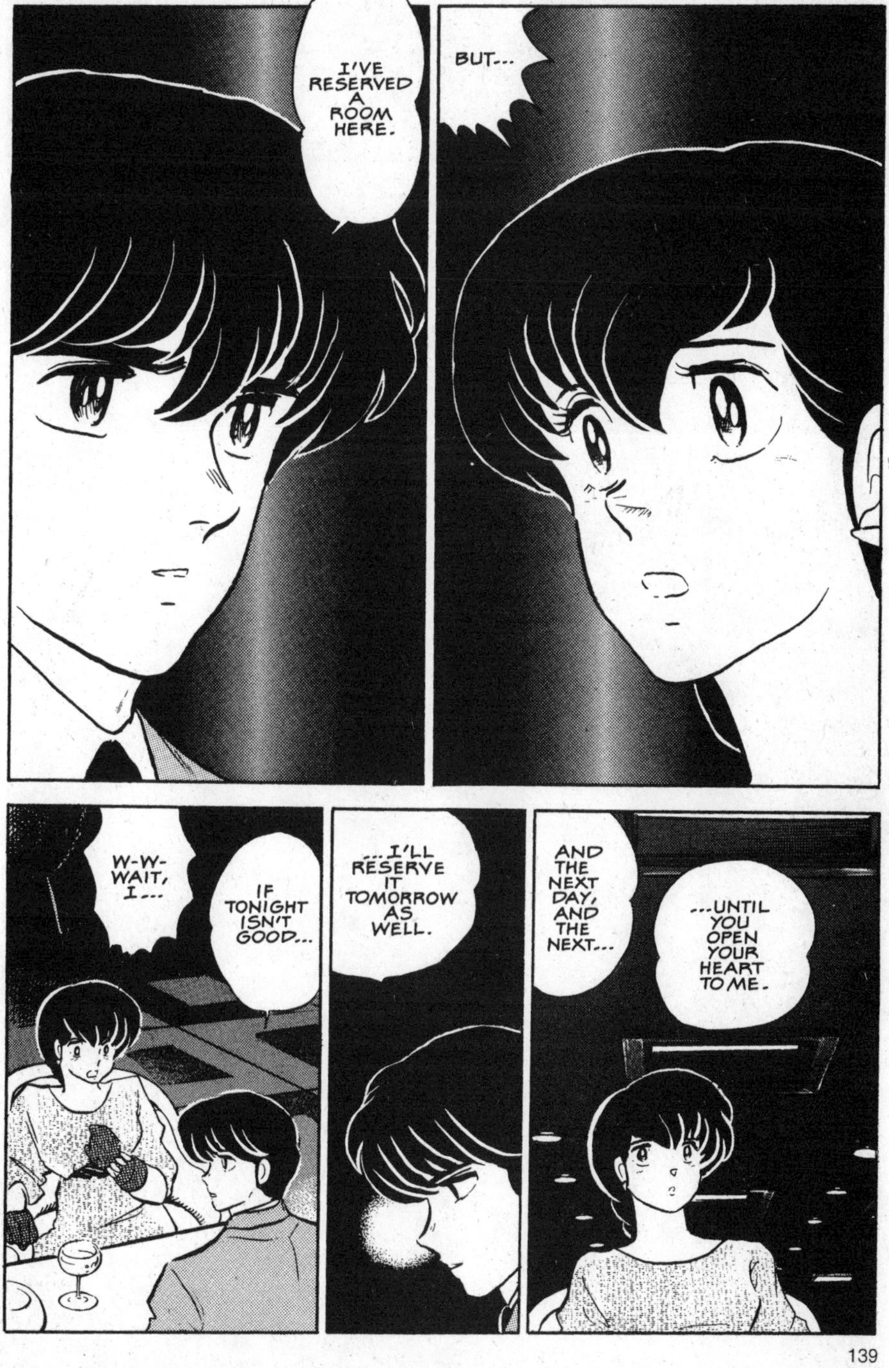
I'VE RESERVED A ROOM HERE.
BUT...
W-W-WAIT, I...
IF TONIGHT ISN'T GOOD...
...I'LL RESERVE IT TOMORROW AS WELL.
AND THE NEXT DAY, AND THE NEXT...
...UNTIL YOU OPEN YOUR HEART TO ME.

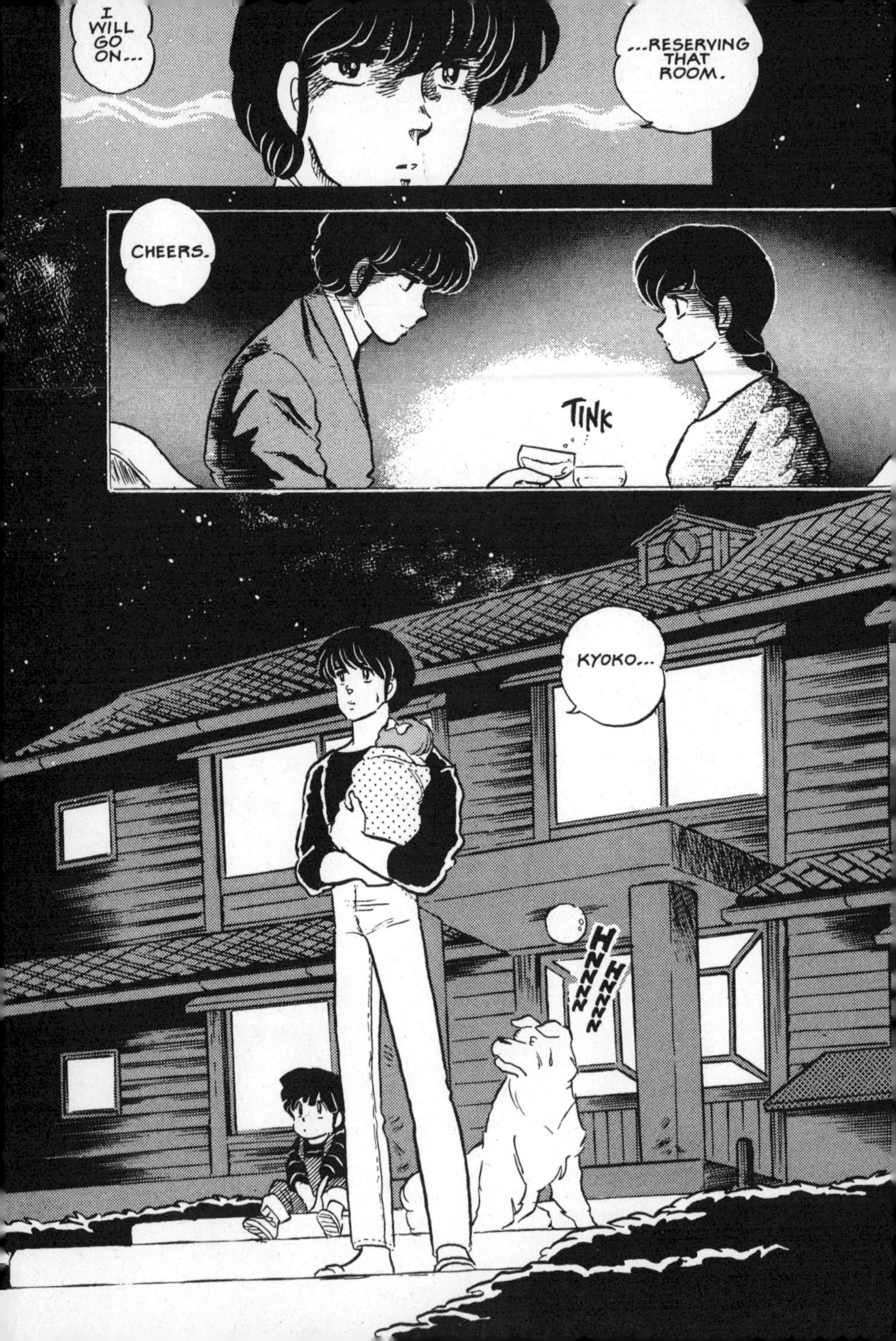
I WILL GO ON...
...RESERVING THAT ROOM.
CHEERS.
TINK
KYOKO...
HNNNNN HNNNNN

PART NINE
NO SLEEP...UNTIL MORNING

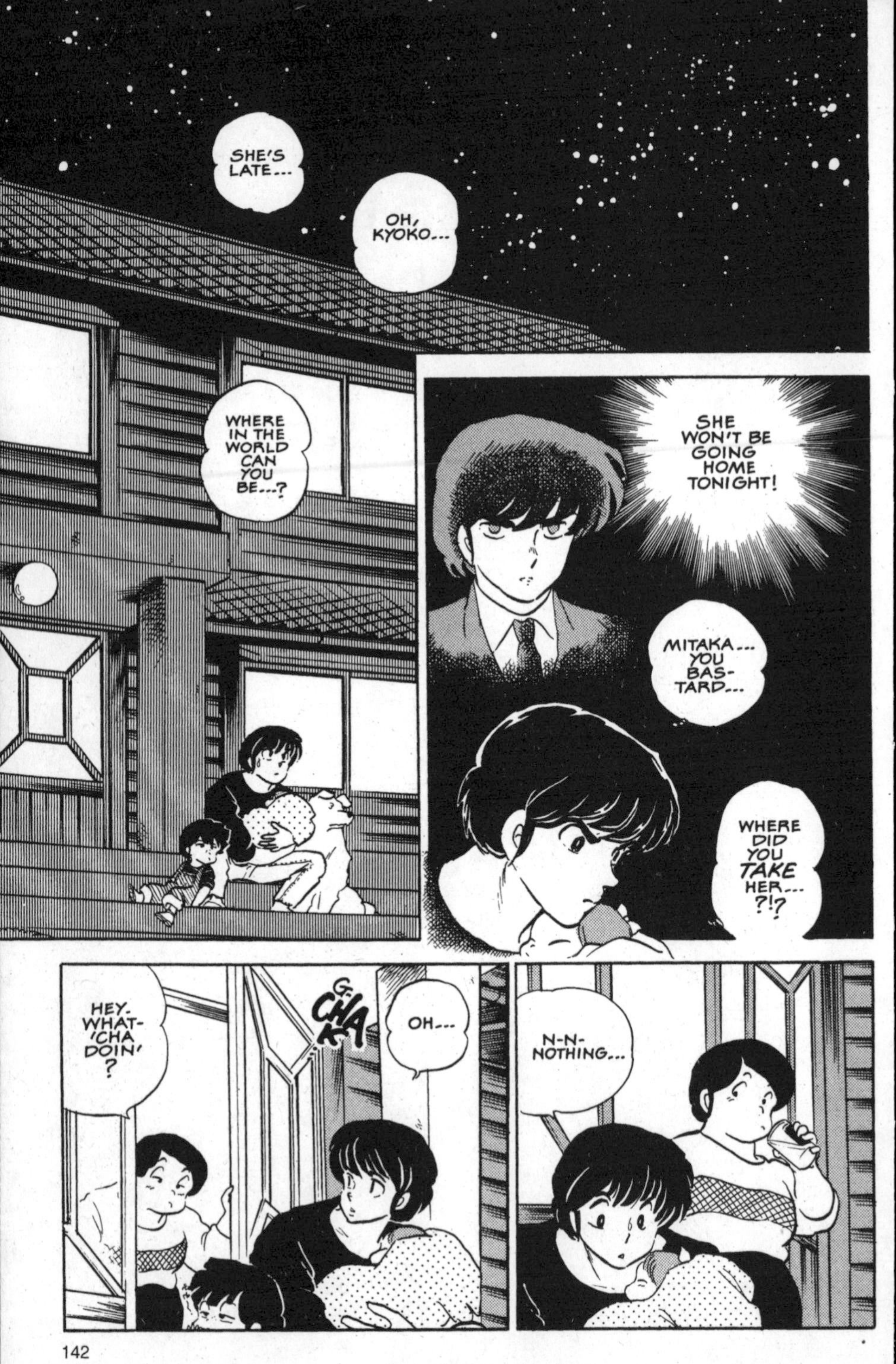
SHE'S LATE...
OH, KYOKO...
WHERE IN THE WORLD CAN YOU BE...?
SHE WON'T BE GOING HOME TONIGHT!
MITAKA... YOU BAS-TARD...
WHERE DID YOU TAKE HER...?!?
HEY. WHAT-'CHA DOIN'?
G-CHAK
OH...
N-N-NOTHING...

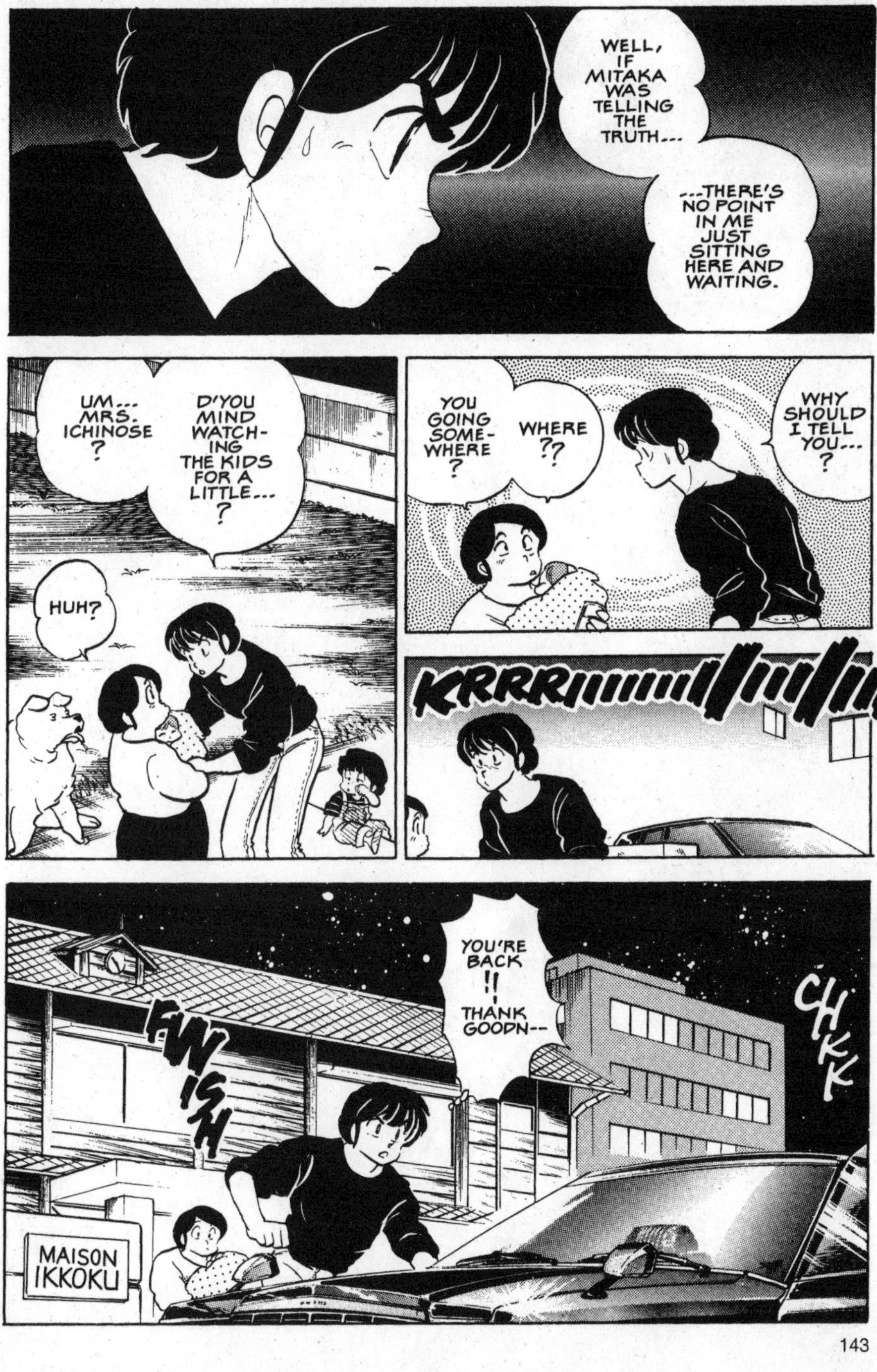
WELL, IF MITAKA WAS TELLING THE TRUTH...
...THERE'S NO POINT IN ME JUST SITTING HERE AND WAITING.
UM... MRS. ICHINOSE?
D'YOU MIND WATCHING THE KIDS FOR A LITTLE...?
HUH?
YOU GOING SOME-WHERE?
WHERE??
WHY SHOULD I TELL YOU...?
KRRRIIIIIIIIIIIIII
YOU'RE BACK!! THANK GOODN--
FWISH
CHKK
MAISON IKKOKU

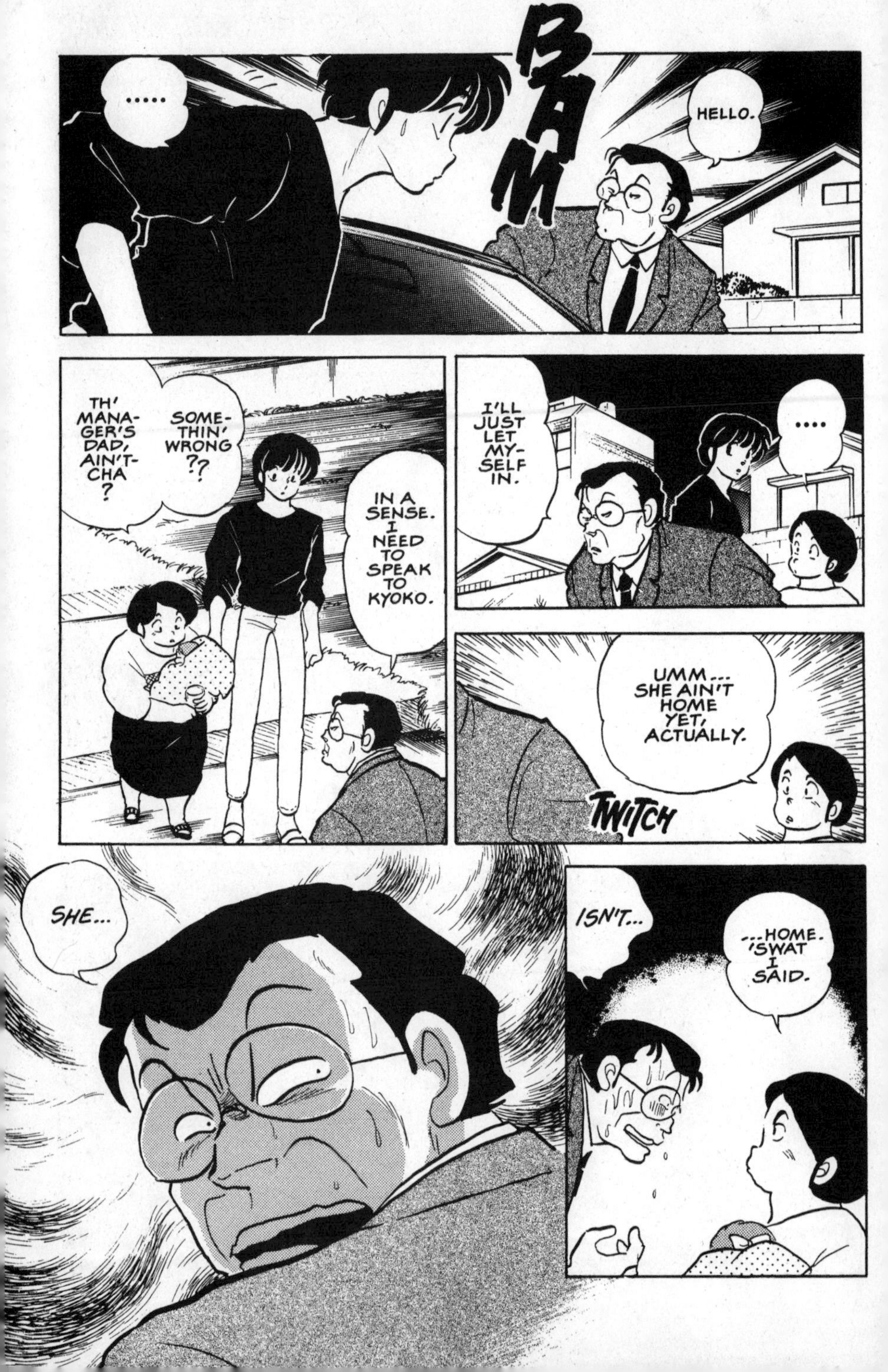
......
BAM
HELLO.
TH' MANAGER'S DAD, AIN'T-CHA?
SOMETHIN' WRONG??
IN A SENSE. I NEED TO SPEAK TO KYOKO.
I'LL JUST LET MYSELF IN.
....
UMM... SHE AIN'T HOME YET, ACTUALLY.
TWITCH
SHE...
ISN'T...
...HOME. 'SWAT I SAID.

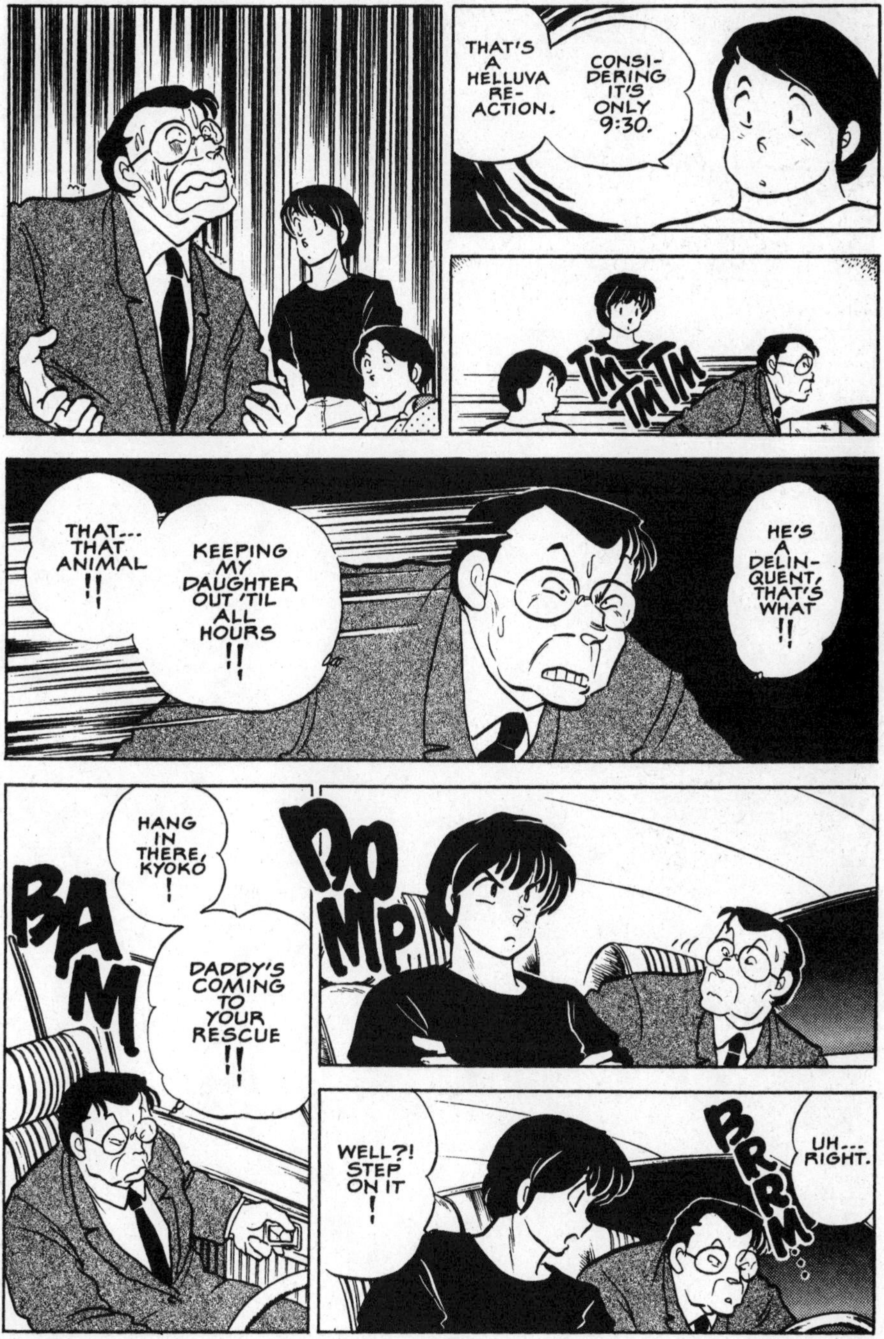
THAT'S A HELLUVA RE-ACTION.
CONSI-DERING IT'S ONLY 9:30.
TM TM TM
THAT... THAT ANIMAL !!
KEEPING MY DAUGHTER OUT 'TIL ALL HOURS !!
HE'S A DELIN-QUENT, THAT'S WHAT !!
HANG IN THERE, KYOKO!
DADDY'S COMING TO YOUR RESCUE !!
BAM
DOMP
WELL?! STEP ON IT !
BRRM
UH... RIGHT.

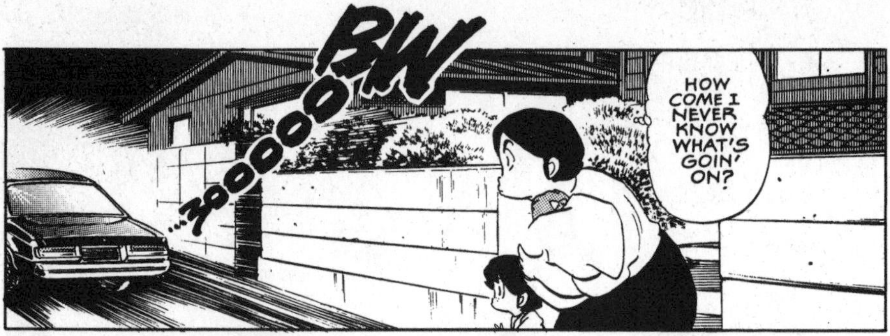
...BOOOOOOOW
HOW COME I NEVER KNOW WHAT'S GOIN' ON?
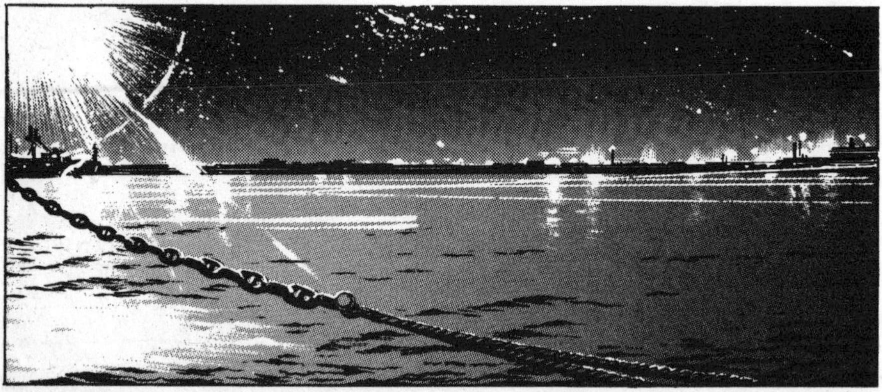
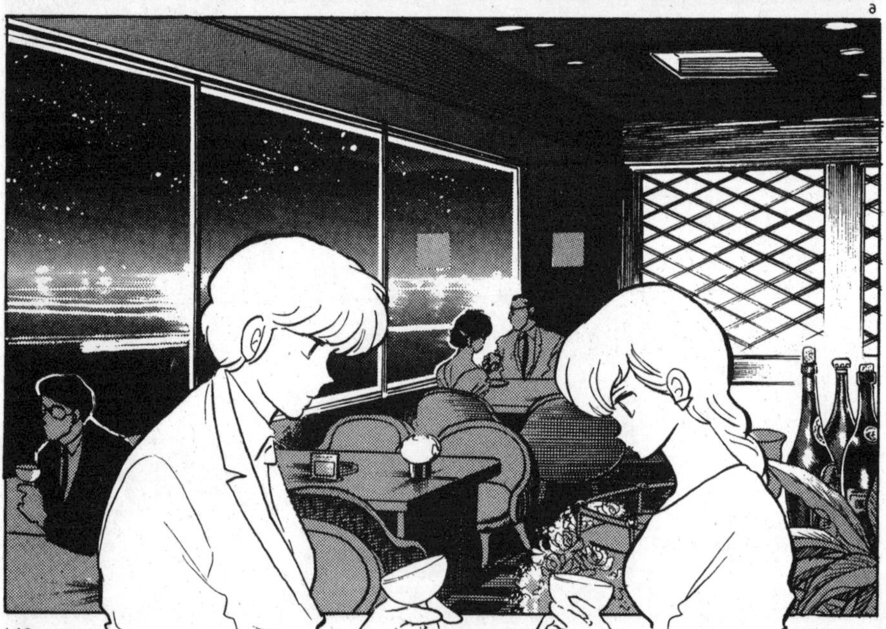

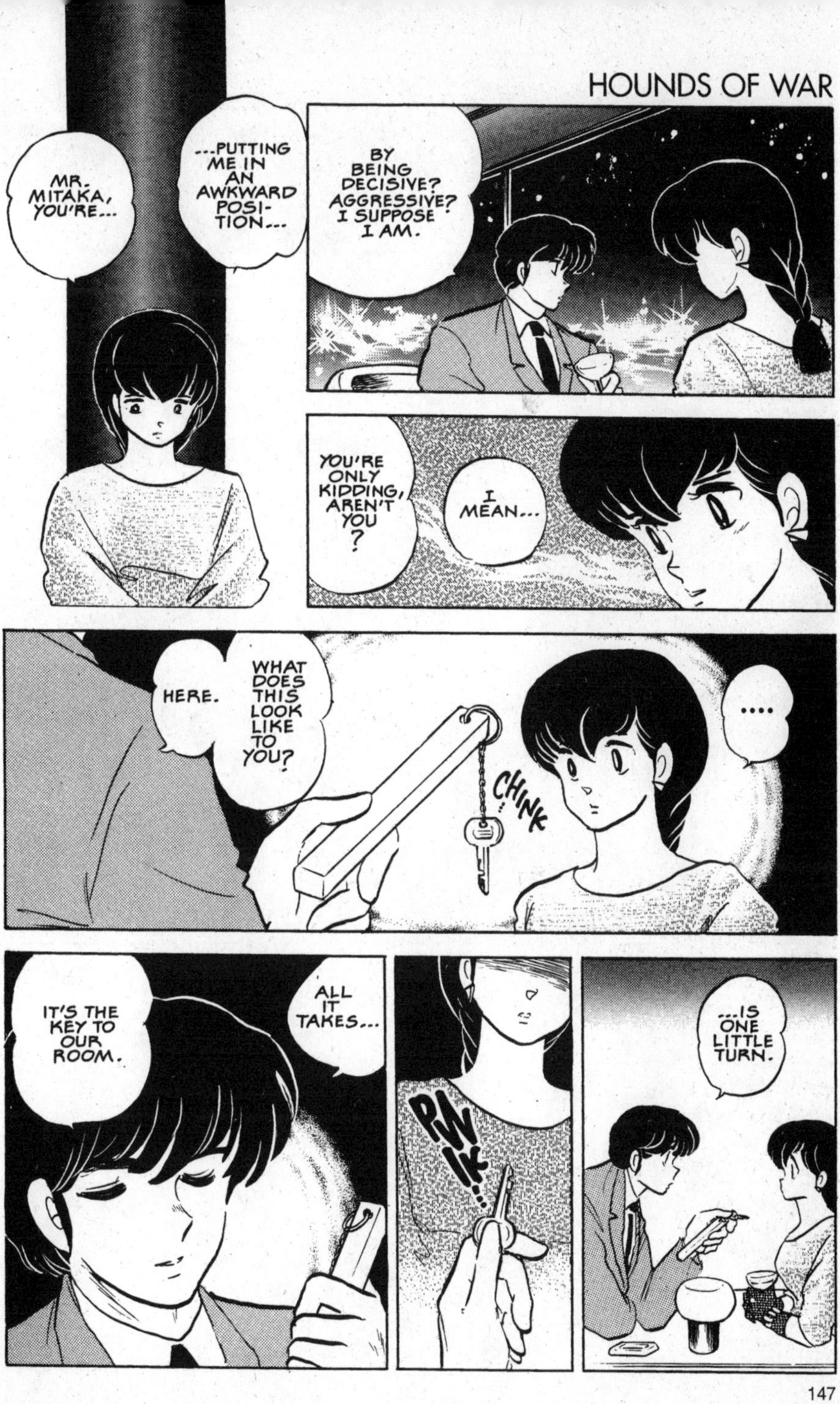
MR. MITAKA, YOU'RE...
...PUTTING ME IN AN AWKWARD POSITION...
BY BEING DECISIVE? AGGRESSIVE? I SUPPOSE I AM.
YOU'RE ONLY KIDDING, AREN'T YOU?
I MEAN...
HERE.
WHAT DOES THIS LOOK LIKE TO YOU?
CHINK
....
IT'S THE KEY TO OUR ROOM.
ALL IT TAKES...
PWIK!
...IS ONE LITTLE TURN.

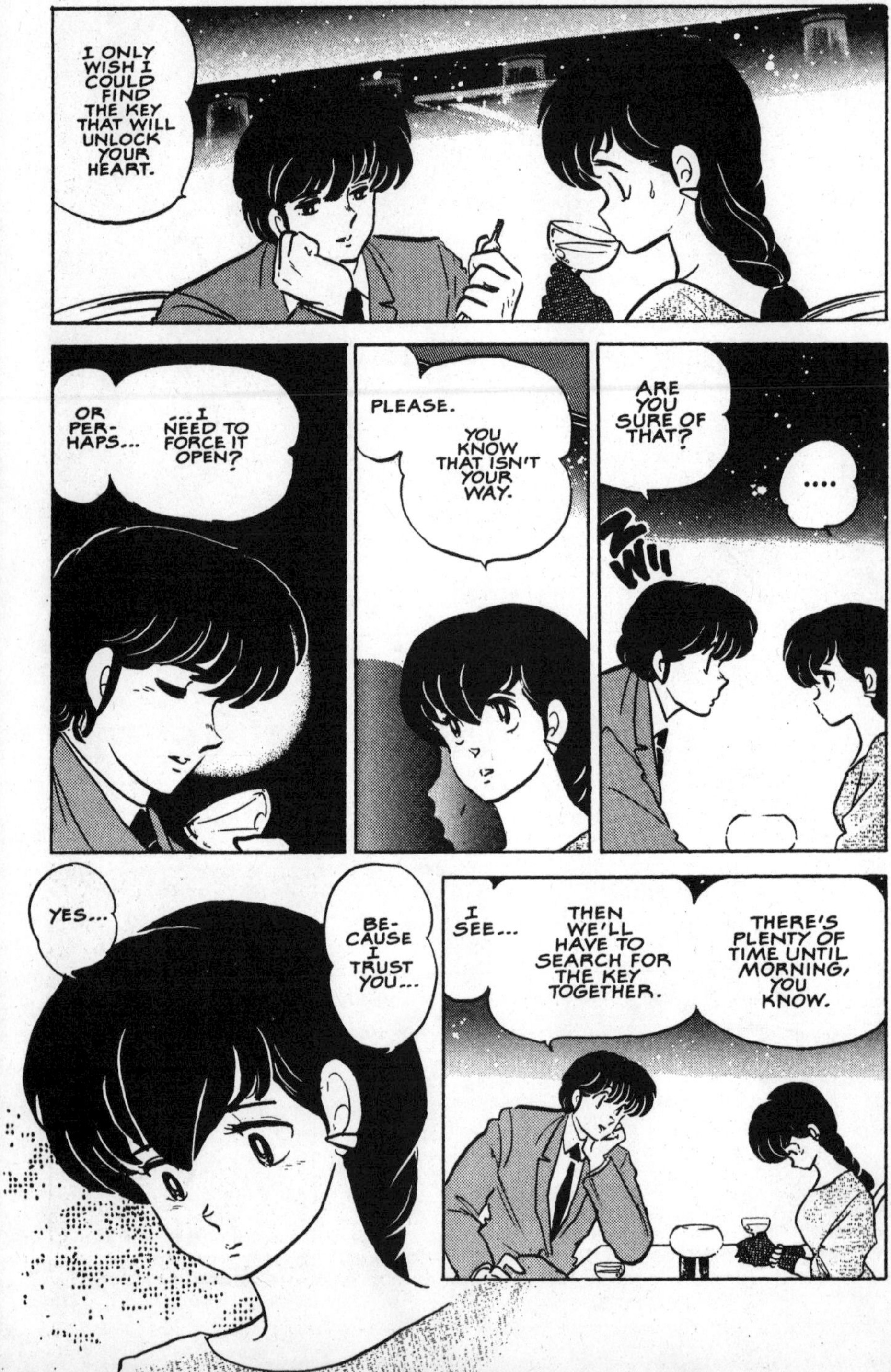
I ONLY WISH I COULD FIND THE KEY THAT WILL UNLOCK YOUR HEART.
OR PERHAPS...
...I NEED TO FORCE IT OPEN?
PLEASE.
YOU KNOW THAT ISN'T YOUR WAY.
ARE YOU SURE OF THAT?
....
YES...
BECAUSE I TRUST YOU...
I SEE...
THEN WE'LL HAVE TO SEARCH FOR THE KEY TOGETHER.
THERE'S PLENTY OF TIME UNTIL MORNING, YOU KNOW.

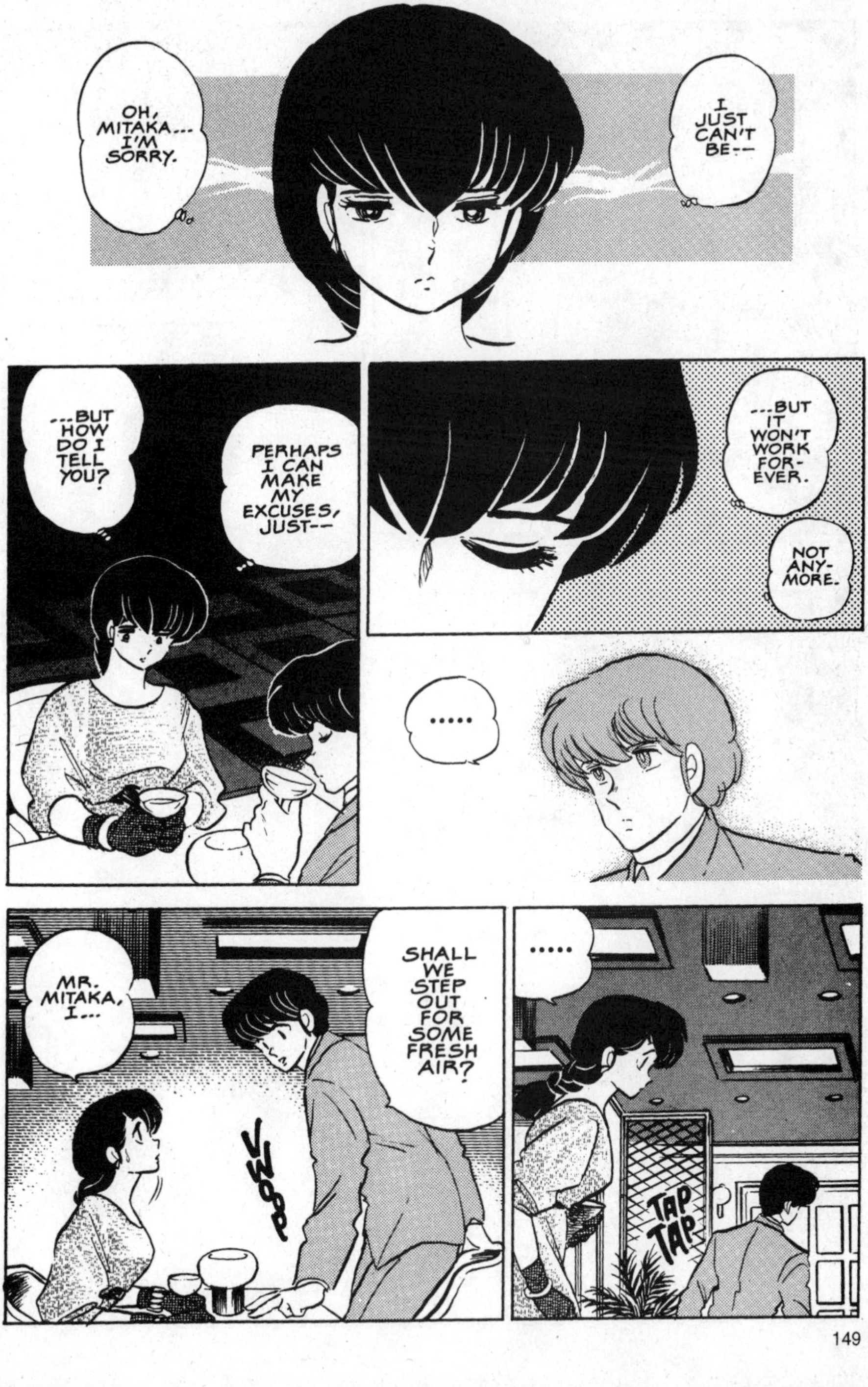
OH, MITAKA... I'M SORRY.
I JUST CAN'T BE--
...BUT HOW DO I TELL YOU?
PERHAPS I CAN MAKE MY EXCUSES, JUST--
...BUT IT WON'T WORK FOR-EVER.
NOT ANY-MORE.
.....
MR. MITAKA, I...
SHALL WE STEP OUT FOR SOME FRESH AIR?
VWOOP
.....
TAP TAP

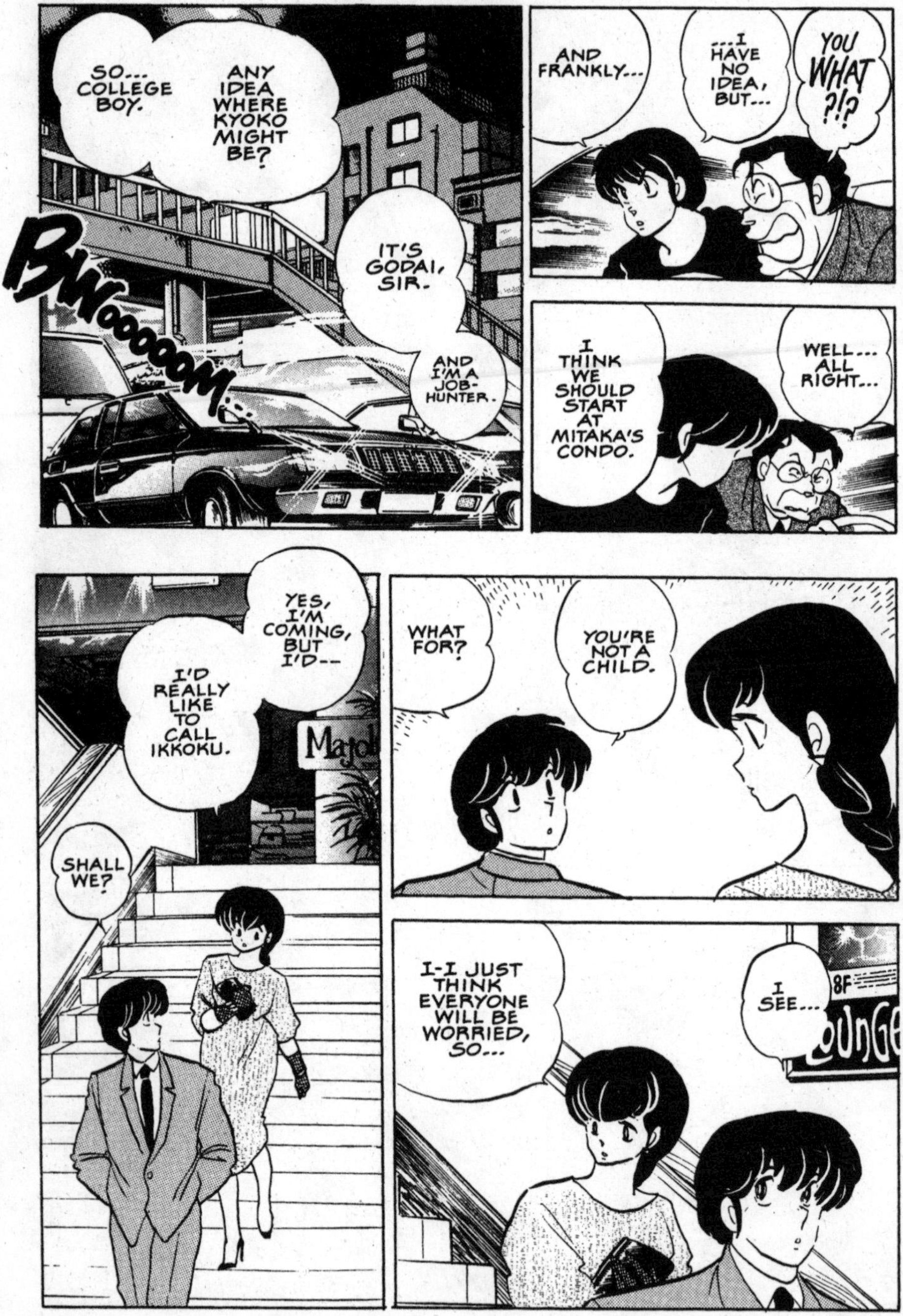
SO... COLLEGE BOY.
ANY IDEA WHERE KYOKO MIGHT BE?
BWOOOOOOM...
IT'S GODAI, SIR.
AND I'M A JOB-HUNTER.
AND FRANKLY...
...I HAVE NO IDEA, BUT...
YOU WHAT ?!?
I THINK WE SHOULD START AT MITAKA'S CONDO.
WELL... ALL RIGHT...
YES, I'M COMING, BUT I'D--
I'D REALLY LIKE TO CALL IKKOKU.
SHALL WE?
WHAT FOR?
YOU'RE NOT A CHILD.
I-I JUST THINK EVERYONE WILL BE WORRIED, SO...
I SEE...
8F
LOUNGE

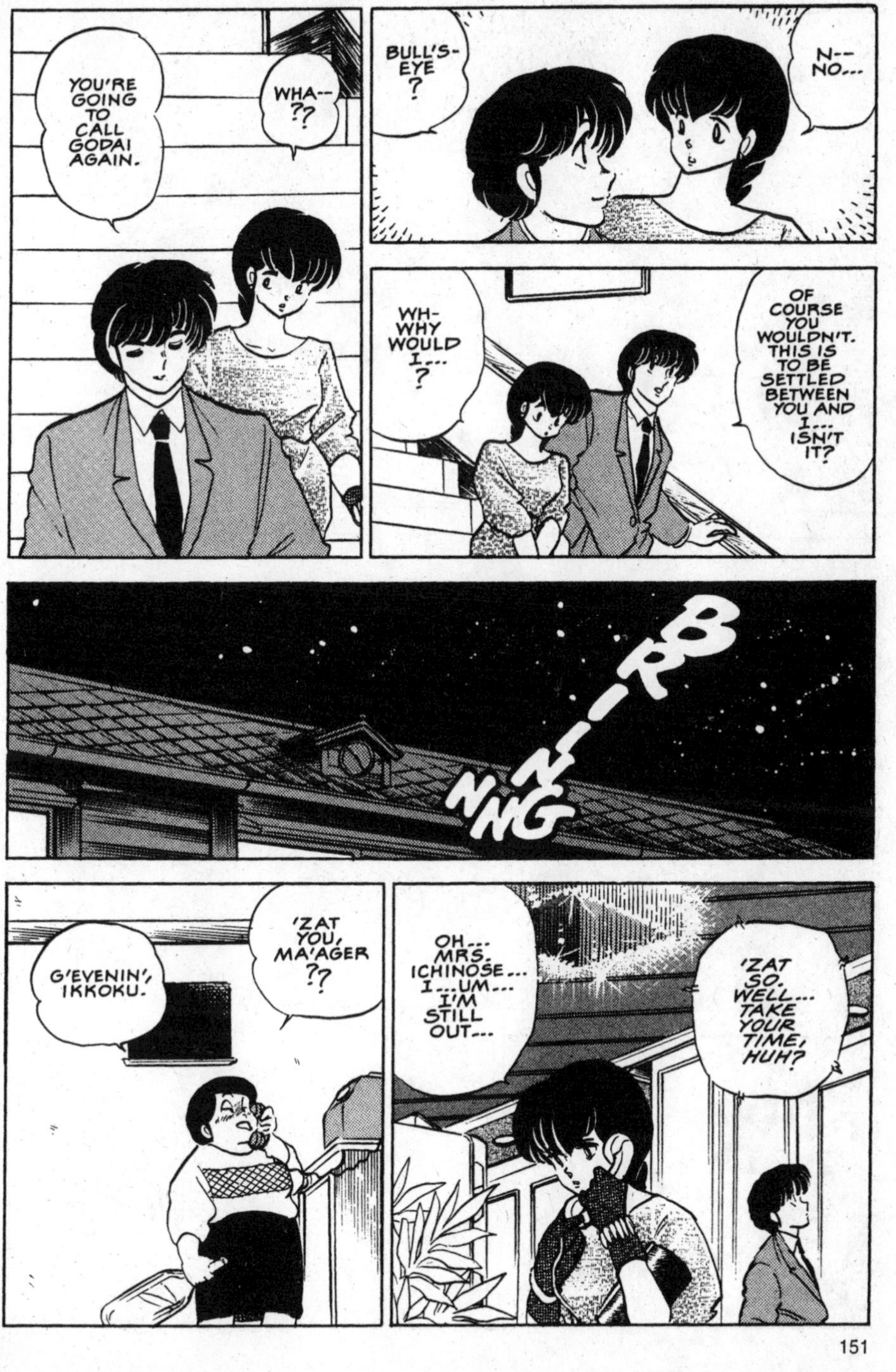
YOU'RE GOING TO CALL GODAI AGAIN.
WHA-- ??
BULL'S-EYE ?
N-- NO...
WH-WHY WOULD I... ?
OF COURSE YOU WOULDN'T. THIS IS TO BE SETTLED BETWEEN YOU AND I... ISN'T IT?
BRI-I-NNNG
G'EVENIN', IKKOKU.
'ZAT YOU, MA'AGER ??
OH... MRS. ICHINOSE... I...UM... I'M STILL OUT...
'ZAT SO. WELL... TAKE YOUR TIME, HUH?

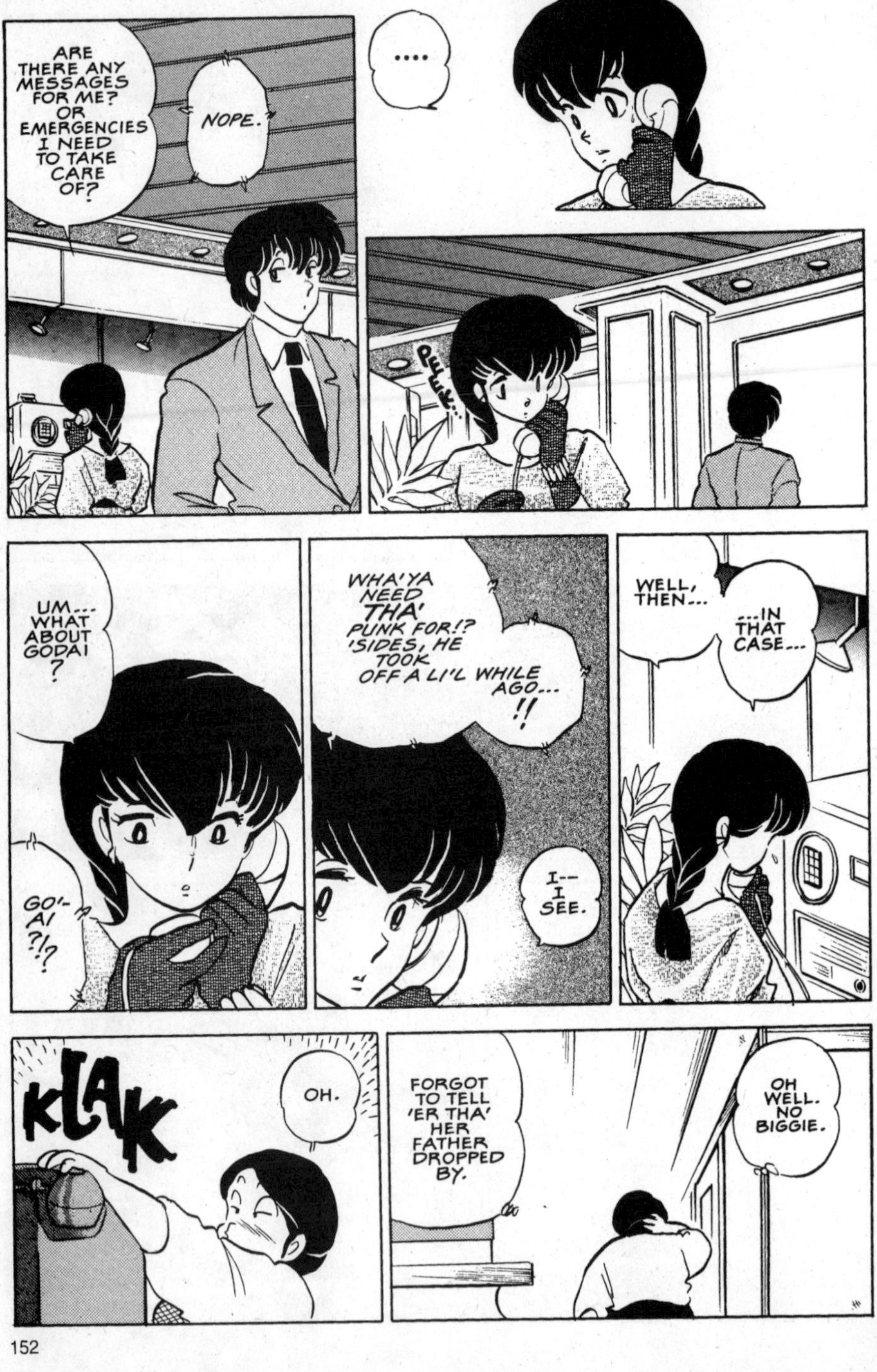

ARE THERE ANY MESSAGES FOR ME? OR EMERGENCIES I NEED TO TAKE CARE OF?
NOPE.
....
PEEK...
UM... WHAT ABOUT GODAI?
GO'-AI?!?
WHA'YA NEED THA' PUNK FOR!? 'SIDES, HE TOOK OFF A LI'L WHILE AGO...
!!
I-- I SEE.
WELL, THEN...
...IN THAT CASE...
KLAK
OH.
FORGOT TO TELL 'ER THA' HER FATHER DROPPED BY.
OH WELL. NO BIGGIE.

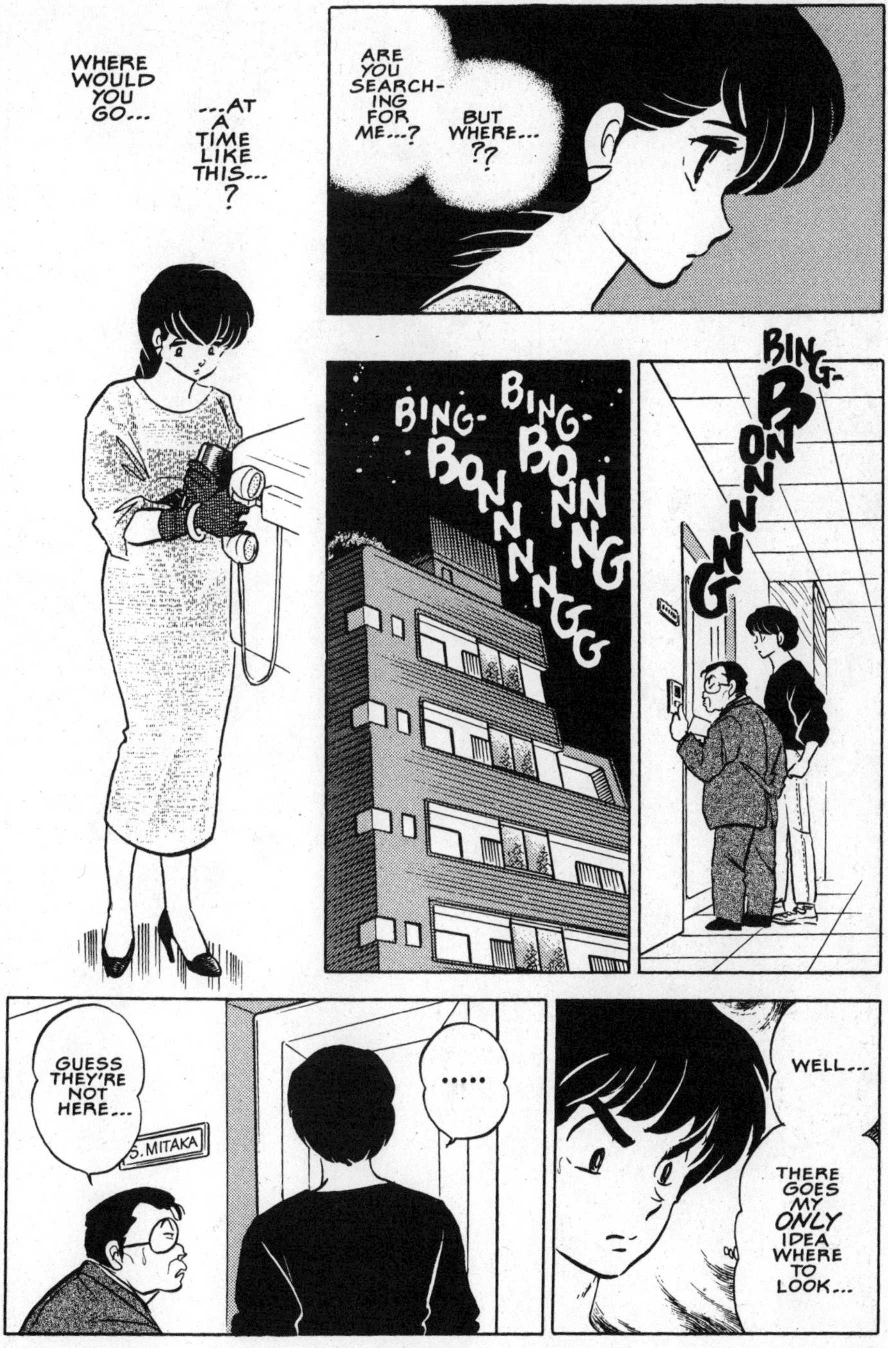
WHERE WOULD YOU GO...
...AT A TIME LIKE THIS...?
ARE YOU SEARCHING FOR ME...?
BUT WHERE...??
BING-BONNNNG
BING-BONNNNGGG
BING-BONNNNG
GUESS THEY'RE NOT HERE...
S. MITAKA
......
WELL...
THERE GOES MY ONLY IDEA WHERE TO LOOK...

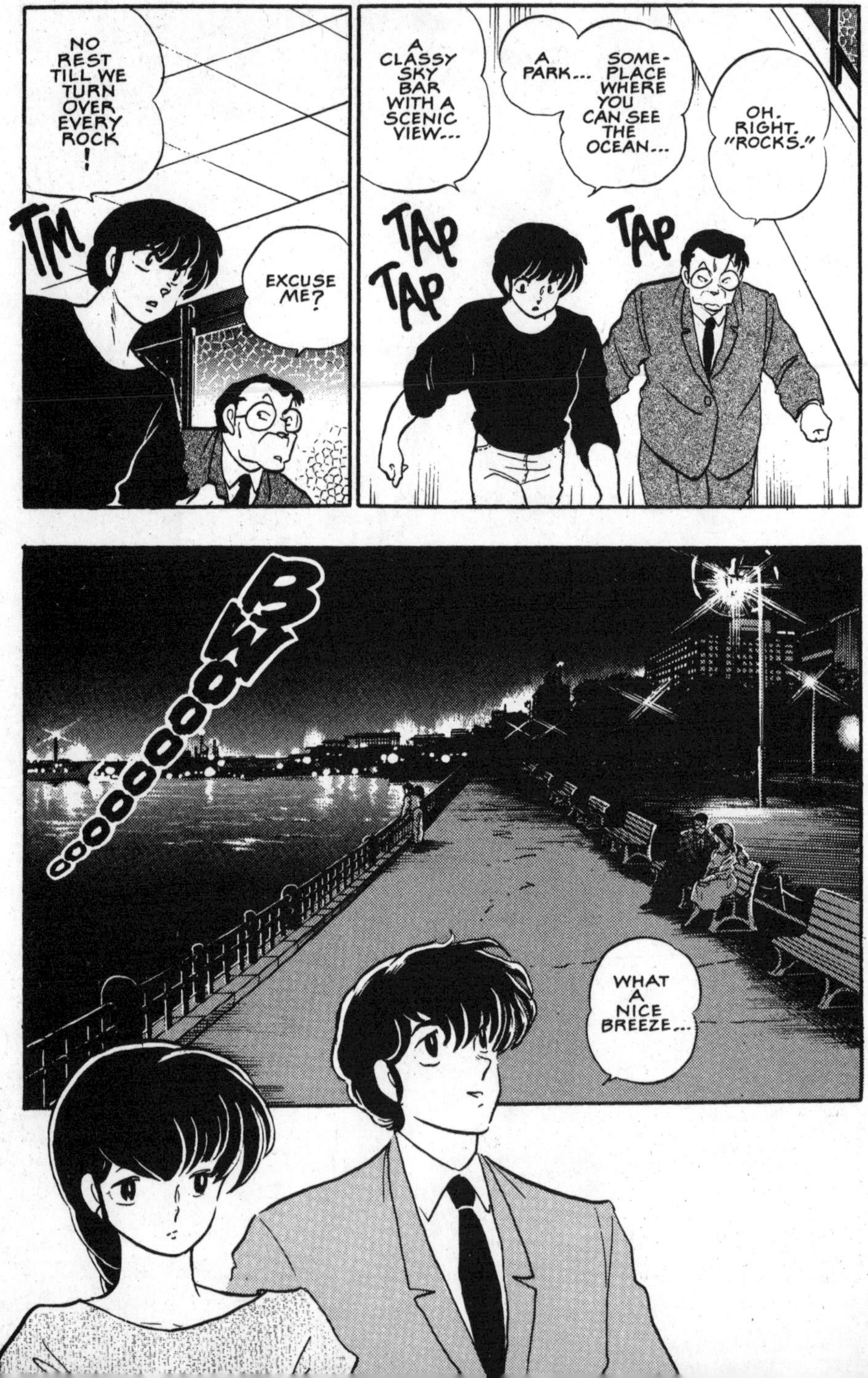
NO REST TILL WE TURN OVER EVERY ROCK!
TM
EXCUSE ME?
A CLASSY SKY BAR WITH A SCENIC VIEW...
A PARK... SOME-PLACE WHERE YOU CAN SEE THE OCEAN...
OH. RIGHT. "ROCKS."
TAP TAP
TAP
BWOOOOOOOO
WHAT A NICE BREEZE...

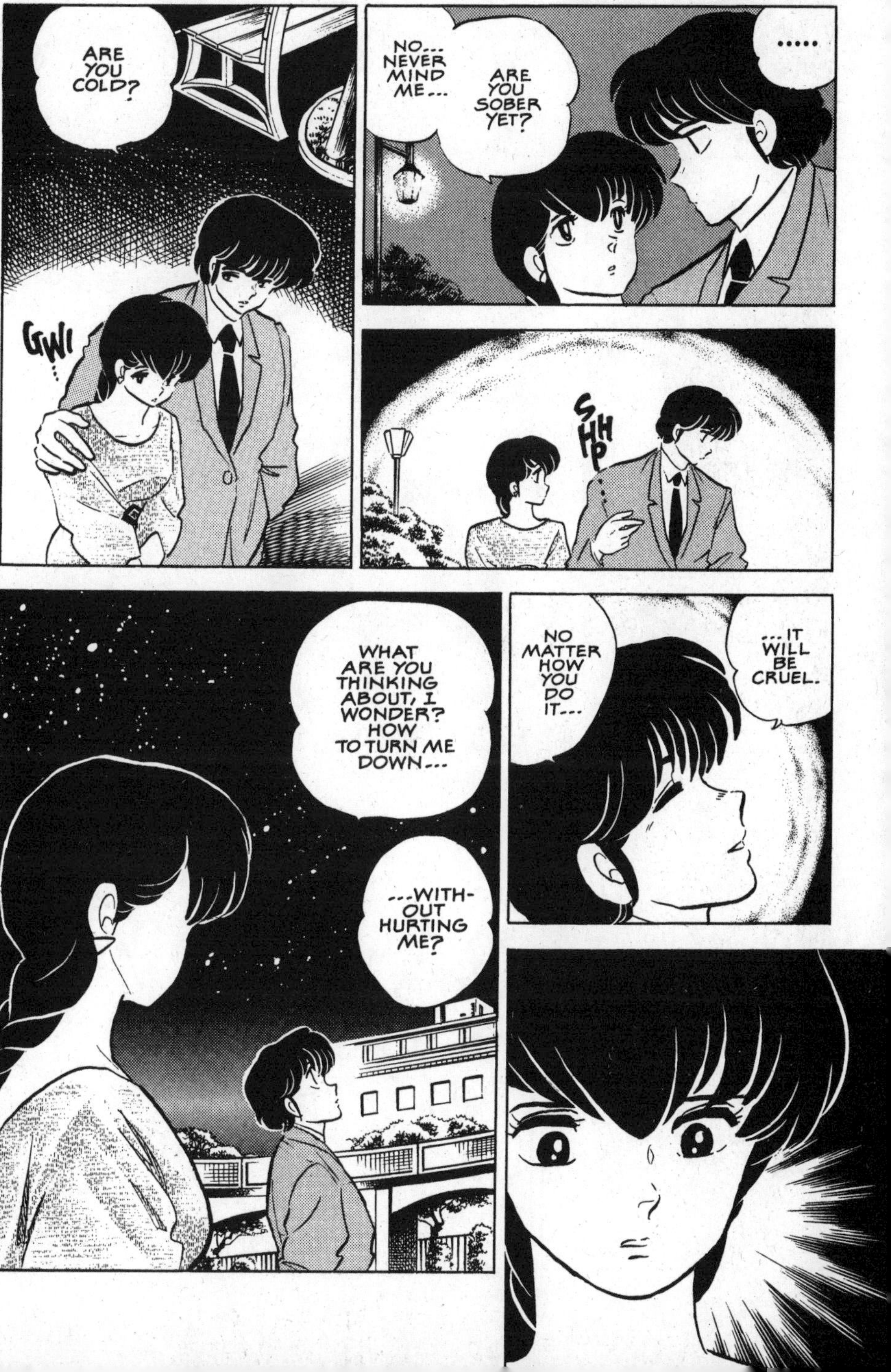
ARE YOU COLD?
GWI...
NO... NEVER MIND ME...
ARE YOU SOBER YET?
......
SHHP...
WHAT ARE YOU THINKING ABOUT, I WONDER? HOW TO TURN ME DOWN---
---WITH-OUT HURTING ME?
NO MATTER HOW YOU DO IT---
...IT WILL BE CRUEL.

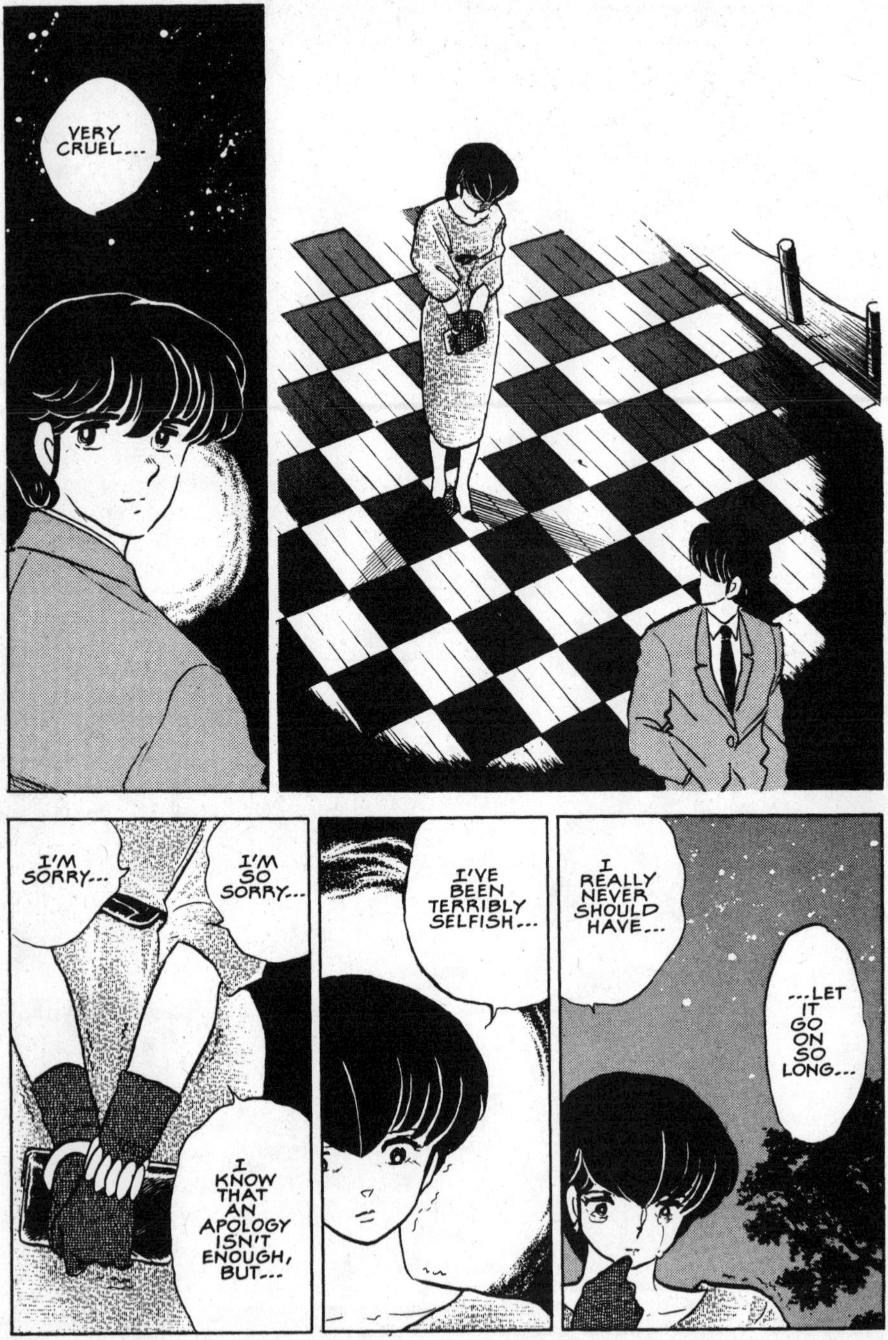
VERY CRUEL...
I'M SORRY...
I'M SO SORRY...
I KNOW THAT AN APOLOGY ISN'T ENOUGH, BUT...
I'VE BEEN TERRIBLY SELFISH...
I REALLY NEVER SHOULD HAVE...
...LET IT GO ON SO LONG...

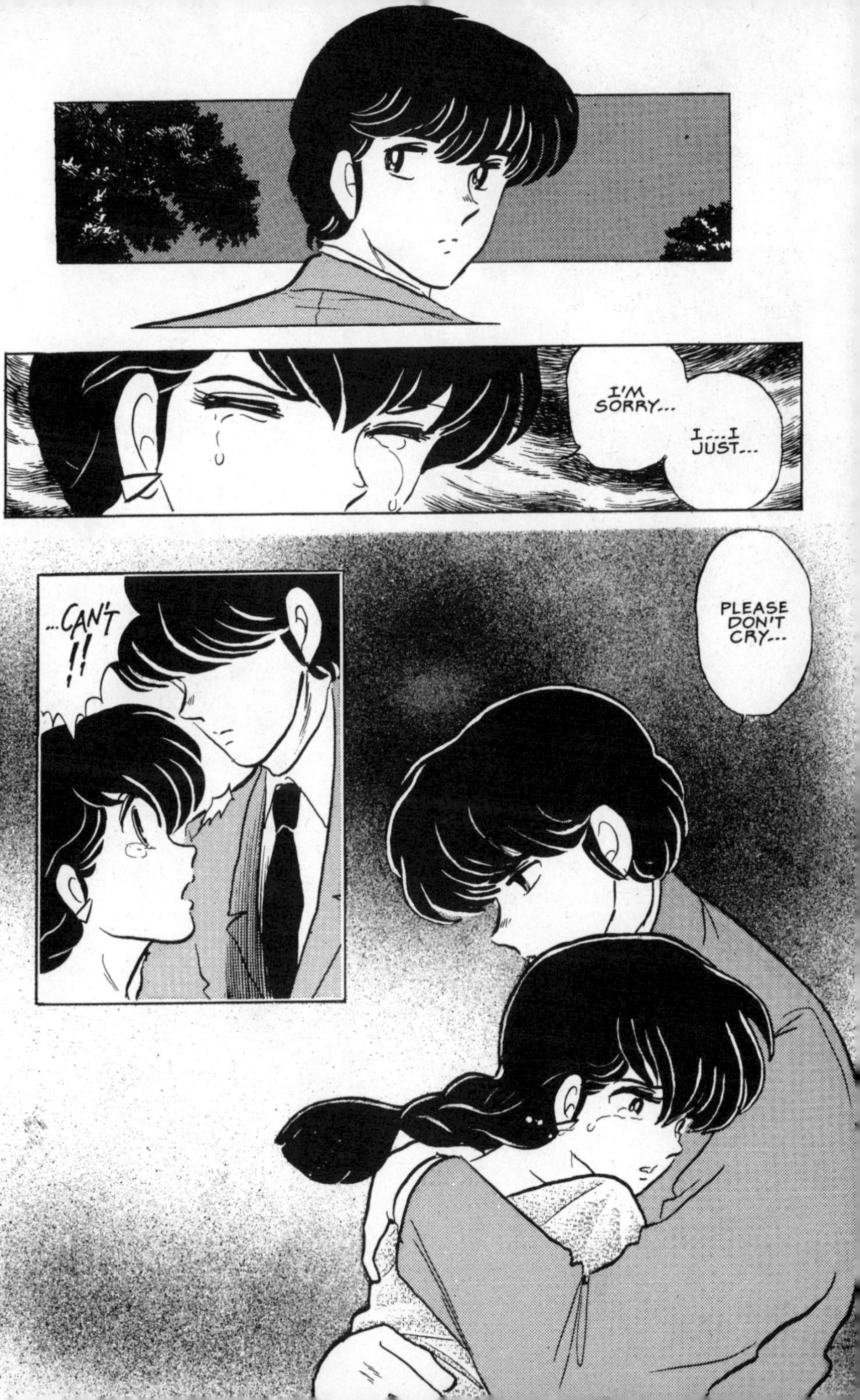
I'M SORRY...
I...I JUST...
...CAN'T !!
PLEASE DON'T CRY...

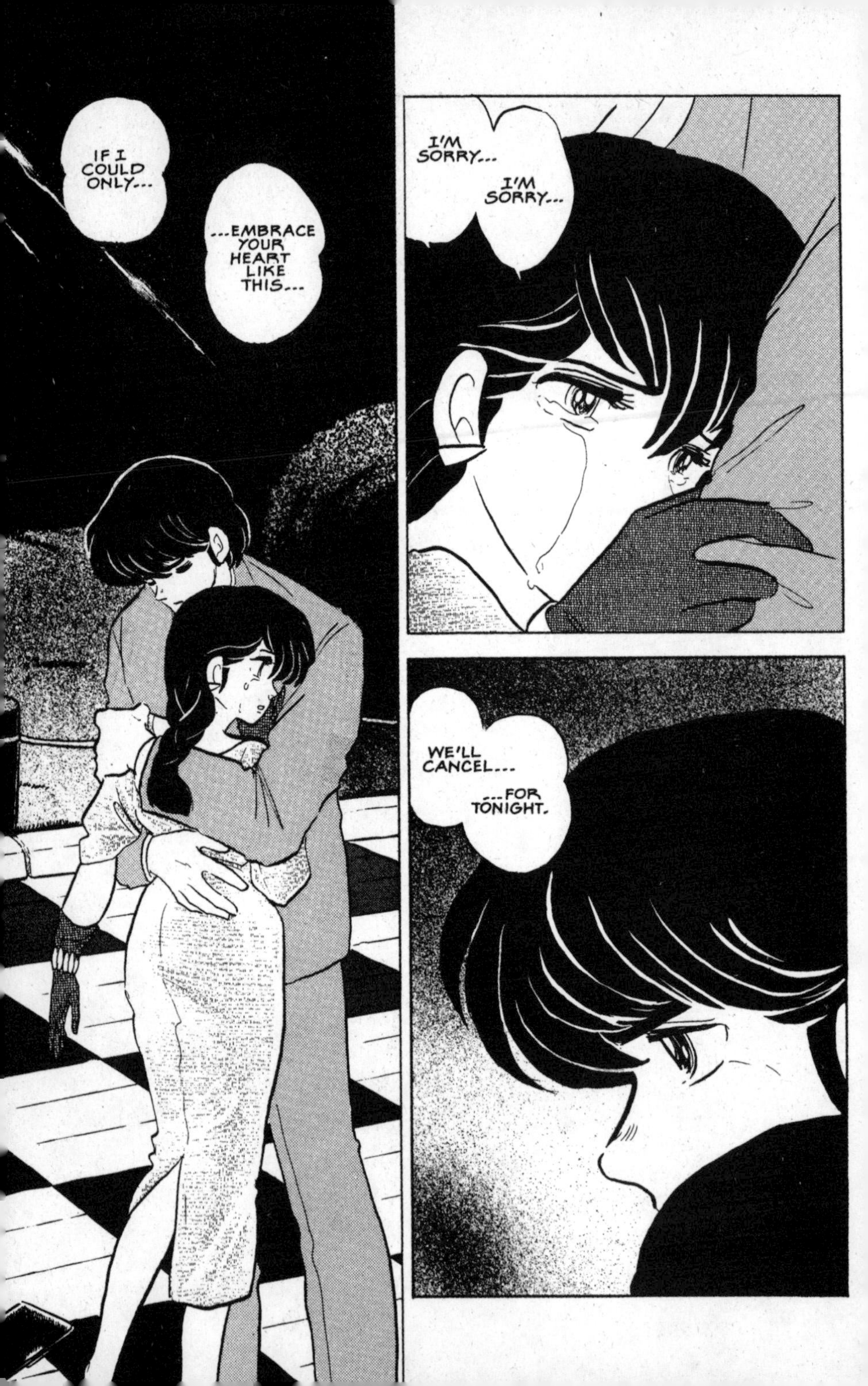
IF I COULD ONLY...
...EMBRACE YOUR HEART LIKE THIS...
I'M SORRY...
I'M SORRY...
WE'LL CANCEL...
...FOR TONIGHT.

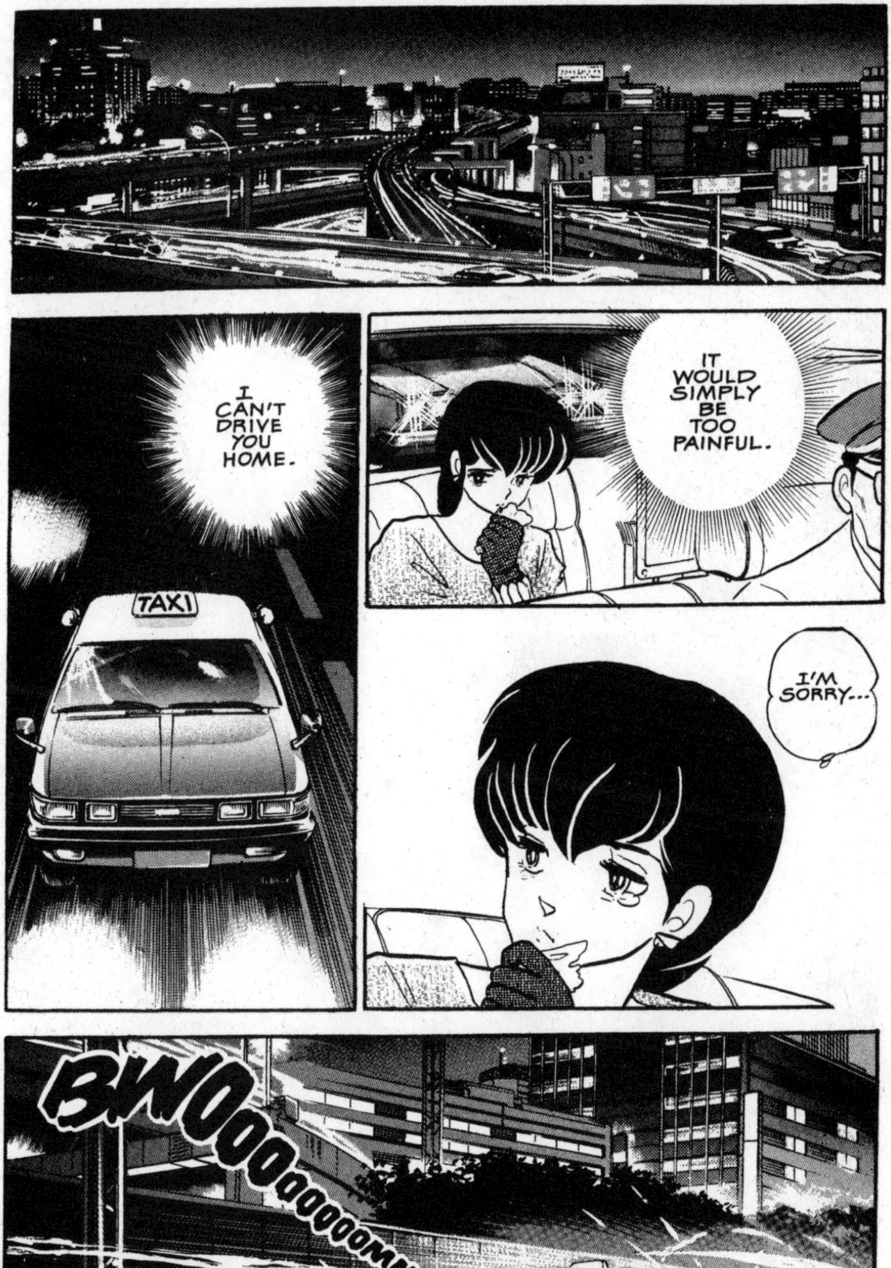
I CAN'T DRIVE YOU HOME.
TAXI
IT WOULD SIMPLY BE TOO PAINFUL.
I'M SORRY...
BWOOOoooooMM...

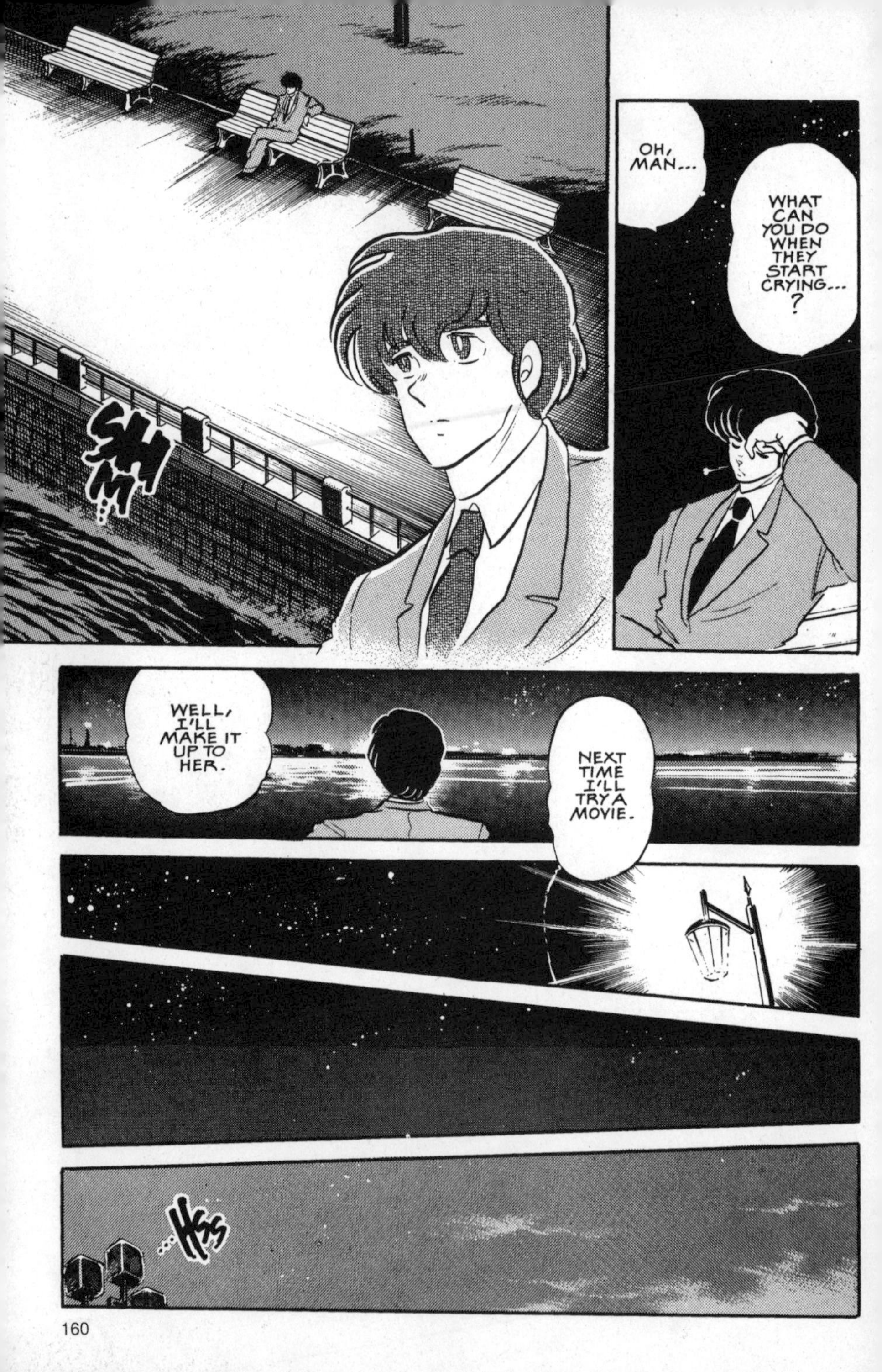

SHM...
OH, MAN...
WHAT CAN YOU DO WHEN THEY START CRYING...?
WELL, I'LL MAKE IT UP TO HER.
NEXT TIME I'LL TRY A MOVIE.
...HSS

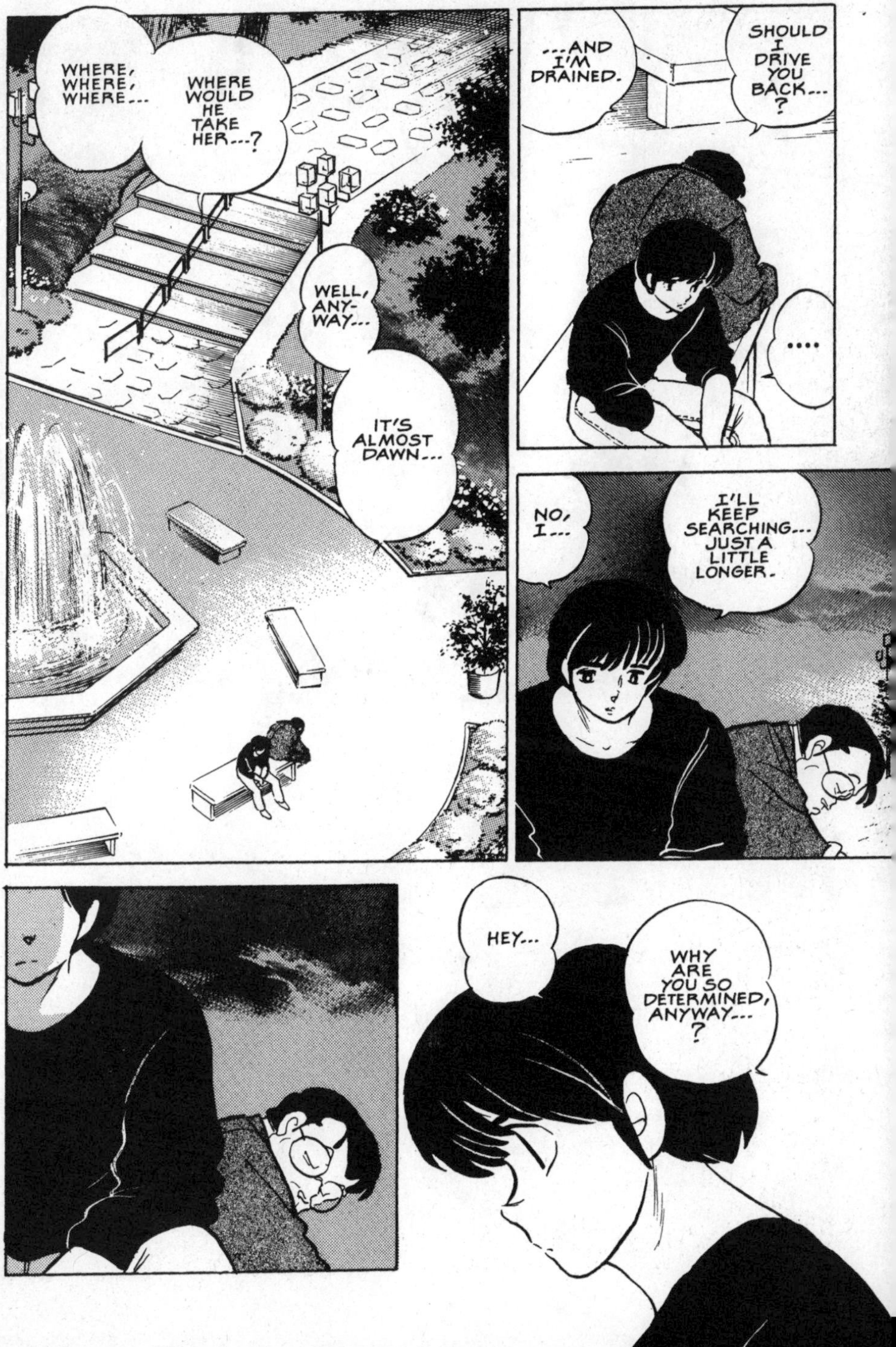
WHERE, WHERE, WHERE...
WHERE WOULD HE TAKE HER...?
WELL, ANYWAY...
IT'S ALMOST DAWN...
...AND I'M DRAINED.
SHOULD I DRIVE YOU BACK...?
....
NO, I...
I'LL KEEP SEARCHING... JUST A LITTLE LONGER.
HEY...
WHY ARE YOU SO DETERMINED, ANYWAY...?

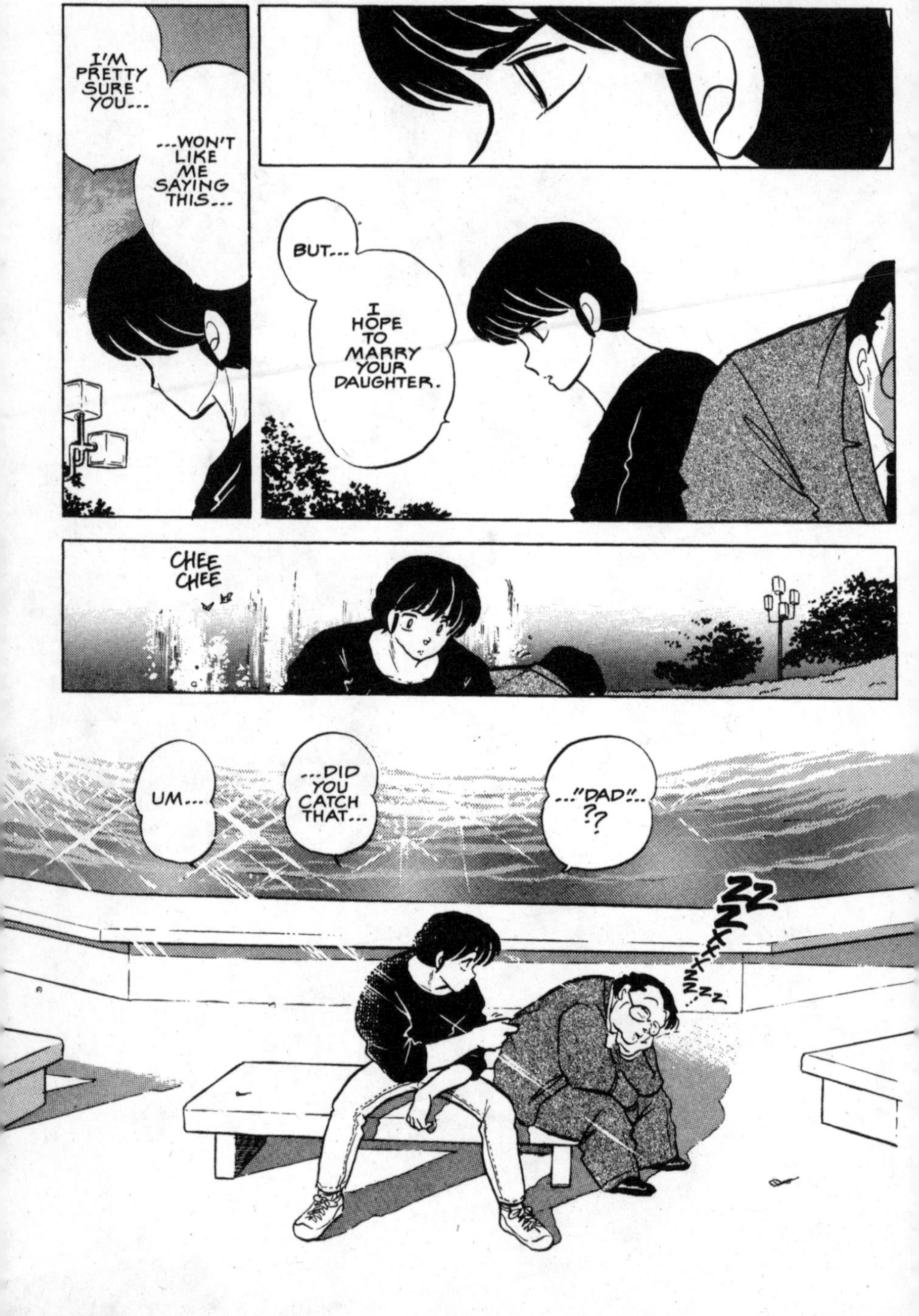

I'M PRETTY SURE YOU...
...WON'T LIKE ME SAYING THIS...
BUT...
I HOPE TO MARRY YOUR DAUGHTER.
CHEE CHEE
UM...
...DID YOU CATCH THAT...
..."DAD"...??
ZZZZZZZZ...

PART TEN

SHADOWS IN THE SUNLIGHT

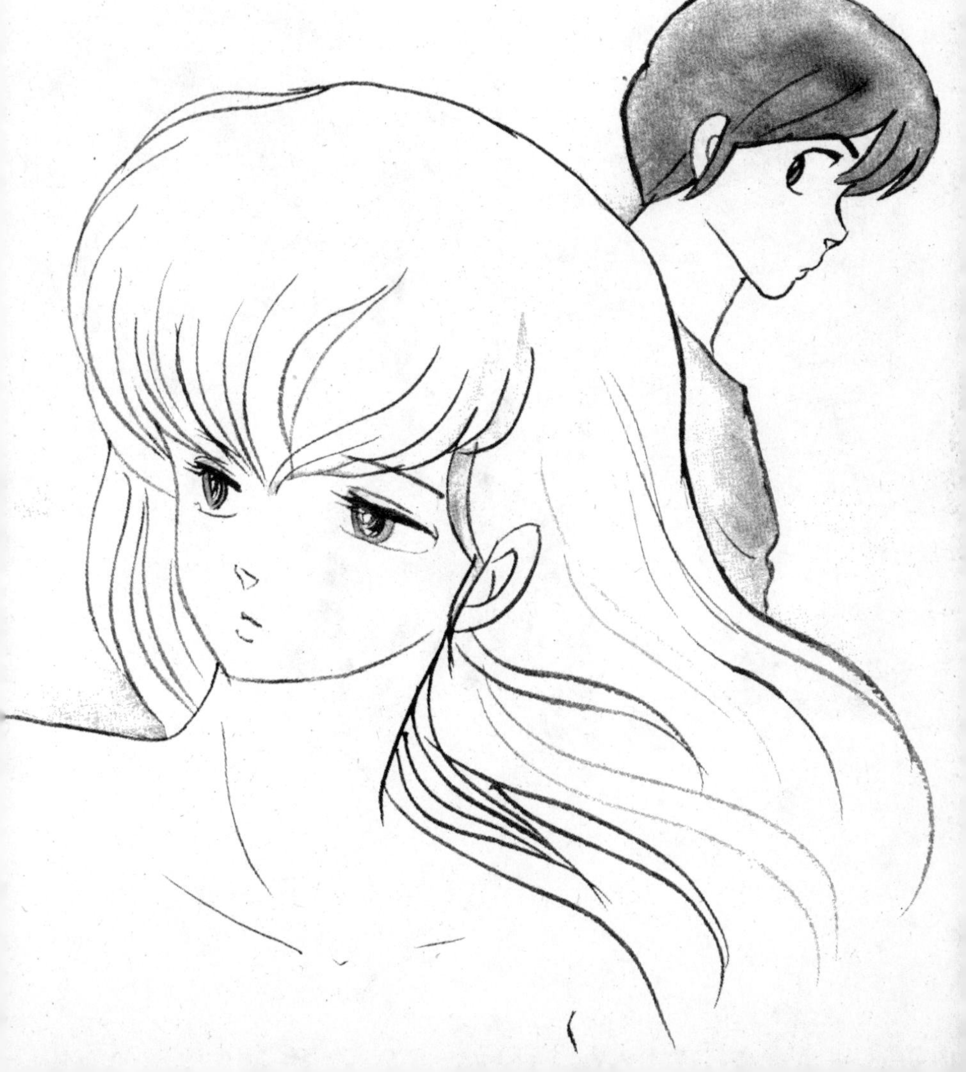

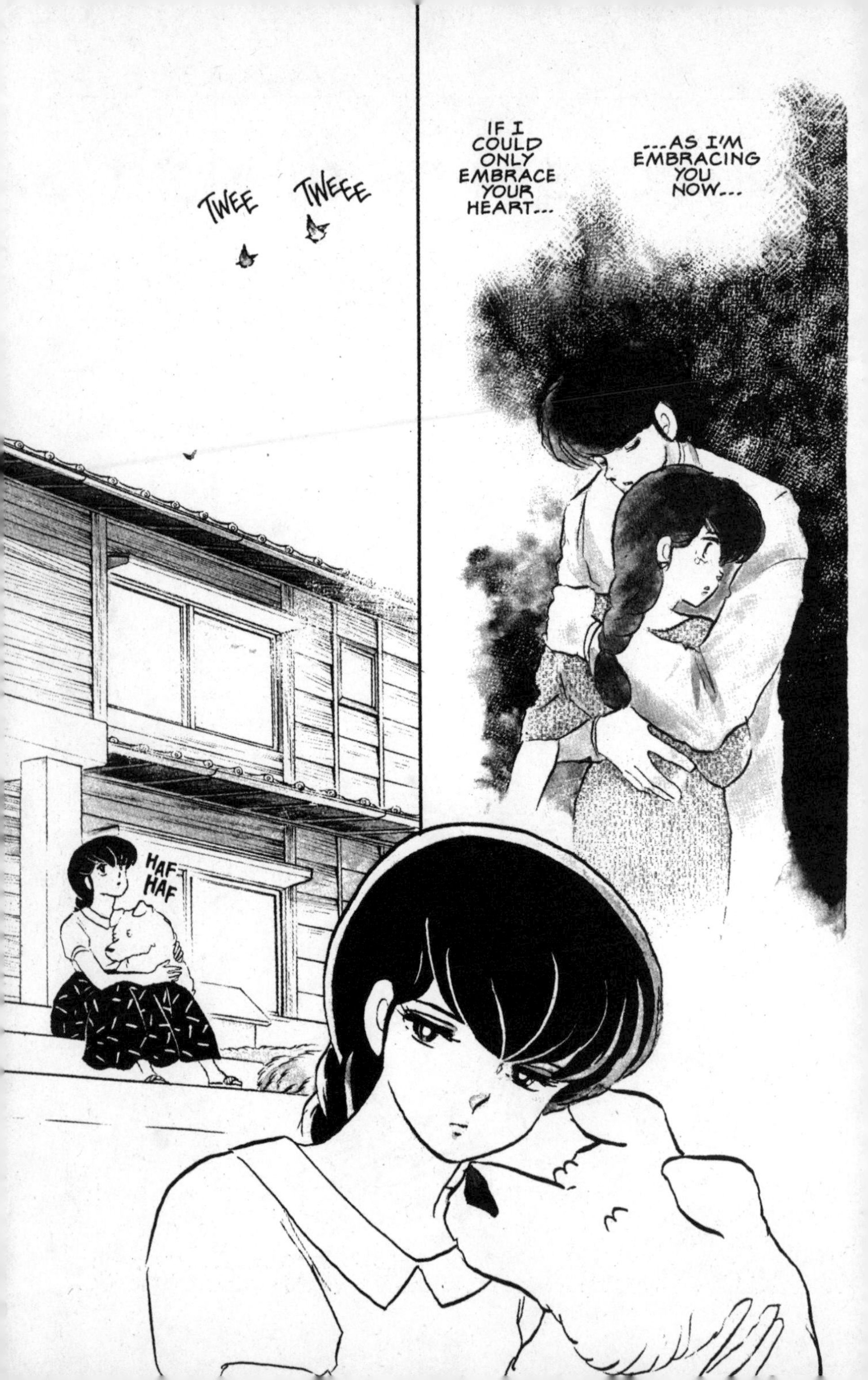
TWEE
TWEEE
HAF HAF
IF I COULD ONLY EMBRACE YOUR HEART...
...AS I'M EMBRACING YOU NOW...

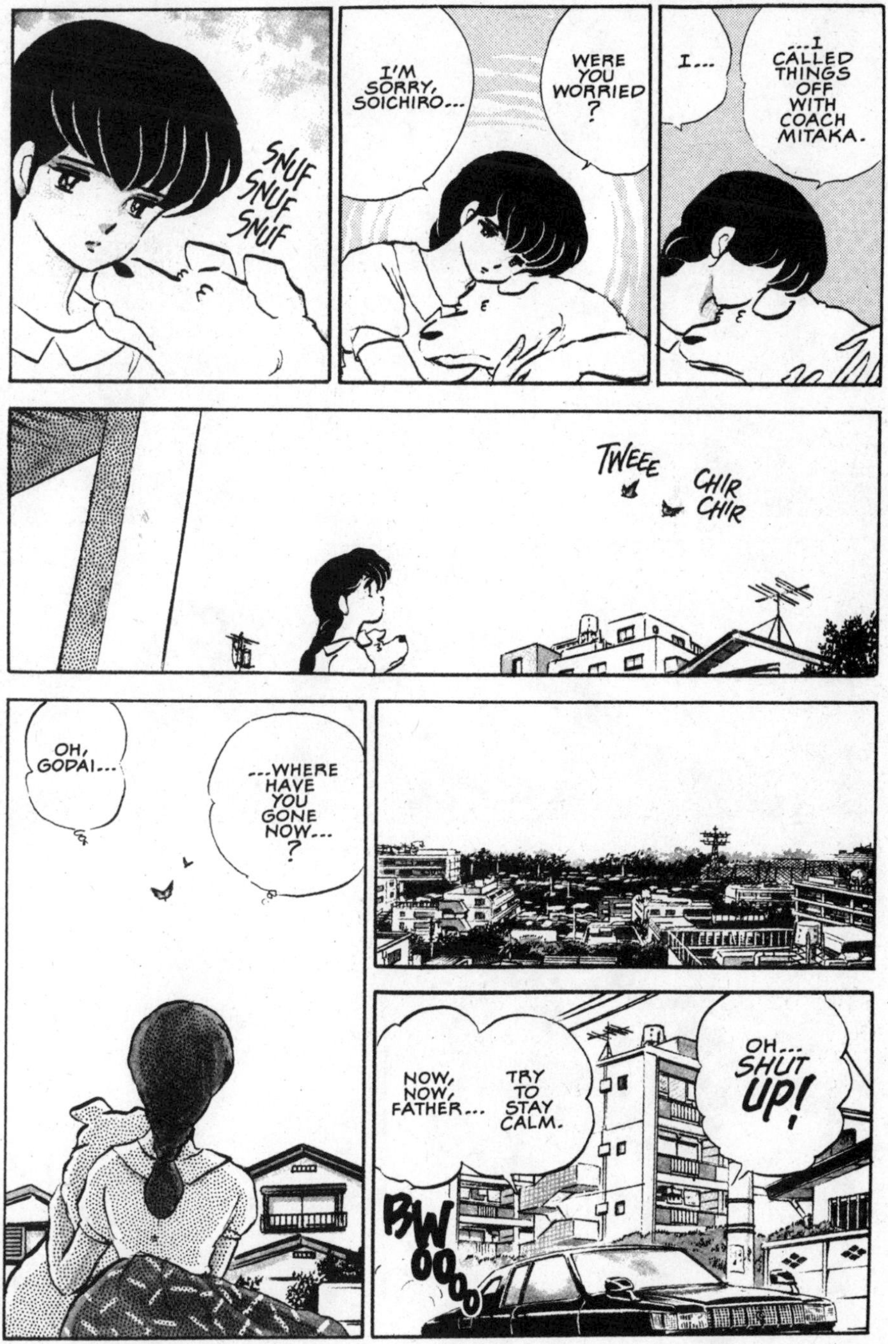
SNUF SNUF SNUF
I'M SORRY, SOICHIRO...
WERE YOU WORRIED?
I...
...I CALLED THINGS OFF WITH COACH MITAKA.
TWEEE
CHIR CHIR
OH, GODAI...
...WHERE HAVE YOU GONE NOW...?
NOW, NOW, FATHER...
TRY TO STAY CALM.
OH... SHUT UP!
BWOOOOO

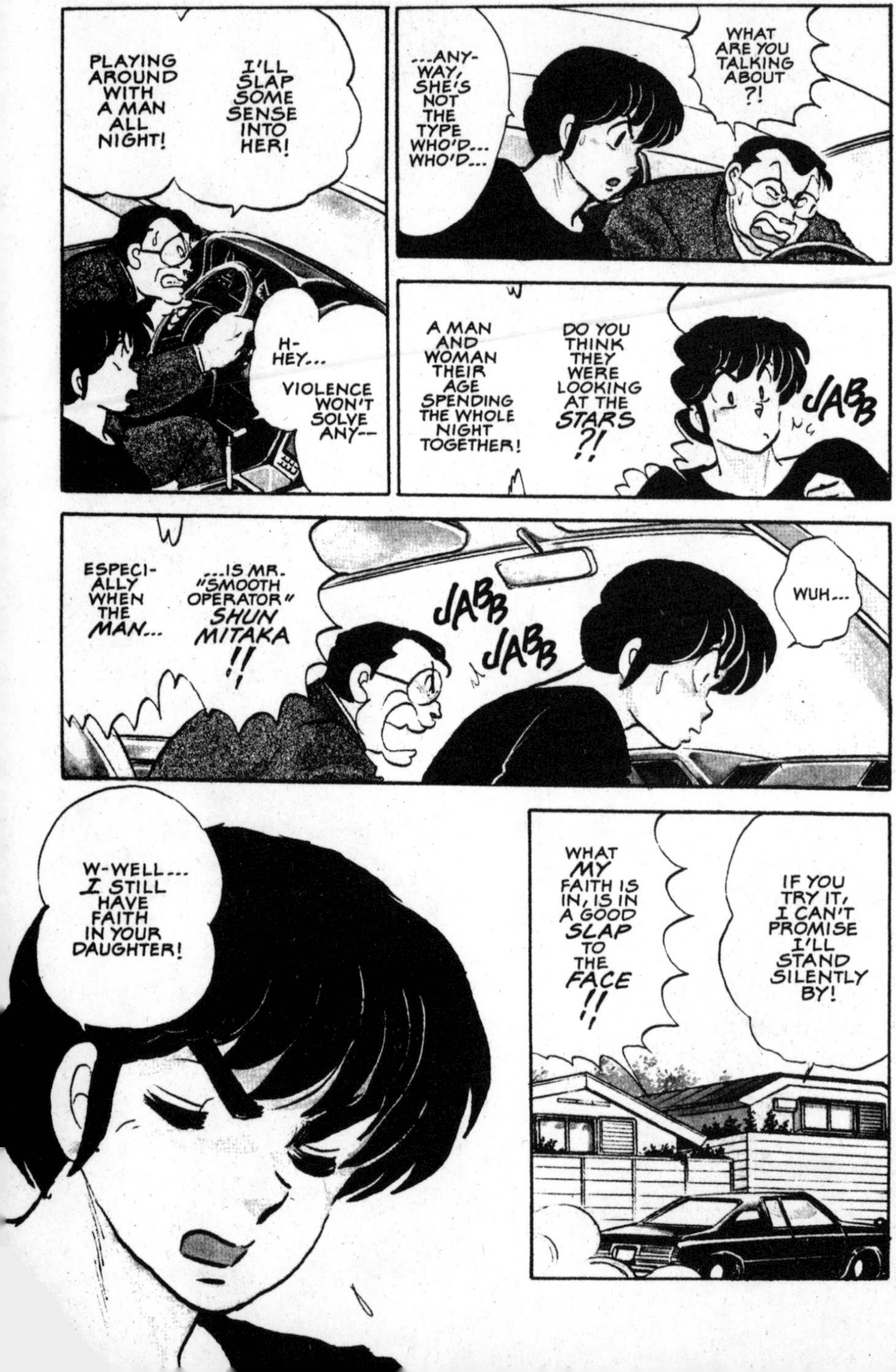
PLAYING AROUND WITH A MAN ALL NIGHT!
I'LL SLAP SOME SENSE INTO HER!
H-HEY... VIOLENCE WON'T SOLVE ANY--
...ANYWAY, SHE'S NOT THE TYPE WHO'D... WHO'D...
WHAT ARE YOU TALKING ABOUT ?!
A MAN AND WOMAN THEIR AGE SPENDING THE WHOLE NIGHT TOGETHER!
DO YOU THINK THEY WERE LOOKING AT THE STARS ?!
JABB
ESPECIALLY WHEN THE MAN...
...IS MR. "SMOOTH OPERATOR" SHUN MITAKA !!
JABB
JABB
WUH...
W-WELL... I STILL HAVE FAITH IN YOUR DAUGHTER!
WHAT MY FAITH IS IN, IS IN A GOOD SLAP TO THE FACE !!
IF YOU TRY IT, I CAN'T PROMISE I'LL STAND SILENTLY BY!

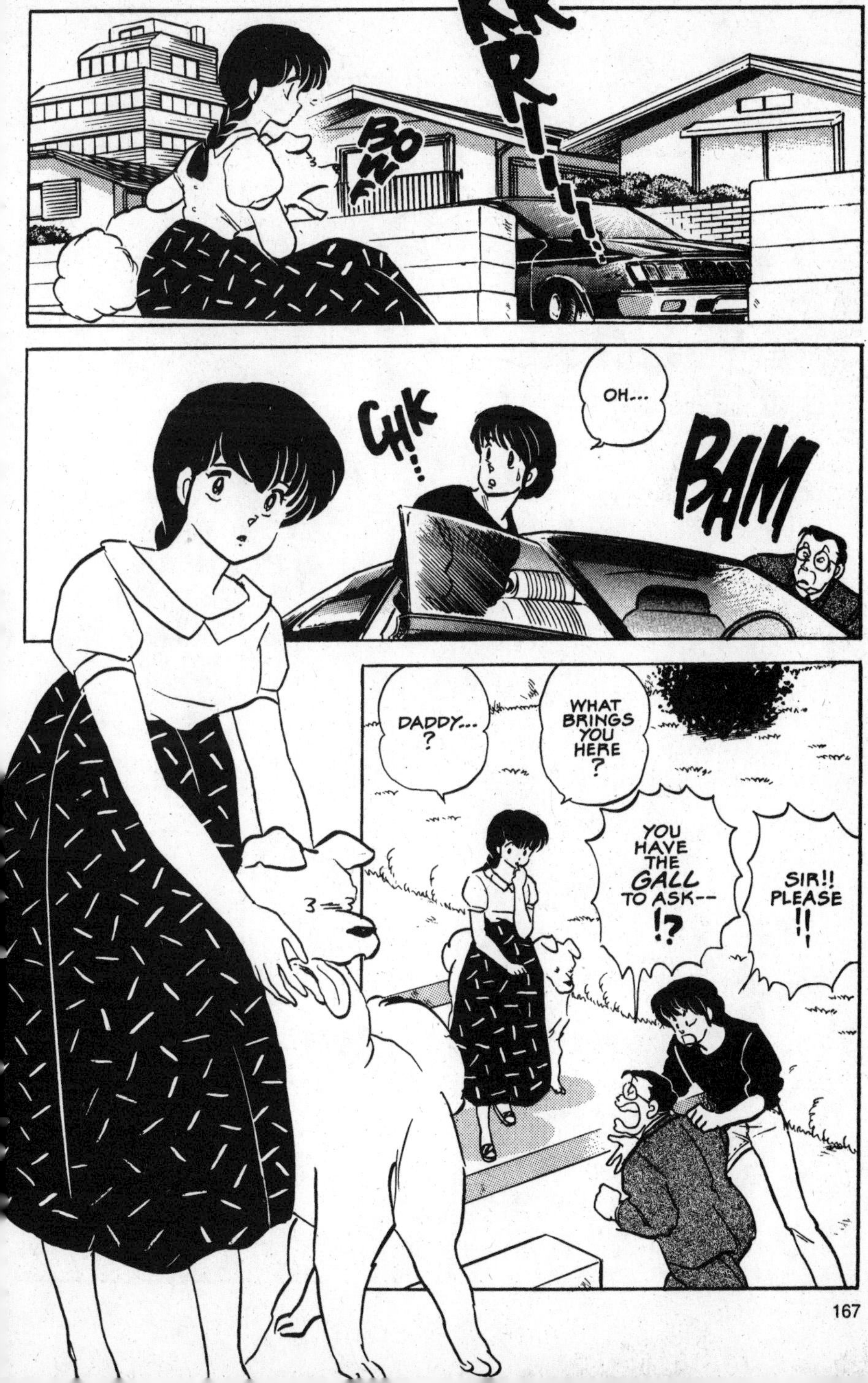
KRRIIII!!
BOWF
CHK!!
OH...
BAM
DADDY...?
WHAT BRINGS YOU HERE?
YOU HAVE THE GALL TO ASK--!?
SIR!! PLEASE!!

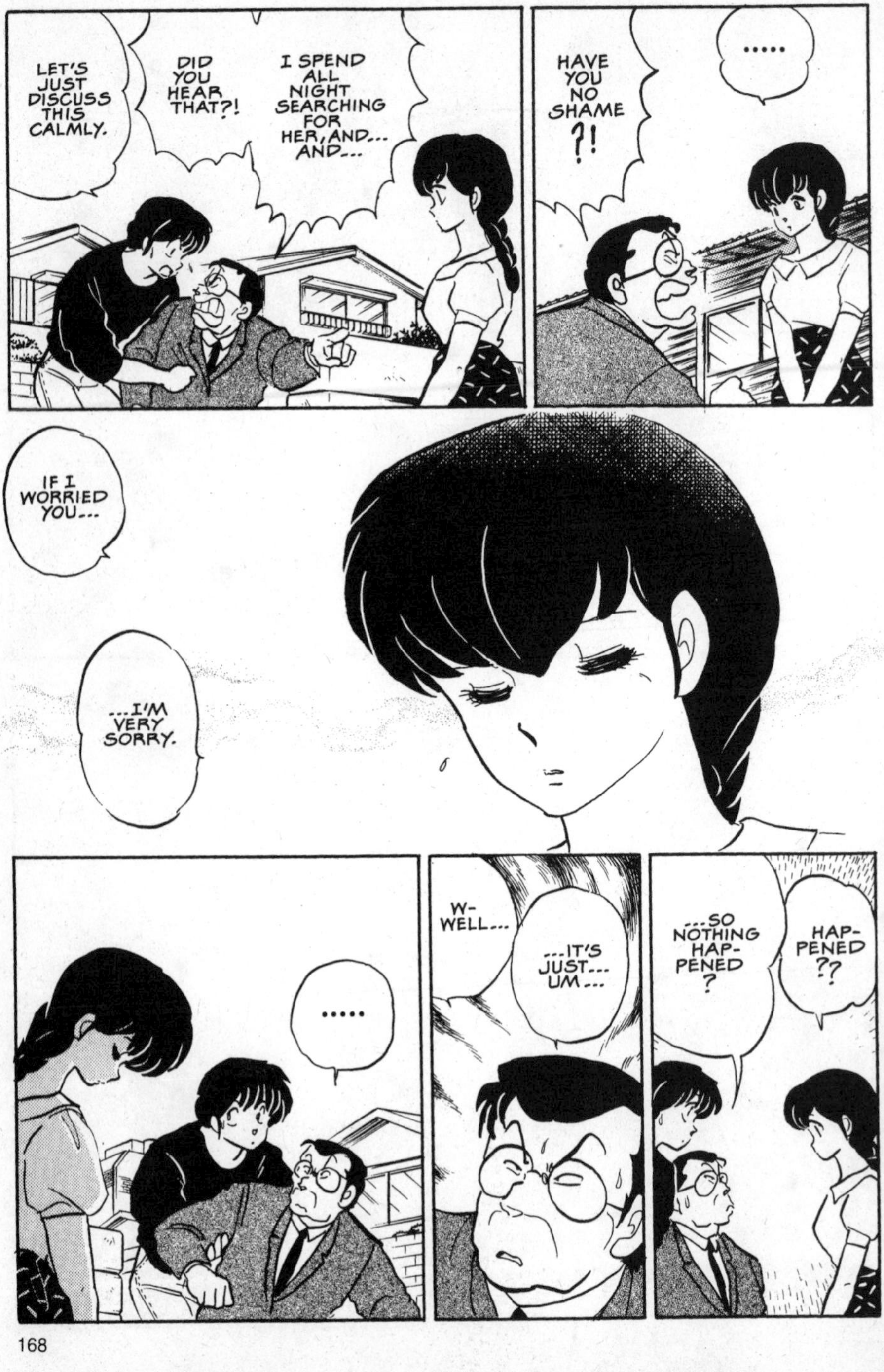

LET'S JUST DISCUSS THIS CALMLY.
DID YOU HEAR THAT?!
I SPEND ALL NIGHT SEARCHING FOR HER, AND... AND...
HAVE YOU NO SHAME ?!
......
IF I WORRIED YOU...
...I'M VERY SORRY.
......
W-WELL...
...IT'S JUST... UM...
...SO NOTHING HAP-PENED ?
HAP-PENED ??

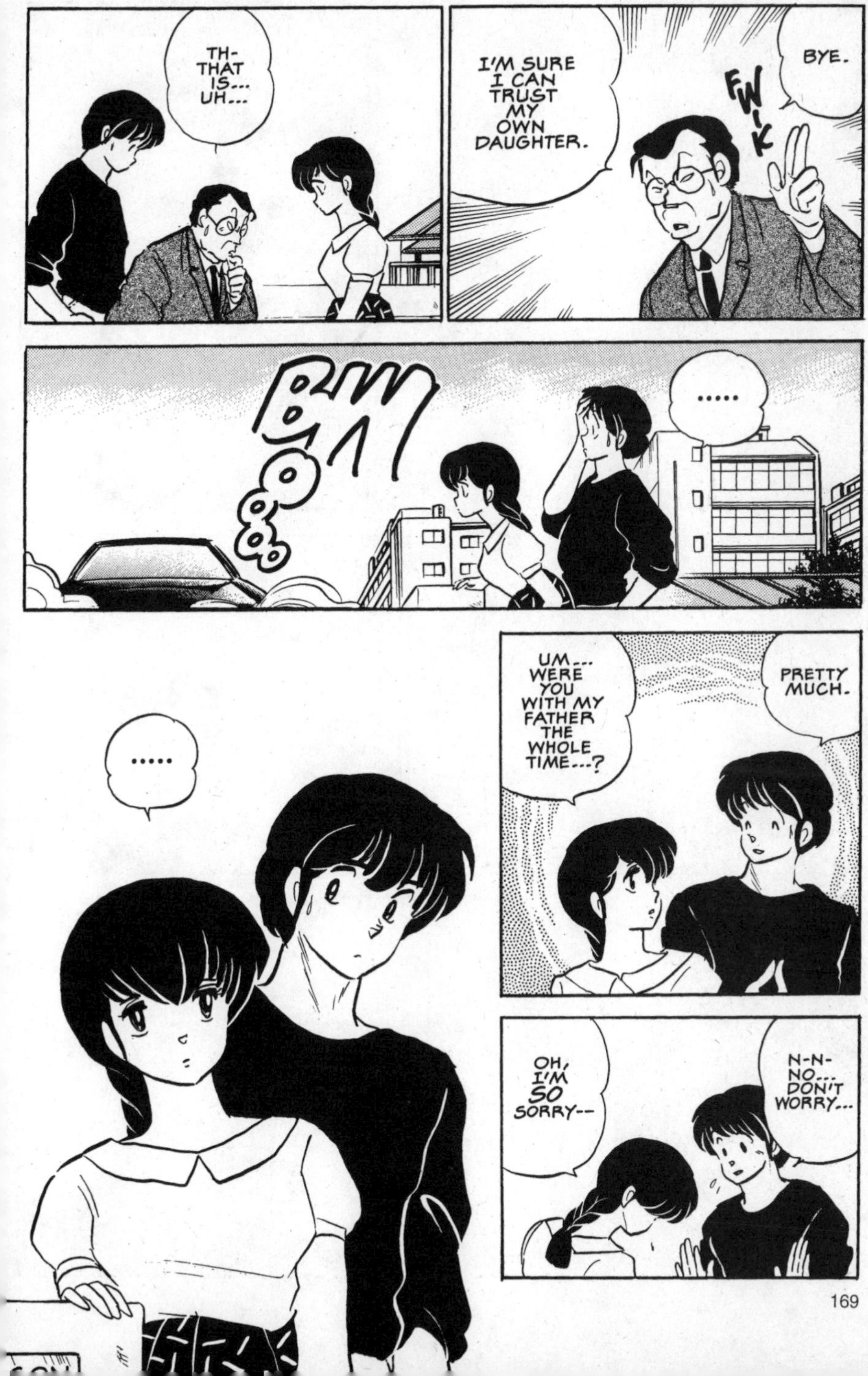
TH- THAT IS... UH...
I'M SURE I CAN TRUST MY OWN DAUGHTER.
BYE.
FWIK
BMM
.....
.....
UM... WERE YOU WITH MY FATHER THE WHOLE TIME...?
PRETTY MUCH.
OH, I'M SO SORRY--
N-N-NO... DON'T WORRY...

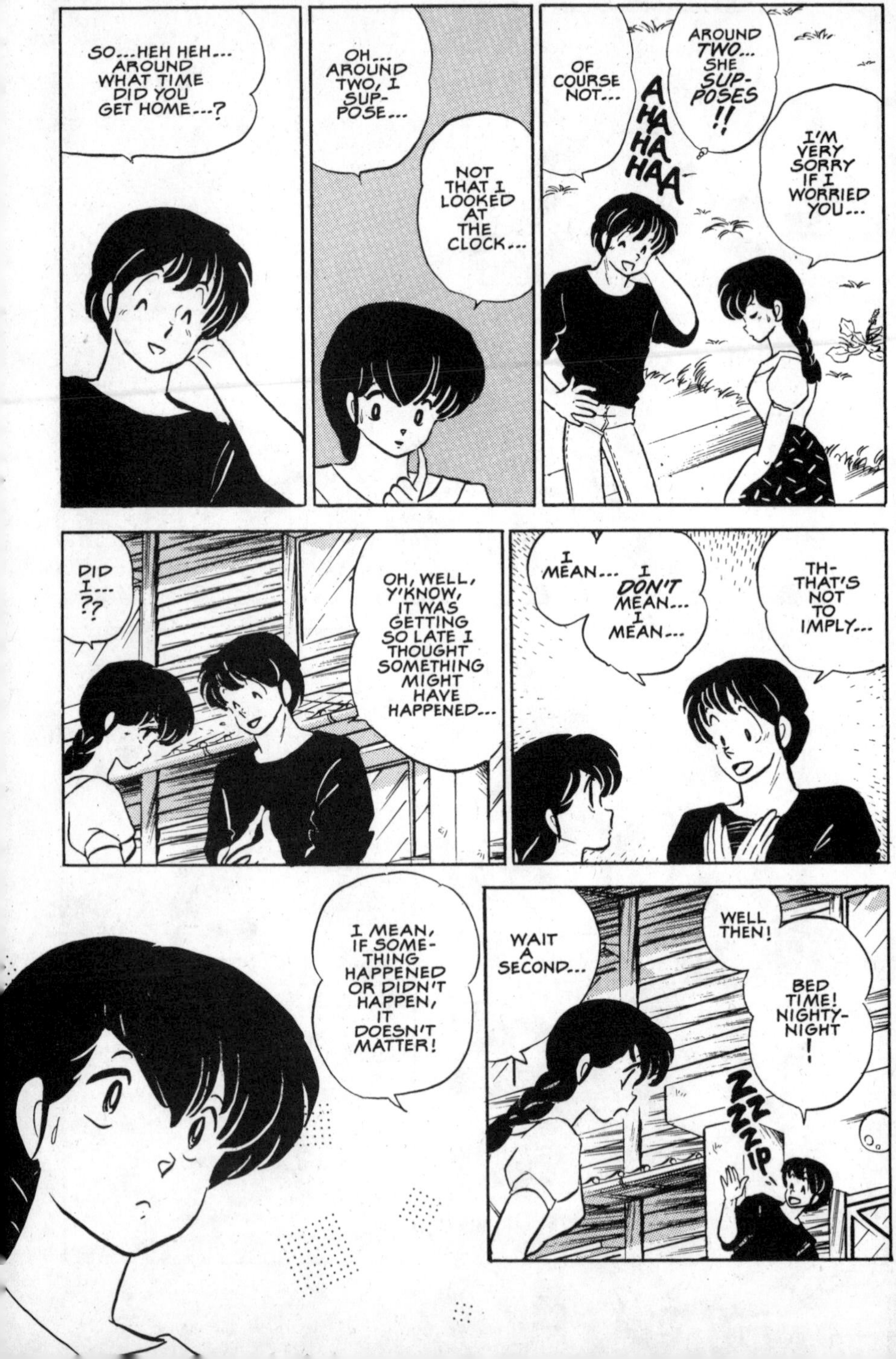
SO...HEH HEH... AROUND WHAT TIME DID YOU GET HOME...?
OH... AROUND TWO, I SUPPOSE...
NOT THAT I LOOKED AT THE CLOCK...
OF COURSE NOT...
AHAHAHAA
AROUND TWO... SHE SUPPOSES!!
I'M VERY SORRY IF I WORRIED YOU...
DID I...??
OH, WELL, Y'KNOW, IT WAS GETTING SO LATE I THOUGHT SOMETHING MIGHT HAVE HAPPENED...
I MEAN... I DON'T MEAN... I MEAN...
TH-THAT'S NOT TO IMPLY...
I MEAN, IF SOMETHING HAPPENED OR DIDN'T HAPPEN, IT DOESN'T MATTER!
WAIT A SECOND...
WELL THEN!
BED TIME! NIGHTY-NIGHT!
ZZZZIP

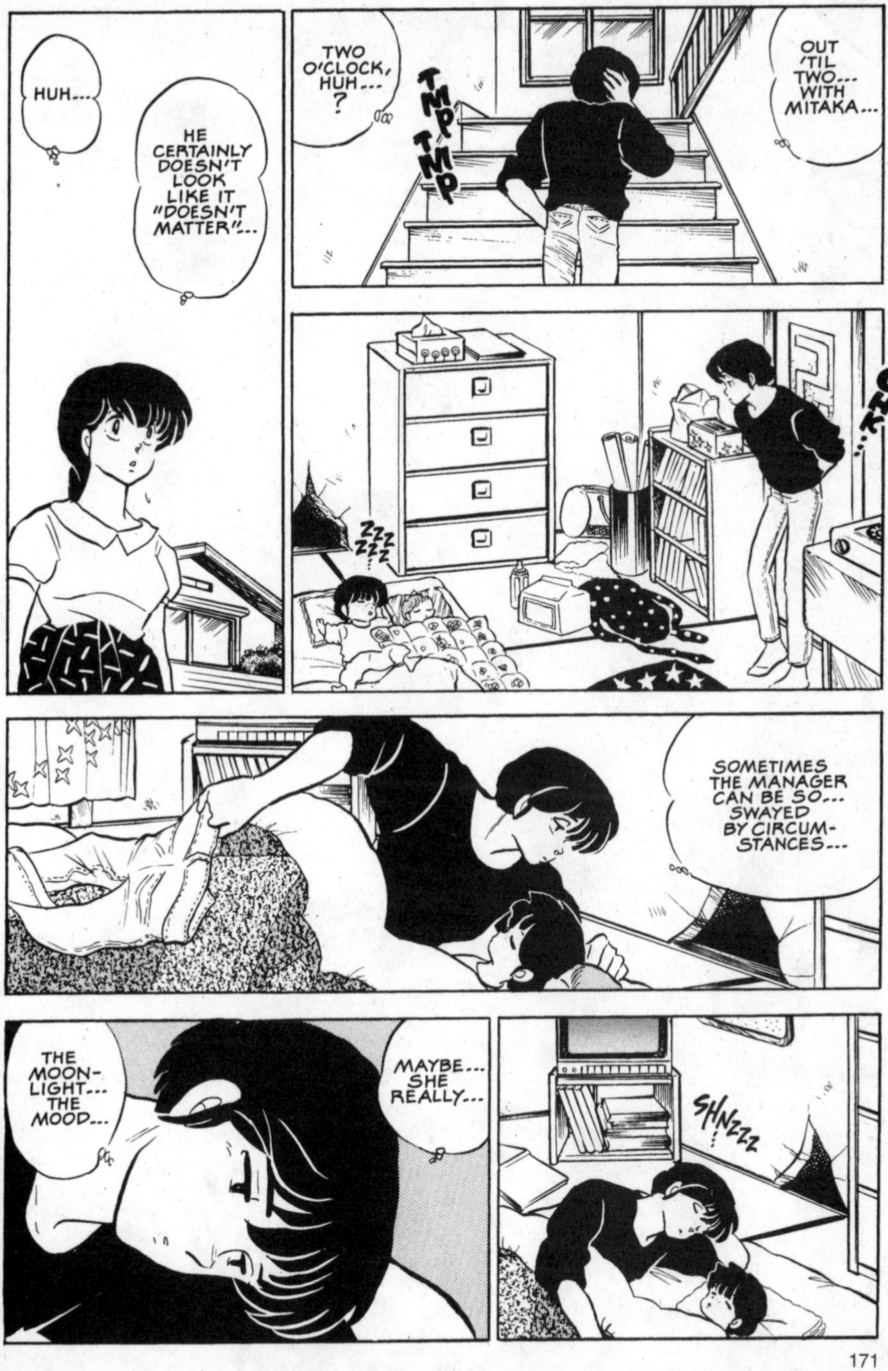
HUH...
HE CERTAINLY DOESN'T LOOK LIKE IT "DOESN'T MATTER"...
TWO O'CLOCK, HUH...?
TMP TMP
OUT 'TIL TWO... WITH MITAKA...
ZZZ ZZZ
CHK...
SOMETIMES THE MANAGER CAN BE SO... SWAYED BY CIRCUM-STANCES...
THE MOON-LIGHT... THE MOOD...
MAYBE... SHE REALLY...
SHNZZZ

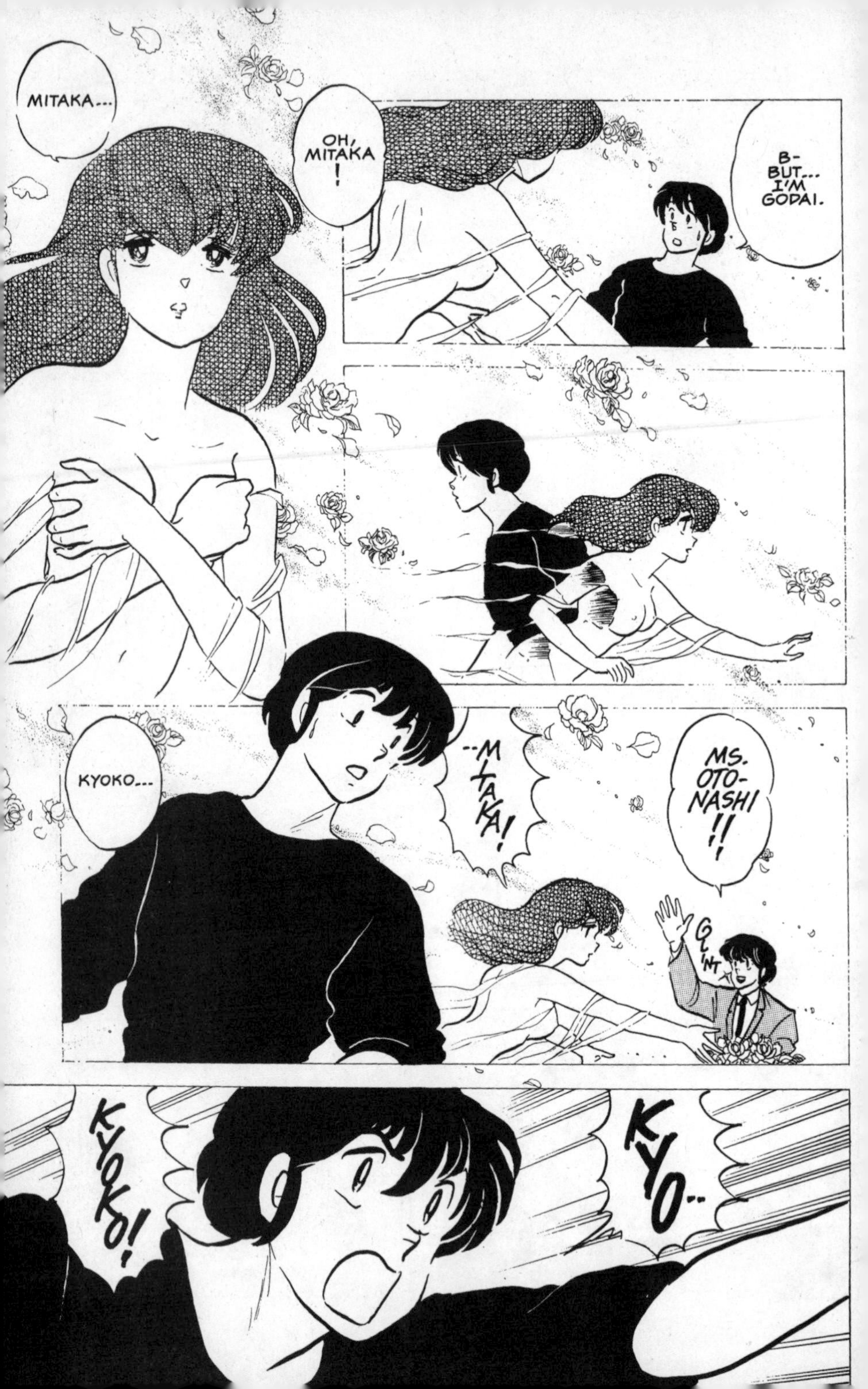
MITAKA...
OH, MITAKA!
B-BUT... I'M GODAI.
KYOKO...
--MITAKA!
MS. OTONASHI!!
GLINT
KYOKO!
KYO..

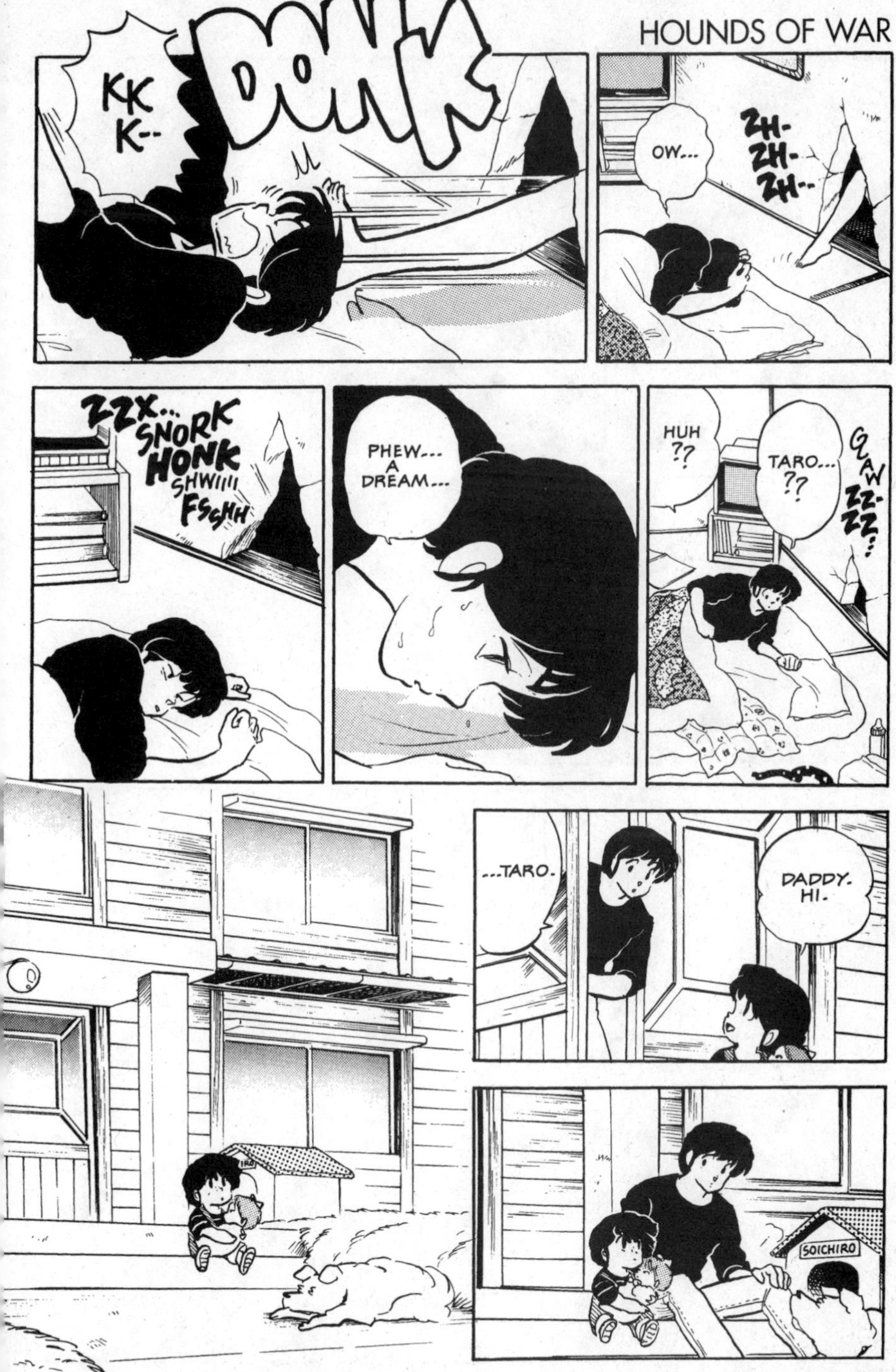
KK K--
DONK
OW...
ZH-ZH-ZH--
ZZX... SNORK HONK SHWIIII FSGHH
PHEW... A DREAM...
HUH ??
TARO... ??
GAW ZZ-ZZ
...TARO.
DADDY. HI.
SOICHIRO

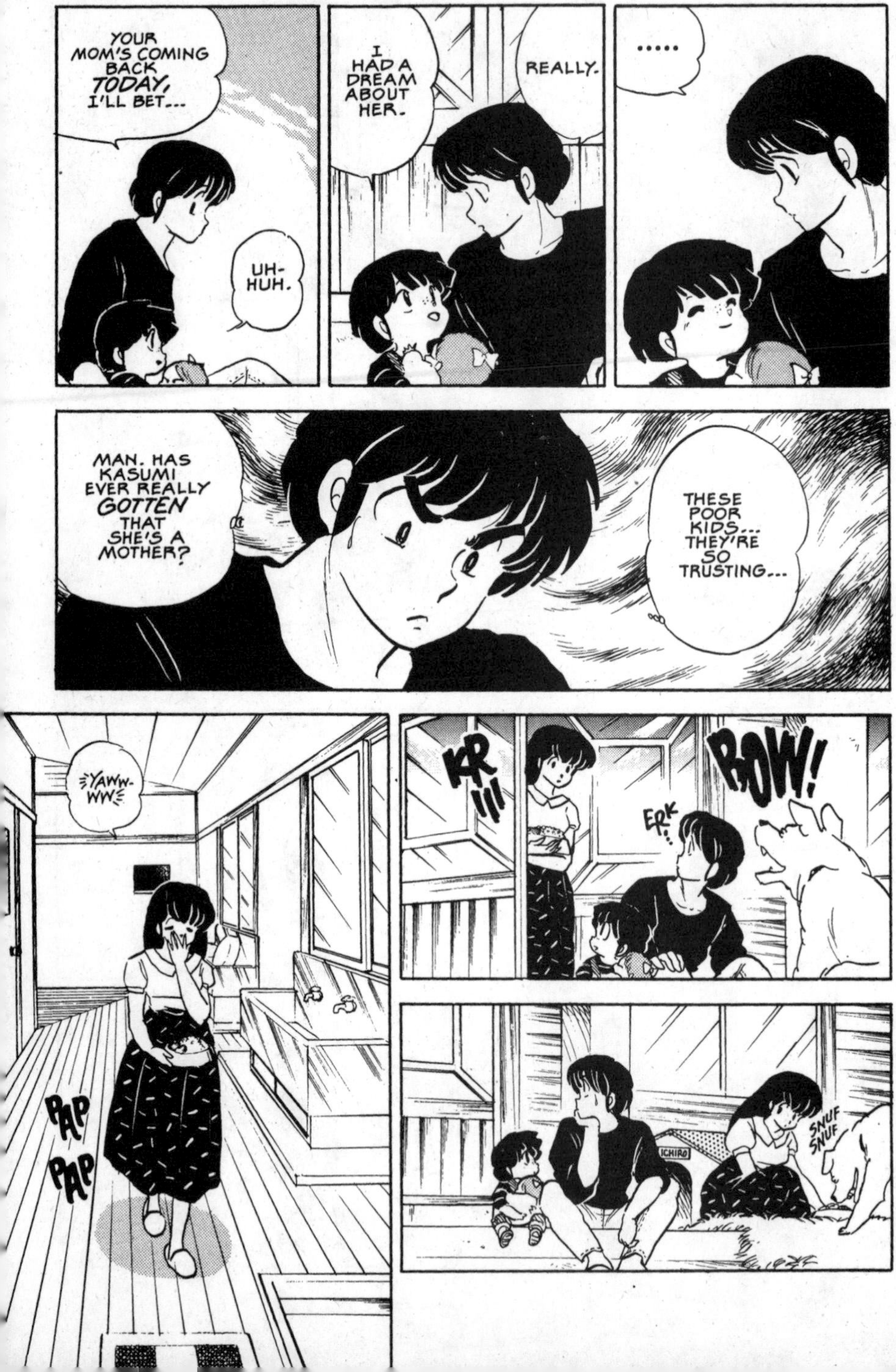
YOUR MOM'S COMING BACK TODAY, I'LL BET...
UH-HUH.
I HAD A DREAM ABOUT HER.
REALLY.
.....
MAN. HAS KASUMI EVER REALLY GOTTEN THAT SHE'S A MOTHER?
THESE POOR KIDS... THEY'RE SO TRUSTING...
YAWW-WW
PAP
PAP
KR
ROW!
ERK
SNUF SNUF
ICHIRO

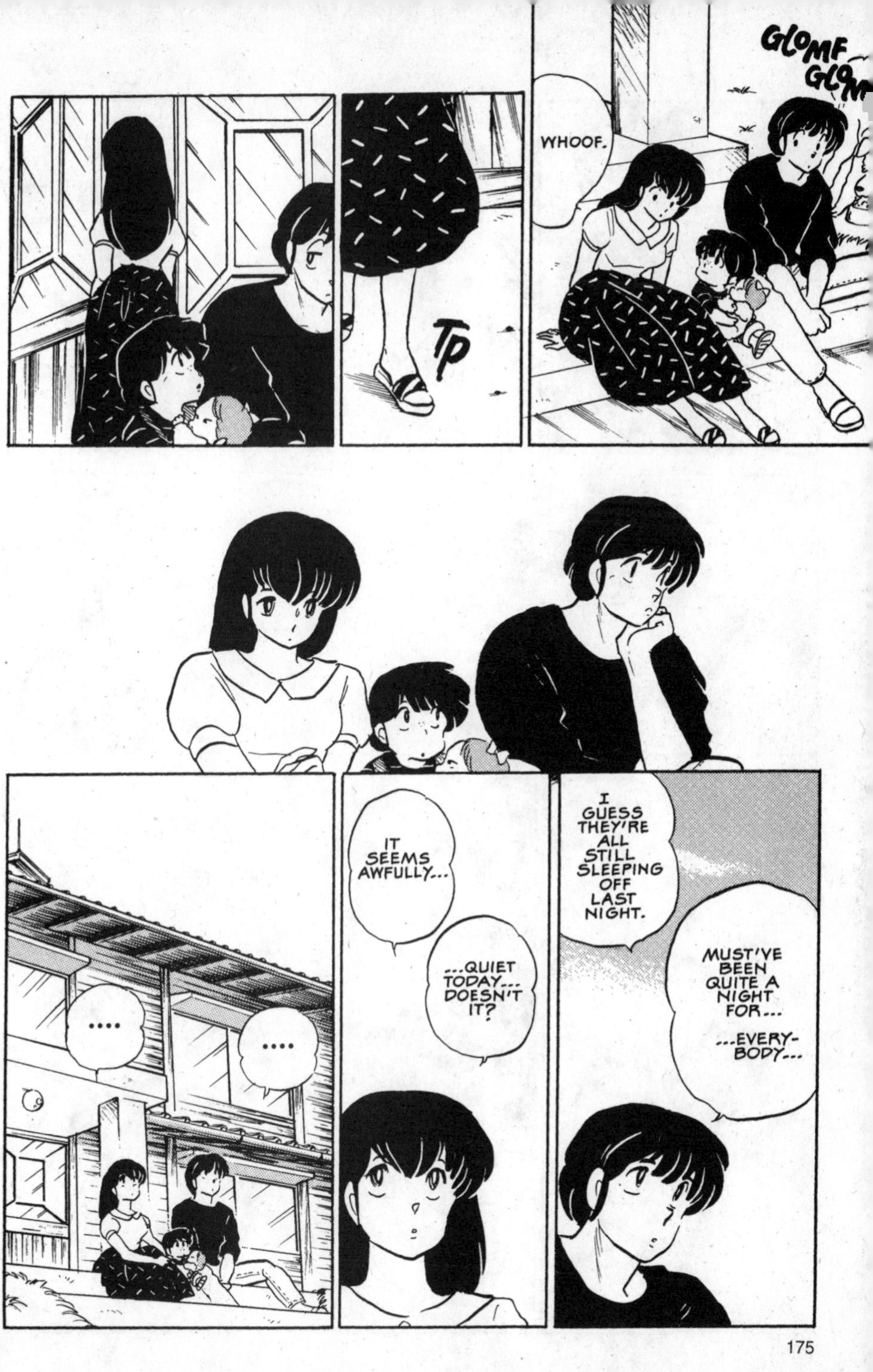
WHOOF.
GLOMF GLOMF
TP
....
....
IT SEEMS AWFULLY...
...QUIET TODAY... DOESN'T IT?
I GUESS THEY'RE ALL STILL SLEEPING OFF LAST NIGHT.
MUST'VE BEEN QUITE A NIGHT FOR...
...EVERY-BODY...

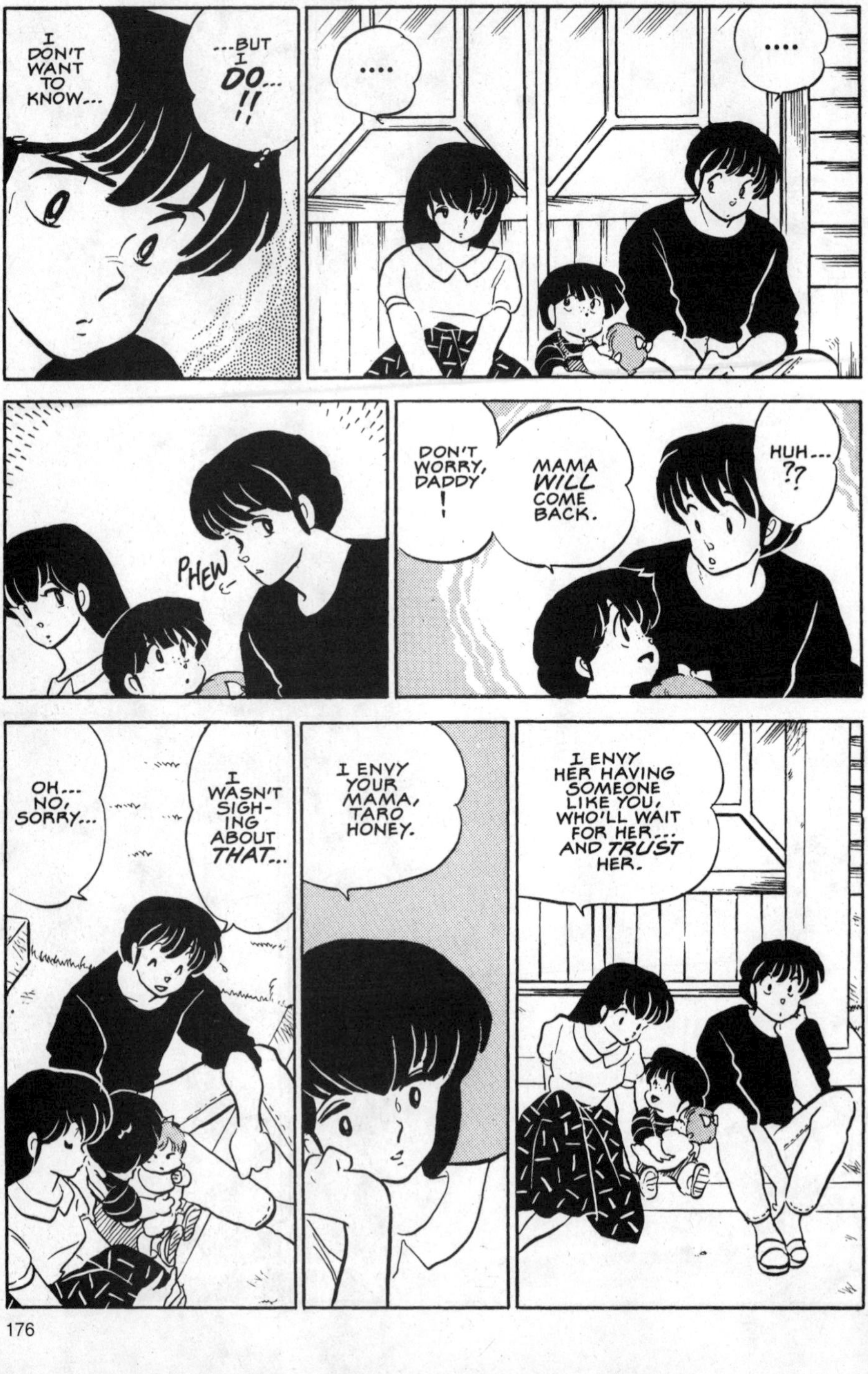
I DON'T WANT TO KNOW...
...BUT I DO...!!
....
....
PHEW
DON'T WORRY, DADDY!
MAMA WILL COME BACK.
HUH...??
OH... NO, SORRY...
I WASN'T SIGHING ABOUT THAT...
I ENVY YOUR MAMA, TARO HONEY.
I ENVY HER HAVING SOMEONE LIKE YOU, WHO'LL WAIT FOR HER... AND TRUST HER.

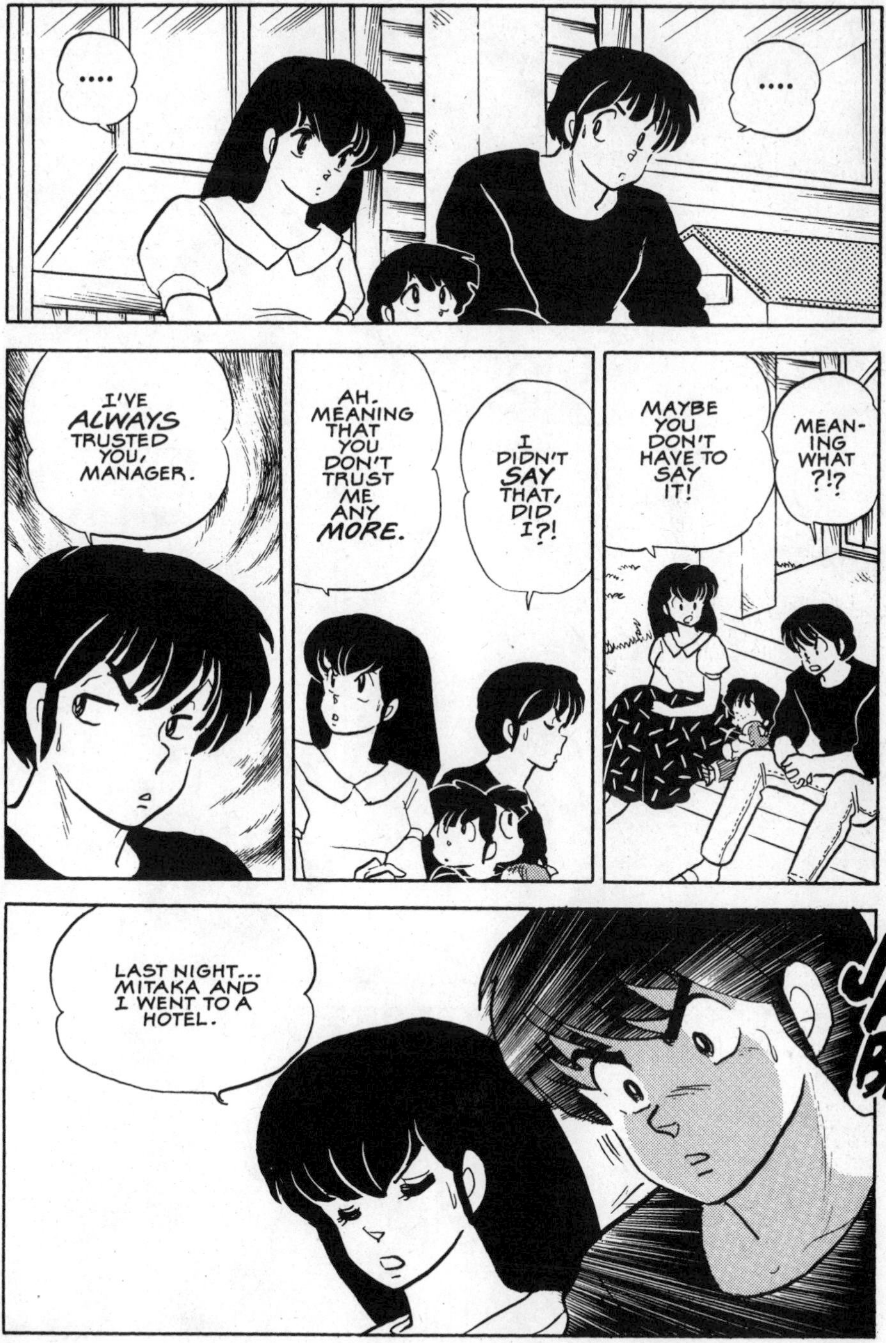
....
....
I'VE ALWAYS TRUSTED YOU, MANAGER.
AH. MEANING THAT YOU DON'T TRUST ME ANY MORE.
I DIDN'T SAY THAT, DID I?!
MAYBE YOU DON'T HAVE TO SAY IT!
MEAN-ING WHAT ?!?
LAST NIGHT... MITAKA AND I WENT TO A HOTEL.
JABB

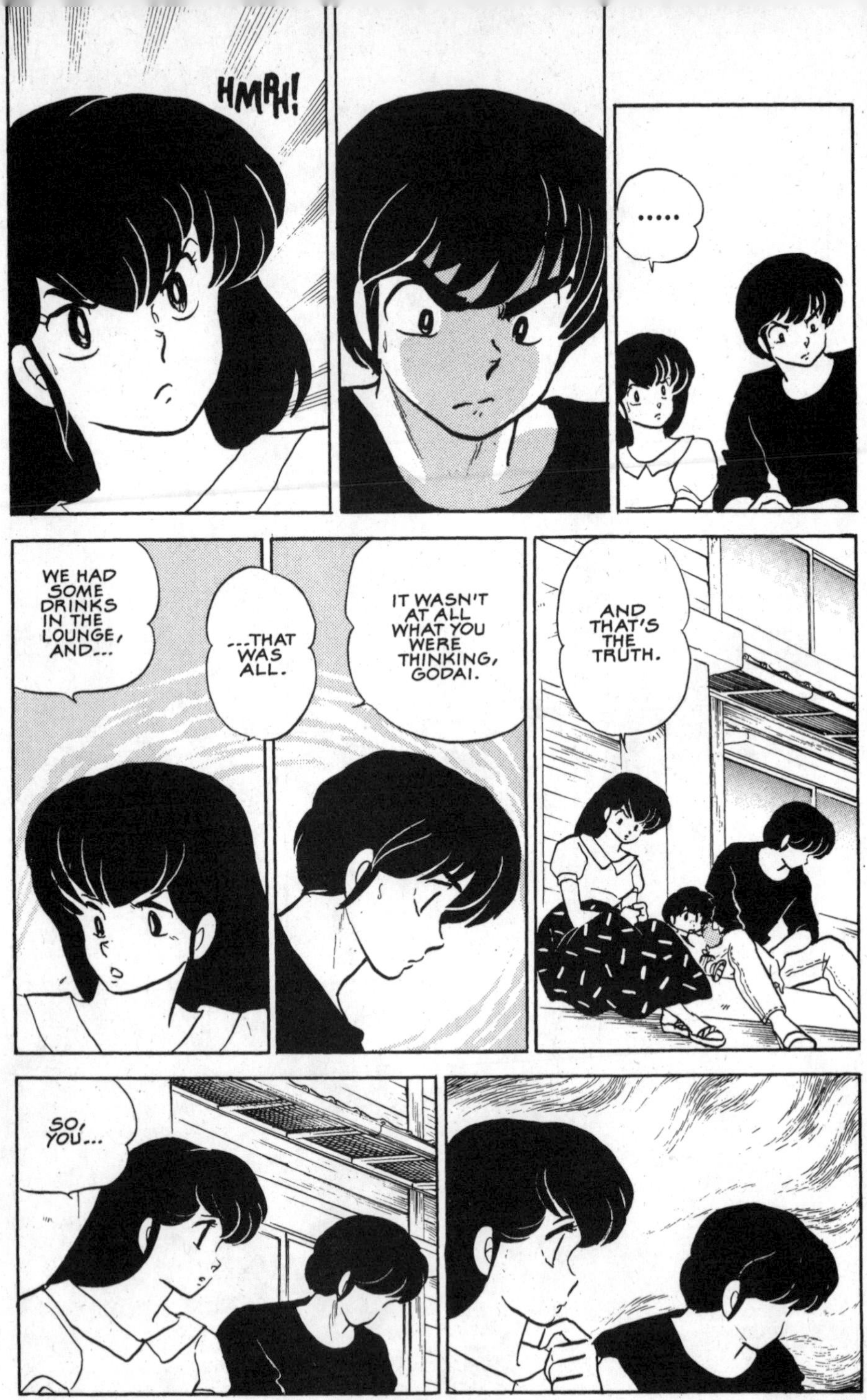
HMPH!
......
WE HAD SOME DRINKS IN THE LOUNGE, AND...
...THAT WAS ALL.
IT WASN'T AT ALL WHAT YOU WERE THINKING, GODAI.
AND THAT'S THE TRUTH.
SO, YOU...

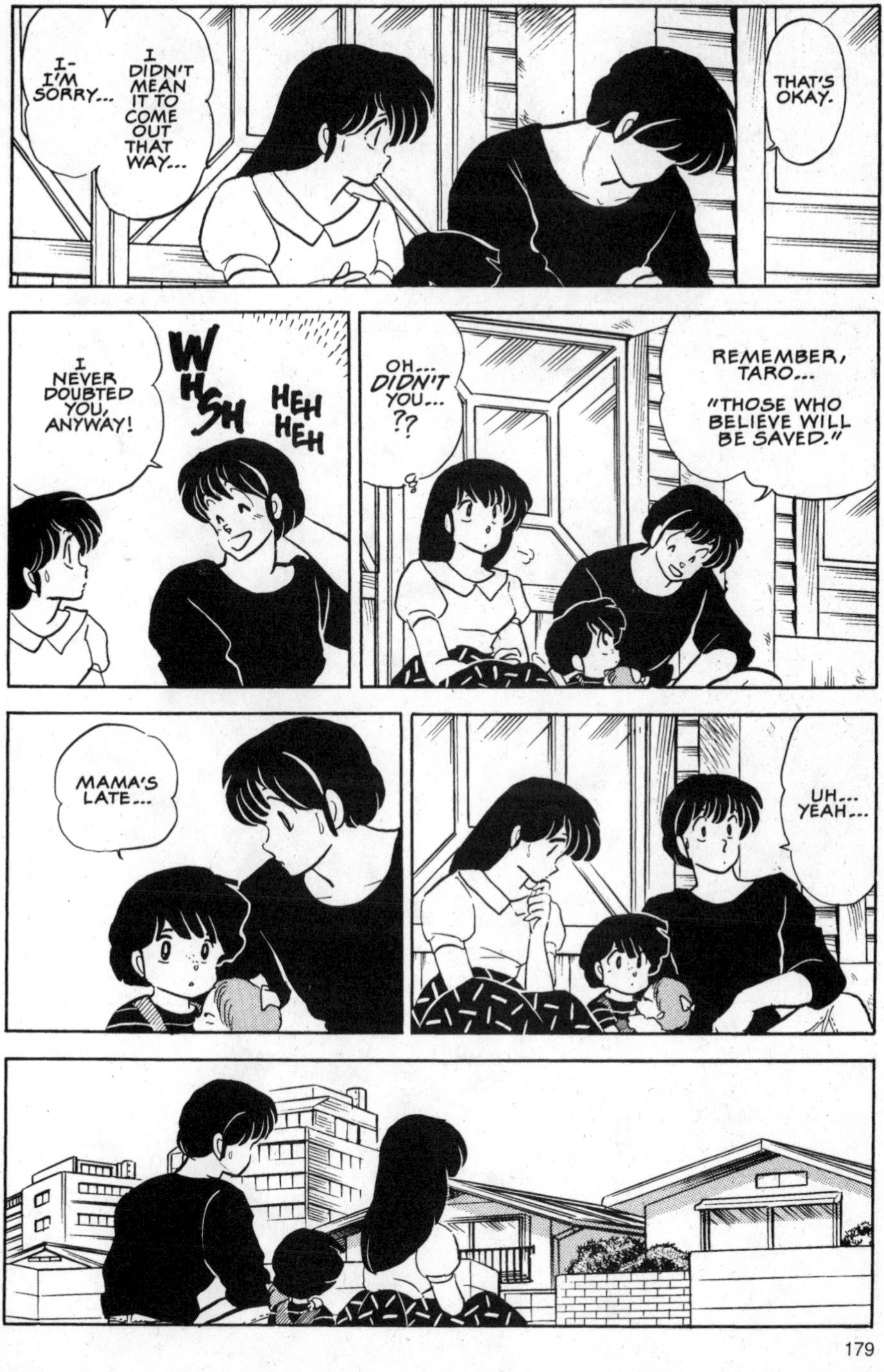
I- I'M SORRY...
I DIDN'T MEAN IT TO COME OUT THAT WAY...
THAT'S OKAY.
I NEVER DOUBTED YOU, ANYWAY!
WHSH
HEH HEH
OH... *DIDN'T* YOU...??
REMEMBER, TARO... "THOSE WHO BELIEVE WILL BE SAVED."
MAMA'S LATE...
UH... YEAH...

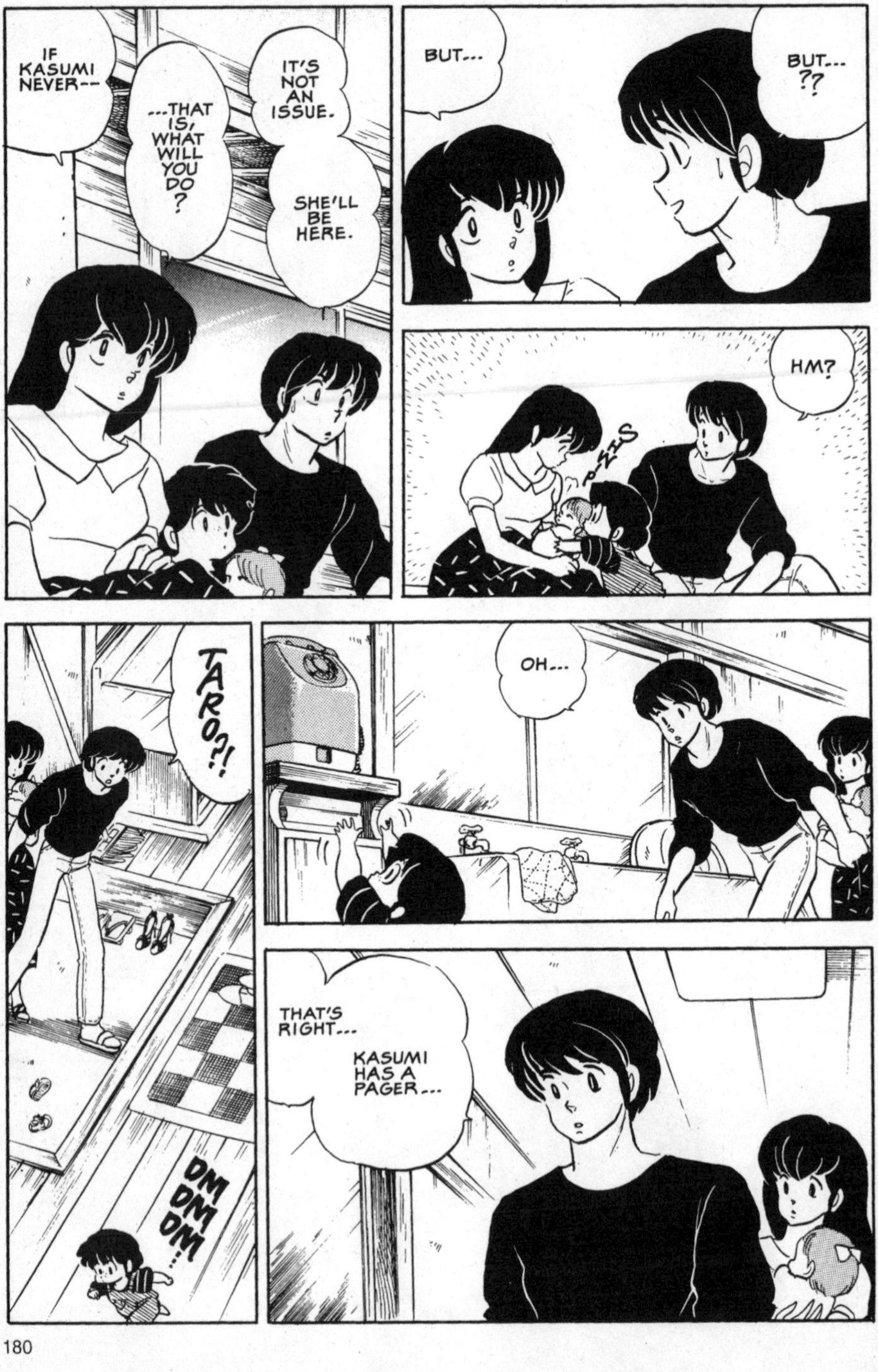
IF KASUMI NEVER--
---THAT IS, WHAT WILL YOU DO?
IT'S NOT AN ISSUE.
SHE'LL BE HERE.
BUT---
BUT--- ??
HM?
TARO?!
OH---
THAT'S RIGHT---
KASUMI HAS A PAGER---
DM DM DM---

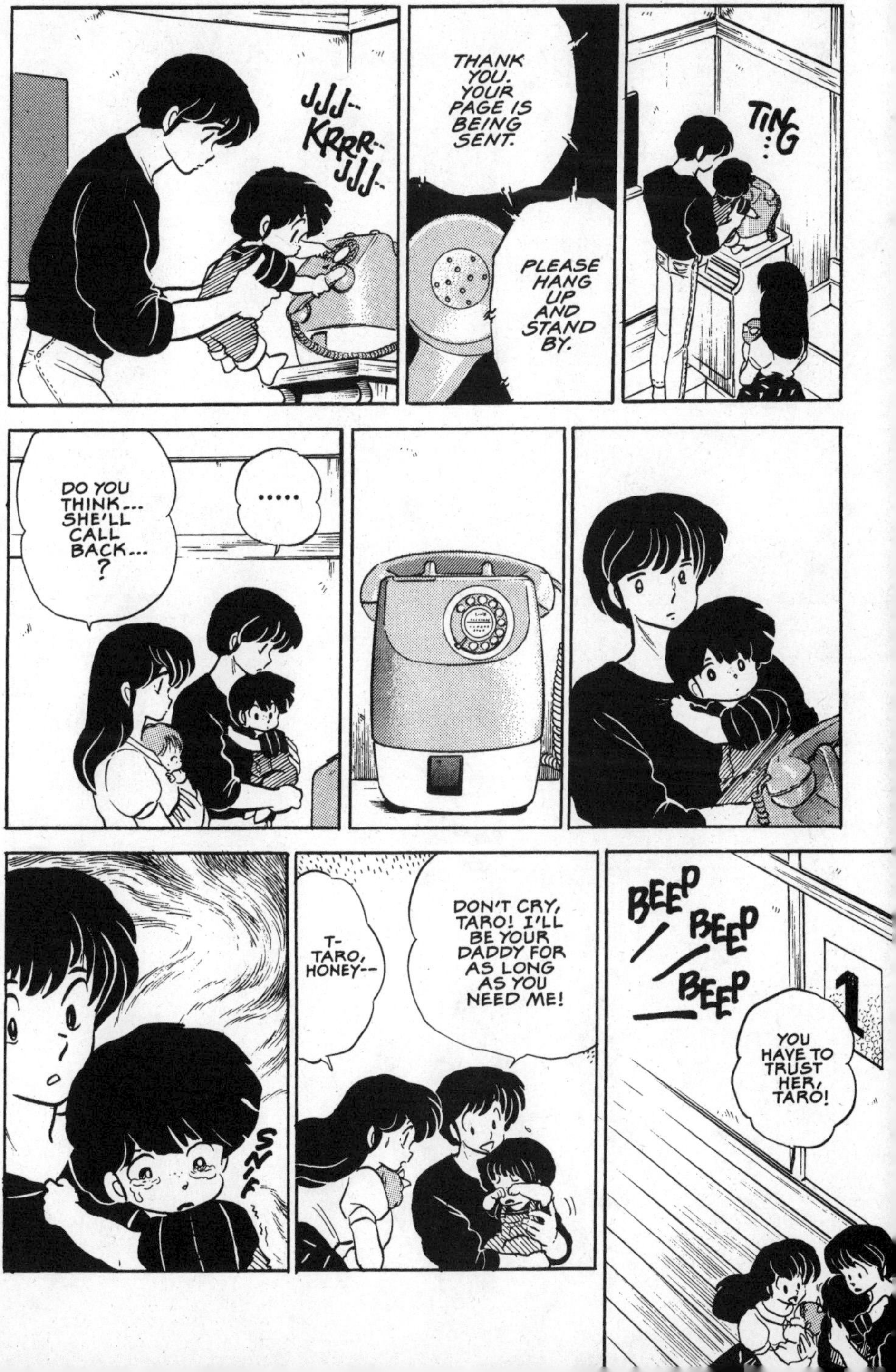
JJJ-- KRRR-- JJJ--
THANK YOU. YOUR PAGE IS BEING SENT.
PLEASE HANG UP AND STAND BY.
TING...G
DO YOU THINK... SHE'LL CALL BACK...?
.....
SNIF
T-TARO, HONEY--
DON'T CRY, TARO! I'LL BE YOUR DADDY FOR AS LONG AS YOU NEED ME!
BEEP BEEP BEEP
1
YOU HAVE TO TRUST HER, TARO!

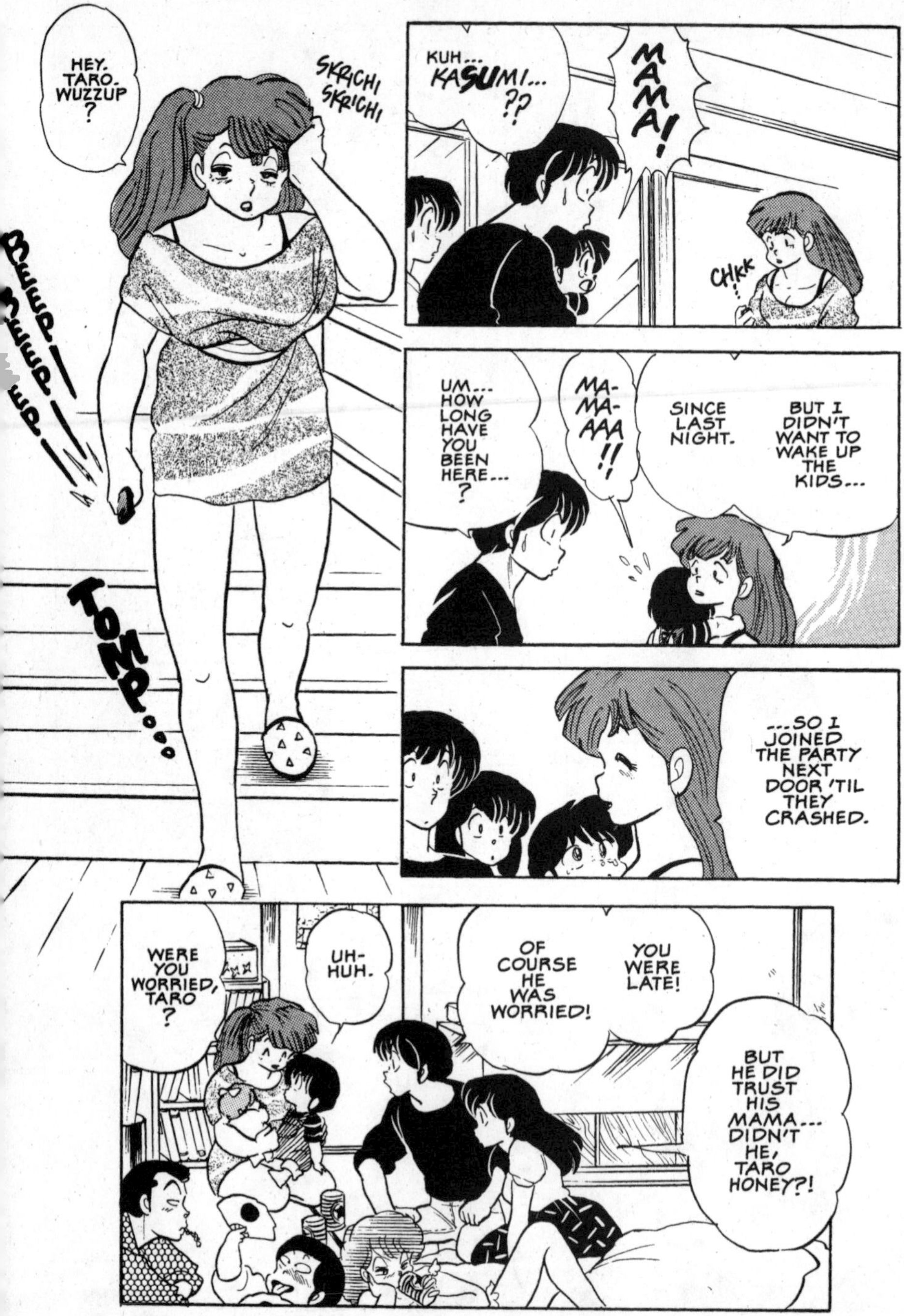
HEY. TARO. WUZZUP?
SKRICHI SKRICHI
BEEP! BEEP! BEEP!
TOMP...
KUH... KASUMI...??
MAMA!
CHKK
UM... HOW LONG HAVE YOU BEEN HERE...?
MAMA-AAA!!
SINCE LAST NIGHT.
BUT I DIDN'T WANT TO WAKE UP THE KIDS...
...SO I JOINED THE PARTY NEXT DOOR 'TIL THEY CRASHED.
WERE YOU WORRIED, TARO?
UH-HUH.
OF COURSE HE WAS WORRIED!
YOU WERE LATE!
BUT HE DID TRUST HIS MAMA... DIDN'T HE, TARO HONEY?!

PART ELEVEN
100% SURE

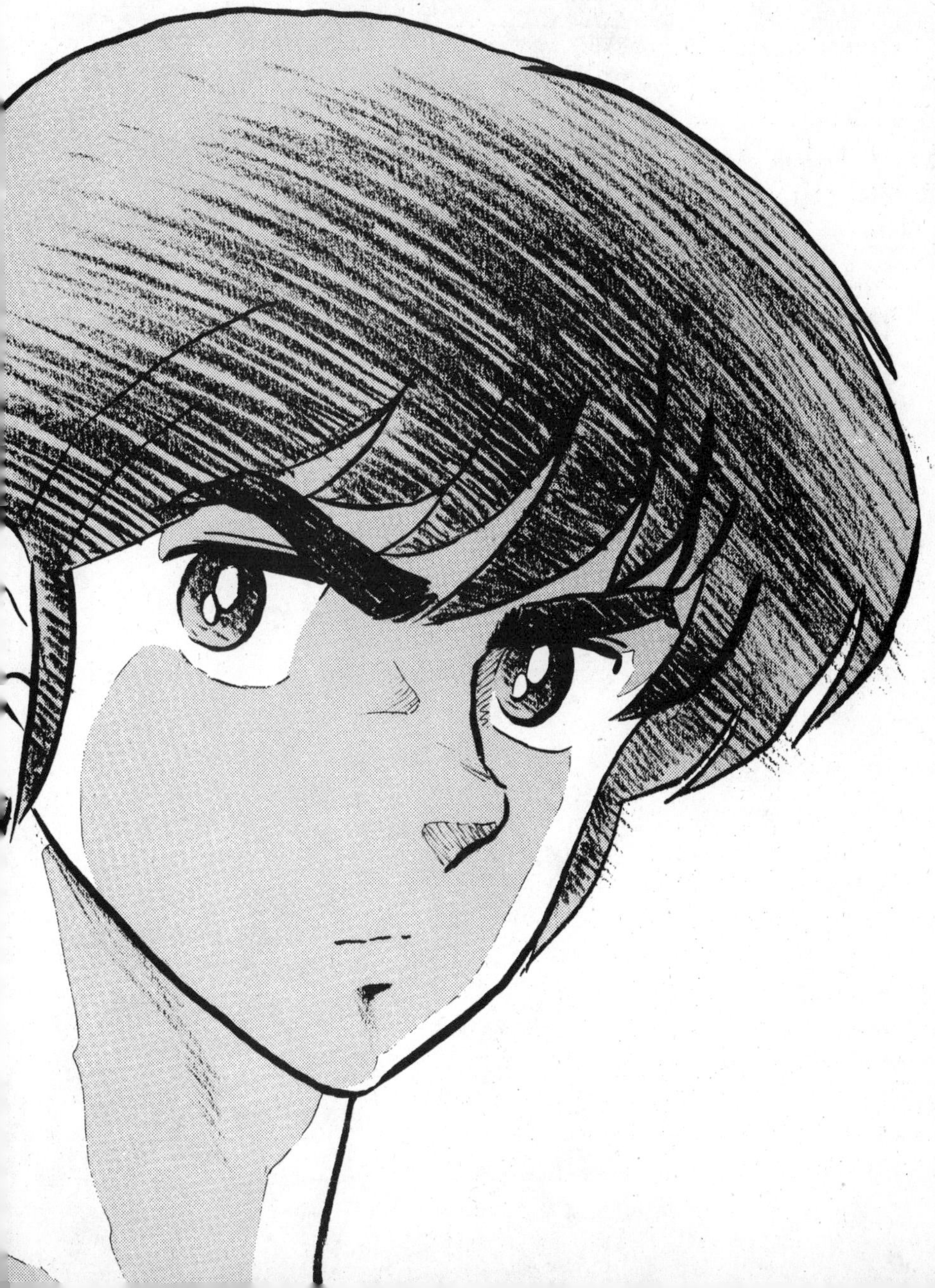

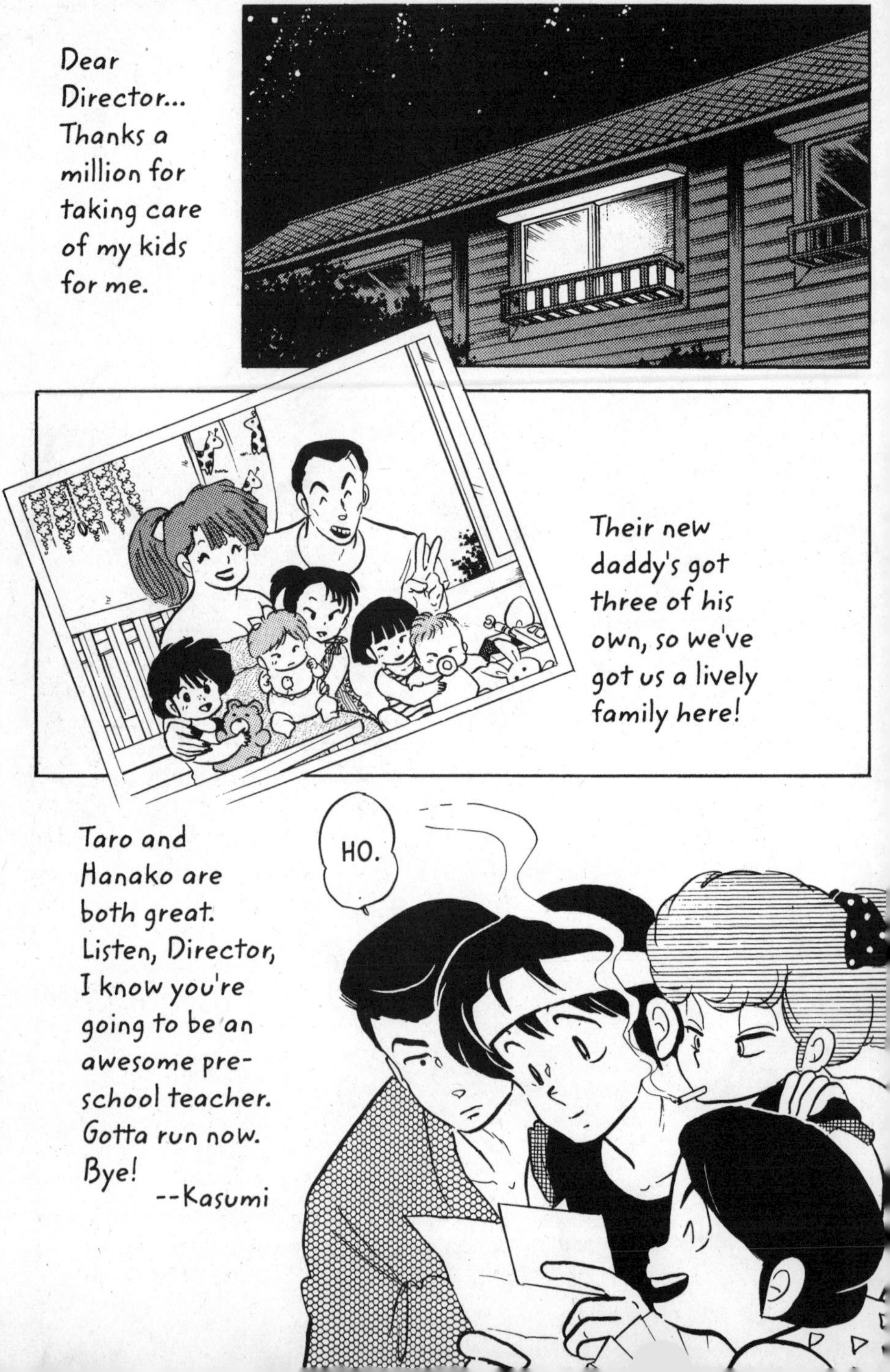
Dear Director... Thanks a million for taking care of my kids for me.
Their new daddy's got three of his own, so we've got us a lively family here!
Taro and Hanako are both great. Listen, Director, I know you're going to be an awesome pre-school teacher. Gotta run now. Bye! --Kasumi
HO.

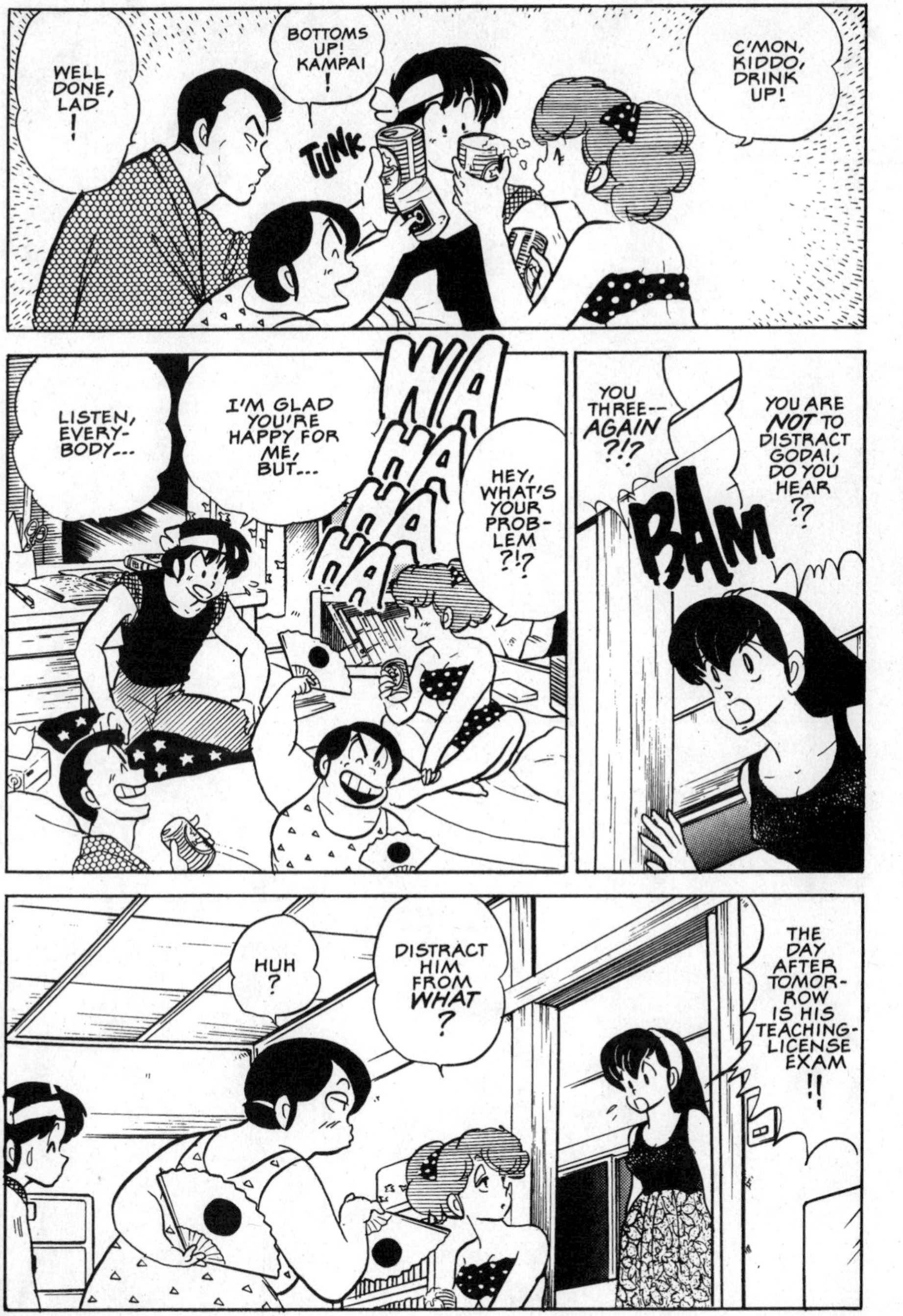
WELL DONE, LAD!
BOTTOMS UP! KAMPAI!
TUNK
C'MON, KIDDO, DRINK UP!
LISTEN, EVERY-BODY...
I'M GLAD YOU'RE HAPPY FOR ME, BUT...
WA HA HA HA HA HA
HEY, WHAT'S YOUR PROB-LEM?!?
YOU THREE-- AGAIN?!?
YOU ARE NOT TO DISTRACT GODAI, DO YOU HEAR??
BAM
HUH?
DISTRACT HIM FROM WHAT?
THE DAY AFTER TOMOR-ROW IS HIS TEACHING-LICENSE EXAM!!

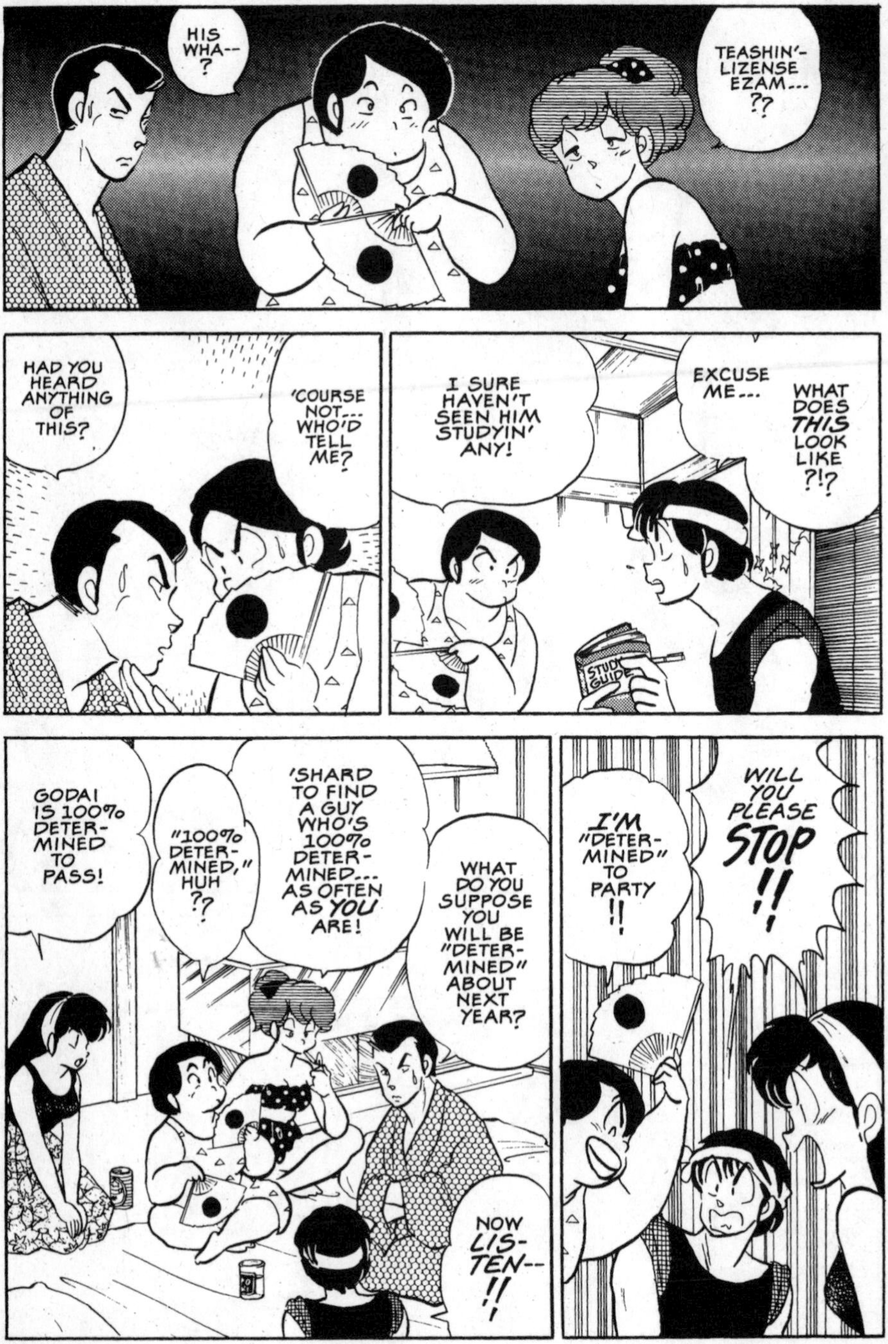
HIS WHA--?
TEASHIN'-LIZENSE EZAM...??
HAD YOU HEARD ANYTHING OF THIS?
'COURSE NOT... WHO'D TELL ME?
I SURE HAVEN'T SEEN HIM STUDYIN' ANY!
EXCUSE ME...
WHAT DOES *THIS* LOOK LIKE ?!?
STUDY GUIDE
GODAI IS 100% DETERMINED TO PASS!
"100% DETERMINED," HUH ??
'SHARD TO FIND A GUY WHO'S 100% DETERMINED... AS OFTEN AS *YOU* ARE!
WHAT DO YOU SUPPOSE YOU WILL BE "DETERMINED" ABOUT NEXT YEAR?
NOW *LISTEN*--!!
I'M "DETERMINED" TO PARTY !!
WILL YOU PLEASE STOP !!

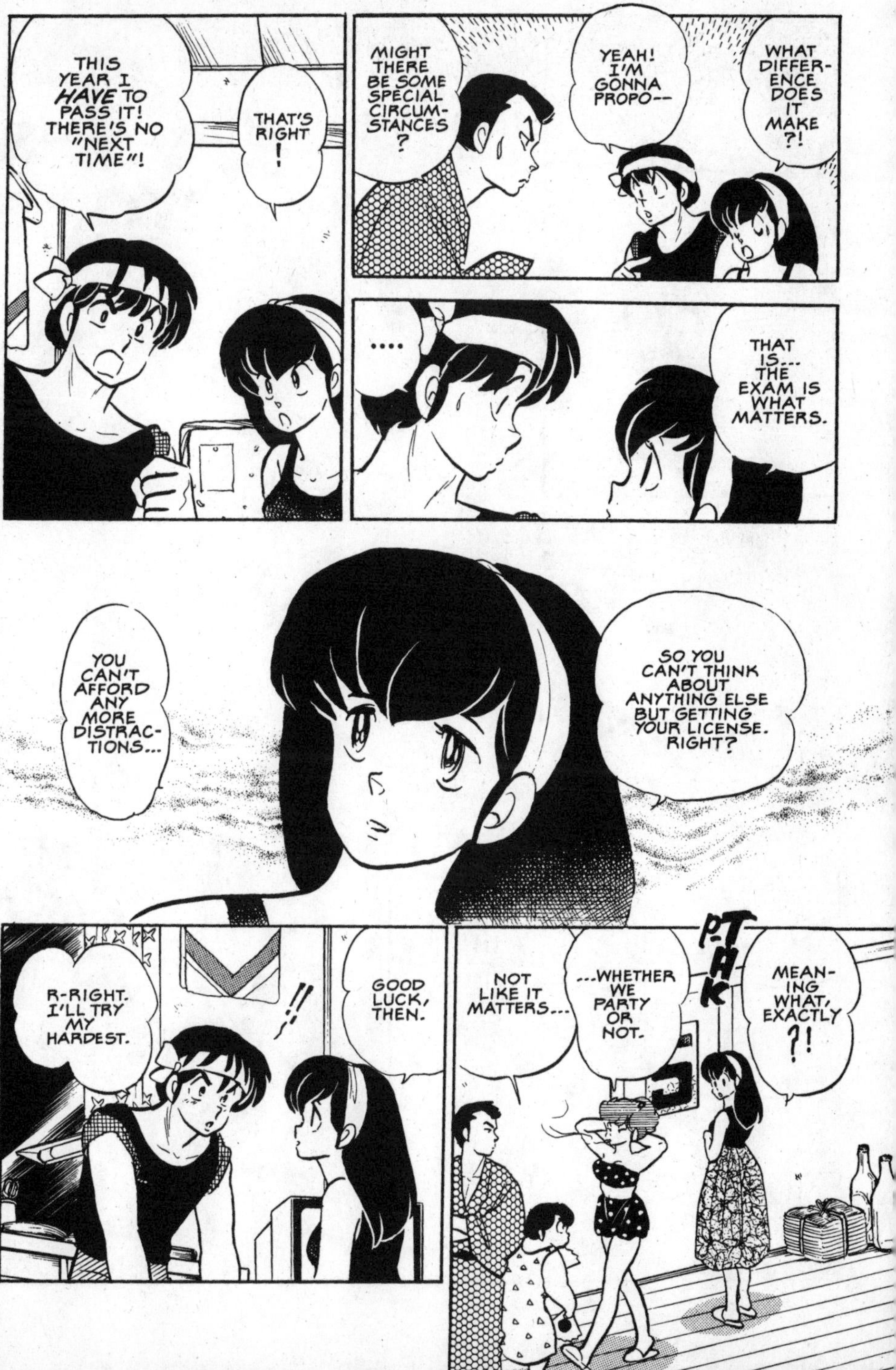
THIS YEAR I *HAVE* TO PASS IT! THERE'S NO "NEXT TIME"!
THAT'S RIGHT!
MIGHT THERE BE SOME SPECIAL CIRCUMSTANCES?
YEAH! I'M GONNA PROPO--
WHAT DIFFERENCE DOES IT MAKE?!
....
THAT IS... THE EXAM IS WHAT MATTERS.
YOU CAN'T AFFORD ANY MORE DISTRACTIONS...
SO YOU CAN'T THINK ABOUT ANYTHING ELSE BUT GETTING YOUR LICENSE. RIGHT?
R-RIGHT. I'LL TRY MY HARDEST.
!!
GOOD LUCK, THEN.
NOT LIKE IT MATTERS...
...WHETHER WE PARTY OR NOT.
P-THK
MEANING WHAT, EXACTLY?!

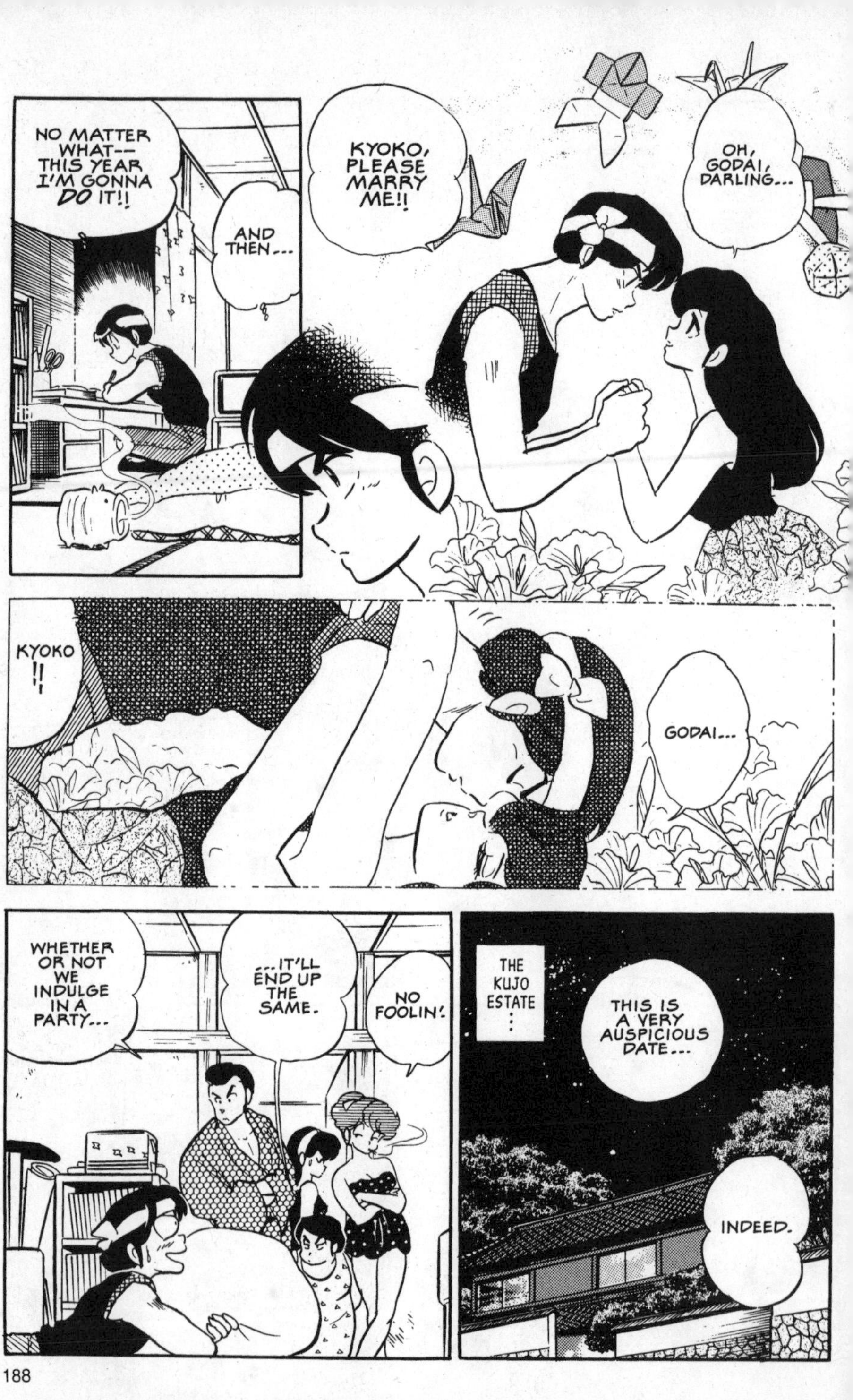
NO MATTER WHAT-- THIS YEAR I'M GONNA DO IT!!
AND THEN...
KYOKO, PLEASE MARRY ME!!
OH, GODAI, DARLING...
KYOKO !!
GODAI...
WHETHER OR NOT WE INDULGE IN A PARTY...
...IT'LL END UP THE SAME.
NO FOOLIN'.
THE KUJO ESTATE ...
THIS IS A VERY AUSPICIOUS DATE...
INDEED.

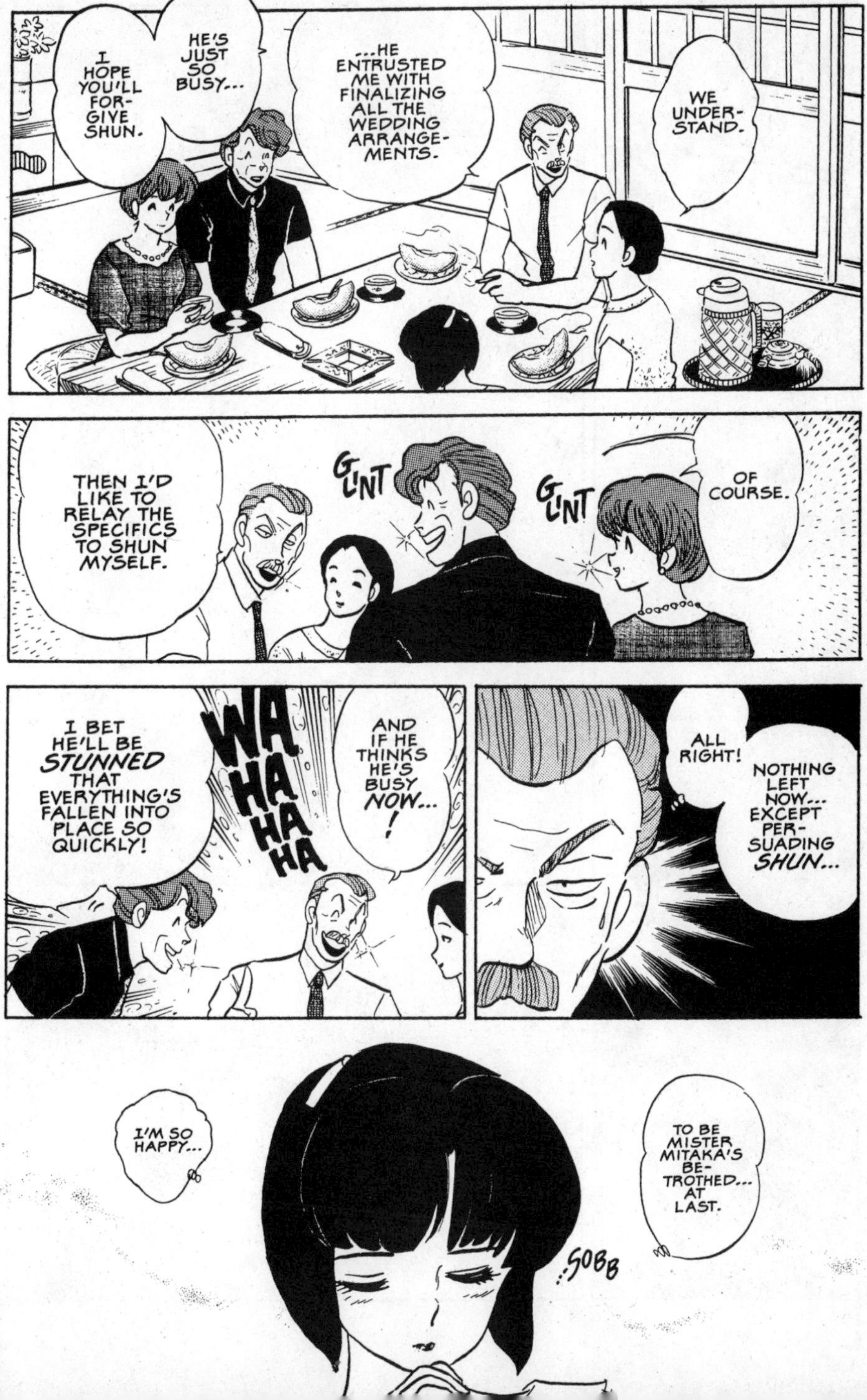
I HOPE YOU'LL FOR-GIVE SHUN.
HE'S JUST SO BUSY...
...HE ENTRUSTED ME WITH FINALIZING ALL THE WEDDING ARRANGE-MENTS.
WE UNDER-STAND.
THEN I'D LIKE TO RELAY THE SPECIFICS TO SHUN MYSELF.
GLINT
GLINT
OF COURSE.
I BET HE'LL BE STUNNED THAT EVERYTHING'S FALLEN INTO PLACE SO QUICKLY!
WA HA HA HA HA
AND IF HE THINKS HE'S BUSY NOW...!
ALL RIGHT!
NOTHING LEFT NOW... EXCEPT PER-SUADING SHUN...
I'M SO HAPPY...
TO BE MISTER MITAKA'S BE-TROTHED... AT LAST.
SOBB

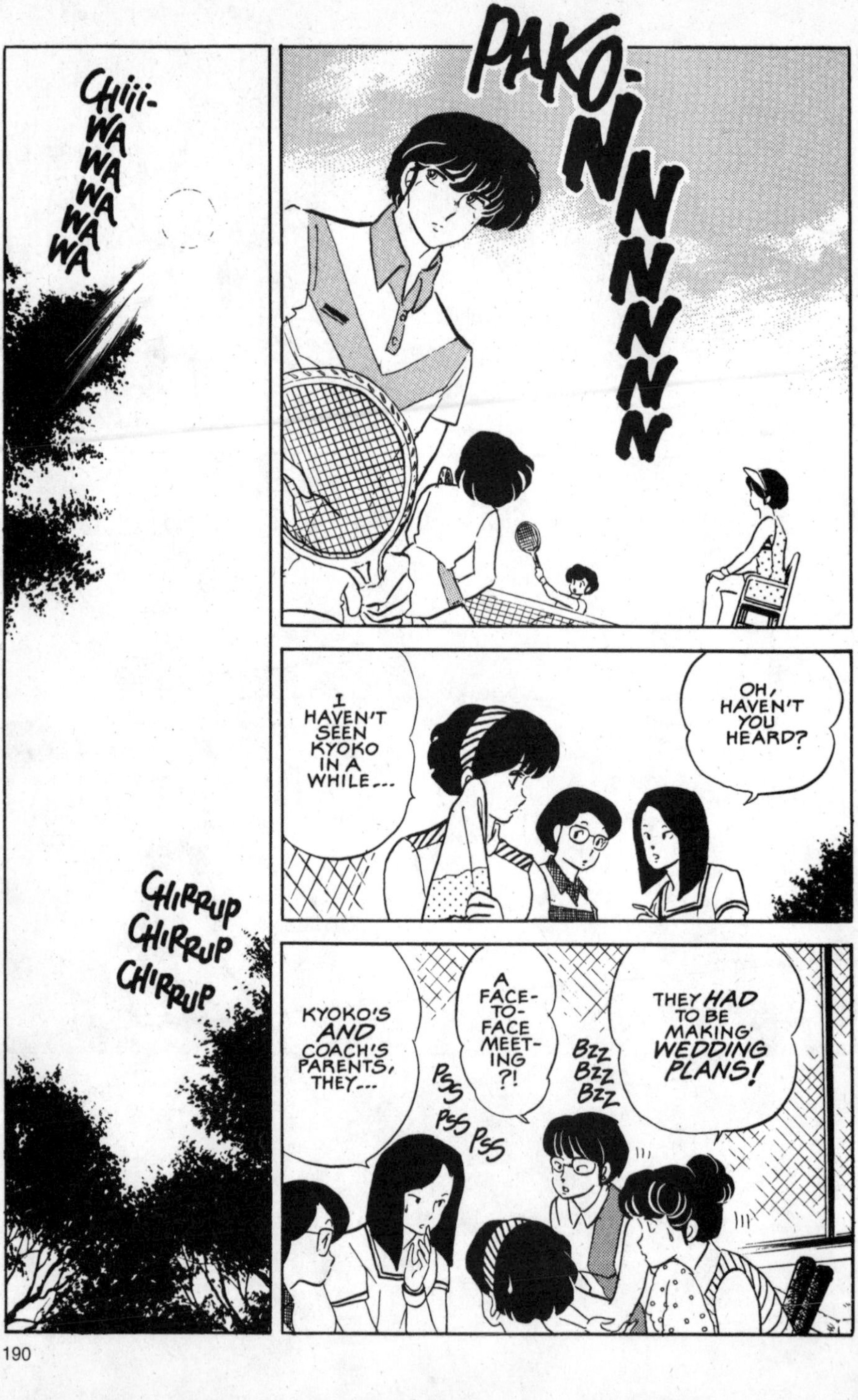
CHIiii-WAWAWAWAWAWA
CHIRRUP CHIRRUP CHIRRUP
PAKO-NNNNNNN
I HAVEN'T SEEN KYOKO IN A WHILE...
OH, HAVEN'T YOU HEARD?
KYOKO'S AND COACH'S PARENTS, THEY...
PSS PSS PSS
A FACE-TO-FACE MEETING?!
BZZ BZZ BZZ
THEY HAD TO BE MAKING' WEDDING PLANS!

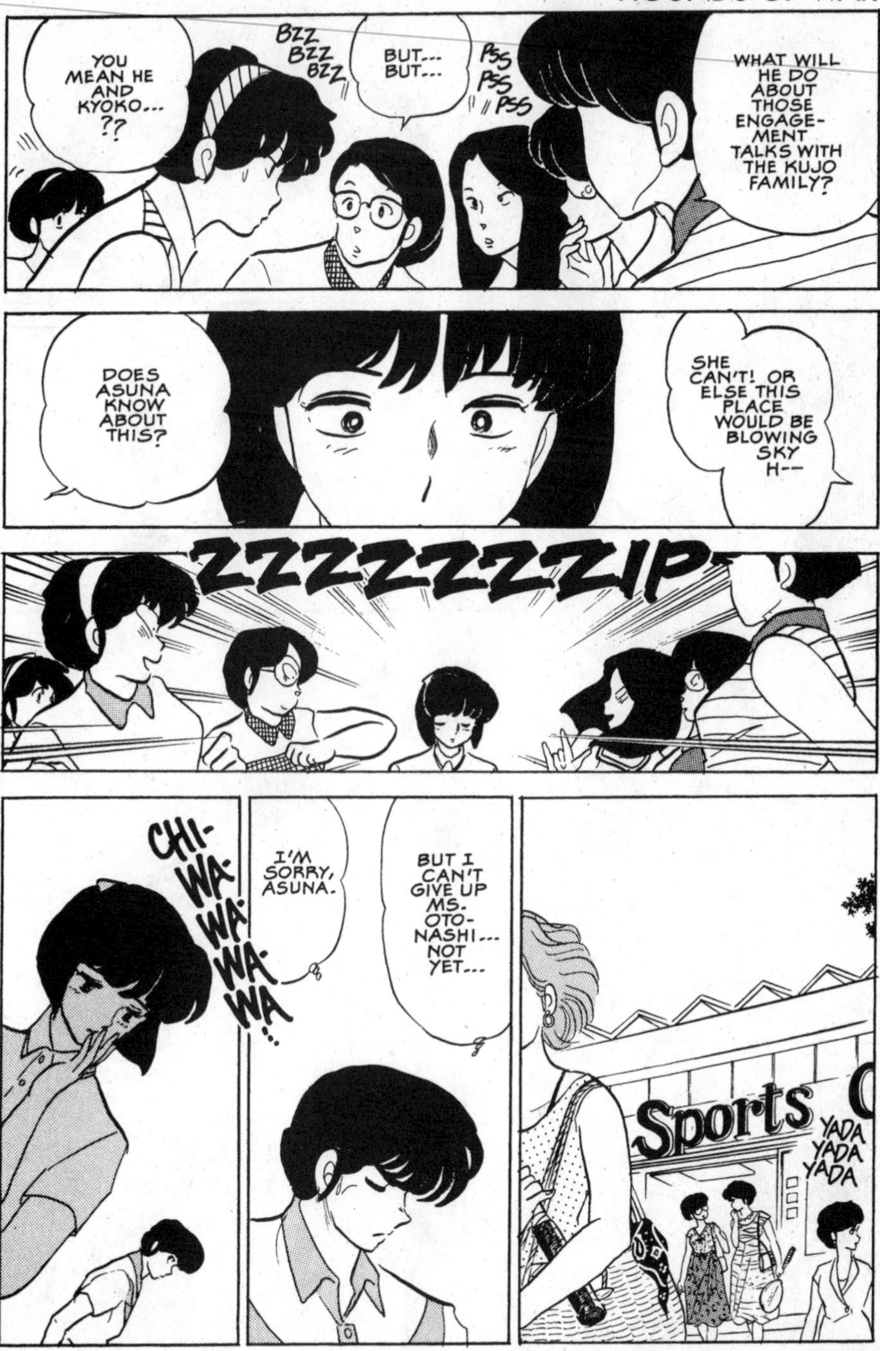
YOU MEAN HE AND KYOKO... ??
BZZ BZZ BZZ
BUT... BUT...
PSS PSS PSS
WHAT WILL HE DO ABOUT THOSE ENGAGE-MENT TALKS WITH THE KUJO FAMILY?
DOES ASUNA KNOW ABOUT THIS?
SHE CAN'T! OR ELSE THIS PLACE WOULD BE BLOWING SKY H--
ZZZZZZZZIP
CHI-WA-WA-WA-WA-WA...
I'M SORRY, ASUNA.
BUT I CAN'T GIVE UP MS. OTO-NASHI... NOT YET...
Sports
YADA YADA YADA

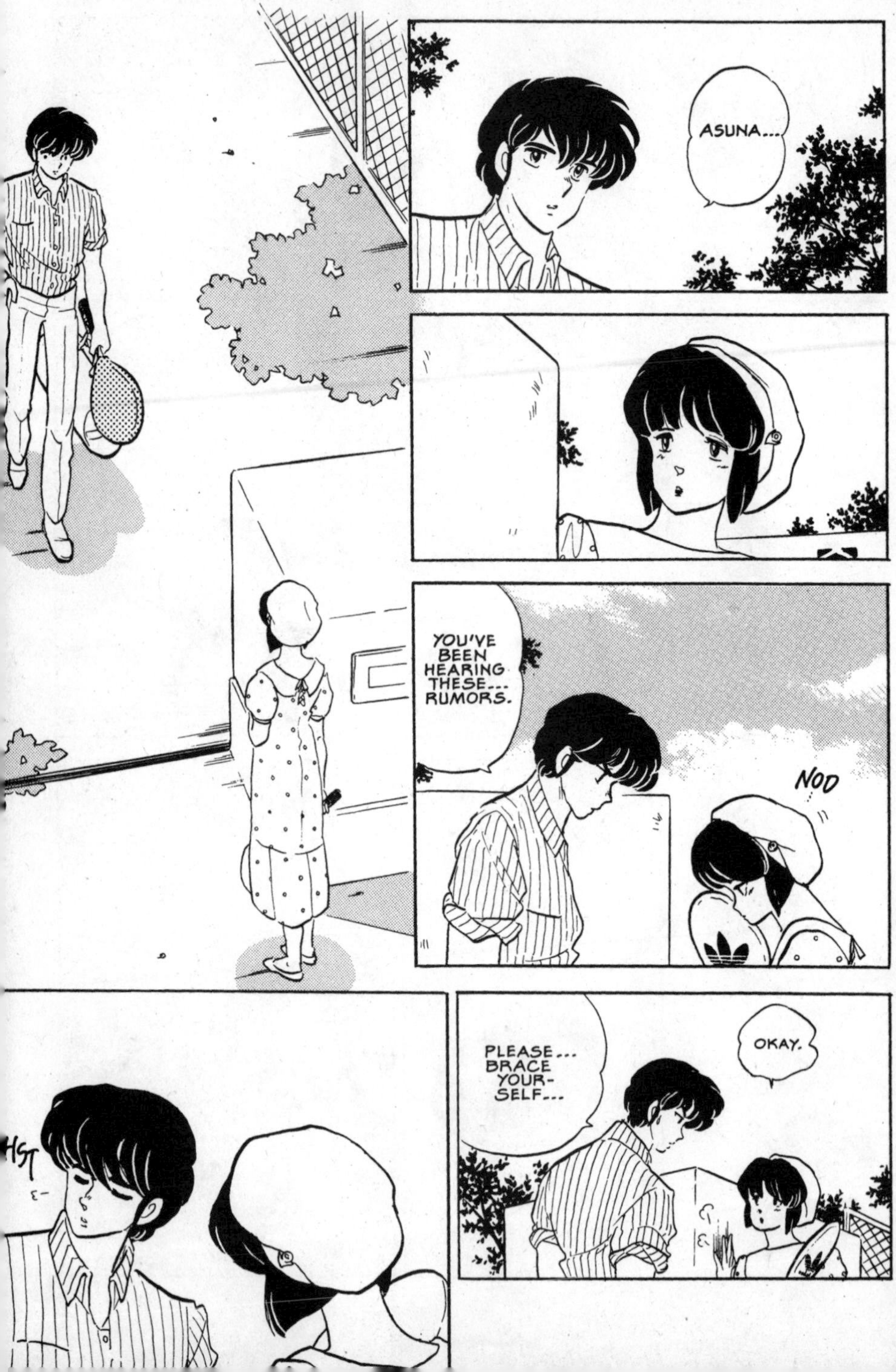
ASUNA...
YOU'VE BEEN HEARING THESE... RUMORS.
NOD
PLEASE... BRACE YOUR-SELF...
OKAY.

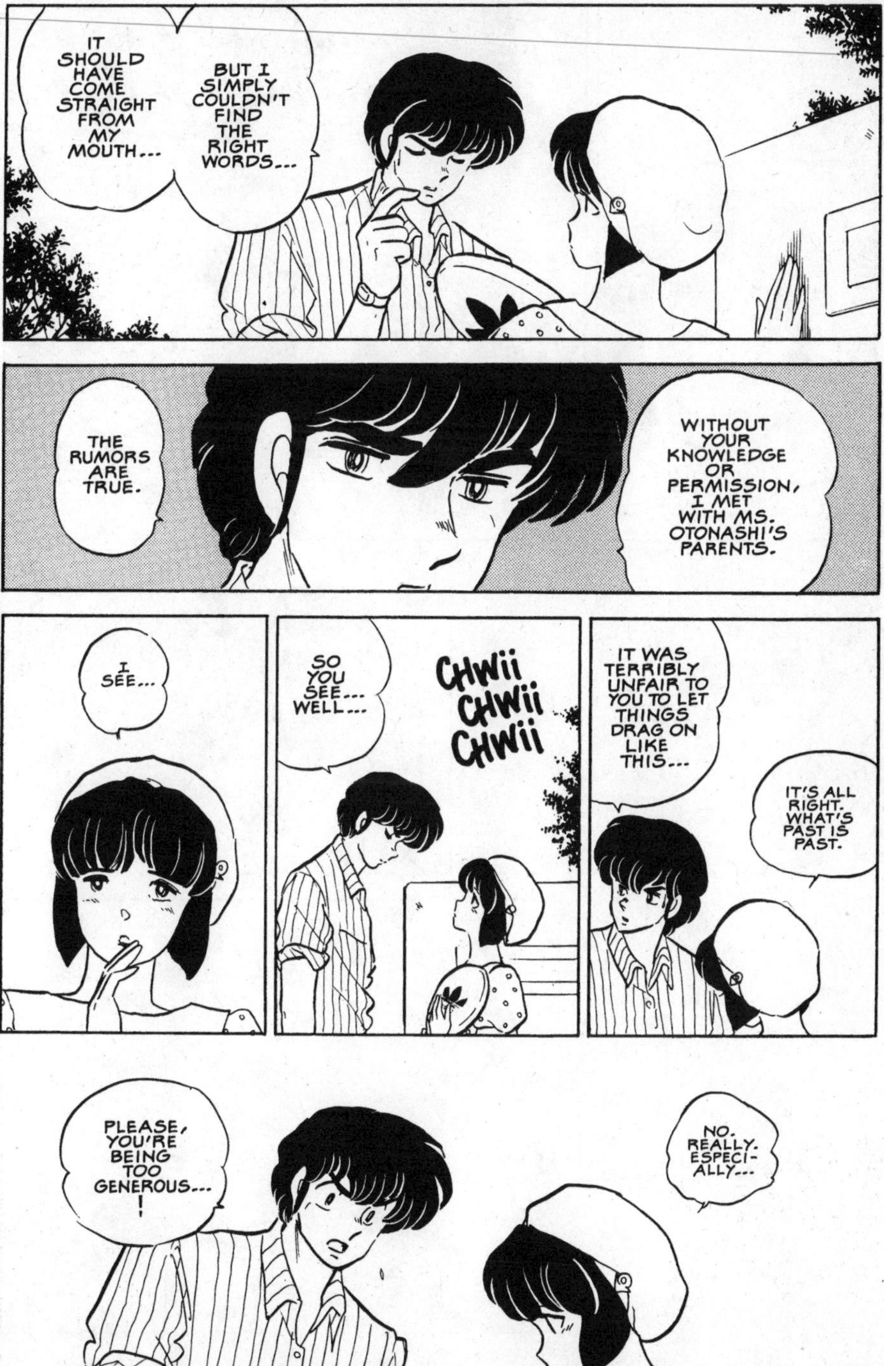
IT SHOULD HAVE COME STRAIGHT FROM MY MOUTH...
BUT I SIMPLY COULDN'T FIND THE RIGHT WORDS...
THE RUMORS ARE TRUE.
WITHOUT YOUR KNOWLEDGE OR PERMISSION, I MET WITH MS. OTONASHI'S PARENTS.
I SEE...
SO YOU SEE... WELL...
CHWii CHWii CHWii
IT WAS TERRIBLY UNFAIR TO YOU TO LET THINGS DRAG ON LIKE THIS...
IT'S ALL RIGHT. WHAT'S PAST IS PAST.
PLEASE, YOU'RE BEING TOO GENEROUS...
!
NO. REALLY. ESPECI-ALLY...

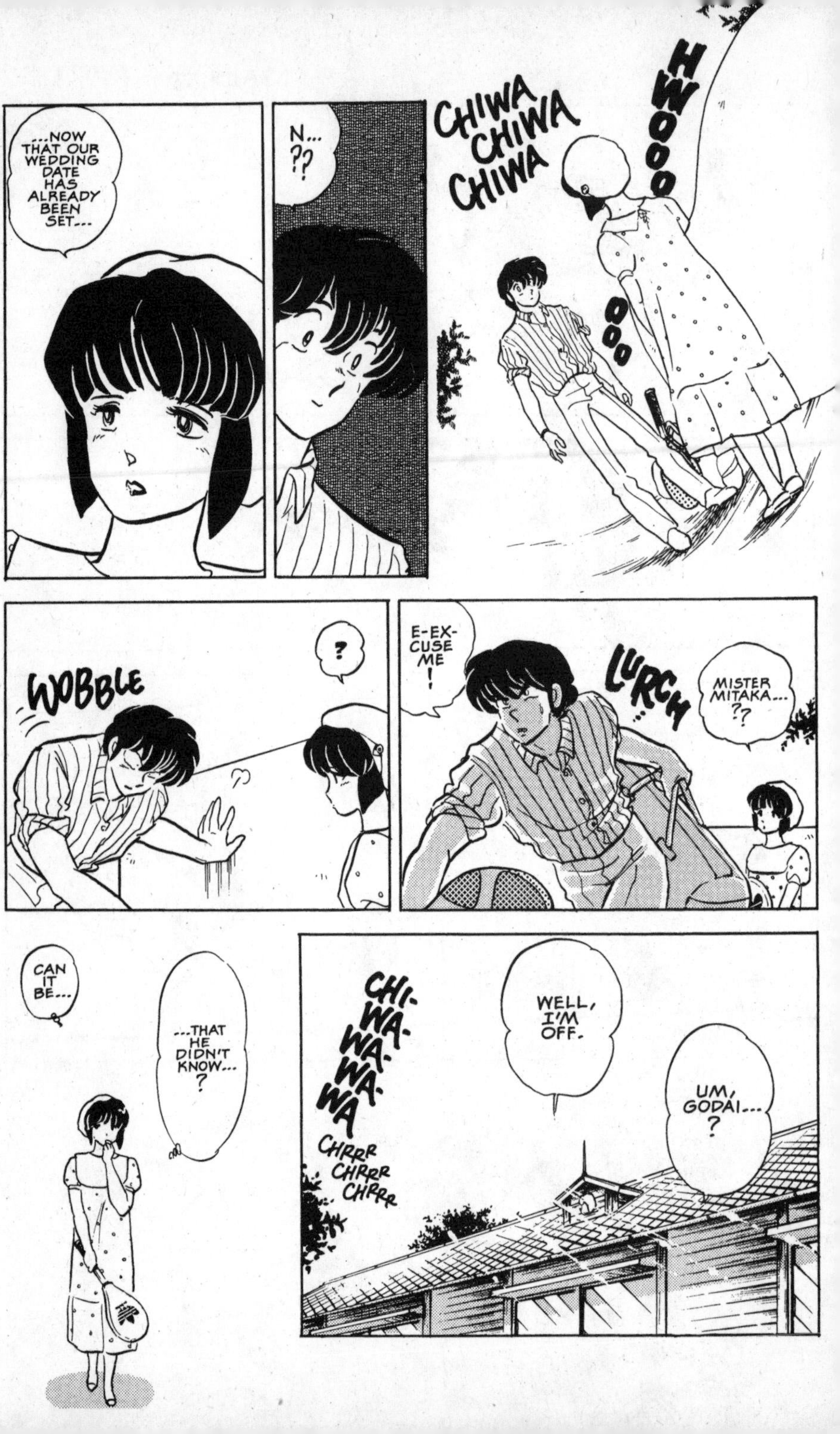
...NOW THAT OUR WEDDING DATE HAS ALREADY BEEN SET...
N... ??
CHIWA CHIWA CHIWA
HWOOOOOOO
WOBBLE
?
E-EXCUSE ME!
LURCH
MISTER MITAKA... ??
CAN IT BE...
...THAT HE DIDN'T KNOW...?
CHI-WA-WA-WA-WA
CHRRR CHRRR CHRRR
WELL, I'M OFF.
UM, GODAI...?

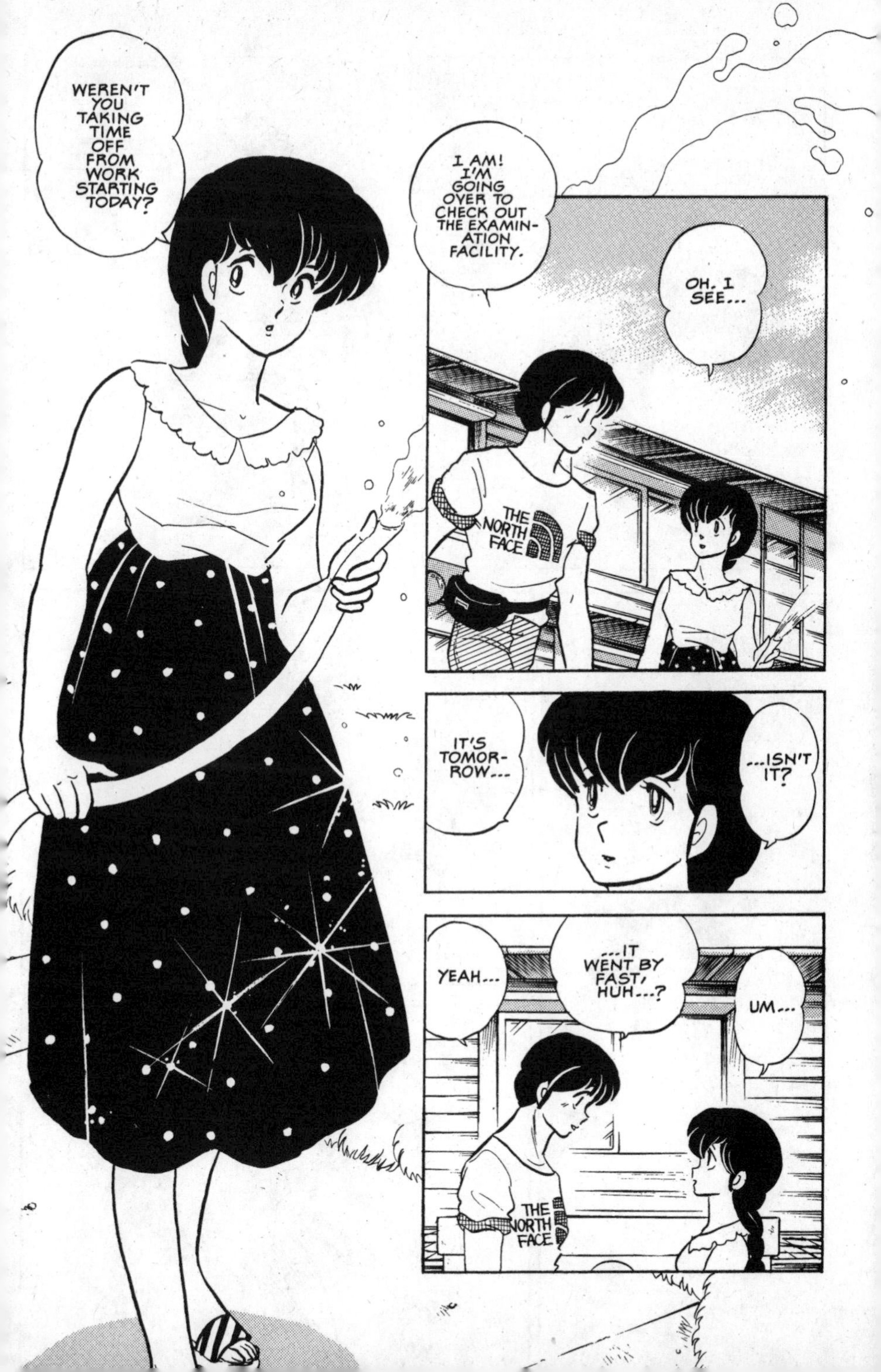
WEREN'T YOU TAKING TIME OFF FROM WORK STARTING TODAY?
I AM! I'M GOING OVER TO CHECK OUT THE EXAMINATION FACILITY.
OH. I SEE...
IT'S TOMORROW...
...ISN'T IT?
YEAH...
...IT WENT BY FAST, HUH...?
UM...

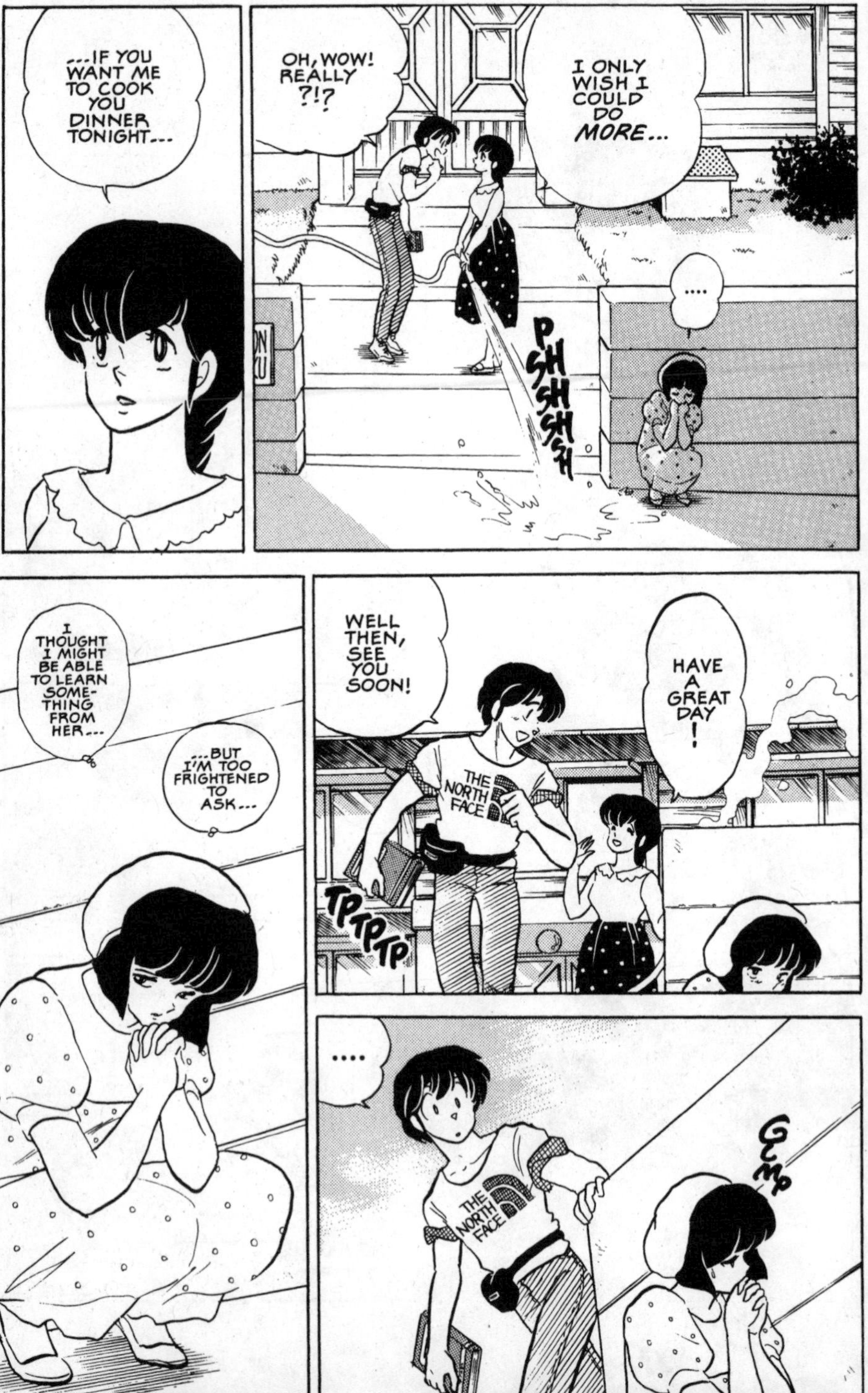
...IF YOU WANT ME TO COOK YOU DINNER TONIGHT...
OH, WOW! REALLY ?!?
I ONLY WISH I COULD DO MORE...
....
PSHSHSHSHSH
I THOUGHT I MIGHT BE ABLE TO LEARN SOMETHING FROM HER...
...BUT I'M TOO FRIGHTENED TO ASK...
WELL THEN, SEE YOU SOON!
HAVE A GREAT DAY !
TPTPTPTP
THE NORTH FACE
....
GLMP
THE NORTH FACE

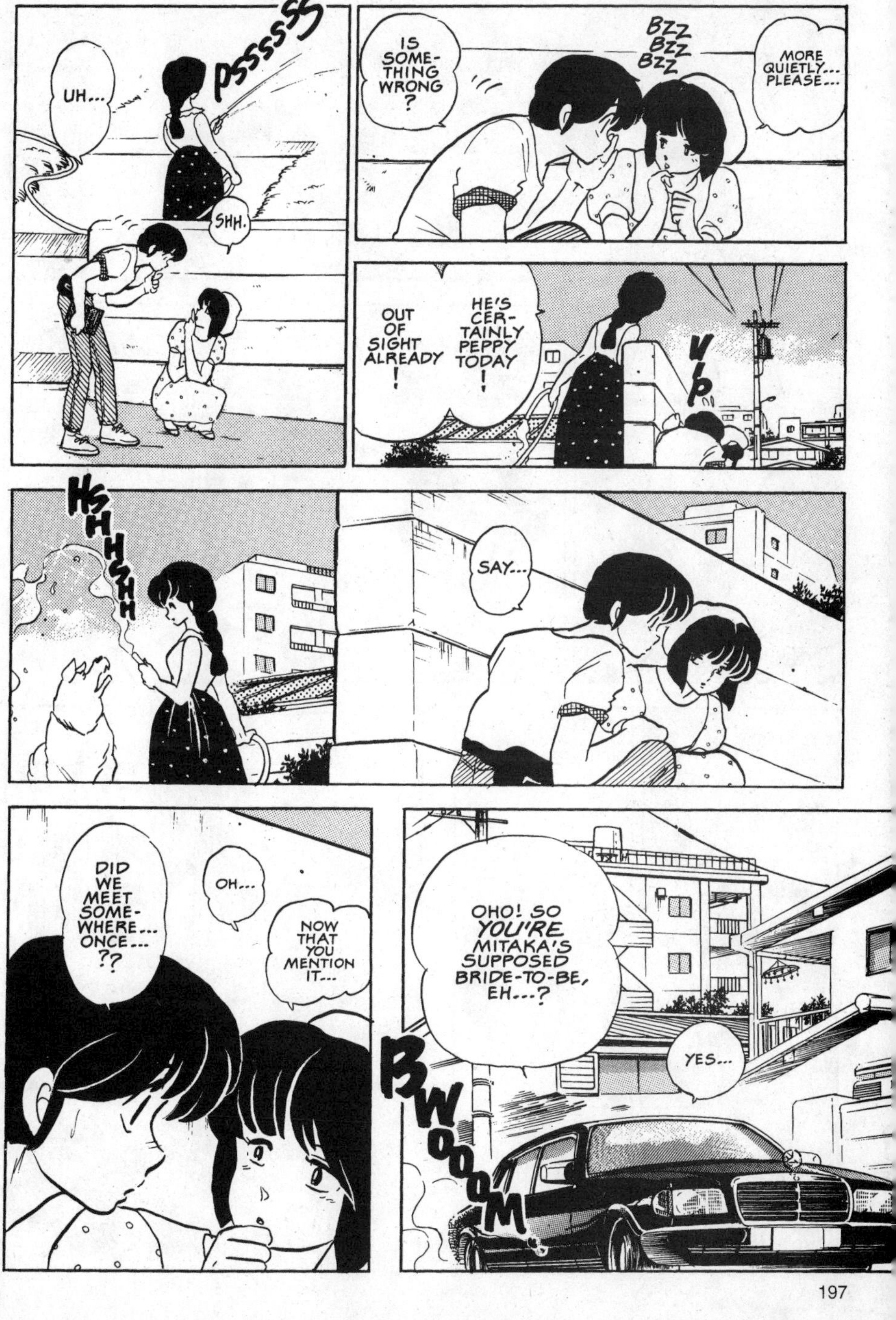
UH...
PSSSSSS
SHH.
IS SOME-THING WRONG ?
BZZ BZZ BZZ
MORE QUIETLY... PLEASE...
OUT OF SIGHT ALREADY !
HE'S CER-TAINLY PEPPY TODAY !
VIP
HSHHSHH
SAY...
DID WE MEET SOME-WHERE... ONCE...??
OH...
NOW THAT YOU MENTION IT...
OHO! SO YOU'RE MITAKA'S SUPPOSED BRIDE-TO-BE, EH...?
YES...
BWOOOOM

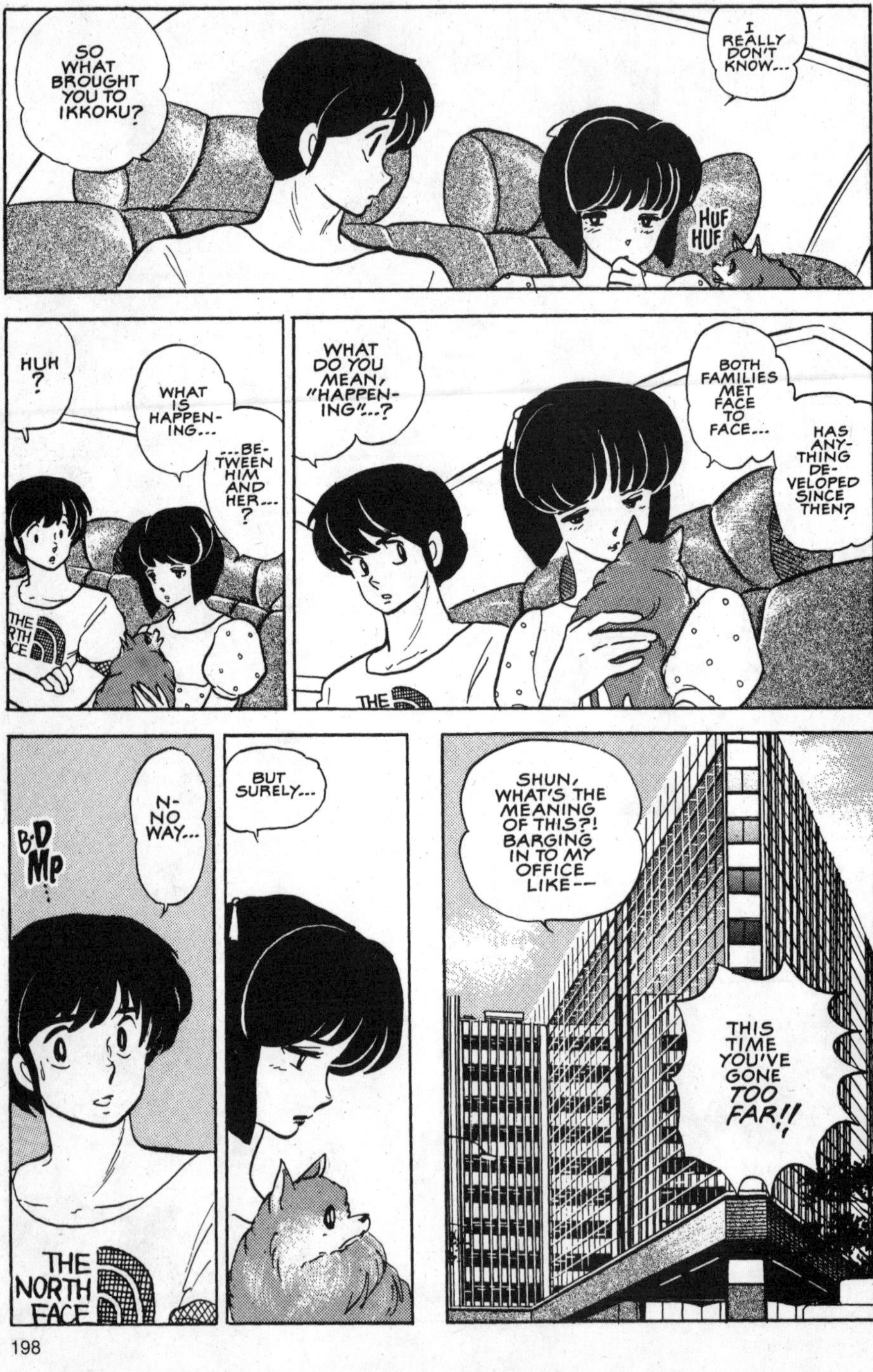
SO WHAT BROUGHT YOU TO IKKOKU?
I REALLY DON'T KNOW...
HUF HUF
HUH?
WHAT IS HAPPENING...
...BETWEEN HIM AND HER...?
WHAT DO YOU MEAN, "HAPPENING"...?
BOTH FAMILIES MET FACE TO FACE...
HAS ANYTHING DEVELOPED SINCE THEN?
THE NORTH FACE
N-NO WAY...
B-DMP
BUT SURELY...
SHUN, WHAT'S THE MEANING OF THIS?! BARGING IN TO MY OFFICE LIKE--
THIS TIME YOU'VE GONE TOO FAR!!

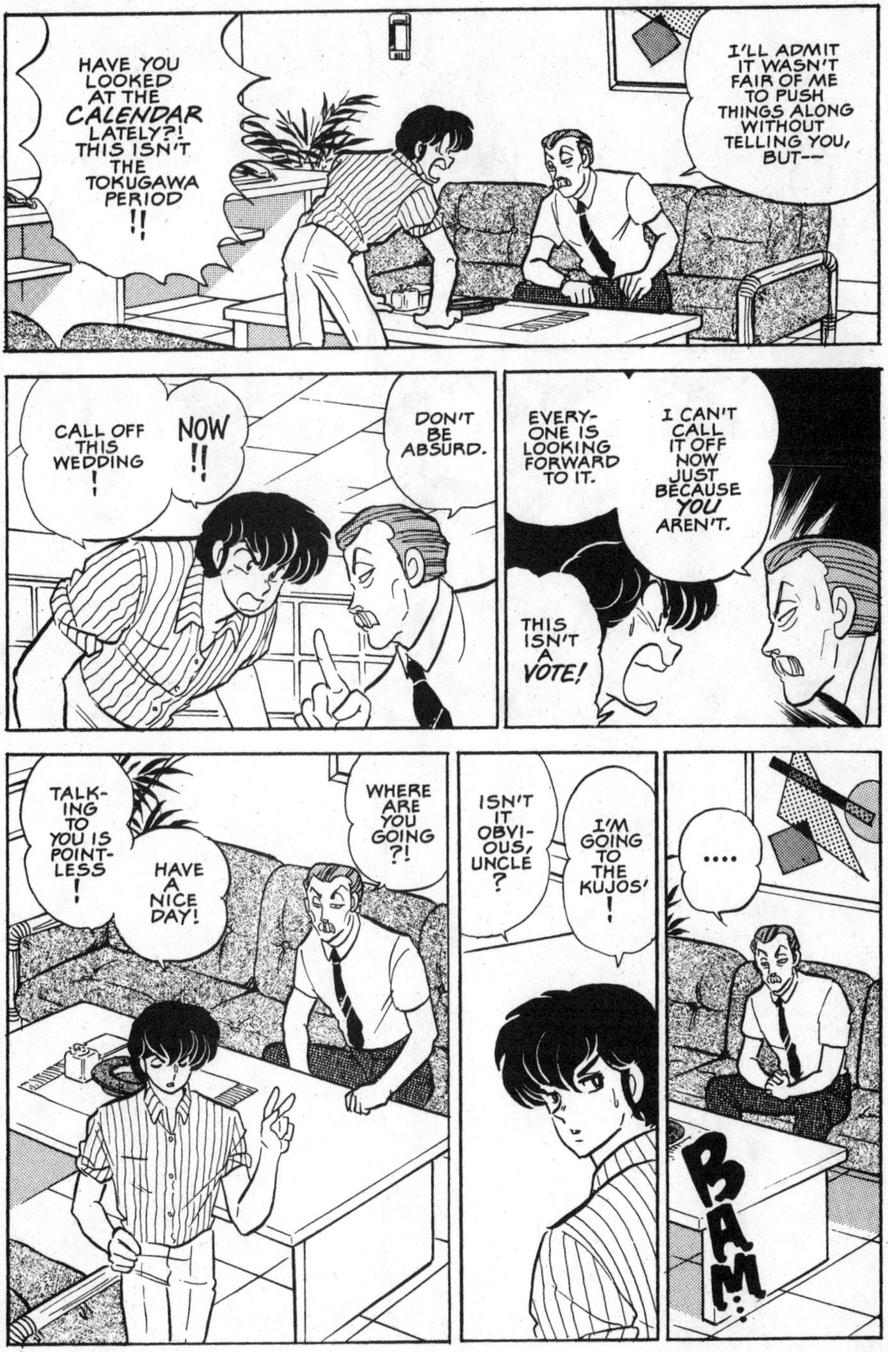
HAVE YOU LOOKED AT THE CALENDAR LATELY?! THIS ISN'T THE TOKUGAWA PERIOD !!
I'LL ADMIT IT WASN'T FAIR OF ME TO PUSH THINGS ALONG WITHOUT TELLING YOU, BUT--
CALL OFF THIS WEDDING !
NOW !!
DON'T BE ABSURD.
EVERY-ONE IS LOOKING FORWARD TO IT.
I CAN'T CALL IT OFF NOW JUST BECAUSE YOU AREN'T.
THIS ISN'T A VOTE!
TALK-ING TO YOU IS POINT-LESS !
HAVE A NICE DAY!
WHERE ARE YOU GOING ?!
ISN'T IT OBVI-OUS, UNCLE ?
I'M GOING TO THE KUJOS' !
....
BAM...

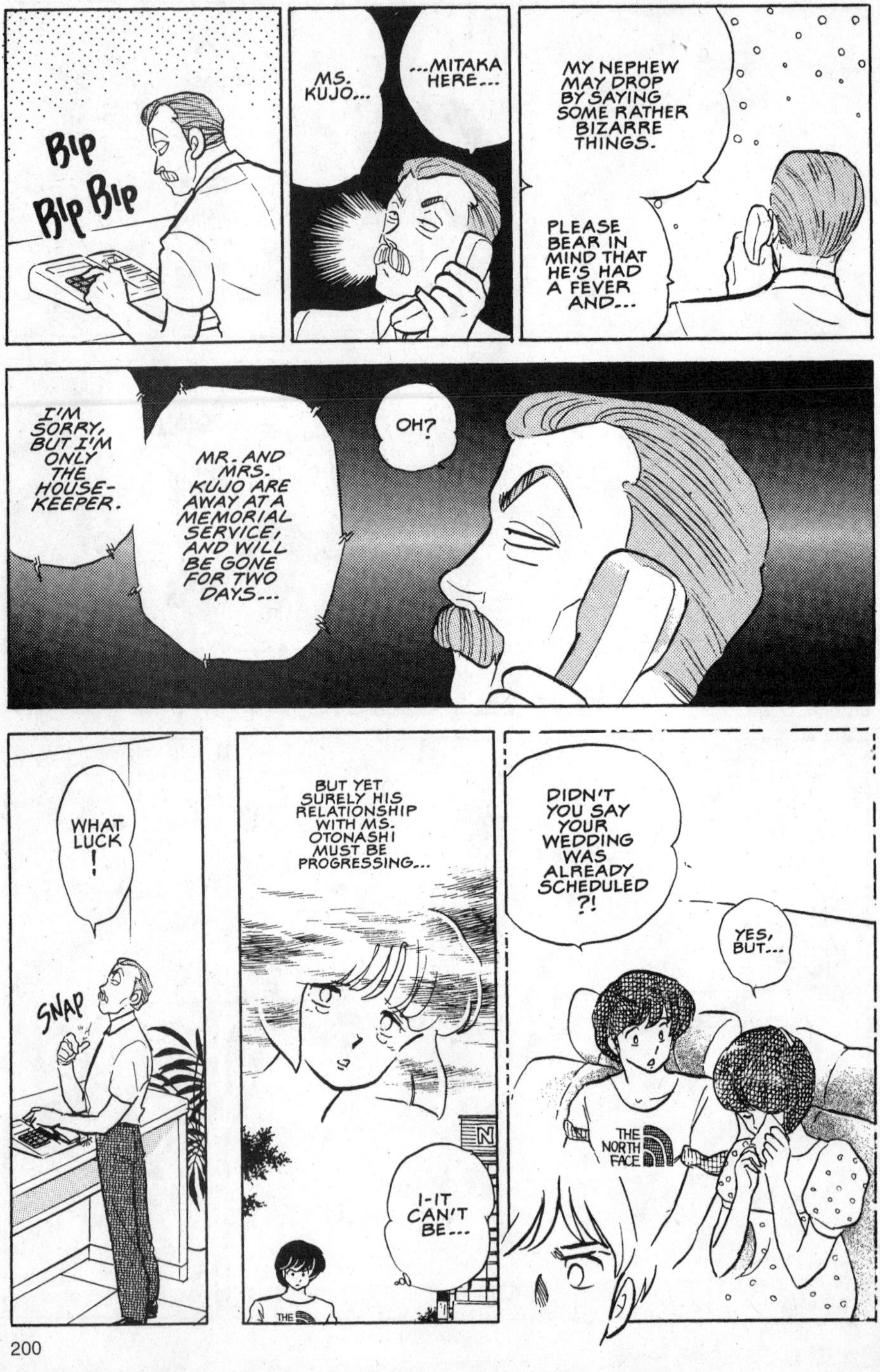
Bip
Bip Bip
MS. KUJO...
...MITAKA HERE...
MY NEPHEW MAY DROP BY SAYING SOME RATHER BIZARRE THINGS.
PLEASE BEAR IN MIND THAT HE'S HAD A FEVER AND...
I'M SORRY, BUT I'M ONLY THE HOUSE-KEEPER.
MR. AND MRS. KUJO ARE AWAY AT A MEMORIAL SERVICE, AND WILL BE GONE FOR TWO DAYS...
OH?
WHAT LUCK!
SNAP
BUT YET SURELY HIS RELATIONSHIP WITH MS. OTONASHI MUST BE PROGRESSING...
I-IT CAN'T BE...
DIDN'T YOU SAY YOUR WEDDING WAS ALREADY SCHEDULED?!
YES, BUT...
THE NORTH FACE

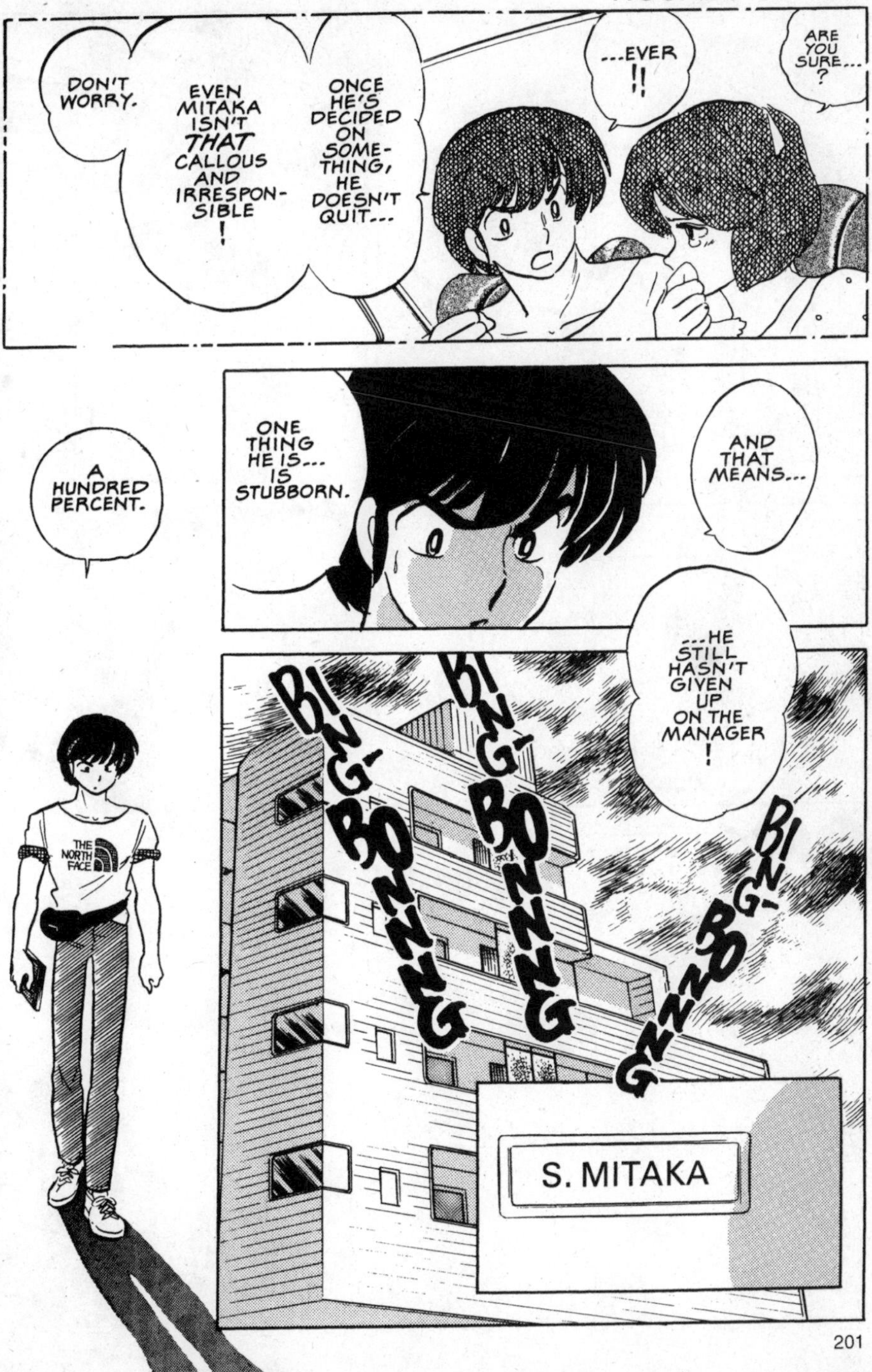
DON'T WORRY.
EVEN MITAKA ISN'T *THAT* CALLOUS AND IRRESPONSIBLE!
ONCE HE'S DECIDED ON SOMETHING, HE DOESN'T QUIT...
...EVER!!
ARE YOU SURE...?
A HUNDRED PERCENT.
ONE THING HE IS... IS STUBBORN.
AND THAT MEANS...
...HE STILL HASN'T GIVEN UP ON THE MANAGER!
THE NORTH FACE
BING-BONNG
BING-BONNG
BING-BONNG
S. MITAKA

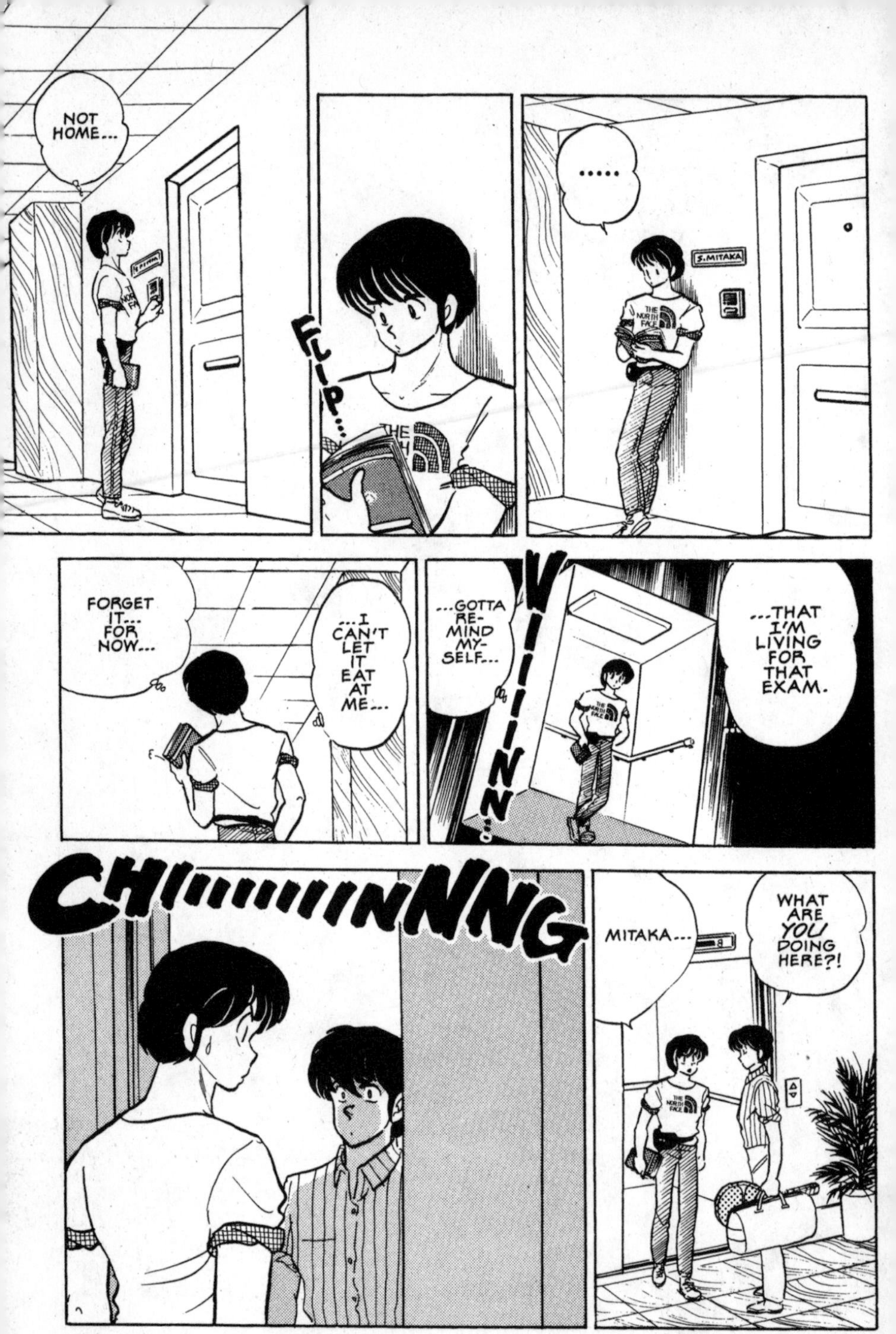

NOT HOME...
FLIP...
S. MITAKA
.....
FORGET IT... FOR NOW...
...I CAN'T LET IT EAT AT ME...
...GOTTA RE-MIND MY-SELF...
VIIIIINN...
...THAT I'M LIVING FOR THAT EXAM.
CHIIIIIIIINNNG
MITAKA...
WHAT ARE YOU DOING HERE?!

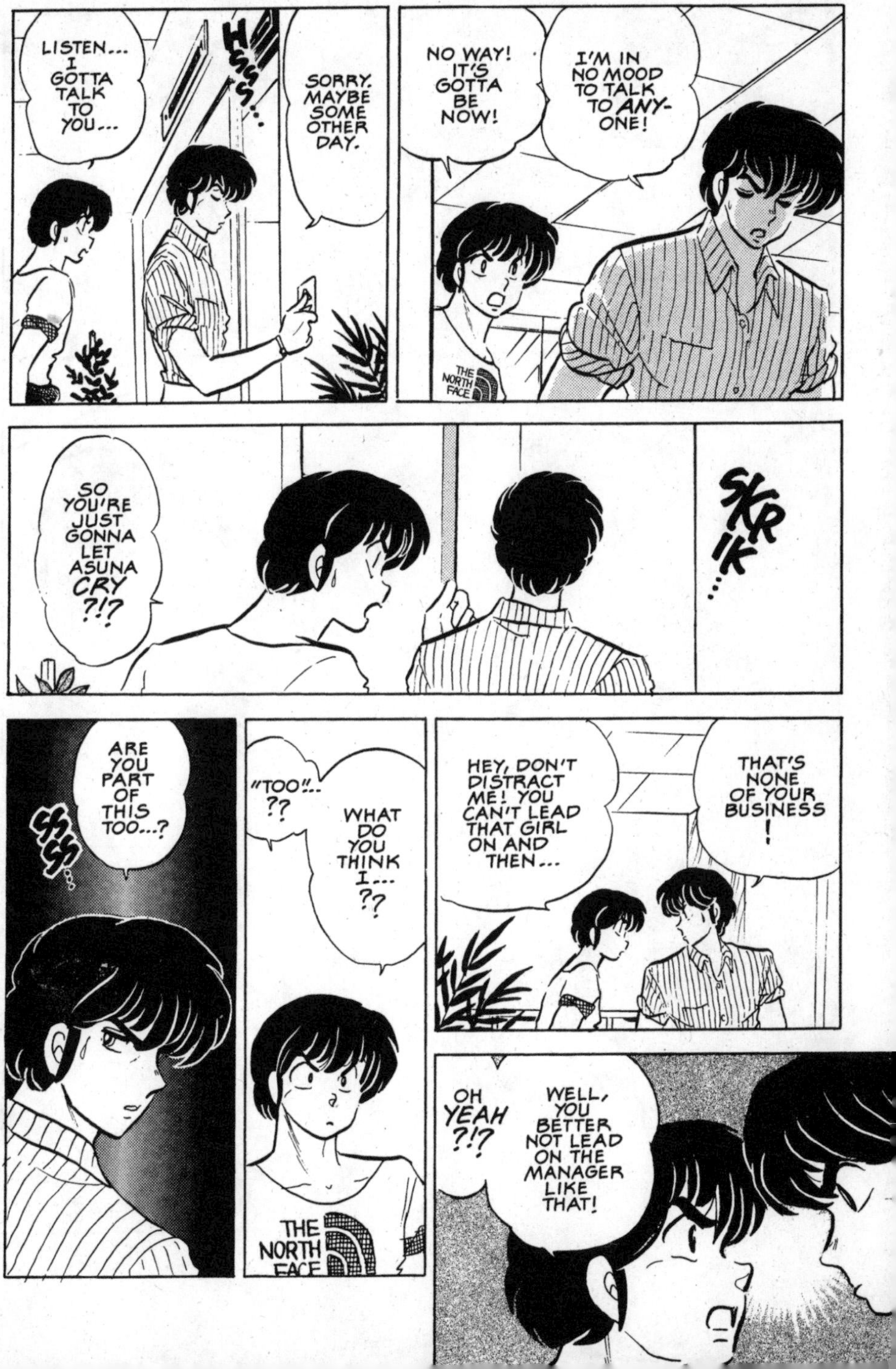
LISTEN... I GOTTA TALK TO YOU...
HSSS...
SORRY. MAYBE SOME OTHER DAY.
NO WAY! IT'S GOTTA BE NOW!
I'M IN NO MOOD TO TALK TO ANY-ONE!
THE NORTH FACE
SO YOU'RE JUST GONNA LET ASUNA CRY ?!?
SKRIK...
ARE YOU PART OF THIS TOO...?
SSS...
"TOO"...??
WHAT DO YOU THINK I...??
HEY, DON'T DISTRACT ME! YOU CAN'T LEAD THAT GIRL ON AND THEN...
THAT'S NONE OF YOUR BUSINESS!
THE NORTH FACE
OH YEAH ?!?
WELL, YOU BETTER NOT LEAD ON THE MANAGER LIKE THAT!

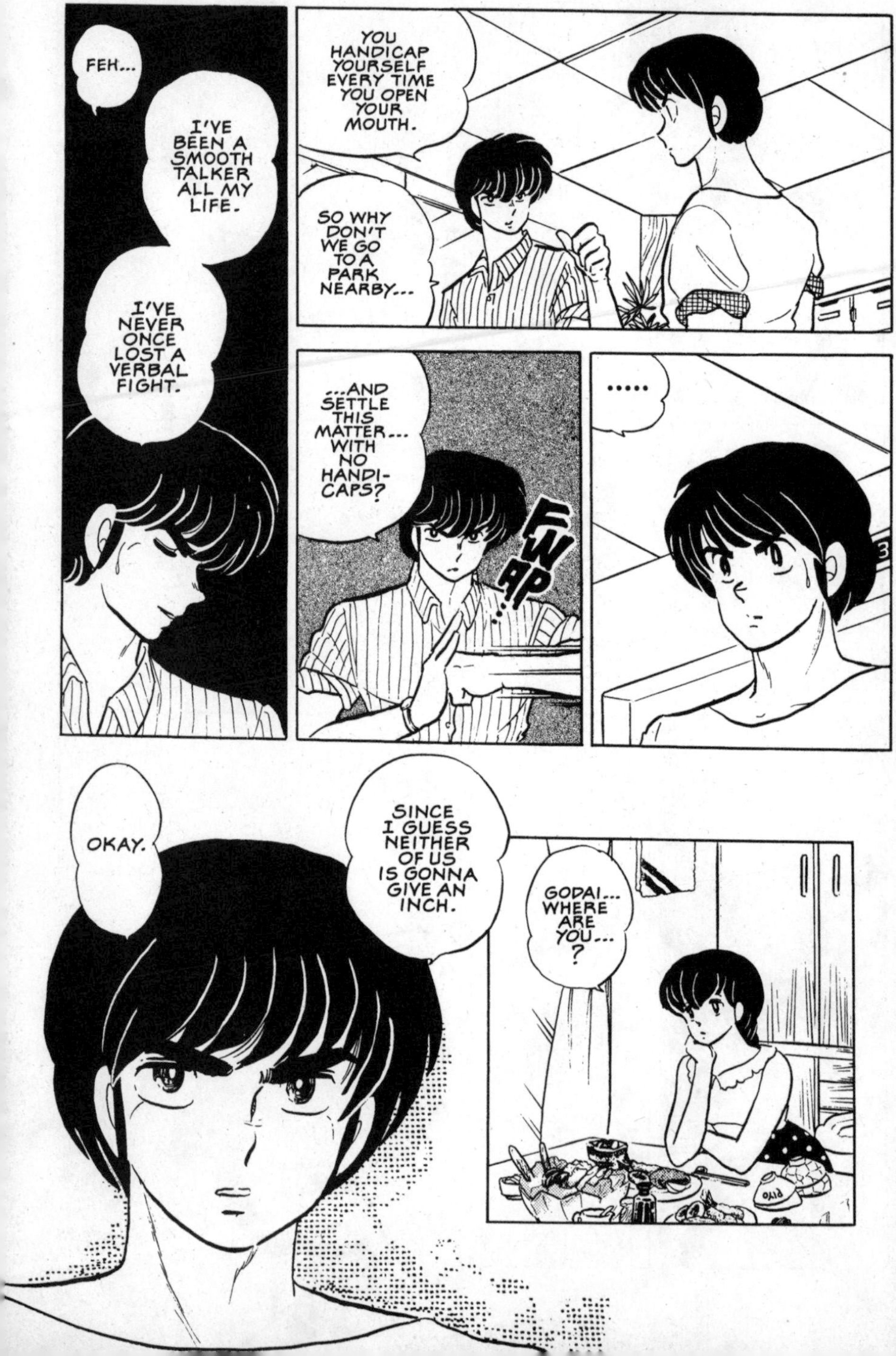
FEH...
I'VE BEEN A SMOOTH TALKER ALL MY LIFE.
I'VE NEVER ONCE LOST A VERBAL FIGHT.
YOU HANDICAP YOURSELF EVERY TIME YOU OPEN YOUR MOUTH.
SO WHY DON'T WE GO TO A PARK NEARBY...
...AND SETTLE THIS MATTER... WITH NO HANDI-CAPS?
FWAP
.....
OKAY.
SINCE I GUESS NEITHER OF US IS GONNA GIVE AN INCH.
GODAI... WHERE ARE YOU...?
KIYO

PART TWELVE

WE HAVE MET THE ENEMY...

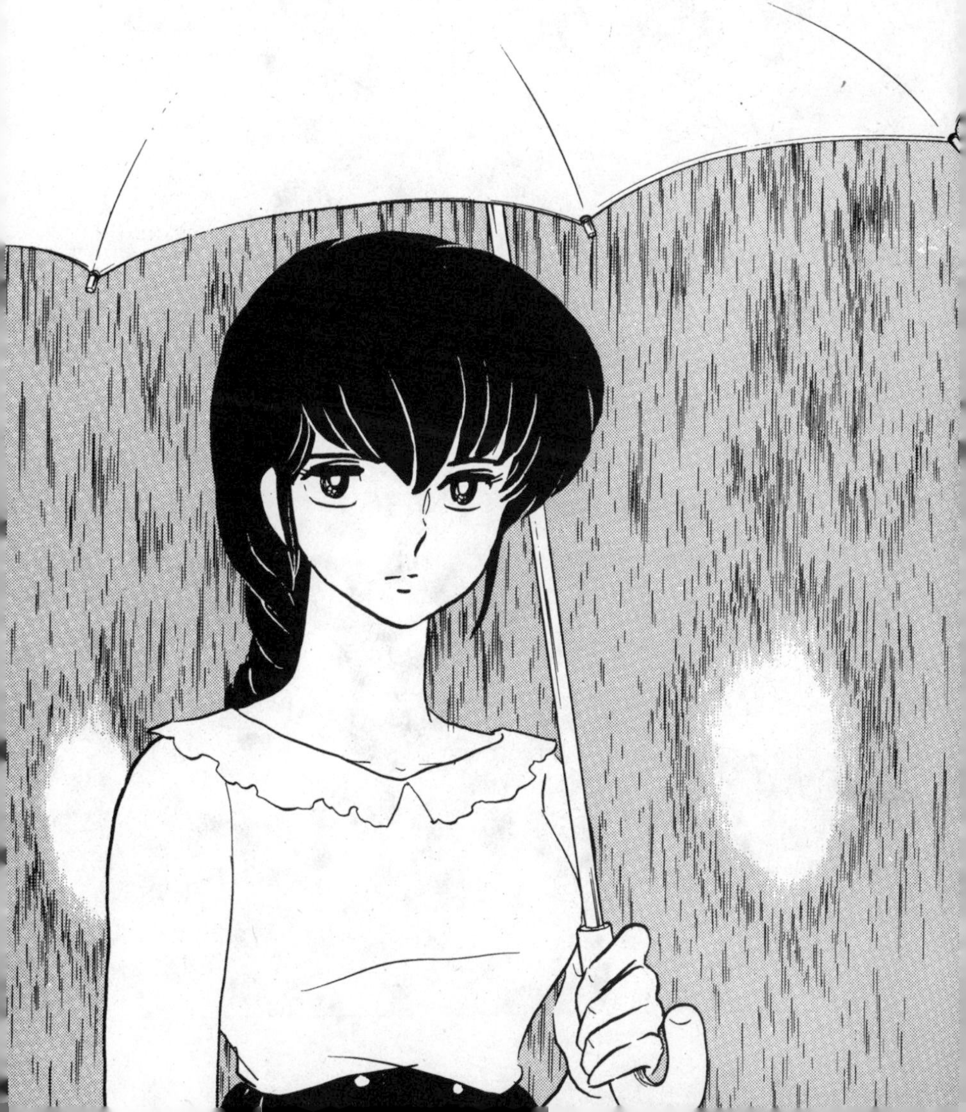

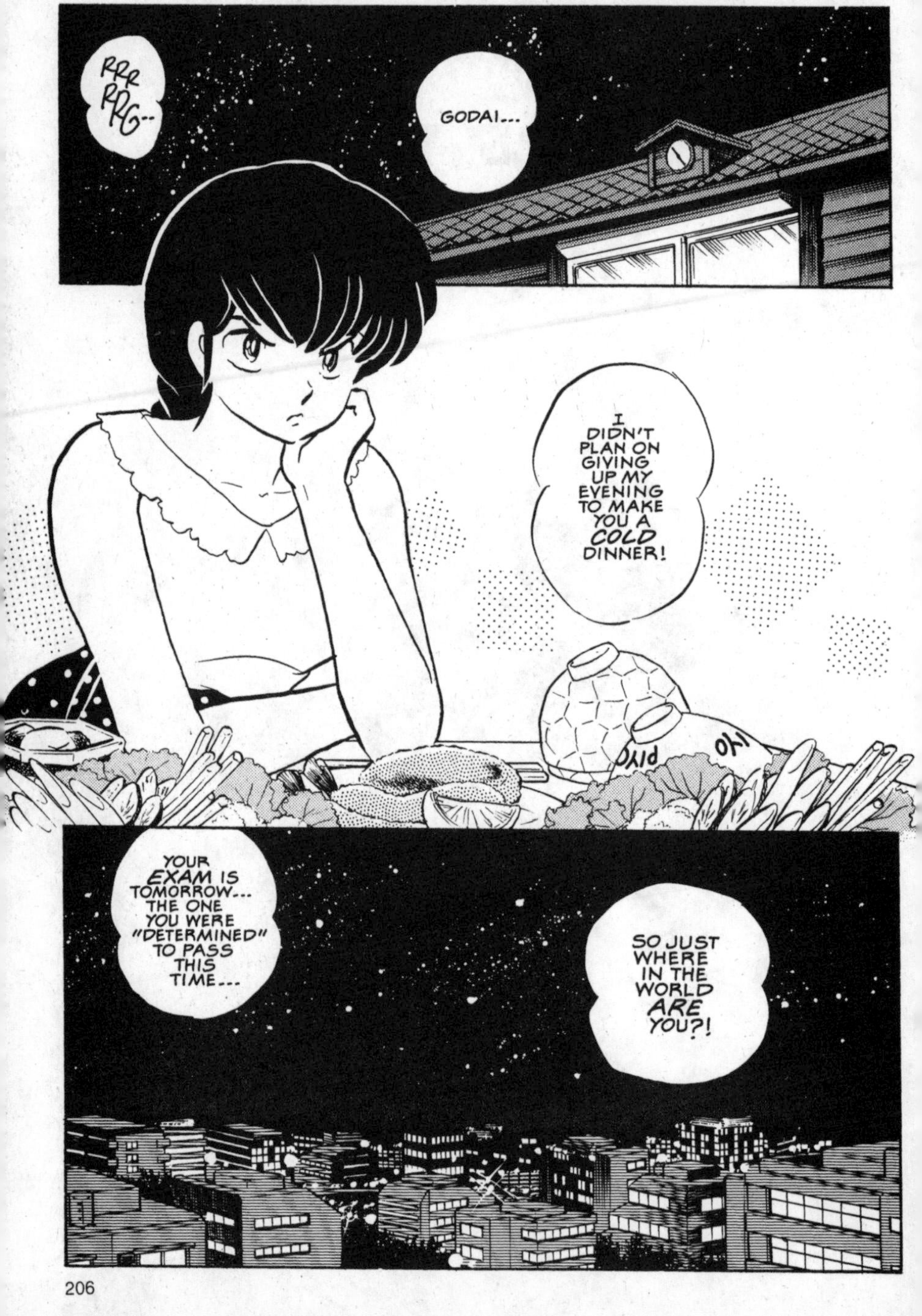
RRR RRG...
GODAI...
I DIDN'T PLAN ON GIVING UP MY EVENING TO MAKE YOU A *COLD* DINNER!
YOUR *EXAM* IS TOMORROW... THE ONE YOU WERE "DETERMINED" TO PASS THIS TIME...
SO JUST WHERE IN THE WORLD *ARE* YOU?!

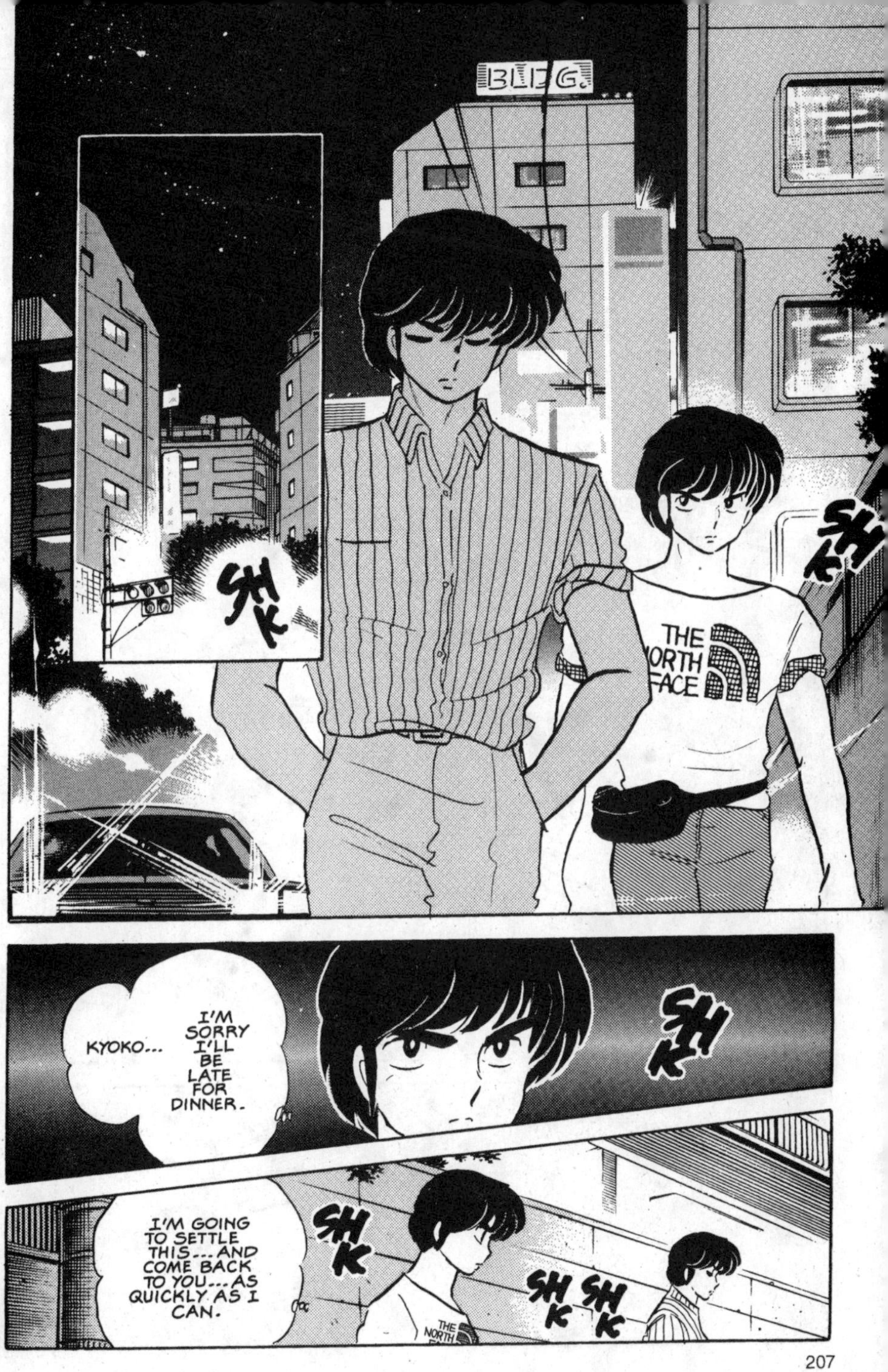
BLDG.
SHK
THE NORTH FACE
SHK
KYOKO...
I'M SORRY I'LL BE LATE FOR DINNER.
SHK
I'M GOING TO SETTLE THIS... AND COME BACK TO YOU... AS QUICKLY AS I CAN.
SHK
SHK SHK

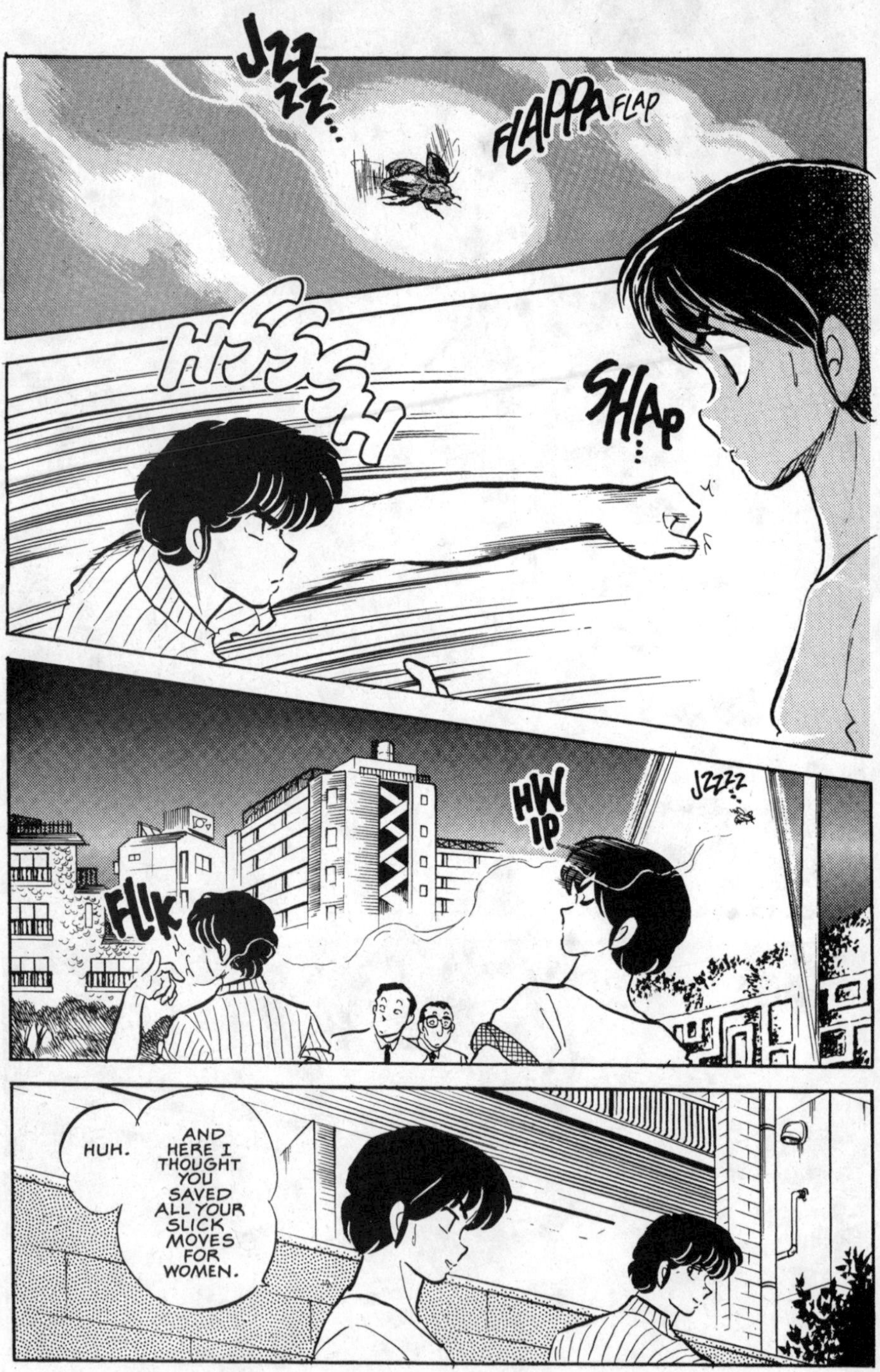
JZZZZZ...
FLAPPA FLAP
HFSSCHH
SHAP...
FLIK
HWIP
JZZZZ
HUH.
AND HERE I THOUGHT YOU SAVED ALL YOUR SLICK MOVES FOR WOMEN.

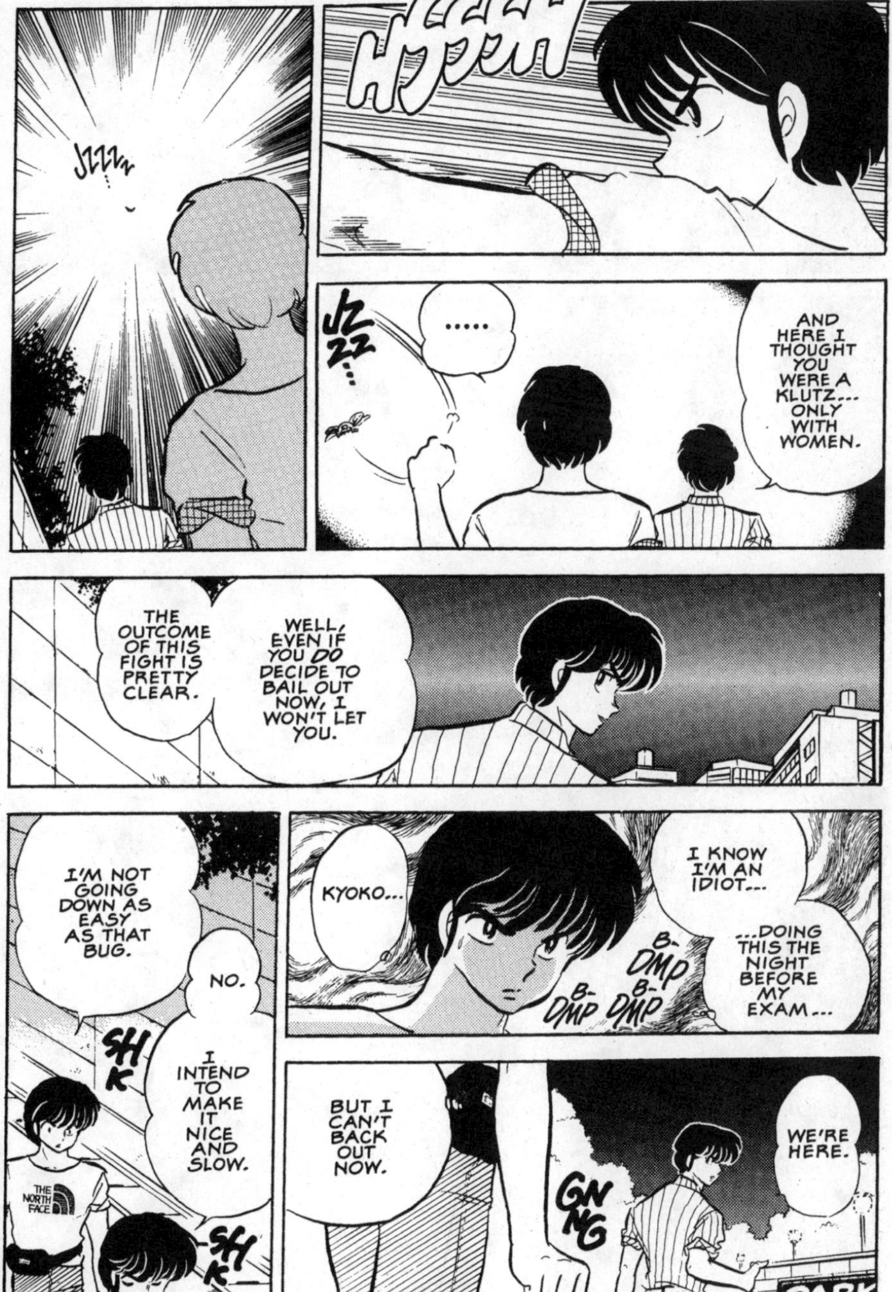
JZZZzz
HFSSSH
JZZZ...
......
AND HERE I THOUGHT YOU WERE A KLUTZ... ONLY WITH WOMEN.
THE OUTCOME OF THIS FIGHT IS PRETTY CLEAR.
WELL, EVEN IF YOU DO DECIDE TO BAIL OUT NOW, I WON'T LET YOU.
I'M NOT GOING DOWN AS EASY AS THAT BUG.
NO.
SHK
I INTEND TO MAKE IT NICE AND SLOW.
SHK
THE NORTH FACE
KYOKO...
I KNOW I'M AN IDIOT...
...DOING THIS THE NIGHT BEFORE MY EXAM...
B-DMP B-DMP B-DMP
BUT I CAN'T BACK OUT NOW.
GNNG
WE'RE HERE.
PARK

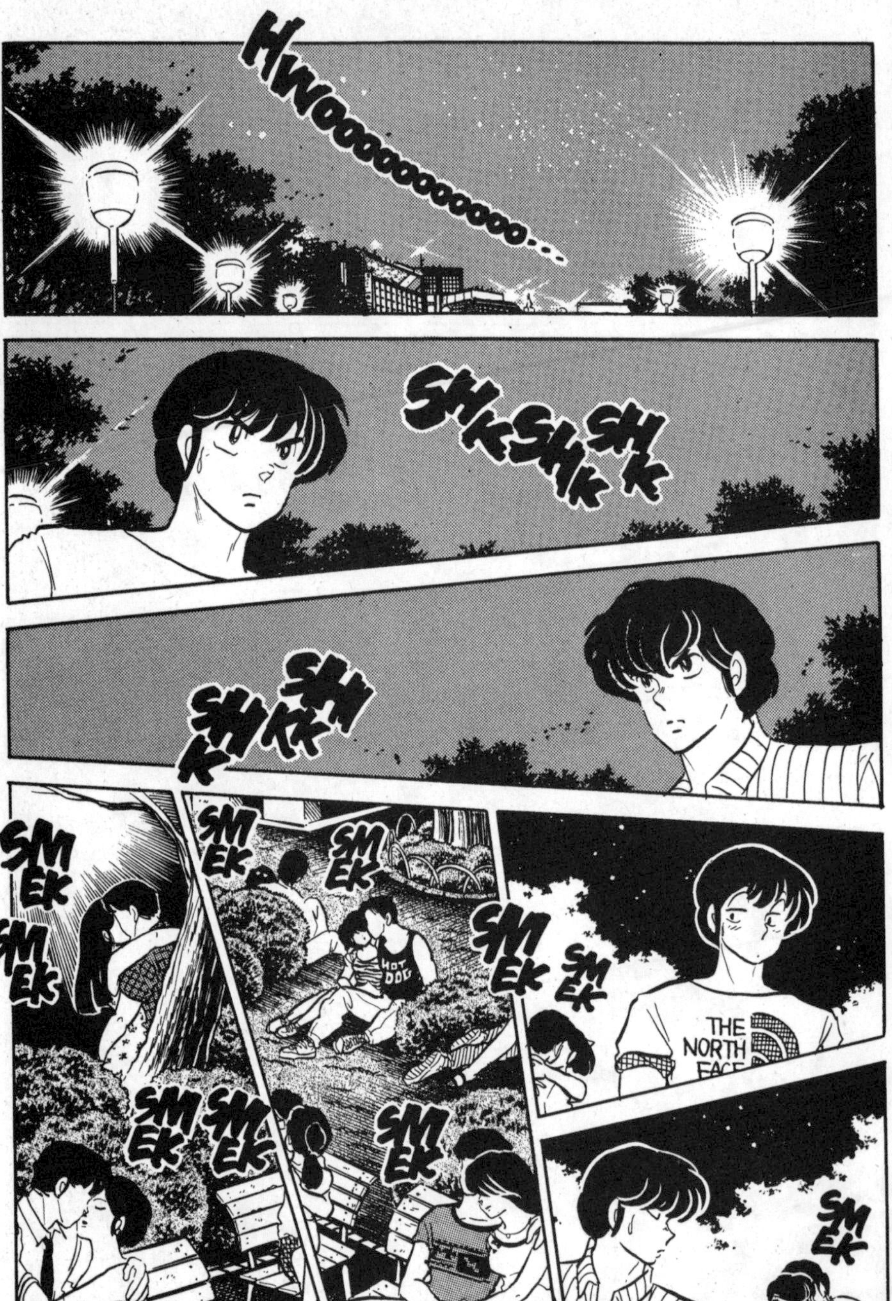
HWOOOOOOOOOOOOO...
SHK SHK SHK
SHK SHK
SMEK
SMEK
SMEK
SMEK
SMEK
SMEK
HOT DOG
SMEK
SMEK
SMEK
THE NORTH FACE
SMEK

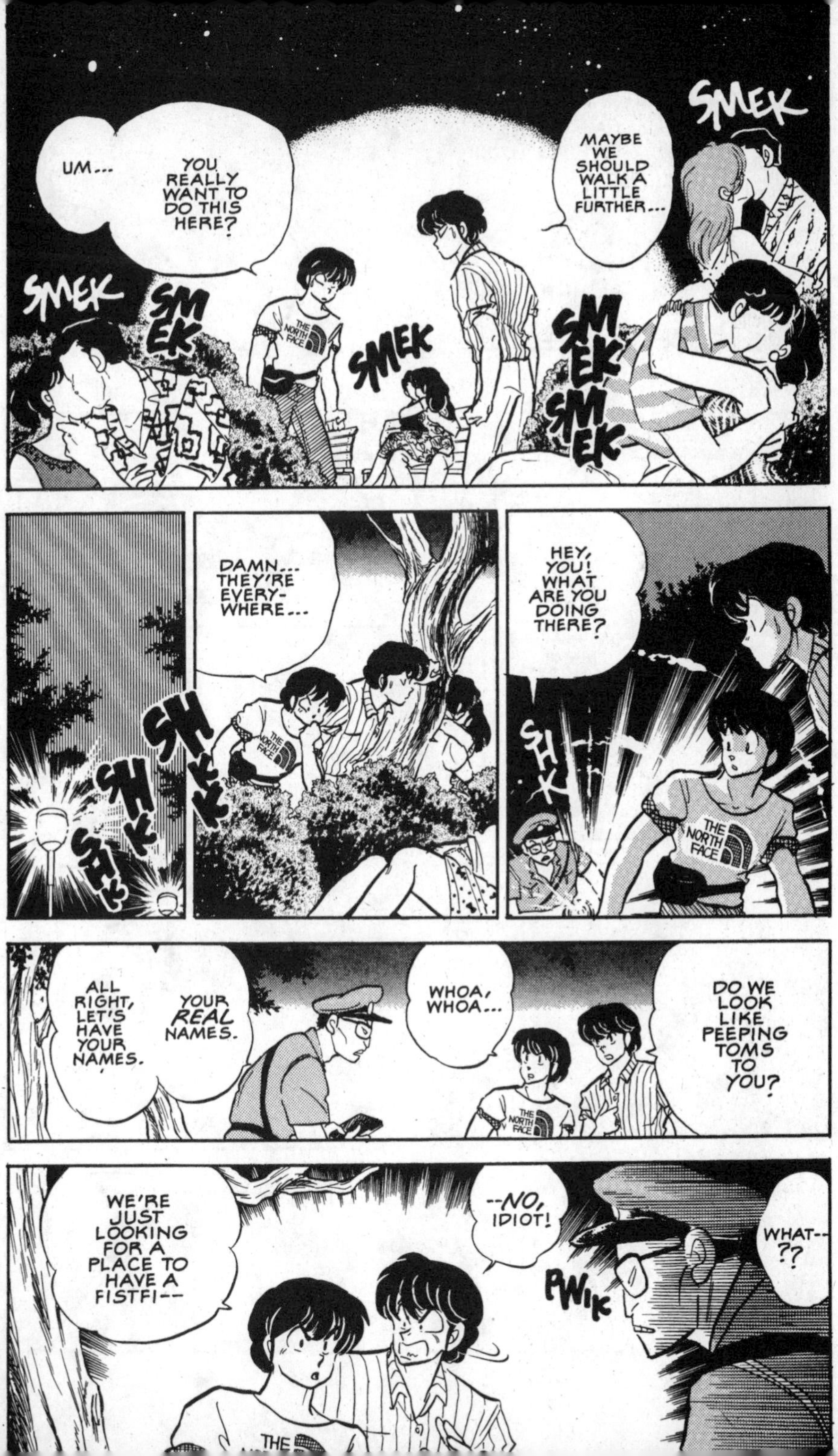
UM...
YOU REALLY WANT TO DO THIS HERE?
MAYBE WE SHOULD WALK A LITTLE FURTHER...
SMEK
SMEK
SMEK
SMEK
SMEK SMEK
SH K
SH K
SHK
DAMN... THEY'RE EVERY-WHERE...
HEY, YOU! WHAT ARE YOU DOING THERE?
SHK
ALL RIGHT, LET'S HAVE YOUR NAMES.
YOUR REAL NAMES.
WHOA, WHOA...
DO WE LOOK LIKE PEEPING TOMS TO YOU?
WE'RE JUST LOOKING FOR A PLACE TO HAVE A FISTFI--
--NO, IDIOT!
PWIK
WHAT-- ??

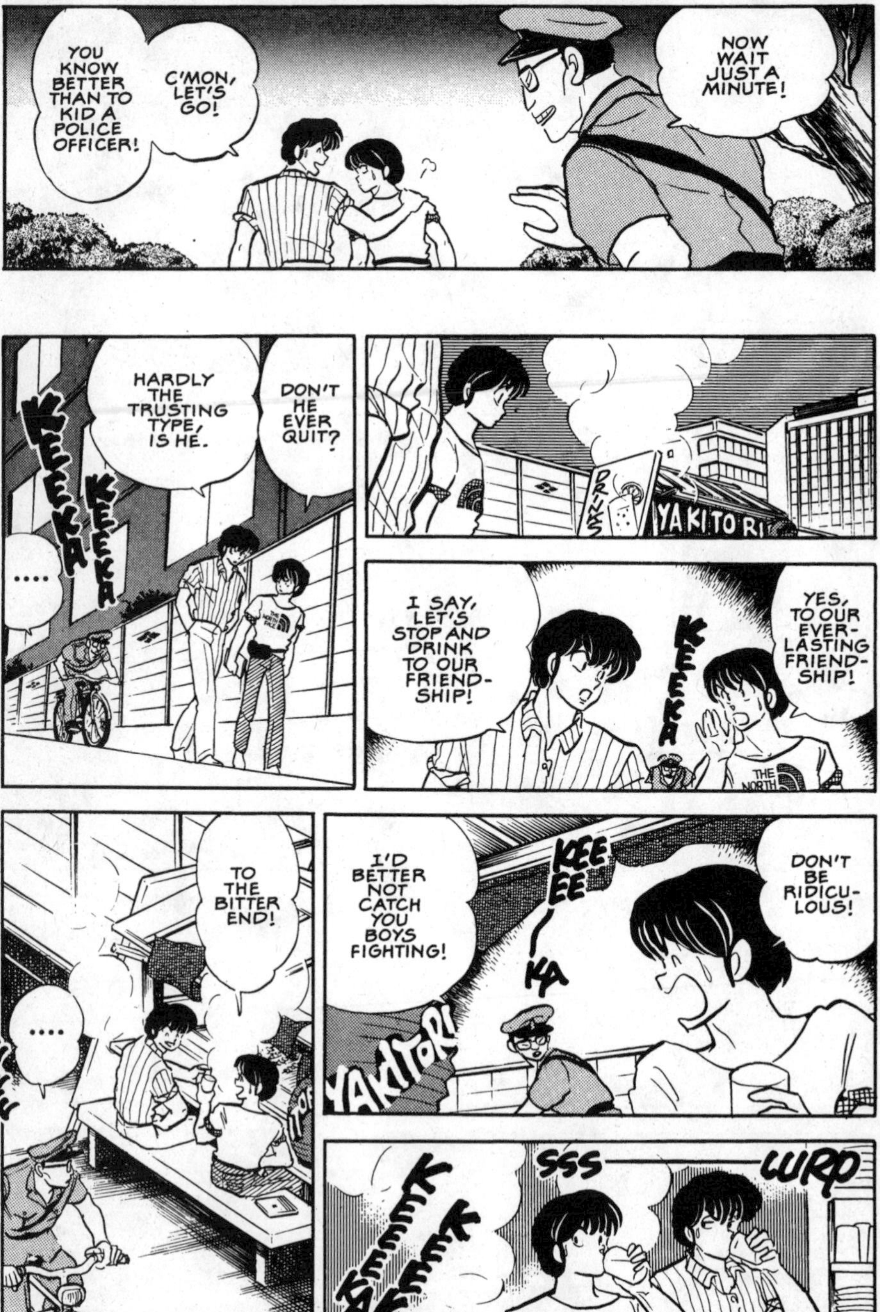

YOU KNOW BETTER THAN TO KID A POLICE OFFICER!
C'MON, LET'S GO!
NOW WAIT JUST A MINUTE!
HARDLY THE TRUSTING TYPE, IS HE.
DON'T HE EVER QUIT?
KEEKA KEEKA
....
DRINKS
YAKITORI
I SAY, LET'S STOP AND DRINK TO OUR FRIENDSHIP!
KEEKA
YES, TO OUR EVER-LASTING FRIENDSHIP!
TO THE BITTER END!
KEEEE
....
I'D BETTER NOT CATCH YOU BOYS FIGHTING!
KEEEEE—KA
YAKITORI
DON'T BE RIDICULOUS!
SSS
GURP
KEEEEK KA TEEEEK

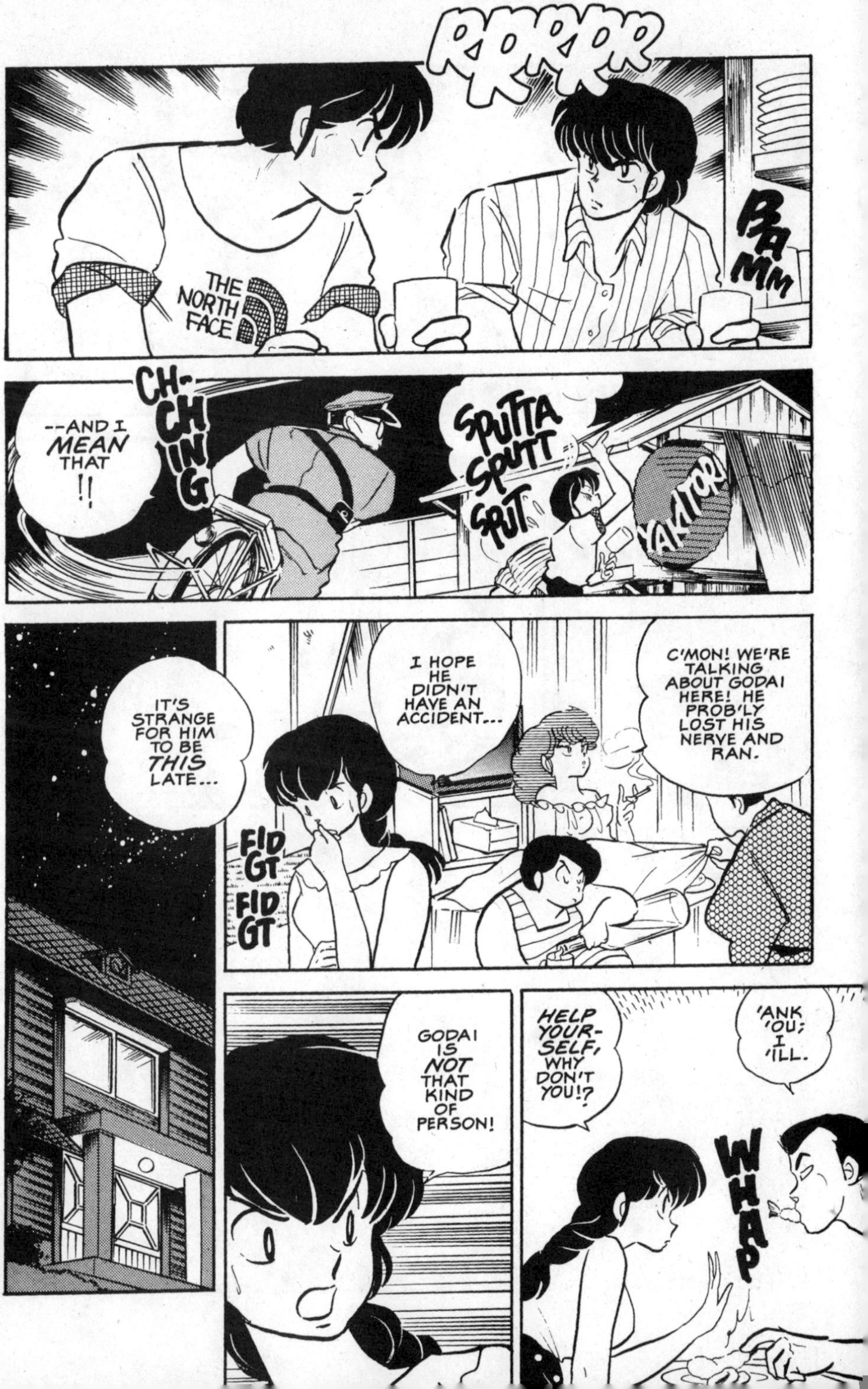
THE NORTH FACE
BRAMM
--AND I MEAN THAT !!
CH-CHING
SPUTTA SPUTT SPUT
YAKITORI
IT'S STRANGE FOR HIM TO BE THIS LATE...
I HOPE HE DIDN'T HAVE AN ACCIDENT...
C'MON! WE'RE TALKING ABOUT GODAI HERE! HE PROB'LY LOST HIS NERVE AND RAN.
FIDGT FIDGT
GODAI IS NOT THAT KIND OF PERSON!
HELP YOURSELF, WHY DON'T YOU!?
'ANK 'OU; I 'ILL.
WHAP

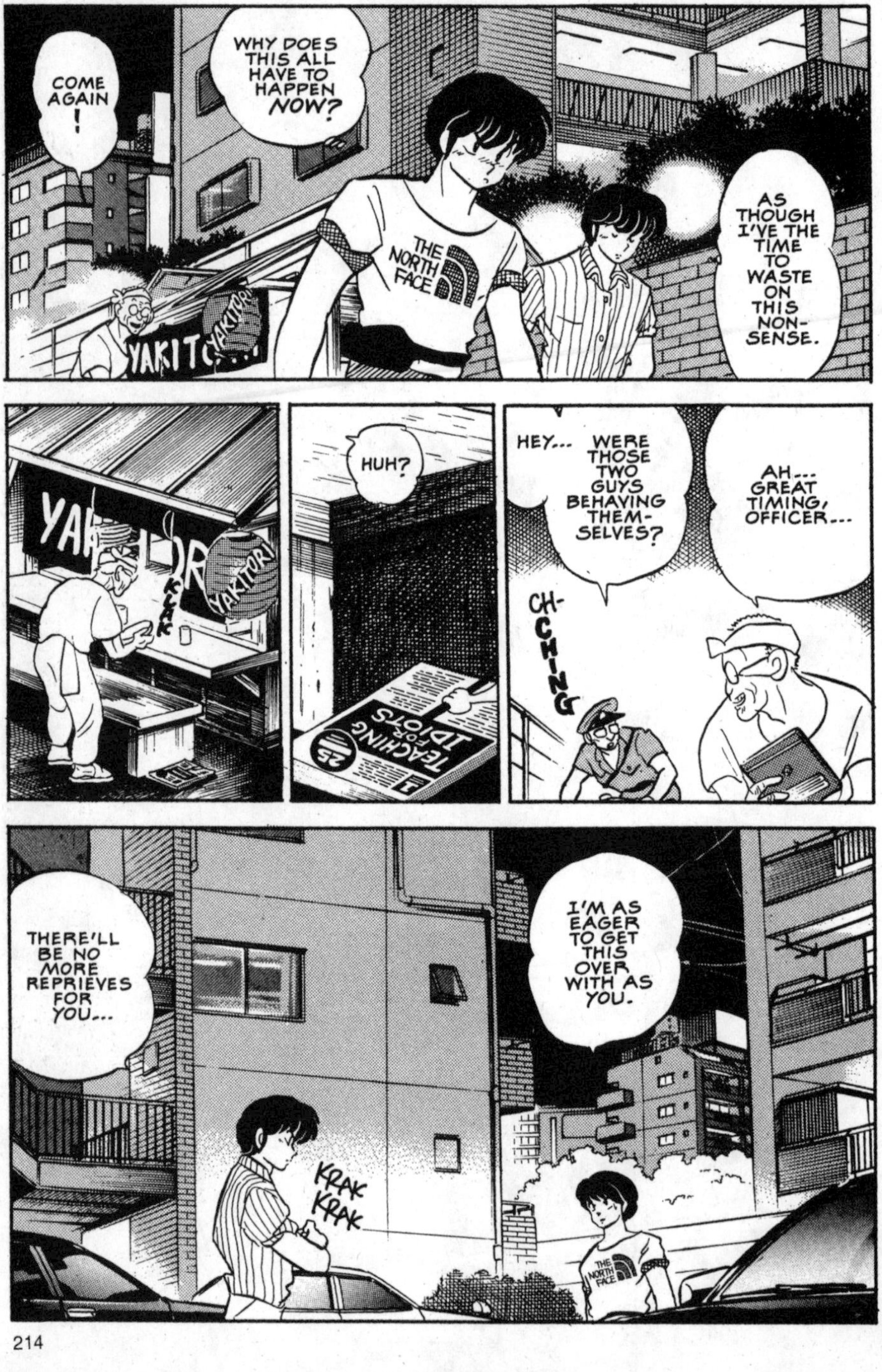
COME AGAIN !
WHY DOES THIS ALL HAVE TO HAPPEN NOW?
YAKITO...
YAKITORI
AS THOUGH I'VE THE TIME TO WASTE ON THIS NON-SENSE.
YAKITORI
YAKITORI
KLAK
HUH?
TEACHING FOR IDIOTS
HEY... WERE THOSE TWO GUYS BEHAVING THEM-SELVES?
AH... GREAT TIMING, OFFICER...
CH-CHING
THERE'LL BE NO MORE REPRIEVES FOR YOU...
I'M AS EAGER TO GET THIS OVER WITH AS YOU.
KRAK KRAK

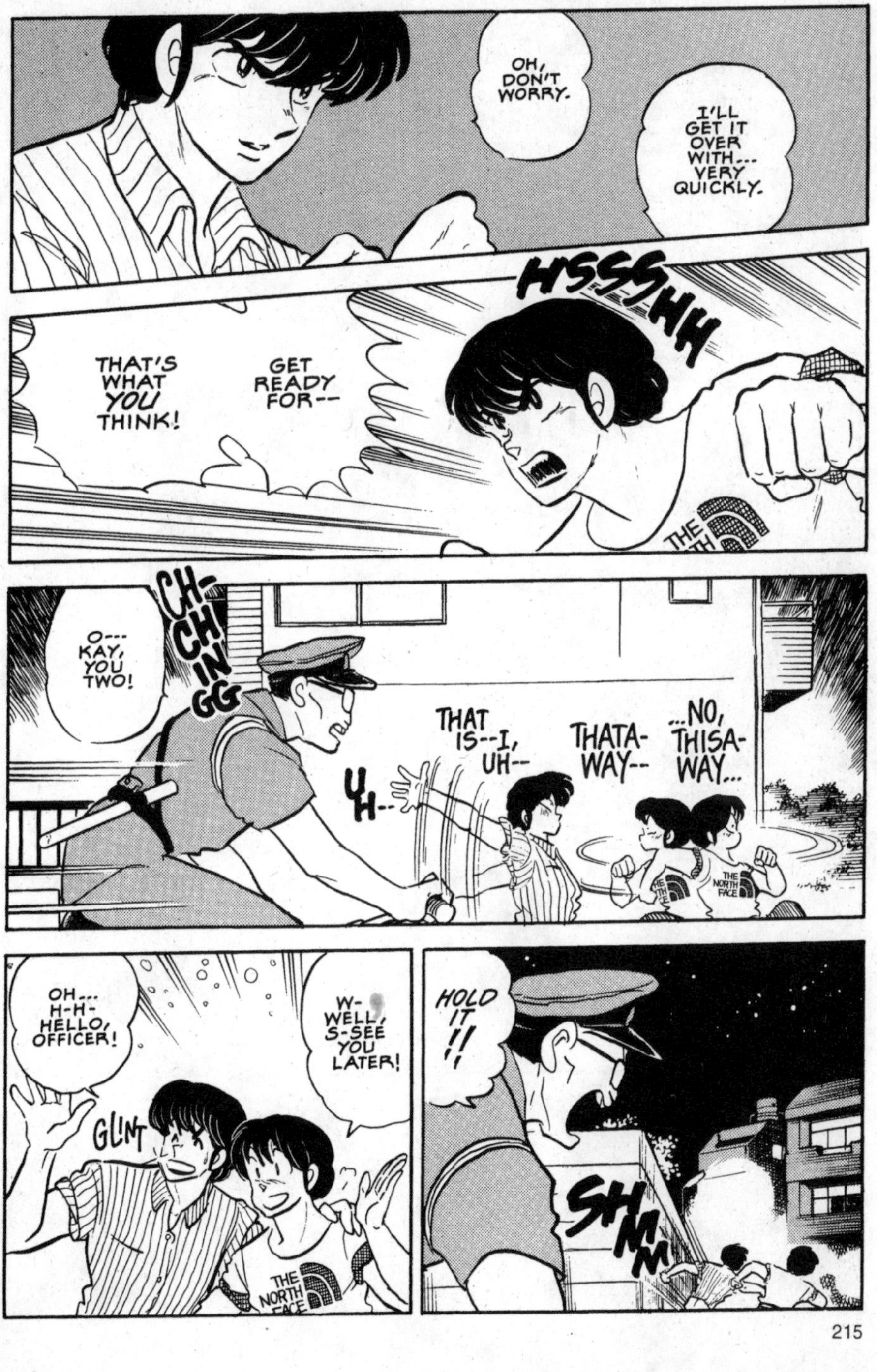
OH, DON'T WORRY.
I'LL GET IT OVER WITH... VERY QUICKLY.
HSSSHH
THAT'S WHAT YOU THINK!
GET READY FOR--
THE NORTH FACE
O--- KAY, YOU TWO!
CH-CHINGG
UH--
THAT IS--I, UH--
THATA-WAY--
...NO, THISA-WAY...
OH... H-H-HELLO, OFFICER!
W-WELL, S-SEE YOU LATER!
GLINT
HOLD IT !!
SHMM

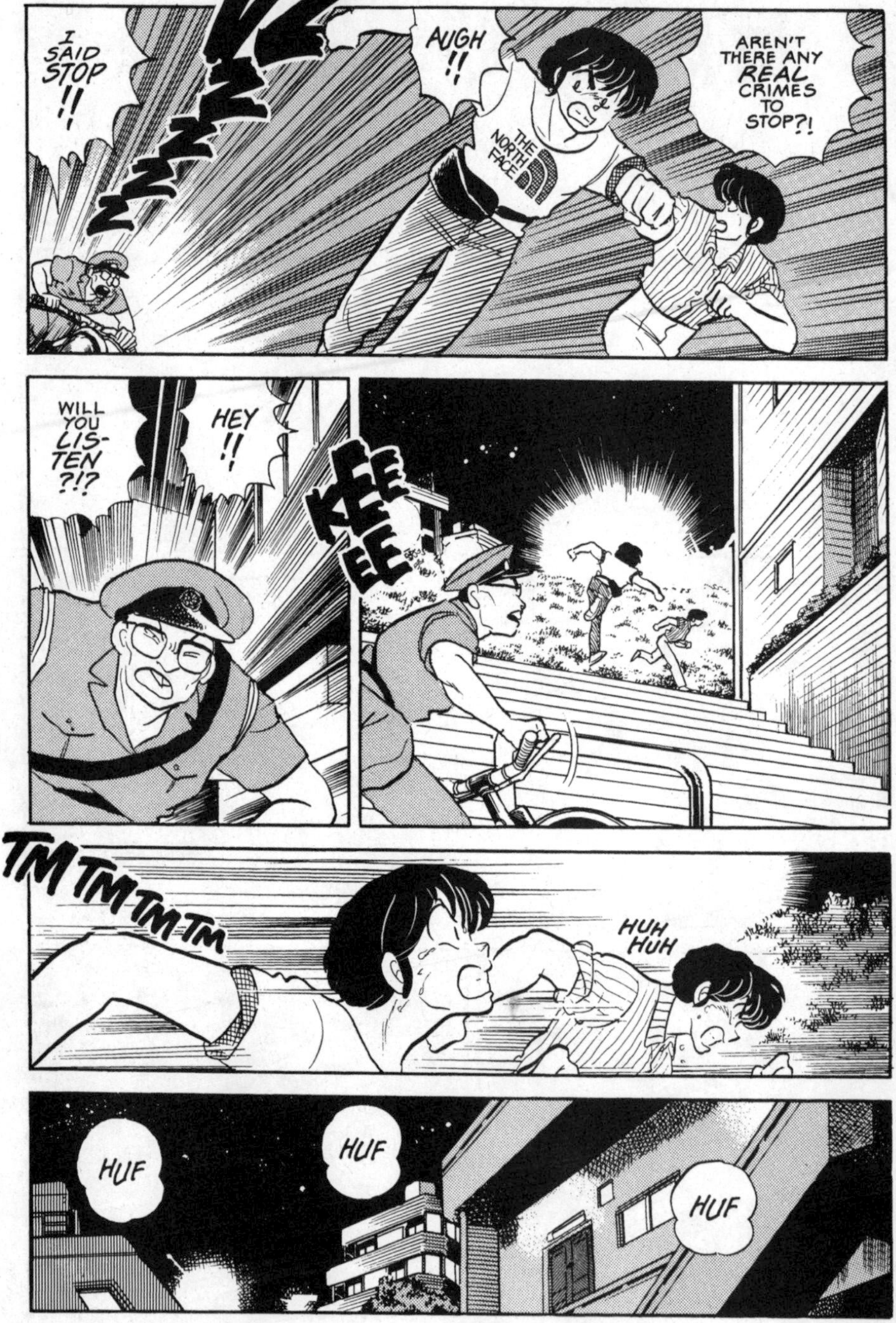
I SAID STOP !!
VZZZZZZ
AUGH !!
THE NORTH FACE
AREN'T THERE ANY REAL CRIMES TO STOP?!
WILL YOU LIS-TEN ?!?
HEY !!
KEE KEE EE
TM TM TM TM TM
HUH HUH
HUF
HUF
HUF

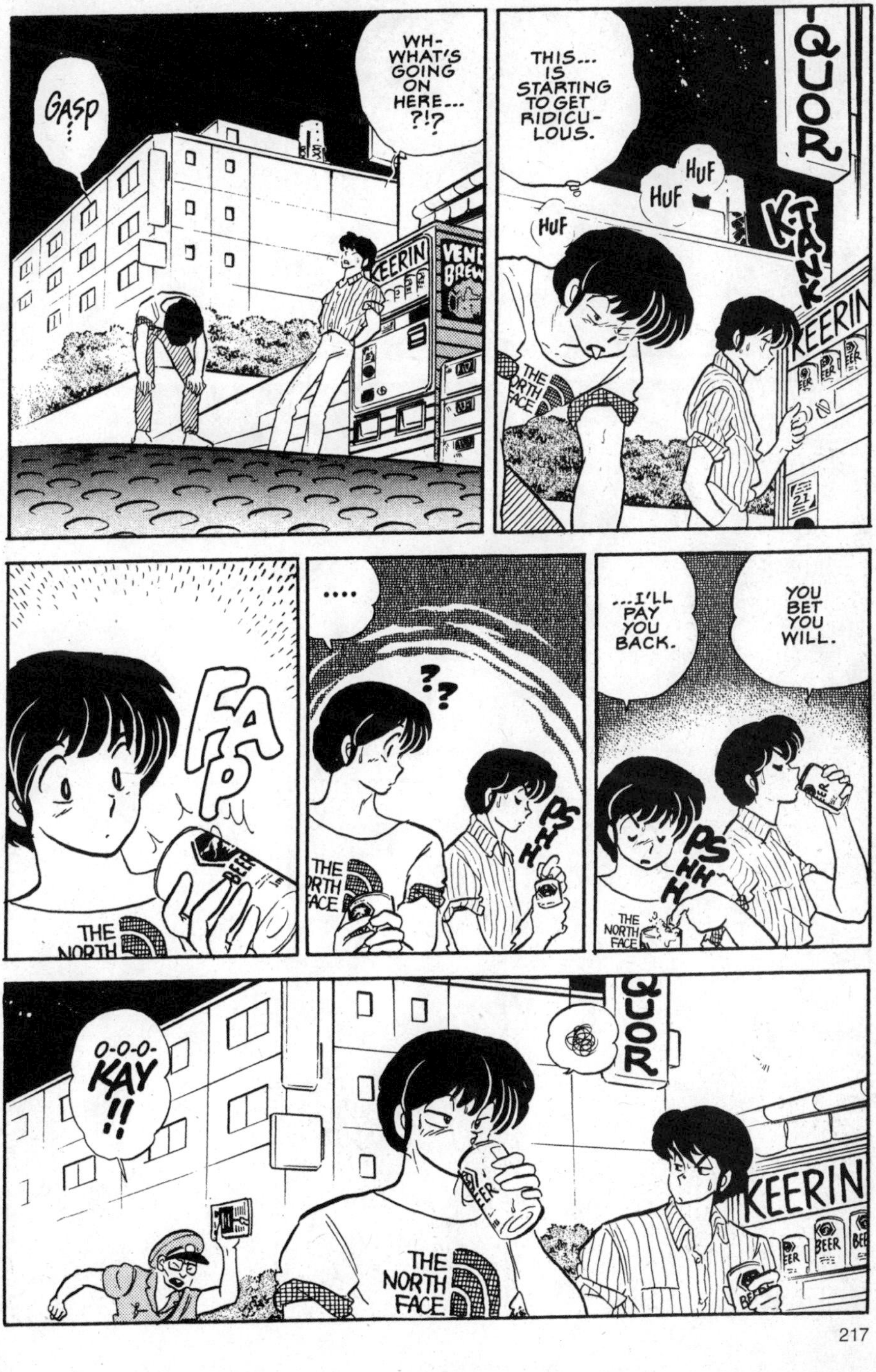
GASP
WH- WHAT'S GOING ON HERE...?!?
VENDO BREW
KEERIN
THIS... IS STARTING TO GET RIDICULOUS.
QUOR
HUF
HUF
HUF
K-TANK
KEERIN
THE NORTH FACE
FAP
BEER
THE NORTH
....
??
PSHH
THE NORTH FACE
...I'LL PAY YOU BACK.
YOU BET YOU WILL.
PSHHH
THE NORTH FACE
O-O-O-KAY!!
QUOR
BEER
KEERIN
BEER
BEER
THE NORTH FACE

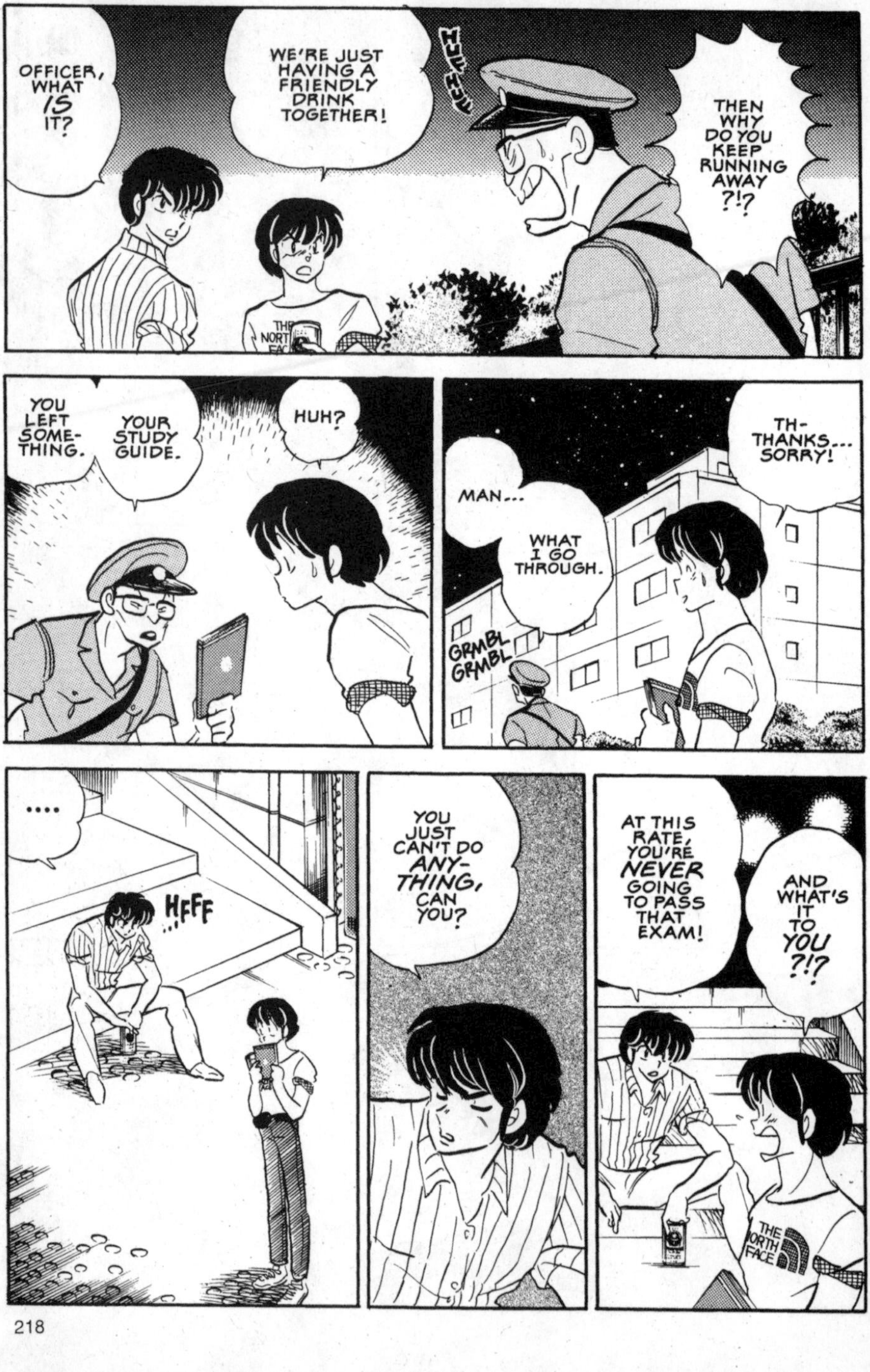
OFFICER, WHAT IS IT?
WE'RE JUST HAVING A FRIENDLY DRINK TOGETHER!
HUF HUF
THEN WHY DO YOU KEEP RUNNING AWAY ?!?
YOU LEFT SOMETHING.
YOUR STUDY GUIDE.
HUH?
TH-THANKS... SORRY!
MAN...
WHAT I GO THROUGH.
GRMBL GRMBL
....
HFFF
YOU JUST CAN'T DO ANYTHING, CAN YOU?
AT THIS RATE, YOU'RE NEVER GOING TO PASS THAT EXAM!
AND WHAT'S IT TO YOU ?!?
THE NORTH FACE

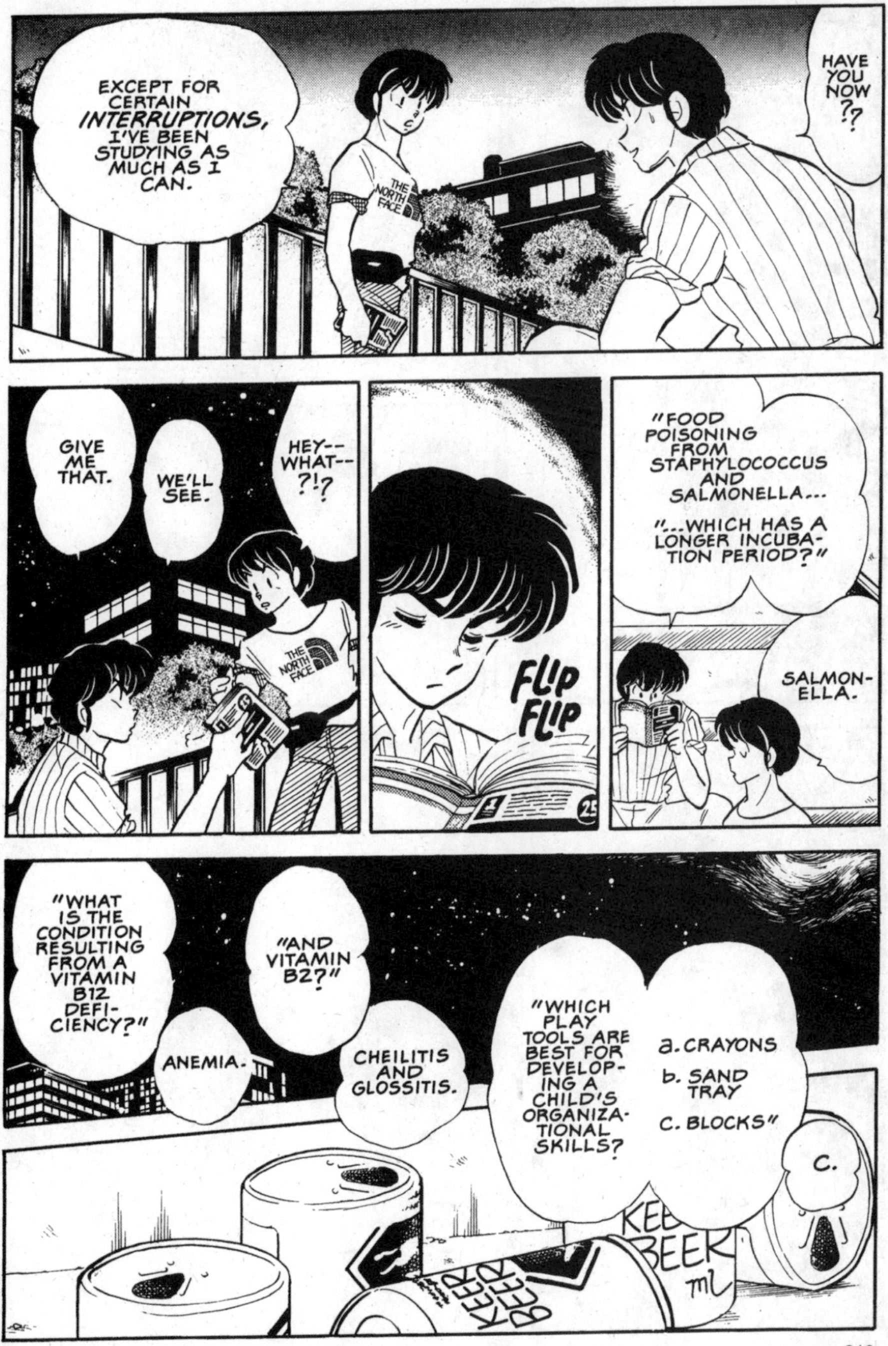
EXCEPT FOR CERTAIN *INTERRUPTIONS,* I'VE BEEN STUDYING AS MUCH AS I CAN.
HAVE YOU NOW ??
GIVE ME THAT.
WE'LL SEE.
HEY-- WHAT-- ?!?
FLIP FLIP
"FOOD POISONING FROM STAPHYLOCOCCUS AND SALMONELLA...
"...WHICH HAS A LONGER INCUBATION PERIOD?"
SALMONELLA.
"WHAT IS THE CONDITION RESULTING FROM A VITAMIN B12 DEFICIENCY?"
ANEMIA.
"AND VITAMIN B2?"
CHEILITIS AND GLOSSITIS.
"WHICH PLAY TOOLS ARE BEST FOR DEVELOPING A CHILD'S ORGANIZATIONAL SKILLS?
a. CRAYONS
b. SAND TRAY
c. BLOCKS"
C.
KEER BEER

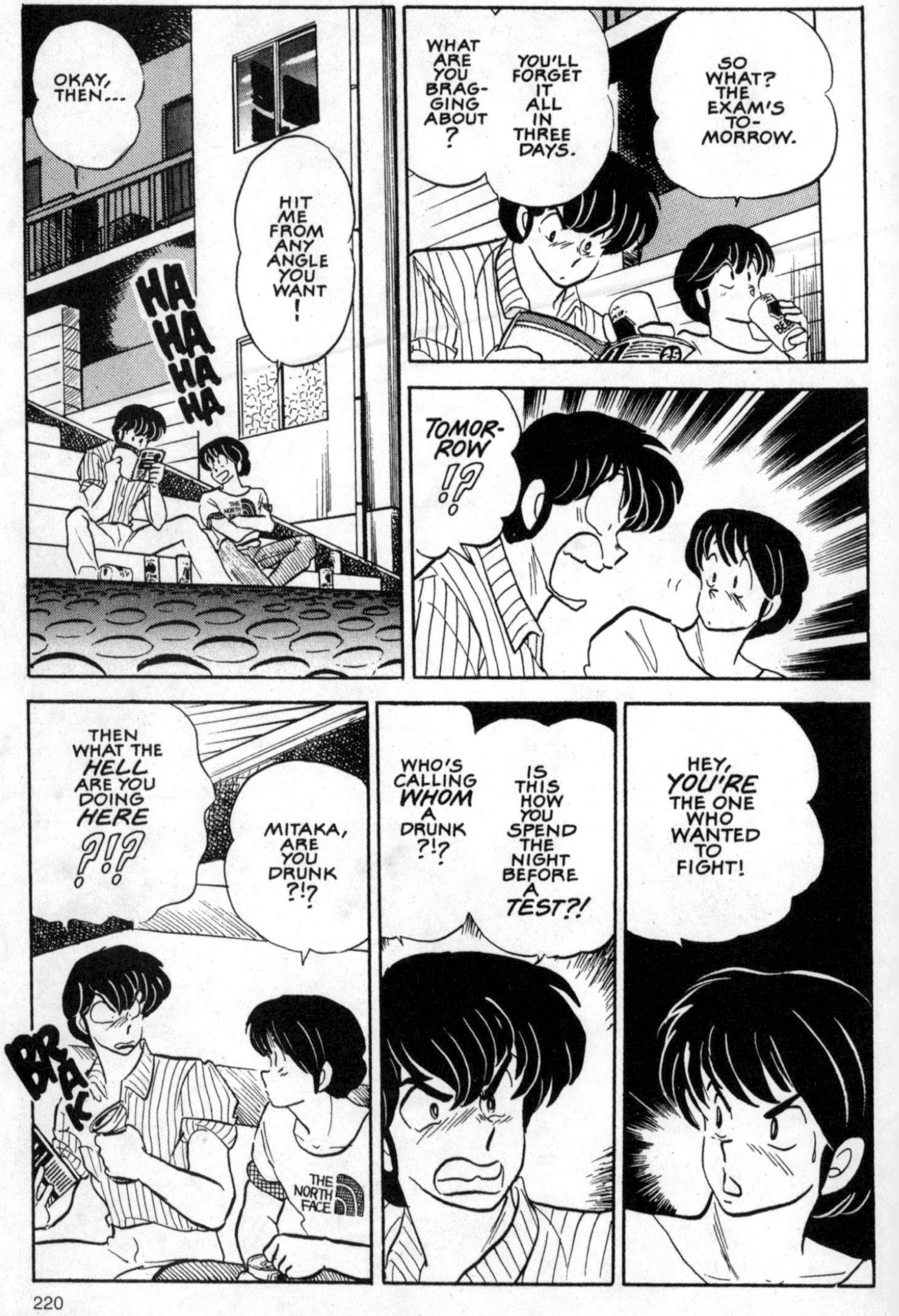
OKAY, THEN...
HIT ME FROM ANY ANGLE YOU WANT!
HA HA HA HA HA
WHAT ARE YOU BRAGGING ABOUT?
YOU'LL FORGET IT ALL IN THREE DAYS.
SO WHAT? THE EXAM'S TOMORROW.
TOMORROW !?
THEN WHAT THE HELL ARE YOU DOING HERE ?!?
MITAKA, ARE YOU DRUNK ?!?
BRAK
WHO'S CALLING WHOM A DRUNK ?!?
IS THIS HOW YOU SPEND THE NIGHT BEFORE A TEST?!
HEY, YOU'RE THE ONE WHO WANTED TO FIGHT!

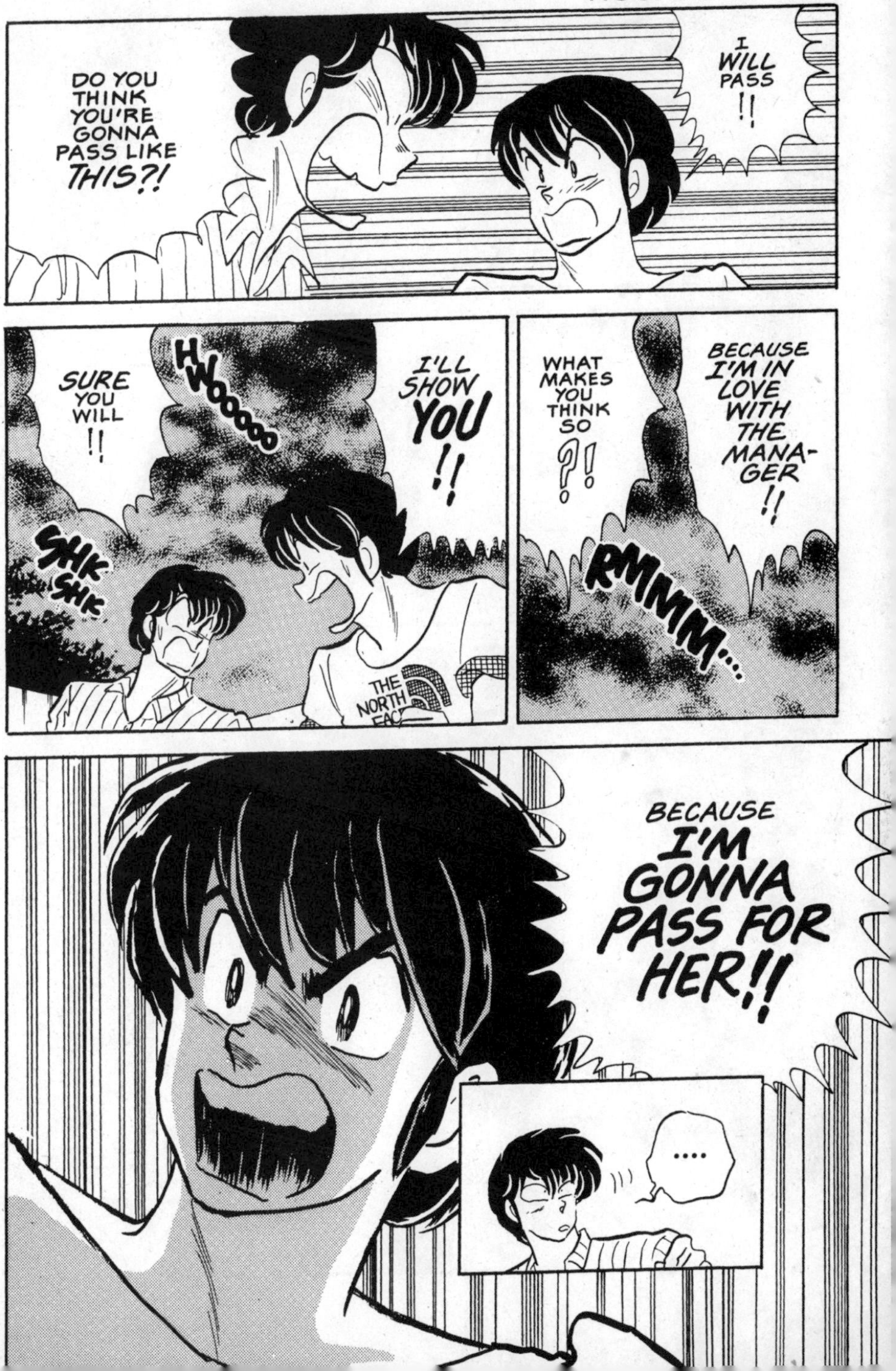
DO YOU THINK YOU'RE GONNA PASS LIKE THIS?!
I WILL PASS !!
SURE YOU WILL !!
HWOOOOOO
SHK SHK
I'LL SHOW YOU !!
THE NORTH FACE
WHAT MAKES YOU THINK SO ?!
BECAUSE I'M IN LOVE WITH THE MANA-GER !!
RMMMM...
BECAUSE I'M GONNA PASS FOR HER!!
....

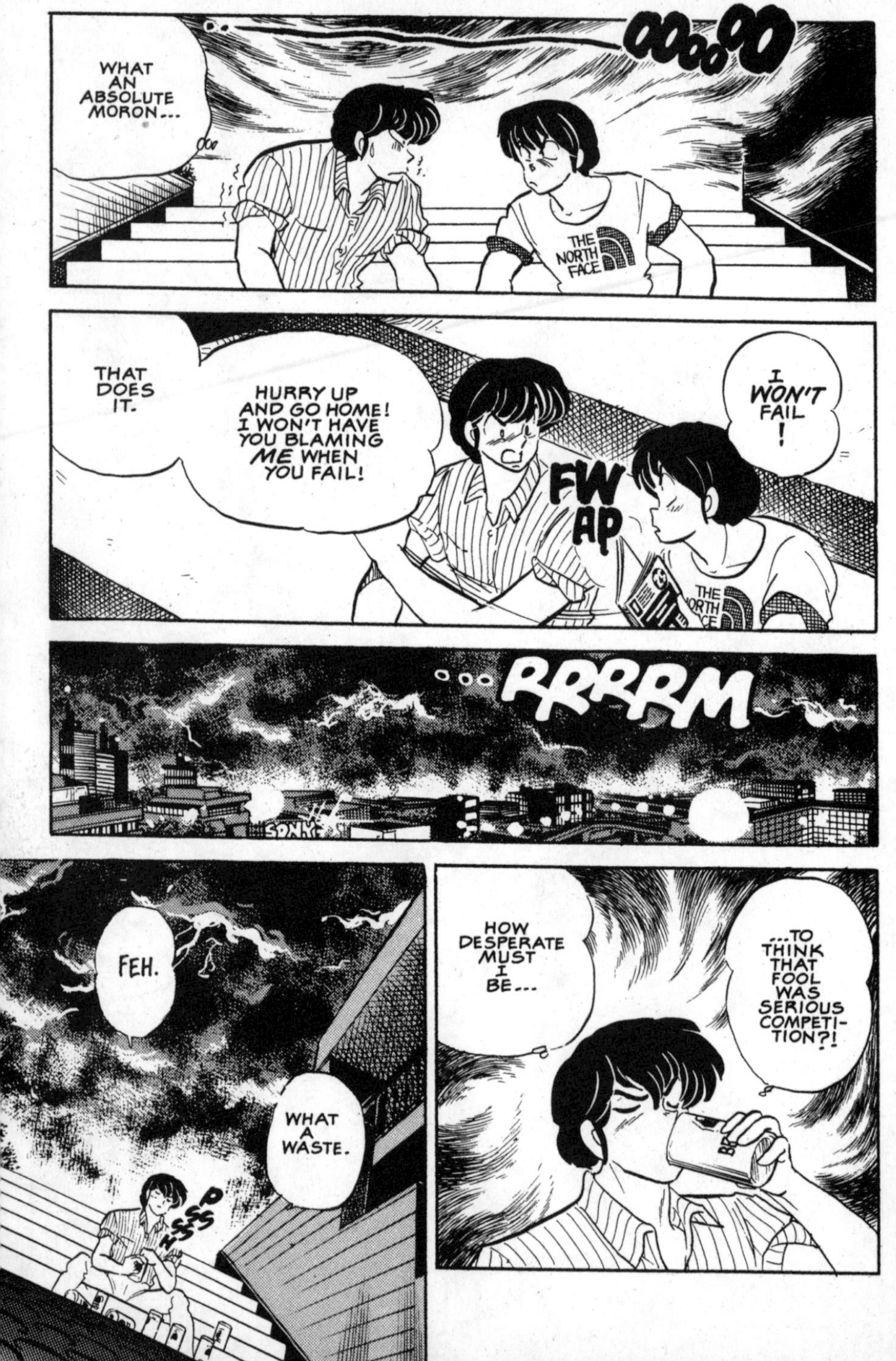
WHAT AN ABSOLUTE MORON...
OOOOOO
THE NORTH FACE
THAT DOES IT.
HURRY UP AND GO HOME! I WON'T HAVE YOU BLAMING *ME* WHEN YOU FAIL!
FWAP
I *WON'T* FAIL!
...RRRRM
SONY
FEH.
WHAT A WASTE.
PSSSH
HOW DESPERATE MUST I BE...
...TO THINK THAT FOOL WAS SERIOUS COMPETITION?!

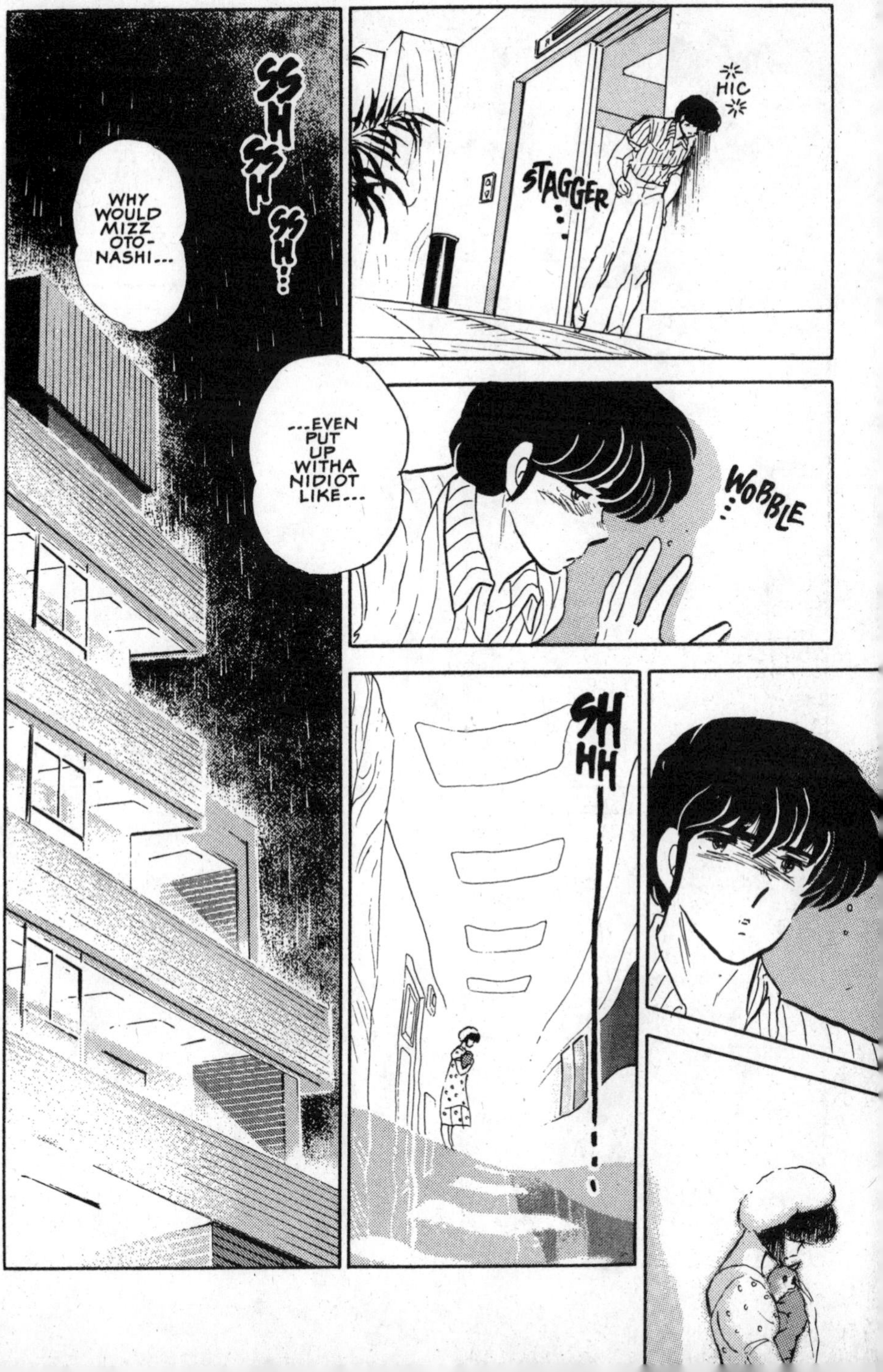
SSH SSH SSH...
WHY WOULD MIZZ OTO-NASHI...
HIC
STAGGER...
...EVEN PUT UP WITHA NIDIOT LIKE...
WOBBLE
SHHH...

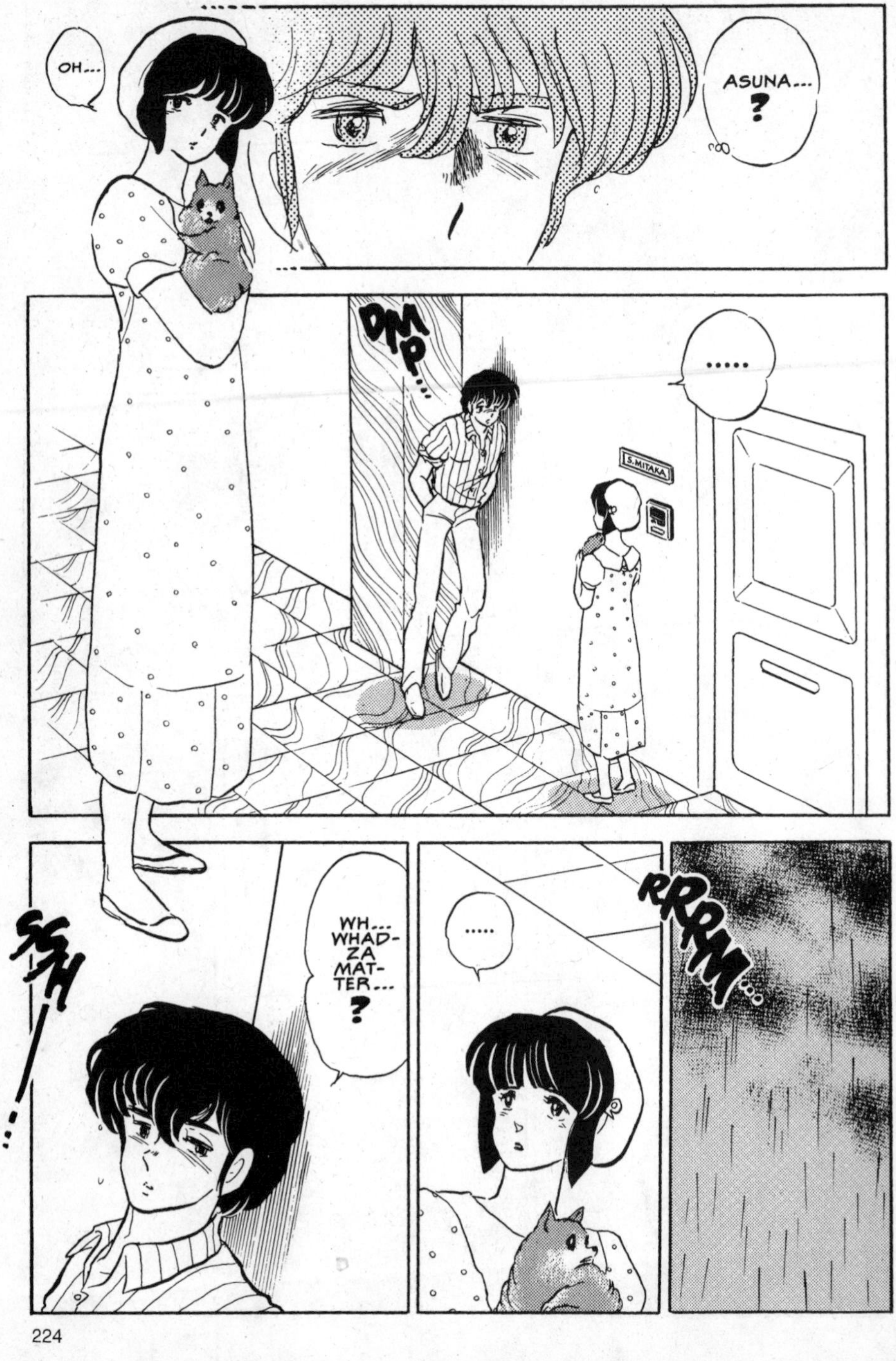
OH...
ASUNA...?
DMP...
.....
S.MITAKA
SCSH...
WH... WHADZA MATTER...?
.....
RRRM...

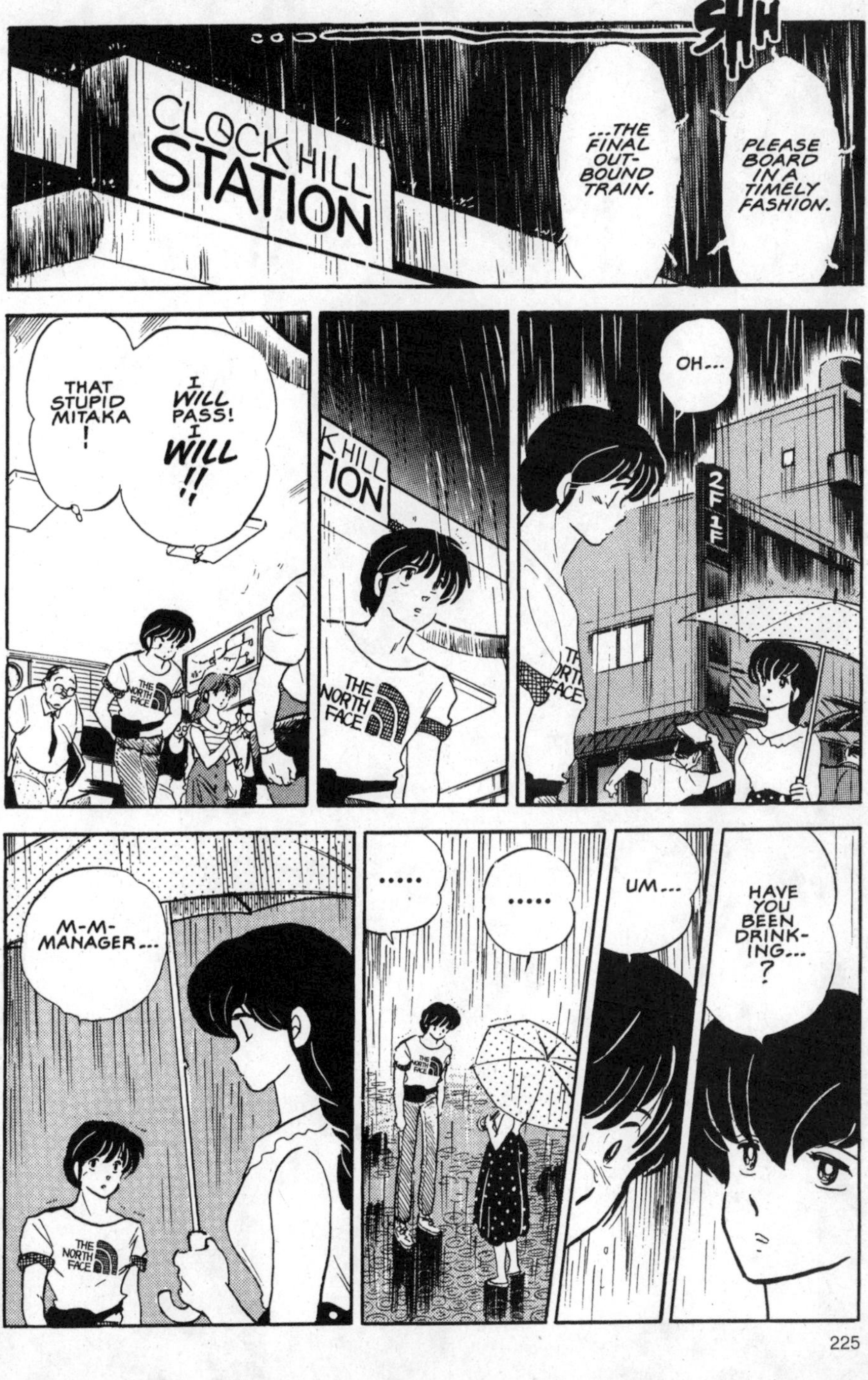
CLOCK HILL STATION
SHH
...THE FINAL OUT-BOUND TRAIN.
PLEASE BOARD IN A TIMELY FASHION.
THAT STUPID MITAKA!
I WILL PASS! I WILL!!
THE NORTH FACE
K HILL
TION
OH...
2F 1F
M-M-MANAGER...
.....
.....
UM...
HAVE YOU BEEN DRINKING...?

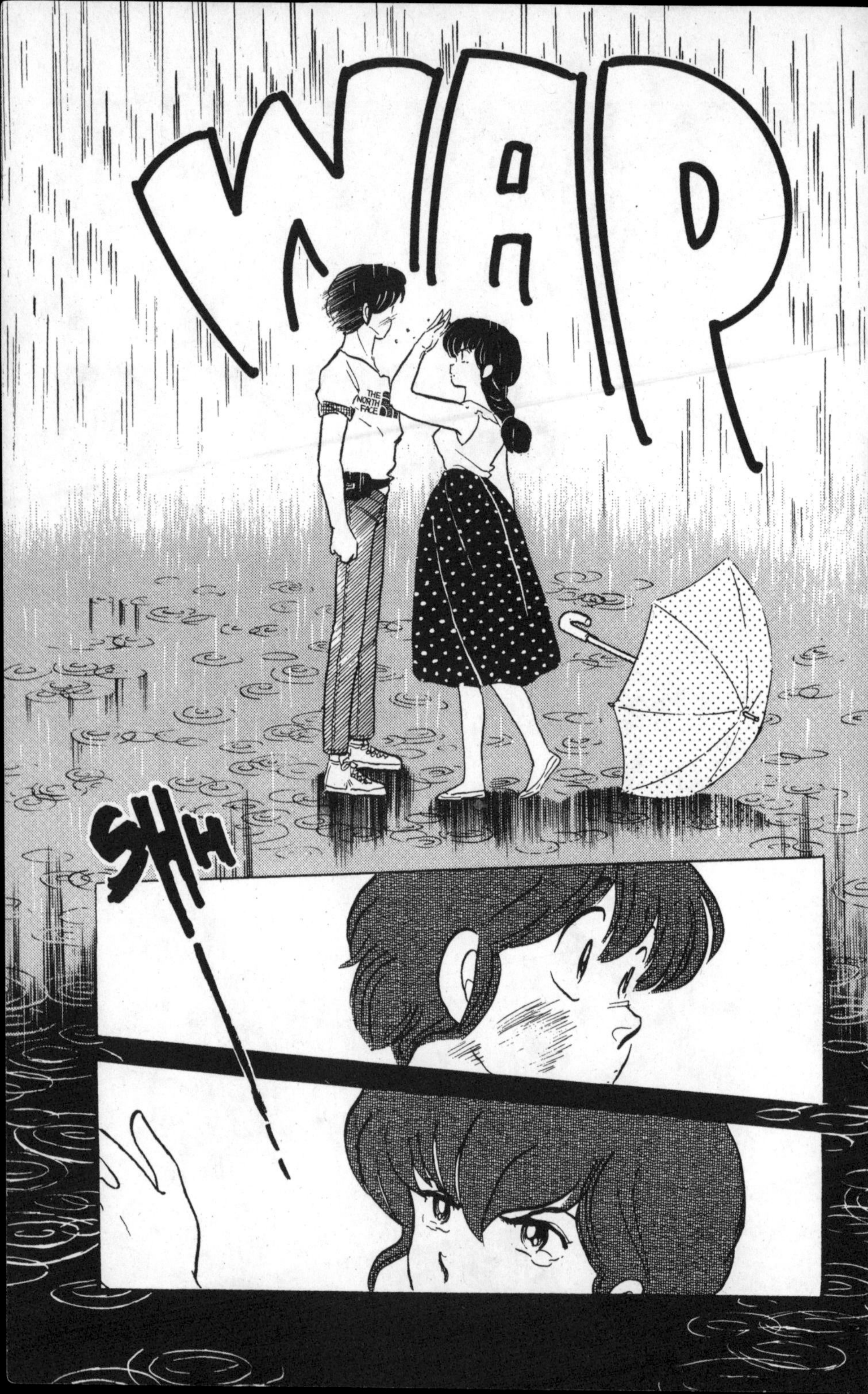
WAP
THE NORTH FACE
SHH

PART THIRTEEN

A FATE SEALED

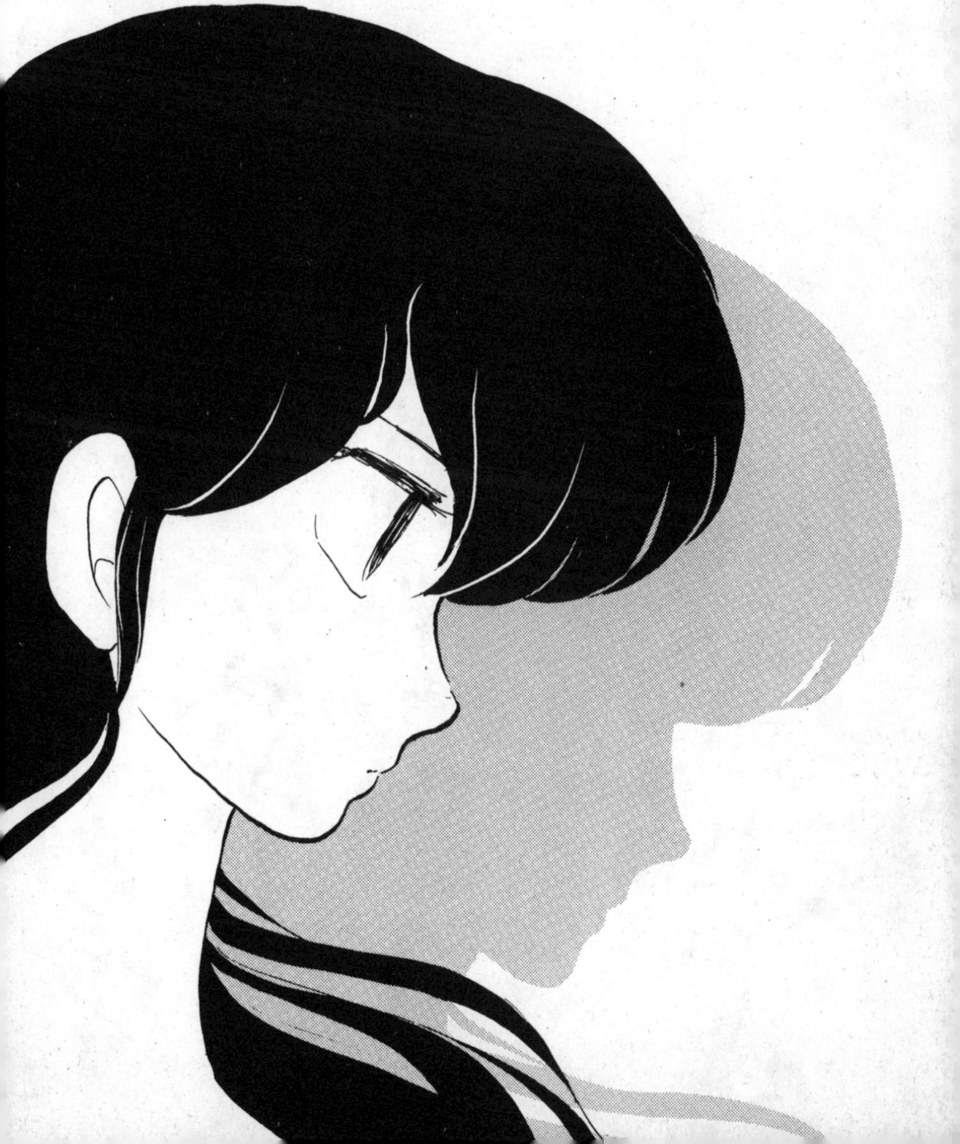

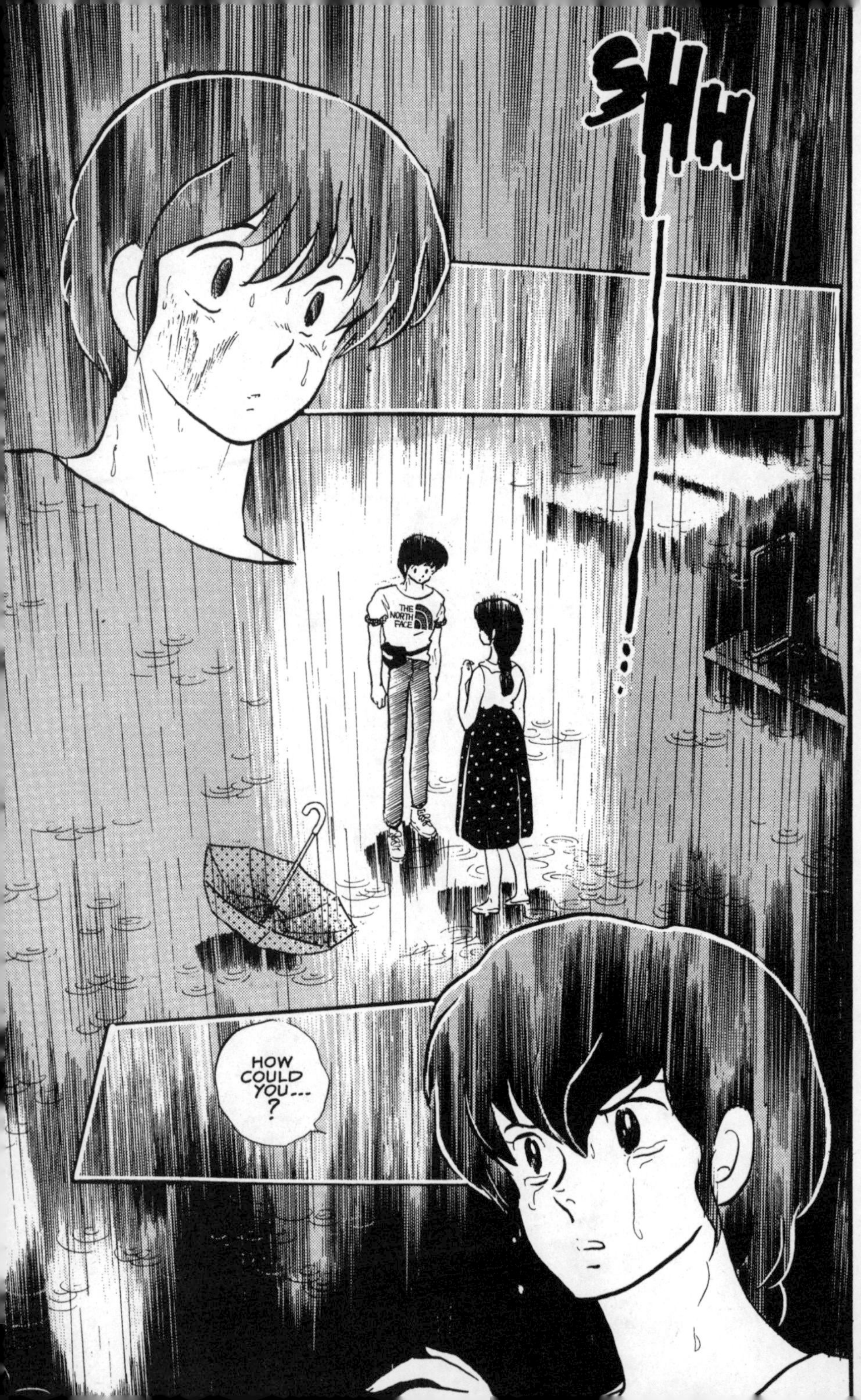
SHH
THE NORTH FACE
HOW COULD YOU...?

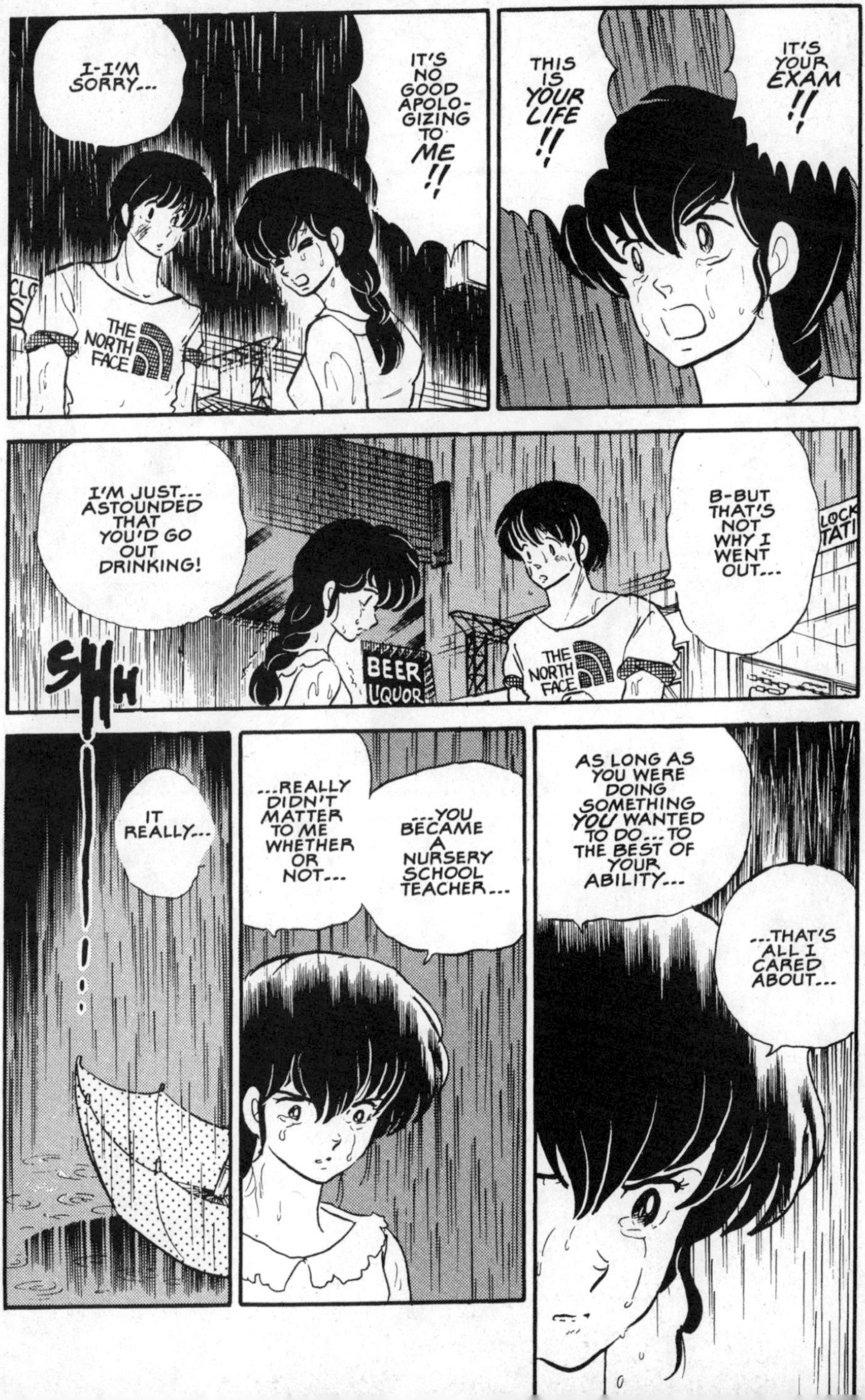
I-I'M SORRY...
IT'S NO GOOD APOLOGIZING TO ME!!
THIS IS YOUR LIFE!!
IT'S YOUR EXAM!!
CLO S
THE NORTH FACE
I'M JUST... ASTOUNDED THAT YOU'D GO OUT DRINKING!
B-BUT THAT'S NOT WHY I WENT OUT...
LOCK TATI
BEER LIQUOR
THE NORTH FACE
SHH
IT REALLY...
...REALLY DIDN'T MATTER TO ME WHETHER OR NOT...
...YOU BECAME A NURSERY SCHOOL TEACHER...
AS LONG AS YOU WERE DOING SOMETHING YOU WANTED TO DO...TO THE BEST OF YOUR ABILITY...
...THAT'S ALL I CARED ABOUT...

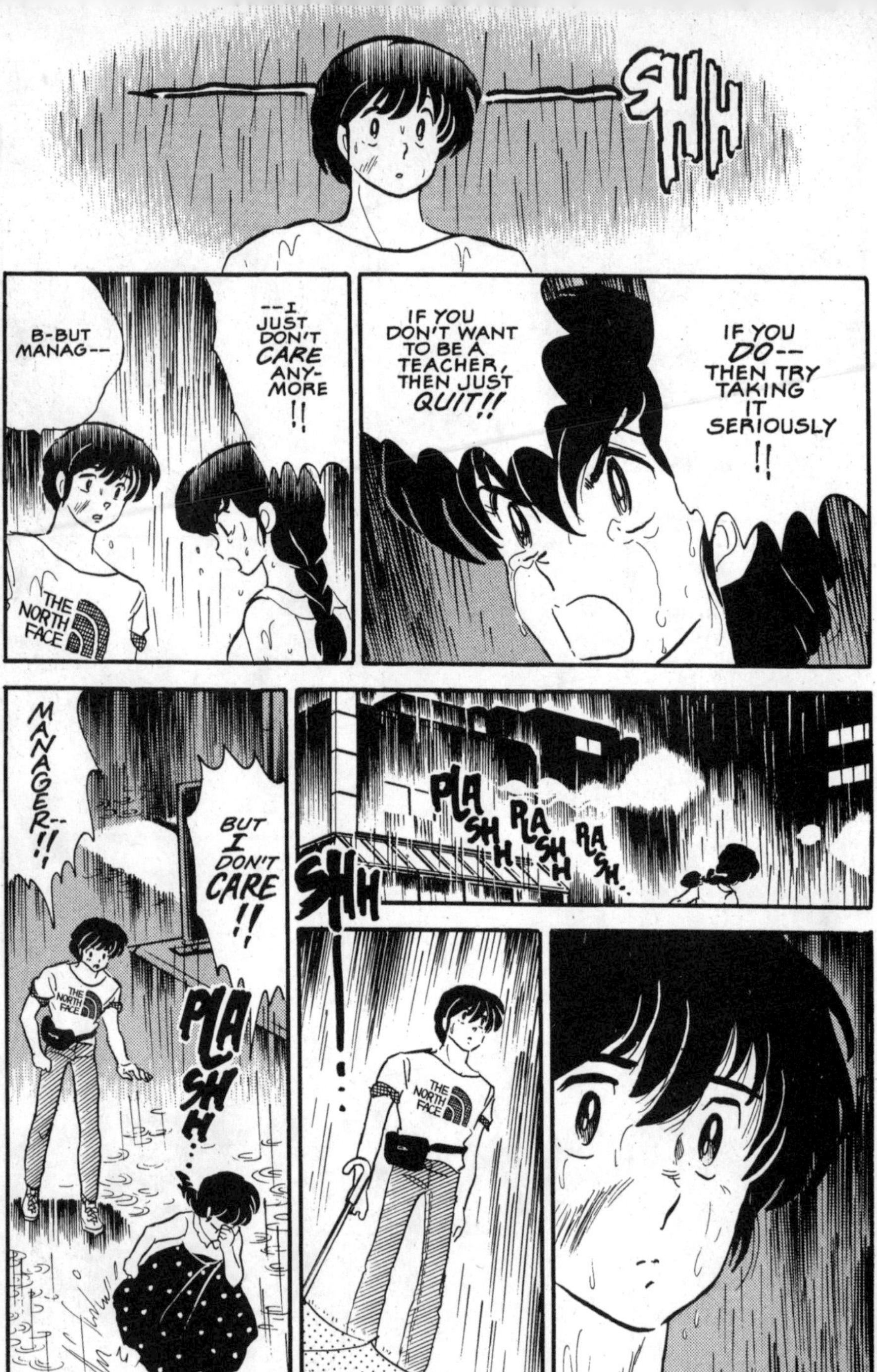
SHH
B-BUT MANAG--
--I JUST DON'T CARE ANY-MORE !!
THE NORTH FACE
IF YOU DON'T WANT TO BE A TEACHER, THEN JUST QUIT!!
IF YOU DO-- THEN TRY TAKING IT SERIOUSLY !!
MANAGER--!!
BUT I DON'T CARE !!
PLASHH...
PLASHH
RASHH
RASH..
SHH
!...

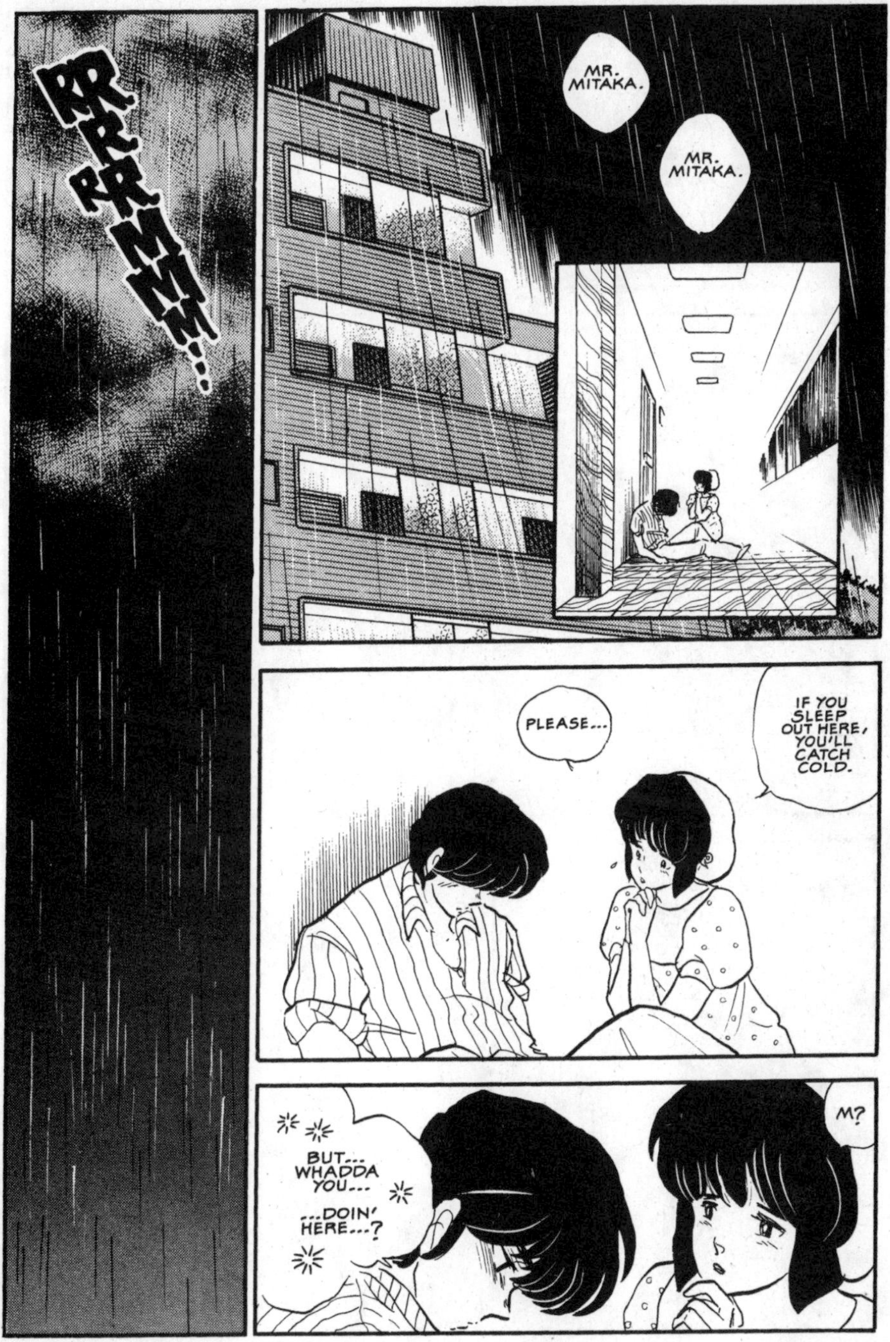
RRRRRRMMM...
MR. MITAKA.
MR. MITAKA.
PLEASE...
IF YOU SLEEP OUT HERE, YOU'LL CATCH COLD.
BUT... WHADDA YOU...
...DOIN' HERE...?
M?

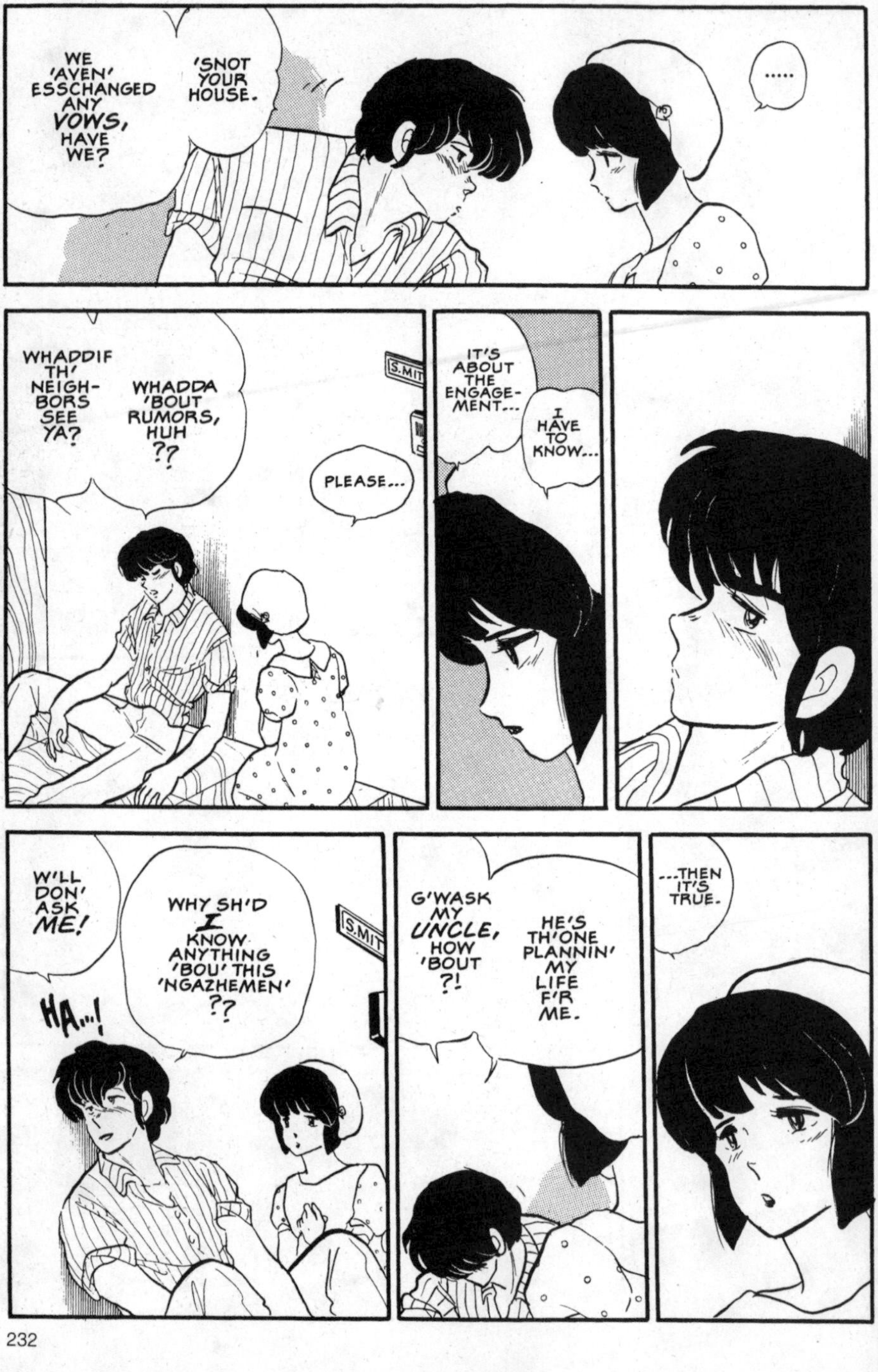
WE 'AVEN' ESSCHANGED ANY VOWS, HAVE WE?
'SNOT YOUR HOUSE.
......
WHADDIF TH' NEIGHBORS SEE YA?
WHADDA 'BOUT RUMORS, HUH ??
S.MIT
PLEASE...
IT'S ABOUT THE ENGAGEMENT...
I HAVE TO KNOW...
W'LL DON' ASK ME!
WHY SH'D I KNOW ANYTHING 'BOU' THIS 'NGAZHEMEN' ??
S.MIT
HA...!
G'WASK MY UNCLE, HOW 'BOUT ?!
HE'S TH'ONE PLANNIN' MY LIFE F'R ME.
...THEN IT'S TRUE.

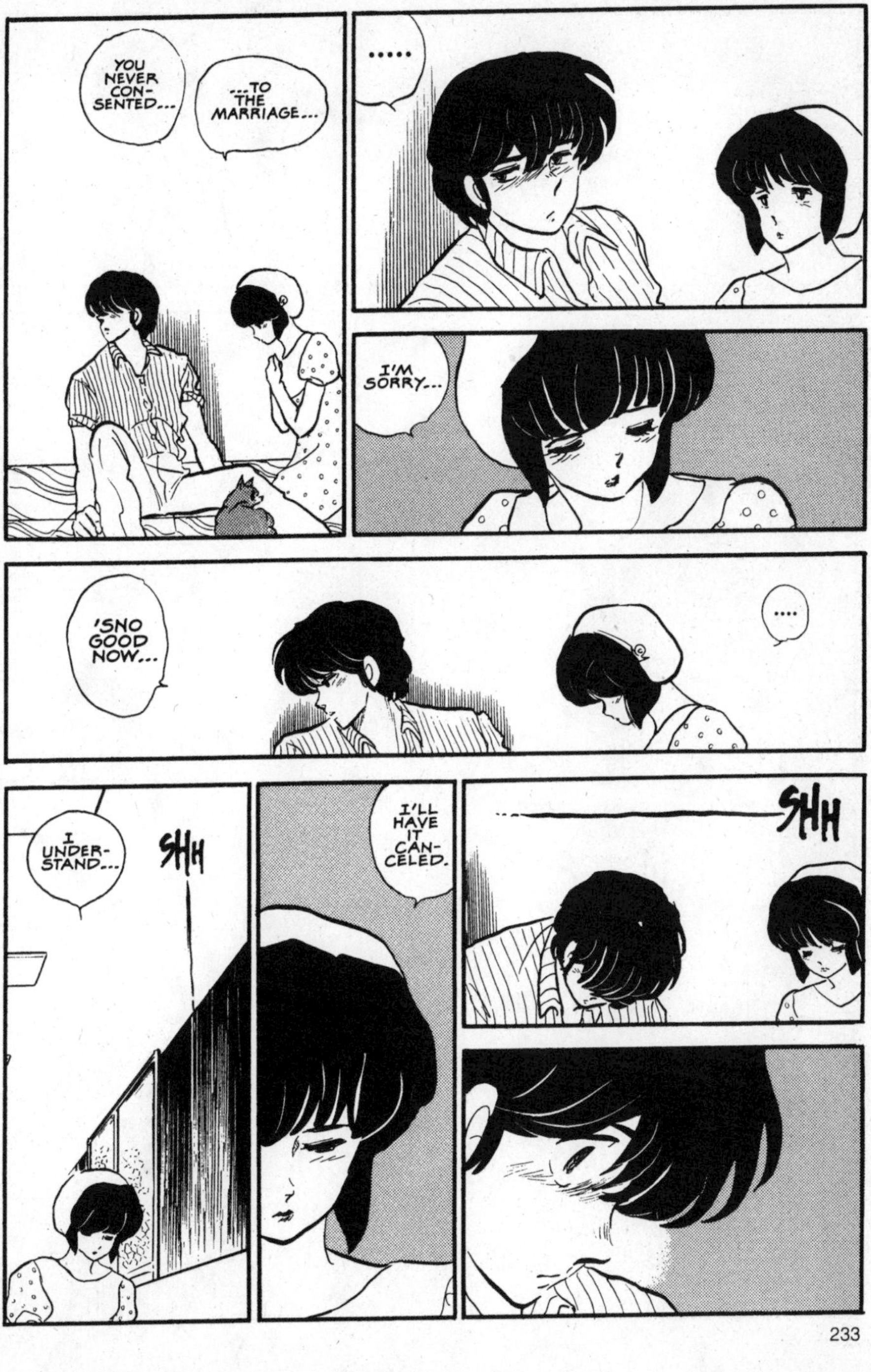
YOU NEVER CON-SENTED...
...TO THE MARRIAGE...
......
I'M SORRY...
'SNO GOOD NOW...
.....
I UNDER-STAND...
SHH
I'LL HAVE IT CAN-CELED.
SHH

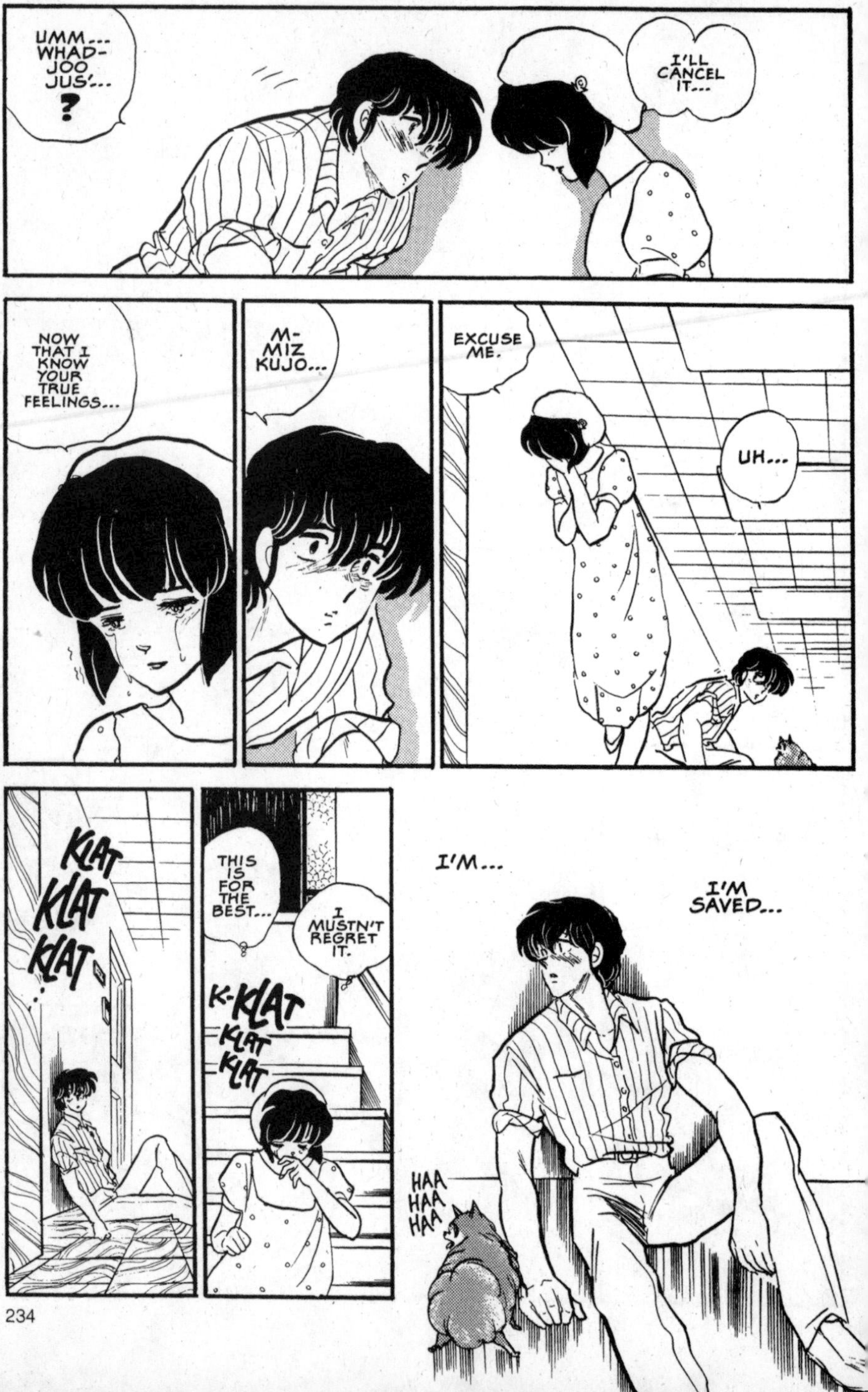
UMM... WHAD-JOO JUS'...
?
I'LL CANCEL IT...
NOW THAT I KNOW YOUR TRUE FEELINGS...
M-MIZ KUJO...
EXCUSE ME.
UH...
KLAT KLAT KLAT
THIS IS FOR THE BEST...
I MUSTN'T REGRET IT.
K-KLAT KLAT KLAT
I'M...
I'M SAVED...
HAA HAA HAA

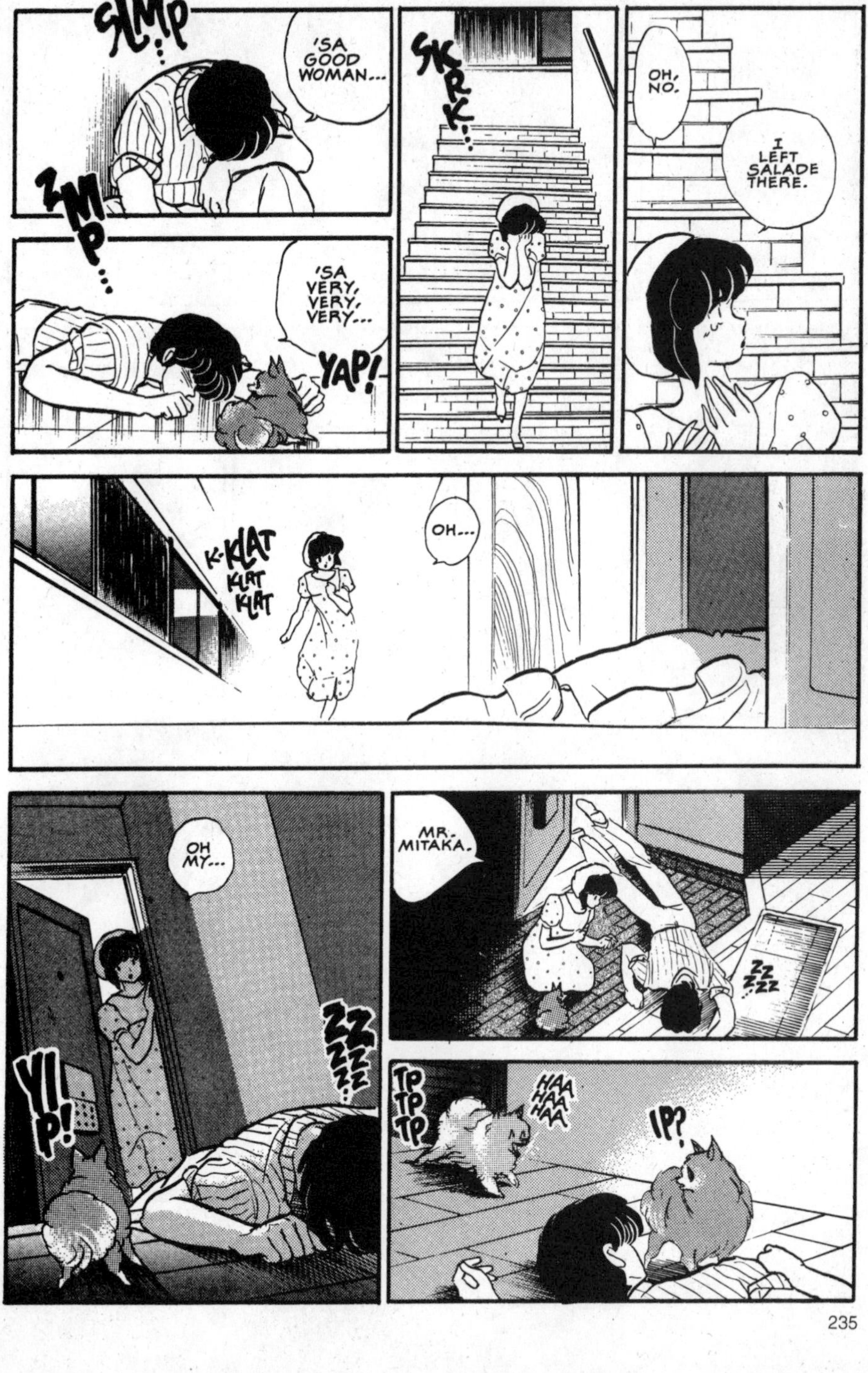
SLMP
'SA GOOD WOMAN...
ZMP...
'SA VERY, VERY, VERY...
YAP!
SKRK
OH, NO.
I LEFT SALADE THERE.
K-KLAT KLAT KLAT
OH...
OH MY...
ZZZZZ
YIIP!
MR. MITAKA.
ZZZZZ
TP TP TP
HAA HAA HAA
IP?

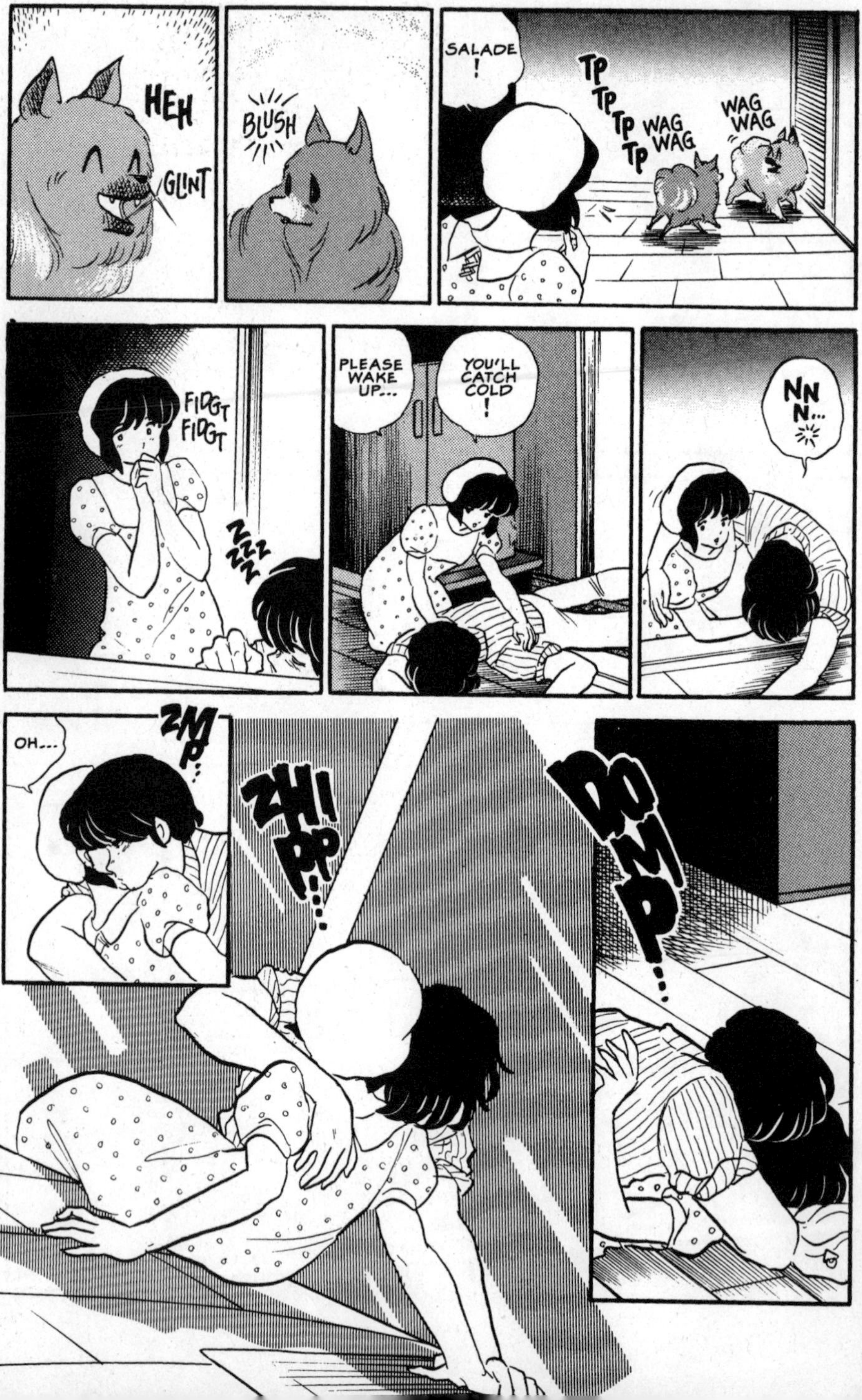
HEH
GLINT
BLUSH
SALADE!
TP TP TP TP
WAG WAG
WAG WAG
FIDGT FIDGT
ZZZZZ
PLEASE WAKE UP...
YOU'LL CATCH COLD!
NNN...
OH...
ZMP
ZHIPP...
DOMP...

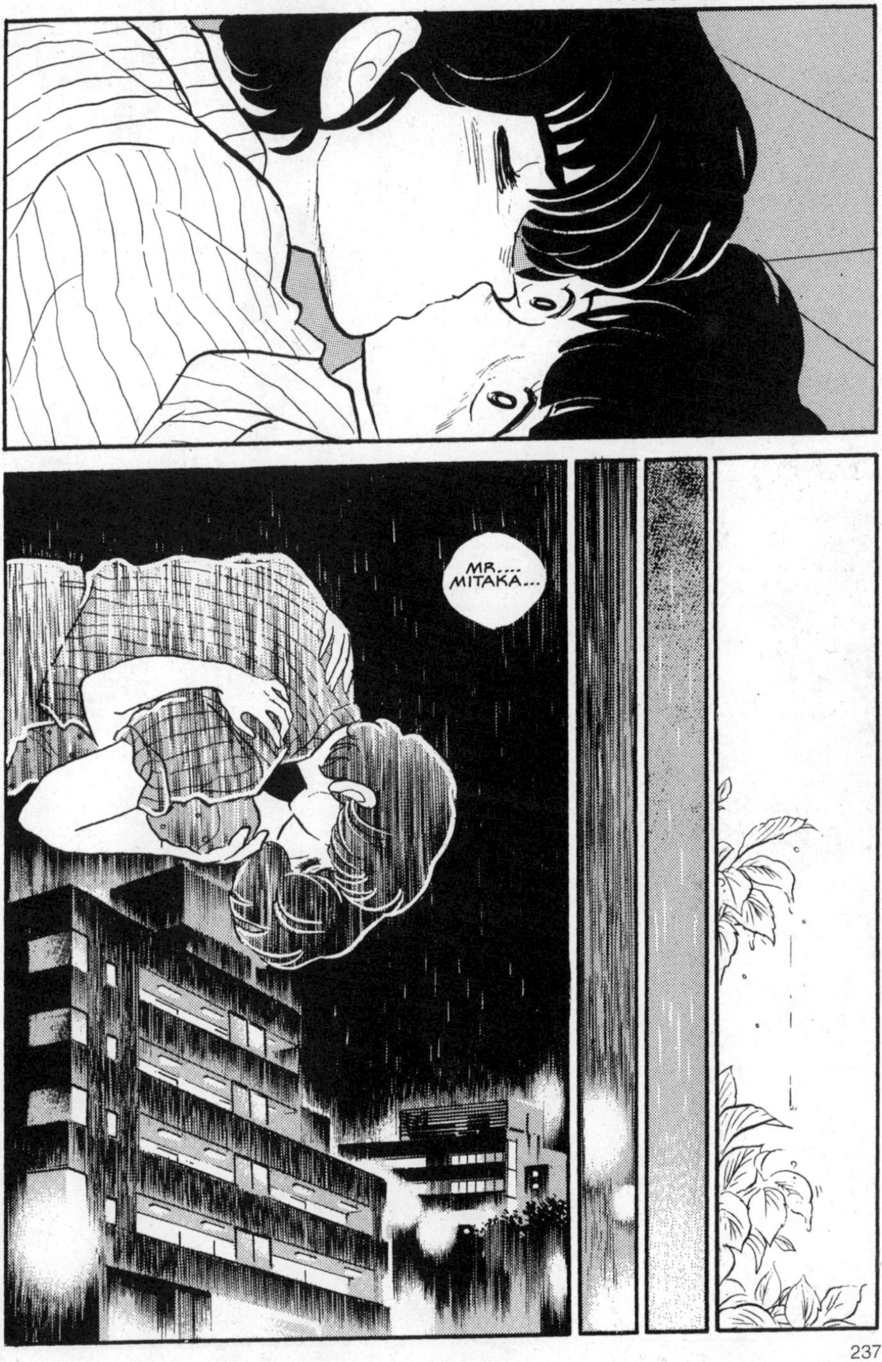
MR....
MITAKA...

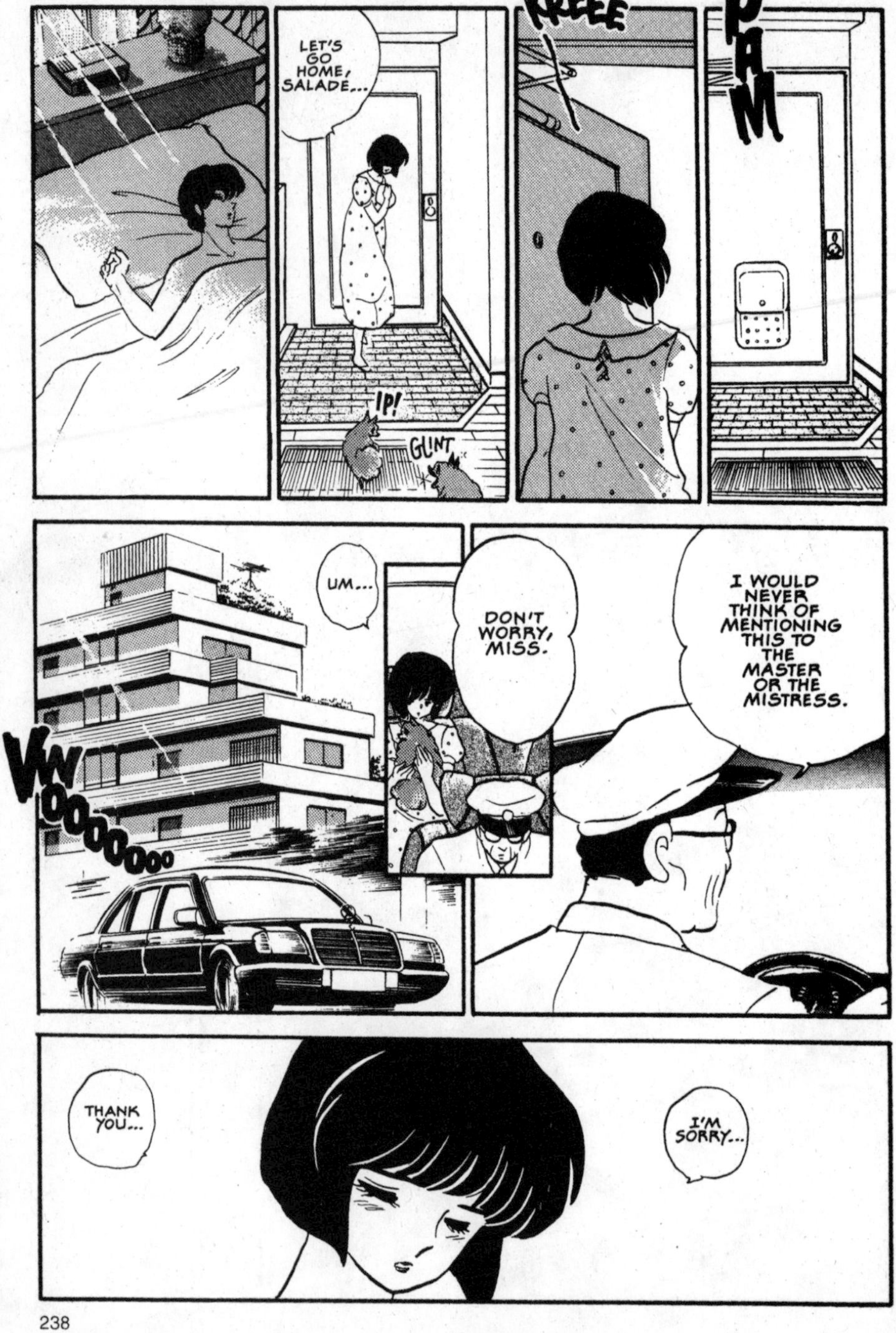
LET'S GO HOME, SALADE...
!P!
GLINT
KREEE
PAM
VWOOOOOOOO
UM...
DON'T WORRY, MISS.
I WOULD NEVER THINK OF MENTIONING THIS TO THE MASTER OR THE MISTRESS.
THANK YOU...
I'M SORRY...

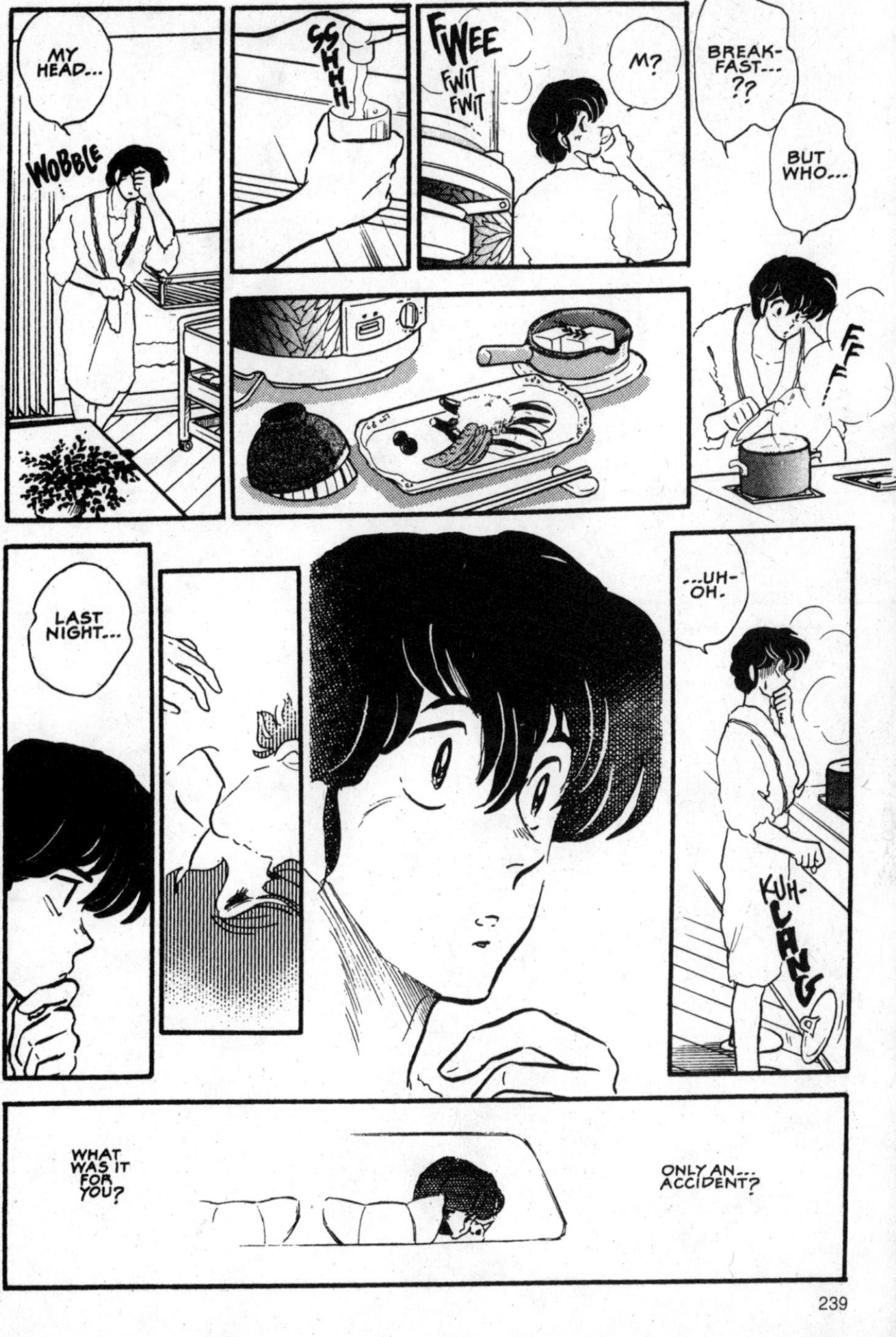
MY HEAD...
WOBBLE
SSHHH
FWEE
FWIT FWIT
M?
BREAK-FAST...??
BUT WHO...
FFF
LAST NIGHT...
...UH-OH.
KUH-LANG
WHAT WAS IT FOR YOU?
ONLY AN... ACCIDENT?

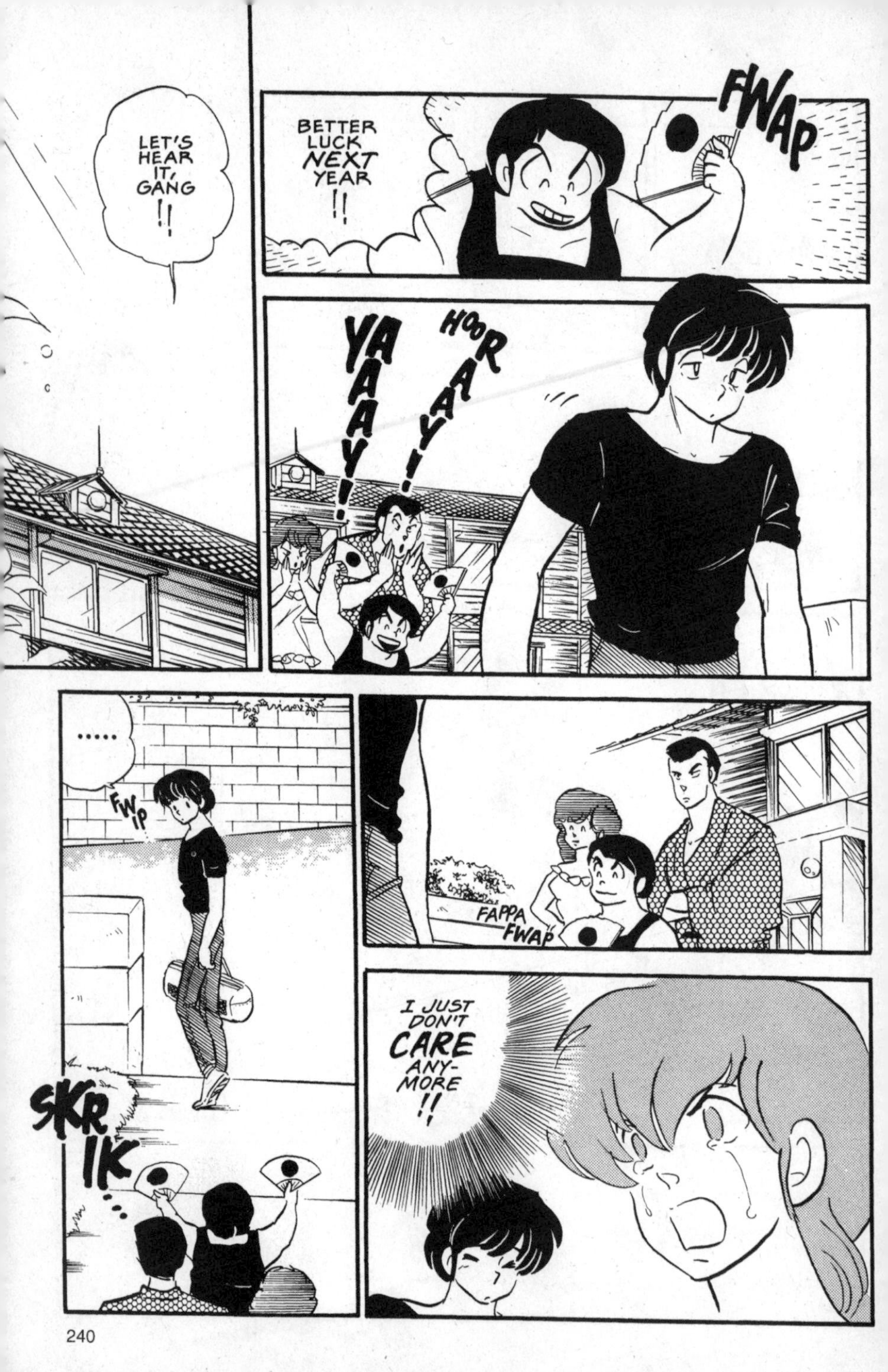

LET'S HEAR IT, GANG !!
BETTER LUCK NEXT YEAR !!
FWAP
YAAAAY!!
HOORAAAY!!
.....
FWIP
FAPPA FWAP
I JUST DON'T CARE ANYMORE !!
SKRIK

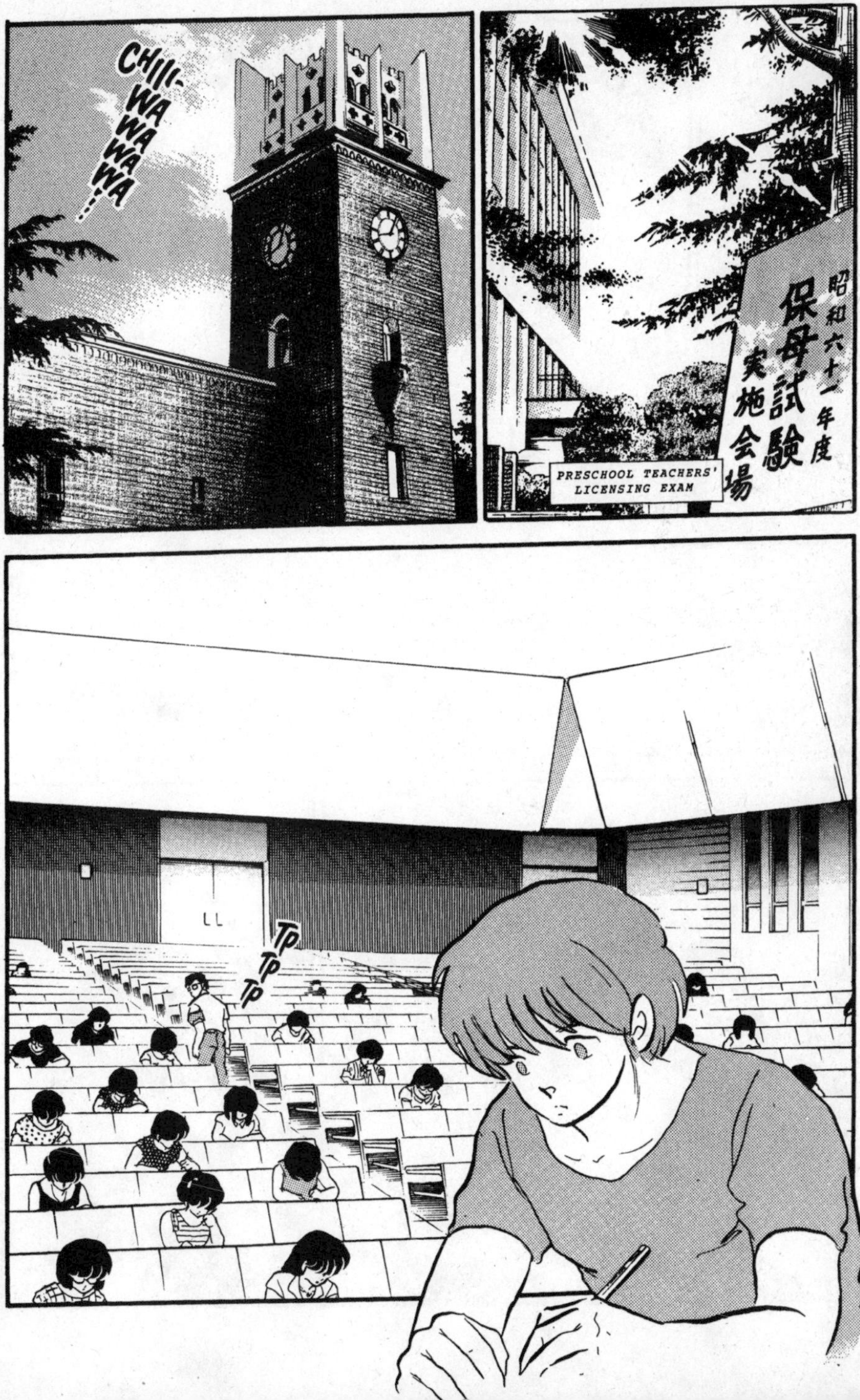
CHIII-WAWAWAWAWA...
昭和六十一年度
保母試験
実施会場
PRESCHOOL TEACHERS' LICENSING EXAM
TP TP TP

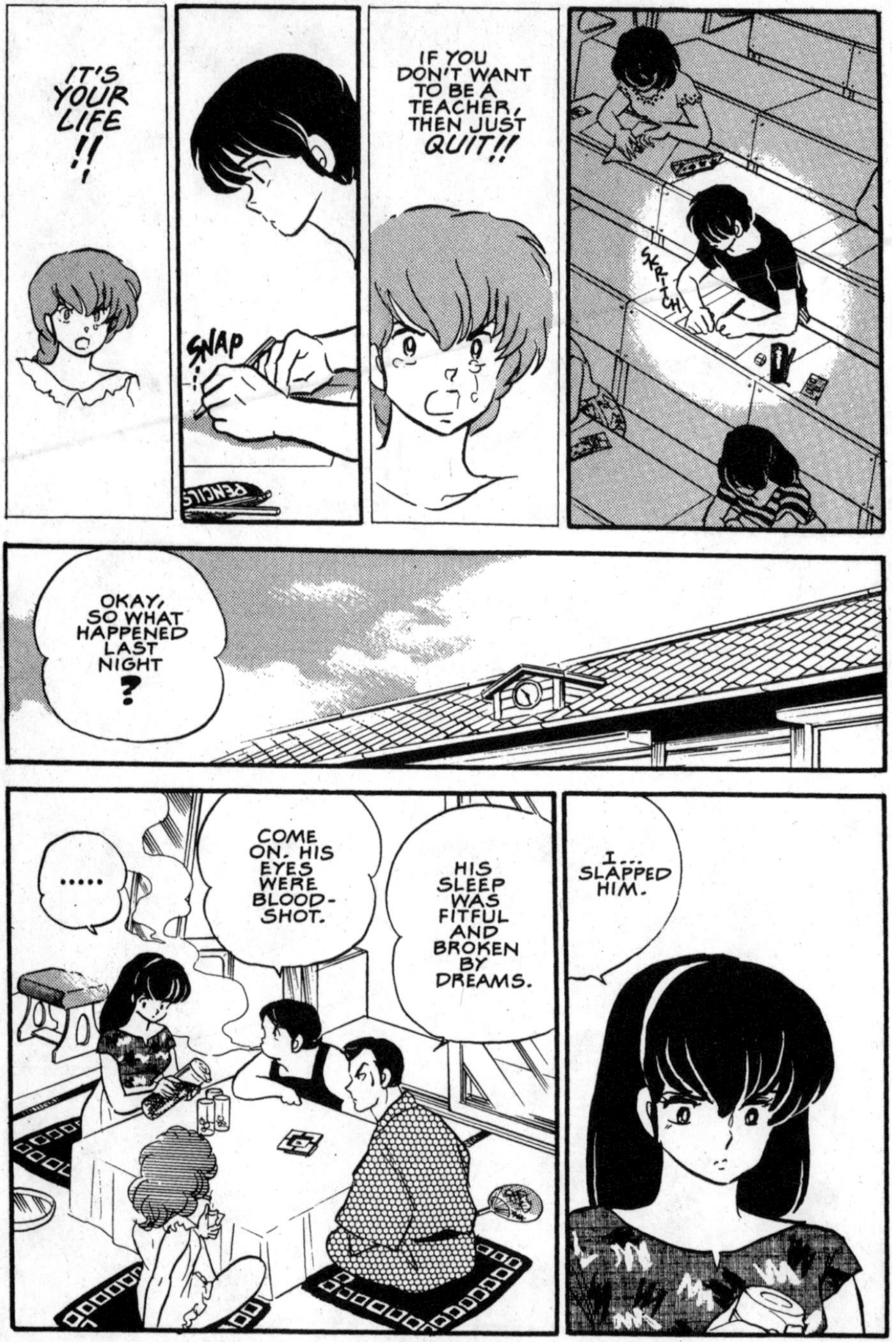
IT'S YOUR LIFE !!
SNAP
IF YOU DON'T WANT TO BE A TEACHER, THEN JUST QUIT!!
SKRITCH
PENCILS
OKAY, SO WHAT HAPPENED LAST NIGHT ?
.....
COME ON. HIS EYES WERE BLOOD-SHOT.
HIS SLEEP WAS FITFUL AND BROKEN BY DREAMS.
I... SLAPPED HIM.

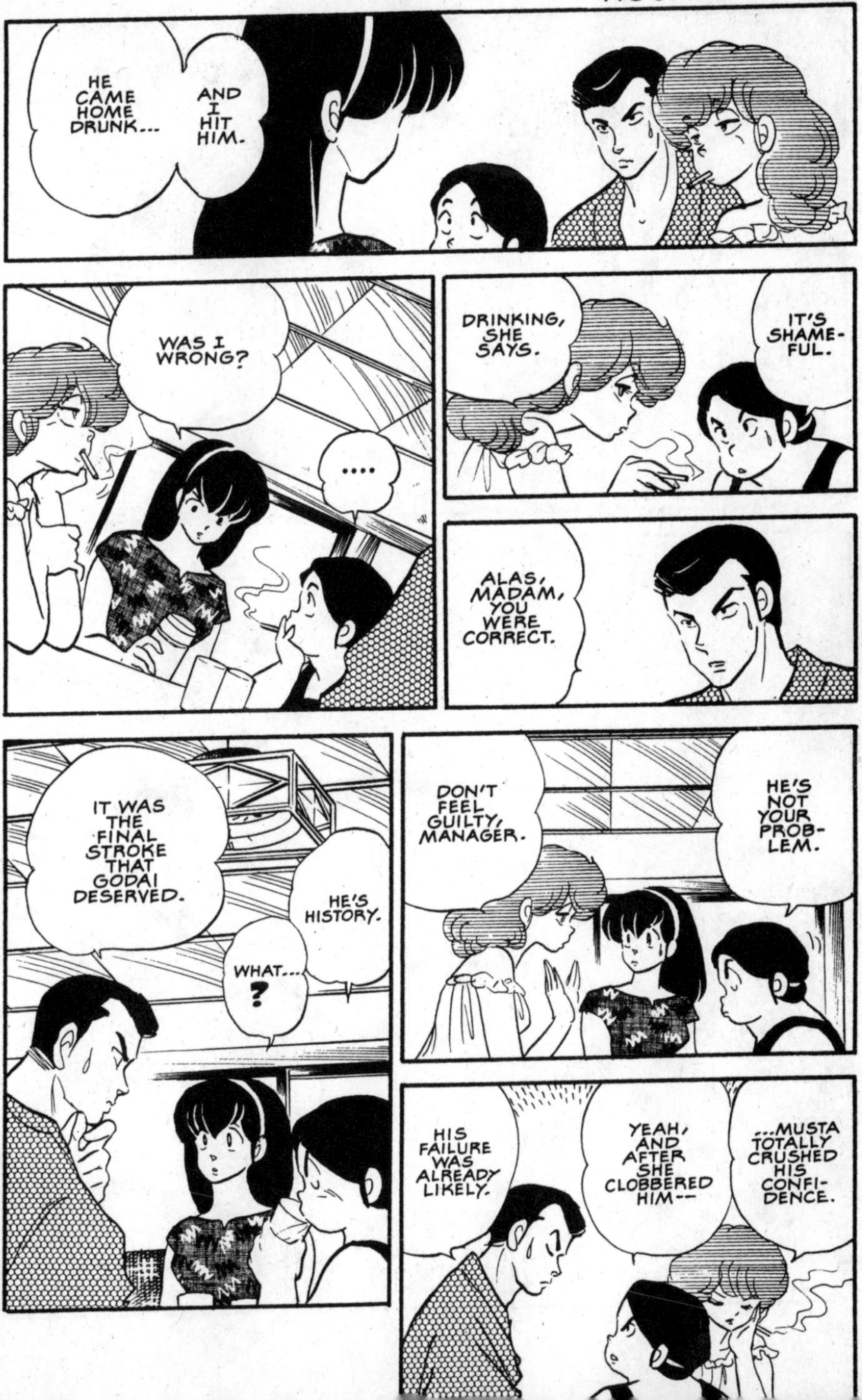
HE CAME HOME DRUNK...
AND I HIT HIM.
WAS I WRONG?
....
DRINKING, SHE SAYS.
IT'S SHAME-FUL.
ALAS, MADAM, YOU WERE CORRECT.
IT WAS THE FINAL STROKE THAT GODAI DESERVED.
HE'S HISTORY.
WHAT...?
DON'T FEEL GUILTY, MANAGER.
HE'S NOT YOUR PROB-LEM.
HIS FAILURE WAS ALREADY LIKELY.
YEAH, AND AFTER SHE CLOBBERED HIM--
...MUSTA TOTALLY CRUSHED HIS CONFI-DENCE.

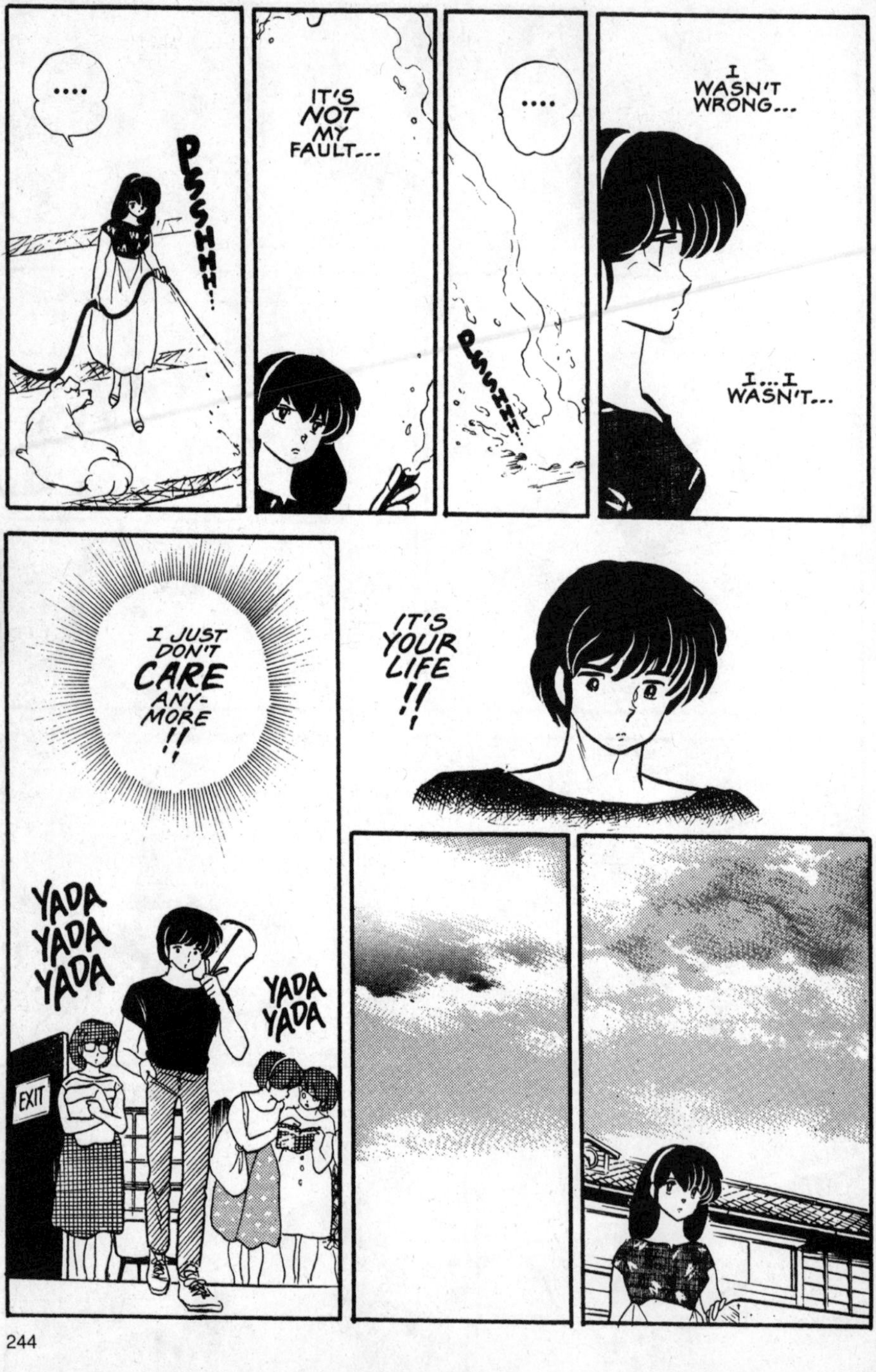
....
PSSHHH!
IT'S NOT MY FAULT...
....
PSSSHHH!
I WASN'T WRONG...
I... I WASN'T...
I JUST DON'T CARE ANYMORE!!
IT'S YOUR LIFE!!
YADA YADA YADA
YADA YADA
EXIT

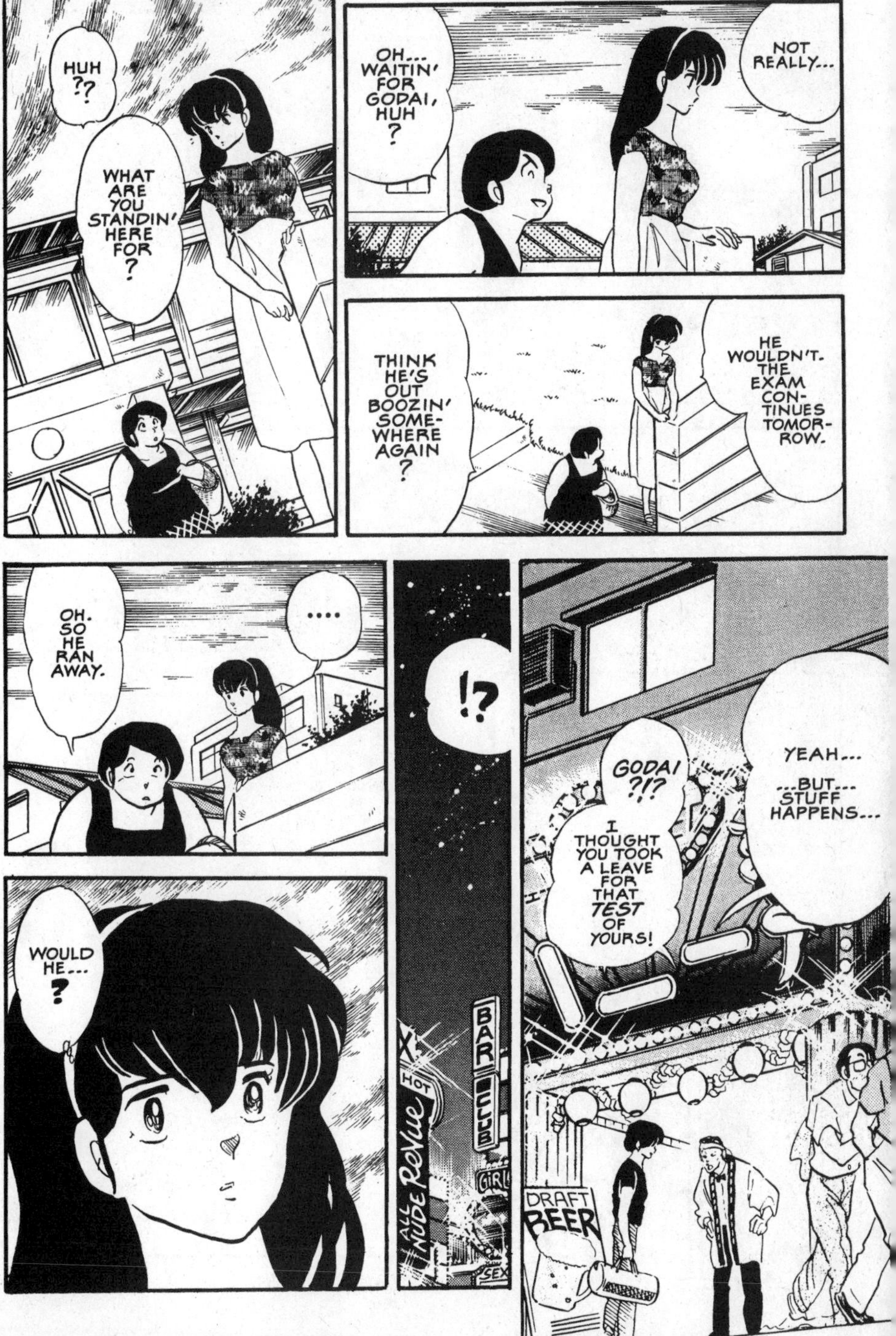
HUH ??
WHAT ARE YOU STANDIN' HERE FOR ?
OH... WAITIN' FOR GODAI, HUH ?
NOT REALLY...
THINK HE'S OUT BOOZIN' SOMEWHERE AGAIN ?
HE WOULDN'T. THE EXAM CONTINUES TOMORROW.
OH. SO HE RAN AWAY.
....
WOULD HE... ?
!?
HOT
ALL NUDE Revue
BAR
CLUB
SEX
GODAI ?!?
I THOUGHT YOU TOOK A LEAVE FOR THAT TEST OF YOURS!
YEAH...
...BUT... STUFF HAPPENS...
DRAFT BEER

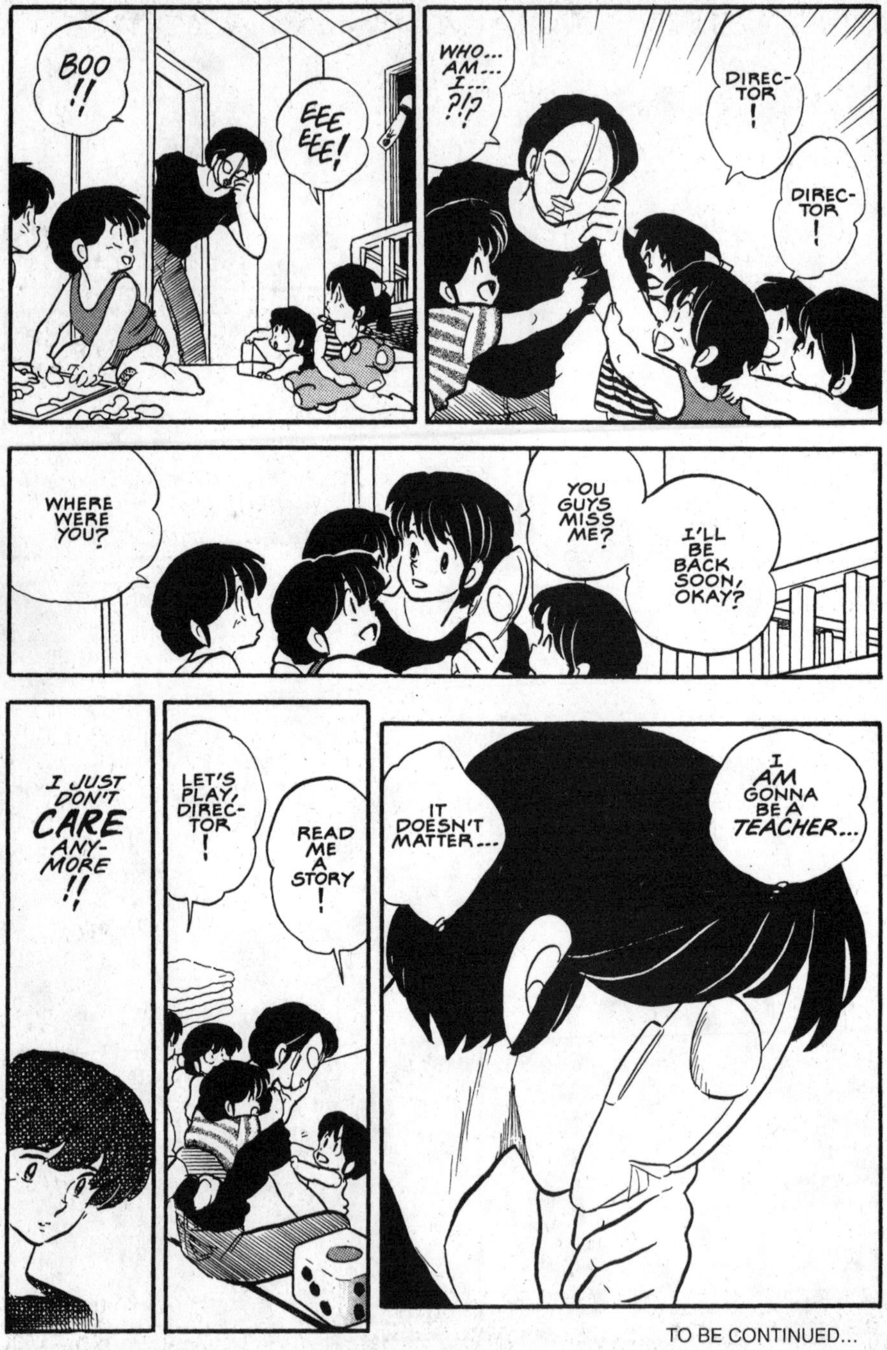
BOO!!
EEEEEE!
WHO... AM... I... ?!?
DIRECTOR!
DIRECTOR!
WHERE WERE YOU?
YOU GUYS MISS ME?
I'LL BE BACK SOON, OKAY?
I JUST DON'T CARE ANYMORE!!
LET'S PLAY, DIRECTOR!
READ ME A STORY!
IT DOESN'T MATTER...
I AM GONNA BE A TEACHER...

TO BE CONTINUED...

The story of a boy who turns into a girl, a father who turns into a panda, and the weird Chinese curse that did it to 'em!

Rumiko Takahashi's Ranma 1/2™

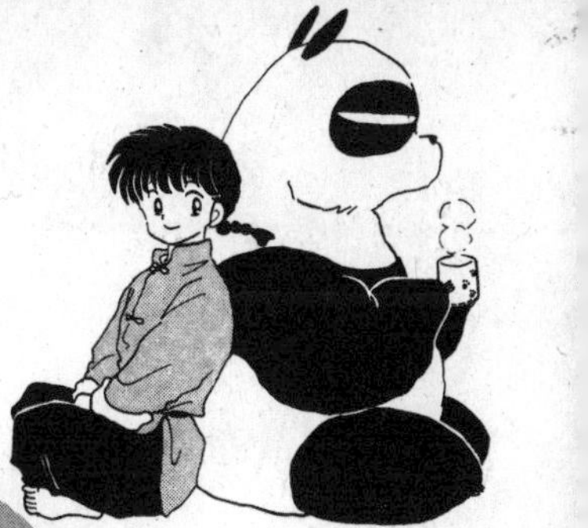

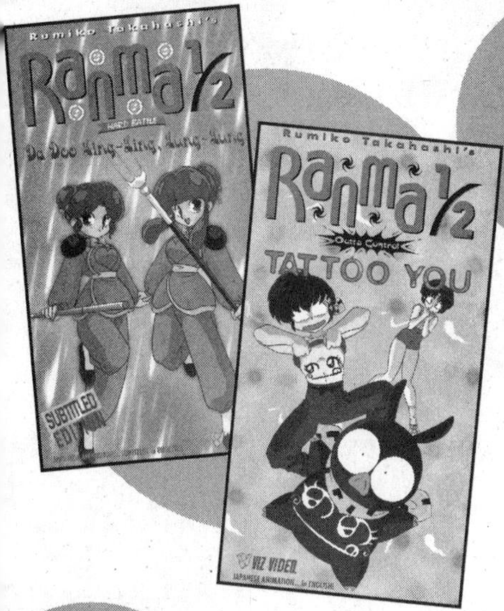
Rumiko Takahashi's
Ranma 1/2
Hard Battle
Da Doo Ling-Ling, Lung-Lung
Subtitled Edition
Rumiko Takahashi's
Ranma 1/2
Outta Control
TATTOO YOU
VIZ VIDEO

Videos!

Four seasons of the anime TV series, plus movies and original animated videos. Available in English or in Japanese with English subtitles.

TITLE	ENGLISH	SUBTITLED
Original TV Series (Vols. 1-9)	$29.95 ea.	n/a
Collector's Edition TV Series (Vols. 1-6)	n/a	$34.95 ea.
Anything-Goes Martial Arts (Vols. 1-11)	$24.95 ea.	$29.95 ea.
Hard Battle (Vols. 1-12)	$24.95 ea.	$29.95 ea.
Outta Control (Vols. 1-12)	$24.95 ea.	Coming Soon
OAVs Vols. 1-6 (Vols. 1-3 are English-only)	$29.95 ea.	$29.95 ea.
Collector's Editions OAVs (Vols. 1-2)	n/a	$34.95 ea.
Video Jukebox	n/a	$14.95 ea.
Movie: Big Trouble in Nekonron, China	$34.95 ea.	$34.95 ea.
2nd Movie: Nihao My Concubine	$34.95 ea.	$34.95 ea.
Digital Dojo Box Set (9 Vols.)	$199.95 ea.	n/a
Anything-Goes Box Set (11 Vols.)	$199.95 ea.	n/a
OAV Box Set (6 Vols.)	$124.95 ea.	n/a
Hard Battle Box Set (12 Vols.)	$199.95 ea.	n/a

Plus!

Graphic Novels: 13 volumes & counting!
T-Shirts: 7 styles available in different sizes!
Music: 6 soundtracks from the anime TV series and movies.
Monthly Comics: Available by subscription or individual issues!
Merchandise: Baseball caps, Cappuccino mugs, watches, postcards & more!

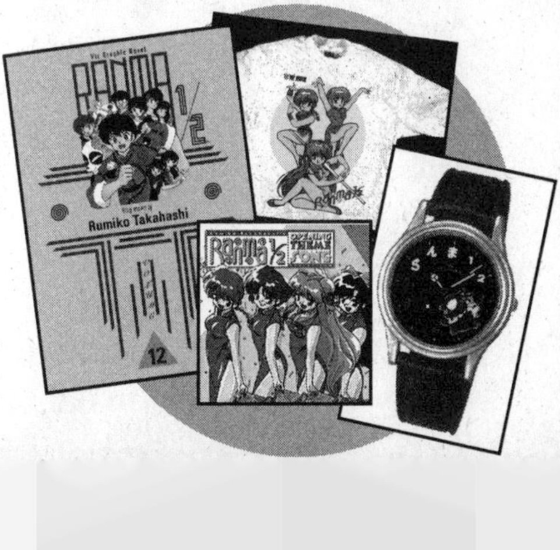
RANMA 1/2
Rumiko Takahashi
12

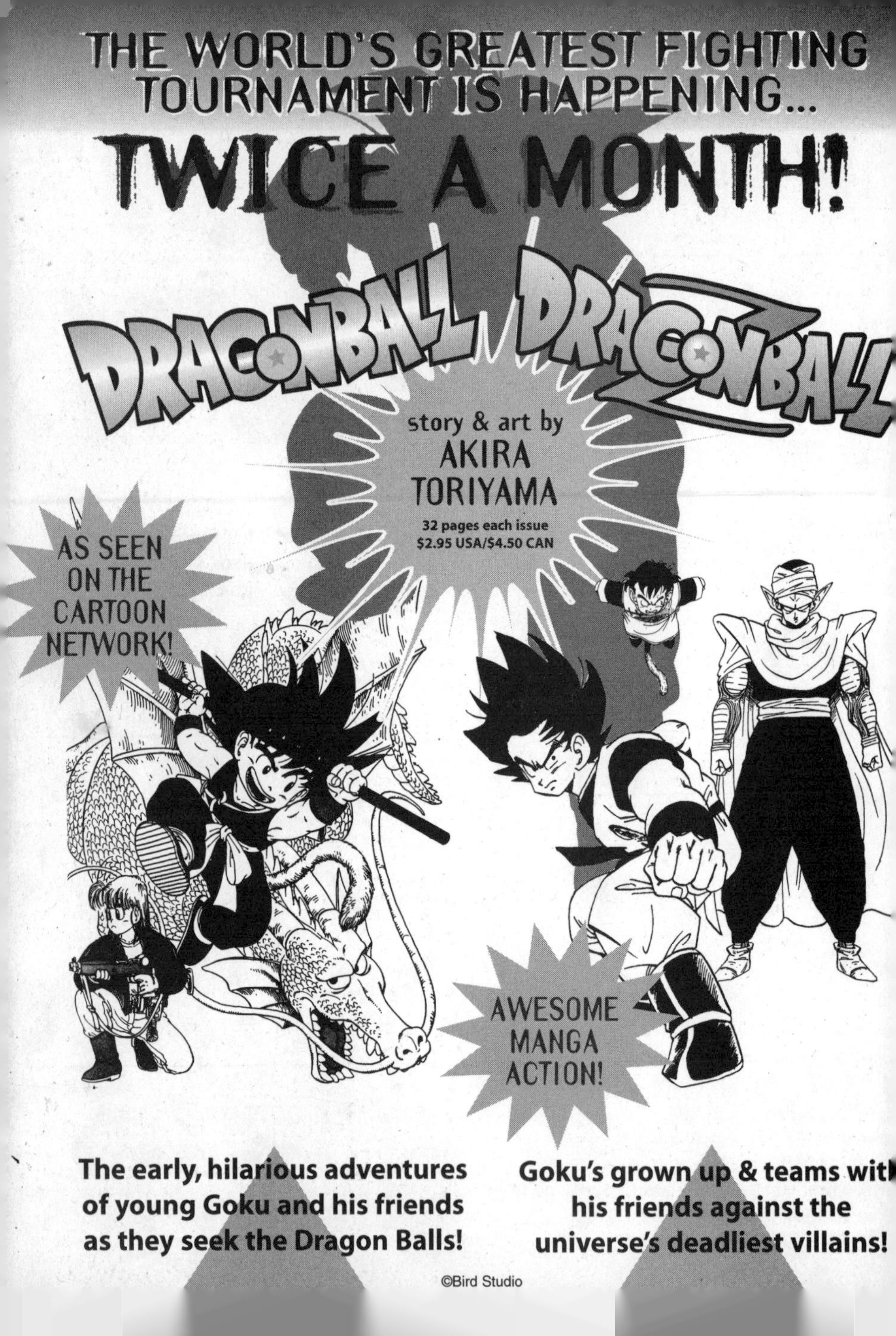
THE WORLD'S GREATEST FIGHTING TOURNAMENT IS HAPPENING...
TWICE A MONTH!
DRAGON BALL
DRAGON BALL Z
story & art by AKIRA TORIYAMA
32 pages each issue
$2.95 USA/$4.50 CAN
AS SEEN ON THE CARTOON NETWORK!
AWESOME MANGA ACTION!
The early, hilarious adventures of young Goku and his friends as they seek the Dragon Balls!
Goku's grown up & teams with his friends against the universe's deadliest villains!
©Bird Studio